NEW ROCK NEW REALM

NEW ROCK NEW REALM

BOOK TWO OF THE NEW ROCK SERIES

For Mat,

RICHARD SPARKS

CAEZIK
SF & FANTASY
ARC MANOR
ROCKVILLE, MARYLAND

＊

SHAHID MAHMUD
PUBLISHER

www.CaezikSF.com

ISBN: 978-1-64710-121-3

First Edition. First Printing. November 2024.
1 2 3 4 5 6 7 8 9 10

An imprint of Arc Manor LLC

www.CaezikSF.com

For Elizabeth

CONTENTS

MAP OF MOURVANIA

THE GREAT WASTE

Map by Jenny Okun

North and South and West and East
Lock the gates and cage the Beast
Seal so none shall ever find
Head and Heart and Soul and Mind

Prologue

I was rooted to the spot in astonishment, staring at the futuristic machine that had risen from below and was now standing on the floor of the cavern. A *spaceship!* Down here, deep beneath and beyond the bowels of Mayport Castle? It was the last thing I expected to see in that magical, pre-industrial world into which I'd been flung when this whole escapade started.

Torches flickered in sconces on the dark rock walls of the chamber. Beyond the transparent dome overhead stars glinted and the moon shone. My battlestaff, Shift, quivered in my hand. She was as shocked as I was. Her thoughts flowed into me as lucidly as if she'd spoken them out loud. "What is *that*?!"

My mouth was dry. I swallowed before replying, silently, *Apparently, it is our reward.*

But... but... My sentient rowan-wood staff was clearly overwhelmed. That was not like her. Shift was always calm and composed, even in the chaos of combat—often more so than I was. I'd grown so used to casting with her that she felt like an extension of myself. She knew what we needed to do the moment I thought it, and she delivered instantly.

"Well?" My other companion asked, interrupting our exchange. "What do you think?"

I turned to "him." Ken—as he'd suggested I called him, short for Kenneth—struck me as odder every time I looked at him. Seemingly part ant and part rhinoceros, he somewhat resembled a bunch of pipe cleaners twisted together, with a proboscis and beak, long antennae, tufts of spiky black and red insect hair, blue tentacles, seven normal eyes of various shapes and sizes and two compound eyes. And with all the beyond-weird rest of him, he didn't look anything like any Kenneth I'd ever seen before, or could even have imagined in my most fevered dreams.

Ken was, he had told me, an Amalgam. His species was part of an Accord of several superadvanced races, all of them Amalgams. Over the millennia they had improved themselves by incorporating bio-enhancements. The treaty between the species was responsible for us being on this planet in the first place—"us" being three humans from Earth: Me, Daxx, and my former online gaming crewmates, Qrysta and Grell.

Qrysta was the dual-wielding, sword-dancing avatar of an Asian American girl, and, Grell the fearsome, battle-axe-carrying Orc avatar of a laid-back Australian. My avatar, Daxx, was a battlemage-healer. A retired British schoolteacher in real life, I'd built Daxx to be everything that I wasn't: Heroic, dashing, and above all, young again. As a team we were the best of the best. We'd proved it. We'd won the online World Championship of Sword and Sorcery, with tens of millions watching us on live stream. After which things had gone very strange indeed—and the next thing we knew we'd been transplanted into a familiar-but-very-different world, separated, lost, and hopelessly unprepared for what followed.

And we were no longer who we'd been before IRL.

We were now, physically, our own avatars. For real.

Beside me Ken gurgled a chuckle at my inability to reply. "I think that you don't know what to think—either of you."

He's got that right, Shift let me know.

I closed my mouth, which had dropped open in astonishment, and swallowed. "It's … really for me?"

"Mm-hmm. You've earned it, Daxx. Much to our surprise. We all thought you were doomed any number of times. This is the least we could do, for the pleasure of seeing those busybody prudes thwarted."

It took me a moment to work out who he meant: His Accord's implacable enemies, The Pure—a coalition of super-advanced species who considered all Amalgams to be abominations. They saw it as their sacred duty to cleanse the universe of any race that undertook bioengineered self-improvement. Which is how humanity had, without anyone back on Earth being in the least aware of it, become their target as soon as our scientists started experimenting with gene-splicing and DNA hacks. As they saw it, we were on our way to becoming Amalgam, and they couldn't allow that. Rather than wage intergalactic war with The Accord, who believed that all intelligent species deserved the chance to grow and develop, a proxy fight was agreed upon.

A real, live war game on a world well suited for the purpose.

Which, for the participants—us three—meant a real *death* war game.

You lose, you die. And so does your species. The price of our failure would have been the extinction of the human race.

The Accord chose us because, as Ken put it, "Who better to represent humankind than its virtual World Champions?"

It had been a close-run thing, but we'd succeeded. With no idea why we'd been thrown into this world and become our own avatars, we'd completed the daunting quest and defeated the End Boss—against overwhelming odds.

Which, from what Ken had told me, was just the first of many.

I reminded him of what he had told me when I first met him. "It's not over, though."

"If only. A stay of execution is all that you've achieved for your species so far."

"So … what's next?"

His peculiar body gave what seemed to be a shrug. "I'm as much in the dark as you are, Daxx. I'd give you all the help I could, if I had any information. The Pure know that, of course, so neither side knows anything in advance. Those are the rules that we've agreed on. The game is afoot, and none of us can interfere with it. It will decide for itself what it is going to throw at you. Whatever's coming will reveal itself soon enough."

He saw the look of concern on my face. "You made it through in the end last time, didn't you? So you might manage to do so again. And maybe you'*ll* eventually save humankind from annihilation once and for all."

I felt a surge of energy up my arm. I looked at Shift. Her red and green tourmaline eye was glowing. *Bring it on.*

Ken waved a feeler towards my reward. "Meanwhile, I expect you'll want to try it out?"

I hesitated, studying the spaceship. "Does it … fly itself?"

"She," Ken corrected me. "Her name's Eydie. And yes, she does."

I

The Incident at Westwich

Qrysta was sore from two long days in the saddle. They had been riding since dawn, through a persistent thin drizzle. If it hadn't been for her weatherproof, niblun-crafted battle leathers, she would have been soaked to the skin.

She was bedraggled enough as it was. It was another gray day, on another muddy road, plodding west through the bogs that lay between the May Hills and Westwich. Behind her trailed the Palace Guard, looking anything but palatial, their fine uniforms quite unsuited to anything other than parading smartly in fine weather. Captain Qrysta had suggested that they might be better off in proper campaign gear; but the officers that she'd been promoted above had made it quite clear, as politely as possible—with, of course, a deep undercurrent of sneering at this jumped-up girl who was now their commanding officer—that "this isn't how things are done in the Guards, ma'am."

"Of course, gentlemen," she'd said. "I'm sure you know best." They'd tried not to preen at their little victory. *They'll learn,* she had thought.

And they were learning now, two days out of Mayport.

Behind the sodden Guards marched four hundred battle-hardened Orcs. They'd started singing the moment the rain had started. It appeared that Orcs liked rain, especially when it was nice, warm—by their standards—southern rain. It hadn't let up for two days, and neither had their singing. Qrysta had heard the playlist so often that she knew all the words by heart.

With titles like "The Wetter the Better," "Pour on the Poor Bastards," "Blood and Thunder," "Storming in the Storm," "Orc'd Lightning," Qrysta wondered if the Orcs loved the rain more than sunny skies. It definitely made for more entertaining songs.

Not for the first time since they'd set out from Mayport she thought of Grell. Why wasn't he back there, shambling along with his fellow Orcs, bellowing out the songs? Where was he? He'd left the Victory Feast not long after Daxx had, following a flunkey off into the castle. Nearly a month ago, that had been. She hadn't seen either of them since. She felt lost without them. Confused. She didn't know what she was meant to be doing. They'd always been a team. The best team. They'd *never* abandon her. Which was why their absence worried her. Were they safe? Did they need her help?

If they did, there was nothing she could do about it. She had nothing to go on. She shook the thought away. At least she knew what she was meant to be doing on this campaign: Leading the Palace Guardsand escorting the Orc army on its mission to set the realm to rights, under the command of the man who was riding alongside her.

She glanced across at him. He was lost in thought, head down, brooding, water dripping from his black-and-gray beard and straggly hair: Jack Blunt, the master-at-arms who had trained Daxx and Grell up from raw recruits—along with the newest member of their crew, Oller, the slippery sneakthief with his deadly knives. *Commandant* Blunt, he now was, head of the Royal Army—but most people didn't call him that. They called him by his nickname, Commandant Bastard. But never to his face.

It was a hard face, Qrysta knew; but, as she studied him out of the corner of her eye, she thought that there was something more in it. Those deep lines had been carved into it by more than just the hardships he'd endured in his life as a soldier. The jaw was clenched, the expression grim, but the dark eyes under the bristling eyebrows were soft. *There is pain there*, she decided. *Suffering.*

Suddenly, she wanted to know more about him.

She wondered where to start.

Home, she decided.

"The Wetter the Better" ended in a raucous, final chorus. Taking the opportunity of the pause before the next Orc war song started up, she turned to Commandant Bastard and said, "Is there a Mrs. Bastard?"

At her question, Commandant Bastard came out of his reverie and looked at her sharply.

"Oops," Qrysta added, realizing her gaffe. "I mean, a Mrs. Blunt?"

Commandant Bastard held her eyes for a moment before calmly turning away from her. "Seeing as you're not one of mine," he said, "I see no need to chastise you."

It was Qrysta's turn to glance sharply. Her eyes narrowed as she studied his profile.

He was staring ahead, expressionless.

Might as well try to read a stone. But Qrysta could read *this* stone now. In that expressionless expression she read him, clear as a book. Commandant Bastard was being funny.

"You're welcome to try, Commandant," she said, turning away to look nonchalantly ahead. Out of the corner of her eyFe she saw him stiffen. *Gotcha,* she thought. She had hit a nerve: Commandant Bastard knew she was his equal. And no one was meant to be his equal. It wasn't right nor proper. He'd have to put this lass in her place.

Only he knew that he couldn't. Qrysta wasn't some recruit in the training yard, whom he could order to use a warhammer, instead of the twin blades she could wield as well as he could, if not better. Which he both appreciated and resented. Respected, even.

So he let the gaffe pass and turned the question of whether he had a wife back on her.

"Why," he asked, "are you volunteering? Our sons would be useful, I'm thinking."

"Daughters," Qrysta corrected.

"Them too," Commandant Bastard agreed.

"No," Qrysta answered, "I'm not the marrying kind. And when, mayhaps in time, I *am* the marrying kind, I wouldn't want to marry someone I can't knock sense into when I need to."

Commandant Bastard's eyebrows rose. "Now why," he wondered, turning to her, "would you want to do that?"

Qrysta frowned. She'd thought she was being amusing. Her quip had been intended as a joshing kind of compliment to his mastery of every fighting skill, both armed and unarmed. He'd made it look foolish by taking it literally. She looked across at his frank, open face and nodded. She understood that she hadn't been "being amusing" at all. *What kind of a relationship would that be, one that involved "knocking sense" into your spouse?*

She nodded and admitted, "I didn't think that through, Commandant."

It was not the confident warrior answer he'd expected. He could see that she was regretting her flippancy.

"Any man who raises his hand to you would be a fool, Captain," he said, to reassure her.

"And," Qrysta said, slowly, "the reverse would also be true. I thank you, Commandant. I'm … well, I don't know how to put it. New to this."

Commandant Bastard grunted. It was a grunt of agreement.

"The older we get, I'm thinking," he said, "the newer we get to everything. My son, now, when he was eighteen, he wouldn't give me the time o' day. Thought I was a silly old fart, he did. A right know-nothing. Couple of years later, when he'd growed up a bit, I overheard him saying to his sister, 'You know, Kitty, Dad's learned a lot in the last two years.'"

Qrysta said, "So there *is* a Mrs. Blunt."

Commandant Blunt went quiet. Eventually, he said, "I hope so."

Qrysta waited.

The Orcs behind them launched into another rendition of "Blood and Thunder."

Commandant Bastard turned in his saddle and looked her in the eye. "I hardly know you, Captain," he said, "and yet, I feel I know you better than anyone, in some way. Mayhaps because you're my equal." He thought about that and shook his head. "I flatter myself," he grumbled. "Twin-blading, you're my master—we both know that. If I had to fight you for my life I'd equip myself different, because I know when I'm overmatched. You and your blades, against me and my sword-and-board: Well, *then* we'd see. Not that I have any desire to." He paused, considering his next words carefully. "What I appreciate, in a warrior, is mastery. I see a master, my heart warms. I don't need to prove myself against him. Or her. That's not the point anymore, at our level. We're not fighting. We're embodying." He smiled, briefly but sadly. "But you asked me a question. There *was* a Mrs. Blunt, and I hope there still *is* a Mrs. Blunt, but gods know where she is, and gods know I've tried all these long years to find her."

He went quiet. They rode on. The Orcs sang on. The rain rained on. The Palace Guards trudged on, soaked and shivering and useless.

Commandant Bastard sighed; took a deep breath and continued, "You may never have loved, Captain, and I both hope you do and hope you don't. It's everything and nothing. Everything, while it's there, and an emptiness you never knew there could be when it goes. Mrs. Blunt stayed home with the babes while I went off to seek our fortune in the far lands; and I found it, but when I came home, she was gone. Which is," he added, his face going grim, "why I am particular keen to knock some sense into His Lordship of Westwich, because this is where it all started."

He stopped and sighed again; and the rain fell, and ran off their helms and the horses' coats; and from the tone of Commandant Bastard's voice, Qrysta felt that the world, and everything in it, was worthless.

"Westwich," Commandant Bastard continued. "Nice town. Defendable, but we'll see to that. It can be supplied from the sea, being a port, but Their Majesties' fleet will blockade it. This job won't take long.

"Westwich was where we lived and raised our bairns, and where I enlisted and trained, and from where I left for foreign parts, where the wars were fiercer and the pay richer, and the promotions quicker for those as could do what was needful. And I rose through the ranks, private third class to lance-jack and corporal and serjeant; and came home with a full purse and a fine future to find my wife gone. She was a good wife, and a good mother, and a good person; and she had a gift.

"Her gift was her voice. It was as beautiful as she was. She sang like a skylark. Well, there's no point in wasting that. With her Mam and her friends and neighbors, she had help enough to leave the bairns for an hour or two the odd night and do what she loved, which was sing. It filled her back up, it did, after her emptying days of toil and motherhood. And her singing filled back up those who watched and listened in the inns and taverns and chapels of Westwich.

He paused and remembered.

And smiled. "Hmh! There was one night, shortly before I left for the wars overseas, when there was a competition, at The Mermaid's Arms, for singers. And good singers came, from near and far. And they sang, and my Jenny did the judging and gave the prize to a high-voiced lad from Athendene, who sang like an angel. And the tavern keeper's wife, who was a jolly soul, said to her, teasing, 'Now how about him,

Jenny? Was he not as good as the purse o' gold he won?' And my Jenny says, 'Good he was, goodwife, but he didn't make them cry.' 'What do you mean?' goodwife says, and my Jenny sighs, and puts down her mug of ale, and hauls herself to her feet, because she was resting after a long day looking after the bairns and didn't need this. And she gets up on the table, and everyone goes quiet, and my Jenny sings "The Maid of the Moorland." One of her sad ones."

"And within a minute, everyone in the room is weeping."

Qrysta was moved. *Wow.* "Mastery."

"Exactly that," Commandant Bastard agreed. "Every song is a story, and every voice is its own, and some finer than others. But even the finest voice, if it doesn't tell the tale, misses the mark. My Jenny never did. No more than you do with your blades, Captain. No. She always hit home. Home to the heart."

He stopped.

Qrysta waited.

The horses plodded. The rain fell.

Commandant Bastard gathered himself and continued. "As I later heard it, there was a smuggler ship in port—Westwich being notorious for the smuggling. And what is the difference, when all is told, between a smuggler and a pirate? Those who live beyond the law, as they sail the nine seas. And the captain of that ship saw my Jenny and heard her sing. And when the smuggler ship sailed, my Jenny was among her cargo."

In the silence that followed, Qrysta whispered, "Gods ..."

"I went looking," Commandant Bastard said, "many years. All over the lands where suchlike sail, west and south and east. I crossed the Northlands too, to the edge of the lands of ice and snow, and they stretch east and west as well. Jarnland's but a small part of this world, and I've seen more of it than many." He paused, remembering, and shook his head. "I heard rumors. Many a time I found a trail that turned out to be a false one, or to run cold. And many a night I've lain in my cloak, under the stars, and watched the scene in my mind, in which I find the man who took my Jenny from me. And there are times she's dead, and times she's alive, because who can know the ending? But there are no times he lives, whether he begs for mercy or faces me like a man."

He fell silent.

"Does he have a name?" Qrysta asked.

"More than one. Bartle, most often. The Skimmer. Skims his cut off the top of everything that passes through his hands. Redchops, on account of his whiskers. Which will be gray by now. As will my Jenny, if she still lives."

"How long ago was this, Commandant?"

"Twenty-four year. My lad would have turned thirty next month, had he come back from his wars overseas. He was five when she was taken. And I'll be one and fifty. Married six years, a living widower for twenty-four. Which is," he added, "why I made myself a master of every weapon and why I keep myself in form. Training my lads, making men of them. And keeping myself in form."

Qrysta knew what for. "Job to be done, still," she understood.

Commandant Bastard's eyes grew hard. "Still to be done," he agreed. "What with these wars, and that excitement of yours in the Undergrounds, I had no chance to go looking this year; but come the New Year, I'll be on my travels again. Mayhaps as I'll find him next year. Mind you ..."

He trailed off, as did the full-throated Orc roar that ended "Blood and Thunder" behind them.

Took a deep breath. Exhaled, slowly.

Continued, his voice lowered, wary. "I've heard rumors. Of how he is protected, now, by dark magic. That he has changed, into something no longer human. He knows I'm looking for him, you see, Captain. That makes him fearful."

"How could it not?" Qrysta said.

"Fearful enough to take risks that no man in his right mind would."

They rode on, in rain and silence, thinking.

"No matter," Commandant Bastard said. "If he can be killed, I will kill him. If," he added, with irritation, "he can be *found* ..."

"If I hear of him," Qrysta said, "I'll seek him out."

He looked at her sharply again, but this time with a different look in his eye.

A look almost of panic.

She knew why that was. Jack Blunt wanted his own closure. "With your permission," she explained, "if I am unable to bring him to you, I would be pleased to end the matter on your behalf."

The Commandant's face, normally so stoic, was a kaleidoscope of tells. Fear, hope, loss, longing, anger, confusion.

Qrysta pointed out, gently, "It's hardly likely."

That seemed to relax him. He barked his deep, short laugh. "About as likely as he'd survive a dance with you, Captain."

She waited as he pictured the scene in his mind.

At which, eventually, he smiled. "Now *that* I'd like to see!" he said. "Yes, Captain. You have my permission. And my thanks for the offer."

A familiar call-and-response number started up behind them.

Call:	*Oh, there's nothing like a battle when it rains*
Response:	*There's nothing like a battle when it rains*
Call:	*Cos rains make—*
Response	*Mud*
Call:	*And hammers—*
Response:	*Thud*
Call:	*And brains go—*
Response:	*Splat*
Call:	*And spurt out—*
Response:	*Blood*
Call:	*And they fall flat*
Response:	*And that is that*
All:	*Rains and brains and mud and blood*
	Splat and flat and that is that
	Ohhhhhhh …
	There's nothing like a battle when it rains!

Beside her, Commandant Bastard chuckled. "Wouldn't mind seeing this little lot in action, rain or no!"

"Think anyone will oblige?" Qrysta, too, thought that a rampaging Orc army would be a sight to behold.

"Our Noble Lords? If they've any sense they'll fling open their gates and welcome us with open arms and feast us till we burst. It'll be their only chance of hanging onto their lands. Lose your head or swear fealty to the crown—or crowns, as it now is in the realm, what with young Queen Esmeralda co-ruling along with old Wyllard." He shook his head, and chuckled, "Never thought I'd see the day."

He considered that, then added, "We'll see how it goes with My high-and-mighty Lord of Westwich. Ideas above his station, that one. If he falls in line, word will spread, and the other Noble Lords will fall in line behind him. And our fine Orcs will be back in the Uplands before the year's out, back to their old ways of quarreling with each other."

As if on cue, "Balls to Them All" started up behind them *once gain*.

The Orcs seemed to need to keep coming back to "Balls to Them All," because the other marching songs were about Orcs versus Everyone Else, and they'd all had enough of that matey stuff after a while, and needed to get back to Orc business, which was having a go at each other. "Balls to Them All" was an improv number. It seemed to Qrysta that the object of the exercise was to be as bizarre, as well as inventive and insulting—if not necessarily as logical—as possible. It would start with, say, a Graycrag round—again, call-and-response, led by G.C, the lone Graycrag Caller, followed by G.R., a general Graycrag Response:

G.C: *Bogginmoor Orcs are as feeble as anything*

G.R: *Blow them a kiss and they'll all of them fall*

G.C: *Can't fight for bollocks and can't even effing sing*

All (Except Bogginmoors): *Balls to the lot of them*
                          Balls to them all!

At which a barrage of jeers and raspberries and back-and-forth insults would follow.

Then it would be the Bogginmoors' chance to lead; and, to show their expertise at this game, and their disdain for the pathetic insults that was the best the Graycrags had managed, they'd pick on another tribe:

B.C.:   *The Orcs of the Stonefields are wetter than leprechauns*

B.R.:   *Blow them a kiss and they'll all of them fall*

B.C.:   *Ask 'em to fight they're pathetic as peppercorns*

All (Except Stonefields): *Balls to the lot of them*
                          Balls to them all!

As always a chorus of hoots and mouth farts and insults followed, from all to all, with Stonefields Orcs sneering about *waterlogged leprechauns*, saying, "What's pathetic, mate, is that forced fucking rhyme! Call yourself a bard?!?"

Commandant Bastard turned to her and grinned.

"Orcs, eh?"

The siege of Westwich lasted less than a day. His Lordship of Westwich rode out with his splendid heralds, and his handsome son, and his honor guard, and made a show of looking over Their Majesties' bedraggled army with disdain.

This sorry-looking bunch was no match for his high walls. Orcs? His archers would turn them into hedgehogs. The feeble old king and this upstart girl who called herself queen had not even had the civility to indulge in the courtesies! Who were *they* to order him around, within sight of his own walls? Who were they to demand four years of taxes, which he had dutifully gathered but kept for himself? And who was this grumpy Commandant, who was clearly common-born, to set him terms? Nothing but a *fool*, he saw with delight, as the man blundered into the trap that he set for him.

They talked of the inviolable rights of the nobility; of allegiance and duty to the crown; of custom, and the needless shedding of the blood of the realm; and, with the subtlety that only comes from high birth and breeding, His Lordship of Westwich mentioned, with regret, the passing of the old way of doing things.

How much simpler it was, he said, in the golden age of chivalry, when matters were settled on the Field of Honor.

And, to his secret delight, the lumpen clodpoll took the bait.

"Aye, My Lord is right," the Commandant agreed, sighing, " 'twas so in the old days—and better days than ours they were, I'm thinking."

"I'd hate you all to have to wait here forever while you besiege my town," His Lordship of Westwich said, all politeness and sympathy, adding, "and in this rain. I'm sure you'd all much rather be back home."

"Indeed we would, My Lord!" the fool admitted, glumly. His Lordship could see all too clearly that the tired old fellow didn't like campaigning. Marching in the rain, when he could be at his fireside, with his dog, and his ale, and his grandchildren …

"Then you are in agreement, sir? That we do this the old-fashioned way?"

The other's slow mind took an age to think it through, his huge, scraggly eyebrows knitting together as he tried to work it out. Eventually, he said, "What is My Lord suggesting?"

"Single combat."

That had surprised the old fool, whose scraggly eyebrows unknotted and rose. "Well. Now. I don't know as if Their Majesties would approve …" he said.

"Are you not here to represent them, Commandant, with full authority to deal with matters as you see fit?"

He watched the man think it over. "Well, yes, my lord is again correct. And that is indeed the Old Way of doing it. But …" he thought; and thought … and then thought himself into a corner.

"Begging Your Lordship's pardon, the Palace Guards can't fight, I am ashamed to admit. Should my lord wish a smart parade—why, they'd be your men! If they could find good washerwomen, to clean and starch their uniforms …. Turn out smart as anything, they would, and march up and down, *by the left,* in step and line, slow and quick, not a hair's breadth between them." He sighed, looking forlorn. "They're not used to campaigning, though. Anyone else of us *not* in Palace Guard uniform—why, they'd be honored to step up to the mark against My Lord's champion!"

His Lordship considered. "It would be an honor indeed. If I were a younger man, I would need no champion to fight for me, I would stand to the mark myself. As, no doubt, you would yourself, Commandant."

The fool looked down humbly and shook his head. "My Lord is a braver man than I am," he mumbled, ashamed. "I would only let Their Majesties down." He straightened up, his decision made. "We're on *your* lands, My Lord, the which—in the Old Way of doing things—gives you the right to name both champion and opponent. As you see, I have four hundred Orcs with me, all of them veterans of the Wars of the Undergrounds. There's not a man or woman of them I wouldn't have full confidence in. And should Your Lordship's champion win—the which I find highly unlikely, I should warn Your Lordship—why, well, we'll turn around and go back to Mayport, and tell Their Majesties we lost, and to leave you alone."

His Lordship of Westwich hid his glee.

As did Commandant Bastard.

They looked at each other with all serious solemnity. They both knew what was going to happen. They had both planned it that way.

His Lordship of Westwich, eventually, nodded. "Very well," he said, "let us see. Your champion against mine. Mine," he beckoned behind him, and a tall figure in full plate armor rode forward on his destrier, "is the captain of my garrison. And as for yours ... I understand that I may choose any of you, except those in the uniform of your Palace Guard?"

"That is correct, My Lord," Commandant Bastard agreed, humbly.

"Then I pick her." His Lordship of Westwich ponted at Qrysta.

Commandant Bastard, Qrysta saw, was a convincing actor. He sat up, looking confused, after a long moment in which he 'digested the surprising suggestion.' Which he'd known, as surely as she had, would be coming.

"That seems hardly fair, My Lord," Commandant Bastard said.

His Lordship of Westwich said, "All is fair, Commandant, in love and war."

"If you say so, My Lord," Commandant Bastard said, inclining his head in agreement. Then, to Qrysta, he said, "It seems we have no choice but to accept, Captain."

Qrysta nodded and swung down from her mount. It felt good to be on her own two legs again—even if those legs were stiff. She bent and flexed them as she drew her blades from the waterproof cloth below her saddle. Gripping their handles, she once again felt their familiar strength flow back up her arms.

The youth beside His Lordship of Westwich spoke up. "Father," he said, "this is dishonorable."

"Quiet, boy!" his father snapped.

The boy would not back down. His fair face bore a troubled expression. "To pick on a woman, sire. It is a low trick; it brings shame on our house—"

"*You* bring shame on our house!" His father rounded on him. "You, with your books and ballads, and singing and dancing. If you were half a man, I'd stand *you* in the lists against her, but I know she'd cut your balls off, if you have any—and while I'd be happy to lose them, I don't want to lose my town!"

The youth dismounted and walked over to Qrysta.

18

"Milady," he said, bowing, "on behalf of my house and name, I apologize."

Qrysta returned the bow. "No need," she said, smiling, "but I thank you."

"I will make sure you are treated with honor, after ..." he tailed off, embarrassed.

"After I'm dead?" Qrysta said. "Don't hold your breath."

The youth did not know the expression. "I'm sorry?" he said, puzzled.

"Yes, you said," Qrysta acknowledged. "Now stop apologizing and move out of the way—there's a good lad. I have business to take care of."

She moved to one side, and waited, blades in hand.

The Champion of Westwich dismounted and clanked towards her.

The heralds raised their trumpets.

His Lordship of Westwich held up a hand to stop them.

"To the death," he said, smiling directly at Qrysta.

Qrysta looked at him thoughtfully. She said, "Is that truly necessary?"

"It is the Old Way," His Lordship emphasized, his smile widening.

Qrysta said, "It may be, but I ask you to allow me to spare his life. He is no enemy of mine."

His Lordship of Westwich did not like being questioned. Least of all by a woman.

"To the death," he snapped.

Qrysta contemplated him, for a moment. Then nodded. "If you insist ..."

"I do," His Lordship interrupted.

"...the death will be yours."

His Lordship's smile faltered.

The Orcs had been away in the north, returning from their battles in the Undergrounds, when Qrysta had dueled with Commandant Bastard, so they had never seen her dance. They'd heard she was good. They were excited that now they were going to get to see for themselves. They were also a little anxious. They didn't quite understand what they were about to be watching. Orcs fight double-handed. Warhammer, or—if you're elite—battle-axe. Thump, chop, slash, whack, jab—block, avoid. They were all damn good at all of the above. They all thought, *Nah, no one with two little twinky swords stands a chance against this big brute in his plate armor, with his broadsword.*

19

Commandant Bastard noticed the consternation on their faces when they glanced at him anxiously.

He winked down at them, folded his arms across his chest, and settled back in his saddle to watch Qrysta at work.

She and the Champion of Westwich raised their weapons to each other in salutation. Qrysta bowed. Her opponent, after an awkward moment of surprise, bowed back.

"For Westwich!" he roared, and His Lordship's retinue echoed the cry.

He charged, broadsword whirling.

Qrysta danced.

Commandant Bastard was the only one among the onlookers who was not surprised to see her smiling.

At first, she only used her swords to deflect the few swipes that came near her.

She ignored the complaints coming from the Westwich delegation that she was not standing and fighting fair. She knew what she was doing. Soon enough, everyone else could see it too.

The Champion's slashes became wilder, then slower and fewer and farther between. Soon there were longer and longer pauses as he gathered the strength to heft his broadsword yet again and drag his plate armor-encumbered body yet one more time towards her. Wherever she was …. He turned his head this way and that, searching for her through the narrow slit in his helm.

Jabs from her blades into his back and legs let him know that he was looking in the wrong direction—which he was again. As soon as he turned, she was no longer there. The Orcs, by that time, were openly laughing. Qrysta's thrusts were striking home through joints in his armor. He was lost, exhausted, wounded, confused. She was toying with him.

She was also making sure that His Lordship understood exactly what was happening. When, at last, he stopped cheering, then urging, then cursing his Champion on, Qrysta stepped behind the exhausted man and jabbed him to his knees with a blur of steel into each leg. He dropped, gasping. His broadsword slipped from his grasp.

Qrysta walked round to face him.

"You fought well, sir," she said. "Do you yield?"

His Lordship of Westwich shouted, "No!"

His Champion hesitated.

Qrysta said, gently, "Can you defend yourself?"

The kneeling, defeated man shook his head.

Qrysta returned her blades to her belt, held out her hands to him, and helped him to his feet. His companions dismounted and came to his aid, ignoring their furious lord.

"That wasn't the way it was done in the old days," His Lordship of Westwich protested. "The bout is null and void. This is an outrage—a disgrace to my Field of Honor!"

Commandant Bastard hung him out to dry while he shouted himself hoarse.

"Your Champion honored you, My Lord, with his courage and prowess. The matter is settled. I will escort you to Mayport, to plead your case to Their Majesties."

King Wyllard and Queen Esmeralda had already decided what would happen, should the man disobey their command. He, like they, knew the penalty for treason. The Lordship of Westwich would pass to his son, a scholarly, artistic lad who was a great disappointment to his stern father. Alaryd was a dreamy, beautiful youth who would rather dance and hear tales and write poems than march to war. It escaped no one's notice that Queen Esmeralda danced with the new young Lord of Westwich, at the ball held in his honor in Mayport Castle, more times than with anyone else.

"You do make a lovely couple," Captain Qrysta said, as her queen resumed her seat at the High Table.

"Stoppit," Queen Esmeralda muttered, but she couldn't help but grin, and her eyes were shining.

Well, Qrysta thought. *Should Queen Esmeralda turn out to be the marrying kind, she could do a lot worse than His New Lordship, Alaryd of Westwich.*

"A distinct improvement on his father," old King Wyllard said to his young co-monarch.

"Indeed," Queen Esmeralda agreed. "For one thing, he has a head."

"And a fine-looking one too. Anything inside it?"

"Lots. Books, stories, ideas, poems, plans. Funny too."

"I noticed the two of you laughing."

"We need more like him," Queen Esmeralda said, and King Wyllard agreed wholeheartedly.

Their realm had had enough of war.

21

2

The Ghost Ship

The ghost ship floated into Mayport long after midnight under a full moon, on the lightest of breezes, over a sea as calm as a millpond. It drifted across the wide reach that spread within the stone arms of the harbor's mouth, silently passing other ships sleeping at anchor, its ragged sails whispering, its wake barely a ripple. At the quayside it settled into its berth as if it had been lying there for days, its lines slipping out and making themselves fast around the wharf's stanchions. There, it waited for the morning.

The day dawned around it, but not on it. Bright early sunshine lit the docks, and the harbor, but not the ghost ship. From crow's nest to waterline it was veiled, shrouded in a lesser light. Shreds of tattered canvas hung from its yardarms, untethered, floating like unwashed laundry in the still air. Nothing moved on its mottled, long-unscrubbed decks. A gangplank led down from its gunwale to the dockside, but no one came down it or went up it, and who had run it out?

No one had seen, just as no one had seen the ghost ship sail in on the last of the night tide. No captain had come from her to present papers at the Tidemaster's lodge, as was the form, and to receive passport, without which neither captain nor crew could leave the docks, nor could any vessel unload cargo.

Tidemaster Pike studied the ghost ship while the early morning crowd on the dock studied her. She knew what they were thinking. *Her father would have known what to do.* Her officers waited around her. All were older than her, and all had been offering plenty of advice but no help at all, until she'd stopped them. Which she had done by asking her father's second-in-command, old Undertidemaster Hurnden, what he would do if he were her.

He'd had no answer.

Well, at least that shut them up, she thought.

"I'm going aboard," she said. "If I'm not back in twenty minutes, send to Queen Esmeralda."

She noted how no one insisted on accompanying her.

She walked up the gangplank and onto the ghost ship.

She looked around, inspecting everything on the main deck carefully—everyone could see her do that, quite clearly, even though the light on the ghost ship was dim—and then turned to walk aft. There was no one above, on the quarterdeck itself, so she did not mount either of the flanking, curved stairways that led up to it. Instead she opened the door between them and went through.

Twenty minutes later Undertidemaster Hurnden sent his fastest runner to the castle.

Within the hour Queen Esmeralda and her retinue arrived at the quayside.

There was still no sign of Tidemaster Pike.

Queen Esmeralda nodded to her Guard Captain, who bowed to her queen and marched up the gangplank.

Once on the deck, she turned aft and went below.

Qrysta made her way quietly down into the hold, listening. She heard nothing but the whispering of the breeze in the lines above, as they tapped against their masts, and the creaking of the ghost ship's boards as she rode the swell in the harbor. She was on alert, ready, but not alarmed. There was no need to draw her blades. That would happen quickly enough, if it had to. Better for her to enter unarmed, and unthreatening. A roomful of crossbowmen? *I'm unarmed, let's talk before you shoot me.*

At the bottom of the stairs was another door. It scraped as she pushed it open carefully. There was nothing moving beyond. Barrels, casks, lockers, chests; a counter; sacks of vegetables; bunches of herbs and roots hanging from the rafters.

A cargo hold, then.

She went in.

She checked storage compartments as she passed them.

She opened another door, into another hold. She slipped in and crouched behind a barrel when she saw that ahead of her there was a light. Within that pool of light there was a form. In the shadows around it there were pale shapes. The form was Tidemaster Pike, standing motionless in the air above a crate. The shapes in the shadows around her were shifting, inconstant. Tidemaster Pike, it seemed, could not move. The shapes surrounding her moved gently, slowly, in small, quiet, untethered motions; up, down, side to side, softly gleaming …

Ghosts.

All facing Tidemaster Pike.

Hovering. Almost waiting.

For what, Qrysta had no idea.

She stayed hidden, peering over her barrel, to see what was happening.

Nothing.

The nothing continued while she watched and waited.

The shapes floated. Tidemaster Pike stood at their center in mid-air, over her crate, her head bowed in the light that shone down on her from a hatchway in the deck above.

It was odd, Qrysta considered, but not threatening.

Just, *weird.*

She decided that nothing was going to happen, however long she waited.

No point in waiting, then.

She stood up and walked towards the light.

No one noticed. No one stopped her or challenged her. Everything, and everyone, seemed to be waiting.

The only sound was the click of her boots on the boards of the cargo hold.

She stepped up to where Tidemaster Pike was standing, suspended. Her feet hung inches above the crate. Floating like the ghosts around her.

Weird indeed.

Qrysta studied her.

Pike was in a trance of some sort.

Qrysta waved her hand in front of her eyes. No reaction.

"Pike," she said, "I'm Captain Qrysta, the queen's bodyguard. I'm going to take you home now."

She waited, to see what, if anything, would happen.

As before, nothing did.

She reached out and took Pike's arm.

It was warm, and soft, and like a perfectly normal arm in every respect but one: It would not move. Nor would Tidemaster Pike. Qrysta pulled a little more firmly. Pike, standing on air, might as well have been a stone statue, on a pedestal sunk deep into the ground. Qrysta knew that there was no point in pulling harder.

She looked again at the ghosts.

Pale, translucent, hovering blobs.

They had no faces.

They gave no clues.

Qrysta crossed her arms and frowned. *A puzzle. But … what sort of puzzle? I've never seen anything like this before …. A puzzle without clues? Maybe the puzzle itself is the clue.*

What does that mean?

It means that the only information I have is what I see in front of me.

Tidemaster Pike, suspended above a crate, surrounded by ghosts.

Is that all I've got? She looked around the hold. *Yeah, pretty much.*

So, what do I make of it?

Puzzles had always been one of her weaknesses. She could never be bothered with the things. She'd get into the ruined crypt, or whatever, and see another damn hotchpotch of slabs that had to be shoved into a certain order, or whatever, and think *screw this*, and just google the answer and rearrange the stone squares on the floor, or whatever, so that she could walk across, and then the secret panel, or whatever, would open and release the zombies, or whatever. Then she could get on with what she was good at, which was fighting things. And now here she was, with an audience of mute ghosts, floating like ectoplasmic balloons, all looking at a dock official suspended above a packing crate. Who wouldn't move. Qrysta couldn't do what she was good at, which was fighting things, because the ghosts were not attacking. And Tidemaster Pike needed rescuing, not fighting.

All of which was a puzzle.

Qrysta looked at the ghosts. They all looked pretty much the same. She thought, *What, I'm meant to rearrange these into the right order?*

25

Well, she realized, *what else have I got?*

She pushed the nearest ghost. Her hand went through it. The ghost didn't move. It just kept bobbing gently there in the air.

Gently, and annoyingly.

She thought, *Daxx would have solved this by now.* Could think around corners, Daxx could. When it came to strategy, he just had an eye and mind for clues. *What would he see here?* Well, he wasn't here, so it was up to her. *Come on, think—it's always obvious when Daxx points it out afterwards! Oh yeah, of course—why didn't I think of that?*

She studied the scene in front of her again: Ghosts, Pike, crate.

And then, she realized, *Oh, good gods above and below …!*

After which, she immediately thought, *Grr, idiot!*

She sighed. How effing obvious can you get?! *Thicko.*

She drew one of her swords and inserted its tip into the seam below the crate's lid. Using it as a lever, she worked the top of the crate open. It gave easily, the nails sliding out of the wood. She pulled the lid up … and, of course, it stopped short against Tide-master Pike's feet.

Pike still wasn't moving, Qrysta knew that, so she worked her way around the crate, nudging the lid off, an inch at a time, until she could slide it beneath Pike's feet. She stood it on the floor away to one side and looked into the crate.

It was empty except for a letter.

She picked it up.

On its outside, in black ink, and careful, neat lettering, was one word.

Qrysta.

She turned it over and studied the seal. It was hard, red wax, impressed with a curious stamp: The figure of a clawed, winged lion-mixed-with-birdlike animal rearing on its hind legs. Its tail was the arrow-pointed tail of a dragon, curled behind it in a circle. The mouth in its long, feathered head was a roaring, open beak.

She needed to find out about it; so, instead of breaking the seal, she eased it away from the paper with the edge of her sword.

The letter was a single sheet of heavy parchment. On one part of its outside was a red stain where the seal had been, above her name. She unfolded it.

On its inside was the message:

26

The Four will come
Across the sea
To break my chains
And set me free

Whoa, Qrysta thought, as she read it. *Interesting ...*

It seemed obvious enough: *The letter has my name on it; I'm part of a team of four. Someone needs our help.*

On the other hand .... *Pretty strange way of sending a message. Ghost ship, crate, suspended Tidemaster Pike ...*

And on the third hand: Four? She was pretty sure she knew who two others of that four would be, and they were missing. *Where in all hells were they?* Grell and Daxx. It had been weeks. They'd just walked out of the banquet, quietly, one at a time, and never come back.

Unlike me, she thought. *I'd just been left here. Ken said he'd see me again, but he never did. Did he see Grell and Daxx? And if them, why not me?!*

And ...

All the other questions.

A wary voice above her said, "Hello?"

Qrysta looked up.

Tidemaster Pike was blinking down at her, puzzled.

"Pike," she said, "are you all right?"

"I think so," Pike replied, hesitant; and then, "yes." And then, recognizing who she was talking to, her eyes widened. "Captain Qrysta. What are you doing here?"

"I'm here to get you. And to take you home."

"Oh. Thank you."

"Can you move?"

"I think so ..."

"Then let's go."

Qrysta watched as Pike took a step in the empty air.

She walked forwards, and, as she did so, she sank, gently, to the floor.

She turned to Qrysta, bemused.

Qrysta smiled at her. "Okay?"

Pike nodded. She looked at the ghosts, still bobbing around them. "Who are they?"

"I've no idea. You?"

27

"No."

"Well. Let's leave them then, to … whatever they're doing. Shall we?"

Pike was clearly relieved to be going. "Yes."

Qrysta had a thought. "Who are you?" she said, to the ghosts.

They just bobbed, slowly, up and down, and said nothing.

Qrysta said, "We'll be back."

They didn't reply, but then she knew that they wouldn't. They were something that would have to be dealt with later.

She and Pike left the hold and went above. When they reached the main deck, the light above them was clear. The shadow had lifted from the ghost ship. The crowd on the dockside, that had been waiting in growing anxiety, saw them emerge and cheered.

Oller was enjoying a quiet ale in The Shanty. Or, rather, not enjoying, because he was feeling down in the dumps. The Shanty was the worst tavern in Mayport, by a long way, and Oller was only there because in every other tavern in Mayport people would buy him drinks, and shake his hand, and want to hear all about the famous quest to the Floor of the World, and the fight to end all fights, and he was fed up with talking about it.

Here, in The Shanty, no one would offer to buy him a drink, because the people who frequented The Shanty were always broke. They might, if they felt bold enough, ask him for the price of a mug of ale; and, because he was rich now, he'd buy them one—if he thought it wouldn't cause a stampede in his direction. But it would be on the condition that they buggered off and left him alone.

They were always happy to accept his ale and his condition. Under the table, Little Guy, a good half-dozen pounds heavier than he'd been when he'd adopted Oller, whiffled and twitched in his sleep, his stomach bulging with The Shanty's finest sausages. Which were exactly the same as its worst ones.

Oller wouldn't eat anything in The Shanty, least of all one of its sausages. Gods knew what was in them. Little Guy's clever nose knew. Rat. Little Guy was partial to a nice bit of rat. Rat had been the highlight of his life, before he'd adopted Oller. Not for the first time that evening, Little Guy's distended gut eased itself in the normal manner, unleashing a bubbling, rat-sausage-scented fart.

28

Oller waved his hand in front of his nose. "Gawds, leave it off, will you?" His foot reached out and found the comatose dog under the table. "Fat little perisher," Oller muttered, rubbing his best friend's plump belly. He sighed, gaining comfort from the contact with the small, brown, sleeping mutt. Without Little Guy in his life, Oller didn't know who he would be. Little Guy was *fat little something* as often as he was Little Guy these days. He answered happily to any name. He didn't mind what Oller called him. He loved Oller. He heard Oller's voice through his dreams of urine-sprayed trees, and winds full of smells, and rat sausages, and other dogs' bottoms, and gently tapped his scruffy tail on The Shanty's sawdust-covered dirt floor in response.

Oller took another swallow of the worst horsepiss in Mayport, grimaced, wiped his mouth with the back of his sleeve, and sighed. Godsawful ale, in a godsawful back-alley dive, but at least, here, he was left in peace. He didn't feel he deserved any better. All his guildies in the Thieves Guild were wary of him now. Hero of the Realm? People with titles like that shopped lawbreakers to the reeve. He tried to reassure everyone that of *course* he wouldn't inform on a guildie! He was TG to the bone! But something had altered in the way they viewed him, from Receiver on down; and there was no going back. Eventually, he worked it out.

No one starts off a criminal. A broke lad, ninth son of some village nobody needs a job. He hooks up with a mob, good or bad—outlaws, or Sir Someone's guards. And he does whatever he has to do: Step on toes, break arms, campaign, whatever. He moves up the ranks and hopes to make a way in the world. But what's at the end of it? If not for himself, then for his children?

A decent life. A place in the community. Maybe an education, a step up…

Oller realized a simple truth. *Every outlaw wants to be an inlaw.* The moment that they can, all bandits go legit. They become lords, by right of conquest. Or reeves, because some smart Clerk of the Watch headhunts them, knowing they could sort out those wrong 'uns better than anyone, seeing as they know them better than anyone. And, given a choice between My Lord's dungeons and a proper job, they turn civilian.

Or if a whipping, or repeated spells in the dungeons, hasn't persuaded a ne'er-do-well to change his ways: Mayhaps a Lord appoints him gamekeeper—he having been that Lord's most exasperating, and elusive, poacher. At which the poacher-turned-gamekeeper gets a nice cottage in the woods, and kennels for his hounds, and a mews for his hawks, and a place with the Lord's other servants in the hall for his meals, and one of the castle lasses to wed, if she so pleases.

And their children grow up among the castle children, having their lessons together, learning to read and write and count, and have advantages in life their father never dreamed of as a child. And then, when he turns twelve, his eldest lad surprises his parents by telling them that, "I'm going to be a *clerk* one day—just see if I ain't!"

It's the way of the world. Everyone wants to go straight, to be a respectable citizen. That's how his Thieves Guild mates looked at him now. Respectable. Honored. A companion of the queen, for all the gods' sakes! How could they *not* think he'd gone over to the other side? No, "not gone over"—*made it* to the other side. The lucky, clever bastard. He was what they all wanted, in their heart of hearts, to be themselves: Legit.

Which was something that Oller had no idea how to be.

Late afternoon sunlight, dimmed by the gloom of the back alley outside, filled the doorway as Qrysta walked in, and disappeared again as she closed the door behind her. The few customers saw her and went still. The Captain of the Queen's Guards, Her Majesty's personal bodyguard? *Here?*

Qrysta ignored their wary eyes and sat on the bench beside Oller. Little Guy woke up at once and shoved his head up between them, and Qrysta scratched his ears. His tail thumped against the leg of the table. He started his Mutt Mind Tricks at once, beaming *rat sausage … rat sausage … rat sausage* into Qrysta's unreceptive mind.

"You're a hard man to find," she said.

"When I want to be," Oller agreed.

"Buy me a drink?"

Oller's eyebrows shot up. "I *like* you, Qrysta! Anywhere else but here, my pleasure—but you know what the ale here's like."

She raised an eyebrow. "Never been in here before."

He handed her his tankard. "Smell first," he advised.

She did. "Ew!" she gasped, her nose wrinkling. "You actually *drink* that?"

Oller said, "There's an inn, back in Brig, where they proudly show you that they have *their own barrels*. 'Look,' the innkeeper will say, 'our own Special Reserve barrels, with our name on it, branded, by My Lord's brewer himself!' And Matty Brewer's ales are famous up our way—people come from all over for them. We *lived* for them while we were training, me and Daxx and Grell. And he's right, the barrels are branded all right, *The Goat's Head, Special Reserve,* in big letters. Only they're not filled with Matty's finest, but with even worse than this piss."

Qrysta grimaced. "You must have been desperate."

Oller chuckled. "Grateful, but …. Yeah. Didn't know no better, did I? See, what Matty puts into them is what in the trade is known as the arse-juice," he explained. "All the leavings from all the drip trays in the inns and taverns he supplies, all jugged up together and brought back to him, and he fills up the Goat's Head *own Special Reserve barrels* with the stuff. Half of which is sour, after being left out for gods know how long in pitchers, and such. He wouldn't want his proper customers getting that muck in a mix-up of barrels, so he brands the Goat's Head barrels in big letters. And he tops them up with a bit of new brewage, and sells his ales for the second time cheap to The Goat.

"Gods …" he tailed off, thinking back. "I used to count myself lucky when I had half a copper in my cly and could buy myself a pint of arse-juice! Only we wasn't allowed to call it that in The Goat, or we'd be banned; *Special Reserve* we had to name it. Once, when I was 'prentice to old Fingers, he'd come across some Southisle rum. Well, a big slug of that added in the arse-juice: Woof, *now* you're talking! Proper good, that was …!"

He was smiling, now, at the memory.

Little Guy sensed the change in his mood and locked onto a new target. *Rat sausage … rat sausage … rat sausage …*

"Oy, Bertha—got any more of them sausages?" Oller called out.

"'Ow many d'you want, love?"

"*Three … three … three …*"

"Three please, darling. Cheers."

"Coming up."

Oller turned to Qrysta. Little Guy's tail thumped the table leg.

"Why d'you want to find me, Qrys?" he asked.

"Take a look at this," she said, handing him the seal she'd removed from the letter that she'd found in the crate aboard the ghost ship.

Oller studied the strange creature on it thoughtfully. "I've seen this before," he said. "Somewhere …" He tried to think back.

31

Qrysta waited.

If Oller knew anything, she'd want to hear it. Bertha brought a bowl containing three steaming sausages over and put it on the table in front of Oller.

"Gravy, love?" she asked.

"Please, Berth."

Bertha poured lumpy, brown-black sludge over the sausages. The smell hit Qrysta like a punch in the nose. She did her best not to recoil.

"Same for you, dear?" Bertha asked.

"No," Qrysta said, managing a smile. "Thank you kindly."

"You just let me know if you change your mind," Bertha said. "More ale? Tankard for you, young lady?"

"We're fine, thanks Bertha," Oller said. "I'll just finish this, and we'll be off." He dropped a silver on the table. "Keep the change," he said.

Bertha beamed. "Thank'ee kindly, Oller. A true gent, you are, as I tell all who comes in here!"

Oller grunted. *True gent. Yeah, that was the damn trouble, wasn't it?! Me, Master Thief, and now a True Gent? Master Thief fits me like a glove; True Gent, I don't have a clue ...*

Bertha waddled off to her kitchen. As soon as her back was turned, Oller put the plate of sausages and gravy under the table. Sounds of happy slurping and growls of pleasure rose from below them. Little Guy always growled with pleasure when eating.

Oller returned his attention to the seal. "No, can't think where I saw this," he admitted, eventually. "I'm sure it was recently, though..."

"It is the seal of the Archon of the Occult Order of Varamaxes," Qrysta said. "I asked around at the College of Lore and Learning. Anyone I showed it to was *not* happy to see it. Didn't even want to touch it, some of them."

Oller said, "Varamaxes? Who are they when they're at home?"

"A once-powerful sorcerer-priest cult that held sway over a number of lands to the south. Lands that no one here that I've talked to seems to know anything much about. The cult leaders weren't kings, exactly, but they were the power behind a lot of thrones, the kings and queens who sat on them being pretty much puppets. And a dark power it was, they told me." She hesitated. "It bothered them to see it. They'd understood that it had died out. The kings and queens down there, in those realms, banded together with some priestly order to wipe it out."

"When was all this?" Oller wondered.

"A long time ago, two or three hundred years—and the cult hadn't been heard of in ages." She leaned forward, her expression growing serious. "Hearing *dark power* and all that, I popped over to the Guild of the Arcane Arts." She nodded at the seal in Oller's hand. "Got the same reaction from anyone I showed it to."

"Bad news," Oller could tell.

"Very," Qrysta said. "They're going to put their heads together, all the guildmasters. I got the feeling they'd rather talk to one of their own than to me."

Oller glanced up at her sharply. "Daxx?"

Qrysta nodded.

"Figures," Oller said. "If this was Thieves Guild business, they wouldn't talk to civilians."

Qrysta passed the letter she'd found aboard the ghost ship across to him. "And there's this," she said.

Oller took it, and inspected it, front and back. "Well now," he said. "Seal was here, I take it?" He pointed to the red patch from which Qrysta had sliced the wax.

Qrysta nodded and pointed at her name. "Addressed to me. Who this is from, who even knows my name, wherever that ship came from—well, I obviously have no way of knowing," she said. "But whoever wrote this clearly does, so, this is not some random thing. A ghost ship, full of ghosts, bringing a message for me, specifically, where I'd be bound to find it? And it's not, I think, for me alone. Turn it over."

Oller read the lines. "Four. You, me, Daxx and Grell, are you thinking?"

Qrysta nodded. "That sure makes four," she agreed.

"Where *are* those two anyway?!" Oller said. "Place is as dull as ditchwater without them around."

"I've no idea," Qrysta said, "but me receiving this makes me think they'll be back."

"I bloody hope so," Oller said.

"The GAA were very helpful. They stressed that we'd be needing a caster for sure, if this," she pointed to the letter he was holding, "was going to take us anywhere. Occult order; powerful sorcerer-priests of the unapproved kind?"

"Job for Daxxie!" Oller agreed, happily.

"That's what they thought. So, they sent him a pigeon."

"Oh," Oller said, "nice."

"They'll let me know if there's a reply. It certainly stinks of magic, as bad as Bertha's gravy. Ghost ship; bobbing phantoms; Tidemaster Pike frozen in midair, unmovable: We'd need more than blades against a power that can do that."

"Hang on," Oller said, as a thought hit him. "Dark power, occult order: Why are they writing to *you*?"

"Yes, I wondered that," Qrysta agreed. "Maybe because I'm Captain?"

Oller grunted and shook his head, trying to figure out where to start. He read the lines again. "Seems pretty simple, right?" he said. "Go and help this poor bugger. Whoever he is. That these Vara-whatses have captured."

"That's the way I'm reading it."

Oller thought it over. "Yeah," he said, eventually, "that's it, though, innit? Seems simple, but what way do we have of knowing that it is? I mean, how d'you know you can trust this?"

Qrysta's eyebrows rose, as she considered that. "Nope," she admitted. "I don't."

"Right," Oller agreed. "Only one way to find out."

"Yep," Qrysta said. "Which we can only do, according to this letter, when there are four of us."

"Well, I'm up for it! I'm bloody stifled here; couldn't half do with a change of scene. Not to mention a little action." A thought struck him—the thought of loot. "Never know what we might find along the way, eh?" He grinned.

Qrysta smiled back. "That we do not," she said. And then added, "I knew you'd be in."

"Are you kidding me? On the road again, you and me and Daxxie and Grell?! Nothing we'd like better, is there, little feller?"

Little Guy's tail went *thump, thump, thump* against the table leg in agreement.

Oller's face suddenly brightened. "I remember now! Him up at Aylsmoor! The necromancer—this seal. I seen it in his tom, when I was searching for the silver key!"

"His what?" Qrysta said, baffled.

"Sorry, thief talk—jewelry. *Tom*, short for tomfoolery, rhymes with joolery. In one of his desk drawers: Old bugger had a ring with a lump of jade in it, carved with this. Lovely jade too—top quality, worth

34

a packet. And he had a big brass seal of it too. With a bone handle. Probably best not to think whose bone. I itched to lift them; set me up for life, that piece of jade would, but I couldn't, of course. If he saw sign of thief, and I was still there, he'd have locked the place down and I'd be shut up in his walls now, screaming …"

The memory of what he'd seen in the necromancer's walls still unnerved him. Marnie had sent word that he had been dealt with. The Conclave of the GAA had raided his tower, with Coven riding shotgun above. The relics that had gone missing from sacred sites had been returned to them, and Marnie's friend released from her prolonged death-agony and laid to rest with full Coven rites. For, as they had all suspected, it had been the creator of the silver key, Marnie's lifelong friend, whom Oller had seen that night in the necromancer's wall. Or what was left of her. The necromancer himself, Marnie had informed them, with grim satisfaction, had been dispatched to join the subjects of his forbidden study beyond the grave.

Qrysta and Oller contemplated the connection with the message from the ghost ship.

They didn't like it at all.

3

The Sacrificial Orc

The Decapitator came for Grell on the fifth morning of his captivity. He was chained and manacled in a sweltering cell not much bigger than himself, with only bugs and the geckos that hunted them for company. The geckos were delightful little things. If he sat still, on the pile of straw that was his bed, they would come onto his arms, in little sharp motions, then freeze, hiding from their prey in plain sight. Occasionally, especially early in the evenings, they would chirrup at each other. The sound made Grell smile. It reminded him of home, back in Oz. He'd lived in a big city, but all his life had taken vacations up on the Gold Coast; first with family, and, when an adult, with friends, or alone. He'd always loved the geckos, and their swift, neat movements, and their chirrups. Here, in this cramped cell, they were the only things keeping him sane. Everything else was so utterly messed up that he didn't know where to start trying to work out what was going on.

Every dawn the captives were whipped out, chained to each other in a coffle at neck and ankle. They were made to stand in a line, facing the sun as it rose over the mountains beyond the brown, parched jungle, their eyes squinting and their skin burning, while the day's victims were paraded, and the drums beat, and the horns bellowed, and the priests chanted, and the Decapitator waited for them at the top of the pyramid, black stone knife in hand. His acolytes stood beside him with their ropes and spears and the gold tray for the heads. One by one the victims, garlanded, resigned, sobbing as like as not, their hands bound in front of them, mounted the stairs, stumbling, dragged and prodded by the acolytes, the drums and horns getting louder as they reached the killing platform by the altar. Spears jabbed them to their knees; hands held their shins to the floor; other hands pulled their arms forward; the Chief Acolyte took two handfuls of hair above the victim's ears and stretched their necks out, while another acolyte hauled back on the rope around the victim's waist. The Decapitator raised the stone knife—which was more like an axe-head without a handle—and slashed it down through the spine at the base of the victim's skull. The Chief Acolyte stepped aside with the head, which he placed carefully on the gold tray, while minions caught the victim's spurting lifeblood in gold basins and the horns blared the climax.

The drums and horns subsided, to a steady holding pattern, while the priests did what they did between victims, their crap ritual bullshit; and then, after a while, they were all in place for the next one, and the drums and horns got to work again. Grell had been watching the Decapitator kill man after woman after child, in his stupid feathered headdress, and gold armbands, and neck plates, his proud, *aren't-I-so-important* expression showing all his inferiors how seriously he took himself, and what a fine, so-important man he was, doing this fine, so-important job so magnificently. One thought, amid all the others that had churned around his head these last five days, had kept coming back to Grell.

I'm taking you with me, mate.

And now here he was, in his feathers and finery, standing outside Grell's cell, staring at him. Grell knew better than to stare back. From the moment he'd found himself there he'd played rope-a-dope. He'd done it convincingly. His captors thought he was weak, scared, cowardly. No threat at all. They'd been wary of him at first, because of his size. He was twice the weight of even the biggest of them and towered over them all. Or he would have done, if he'd stood upright; but he'd been working on his cringe, dropping a good two feet off his height. The acolytes opened his cell, fearless now that they knew him to be a coward and a weakling, no better than a whipped animal. They strode in, glaring down at him on his bed of straw. They jerked on the ropes that bound his arms, to get him upright, and Grell hastened unsteadily to his feet, where he crouched, trembling. He didn't say anything. He'd tried that, the first time he'd seen his captors, pleading for common ground. *Quetzalcoatl. Huitzilopochtli.* Nothing. *Chichen Itza.* A backhand across the face had shut him up. He hadn't tried again.

They brought him out of his cell to face the man who was going to kill him. Grell shuffled, respectfully, and cringed a low bow.

The Decapitator nodded. Half a dozen acolytes pulled and goaded, and Grell gave no resistance as he dropped to his knees. They stretched him between their ropes, the way he had seen them do with the other victims. Grell's skull, covered as it was with short, brown-gray Orc bristles, gave the Chief Acolyte nothing to hold onto but Grell's ears, which he grabbed and hauled on. Grell tested the tension in the various ropes that were holding him, remembering to whimper. *Yes,* he thought. *But not now. He doesn't have his ceremonial knife; he hasn't come to kill me.*

Sacrifice, Ken had said. Which meant that he'd kill me at the ritual altar, not in a cellblock; he's just come to size me up, to see if he thinks my neck will part like anyone else's. They've obviously never seen an Orc bef—

Grell flinched, and squealed, as he felt a blade bite into the back of his neck.

Just a small cut, but even so …

He hoped for the best and kept up the whimpering, and flinching, and feigning terror.

He heard grunts as they spoke in their guttural language.

He was prodded and hauled upright again.

The Decapitator looked him in the eyes and nodded.

Grell blinked, pathetically, in meek surrender, as he understood the message.

Tomorrow.

Okay, pal, Grell thought, as the cell door was bolted behind him again. *Tomorrow it is. I don't know where I'm going, but you're coming with me.*

If his captors had had metal weapons, Grell had decided, then he'd have stood no chance. Not because metal weapons were sharper than their black stone blades and spearheads—which were as sharp as any steel but niblun steel—but because it would then have meant that they had discovered iron smelting; in which case, they wouldn't stop at arrowheads and such. They'd have iron chains. And there was no way that even he could break halfway-decent iron links. He'd have had to die like all the others. But he was bound with rope. Tough rope, to be sure, but fiber, not iron. This fact was the single thing that had given him hope, and had led him to think up his simple, probably doomed, certainly suicidal plan. Yet again, he went over his checklist: Wrists bound tight in front of him; legs hobbled so that he could walk but not run; rope halter around his neck; rope belt around his waist—to all of which they would tomorrow attach longer ropes, to drag and guide and restrain and, finally, stretch him. They'd given up checking his leg and wrist bindings—he'd made sure not to touch them in any way. They'd have been wise, he knew, to have taken a closer look at his toenails and tusks. The toenails were more like claws than nails, long and sharp, and those tusks weren't just decoration. If wild boars could disembowel hunters with their tusks—well, he was looking forward to seeing what Orc tusks could do, given the chance. He would find out tomorrow. *Bring it.*

Sacrifice.

Thinking of that word, the word Ken had used, his mind went back, yet again, to Esmeralda's Victory Feast. He remembered Daxx getting up and leaving, following the flunkey who had whispered in his ear. As he passed, Daxx flashed him, and then Qrysta, secret grins: *Here we go, guys ...!* And he disappeared. Qrysta reminded Grell that Ken had said he'd see them again soon. And then, said "*Reward ...*"

There was more food, more scraps for Little Guy under the table, who always knew when to appear, and more ale. More singing, more laughter.

Then the flunkey reappearing, whispering in *his* ear, and him getting to his feet and following him out. Qrysta seeing him off with, *Have fun, Grello!* Him replying, *You too, mate. Bet my reward is better than yours!* Following the flunkey through the castle, to the door at the end of the corridor where the servant knocked. Ken's voice coming from the other side, "Enter."

The flunkey closing the door behind him, leaving them alone. Ken congratulating him on their task well completed.

And then the good news and the bad news.

He and his crew had, if only temporarily, saved the human race— though no one back on Earth had the slightest idea about it. So far, so good. Next up was their new task: To keep on keeping on, until they had completed the job.

No, Ken told him. *It wasn't over. Far from it.*

They had won the first round, which meant that The Opposition got the next move. Grell believed that he pretty much had his head around it. The easiest way to look at it was that they were in a game within a game. He and Qrysta and Daxx, and anyone else in that world, were three-dimensional, living players, with minds of their own, all of them making their own decisions and moves, while war games way above their pay grade played out where they always do: In the Situation Rooms, and the Diplomatic Missions, and Parlays and Conferences— where rank and filers like them never get to know what's going on.

Just keep your head down, and do your job, he figured.

It would all become clear in the end, Ken had promised. Just not at the beginning. *I'm not your Quest Giver, Grell. You'll only see me afterwards. I hope we meet again.*

Okay, if that's the way it is, then that's the way it is. He hadn't had a clue about anything when he'd landed in Jarnland. Nor had Daxx, or Qrysta. Gradually, the world had revealed itself, and the situations, and the possibilities, and the choices. And they'd made it through. There was no reason they couldn't do it again. It was what they were good at, after all.

And then the bombshell.

The next move the Opposition had made was a sacrifice.

No, Ken explained, *not like in chess, where you sacrifice one of your own pieces. You tell the other side to sacrifice one of theirs.*

Most of his questions about that tactic had led nowhere, into that void where answers were evasive. One question, though, had yielded a firm response.

Why me?

"I'm sorry," Ken replied, "but that's our choice."

The next thing he knew he was waking up in a stifling hot cell in a brown, bone-dry jungle, thirsty, confused, and bound hand and foot.

It had taken him several days to realize that Ken hadn't answered the question.

The cockerels crowed. A nice, random sound, of nature doing her thing. He didn't need to sleep, so he didn't mind. He lay back, on his bug-filled straw, calmly waiting for the day. It was, Grell felt, like those moments when the three of them conferred before an onslaught. They had a joke, the three of them that had made up their online gaming group, the Pilgrimz of Pain: *Onslaught, onslaughter, onslaughtest. Kill 'em all.* Or, if that clearly wasn't going to work, kill as many of the bastards as possible, and then hightail it out of Dodge *A S A effing P.* Many was the time the three of them had run whooping and laughing from angry mobs of heavily armed incompetents, and then dropped into stealth and watched them all rampaging off in the wrong direction.

He smiled at the memories. He would make Qrysta and Daxx proud. He wasn't going down without a fight; no way. These little feather-hatted farts had no idea what was about to hit them. How many could he kill, he wondered? Didn't matter. One was all that counted. That Decapitator. What a dick, to do what he does. Hacking people's heads off, in offering to some daft god?

Grell concentrated on what was going to happen. It was going to be sweet.

If brief, and then terminal.

No one fucks with the Pilgrimz of Pain. We don't die easy.

The tinkling of the bells on their arms and legs announced the arrival of the acolytes. Grell went into Hollywood mode. Fear, confusion, weakness, pleading. They roped him, jabbed, and hauled, and prodded; and, herded by them, he lurched out into the sun, blinking and whimpering. Inside, he could feel the Orc songs singing to him. *Here we go.* It was hard not to grin. *You're So Pathetic.* A fine day to die. A fine way to die, against all the odds, while smashing arrogant unsuspecting fuckwits.

It appeared that he would be the last, this morning—the Big Climax. The other eight victims were lined up ahead of him. He wasn't having that. They didn't deserve to die any more than he did. *Sow confusion,* he thought.

Panicking like the coward they all knew he was, he blundered to the front of the line. Once there, he wouldn't move, despite all the hauling and prodding. He just dropped to all fours and sobbed. He curled up in a ball. And, while the jabs and slaps rained in on him, he finished off the work he'd done in the night on his ropes. He'd been careful to disguise the bites and gouges he'd made in them. From now on it would be all action, and they wouldn't be looking closely at them.

He heard the sharp bark of the Decapitator's voice above him, and all the goading ceased. He would be first. He pretended to not know where he was or what he was doing. They herded him up the steps. He whimpered and staggered, twisting this way and that. They drove him to his knees and began the stretching. They couldn't manage it, because he froze tight like a rock, curled up into a ball again. While the acolytes heaved and hauled he bit through his wrist ropes, dug his toenails into his ankle ropes—and, when he felt them parting, exploded upright, roaring.

He grabbed two of the slowest acolytes, one in each hand, and flung them at the others, howling and exhaling his ferocious breath in their faces. Others fell, two of them off the killing platform and crashing to the ground below. The Decapitator, startled, backed off like the others, but Grell was on him before he could turn and run. Grell grabbed his throat and slammed his head back on the altar, breaking his neck on its edge. The Decapitator's head burst open like a melon. Archers charged up the steps, feathering him with arrows as he seized or slashed anyone within reach. Grell didn't mind. He'd been filled full of arrows before. He was going to die. Who cared about a few arrows?

He seized the Chief Acolyte by his hair and shoved him face-first into the Sacred Flame, where his head sizzled while the Chief Acolyte screamed. Grell held him there with one hand while smashing his underlings with the other. They were all gone within seconds, as the Chief Acolyte's screams turned to gasps, and then silence. All the while, the archers continued to feather him with arrows.

Yeah? Grell thought, and flung the half-cooked Chief Acolyte at them, and then hurled himself down the steps off the killing platform into their ranks. Archers scattered and fell, and Grell's claws and teeth and hands killed any within reach. To his surprise, his joy, he found that he was singing. He didn't know the words, or the tune, but his battle roar was a hymn to their death, and he gloried in it.

Bristling with arrows like a porcupine, he chased anyone who still had a bow in his hands. The crowds who always assembled—*had* to assemble?—scattered and ran for the cover of the jungle. With tooth and claw, Grell slashed the ropes that bound the other victims and, while they fled, turned to face the remaining enemy.

None remained.

Grell looked this way and that, panting, and bleeding.

No one.

Nothing.

Well then. Only one thing for it.

He trudged up the steps to the killing platform again, feeling, suddenly, very weary. And a bit prickled by all the arrows sticking out of him. Oh well. No gain without pain. He reached the top and looked down at the Decapitator. Crumpled like a rag doll. *No longer Mr. I'm-So-Important, are you, huh? What a wanker,* Grell thought. He lifted the dead body and dumped it on the altar. He picked up the black stone knife and cut the Decapitator's cock and balls off with it. Then he urinated over his dead, shocked, pulverized face. "Take this to your stupid gods," he grunted.

Then, as exhaustion hit him, he slumped to the ground.

Well, he thought. *I suppose that is that. And this is it. Full of arrows. Time to die. Took 'em all with me, though.*

Sitting there, cross-legged, head down, dying, he noticed something as his vision faded.

The stone squares that formed the floor of this platform …

There seemed to be …

… something in the middle of them, up here?

He hauled himself, wearily, painfully, over to take a look.

Shapes within a shape. Interesting ….

He felt around and found the recessed handholds. He inched himself to his feet, in a weight lifter's crouch, and hauled.

The trapdoor opened. Not wide enough for him to enter.

Feeling fainter by the moment, he shuffled across and hauled on the other half of the trapdoor. It was an effort that he nearly couldn't make. The slab crashed open onto the floor beside him. Everything swam before his eyes. Weak from lack of blood, he dropped forward into the black hole that he had opened.

"Well," Ken said, as Grell eventually opened his eyes, "I don't think Qrysta or Daxx could have managed that, do you?"

Grell was lying in a warm bed, in a proper hospital room, with real drips and readouts and medical equipment all around. Ken was beside him, his gills and fins and feelers waving happily.

Grell found focus on him. "Ha!" he said, weakly.

"Yup," Ken agreed.

"*Your* choice," Grell said, putting it all together.

"Seems we made the right one," Ken said.

"Strategy."

"That indeed."

"Sacrifice," Grell said, understanding, "didn't mean inevitable."

"You ever do any martial arts?" Ken asked.

"No. Why?"

"There's always a countermove to every move," Ken explained.

"There is? Then how do fights ever end?" Grell wondered.

"When one fighter makes a move that the other doesn't know how to counter. Our opponents chose sacrifice. Our counter was, we picked what *kind* of sacrifice."

"They didn't find your choice … fishy? Didn't realize I had a chance to survive?"

"Who knows? They didn't have a choice. It was one of you against a well-drilled, expert killing machine. Which we picked from the many available choices after running your stats and looking at the options. We believed we'd spotted a countermove. So: Well done, sir!" He paused, his fluttering appendages settling into what seemed like a shrug. "Of course, now they'll be really irritated, so your next steps are likely to be challenges. Well, what will be, will be, no? Keep your wits about you, and do your best to overcome them."

Grell looked at him and, even though most of the muscles in his body were on strike, managed a smile. "I'm beginning to understand this game."

Ken's gills and fins and feelers stopped waving.

"It's anything *but* a game, Grell!" he said. "It just resembles one. From where you're standing."

"Lying," Grell corrected; then added, "Did I get them all?"

"Yup," Ken said.

"Good." He closed his eyes and drifted off to sleep on a cloud of whatever was being infused into his arm.

He couldn't think where he was when he woke up. A big, soft bed—a four-poster no less—and crisp, clean bed linen, and a fresh breeze blowing in through the open window.

He sat up, gingerly, and looked around. He was in his guest room in Queen Esmeralda's wing of Mayport's Royal Palace.

Hah! he thought. *Thank all the gods that's over. Can't wait to tell the others.*

He flung back the covers and swung his legs out of bed.

Not a scar on them anywhere. They'd been full of arrows the last time he'd seen them. And he'd been exhausted, dying from loss of blood, hauling back the stones, and falling into the void below the killing platform.

Whereas now he felt full of life and energy.

He padded across to the clothes chest and looked out of the window above it. It was a lovely autumn afternoon. *Time to find Daxx and Qrysta and Oller.*

Some food would be nice. He wouldn't need his niblun plate armor. It would be too hot, anyway. He'd had enough of being too hot recently. And too thirsty. A mug of ale to go with that food? *Yeah. Several.*

Things were looking up. There were Orc-sized clothes ready for him in the chest. Leathers over linens. Excellent. And just about the best boots he'd ever seen. All of which fitted perfectly. The niblun cobblers and tailors must have measured him while he slept. *How long had that been?* he wondered. Long enough for his wounds to mend and for him to get his strength back.

The leather boots came up to his knees. He buckled them above the tops of his calves. They were as supple as dancing pumps, and as sturdy as his iron, hinged Orc sandals. He could hardly be sure, but it seemed that there were thin, flexible cables within them … he felt around, and decided that they were there indeed. If they were made of niblun steel, those cables would stop any blade. *Right*, he thought, *I'm keeping these. Can't wait to battle-test them.*

He strapped his battle-axe Fugg to his back and checked himself in the wall mirror. He didn't think he'd actually need Fugg today, but there was no way he was letting her out of his sight. He studied his reflection.

He grinned. *Yeah, that'll do nicely.*

Late afternoon sunlight, dimmed by the gloom of the back alley outside, filled the doorway as Grell flung the door of The Shanty open, and then disappeared as Grell's massive frame blocked the entrance. The Shanty's few customers jumped in alarm, and stared as he walked over to Oller and Qrysta.

"You're a hard man to find," he said to Oller.

Oller leaped to his feet grinning and whooping. "When I want to be. Good to see you, Grello!"

"You too, mate," Grell said; and, to Qrysta, "Hey Q. What's up?"

"Hello, gorgeous!" Qrysta said; and then, "A lot."

"Ale!" Grell called. "Ale for everyone, and keep it coming!"

"But not here," Oller said quickly, "Sorry, Bertha, we have to go—queen's business. Ale for all, indeed. Keep the change." He dropped a couple of silvers on the table, and headed out. Little Guy still hadn't finished greeting Grell, but, when Oller whistled, trotted off happily, wagging his bogbrush tail.

"Well," Oller said, as they settled down at a table in the back bar of The Bosun's Locker, "seems there are advantages to being Captain of the Royal Guard!"

Qrysta had quietly told the tavern keeper that they wished to be private, on Her Majesty's business, and *so the back bar was all theirs, yes ma'am—no one would be let in.* It had been empty anyway, apart from the landlord's fat old cat, which lay on the mantelpiece and gazed disdainfully down at Little Guy. Little Guy knew that he was under manners, so contented himself with a low growl, which the cat ignored. It closed its eyes and went back to sleep. Little Guy trotted under the table and sat, ready for action. He'd heard Grell use the word "food" several times. Mugs and a jug of ale arrived, and the door closed behind the departing tavernkeeper. Soon, delicious smells began wafting in from the kitchen.

"Gods!" Qrysta said, when Grell had finished his story.

Oller was, predictably, mystified.

"How'd you get there, then?" he asked.

Grell said, "Dunno, Ols. Magic?"

"Yeah, but ..."

"Got a better explanation?" Grell wondered.

"No. Magic sounds about right, but ..." Oller shrugged. "Well, what else could it be, eh? No, what I was thinking is, but *why?*"

"Some kind of test?" Qrysta suggested. "Like, maybe that's what Daxx is going through, which is why he isn't here? Come to think of it," a thought struck her, "maybe that's what the duel at Westwich was for me." She didn't sound convinced. But then, she couldn't tell Oller about Ken, that would *really* make no sense to him. Still, why had Daxx and Grell met Ken again, and she hadn't?

46

Well, that was up to Ken, not her. If he wanted to see her, or to explain, no doubt he would. He knew where to find her. What she didn't know was where to find Daxx.

Time, she decided, to change the subject.

"While you were off enjoying yourself," she said to Grell, "we had a visitor."

Grell, between mouthfuls of his second huge plate of excellent fish pie, said, "Yeah, 'enjoying myself'—*riiight*. Actually, the last bit was fun. What visitor?"

Qrysta told him about the ghost ship. And handed him the letter she'd found aboard it.

While Grell examined it, she filled him in on what else she'd found out, from the authorities at the College of Lore and Learning and the Guild of the Arcane Arts.

"Seems to me," Grell said, as he put what he couldn't finish of his fish pie under the table, "that we'll be on our way again when Daxxie gets back."

Slurping and happy growls came from below his knees.

"Yeah!" Oller said. "That's what I want to hear! Can't wait, me. I'm fed up of sitting around here twiddling my thumbs."

"Wonder where he's got to," Grell said. "Hope he didn't have to go through anything like I did."

4

The Reward, Part Two

A friendly voice greeted me as I stepped off the gangway into the cockpit of my very own spaceship. "Welcome aboard, Daxx. I'm Eydie, it's nice to meet you."

"It's nice to meet you too, Eydie. I must say, you are"—I looked around at the wondrous display of screens and dials and readouts—"amazing."

"Why, thank you. Ken said you might want to go for a little ride?"

"I most certainly do."

"All right, why don't you take a look around while I get us out of here."

"I don't need to strap in?"

"You'll hardly know I'm moving."

She was as good as her word. I felt no motion at all as I left to check out the living quarters. They could not have been more perfect. There was a galley to one side and a lounge area to the other, facing a long, transparent wall, through which I could see the world below dwindling into the distance and, within minutes, all the wonders of space. The view was mesmerizing. I stood there for a while, gazing out, letting my mind wander to what I was seeing. It was all out there, ahead of me, all around me, stars, planets, galaxies. I felt that I could go anywhere, do anything.

Alongside the spacewall an armory was filled with futuristic-looking ordnance. Eydie explained what all the weapons were as I examined them, one by one. They were as advanced and imaginative as anything I'd seen in any game. I couldn't wait to try them out and told her so.

"*Ummm* ... you're not quite up to handling even the simplest of these, Daxx."

That puzzled me. "So ... why do you have them?"

"For later. When you're more qualified."

I felt that I was being belittled. "I'm a quick learner."

"I believe you. And you should believe me."

I wasn't going to back down. "So tell me, how can I learn without hands-on experience?"

She took a moment to consider that.

"Okay, we'll do this your way. Seeing is believing, right? I'll head for the nearest level zero Beta planet. You wouldn't stand a chance anywhere more advanced. It'll be all the challenge you can handle: Countless horrible life-forms, from super-intelligent to thick as bricks, all guaranteed hostile."

That brought me up short. "Er... I don't want to actually *kill* anything. Drop in on some unsuspecting planet and start firing away at the inhabitants? I mean—what have they ever done to me?"

"It's a *Beta* planet. For beta testing. Bioforms, biowarfare, military hardware, and tactics. No amount of war games can teach you what combat can. And no creatures are killed in the process. Enraged, certainly. They don't appreciate people turning up and unloading on them, so they will fight back, and hard. If you manage to take one out ,it doesn't die, it enters stasis. And stands there, immobilized, glaring at you. And you'd better make yourself scarce before it wears off, because it'll be doubly enraged when it does, and they're not the forgiving kind."

"Oh, well, I suppose that's all right then."

"Let's hope so. I am a fully equipped A and E suite, so I'll be able to put you back together—as long as you still have a pulse."

She was, I thought, hardly being encouraging. "I thought you said no one dies."

"No *creatures* are killed," she corrected me. "They're a valuable resource. Any grunt who can't handle a little light combat is no good to an army. Weed out the losers and you know the survivors are competent."

"That's a little ... callous.

"It's *war*. So, if you're sure about this?"

I didn't know that I was sure any longer, but I didn't want to chicken out.

"Yes. As long as it's a little *light* combat, I'm game."

"Right, pick your rig-out and I'll program a few sims. You'll need the practice; it won't be long before you're on the ground and running a sortie for real. It's only 36.2 light-years away."

That had my head spinning. "Thirty-six years isn't long?"

"We'll be using Worm Drive. Forty, forty-five minutes."

"Ah," I said. "Dimensions?"

"Dimensions," she agreed.

Eydie initiated the Worm Jump. As I watched, everything beyond the spacewall blurred and then grayed out to black. Apart from that, there was little difference from how we'd been cruising before—but it felt different. The ship occasionally made tiny lurches under my feet, popping sideways and taking me with it, or pushing up or dropping down an inch or two. It felt like standing on a rug with a mind of its own.

Less than an hour later I was in the hold putting on my helmet. It automatically fused itself to my battlesuit. The Heads-Up Display in my visor told me everything I needed to know about every weapon I was taking with me. Shift, I could tell all too surely from the grumpiness coming from her up my arm, did not appreciate being left behind. *I'll be fine*, I assured her. *Don't worry about me.*

Worrying about you is my job! she shot back.

I put her down on the floor of the hold. I didn't want to argue with her. We were a team. We worked in harmony. I knew that I'd hurt her feelings. But I already knew what she could do. It was these new weapons that I needed to learn how to handle.

Eydie had thrown a number of different sims at me in my 3D training runs, offering advice as I selected my rig-out. My main would be a Variable Assault Rifle. It didn't hit as hard as the Plasma Cannon but was a lot more maneuverable, and, as its name suggests, was adaptable, and could swiftly change modes, from bullets to bombs to beams. I had a Stingray pistol on each hip, a belt full of various kinds of grenade, and a rocket launcher on my back.

All weaponry was sync'd to my battlesuit and would respond instantly to voice command, so I wouldn't have to fiddle with switches.

Eydie told me I should assume that everything out there would attack on sight, but that, also, this would be a good opportunity to work on my stealth. If they didn't see me, I didn't have to open fire—which would give my position away and might attract unwanted attention. The battlesuit would camouflage itself to blend into whatever terrain I was on and would also keep an eye on my six, so nothing could jump me from behind. A rear view was permanently displayed in a corner of my Heads-Up Display.

Eydie would keep me continually informed, and tracked, and a map relating her position to mine would reveal itself as I progressed. She had told me on no account to go more than a mile from where she landed. It sounded as if I'd get all the action I could handle well before I got that far. We'd see.

The gunsled looked like a cross between a jet-ski and a hoverboard. Eydie had run me through a tutorial on how to handle it on a sim in the cockpit, as we descended, cloaked, to the Beta planet's surface. I settled into its saddle, and it felt like an old friend already.

"Suggestions?" I said.

In my helmet speakers, Eydie said, "Anywhere but south. Group of Fifteens that way."

"*Fifteens?!* Gods …!" The life-forms on Beta planets had names, but no one used them in combat. All that mattered was their level, and their methods of attack and defense. Eydie had drawn my attention to the C-o-S stat on the readout that explained all about each of them. C-o-S stood, she informed me, for Chance of Survival. Against anything above a Three, I was less than even money—a Four or above, I'd be a big underdog. Fifteens would cream me in seconds.

As the ship's hold opened and the gunsled lowered itself to the ground, I checked the beings that were listed in the Fifteen category. A swarm of fast, tiny, ferocious flying things with drills instead of beaks. The bastard offspring of a camel and a gorilla. A tanklike brute resembling a snowplow with massive kangaroo legs, and antlers that fired live bugs that ate their way into anything they hit. Some kind of leather-winged squid, marked *highly intelligent and armed to the teeth.*

Yes, I thought. *Let's avoid those.*

I turned the gunsled north and opened the throttle. We were flying in stealth, so it was a silent, gentle acceleration rather than the bowel-loosening slam of g-force that the gunsled would unleash in rocket mode.

Even so it gained speed fast. Eydie kept me updated every step of the way, talking quietly in my ear, while I, in concert with my battlesuit, scanned the terrain. Little colored dots flashed on my HUD to indicate life-forms in the vicinity. Blue, which meant Ones; green, Twos, both fine; a few yellow Threes. Nothing orange or red, Fours or above. I banked the gunsled left towards a lone blue and throttled back as I neared it. When I was within a hundred yards of it, I slid off and directed the gunsled to circle around and flank it while I moved in on foot.

Well, if that thing was a blue, I didn't want to be around to tangle a green. I had it covered on one side, the gunsled on the other. It had no idea either of us were coming in on it in a pincer movement—and when it did find out, as the gunsled and I opened fire on it simultaneously, it howled with fury and attacked, seemingly in both directions at once, smashing the gunsled into the middle of a swamp with one horrendous bronco kick, and then turning its attention on me. Imagine a truck-sized centaur with the head of a triceratops, massive arms ending in fists like hammers, and the fury of a nest of hornets. It charged at me, bellowing, the slugs from my VAR bouncing harmlessly off its massive headshield. And, gathering speed with every step as it charged, it lowered its nozzle and hosed me.

A wall of acidic sludge the consistency of oatmeal splattered into me, knocking me backwards into a large bush. The bush took exception to having me fired into it. It immediately started thrashing a dozen limbs at me, while a dozen others grabbed and shoved and trussed me. The oatmeal sludge, on contact with its target—me—instantly solidified into mud that contracted around me like an anaconda. From the waist up, I was glued inside a rancid prison, being pummeled black and blue by a demented shrubbery. Meanwhile, the raging One attempted to fight its way into the bush to pulverize me. That, thank the gods, distracted the bush, which turned its attention too its new assailant. I could neither see nor fire my VAR, as its trigger was now encased in concrete. I could, thanks to my battlesuit, still breathe. And scream for help.

I'd be dead if it hadn't been for Eydie. She righted the gunsled and aimed it at the One, Klaxon blaring and machine guns blazing. The One, incensed at the challenge, turned on it. Eydie yelled "Roll!" at me, and I was on my belly and rolling for my life while the gunsled zipped around, luring the One away from me.

52

I kept rolling, blinded, trussed, feeling five times my normal weight, and, somehow, made my way out of the bush at ground level before the brute gave up its chase of the gunsled and returned its attention to me. It closed in on me in seconds, snarling and shrieking, its hooves and fists smashing the ground where I had been a split second earlier. I scrambled backwards, turned onto all fours, rolled again when Eydie told me to, just in time to avoid a pounding, then got to my feet and ran. Eydie guided me with calm *lefts* and *rights* and *jumps,* the damn thing charging after me screaming blue murder while Eydie distracted it by buzzing the gunsled around it. Suddenly I was in the air, as my battlesuit sync'd with the gunsled to jump me onboard, and we were off and away, full speed ahead and stealth be buggered.

Eydie piloted it remotely as I clung on, still blinded by congealed muck. All I could see was the HUD readout on the inside of my visor, as we wove in and out of trees and clumps of foliage and gods knew what all else, me clinging on for dear life, and all the time the blasted One—*One!!*—chasing me like a rhinoceros charging an idiot tourist. Which is what I felt like as we shot into the ship's hold, and the bay doors slammed shut below us while the frenzied creature shook and battered the ship, roaring. Eydie got us airborne within seconds, and I collapsed off the gunsled and lay there, on the floor of the hold, heaving for breath.

Eventually, when I could sit up, Eydie said, "I told you that you should believe me."

I had no reply. Weakly, I groped for Shift, raised her, and cast all the Heals she could manage over myself. As her green bubble bloomed around me and her reviving warmth poured into me, I felt something else coming from her, as plain as if she'd been laughing out loud. *Okay,* I admitted. *You were right.*

Aren't I always?

I didn't bother to answer. We both knew who had won that round. I hauled myself to my feet. The sludge encasing me was wearing off, and I was able to reach up and take off my helmet. I unpeeled the battlesuit and tottered through into the cockpit, where I dropped into the pilot's chair. "Can you clean this all up?" I said.

"Just throw it in the laundry chute. So, where next?"

Before I could reply, there was a muffled BANG as a whirling ball of feathers trailing black smoke shot out of a small compartment in the lower level of the console and flew around the cabin, screeching, firing off shards of ice and bolts of lightning and multicolored sparks, like a fireworks show in a mad magician's aviary.

"FAAAAARK!!" it shrieked, whatever it was—it was moving too fast to make out, not to mention bouncing off walls and floor and console and screen. Its squawks filled the air, along with the stench of burning feathers, and blobs of some kind of white stuff that splattered against everything and smelled like an explosion in a toilet.

"AAAH! GAAAAHHH! FAAARK!! GODS, WHAT IN THE FUCKING FUCK. *AAARGH*, I'M ON FIRE. SHIIIIIIT, WATER, WATER!!! FAAAAARK, I'M"—*zzzappp!*—"AAAHHGGZZ!!!, LIGHTNING, I'VE BEEN HIT BY LIGHTNING! I CAN'T FEEL MY LEGS! *GAAAH*, SHIT, MY WINGS ARE FROZEN! WHERE ARE MY—"

Unable to feel its wings, the pigeon—for such, I could now see, it was—smacked into the spacescreen and dropped onto the instrument panel. It lay there, legs up, sparking, sizzling, smoldering, snorting icicles from its nostrils, and emitting more bursts of that malodorous white stuff from its other end. Apart from that, it didn't move.

Was it dead? I reached out and put my hand on it to see if there was a pulse—and immediately wished I hadn't. My hand froze and burned simultaneously, while electric shocks jolted into my arm. I jerked away, waving my frazzled hand, then hugging it under my armpit, and thought, *Well, there's no way anything could live through that.*

I was wrong. Eydie gently hosed it with analgesic mist from her circulation system, and, after a few final pops and flashes and snowflakes, what remained of it actually resembled about 70 percent of a singed, shocked, and flash-frozen pigeon. The other 30 percent was scattered about the cabin, some of it still fluttering gently to the floor. Suddenly, the pigeon coughed, twitched, jerked spasmodically a couple of times, twisted around, and lurched to its feet. It stood there, swaying, staring around with wide, horrified eyes that seemed bigger than its head.

It opened its beak, croaked, "What the … what the …" tottered a couple of steps, and unleashed a cataract of steaming, buff-colored puke onto the instrument panel.

It swallowed. Belched. Puked briefly again; hiccupped, saw me.

"Message for Daxx," it gasped, "and there'd better not be a fucking reply!"

"What's the message?" I asked.

"Qrysta says come at once," the pigeon said.

"That's it?"

"Yeah, I know! *All that* for five lousy words—what the fuck *was* that anyway?! Never known anything like it …"

I didn't think it would mean much to the pigeon, but I thought it deserved an answer after what had plainly been a bumpy ride. "It's called a Worm Jump," I said.

"Huh? Worms don't *jump*!"

"This one does," I said.

"Well, where is the bastard? I'll have him! No fucking worm's gonna do that to me and live!" The pigeon stared around the room furiously, looking for its tormentor.

"It … jumped away," I said, managing not to smile.

The pigeon turned its angry glare on me. "Fucking coward!" it muttered. It tottered a couple of more steps, swayed, groaned. "I need to lie down," it announced, and dropped like a stone, its eyelids slowly closing. I picked it up and put it in the compartment from which it had made its surprising entrance. It was a compartment that clearly was, I saw as I looked at it more closely, a pigeonhole.

"Well," I said, "there's your answer, Eydie. Back to where we started."

"You got it. I suggest a shower and a rest in the massage pod."

Eydie drifted into the spacedock under cloak, silently. We didn't want to scare the locals. The transparent dome opened as we approached and closed above us as we settled onto the stone-flagged floor. The torches on the cavern walls were still burning, their flames throwing a warm, familiar light.

Eydie powered down and lowered the gangway.

I said, "Do you just wait here? Till I turn up again?"

"Yes," she said.

"You'll be safe? I mean, no one can steal you, or anything?"

"I'm sync'd to you, Daxx. Only you can fly me. Anyway, no one here can find me, because this dock isn't exactly a part of Mayport Castle, even though that's how you get in and out. And only you can open the doors."

"Glad to hear it." I put on my niblun-crafted cloak and slung Shift on my back. It felt good to be back in my familiar gear.

A thought struck me. "Can I take the gunsled? The VAR, Stingrays?"

"That would cause a stir, huh? I'm afraid not, Daxx. That tech is incompatible with this environment."

"Oh," I said. "Pity."

She didn't answer.

"See you later, then," I said.

"I'll be here."

I walked down into the cavern, and Eydie raised the gangway behind me. She settled into sleep mode, the floor below her beginning to sink as it took her back down into her hangar. The heels of my niblun boots rang on the stone flags as I crossed to the door, the shadows thrown by the torches in their sconces crossing and uncrossing in front of me.

I touched the wall by the door, as I'd see Ken do when he'd brought me in there. The door opened, and I was in the first of the corridors that would take me back into the castle itself. As before, it all looked like any other part of Mayport Castle. As before, it was empty. No people, no sounds of people. Eventually, after climbing many stairs, and crossing halls and galleries and courtyards, I came to the chamber where Ken had been waiting for me.

He wasn't there. I wasn't expecting him to be. I checked the room thoroughly, to see if he'd left anything for me. He hadn't, as far as I could see. I wondered if Oller would have been able to spot something.

Oller. It would be good to see him and the others again.

As soon as I opened the door at the far end of the chamber I heard sounds of life. Voices, feet walking and running, the distant, busy kitchens. I kept going, towards the Great Hall. Servants hurried past in all directions, laden with trays, ignoring me. I heard a roar of laughter, and the clattering of pitchers and trenchers and mugs and glasses, and the hum of voices, getting louder as I got closer to the hall. I was eager to confer with the others, to find out what their rewards had been. I was happy. I was back where I belonged.

I was hardly into the hall before I was noticed. The tone in the voices changed abruptly. Heads turned to me, the volume rising, shouts of *there* and *look* and *he's back!* Something brown and hairy, and—I soon saw—a lot plumper than I remembered, shot out from under a table and leaped at me, yelping and wagging. Then it was applause, and cheers, and tankards raised in my direction, and Oller and Qrysta and

Grell surrounding me and high-fiving, and pumping my hand, and slapping me on the back and laughing, and demanding where in all hells I'd been all this time?!

I said, "What do you mean 'all this time,' it's only been a couple of hours."

They stopped pumping and slapping and stared at me.

"You've been gone over a month, Daxx," Qrysta said.

"What?" I said. "The feast's still going on."

"This is the *Coronation Feast*, mate," Grell said. "Took time to organize. People had to come from all over the realm for it. You missed a hell of a show."

I looked around; and saw that, indeed, the assembly was different, and that all were dressed in their finery.

"Ah. Yes, well. I'll explain later. I'd better pay my respects ..."

I headed off towards Their Majesties, thinking, *A month? Well, I suppose that's dimensions for you.* I got a huge smile from co-Queen Esmeralda when she jumped down from the High Table to give me a hug, and a regal inclination of his head from old co-King Wyllard the Seventh. They were both wearing their new, Neva-crafted halfcrowns. Esmeralda looked, if possible, even more radiant than ever. She was off to Downbury soon, she told me, to take her seat there.

"Qrysta wanted to go with me, as Captain of my Guard, but I told her that she had a ghost ship to sort out first."

I had no idea what she was talking about. "A what?"

"You'll see. We believe it's for you and the others. I'll be fine—half the Orcs have volunteered to escort me. Well, they *all* did; but some were needed back at their strongholds, obviously, so the tribes drew lots, and half of each are my new army."

"I can't imagine anyone messing with them," I said, and she laughed. "Are you okay? About going ... there?"

Her smile faded. "Well, it's my job. We're all putting the realm to rights—you just ask Qrysta what she's been up to."

I shot an enquiring look at Qrysta, who smiled back. "Just a little dancing, Daxxie."

I smiled back. I could guess what kind of dancing. Sword-dancing—the kind she did better than anyone. "And I do want to help," Esmeralda continued. "I'd rather not go, obviously, because .... Well, you saw what it's like, on our way up from the Undergrounds."

I had. A dark, gloomy place, a haunt of sorrow and shadow. I couldn't imagine living there. It would drain the joy out of anyone. I could see the demands of her new responsibility weighing on her.

But, I thought, *Perhaps, this radiant girl is the right person for the job. The loveliest life there ever was or ever would be.* Why should she not be just what that sad city needs?

"I'm sure you'll sort it out in no time," I said, to encourage her. She was, after all, only sixteen.

She managed a smile, and nodded. "The murk's gone," she said, "that used to hang over it. They're no longer the Darklands. So ... we'll see." She brightened, and added, "And you'll come and see me there when you get back."

"Get back? Where from?"

"Wherever you four are going. Safe journey, and good luck!"

"You too," I said, still baffled by *going*. I remembered who she was, now, and added, "Your Majesty."

She laid her hand on my arm and said, quietly, "I prefer *my friend*."

Commandant Bastard raised his glass to me with a nod, which I returned with a half salute and a bow. And then it was food, and drink, and conversation, and catching up; and it was quite clear from what Qrysta and Grell and I were *not* saying that most of the catching up between the three of us would have to wait until we were alone.

I'd never felt better. My people. My friends. My home.

Though, from what Qrysta told me about the ghost ship, it seemed that we'd be leaving soon enough.

"Two things any leader can do," Commandant Bastard said, "whether he's a lance-jack leading a patrol or a lord leading his army: Prepare, and run a happy ship. Any idiot can do those. It's surprising how few do, though."

It was the next morning. We'd sought him out, in his quarters above the guard room, and fine quarters they were too. We sat around a roaring fire, for the day was cold, while Little Guy had his head on Commandant Bastard's lap, staring at him and hoping for biscuits. "Happy soldiers will follow you, fight for you," he said, stroking Little Guy's head. "They'll take pride in who they are and who they're following. Miserable ones will desert. Or stab you in the back and *then* desert. Prepare, Pay, Pride. Remember them three words, and you'll think before you act."

"So how," Qrysta said, "would you prepare for this?"

Commandant Bastard read the verse on the letter that she'd found in the crate below Tidemaster Pike.

"Seeing as I can't make head nor tail of this," he said, "I'd look at what else I can see."

Curious, she asked, "What else can you see?"

"That ship. You took a good look at her?"

Qrysta frowned. "I could take a better," she realized. "My concern was Pike, getting her to safety."

"Tell us what you noticed," he suggested.

"Sails were rags. Deck was dirty."

"Lines?"

"Gray."

"Frayed?"

Qrysta thought back, frowning. Eventually, she said, "No."

"Below decks?"

"Holds. Full of cargo. Barrels, chests, vegetables hanging from the rafters, and such."

"Rotten?"

Qrysta examined her memory. "No."

"And this," Commandant Bastard said, "is a ship with no living souls on it? Just ghosts, as you call them."

"Yes."

"Then tell me, Captain," he said, "what use do ghosts have for fresh vegetables?"

Qrysta had no answer.

"And barrels, and chests?"

She said, "None, that I can see."

"Seems to me, then," Commandant Bastard said, "this ship o' yours may be crewed by the dead but is provisioned for the living."

We exchanged glances.

"Lines nice and whole, ready for running out the sheets. Seems to me," he continued, "it's come to Mayport for a purpose."

I said, "To deliver the message?"

"That," he replied, "and to *take* the reply."

We waited.

He didn't elaborate.

Grell saw the answer first. "The reply being us."

Commandant Bastard nodded. "So, if you intend to take that reply, to the sender, my advice is, *prepare.* Everything you need, everything you can think of. Get all the knowledge you can, from them as know. Because this," he picked up the seal that Qrysta had separated from the letter, "is trouble."

Qrysta said, "You know it?"

Commandant Bastard nodded, studying the seal. "Twenty-five or more years ago, now," he said. "Old Birdbeak, we called him. Anytime we saw this sign, we knew there was trouble ahead. Meant to have been wiped out, him and his lot were, but whoever had done the wiping did a poor job of it. The local king knew this only too well, them spreading their grip across his realm again. So, he hired us to take care o' things. I was no more'n a lance-jack when we set out north into the Great Waste, but we lost so many I was serjeant by the end of it."

He shook his head and sighed, remembering. "Gods, it was a mess. We cleared out a couple of nests of them, on the way, and were beginning to think it would be easy, and were planning how to spend the bounties that the king had promised us. Well. A nest is one thing—no more'n a picket really. An HQ of the buggers, that's a different matter. They wouldn't die, see? Even those as were dead before they came at us. Bad magic; the worst. Powerful. Our own casters were babes by comparison. Good as useless. They couldn't even scry out what we was walking blindly into.

"We knew where the temple was; everyone did. The lands had been ruled from there for ages, before the old alliances drove them back. Sealed it up, they did, the old kings and queens. But if they'd thought that had finished the job, we found out the hard way they was wrong. A long way into the desert it was, far to the north, and day after day of a hard, dry march we had to get there. Then deep down into the earth, the way such cults always bury themselves away, I've found. Nearer to whichever hell they serve, is how I see it. And we walked into it, just to check it was empty, like we'd been led to expect.

"Our commanders didn't bother with scouts. There was no sign of anything living. Of course, as it can be in such cases, it wasn't 'anything living' that was the problem. We began to feel more and more uneasy the deeper we went. The men were on edge, not talking, not liking the smell of the place. The seal, when we came to it, was different to what you might expect: Not a walled-up door with our Wards on it, keeping them out. It was a rift. The Sorc who'd done the sealing, back in the long ago, did it by blasting a crack into the floor, right down to the fires of that hell I mentioned, thirty feet wide at its narrowest. Looking down into that spouting, boiling rock, I remember thinking, whatever's across that needs to stay there. And we'd stay this side of it, if we have any sense.

"We didn't. Our sappers set up the winches and pulleys and lowered two plank bridges across, with rope handholds. And over we went and felt both relieved and worried when we made it over the fire trench to the other side. Where we formed up, and moved out, and began to breathe easier after a while, as time passed, and nothing changed, and nothing happened.

"And then there was light ahead. We thought, well, another crack in the earth, and that light is the fires of the hell again. It wasn't. It was the temple, lit from all sides and above, and as tall as Rushtoun Castle, way underground but never touching the roof of that chamber. And front and center, a great statue of Old Birdbeak, just as he is on yon seal, rearing and roaring—only in each of his front claws, a writhing body, screaming in pain.

"And we came in, and looked around, and followed our captains; and even though the place was deserted, we was all as taut as bowstrings. Even so, our thoughts turned to loot, as soldiers' minds do in such places, deserted or no. Could be some fine old treasures down here, we thought. And we headed on; and as the first of us passed the statue, blow me if it didn't let out a screech such as I never heard, and hope never to hear again. And then they were on us, from all sides, pouring out of doors and crypts and tunnels ..."

Commandant Bastard tailed off.

"What happened?" Qrysta prompted.

"We ran."

We were shocked.

We couldn't imagine Commandant Bastard running from anything, alive or dead.

"*Feared,* we was," he said. "Never knew terror like it, up through our legs and turning our guts to water. Men were throwing their arms and armor away to run faster, never a thought of standing and fighting.

You *couldn't* think. It was a nightmare, us all scrambling over each other, and shoving past each other up the tunnel again, all you could think of was: The bridges, have to get to the bridges!"

Jack Blunt shifted on his seat, uncomfortable with what he was about to tell us. "The which we'd never have made, and I wouldn't be sat here nice and cozy talking to you now, if it hadn't been for the bravest man I ever saw. Ever had the privilege to follow. Young 'un, he were; not much more'n twenty, third son of some Norhaven knight, making his way in the world. He stood, and turned, and hefted his shield, and roared orders, and we ran past him, thinking: That's right, son, you just hold them horrors off while we make the bridges. And the next thing we knew, we'd turned, a few of us, and were beside him, forming a wall. And most others ran through and away, and some others stopped and stood with us. And blow me down if we didn't block the tunnel, edge to edge, and stage as fine a fighting retreat as you'll ever see. Men were going down all around, as the hordes of living corpses swarmed us, biting and slashing and tearing, and us hacking away as best we could.

"And we made it to the bridges, backing up slow and steady behind our shields, thanks to our young captain; and those of us left with stripes on our sleeves herded our men across. But the more that crossed, of course, meant the fewer left to hold the bridgehead."

He paused and shook his grizzled head. "I am ashamed to say I did not disobey his order to cross once our men had made it. Many's the time I've wished I died alongside of him. Instead, what died of me that day was my pride."

He filled his lungs with a deep breath, held it, and, deflating, sighed. "Our sappers flung the first bridge off into the flames, and the few of us still with the lad captain backed towards t'other, shields locked, always facing the foe, him in the middle, sword working tirelessly. And then he orders us in from the wings, and the screaming corpses came in after them to get at us, and one by one we made it across, till there was just the two of us …"

Commandant Bastard stopped.

None of us listening moved.

"And then this young sprig yells at me, 'Get across that bridge, serjeant, *now*, and that's an order!'" His voice faltered. He was looking at the tabletop, but not seeing it.

Little Guy, on his lap, sensing his discomfort, wagged his tail.

Commandant Bastard ruffled Little Guy's ears.

We all waited, suspended in the moment.

"An order I was never more pleased nor more sorry to hear," Commandant Bastard admitted. " 'I'm behind you, never you worry, Jack Blunt!' he shouted, and I did as I was told, and turned, and … *ran* … "

He faltered, and then swallowed, and continued. "And arms hauled me off the other end of the bridge as the lad kicked his end aside, into the abyss, and turned back to his killing work as our sappers cut the ropes. And then he was swarmed, and gone, falling with his arms around a group of them fiends, taking them with him. Others fell both sides of him, the bridge and bodies plunging into the boiling fires of that hell.

"There was still a mob of them over there, leaping and howling at us across the chasm. Still there, I've no doubt. We didn't finish the job. Not by a long chalk."

He fell silent.

None of us knew what to say.

Commandant Bastard stroked Little Guy's head thoughtfully. He was still, we knew, remembering his shame.

Qrysta had the right response. She said, simply, "Thank you, Commandant."

He glanced at her sharply, frowning.

Their eyes locked.

He studied her and eventually nodded.

We each came, in our own time, to understand what Qrysta had understood.

We'd all heard soldiers boast. They do it all the time. They rarely tell of their failures. It takes a brave man to own himself a coward. Which is a name no one in the realm would dare give Commandant Bastard.

5

Looking Back, Looking Forwards

On our way through Mayport Castle that afternoon, Grell and Qrysta filled me in on what they'd been up to. *Jeez,* I thought, when I heard what Grell had been through: He's *really* going to be annoyed with me when he sees what I got as my reward …

I led them into and out of the chamber where I'd met Ken, and all the way down through all those courtyards, and corridors, and hall-ways, to the door to the cavern, where we halted. They kept asking where we were going, and what was going on, but they weren't going to get anything out of me. All I said was, "You'll see."

I put my hand to the stone panel by the door. It slid open and we went inside. Looking up, and around—hesitant, disbelieving, jaws dropping—they took in the huge spacedock, the stone-flagged floor, the torches flickering on the walls, the transparent dome, and the bright sky above. They had not expected anything like this. I touched the controls in the wall, where Ken had poked his … poker. The floor began to split. Lights shone up from below as my spaceship rose from her underground hangar.

I watched them, enjoying their astonishment.

Qrysta was the first to find her voice. She whispered "Are, you, *kidding me …*??!"

I said, casually, "Nope."

"You get *this*," Grell growled, "and I nearly get my damn head cut off by some dickwit cultist?!"

"Yup."

He turned and glared at me.

I shrugged, smirking. "You lived."

"Yeah," he snarled, "while you were cruising around space enjoying yourself!"

"Ah," I said, my smirk disappearing.

I knew what they were about to see, and the shit they'd be joyously giving me.

Oh well. I'd just have to grin and bear it.

"Well, as to that …" I said, "come with me."

Once we were all aboard, I got Eydie to play her vids of my ignominious failure on the Beta planet. She'd had drones above and around me recording everything and had cut it all together with POV shots from cameras in my battlesuit. Qrysta and Grell, laughing their heads off, insisted on watching it several times. *And* on freeze-framing the most humiliating parts. They particularly loved the splattering volley from the One's hosepipe, which blinded me and gummed me into an oatmeal-sludge-bound statue. They couldn't get enough of it.

"Looks like you could've used a little help there, Daxxie!" Grell managed, when he'd stopped hooting with laugher.

"No kidding," I agreed, ruefully. "I was in way over my head. I doubt if even Shift could have helped me." A *thump* on my back told me that my battlestaff begged to differ.

Eventually, they stopped ribbing me and we got down to business. Yes, we could all use Eydie and head off into the wide blue yonder, leaving this rock behind us. No, it would be a bad idea to do that for a while, because … well, look at how pathetically I did on a *zero*-level Beta planet. Even with three of us—were we up to it? We'd have to think not. We all wanted to get up there and play among the stars, but until we were good enough to deal with what we might find up there, maybe it would be wise not to bite off more than we could chew.

We were good at what we did, and one thing we knew was that you never want to be overmatched. Be smart. Are we noobs or champions? Exactly. We *were* champions—as a result of which we are now noobs, pretty much. Let's not get ahead of ourselves.

Meanwhile: From what Commandant Bastard had told us, it seemed that our *little local difficulty* would be challenge enough.

Old Birdbeak.

The Archon of the Cult of Varamaxes …

Prepare, he'd told us.

Well, we knew we'd definitely be doing that before we headed off. This wasn't our first rodeo. We'd be ready.

Before we took our next steps, though, I needed to run something by them.

"I have a theory," I said.

Grell said, "Oh, ah?"

I said, "It's not so much to do with what comes next—although, of course, in a way it is, because it will inform the way we proceed—it's more about the way we look at things."

Qrysta said "Meaning?"

"Meaning *think outside the box.* Here's my thought: You know what we always complained about? And not just us three, but every gamer? In every game? That there are only two kinds of quest?"

"Kill or FedEx," Grell said.

"Exactly. Go kill something, or go fetch something. That's the limitation of every game. It's like … you hear people saying about movies, or books, that there are only five stories, or seven stories, or whatever— that, if you boil them down, they reduce to the same few ideas. Which, by the way, is irrelevant, because there are an infinite number of *plots,* so saying there are only x number of stories is like saying there are only twelve notes, so that's all the music there'll ever be."

Qrysta said, frowning, "What's the difference?"

I said, remembering how I'd taught my pupils on this very point, "Stories are emotional, general, and constant. Plots are physical, specific, and ever-changing. The Lord of the Rings is, from first page to last, always the story of The Little Guy with the Big Burden, *aka,* The Reluctant Hero.

"What makes it unique is that it is the plot of *this specific* little guy, Frodo, with this *specific* challenge—head off against overwhelming odds and throw this evil ring into the Crack of Doom—who at one moment is *here,* and later on *there,* from page to page, in all sorts of predicaments doing *different* things, facing different challenges and in different physical states. We don't know what our story is. No one ever really does. And we certainly don't know the plot we're going to go through. But here's what's different from anything we've ever done before: We're not limited by human tech, and human devs. No one has set us boundaries that we can see or understand. So, if we think, 'Well, is this a Kill Quest or a Fetch Quest?' we're behind the eight ball. It's a *'What the Fuck is This Quest?* Quest'."

They thought about that.

Grell said, "How does that help us?"

I said, "By making us think differently."

I watched them puzzling it out.

"Gods, guys!" I said, "Think about it. Didn't we all wonder what it would *really* be like, to *really* be these avatars we built for ourselves, in a world like what we ran in together, in our games? For real? And now, here we are. Well? We have to stop looking for the rules. The limits. The edges. Guidance. *There isn't any.* We're in a *'What the Fuck is This Quest?* Quest.' We're not used to that. We're used to feeling safe. You die, you respawn. You go and get a beer and try again. You get confused, you get help. It's not like that here. We're not on the outside looking in, we're on the inside, living it. Look at what we just went through. We all thought, once the picture eventually became clear, that the quest was Jurun. Well, that was the *apparent* quest. But it didn't stop there. The *actual* quest was the step beyond that."

I stopped, abruptly.

I remembered that I hadn't told them what had happened inside the Tree of Life, between me and Time, before I discovered that he was Ken.

They were both studying me, waiting for me to explain.

I couldn't see how I could hide it anymore. So, I told them.

I told them that I had used Oller's silver key to open the Tree of Life and had gone down into it to bargain with Time. My life for Esmeralda's. Not knowing, of course, that that was the final step of the Actual Quest.

I'd meant it, the offer I'd made. The finality of my choice hit us all. I stopped talking.

Neither of them said anything for a long while.

Grell was staring at me, his mouth hard.

Qrysta, eventually, nodded. "I knew it!"

I said, "Well, it … I …"

She was also staring at me, and also not kindly. "That's just the kind of dumbass thing you'd do, Daxx!"

I couldn't think how to respond.

"Why?!" Grell demanded.

I said, when I could find my voice. "I just *had* to. Once I'd worked it out. I couldn't *not*."

"You hardly knew her!" Qrysta said.

"I know," I admitted.

"And what about *us*?" she challenged. "You *know* us. We're your *friends*. Your *best* friends—in this world, or any other."

Again, all I could say was, "I know."

"You'd do that to *us*?" She sounded angry, but she looked mortified. Disbelieving.

I looked her in the eye. "If I hadn't, Qrys, you'd never have forgiven me."

She frowned. Shook her head. She was still upset with me.

Grell said, eventually, "He's right. We wouldn't have."

Qrysta turned her glare on him. We both let her take her time. She took a deep breath and exhaled. Swallowed. "I suppose," she said, when she'd thought it through, "that's what comes of being so damn good with puzzles. I'd never have worked it out."

"Nor me," Grell agreed.

"And she'd be dead," Qrysta said. "And we'd still be down there, probably. Slogging our way back topside. We'd never have made it, without Ezzie flying us back up on her throne; I was all in."

Grell said, "Me too."

We all fell silent.

"But still," Qrysta said. "Helluva stupid thing to do."

She was right. We all knew that.

I said, "*The loveliest life there ever was or ever will be.* I didn't want to live in a world without that."

Qrysta just stared at me.

I added, "I was all in too, Qrys. Done. I thought, I'm on my way out, might as well. So, this one last thing. You know? Trade it in for something better. There was no need for me anymore. But Ez …. She was needed."

Another silence fell.

"Crap," Qrysta muttered. "It's all very well coming to decisions like that in a *game*, when you know you can rezz if you screw up and die. But IRL?" she stopped. "Daxxie, you have to be …" She tailed off, not knowing where she was going with that.

Nor did I. So I didn't try to finish her sentence for her.

Eventually, she said, slowly, "Hmmm ... I was going to say *nuts*; then I was going to say *tired of living;* then I thought, *completely convinced.*" She shook her head, then looked up at me and held my eyes. "You'd reached the end, hadn't you?" she said. "*Game Over.*"

I said, "Something like that."

She leaned forward and took my hands in hers. "So when it's my turn, I now know what to do."

When I realized what she was saying, I said, "Come on, Qrysta, that won't happen."

She challenged, "How do you know?"

"Well, I don't," I had to admit. "But we're not going to be facing the same problems all the time, so chances are ..."

She tightened her grip, digging her sharp nails into my hands. "Chances are I won't have to lay my life down for you? Or for Grell, or Oller, or Esmeralda, or who knows who else?" She gave a last, emphatic squeeze, then let go of my hands, and sat back. "Good," she said, "I'm glad to hear it. Let's hope you're right. Let's hope none of us has to."

Grell said. "I'll second that."

They waited for my response. Eventually, I said, "Thanks, guys. Thanks for understanding."

"No worries," Grell said. "Just don't do it again."

"I won't" I said.

Grell snorted. "If you do," he said, "you and I are going to have words."

Qrysta grunted agreement. "You and me too," she said, and, to my relief, abruptly changed the subject. "So, are we going to do this, or what?"

"I dunno," Grell said, "I mean ... Daxx? How are you reading this?"

"Mysterious message, addressed to one of us by name, on a ghost ship? Sounds like a quest starter to me."

"Yeah, but—who uses a seal, eh?" Grell said. "On any letter. The owner of it, right? This Archon of Varamaxes—we're meant to rescue him? Everything Qrysta's heard about him sounds a shitload of trouble. Why would we want to get involved with that?"

"Well," I said, "we don't *know* it's him ..."

"No," Grell said, "we don't know anything. You think we should just head off into the unknown, on one weird-arse ghost ship, not knowing anything, and see what happens?"

"I get your point," I said. "For sure, we should do our research. But think—what were we just saying?" I waved a hand around our spaceship's living quarters. "We want to be able to use this beauty, right? And we know, from what you saw of me getting my butt kicked on a *zero* Beta, that we're nowhere near up to it yet. We need to get *good*. What's the way we usually do that?" I answered my own question. "By questing."

"Yeah, but …" Grell was still doubtful, but tailed off.

"Gain XP. Level up. And also," I added, "what else might we find along the way?"

Quests mean loot.

"Fill the coffers," Qrysta mused. "It'd be good to have a decent war chest. The higher you get, the more it costs, right?"

"Right," I said. "And there's another thing. Suppose we walk away. Which we could; we could just settle down here and, I dunno, put our feet up. Retire. That would be kind of letting Ken down, don't you think? I mean," I indicated our futuristic surroundings, "seems like a shitty way to say thank you for this."

The others nodded.

"They've thrown us a challenge," I went on. "Not one I like the smell of, I have to agree, but—isn't this what we do? And besides," I added, "you help someone out, he might just give you a nice reward?"

Grell grunted. "Who are we kidding? We all know we're going to do it." He looked up at the ceiling, and said, loudly, "My next reward had better be better than the last damn one! All right, Ken?"

His challenge echoed around the cabin.

He looked back at Qrysta and me.

He was right.

And, as he said, we all knew it.

Prepare, and run a happy ship, Commandant Bastard had told us. Well, we were going to take his advice, no question about that. Yes, we were itching for adventure, but we weren't going to go ignorant into the unknown. We'd had enough worrying hints, in the little that we'd learned so far, to suspect that what lay ahead might well not be easy, and might equally well involve some unappealing characters, and some serious challenges. We needed to find out as much as we could before setting sail on the ghost ship.

Which is why I found myself, a couple of evenings later, in the study of the Arch Historian of the Faiths, Eldress Quen, in the Mayport Priory. I had already conferred with the Conclave of the Guild of the Arcane Arts, and the Faculty of the College of Lore and Learning, and with Marnie and her Covensisters. None had been able to tell me much, other than they didn't like the smell of it, and to be careful, but all had told me to consult with Quen. She, I'd been told, knew more about the various religions of this world than anyone.

She was in her late seventies at least, but sharp, and sprightly, with long, fine hands, and a slight frame. She wore nothing on her bunched white hair, but her white habit was adorned with a number of intriguing badges and designs, of wrought metal, and carved, rich woods, and finely embroidered, brightly colored cloth. Her eyes were dreamy, a mix of gray and green, and seemed to be focusing on things outside this room—until she turned them on me, when her stare was shrewd, and her voice penetrating. She looked *into* me, it felt, rather than at me. I thought, I would *not* like to be interrogated by Eldress Quen, especially if I was trying to hide something from those all-seeing eyes. I didn't think I'd be up to it. And then, the next moment, those eyes would be mild and unfocused, staring off, her mind on whatever she needed to consider, however far away or long ago that might be; and her voice, when she spoke, would be lost and distant. We sat across the hearth from each other, sipping at her strange herbal tea, a fat old black-and-white cat sleeping on her lap.

"Gods, demons, playing their games with each other, challenging each other?" she said. "Who can begin to know their divine minds and plans?" She tailed off, gazing through the ceiling.

I had no answer, of course, so kept quiet.

"Why are they here, on this mortal plane? Far from whence they came?" She sighed and shook her head. "We pray to them. Or, worse, sacrifice our fellow mortals to them. Why? So many reasons. We crave their approval, their aid. We wish to avert their wrath. We appease. We praise, flatter, cajole, beg—yearn to hear their divine wisdom. How we wish for them to manifest themselves among us; to take away our pain, to lift our burdens, to show us the light of their grace, or to turn their wrath against our enemies. To solve our problems, and bring us bliss, or triumph, or revenge …"

She fell silent, and listened for something, it seemed. She shook her head. "But what do *they* want? Our mortal answers seem so small and foolish, when you consider them. They want our worship, we believe. Why? What good does that do them? Does it improve their status, among each other? Why would it matter, that they have four or forty or forty thousand devotees—what difference could it possibly make?

"Those of us who have studied the histories of this world's beliefs question whether we are considering this aright. We think that they want such and such; but we're only humans, we're only thinking like humans. Surely, they want what gods and demons want, and why should that ever be vouchsafed to us?

"And yet, here they are. On this mortal plane. Locked in their eternal struggle. What are they fighting over? Over us? Or over something far above anything we mortals can ever know?"

She stopped and gazed into the fire.

I said, "How do we know they are here?"

She turned her sharp eyes on me and pointed at the seal I'd shown her. Old Birdbeak. As if to say, *obviously.*

She turned her gaze away from me, back to the flames in her hearth, and drifted off for a moment—and then frowned and looked back at me. "You're not a believer."

I said, "No, I don't think so." I didn't want to offend her, so added, "I'd be happy to be proved wrong, though."

She held my eyes.

Slowly, a smile grew on her face. "*Would* you now?" she said. "I suspect it would be anything *but* happy." She laughed, and rocked in her chair, stroking her fat old cat, who raised his head and looked up at her with sleepy, yellow eyes.

I didn't get it. "Why not?"

She nodded, several times, slowly. "Gods are busy," she said. "They don't have the patience to explain, once again, what they've already explained to so many other mortals, over the ages. If we didn't listen the first, or first hundred, times—that's our problem. We have been warned. Obey the rules or suffer the consequences."

I tried to make sense out of that. "So we're not their first priority?"

She chuckled. "We're just in the way," she said. "They don't need us."

"Do we need them?"

Her eyebrows rose. "That is, indeed, the question that many of us are wrestling with. If you have a couple of months I could give you the basics of our various positions on that. But that wouldn't matter to you, because you don't believe."

She lost her thoughts in the flames dancing in her hearth.

I waited.

Eventually, she inhaled, and sighed. "And who knows?" she said. "You may be right. And we've all been wrong, all these long years. We've all been believing in phantoms. Delusions. It would seem that this is your chance to find out." She looked at me again, and studied me, with her strange, gray-green eyes. "You don't have to take it," she added, quietly.

But we both knew that I would. I wasn't in the habit of backing off from a challenge, any more than Grell and Qrysta and Oller were. Our motto was, basically, *bring it.*

Eldress Quen nodded, clearly reading my mind. She pushed her old cat off her lap and hauled herself to her feet. She shuffled over to a bookshelf and took down a small, black leather-bound volume. She leafed through it, grunting. She came over and stood beside me and held it out to me.

"I can't let you take this," she said, "it's the only known copy in the realm."

I took the book and looked at its cover. The gold letters on it spelled out its title.

Of Gods and Demons. A Guide to the Known Heavens and Hells. With Star Maps.

"You're welcome to study it here, for a long as you wish," she said. She pottered off into her kitchen, saying, "I usually have a nip of apricot brandy at this time of night, I expect you'd like one too?"

"Yes, please," I said, already turning the pages of the book. "Thank you."

Of Gods and Demons, I thought. *Let's get the information.*

I opened it and unfolded the star chart that was attached inside its front cover. I studied the various constellations mapped out on it. All had names that I didn't recognize. The Swallow. The Hunter. The Lord of Shadows, also known as The Thief. The Willow Tree. The Demon. The Dancer. The Lamb. The Fisher. The Protectress. The Whale. The Lovers. The Urn.

I began to read.

6

Shipwreck

Qrysta was first up the gangway onto the ghost ship. We'd stocked up with everything we could think of—buffs from the GAA, potions from the Mayport apothecary. Our niblun backpacks could hold far more than would seem possible, but that's nibluns for you.

We'd all said our goodbyes. Queen Esmeralda gave her a last hug, and a kiss on both cheeks and whispered something private in her ear. Qrysta held her shoulders, and smiled, a private smile, then formally bowed and kissed her sovereign's hand.

We all did the last part, Grell tenderly, taking Esmeralda's dainty hand in his massive paw; then Oller awkwardly, wiping his hand on his leather jerkin before taking hers, and wiping his mouth on the back of his other hand before kissing hers, after which she kissed him on the cheek with a lovely smile, and he blushed, and grinned like an idiot—and turned his hands over, and opened them, to reveal the rings he'd filched from her fingers, and she laughed with delight. Little Guy sat and held up a paw, which Esmeralda took and shook solemnly. And then, because solemn wasn't Esmeralda's default mode, she borrowed a sword and knighted Little Guy. "Arise, Sir Little Guy!" And the curse was taken off our parting as the crowd applauded. I thought, *She just knows.* Knows how to do the right thing, how to handle situations.

74

Oller and Grell each took an end of the iron-bound trunk that contained their bows and Qrysta's, and their quivers, and enough arrows to start a small war, and hauled it up the gangplank. I had a fair idea of what would happen. When the others were safely aboard, Little Guy at Oller's heels, I thanked Esmeralda, and bowed to kiss her hand, and she said, "This will always be your home. Come back to it, safe and sound."

"I will, Your—"

It was a public occasion. It would be expected that I would use her formal title.

All that Correct Form/Public Occasion stuff was her burden to bear. She bore it with grace and patience. It would never leave her shoulders. It was expected of her. She had made up her mind that she would deliver on those expectations, whatever the cost.

But I remembered her words at her Coronation Feast.

I bowed, and said, "I will, *my friend.*"

I heard intakes of breath from the assembled grand personages. Well, I was a rank-and-file deserter, and an ignorant foreigner to boot. How could I be expected to know proper court manners? Esmeralda smiled at me, in gratitude, and there were those pixies, and unicorns, and bunny rabbits and tweety birds dancing around her radiant head …

… I would probably still be smiling at her, in that lovely mutual understanding, if she hadn't said, "Can I have my hand back now?"

I reanimated abruptly, dropped her hand, bowed, turned, and walked up the gangway, thinking, *Oh that was so lovely, why did it have to stop,* and, *What an odd thing it must be to be royalty.* With Ez, though, it just seemed that she was the most normal person of all of us. Only lovelier. I wondered what *she* found lovely. Pixies? Unicorns? Well, no, *hardly:* She loathed the things. I thought, *When I come back, I'll have to ask her.*

I'd decided that I would go aboard last, as I wanted to make sure that Little Guy was coming with us. I'd thought that, if Oller boarded the ghost ship last, then maybe Little Guy would be prevented from following him, somehow, once the head count was four. Oller would *not* have been happy about that, and would have spent the rest of the voyage, and whatever lay beyond it, fretting. We needed him engaged, looking forward, not back—fully alert, fully with us, not thinking about the friend he'd left behind. Well, Little Guy was safely up there, at Oller's side.

So, I joined them. And, as I'd anticipated, the moment I was aboard, the ghost ship set sail. The gangway drew itself up and in. The lines mooring us to the dock's stanchions unwound themselves and whipped in and settled into coils. The bow eased away from the wharf, as if fended off by invisible poles. Ragged sails slapped down from the spars and hauled themselves taut to catch the wind. She leaned as she gathered its power—although how those tattered scraps of canvas held the wind it was impossible to say.

The wheel on the quarterdeck turned itself, and the rigging trimmed itself, and the wind picked up where there had been no more than a gentle breeze before, and we were away, off across Mayport Reach, and tacking into the mouth between the great stone arms that guarded the harbor from the ocean. When the ghost ship breasted the swells that waited beyond our haven, she rode into them hard, down and up again, urgently, as if relishing the challenge and the voyage ahead. The whale's way, the swan's road. The open sea.

We relished it too. We walked around the decks, inhaling the sea air, the wind of our passage blowing in our hair, the waves chomping and banging at our hull as it strode through them, urgent. We checked everywhere, above and below. Supplies. Chart lockers. Cabins. We had, it seemed, everything we needed. Except any kind of clue as to where we were going, who was steering, how it was all working, and *what the fuck the quest* was. We were fine with that.

Leaning over the rail with Qrysta, as we dipped into and up and over the swells, the sharp salt spray spattering our faces, I shouted, above the wind, "Another ship steering itself."

She looked at me.

"Eydie did the driving to the Beta planet," I explained. "No idea who's driving this thing. At least *we* don't have to do it, huh?"

She shouted back, "Would you know how?"

"Not a clue!"

She laughed. She was enjoying herself. As was I. "Me neither," she agreed.

Grell joined us. Oller joined us, with Little Guy. We watched the gray rollers, white-topped above the ink-black sea, foaming, charging at us, as we drank in the movement, the power of the waters beneath us, the cold salt air above, wondering what lay ahead. We'd find out soon enough, we all thought.

If we'd known, we'd have done anything we could to turn the ghost ship around and run whimpering for Mayport.

But we didn't know, thank the gods. And we'd have had no way of turning back. We weren't in charge. We were passengers. Sent for, by ... well, who knew? But there was definitely a disturbing shadow in the background. The Archon of Varamaxes. What was his role in this rescue mission? The ghosts below gave no further clues. I began to wonder if they were indeed ghosts. Or just illusions, things put there to convince us. There they were, floating, bobbing weirdly, doing nothing. Completely useless, really. It would have been more reassuring if they'd fizzed into action once we'd boarded and hauled on lines, and manned the wheel, and—I dunno, played the concertina and danced a hornpipe and *yo-ho-ho'd.*

But they didn't. And we plowed on into the gray-black sea, into the salt spray, into the gathering dusk, southward and eastward, the sun sinking eventually in a red haze behind dark clouds that gave the promise of a nasty night.

I'm no kind of sailor. None of us were. The only one who didn't heave the day's meal into the sea was Little Guy. He heaved his onto the deck. And ate it. And heaved it up again. Twice. At which point, even a mutt who'd spent most of his life starving gave up.

We no longer cared where we were going. All we cared about was that this misery should end. We swore to all the gods that, if they spared us, we'd never get on another ship again as long as we lived. They can't have been listening. The misery lasted another six days.

I call them days, but the hours of daylight were almost as dark as the hours of night—and no more comforting, because we could see our equally miserable companions. There were bunks below. They were more like trampolines made of concrete than beds. They flung us up and around and hit us from all angles when we thumped back onto them.

I doubt any normal ship could have lived through that storm. But it felt like small comfort to think that. We were in hell, in a ship from hell. We just knew this had to get better. Or why would they send for us, only to drown us? And then the treacherous thoughts crept in, *Well, maybe that's the whole point. Maybe, with us no longer around, they ... whoever 'they' are ... would have a clear path to ... whatever goal it was, without us to stop them .... Did they sucker us into this? A cryptic*

77

riddle, in a chest under an innocent, immovable victim, just to tease our interest, to lure us onboard this death trap, and get us out of the way?

It felt, at last, that anything we could do was irrelevant. I spent most of my time casting Heals on all of us. We were in such a state of disarray that it was all that Shift could manage to keep us even halfway functional.

We got colder, weaker, more exhausted. Shift was drained more often than not. I couldn't understand why. She had always had deep reserves of power. But now, whenever I used her, her tourmaline heartstone would fade from its usual bright red-and-green to gray within seconds. And it would take her many long minutes to regain her strength.

We all thought ourselves into the same state of despair. Why had we been so stupid as to walk blithely into this?! With the crowd cheering, and Esmeralda seeing us off with her usual calm? All that confidence. We'd all fallen for it. *It must be all right, if Ezzie is happy. Off we go. How interesting, how exciting. Wonder what's coming next.*

Just the naivete of it. Our sheer stupidity. Walking into this catastrophe.

Some unknown person sends us a riddle, in a crate. So, we think: Right, we have to set off—unprepared, unknowing—and everything will miraculously reveal itself, and we'll figure it out, and go on and do what was needed, tra-la-la ...

Why in the world had *that* made sense?

We were on a ghost ship, with a few bobbing ghosts, in the middle of the mother of all storms, the wind shrieking like a banshee, and the hull groaning and creaking, and we were complete fools because the only possible outcome was disaster.

Six days and nights of roaring and banging. The last shreds of hope disappearing. Thinking, *This is obviously a magic storm, someone whipped this up to drown us, this isn't normal weather* ... and then, *Well, why not get it over with? Why put us through six days of this misery? If you want us out of the way, why not get the hell on with it?!* And then, hope creeping back in again to taunt us, *Well, maybe it is normal weather, in this part of the ocean, and it's fine. Maybe we'll come out the other side of it, because if they wanted us dead, they'd have done it by now. Wouldn't they? And they haven't, so ...*

Every now and again someone would lurch up onto the deck, to look for land, or lights, to check the horizons for any sign of a break in the storm. And would find nothing but the howling wind, and the stinging rain, and would stagger back below again, soaked, shivering, more dispirited than ever, and tell us nothing that gave us any hope.

The last one to make that wretched trek was me. The horizons invisible behind dark clouds. The rain driving harder than ever, colder than ever. The deck under my feet rearing and bucking and rolling. Back down below I went, awkward handhold to invisible foothold, down into the cargo hold, heading for our cabin, in which we'd camped because, being on the waterline it was the least thrown-about place in the ship.

Sick, exhausted, I looked up and saw that the ghosts—those silly, pale balloons that had been doing absolutely nothing up to this point—were now moving around.

With, it seemed, some kind of purpose.

They were getting into position, weaving in and out of each other, faster, surer.

Until they found where they should be. Where they settled.

They altered.

They began to glow. Dull, at first, then cycling through the colors of the spectrum until they all turned gold. They held that gold glow as it brightened. Then they merged.

Where there had been nine pale bubbles, now there was a single, large golden one.

The ghosts faded.

The bubble held.

It expanded out, in all directions, from the hold to the decks above, and beyond.

Beyond the hull. Beyond the confines of this eerie ship.

Meanwhile above, as it had for the last six days, the storm raged. And then, suddenly, it didn't. I felt the deck tilt sharply downward beneath my feet. I knew at once that things had changed. I hurried, as fast as I could, on awkwardly angled boards, to rouse the others. We grabbed our clothes and packs and weapons. Clearly this was it. We were going down with the ship, *down and down*—but weren't drowning. We were still standing, still breathing.

79

We all knew that we weren't on the surface anymore. There wasn't a storm—at least not down here where it could affect us. No more shrieking wind, no more bucking and rolling deck beneath our feet. We all thought, *What has happened?*

We all tried to talk at once and found that we couldn't. We could move our mouths, and I could feel the vibrations in my throat, but none of us made a sound.

Uncertainly, confused, pointing up, and agreeing, we made our way above.

We emerged into a gold bubble. It surrounded us, and the entire ship, as we and it sank into the depths.

We stood there, on the steeply tilting deck, clinging onto whatever we could grab hold of.

Watching.

Thinking, *What in all hells is going on,* but also, eventually, *Well, there's not much we can do about this.*

So we'll just have to see.

We could breathe, and wonder, and watch, while our ghost ship, held within its gold bubble, gently sank to the ocean floor, where, eventually, it stuck, and settled. The golden bloom from our bubble lit the seabed around us; and, as we peered out into the murk, it began to shrink in towards us. That did not seem good. It was collapsing. The seawater would burst in on us and it would be all over …

But when the bubble shrank towards us, it separated back into individual bubbles and closed in around the five of us, each in our separate, glowing gold sphere. Which all started moving. We floated off, one after another, into the ink-black sea, Grell first, then Oller, then Little Guy, then Qrysta, then me, like a line of ducklings following their mother. One by one we found that the most comfortable position was to sit cross-legged. Little Guy simply sat.

Off into the deep we drifted only yards above the ocean floor. Strange, pale fish appeared around us as the soft light we cast illuminated them. They swayed their tails and slid off into the gloom. Our file of bubbles followed Grell's, rising over the bones of a whale, then gliding along to … wherever we were going.

A squid the size of a sofa, black eyes glaring at us before moving slowly away. A ghost-white, snaggle-toothed shark, moving even slower. Crawling things on the seabed. Wafting things that poked out of the mud and undulated in the current. Everything at this depth slow, conserving energy.

I thought, *The pressure down here must be ridiculous. And we're in glowing gold bubbles, behind wafer-thin membranes? How are they holding together?!* And wafer-thin was how I felt myself after the battering the storm had given us. It was as if every emotion I had ever felt was coming and going as it pleased, and there was nothing I could do about it. I was jazzed on adrenaline and confused by a jumble of conflicting thoughts, while my body just longed for the sleep it knew was never coming. Not while this weirdness was going on.

We bobbed along the featureless ocean floor until a feature presented itself—a black slope, up which we glided. The slope steepened and became a cliff, a mountainside: The roots, presumably, of some island rearing above us.

Thank the gods, I thought: *Land; the open air.*

I was wrong. Our bubbles rose for a while, and I kept craning my head back, to look up, for any hint of light from the sky above, knowing of course that it was the middle of the night, but there might be a moon up there—but we were still far below the surface when we followed Grell inward, into the mouth of an underwater tunnel that led not up but back down again.

It was a long, narrow tunnel, dark everywhere except for the passing patches of gold light thrown by our bubbles. Down. Down didn't feel good. None of it felt good, except the not-freezing-and-drowning part. I thought, crazily—and this shows how lightheaded I was becoming—*What's the opposite of out of the frying pan, into the fire?* Out of the ice tub, into the morgue?

I racked my brains for any kind of magic I might know that could … do what? Break this spell? Then—no more bubbles. And we'd implode, and our corpses would be food for those languid, snaggle-toothed sharks, and the giant squid, and the crabs. I could … do what? Fireballs? Lightning?

Underwater?

Nope, I told myself: Just deal with what you can deal with. There's no point in banging your head against anything else. You can't control things outside your control.

We emerged at last into a large cavern and floated down to its floor, and along—and eventually up—another long, gentle slope.

Ahead of us, after many minutes of climbing, a light appeared, hovering, waiting for us. It resolved itself into another gold bubble. There was a dark shape inside it. As we neared it, we could see that the dark shape was a man.

We all stared at him, of course, wondering who he was, and what was going on, but he was strangely difficult to see. The light in his sphere somehow diffused him, making him a blur, as if he'd been scribbled out. He was completely black, as far as I could tell: Hooded, dressed head to foot in black robes, sitting cross-legged inside his bubble, his features indistinguishable. There was a smaller shape beside him, I saw, standing on two thin legs. It turned its head and looked at me.

I didn't like the look. *Imp*, I thought. Which was bad. A small, thin body, below a heavy head, its red eyes burning into me. I felt it look through me, as if I was nothing but a sack of meat to it. *Malice*, I thought. Magic—the wrong kind. Its bubble turned, leading ours away up the slope. I was relieved to be no longer on the end of that unnerving stare.

Our bubbles followed, up, and up. I was thinking, *We're going to bump up against the bottom of the island .... No, that doesn't make sense, there must be a lake up there, a saltwater lake connected to the sea.*

Once again I was wrong. We broke the surface and floated ashore, then rose above the land and kept on floating, as if we were aboard hovercrafts—but ones made of glowing gold bubbles. We were moving across an island beneath the island, above a calm, inland sea that was not disturbed by the storm raging beyond. And we were moving in absolute silence. It was more than very peculiar, and more than a little disturbing—especially as, no matter how hard I strained, I couldn't really make anything out in the little pools of soft light cast by our bubbles.

I was far from confident that this was going to end well. I was even less confident when, after a few minutes of floating after our mysterious leader, I could make out the building ahead of us, which was plainly our destination.

Well, it had been a building *once*. Now it was a ruin. The ruin of something that looked distinctly religious. And not in a good way.

As we neared it, I saw that it was some kind of ancient, battered temple. Bits of its pale walls still stood behind the bits of outer fortifications that had once encircled and protected it. We drifted through gaps in those, and through gaps in the inner walls, and into the ruined temple itself. There was faint light inside: A dim, blue light like a summer night in the far north. It was not coming from any source that I could see.

Tall, spectral marble pillars reared high, supporting what remained of the ceiling. We drifted through archways, past side chapels containing marble screens, and around rows of marble pews, and altars, always at the same steady pace. We came, finally, to a door, where we halted. Points of light glinted in walls and ceiling. The place still felt hallowed. Revered. And, again, not in a good way.

I was feeling more and more apprehensive.

A hand reached out of the leading bubble. A small, dark hand. The imp's. Holding a key. The key turned. The door opened. We glided in.

Beyond the temple itself, it seemed, were living quarters. For the … priests? Monks? Devotees? Well, for whoever had once lived here, presumably. We had entered into the corner of a large library. Bookcases filled the marble walls, and scrolls poked out of cubbyholes. It looked both ordered and disorganized at the same time. There were benches, and alcoves with chairs, and, towards the end of the room, a long table, below a dais, on which a lectern stood. Burning torches stood high on the walls, and at last we could see clearly.

One thing we all saw right away was the central figure, carved into the end wall above the dais. Other figures surrounded it, on the other walls—all, we later saw, disturbing enough. But none were as large, or as disturbing, as the one that caught our eyes immediately.

There he was, rearing from floor to ceiling on his clawed feet: Body of a lion, arrow-tipped tail of a dragon, huge, feathered head, beak agape, roaring, in each of his claws a broken body dripping blood.

Old Birdbeak.

Abruptly, our bubbles burst, and we were standing on the marble squares of the library's floor, onto which our weapons clattered around us. The little man in his hooded black robes didn't bother to turn around. He headed on, leading us towards the far end of the hall. He either knew that we weren't going to lunge for them or didn't care if we tried. Which suggested that he was confident he could handle anything we might throw at him.

Grell reached for Fugg, Qrysta for her twin blades, Oller for his knife belt—and I tried to get my hands on Shift. Our feet wouldn't take us where we wanted to go. Grell's feet pointed towards where Fugg lay, just out of his reach, but they carried him, almost tripping over each other, in the direction we were all, inexorably, going.

Grell fought the invisible binds and tried again—but his course was set.

We stumbled past our weapons and went where our feet carried us. They weren't obeying us; we were obeying them. It was a worrying feeling, being walked rather than walking. As long as we went where we were meant to be going, we were unrestricted. Little Guy padded up to take his usual place at Oller's heel. Oller glanced at him, reached down, and ruffled his head. Little Guy's scruffy tail wagged contentedly.

When he reached the end of the table, the little man in the hooded black robes sat in the chair at its head. It was the only chair that had arms. *The boss's chair.* The imp clambered up onto the back of it and stood behind him, red eyes burning. Slowly, two reptilian wings spread out behind it from his shoulders. The little thing radiated menace, and power—and we, I knew, were helpless. We sat where our legs stopped us, Qrysta and Oller on the hooded man's left, Grell and myself on his right.

We waited. There were scrolls and sheaves of paper and parchment on the table in front of him. He reached up, drew back the hood of his robes, and looked at us.

I felt my bowels turn to water.

He had no face.

Then—but—how did I know he was looking at us?

Because his *no face* turned as he examined us, one after the other. I could see the shape of it shifting above his neck. Another bubble; another indistinct, foggy outline, like the ghosts in the ghost ship. And yet we knew that he saw us. Studied us. There was something there all right, even though we couldn't see it.

Beside him the imp stared, red eyes burning, unblinking. *We're just sacks of meat to it,* I thought again. *Contempt.* No, we didn't merit even that. We were as insignificant to it as victims to a torturer.

The black-robed man with no face studied us for a while. Grunted, at last. "Well, this is not what I've been expecting."

Automatically, I asked, "What have you been expecting?"

But no sound came out of my mouth. I looked around, at the others, and saw their lips moving too. And heard nothing.

We were, we realized, powerless.

He sighed. "So long to wait." He inhaled, and sighed again, and shook his bubble of a head. "All this time, and everything I thought was wrong …"

It was our turn to wait. "No," he decided, "it can't be."

He studied us, again, with his invisible face, turning it this way and that, to examine each one of us in turn.

Eventually, he said, looking at Little Guy, "I don't understand the dog." He frowned. "I'll have to kill it, I think."

Oller stiffened and attempted to jump to his feet. Constrained as he was, he could not move. The man with no face turned to look at him.

"You wouldn't like that," he said. It was a statement rather than a question.

I could see Oller doing all he could to convey the message, *You're damn right I wouldn't, and I'll hunt you down and kill you if you harm a hair on my dog's head!*

The little, black-robed man without a face said, "Hmmm."

We couldn't speak, so didn't try.

He drummed his fingers on the table. "Thief, yes?" he said to Oller. "I suppose you stole him."

I could just feel Oller bulging with annoyance. And something inside me worked loose. I wanted to laugh. For two reasons. First, I'd never heard Oller not speak all he wanted whenever he wanted to, and second, because—was he annoyed that his professional pride had been insulted? *What, me, a Master Thief, steal a scruffy little bugger like this?! If I wanted to steal a dog, mate, I'd steal a prize one, thank you very much*—

The pale, no-face turned to me sharply. "You think this is funny?" he demanded.

Gods, I thought, he can read my mind—

"I can indeed," he said. "All of you, all at once. There's a lot going on in your heads that I don't understand. But I will—I will, soon enough."

The way he said that, dryly, was unnerving.

How? I thought.

"I have my methods," he answered. "So does he," he added, tilting his no-face at the imp beside him. Who was staring at me again with those unblinking, basilisk eyes. And giving me the distinct feeling that it would enjoy using those "methods" on me, and that they wouldn't be pleasant.

"He would, and they wouldn't," the no-face man agreed. "As for killing the dog, it wouldn't surprise me if you didn't think he'd been the lucky one, where you're going."

The imp turned its heavy head and stared at Little Guy, who was sitting between the no-face man and Oller.

It then looked at the no-face man.

His master, I assumed.

"Yes, you can have him, if I decide to," he answered the question that none of us had heard the imp ask. "You'd enjoy playing with him, wouldn't you?"

The imp turned to look at Little Guy again and nodded.

Hungrily.

Little Guy's ears flattened back against his skull. Dogs read people well—much better than people read dogs.

Not that this imp was *people,* clearly.

But it was, also clearly—and to all of us, as well as to Little Guy— readable. It wouldn't be the sort of "playing with" that a child might do with a puppy.

We couldn't let that happen to Little Guy …

The no-face turned to us, one after the other. "Interesting," he said. "All four of you with the same thought." He turned to look down at Little Guy. "You have some loyal friends, dog."

He reached out a hand, and I felt Oller tense again. The hand stroked Little Guy gently on the head.

We waited, frozen in place and speechless, until he'd finished.

It was a long, slender hand—delicate even. I thought, *At least it's a real hand, not a blob of pale nothingness like his head.* I wondered how that could be.

"Long story," he explained. "Which we don't have time for now. We hardly have time for you to be about your task. Quite why it took you a month to set sail … well, I'll be interested to find out. All in good time. Which, to repeat, we don't have enough of at the moment, so that will have to wait. I believe you know who I am."

He waited. Watched us.

Yes, we all did.

The no-face nodded. "Mm," he grunted. "Well then. You will also know why you are here." He reached for a piece of parchment on the table in front of him and studied it.

I believed that I knew what was on it. I thought, *Well, if he can read our thoughts, let's give him something to read.*

I recited, in my head:

The Four will come
Across the sea
To break my chains
And set me free

That chilling no-face turned to me abruptly. Studied me. "Caster," he said, eventually. "The one who is good with puzzles."

I saw no reason to hold back. I said, in my mind, "I'd hardly call that a puzzle. Seems pretty obvious to me."

"Oh, it does, does it?" he challenged. "And how, exactly, are you going to do what it says?"

I said, casually, "I don't know if we are."

He went still. He stared at me, from his no-face, the parchment frozen in his unmoving hands.

Good, I thought. *I've touched a nerve.*

"You have indeed," he said, and his voice was acid. And then he added, "But I'd hardly say that that was *'good.'* I'd advise you not to challenge me."

I waited.

"And why," he went on, when he saw that I wasn't going to say anything, "don't you know if you are?"

I shrugged. *It's your problem, not ours. Why should we? What's in it for us?*

I was feeling pleased with myself, I must admit. I'd shown him that I wasn't going to be pushed around.

A moment later I was flat on my back, screaming. Except that my voice couldn't make a sound. Such pain as I'd never felt jabbed at every nerve in my body, so fierce that I could think of nothing else.

Until, eventually, mercifully, it subsided.

"Does that answer your questions?" he said.

I sat up, groggily.

The others, I saw, were still frozen, immobile, their faces masks of horror.

"My problem is your problem now," he stated, as if he'd just proved it. "And as to what is in it for you, shall we start with an absence of *that?*"

I knew what he meant. The unbearable pain.

"Do I need to show your friends?" he asked.

In my head, I begged, "No. Please. We're listening."

"Good," he said. "Now, here's what you're going to do."

7

The Proof

Ah, I thought, as I got unsteadily to my feet and sat back down. *Finally we'll get an explanation.*

Bubblehead looked up at me sharply. "An explanation?" he snapped. "No, I'm afraid that will have to wait. First we'll have to see if you're up to the challenge. All I will 'explain' at the moment is where you are and why the challenge starts here. It starts here, because *here* it is hidden. No one living knows of it. Plenty of the dead do, but they're not going to tell anyone. You are in a Temple of Varamaxes. Within which I have, as you have discovered, considerable power. And within which, for far too long, I have been confined. Should I go where you're going, I'd be weaker than your dog. You're going to change all that. Which is why I sent my ship for you. And also why I wrecked it."

He paused. "I wrecked it so that my enemies will think that you drowned. I will explain who they are, and why I did that, if you survive your first challenge. Above us, on the island, there is a portal. It is located at the end of a very long, very dangerous delve. You will attempt to reach that portal. If you do, you will pass through it. There you will be in another place altogether, another *state* altogether, and you will have to work your way through that, under conditions very different from any you have ever known. At the end of that journey

89

you will find a helldragon. She has something of mine which I would like back."

He was about to continue, but stopped, and turned to me. "Let's see if you are indeed good with puzzles. I won't tell you what it is that you need to bring me. Should you succeed in defeating her, feel free to loot her hoard. She's been gathering it for a long time now, from every corner of this world, so you might find some things you like the look of. She has nothing of any value to me, apart from that one small," he hesitated, "shall we say, rather *ordinary-looking* object. The only thing of value to me is my freedom. Which is what I will send you to achieve if you defeat her. Because then you'll have shown to me that you might, just, have the capability to do what must be done."

I didn't know what to think.

"No," he answered, "neither do I. And let me inform you what will happen should you succeed. You will go back out into that storm, which will still be raging—I will make sure of that; I summoned it in the first place—and you will have a few spars to cling to, and some barrels, and so on, which you 'have managed to lash together'; and then you will be thrown about in the waves, until you are nine-tenths dead, and will finally wash up on the shore, and it will begin."

So, I thought, *Assuming we pass our trial,* what *will begin?*

"The task for which I brought you four here, on the slender chance that you are the Four I have been awaiting all these years. About which there's no point in telling you now," he said. He considered. "You'll all probably die up above on the island during your trial. You don't look very impressive to me. My guess is that you won't make it to the portal, let alone to the helldragon, and that I will have to wait another few centuries for the actual Four to appear."

I thought, *Well why does he think that? We're good.*

"You'll need to be," he said, dryly.

I thought, *When we bring you her head, you will owe us!*

His eyebrows rose. Or no, they didn't—he had no eyebrows—but it seemed from his body language—his *no-face* language—that they did.

He said, bemused, "Owe you what?"

I thought, *Respect.*

There was a pause. He hadn't been expecting that. "Interesting," he said. And then, he said, "I'll tell you what I'm going to do."

The Proof

We waited.

"I'm going to let your dog live until you come back. And if you don't, I will give it to him."

He gestured at the imp.

Who shifted on his haunches, and turned his bleak, red gaze on Little Guy.

The no-face man in the hooded black robes said, "He's very patient. Your dog will take a very long time to die."

I thought, with a growing swell of confidence, *That won't be your problem, pal.*

"Meaning?"

I actually laughed, inside. *Meaning,* I thought, *I'll kill you and that little gray piece of piss as soon as I possibly can.*

He chuckled. "Well, that won't be anytime soon," he said.

I thought, *I can wait.*

He went still at that. His no-face stopped blending and moving. He was staring at me.

I thought, *No answer?*

He said, eventually, and calmly, "I'll think of one. As will my companion here."

Okay. Tortured to death. Let's not do that.

He chuckled again. "No," he said. "You will either please me, by succeeding, so that you have proved that you might be capable of attempting the task, or you will please my companion here by failing."

We all looked at the imp. Who smiled. It was a smile that made my blood run cold.

"And if you fail, well," the no-face man added. "If your bones are ever found, as far as anyone will know you were just four foolhardy adventurers, who took the miscalculated risk of exploring the wrong delve."

I said, in my head, "I have a question."

"Which is?"

"What are you going to do if it turns out that we're not—whatever you'd hoped we were?"

"Continue to wait," he replied. "Which is what I've been doing since they thought they'd got rid of me. Wait here, as long as it takes, until the Four appear."

"So ... where do 'they' come into it?" I said. "Your enemies?"

"You can't work it out?" he replied. "I thought you prided yourself on being good with puzzles. It's very simple. I suggest you think about it. And when you come back, if you haven't worked it out I'll tell you."

We felt the invisible shackles break. We could move, wherever we wanted. Hesitantly, at first, we got up, exchanging glances. We retrieved our weapons. The no-face man and the imp watched. Surreptitiously, I fired up a glow from Shift, to pop out and hover above us.

Nothing popped or hovered.

Right, so there's no use aiming her Damages at these two. This was their turf, not ours. The no-face man led us out, through the pale, marbled halls and corridors, past the ruined walls, and into the darkness of the island under the island, the imp padding along beside him. We didn't even need to speak about it. We knew there was no point in trying to attack them. Not here.

The only things that grew down there were various kinds of fungus. Some formed little patches and clumps that we walked through. Some reared above our heads, as tall as trees. Some glowed, lighting our way. Some stank. Some hummed with an eerie music. Abruptly, the no-face, black-hooded man stopped. He pointed at Little Guy, who froze, staring at us, crouching, his eyes round in alarm, and his ears flat back against his skull.

"This is where we part ways," the no-face man said. "You go on, and up, and out, and in, and we go back. With your friend."

None of us went on. We stared at him, our weapons in our hands.

He smiled. He knew what we were thinking. "You're welcome to try," he said.

Oller was bristling with fury.

"Yes, yes, yes," the no-face man said, dismissively. "Off you go. We'll be here if you make it. If you don't, well—your friend won't make it either."

We looked at each other.

"One more pace and you can say your goodbyes," he said.

I took another step and realized that I could speak again.

"Over here, guys," I said.

They joined me beyond the invisible barrier.

Little Guy tried to follow but couldn't. He looked at Oller, pleading, confused.

Oller knelt down. "You stay here, little feller," he said, his voice as reassuring as he could make it. "We'll be back quick as quick; don't you worry about that! And I'll bring you a nice treat."

Little Guy was shivering with fear.

Oller reached out through the invisible barrier and patted him.

"You just be a good boy, and have a nice rest, and we'll see you in a bit. All right?"

He looked up at the no-face man. "He's not a fussy eater," he said, "anything, really, whatever you've got, but he hasn't eaten in days 'cos of the storm, so he'll be hungry."

"Oh, we won't be feeding him," the no-face man said. "Or," he added, pointedly, "*on* him."

Oller stood up, slowly, and stared at him. He was only a shrimp himself, Oller: No more than a human version of Little Guy. But you didn't fuck with him. Because Oller always fucked back.

"You harm a hair of him," he said, "and I'll cut you to pieces."

"Out there, yes; in here, no," came the dismissive reply. "I hope you succeed," he added, "for your little friend's sake, as well as for mine. Now, let's not drag this out—off you go."

The others were on edge, tense, ready to attack.

I had an idea.

I hefted Shift and unleashed a barrage of spectacular, loud attacks at the no-face man, Fireballs and Lightning and Thunderclouds and Ice Shards, all at once.

As I'd suspected, they hit the invisible barrier and died, unable to pass through it.

"Very pretty," the no-face man said.

There was nothing more to be said or done. We turned and headed off, and up, and out. I don't think I'd ever heard a sound as heartbreaking as Little Guy's crying. The no-face man must have unmuted him just for that purpose. Oller, beside me, was muttering, enraged. We couldn't help looking back. Little Guy was heading away in the other direction, his tail between his legs, dragged along by his own unwilling feet. He too was looking back at us as he shuffled awkwardly along between his captors.

We hurried.

The sooner this was over the better.

It was a dull, blustery, wet evening when we emerged into what was left of the daylight. A dozen giant spiders had been unfortunate enough to have us pass through their nest on our way up, and stupid enough to attack us. We weren't in a forgiving mood. Killing them relieved some of our frustration. They clearly hadn't eaten in a while. The corpses in their few cocoons hanging from the ceiling had long been drained dry. Some poor weapons dropped when we opened them, and a few copper coins. Even Oller didn't bother scooping them up.

We'd forgotten about the storm. We heard it echoing down towards us as we neared the cave's mouth. We felt wind, and rain, and soon emerged into air that was more brown than gray, air that seemed like the worst combination of a dust storm and a rainstorm. Everything smelled of mud and mold.

The cave opened onto a high, barren hillside. Rocks studded it, and stunted trees grew where they could find shelter in the gullies that ran down the slope towards a cleft between ridges. Below us lay a long horizon, fading into a gray sky. Much as we'd expected, really. A bleak, unwelcoming place, chilly, wet, desolate.

What we hadn't expected was to see firelight in the distance. It was faint, as it was coming from a long way away, and it was still daylight, being late afternoon, so we weren't quite trusting our eyes at first; but the light was certainly coming from flames, which flared up briefly, then died away.

Fire? In *this* rain? And what was more, around the fire there were roofs.

This island was inhabited?

Well, we thought, why shouldn't it be?

We knew which way to go. We'd been given directions. The settlement ahead of us wasn't much out of our way. We'd all been debilitated by seasickness for six days and hadn't managed to hold onto much of what we'd eaten in that time. We were running on empty. Whatever a helldragon was, it was a good guess that we'd be well advised to refuel before taking one on.

The inhabitants might not be friendly, of course. If that were the case, the four of us were capable of being unfriendly back. *Let's take a look, then,* we decided. It would seem odd if we appeared out of this miserable weather dry and warm, so I didn't cast Orbs of Warmth and Shielding on us as we headed down towards the village.

It didn't look like the sort of place that would maintain an army. Or even guards, or a decent watch. It actually seemed, as we made our way towards it, quite peaceable, in an isolated, beaten-down sort of way. There was decent farmland. Sheep and goats on the hillsides, cattle in fields. Pigs, ducks, chickens.

Children were in the barns, under shelter, playing. They stared at us as we strode into the village, and then ran off in all directions. Soon we came to the source of the fire: An open-sided smithy, where the bare-chested smith was hammering while his apprentice worked the bellows. They stopped and watched us as we passed. Adults appeared in doorways, peering at us through the rain. Simple village folk. Peasants, but prosperous enough; well fed, well clothed in homespun wool. We nodded at them, and got nods back, and a shy wave or two.

Hovels gave way to cottages, and to a square, in the middle of which was a low platform. On it was a still, small, forlorn figure sat in the stocks, hunched under sodden clothes, bare, dirty feet sticking out towards us. *Poor guy,* I thought.

Then, *No, wait—poor girl. Wonder what she's done to deserve that …*

At the sound of our arrival, she looked up at us, bedraggled, through soaked brown hair. Gods, she couldn't have been more than ten or eleven. She looked cold, and thin, and miserable. More than anything, she reminded me of Little Guy. We could see the village inn ahead of us, across the muddy square, but I veered off towards the girl.

She watched me warily as I approached.

I said, "Hello."

No reply.

"What's your name?"

She swallowed. Looked around. Looked back at me.

I waited, eyebrows raised, unthreatening.

The girl mumbled, "Jess."

I said, "Nice to meet you, Jess, I'm Daxx."

She frowned.

Did she think I was taunting her?

The others had gathered around me by now.

Qrysta asked, "Why did they put you in there?"

Jess looked from one face to another. Finally she looked back at Qrysta. "I stole."

Oller said, this being his field of expertise, "Got an uncle here?"

The girl looked at him, puzzled. "Huh?"

Oller grunted.

I thought I knew what he'd done: Used thieves' slang, and she hadn't understood it.

I said, quietly, "TG?"

Oller shook his head and muttered, "amateur."

I couldn't quell my curiosity. "What did you steal, Jess?"

"Scraps."

"From?"

"The inn. They were throwing them out, honest, in a bucket out the back door. I didn't know they was for the pigs. I only picked a crust o' bread. They caught me. Said I had to sit here until I pay up."

I said, "How much?"

"Half a copper."

Oller snorted in derision. "Half a copper for a crust?! *That's* thieving—not what this lass did! I spec' you was hungry?"

Jess nodded.

"I spec' you still are?"

Jess nodded again.

We could see, now, that the water running down her face was not just rainwater.

Qrysta said, "You not from around here, Jess?"

Jess shook her head.

"Where are you from, then?"

Jess didn't seem to know how to answer that. Eventually, she said, "Home."

"And where's home?" Qrysta asked.

Jess said, "I don't know."

"How can you not know where home is?" Oller said.

"I don't know," Jess said. "I don't know where here is."

We didn't follow. We didn't want to interrogate her; the poor thing was miserable enough.

I looked at Qrysta. She'd think of something.

She crouched by the shivering child and asked, gently, "Do you have a family, Jess?"

"I did," Jess said, in a small, dulled voice. "But I don't anymore. They're all dead."

We all went still.

"What happened?"

Jess hesitated, then said, "Pirates." Then her self-restraint broke, and she started weeping, her thin shoulders shaking.

I said, "Grell, see what you can do with those stocks."

Grell unslung Fugg from his back, growling. "Right you are, mate!"

Jess looked up at his growl, startled. Well, wouldn't you be? A little, shivering, hungry girl, clapped up in the stocks, in the cold rain, and now a huge Orc bearing down on you with his battle-axe …

I said, "Don't worry, Jess, he won't hurt you."

Her scrawny legs were free by the time I'd finished saying that.

Qrysta reached out a hand and helped Jess to her feet. "Come along, love," she said, with a smile. "We're going to pay your debt and get this all squared away. First, though, we're going to make it a lot bigger. We're all as hungry as you are!"

Jess didn't know what to say. We hung back, and gave her and Qrysta space, thinking, *Three heavily armed, strange men have got to be worrying to the kid; best not crowd in on them. She'll feel safe with Qrysta.*

Qrysta led her across the square to the inn, and we followed a few paces behind them, as the light closed in, and the wind strengthened, and the cold rain drove harder into our backs, and we heard the first grumbles of thunder over the hills behind us. No one should be out on a night like the one that was coming. Not even a thief who had stolen the enormous sum of half a copper.

The inn was small and bare, but snug, and warm, and well lit by candles and lanthorns. The candles guttered as we entered, and the wind blew in with us. The low murmur of rustic voices died to silence. A quick look around told us that there were no fighting men there. Farmers, peasants, fisherfolk, craftsmen, and women. They stared at us in shock. And, I soon saw, fear.

There was no need for that. "Good evening, good folk," I said, quietly, and let my voice sound as tired as I felt. "Don't let us disturb you. A meal and a mug of ale, and we'll be on our way. And we owe someone here our thanks, for rescuing our friend here, young Jess. Innkeeper?"

I'd already identified her: A middle-aged, middle-sized woman wearing a food-stained apron, with a shock of unruly red hair and a tired, wary face.

She came forward and curtseyed and whispered, "Yes, m'lord?"

"I'm no lord," I said, with a smile, "just a hungry traveler. Five mugs of ale, if you please, and I hope you have hot food ready?"

"Mutton stew, if it please you, sir, and bread fresh-baked this morning, and a mash o' neaps and parsnips, and butter-fried cabbage would be all I have, sir, but plenty of it."

I could smell it. My mouth was watering. The others were groaning, from lack of food as well as from anticipation.

I held out a gold piece to her. Her eyes grew round. "I ... I could never make change for that, sir!" she stammered, unable to take her eyes off the gold. "Some few silvers or coppers?"

I said, "It's yours. Just keep the food and the ale coming. If it tastes as good as it smells, we have a bargain."

It did.

Gods it felt good to eat.

We fell onto the stew like flies onto a corpse. Oh, we'd have eaten anything—but *this?* Heaven. No one had the strength, or the time, or the slightest inclination to talk. All we wanted to do was shovel. And gulp.

Jess hung back until she saw that no one was watching her. Then she was as absorbed in her eating as the rest of us. I had a vague impression of the other guests in this tavern watching us with confused, but not hostile, interest. I saw no one slip out to run off and tell anyone about us—any reeve or Clerk of the Watch.

I beckoned the Innkeeper over, between mouthfuls of her mutton stew, and ordered ale for all. And went back to my shoveling. And all in the little room took their ales, when the boy and girl delivered them, and thanked us with wary nods and raises of their mugs, and shy, "Thankee's", and returned to their own business.

When we sat back, after eating our suppers, and put our feet up, and saw the steam coming off our clothes in the light that was flickering from the fire in the hearth, all felt well. Oller and Grell moved off and struck up quiet conversations with the other guests. None of them had ever seen an Orc before and were both wary and interested. Oller was far more of a threat, but they had no way of knowing that. He just seemed like a normal little bloke, like the rest of them. Qrysta and Jess conversed, on a bench in a corner by the fire, in low voices. I heard Jess sob, and then sniffle, and then pull herself together. We weren't in any kind of danger there, clearly. But we didn't have the information. *Where, who, what.*

I signaled to the Innkeeper to join me. I thanked her for the excellent food, at which she seemed less overawed by us. I asked her simple questions, about the place and the people. I got simple answers. This was a poor island, an uneventful island, of few people; an independent island, not owned by any grand lord, they thanked all the gods. They fished, and farmed, and gathered crabs, and shellfish, and samphire, and harvested, and crafted, and traded.

Who with?

At that, she became uncomfortable. "With them that comes to trade," she said.

Ah, I thought. So that's where the power lies. Smugglers.

No point in pushing it.

Her name, I learned, was Sallen. "Sally-Ann for long, sir, but it's been Sallen to one and all, since I were a babe." She was shocked by what I told her about Jess, and the stolen crust, and the stocks. She'd look into it, she said, to see which of her girls had done that.

Her family were all dead, Jess had said, but the village folk might not know that. And even if they did, instinct told me it was important that they knew Jess had people to protect her. "Don't punish your lass, Sallen. Jess would have run away, and we'd never have found her. We'd still be out looking for her, in this thunderstorm."

"She's not from around here," Sallen said, looking at Jess.

"Nor are we," I said.

She seemed satisfied with that.

No, they had no reeve on the island—no constable to serve any lord's justice. The islanders dealt justice as they saw fit. A crust, a crime, an hour in the stocks. Sallen didn't make the rules. She was glad that the poor mite had found her friends again and had a good meal in her belly.

Jess had said she was not from around here. And now we knew she had been here less than a day.

Where had she come from? And where was she going?

8

Jess's Tale

Oller, of course, wanted to be heading off that night. We pointed out that we all, including him, needed sleep as much as we had needed food. He saw the sense in that. He was as exhausted as we were. We wouldn't be expected back for a day or two. Yes, Little Guy would be starving, but he'd starved and survived before, often, in his hard life on the road.

They rarely saw outsiders here, Sallen told us. The only travelers who passed this way were farmers and traders, who might sometimes need a bed for the night before heading on. She had two small rooms, both, as usual, unoccupied. We took both, one for Qrysta and Jess, the other for Grell and Oller and me.

Jess seemed quietened, now, when I looked across at her and Qrysta, talking softly in their corner by the fire. I wondered what Qrysta had learned. I also wondered what in the world we were going to do with Jess. We could hardly abandon her. Nor could we take her through a nasty-sounding delve and whatever this "portal" was, to face off with a helldragon.

We slumped down on our beds, which were thin mattresses stuffed with straw. Sleep was as welcome as our supper had been. Grell was snoring the moment he was horizontal. Shift and I popped some Orbs of Warmth around us, and the last of the rain evaporated from our clothes.

"Gods, that's good!" Oller muttered in appreciation.

I said, "What are we going to do about Jess?"

"No idea," he said, and turned over and went to sleep.

I tried to think, but the next thing I knew, it was daybreak. A rooster was informing us of that fact, loudly and repeatedly. Others, more distant, echoed their challenges back at him. *Fu-uh-huck you-hoo, ooh-ooh-oo!*—Yeah?? *Fu-uh-huck you too, ooh-ooh-oo!* We'd had a good eight hours of sleep or more, on full stomachs. A long day lay ahead of us. None of us minded rising with the dawn.

Sallen fed us, an enormous cheese omelet full of onions and carrots, no doubt made with eggs supplied by our alarm clock's wives, and loaves fresh out of the oven, slathered with her home-churned butter. She made us packages of food and supplied us with flasks of ale for the journey.

Qrysta told me what to do about Jess, and I, in turn, told Sallen that she was to look after the girl, who would work willingly, she'd agreed, and that we'd be back for her in a day or two.

I gave Sallen another gold coin, for Jess's bed and board.

She took it, trembling, and curtseyed again, and said, "You'll be welcome here, Miss Jess," as if Jess were some young noblewoman.

Jess thanked her, and said she was very kind, ma'am, and that she'd be a good girl. She thanked us, solemnly, but was clearly nervous to see us go. We all gave her smiles and farewells, hoping they didn't seem fake. After all, who were we to her, and who was she to us?

We'd find out some of that soon, Qrysta had hinted. She'd had a good, long chat with Jess, after supper in the public room of Sallen's inn, and later in their bedroom. I could tell from the way she said it that what she had learned was interesting. She gave Jess a last hug, and a kiss on top of her head, and said, "Well, at least you'll be nice and dry here, while we're out there getting drenched!" It was still awkward, but we felt the ice was breaking, somewhat. And what had to be done, had to be done.

We shouldered our packs, and hefted our weapons, and left into a gray, drizzly morning. We were soon soaked, but we didn't mind that. We had a job to do. And, the moment we were away from the village, and away from anyone watching, I opened Shift's eye, and felt her wake up with her familiar *hullo* up my arm and raised her to cast Orbs of Warmth and Shielding on us all, and we marched on, drying out inside them, as the rain fell steadily all around, on everything but us. We knew it was another half a day's march to our destination.

Which gave us plenty of time to talk.

Jess had been helping her mother with the laundry, Qrysta told us, when the attack came on their remote coastal cottage. It came out of the blue and was on them before they knew it. Or rather, it came out of a blanket of sea fog, early on a cold morning.

Several days before, that had been, we gathered. The only reason Jess wasn't killed or captured was because her quick-thinking mother had pushed her to the ground and piled the dirty laundry on top of her, urging her to lie still and be quiet. Jess—"who had been sobbing as she told me," Qrysta said—had heard what happened to her mother. Slaps, and rough male laughter, and her mother pleading, and then crying out in pain, and then the sounds of clothes being ripped, and more rough laughter, and grunting, and mockery, and her mother's muffled voice, sobbing.

Eventually, long after all sounds had died away, Jess had emerged from her cover. The fog had lifted. Her mother was naked, her throat slit. Her father's body she found on the shore, slumped over his upturned fishing boat, arrows in his back. They must have shot him the moment they saw him through the fog, to stop him raising the alarm.

Her two-year-old brother and infant sister were missing. There was a ship halfway to the horizon, hardly moving in the still, clear air. As Jess watched, the ship lowered a tender, men piling into it. She had sharp enough eyes to see that they were looking at her. Something glinted. The end of a telescope, pointed her way. They'd left a valuable piece of merchandise behind and were coming back for her.

She ran, not stopping for food or clothes, but only to bolt the cottage door from the inside and then wriggle out through a back window. She hoped they'd think she'd barricaded herself inside and would waste time breaking the door down and searching the house for her, while she fled. She knew the surroundings well, which the pirates didn't. She worried that they'd have a dog that could track her.

The land was wooded, and she was soon hidden in the trees. They wouldn't even know which direction she'd run in. She thought about hiding up a tree, or watching to see which way they went, and then going another—but then, maybe they'd fan out and search in all directions. Better to put as many miles between herself and them as possible.

"I'm a good runner," she'd told Qrysta. "Ma or Da was always sending me on errands. And I'm stronger than I look, I could carry a creel full of fish on my back all day."

She'd had plenty of time to think as she made her way inland. Most of the places she went on her errands were near the coast, where the pirates might call next. She could go and warn people, she thought. But then she might walk into another raid. What she'd seen was nightmare enough to put her off risking that.

She walked away from the coast, always heading inland, and by nightfall was in a place she didn't know. She was cold. It began to rain. She was hungry. She kept walking, until she could walk no longer. She huddled under a tree and eventually slept, fitfully. At least she had plenty of water.

The next morning she was up and off again. She didn't hurry. She wanted to preserve her strength. She was hopeful that she'd lost her pursuers. She was hopeful that they wouldn't go too far from the shore and their ship. They'd give up, surely, and go off with what prizes they already had. She walked through the woods, over the following days, until she came out of them to the village, where, starving, soaked, shivering, we had found her, clapped up in the stocks.

Qrysta had done her best to comfort her.

"She's a tough little thing," she said. "She just told it like it was. She held back the tears as much as she could. If it hadn't been so horrible, you'd have thought, from the flat tone of her voice, that she was telling something dull. Ordinary, even. That was somehow worse. It sent shivers up my spine. Made me wish I'd been there, to even things up a bit."

"You mean, *we'd* been there," Grell said.

Qrysta grunted her agreement.

The four of *us*, against a few scruffy sea-reavers …?

Jess would still have a family. And a home.

"She's not going back, she told me," Qrysta said.

I said, "So where will she go?"

Qrysta looked at me, and said, "Wherever she wants. I'll see to that."

I agreed. "Yes, we will."

We saw no one on our way. Jess had told Qrysta that not many people lived on the island, and of those that did, almost all lived by the sea. Clearly, no one ever went where we were going. It was past midday, after a gloomy morning's march, by the time we reached our destination. *You can't miss it,* the no-face man had said. We couldn't.

The mouth of the cave was, indeed, a mouth. The cave itself sat below what looked like a skull made of bleached rocks in the cliffside ahead. Deep holes made two lopsided eye sockets. Someone had carved out an arch of teeth above the entrance. *Very welcoming,* we thought. There was no path leading up to it. It seemed that this place was avoided by one and all. I couldn't blame them. Only the foolhardy would enter somewhere as forbidding as this. Unless, of course, they had to.

We contemplated the dark cave entrance.

"Pity our bows are at the bottom of the ocean," Qrysta said. "It'd be nice to have the option of ranged attacks."

"Just have to spray 'em with everything you've got, then, eh Daxxie?" Grell said, as we unslung our weapons. "While we three get up close and personal."

"I'll do my best," I promised.

"Right," Oller said, "let's do this."

He led on, padding ahead on his almost-silent boots. Oller never seemed to make a sound when he moved, certainly if he didn't want to. Grell, on the other hand, sounded like trouble coming from a long way off with his menacing, thumping strides. We let Oller scout ahead, and followed in silence; me, Qrysta, Grell bringing up the rear. I wasn't about to throw up any Glows to light our way. We knew this place was inhabited, and we didn't want to give warning of our approach. I cast Reveals on the passages ahead, and we walked on, and down, the tunnel twisting this way and that, stopping occasionally to listen. We heard nothing. Oller saw nothing. No hidden life was revealed.

Suddenly, I nearly bumped into him, invisible in the dark ahead of me. He had stopped and was holding up his hand. He'd spotted something. He listened. The others arrived and halted behind us, breathing as quietly as they could. My Reveals showed nothing. Well, nothing of interest: Just a few small, fuzzy red outlines, scuttling along the floor going about their business.

Peering ahead, motionless, Oller listened. He lowered his hand to his knife belt, and raised it, a blade between thumb and finger. His arm blurred. The knife flew. There was a thump, and a squeal, and a mutter from Oller of, "Gottim!"

He trotted on down and picked up the large, dead rat.

He cleaned his knife, carefully, and replaced it in his belt.

He held the rat up by its tail and inspected it. It was a big, heavy brute, a pound in weight or more.

Oller grunted, pleased, and placed it in his pack.

I said, "Oller?! Your food's in there!"

"So's Little Guy's, now."

I stared at him as if he was mad. "Are you serious?"

He stared back as if I was. "He'll be starving! Dead partial to a nice bit of rat, he is."

Grell said, "Mate … you're going to attack a helldragon, carrying a dead rat?"

"He'll love it!" Oller protested.

Qrysta said, "We'll be coming back this way, you know."

"So?"

"So, we can kill all the rats you want then."

"How d'you know?!" Oller challenged.

Qrysta retorted, "Well, it's kinda obvious, isn't it?"

"No?"

She turned to me. "Daxxie, any more rats around here you can see?"

I refreshed my Reveals. I could see four little scuttling glows. "Several."

"Is that so?" Oller said, suddenly interested. "You wanna Ice Trap them for me, Daxx? The more the merrier!"

I put my hand on his shoulder. "Oller," I said, "killing rats is *not* going to be a problem. Surviving, so that we can come back and kill rats, is the problem. So, I suggest you forget about rats for the moment, and drop the one you're carrying with all your food because that's not hygienic, and—"

"I'm not leaving it here!" Oller protested.

I thought, *what?*

Qrysta said "You can get food poisoning from having a dead rat near your food."

Oller objected, "It'll get eaten!"

"What by?"

"Rats! Rats eat rats, everyone knows that—they'll eat anything. Or spiders and such. I'm not leaving his dinner here to be eaten by rats!"

He was not, we could see, going to change his mind.

"Fine," I said. "On we go. Only no more rat-hunting, all right? Leave that for later."

"Umf," Oller snorted and trotted off, on point ahead as always.

He had no more than half a dozen dead rats in his pack by the time we reached the portal. This was because we were in combat much of the way, rather than because he was keeping an eye out for more food for Little Guy. We'd run into a mob, of ghouls or zombies or slime-lizards, and when the smoke cleared there was sometimes a rat among the dead, which had been collateral damage to the Area of Effect attacks I'd laid down. Occasionally those were Flamefields, so the rats were already barbecued by the time Oller harvested them. He was more interested, I think, in picking up dead rats than he was in slaughtering whatever it was that was attacking us.

It was hard work. The things were a lot tougher than they looked, all of them. We should have routed mobs like these without breaking a sweat. Were we out of practice? Maybe. Whatever, it was a tough grind reaching the portal. It was guarded by four tall, iron pillars, between which ropelike strands of lightning crackled. I couldn't work out how to take them down, so we just ploughed through them, yelping as they shocked us, and then the pillars jerked into life, becoming sizzling, sparking, lightning creatures that threw everything they had at us. And everything they had was a *lot*.

Qrysta danced. Grell roared and slashed. Oller slipped and stabbed, and nothing that any blade did to them had any effect. Meanwhile, the tall lightning creatures were draining us of strength and jabbing us with bolts of pain that threw us around like leaves in the wind. Anytime that they managed to grab one of us with what I suppose must have been some kind of "hand," the person in that grip froze, jerking and screaming, and heating up like a mouse in a microwave. It was all I could do to Ward and Heal and Shield. There was no chance of unleashing Shift's Damages on them.

Until Grell had an idea. "Olz, Q! Focus the other three! Keep 'em busy."

Bellowing, he stalked up to the nearest creature and slammed Fugg through it—to no avail, except to get his arm gripped. He stood, howling with pain and defiance, while the other creatures ignored Oller and Qrysta and closed in.

I thought, *What in all hells is he doing? I can't deal with all of them at once on him—*

And then I felt Shift's surge of excitement.

As so often in combat, she was ahead of me. I'd long since stopped wondering what she was thinking when she reacted like that. I knew she'd let me know any second.

Her surge became a jolt, and then another, until my arm felt as if it was sizzling. Normally I'd have dropped anything that did that to me and shaken the pain out of my poor fried hand.

Instead, I got the message. I pointed her at the four lightning creatures that were pouring their bolts into the howling, writhing Orc. Shift had seen that ice didn't work. Against fire, maybe not—but lightning?

She was throwing up the heaviest Cloudburst that she could manage as what she had seen became clear to my slow brain.

Black thunderclouds filled the air above us and broke. A deluge of water poured out of them, and an eerie, very short, very dazzling fireworks display erupted in front of our eyes. The lightning creatures short-circuited and exploded. Oller and Qrysta were thrown backwards, gasping. Grell dropped to the ground like a statue falling off its plinth, face down, stiff, his bristly Orc hair sizzling, smoke coming out of his ears.

After the cacophony, silence.

And Grell's ominous stillness.

"Grello?" Qrysta shouted, scrambling to her feet and running over to him. "You okay?"

I could tell from her tone of voice that she was worried. Between us we rolled the rigid, sizzling Orc onto his back.

He lay there, eyes empty, staring up, expressionless.

I didn't bother looking for signs of life. I hit him with every Heal I could think of. Qrysta pumped his chest and blew into his far-from-fragrant mouth and urged and cajoled, while he lay there, as still and lifeless as the stone statue he resembled. The longer he didn't respond, the harder she worked, and the more frantic she sounded. "Don't you dare die on me, big boy …!"

Thoughts just as frantic were passing between me and Shift. Nothing we did seemed to have worked. And we had tried everything we knew. Oller was hopping from foot to foot, asking me, *What d'you think, Daxx?* And, *He'll be all right, won't he?*

It was an age before he coughed, and gasped, and sat up, and coughed again, and swallowed, and looked about himself in confusion, and saw us without seeing us, and threw up all over Oller.

It took us all a long while to recover.

And that, we all thought, hadn't even been the End Boss of this delve.

Helldragon.

That didn't sound good.

We'd damn nearly been overmatched by the lightning creatures.

A leathern flask of Sallen's ale was opened and passed around. Slumped on the ground, we ate cheese and bread, and pickled onions, and the remains of the previous night's cold mutton stew.

It was a long time before anyone had the strength to speak.

Eventually, Grell hauled himself to his feet.

"Right," he said. "Let's go."

We picked ourselves up and followed him to the portal. It was an arch, made of some kind of woven bone, between which an opaque sheet of blue and white energy crackled. We inspected it, from front and back.

"What do you think, Daxxie?" Qrysta said.

I cast Divination on it.

Nothing. It gave me no clues. "I've no idea."

It was here. What was beyond it, we would only find out by going through it.

Which, in our usual order—Oller, me, Qrysta, Grell—we did.

As I stepped through it, everything faded out, and, slowly, a very different everything faded back in. Where before we'd been heading downwards, on the steadily descending dirt floor of the cave, now the path spiraled up and away from us, and it was a path of sky-blue light, twisting among other ribbonlike paths of other colors that led from nowhere to nowhere. The spaces between the paths were a deep indigo that was almost black, in which points of light flickered and glinted like stars. The paths, including ours, were continually moving, undulating, writhing as if alive.

Grell, arriving last, said, "Bugger me …"

We all took a few moments to take in our strange surroundings.

"Well," Qrysta said, eventually, "keep going forwards, right?"

We did, in file, as there was no room on the path for us to walk abreast, Oller leading the way. The path, somehow, seemed to know that we were there. It bunched around our feet as we stepped along it, as if feeling us out, trying to find out what we were. It also, always, twisted; but whichever direction we were standing in was always "up"; so when, looking back, we could see the portal behind us, we felt that we were the right way up, but could see that it was now, compared to us, upside down.

No point in trying to be stealthy in here, I thought, so I popped some Glows up, to move along with us, and those were comforting. They also floated overhead, whichever way up we actually were, so their "above" was the same as ours. The further we went, the nearer the little points of light became. We could, before long, reach out and touch them.

Qrysta brought one in, on her hand, where it hovered, like a glowing snowflake. It also hummed, an ethereal, glassy sound. The other little starflakes around us hummed too, not exactly in harmony but certainly in concert. It was a strange, unsettling, jangling music—in a strange, unsettling place.

We stared at it slowly rotating above Qrysta's palm, its light fading and brightening.

Grell said, "Daxxie?"

I shook my head. "No idea."

"It's beautiful," Qrysta said, but her tone was wary.

She released the starflake and it drifted back to hover among its companions. We kept going forwards. No one spoke. We were on alert, listening through the brittle humming of the starflakes for any hint of any other sound.

Our path, abruptly, divided.

One moment we were walking up and down and along, and the next, there we were, as the sky-blue path split ahead of us and separated into a fork, slowly, as we watched.

We stopped. Well, which way?

"When you come to a fork in the road," Grell said, "take it."

Oller had never heard that cliché before. He turned and frowned at Grell, and said, baffled, "Eh??"

"It's a joke," Grell said.

Oller frowned. "Bloody silly one, if you ask me."

Grell said, "Yup."

"So, what d'you think, Daxx?" Oller asked me.

"I think Grell's right. We take it. You and Grell take the left, Qrysta and I'll take the right."

Qrysta said, uncertain, "Divide our forces?"

Grell said, "What if it divides again?"

"Split up again," I suggested.

None of them seemed sure about that.

I said, "Look, I'm not happy about this either. But I can't see what else we can do. It could keep dividing forever, and we'd be going around in circles."

Qrysta said, "Yeah, but without comms, Daxxie, we're on our own. At least we'd be going around in circles together."

I thought about it. "I don't think so. I think that's what it wants."

Grell said, "It?"

"The path."

They looked at me quizzically.

"Well?" I said. "We've all noticed it writhing and grabbing our feet as if it's feeling us out …"

I had an idea. I turned around and aimed Shift at the path behind us.

I fired a Flameball at it. The path did *not* like that. It writhed, and bucked, and shivered, and we were tossed into the air, landing on our backsides, and grabbing the path's edges to prevent ourselves falling off. Eventually, it stopped bouncing.

Behind us, I saw, the rest of the path had disappeared.

"Fuck," Qrysta said.

I grinned at her.

"What's so funny?!" she challenged. "You've cut off our retreat!"

"There's no going back, Qrys," I said, "you know that. As for what's so funny, let me show you. Left or right?"

"Huh?"

"Left," I repeated, "or right?"

She shrugged, having no idea, and eventually said, "Left."

At Shift's glow of confirmation, I said, "Good guess. Stay down, guys, and hang on tight." I raised Shift and blew a Flameball at the left-hand path ahead of us.

Once again, the path under us bucked and writhed, and once again we were trampolined, flat on our sides and clinging to the path's edge.

And when that stopped, there was only one sky-blue ribbon ahead of us, leading away into the indigo void, the burnt stump of the other fork hanging limply off it.

"What if you destroyed the right way?" Qrysta exclaimed.

"I didn't."

"How the hell do you know?" Grell challenged.

I felt Shift preening and her merry warmth spread up my arm. She loved to make mischief. "Let's just say that I have wide experience with, uh … *shifty* magical constructs, Grello."

Qrysta was the first to work it out. She glanced at Shift, and then at me, and grinned.

"Smart friend you have there, Daxx."

Her smile lit me up from the inside. It was as refreshing as any of Shift's Heals.

"We all have our uses. Shall we?"

We did.

9

The Helldragon

After a while, and a few more Flameballs—and we all made sure that we were lying down, and clinging on, before I cast them—the path gave up trying to challenge us by dividing, and setting us the problem, *now what?* It knew when it was beaten.

Our mood lightened. As I fired one of my last Flameballs, and the path under us kicked and writhed as its fork blew away, Qrysta said, "Talk about Player versus Environment!" which made me smile.

We'd never had to fight the actual *landscape* before—the environment itself. Things were, indeed, very different here.

As we marched on, Grell sang, in a hideous Orc falsetto, "Daxxie, the Puzzle King," to the tune of "Gypsy, the Acid Queen." Which was, of course, a song Oller had never heard, and he said, "Gods above and below, Grell! What a bloody *din!* Is that what passes for bardsong among you Ozgaroos?"

Grell said, happily, "Yep."

Oller grunted, and said, "Remind me never to go to one o' *your* hoolies."

"Our what?"

"Hoolies? That's what we call them, when we all gather round and sing. The old songs, usually. Sad ones, love ones, comic ones. We all join in with the choruses; bawling them out by the end of the night, drinking too much, only to wake up with sore throats and sorer heads. Sometimes you have proper bards, who might be local, or passing through, with harps and lutes, and pipes and tabors and such. They all know all the tunes, whatever they throw at each other. You should hear 'em, passing the melody round to each other, and taking off, and playing fancy buggers with it. Whip us all up, they do, and before you know it, you're dancing."

I said, "Jam session."

Oller frowned at me. "Jam? We're not bloody stewing fruit, matey, we're throwing a hoolie!"

"That's *our* name for them," I said. "Jam sessions."

Oller stopped and turned around and stared at me. "Fuck me," he said, "you foreigners really are a weird lot. *Jam?!* Why jam?"

I thought about it. I had to admit that I didn't know. "No idea."

Oller was still staring at me, mouth open. "You give it a stupid name and you don't know *why?*"

I said, "That's about right, Oller."

"Uhh," he grunted, dismissively, and shook his head, and led on.

Twisting around, and above, and below us: Orange ribbons, yellow ribbons, green and red, our sky-blue ribbon-path among them, leading us plodding on towards—well, we supposed we'd find out soon enough.

The starflakes hummed their glassy not-quite-harmonies around us. The indigo depth of the distance beckoned to us. It was, strangely, beautiful. Even though we didn't want to be there. Why was it like this? Where were we going? What lay ahead? All we had was a ribbon-road of sky-blue light and the discordant music of our tiny, floating stars. Odd. All, very, odd.

And then, odder.

We came up over a curve, where our blue ribbon undulated onto a circular platform. On the platform was a black shape. Which, as we approached, resolved itself into a clerk, perched on a stool behind an upright desk.

An elderly, very old-fashioned clerk, in very old-fashioned clothes. He was dressed in a long, black robe, its lace collar laced up under his chin. A cloud of white hair stood out around the edges of his bald head. His fingers were ink-stained, his thin back stooped from a lifetime of pen-pushing.

He looked up at us as we arrived, peering at us with pale, watery eyes.

"Names?" he asked, in a voice as gloomy as the void behind him.

We gave them: Daxx Pytte, Oller Pinches, Grell Ozborn, Qrysta Orange.

He wrote them down, slowly, using a quill which he dipped in an inkwell, checking the spelling of each word before he did.

"Pleasure or business?"

Well, you never say *business* or there's all sorts of crap they ask you.

I answered, "Pleasure."

"Tourism?"

"Yes."

"Please fill out this form."

He handed us a form. It was several pages long, made of beige parchment and bound with red ribbon.

Actual, genuine red tape.

The others passed it to me.

"Puzzle," Qrysta said.

It took me ten minutes to complete the damn thing. And I had to complete it with mostly lies, so …

… let's see what this geezer comes up with.

He studied everything I had submitted. Slowly.

Every time he came to the end of a page, he licked his left thumb, and applied it to the top right-hand corner of the page, which he turned, slowly. Only his rheumy old eyes moved. He gave off no clue as to what he was thinking.

He finished.

He reached for a large, round stamp, and pressed it into his ink pad.

He stamped the document; footled around amonth the clutter on his desk; found another folder; took out form it four small pieces of paper and gave us one each.

They read, *Admit One.*

He looked up at us, his face a mask of bureaucratic solemnity. "Don't lose them," he said. "They'll need to be stamped on the way out."

I said, "What if we do?"

"No ticket," he said, "no exit."

And that, it seemed, was that. His job was done.

"Have a nice day," he intoned, and waited for us to leave.

"You too," I said.

Oller led us on across the platform, and we fell in beside him. "Nice day?" he sneered. "If it's as nice as him it'll be bloody miserable."

"I think," I said, "all this is designed to disorient us."

"Dis—what?" Oller did not know the word.

"Confuse. Unsettle. Bamboozle."

"Ah. Well. I've no idea what's going on," he agreed. "So you've got that right."

I said, "I expect we'll find out soon enough." I looked back at the clerk.

He, and his desk, had gone.

"Uhh, guys …"

They all stopped and looked back. No desk, no clerk.

"Environment's certainly dicking with us," Qrysta said.

"It is that," I agreed.

"Best be on the alert, then," Grell said, as we moved on again, down another sky-blue ribbon-path.

We heard the sounds of trouble ahead long before we could see what was causing them—and long before whatever was making them could see us. Intermittent growling, and rumbling, then silence; then more deep, sinister sounds, as if all the giants in creation were snoring after some drunken feast.

And then, as we got closer, other noises. Deep, barking coughs. Snarls, answered by other snarls, as if several of the biggest cats ever born were taunting each other—and I don't mean domestic cats. Sabercats, at the very least. And then, suddenly, a chorus of roars. Coming from it was impossible to tell how many throats.

Whatever was up ahead of us wasn't alone. And that wasn't particularly reassuring.

I cast Reveals, and when I saw the fuzzy red outlines ahead, muttered, "Fuck me …"

Grell said, "What is it?"

"It's not an it. It's a *them.*"

The glowing red outlines that my cast had revealed were enormous. Where Oller's rats had been trotting along the floor, barely noticeable, minding their own business, my Revealed view ahead was filled with huge, red-framed shapes, crowding each other out.

Whoa. Talk about a mob …

I thought: *The no-face man had said helldragon.* Nothing about a menagerie of monsters. There wasn't just one brute ahead that we'd have to deal with; there was a swarm of the things.

I told the others. None of us liked the spot we were in. There was no going back, obviously. And ahead lay a world of trouble.

"Can you tell anything about them?" Qrysta asked.

"Only that they're massive," I said. I cast Divination but got no result. Either we were too far away or my skills weren't up to learning anything about whatever this lot were.

Grell said. "How many?"

Shift and I refreshed Reveals and tried to count. I could feel her nervousness up my arm. She didn't like this one bit. There were so many huge shapes moving around it that was impossible to be sure. And some smaller ones at the edges ...

"At least six big ones," I said, "maybe more. And a number of others. *Gods* .... If we didn't have to do this, I'd seriously consider sneaking past. If that's even possible."

"My guess is that it isn't," Qrysta said. "So, we're going to need a plan."

"It's never easy coming up with a plan without information."

"Well, who said this would be easy?!" she retorted. "Come on, Daxx, you're the strategy guy. What have you got?"

I thought. "We have no ranged attacks except mine. Not that arrows would have much effect on ... well, whatever those things are. You guys are close-quarter artists. Yes, you might be able to get among them and deal some damage, but equally you might get stomped on. I mean—*helldragon*? You'd think that might involve fire, wouldn't you? Okay, you're in good niblun gear, but getting up close and personal with a flamethrower ..."

I really couldn't think of anything.

Grell said, "Well, let's take a look at the arena anyway."

We moved on, towards the roaring and thundering, and, now, occasional shrieks and squeals. The closer we got to the sources of them, the louder they grew. The sky-blue ribbon-path twisted, and spiraled, and rose, and fell, down and around, ending at a stone floor that led to the mouth of a tunnel. When my Reveals filled my vision with the fuzzy red outlines of huge lumbering blobs, I stopped and motioned to the others to get down.

There was no point in attempting to speak. We'd never have heard ourselves above the cacophony that was filling the air and making our bodies vibrate. We dropped, and crawled into the tunnel, and came to a ridge, and looked down at the scene below.

Ah. So, they weren't moving around each other as I'd thought.

They were moving in and out of each other.

Literally.

Down there it was mating season.

We were looking down at a large, circular stone floor, which was hosting the biggest orgy of the biggest things we'd ever seen.

And at the center of them, the helldragon.

Who made the others around her seem like shrimps, while they clambered all over each other, and fought with each other—all to get the chance to clamber all over *her*.

We watched, amazed. And wondered what in all hells to do.

Wait until they'd finished?

What would that achieve? They'd all subside and sleep it off? And then we'd, what? Go for the boss, and—yeah, right, kill her without waking her, um, "mates" up?

And anyway, how long would that take?

We could be waiting here for days.

Nope.

We were going to have to hit them while they were … otherwise engaged.

And that would piss every one of them off—especially any that hadn't yet had his, or her, jollies.

Indeed. But … so?

Better to catch them while they, so to speak, have their pants down, than to give them a chance to organize. Look, it's chaos down there, right? They're busy. We can use that to our advantage.

How? *I'm thinking, I'm thinking …*

And how long d'you think it'll take them to realize they're under attack before they attack back? Probably not very long.

Okay, so you have "not very long" to do this. Act now, while they least expect it, and act fast.

Yes, I thought. Time for a little coitus interruptus.

By yelling in each other's ears, we got our strategy sorted.

It was a pretty straightforward strategy. First, surprise assault, take as many down as possible. Then, at my signal, a red flare: *ITA, FTB.* Ignore the Adds—meaning, the other, er, fuckers—*and Focus the Boss. Grell front and center as always, taunting and enraging, getting the bulk of the attention. Qrysta dancing and striking, Oller slipping and slicing, both with license to roam as well as to kill. Shift would keep Shields up on them all and would be healing as hard as she was hitting.*

They knew what to do. And they would do it.

I set about planning my attacks. Everything I cast would have to go off one after the other, at speed and in sequence. It took a while, but eventually I was satisfied.

Traps: Ice, Fear, Cage.

Distractions: Illusions charging them—Specters and Ghouls, and so on—Barkers and Screamers overhead, Flashbombs.

Area of Effect attacks: Ice Field below and a Cone of Sheet Lightning from above, just to root them in place and occupy their attention.

Fragbombs: Every seven seconds, another wave.

And my *pièce de résistance* (taking my cue from how we'd killed the lightning creatures): Tempest. Wind, rain, and as much shock power as I could load into it.

Shift needed a few moments to digest all the instructions I'd given her. She closed her red-and-green tourmaline eye. She'd let me know when she was ready to rock.

When she did, I let slip my dogs of war.

There's not much point in screaming orders in combat when there's far too much noise in the air already, but I do it anyway. My words and my body language work together. And my crew is smart—so smart that it sometimes seems that they can read my mind. They can't. I wish they could. But they can read my lips and my expressions and my gestures. And I can read theirs.

As my AofE's and traps sprang up around the clusterfuck ahead, and my Shrieks and Barkers and Whizzbangs had them all looking up in alarm, Grell and Oller and Qrysta charged.

They killed everything that was trapped, and ignored everything that was Feared or otherwise distracted. Those were either fleeing in terror or busy swatting off nonexistent ghouls, so were no threat. The three of them herded everything back into the Icefield, where they slowed and stuck. They danced around the Cone of Lightning where our foes sizzled and exploded.

We'd made a good start with our surprise assault, but there were still too many of the things left. My bombs took out one or two, but these brutes were *tough*. Much sooner than I'd hoped, I heard Grell yell, "Boost!" I poured Heals into him and refreshed his Stamina to the max, and he turned back to his work with fresh energy.

He'd needed it sooner than I had expected.

Not good.

I did a quick calculation. Shift would only manage a few more minutes of this. Fugg didn't seem to be nearly as effective as she'd been back in Jarnland. A massive slash at a leg or a trunk, that you'd have thought would have sliced the target in two, seemed to have little effect. A few nicks, a little blood. Qrysta, too, was jabbing her attacks home and getting poor results. Why? Oller and his knives fared no better. The hides on these things were ridiculous.

I shouted, "Ols!"

He glanced at me.

"Work with Qrysta! Same target, double-team!"

He nodded, and a second later was skewering the other end of Qrysta's foe. The new tactic seemed to work. Beasts dropped, they moved on. The trouble was that there weren't enough of us and there still were too many of them.

All the while I kept glancing at Shift's tourmaline eye while throwing as many Heals and Shields and Wards at my crew as she could. It was clearly fading. She knew what I was thinking: Normally, she'd have anticipated my question with a, *Don't worry, we've got this.*

It was no time to bother her with questions. She needed all her resources for her work.

Up to me, then.

I let her get on with it while I reviewed the situation.

Her Heals were helping, but they weren't holding; not the way I'd expect them to. They frayed quickly, and dropped, and we had to recast them much quicker than I'd anticipated. I began to get the sinking feeling that we were overmatched. And by what? Very large, very angry, very aggressive creatures who seemed to be all teeth and claws and horns and spiked tails, with hides like reinforced steel. Yes, we'd taken some of them down, but there were still a lot of them, and they were fighting back, hard. And, at the center of it all, aware now of what was happening, the helldragon: A horned lizard the size of a whale, with a huge, crocodilian head, leathery wings rearing from her shoulders, and spiked hide as tough as stone.

And she was enraged. It was not looking good.

All-or-nothing, then. Now or never.

"Change of tactic," I told Shift.

I felt her *Over to you* response. It was clear, but tired. And her eye was dimming.

I had to leave off Heals and put everything into Damages. I just hoped the others would survive without my aid. I laid down a Flame-field, threw Tempest over the arena, and popped up my red signal flare. Then I was firing as many shock attacks as I could at the helldragon. *Ignore the Adds, Focus the Boss,* just as the others were doing.

As I'd anticipated, the Flamefield melted all the Ice I'd laid in my first macro attack, which, coupled with all the rain blasting in from Tempest, meant that the battle was raging in a foot or more of water. The shock attacks struck home, from the storm above and the Cone of Lightning surrounding us, while Shift poured on more from the last reserves of her heartstone.

Water and electricity: Not a good combination. Our foes shrieked, and sizzled, and fried, and juddered, and dropped; and, with more than a little help from my friends, died. At least, most of them did. The biggest didn't seem affected in the least by what we were throwing at her. At least, not physically.

Her mood, though, had not been improved.

And that mood, we could all clearly read, was towering anger. I have no idea to this day if helldragons have a language, but it was only too obvious what she was thinking as she stomped around the cavern, crushing her mangled exes under her claws.

You worms think you can crash my party?!

Well, you don't taunt an Orc in battle unanswered.

Grell's shoulders squared, and he drew himself up to his full height. I cast a Shield of Protection around him, and as it bloomed bright green, he bellowed, "Party? This isn't a party, fartbreath. It's a bloody *wake. Yours!*"

They read each other loud and clear. We focused on the Helldrag-on. She focused on Grell. Shift had no reserves left for anything but

Heals, which grew weaker and weaker by the second as my crew set about their business with the last of their stamina. Wherever the helldragon breathed her blasts of fire, Oller or Grell or Qrysta suddenly wasn't, and the other two were behind her, dealing damage.

Her armored tail was, if anything, more dangerous than her jaws and flames, even though she was just thrashing it about blindly. Being away from her head meant being in range of her tail. Grell, slower than the others, got caught by it a couple of times. It takes a deal of force to throw someone as large as Grell twenty feet through the air. If he hadn't had my Shields on him, he'd have had every rib in his body broken, niblun armor or no.

It was Qrysta who ended it, and in typical Qrysta fashion—with, speed, smarts, and that courage of hers that bordered on insanity. When the helldragon's tail was still for a split second, she sprang onto it and clung on. As it thrashed her from side to side, she hauled herself up it, until she could at last get to her feet. She crouched, waiting. Oller happened to be by my side as we both saw what she was doing.

"Gods above and below!" he muttered, breathing heavily.

"Go on, Q!" I urged. "You can do it …"

Abruptly, Qrysta ran along the monster's back, almost disappearing from sight as she ducked behind spines that were taller than she was.

Oller's mouth was hanging open, and he was shaking his head in disbelief. "Never seen the bloody like …"

The brute had no idea she was on top of her. It probably couldn't feel anything through its bony carapace. When she got to its neck, Qrysta paused, one arm around its neck frill, timing her moment. The helldragon's head was swinging from side to side, looking for its tormentors among the Distractions I was firing at her.

"Over here, ugly mug!" Oller yelled, jumping into her sight line.

Grell, seeing Qrysta up there, suddenly stopped dodging and weaving and roared defiance, spreading his arms wide in challenge. "No, over *here*, bugshit-for-brains! Ignore that little squeaker—think *that* can hurt you?"

The helldragon spotted him and took aim. As her mouth opened to douse Grell with fire, her head was momentarily still. Qrysta danced down it and plunged her niblun swords into the monster's eyes up to their hilts.

The flames that would have incinerated Grell if Qrysta had been half a second slower died in the helldragon's throat.

I was watching from a safe distance, popping off what few weak Heals Shift could still manage. As the huge beast tottered and fell, as slowly at first as a giant tree, I was alarmed for Qrysta. Wouldn't she be crushed as the thing hit the ground and rolled on her …?

Calmly, Qrysta held onto the hilts of her swords and braced herself. She rode the helldragon's head down as the monster collapsed, then shoved off them just before it hit the ground, pushing herself well clear of the body and landing off a handspring onto her feet.

I could hear Grell muttering, "Show-off," as I walked over to join them, feeling the usual after-combat combination of exhaustion and relief. He and Oller were both panting hard.

Oller snapped at him, annoyed, *"Little squeaker?"*

Grell chuckled. "Why piss one off when you can piss off two for the price of one, mate?"

Qrysta stepped aside as a long wing crashed beside her, then pulled her swords out of the helldragon's eyes and set about cleaning them.

Grell appraised the corpse thoughtfully. "You said something about bringing the head back?" he said. "Don't think I could carry one this big. Even if I could hack it off."

I saw his point. The head was bigger than he was. He managed to lift it a few inches but couldn't hold on, and it thudded back down.

"No way," he said.

"See if you can get that horn off," I said. "That should convince him."

A couple of chops from Fugg and the horn clattered to the ground. Grell picked it up.

"Right," Oller said, wiping off his knives and settling them back in the pouches on his knife belt, "let's get back and give Little Guy his dinner."

"Bubblehead mentioned a hoard," Qrysta pointed out.

"Oh, yeah, right," Oller remembered, surprised. It wasn't like him to ignore an opportunity for a good looting.

"Don't see anything," Grell said, looking around.

"Maybe she kept it somewhere less public," Qrysta suggested.

I checked Shift's tourmaline eye. It was glowing again. I cast Area Heal All, and Shields of Revival on each of us. Grell straightened up immediately as the warmth of his own private green bubble bloomed around him. A big grin lit up his face. "I love these," he said, slinging Fugg on his back. "Thanks, Daxxie. Thanks, Shift."

Qrysta settled her twin blades in her belt, and we kept going forwards. That involved stepping past several of the corpses we'd harvested. We assumed that we'd beaten the End Boss of this particular delve; but, as always, you never knew. There could be some sting in the tail of this one, I thought, so I kept Reveals up as we walked and cast Glows up above our heads to light the way.

And there it was: A black hole, off to one side in the cavern wall where it narrowed down towards us from the high ceiling. I lit our way into the side tunnel, and our Glows moved along above us. It wasn't a long tunnel, but obviously well used—massive prints and scrapes were evident where the helldragon's claws had chewed up the hard, dirt floor. The tunnel stank—and stank worse the closer we got to the end of it, a rotten, swamp-like smell. Was this her midden, rather than her lair?

As it turned out, it was both. We emerged into a double chamber, one side of it filled with enormous lumps of dragon dung congealing into a waste pile that had been decades, perhaps centuries, in the making.

"Lovely," Qrysta muttered.

Grell said, "I dunno, en-suite bathroom? Convenient."

The other half of the chamber was where the helldragon had slept. And where she kept her shinies.

IO

The Shinies

Gold. As much as we could carry. We wouldn't be short of funds for a long while. The hoard was, indeed, immense, its treasures scattered all over the chamber in haphazard mounds. Rings, torcs, necklaces, circlets, brooches; many of them set with gems, which Oller sorted through with a practiced eye.

"I could pop this lot for a fortune!" he told us. "Proper stuff, this." He was admiring a large, solid gold chalice set with red and green jewels. "Them's rubies and emeralds! Mateys, this alone is worth more'n us lot put together."

I wondered what, if anything, in this lot was magic. Nothing stood out. But then, magic items often look ordinary. We don't like to call attention to ourselves. People are wary of casters—which is why I keep Shift's eye closed most of the time. *Better to be just an ordinary traveler, with an ordinary wooden staff.*

I looked over the helldragon's hoard. In the warm light of my Glows it all glittered, beautifully, enticingly. Right, so: What am I meant to be looking for? I knew that I had to find it. If we went back to the ruined temple without it, I didn't like Little Guy's chances. Nor ours, really. We wouldn't be stupid enough to cross the invisible barrier to try to rescue him. We knew that we wouldn't stand a chance in there, where the no-face man could have us all screaming in agony just by thinking into us. In there, we wouldn't be able to speak, or walk of our own volition, let alone fight. If we went in, we were dead. And if we stayed outside … Little Guy would still be in there. While we stood outside and watched. We wouldn't be able help him.

Little Guy would be given to the imp, to play with; and we'd just be tossed aside. Abandoned, having failed to be who he wanted us to be. And would then have to fend for ourselves on this way-out-of-the-way island.

So—no question about it. I needed to succeed here.

I said, "Guys, hold up. I need to find 'that one small, rather ordinary-looking object.' So, don't disturb anything just yet, all right?"

The others stopped picking through the helldragon's hoard and waited for me to do my job.

I looked around at the treasures heaped everywhere.

Gem-encrusted salvers and ewers and goblets; gold and silver and enameled boxes and candlesticks. Weapons of all kinds, from the jewel-hilted great sword that Grell was checking out to a small, dainty whitewood bow that Oller had found. With it was a quiver of soft doeskin, filled with lightweight but sturdy arrows, well-fletched and with sharp heads. *Slight but deadly,* I thought.

Items of armor: Helms and gauntlets and spurs. Lockets and chests, some open, some closed. A dark brown, almost black staff of weirdly twisted wood, with a head of twigs that looked like a hand of a dozen crabbed black fingers around its thumb notch, which was set with a heartstone I couldn't identify. If Bubblehead was a caster, "it" could be that? This staff was hardly "ordinary" though; I'd never seen a stave like it. I'd definitely want to examine it, so that was coming with us.

What had he said?

One small, rather ordinary-looking object …

There were plenty of small objects, but I wouldn't have called any of that jewelry "ordinary." Where to start? Everything was just piled at random. Anything small and "ordinary" wasn't going to stand out in this lot, with its jewels and silver and crystal and gold fascinating our eyes wherever we looked. And *it* could be buried at the bottom of one of those many heaps. Were we going to have to sift through everything, methodically, looking for something we didn't know we were looking for?

I cast Divination over the area, but I wasn't hopeful that it would locate anything. Divining is a very elusive skill, which needs to be properly focused on one particular object, or place, or person, and takes time and concentration—and even then often doesn't yield results beyond, *Yes, this is Imbued,* or, *Trap below.* Imbued with what? No answer. What kind of trap? No answer.

Divination was among my weakest skills and wasn't nearly up to that kind of advanced result. My cast of it at the hoard produced only one noticeable result: One of the chests in one of the piles began to glow with a rich, distinct shine.

I clambered over to it and opened it. It was full of large gemstones, all glowing like the box itself, their glows slowly fading as the Divination spell wore off.

"Bloody hells!" Oller breathed. "Look at the size of that diamond …"

Well, beautiful though they were, none of them was what I needed to find. You couldn't call any of those gems "ordinary-looking." I gazed around at the piled masses of objects and felt my heart sink at the task. We could search through this lot forever, and still not find it, whatever it was.

It was Oller, of course, who pointed me in the right direction.

Oller was good at finding things, as he was always reminding us. His professional eye had noticed something that I'd overlooked.

"I'd take a look over here, if I was you, Daxxie." He padded over to a small, nondescript pile that had, I now saw, clearly been carefully set to one side.

I joined him to inspect it. Nothing in it seemed very interesting, though. A clay cup, not particularly well made, and fired with dull green and brown colors in it that had run together haphazardly, making it look like something a child had made at her first attempt. A round hand mirror in a simple hoop frame. A wooden box inlaid with slender spirals of marquetry. It smelled fragrant when I picked it up.

Sandalwood? I couldn't tell. I opened it. There was nothing in it but a white feather and a loop of hair that might perhaps be a bracelet. A memento? A charm?

I sorted through the rest of the pile. Some rings, none of them as pretty as the ones Oller had picked out. A cheap tin tray. A bundle of thin sticks that had obviously been carefully tended and tied together with green thread. A bone-handled folding knife, blunt, with a dull, rusting blade. A latticework cloth, nothing but cheap homespun. A scruffy old glove. An enamel pillbox, empty. A length of dirty silk. A brass bowl. A plain iron bracelet with a deep groove running around its center. Why was this lot put aside, as if valued?

I cast Divination on each of them, in turn, and got nothing from any of them. The iron bracelet sparked and fizzed, briefly, clearly a reaction to the casting—and I felt Shift jump in my hand in response. A magic item, then, this dull, dark gray hoop. I turned it over and over in my hands but learned nothing further about it.

And that was what I needed to do. Learn. Identify which was the *small, rather ordinary-looking object* we'd been sent to find. We didn't need money now. We needed information. Had we been expecting some fabulous prize to drop from the helldragon when we killed her? Probably. And that was because we were still, reflexively, thinking in the old way. *Kill the Boss, grab the shinies.*

It wasn't like that here. It wasn't like that at all.

It was, always, *think.*

Think.

I had never felt so open to whatever was out there. I didn't know what I was looking for, but I did know that I needed to readjust my attitude. It was no longer simply *wade in and fight, and win, and loot, and move on.*

It was, and, I had the growing suspicion, always would be, from here on in: *What the Fuck Is This Quest?*

So, only one thing for it then. Go through this lot carefully, one at a time.

Box, nothing; folding knife, nothing; bundle of sticks, no idea what kind of wood, so, as of yet, nothing; rings, nothing; mirror …

It was a plain, slightly mottled mirror. Ordinary, indeed. But something about it made me stop and look again. I peered at myself in it. It was me all right, but my reflection didn't seem, somehow, quite right.

The others saw me frowning at it and crowded around behind me to look. What I could see of myself was quite dark, but that was from the poor quality of the silvering behind the age-dulled glass rather than from the lack of light. I couldn't work it out.

It was Qrysta who solved it. "Well now," she said. Her reflection smiled at me, beyond my baffled one. "See it?" she said.

I didn't.

"Puzzle King, huh?" she mocked.

She reached out from behind me and tapped me on the right side of my forehead with her right forefinger.

I could see my reflected eyes grow round in astonishment and my scalp flatten.

In the mirror, her left forefinger was tapping the left side of my forehead. The mirror was showing me *as I really was*, not a reversed reflection of myself, as in a regular mirror.

"Which is why we never really see ourselves in mirrors, right?" she said. "And we think photos look wrong to us, because we're so used to seeing ourselves in reverse in mirrors."

We couldn't help playing with it, turning our heads this way and that, and waving, and leaning out of one side while our reflections waved across from us, and leaned out of the opposite side.

Grell said, "Is this it, do you think?"

I said, "Could be."

We had Little Guy's fate to consider, so we went through everything in that pile of oddments. None of us found anything that stood out as being "it." *One small, rather ordinary-looking object.* Well, the mirror was ordinary-looking. But not ordinary. He hadn't said *ordinary*, though, had he?

Ordinary-*looking*.

Was that his little joke? Ordinary-looking, as in looking glass, like in Alice? And the way he'd said, it, with that little hesitation, "that small, shall we say—rather *ordinary-looking* object ..." knowing full well that the way this looking-glass "looked" was the exact opposite of ordinary? Or, more than that, that it looked at its subjects *as they really were*—and what could be more "ordinary" than the way the rest of the world sees you?

Yes, I thought. This is probably it.

But to be on the safe side we took everything else in the little, separated pile where we'd found it.

We also, of course, took all the loot we could carry, including a gold chalice, the chest of gems that had glowed under my Divination spell, a huge amount of jewelry and gold—and the small whitewood bow, which Oller tested. He nocked an arrow on its string, drew, and loosed it at an empty wooden chest in the hoard. The arrow pierced through one side before burying its head in the other. Sharp indeed. Dainty the little bow might be, but it was also lethal.

"Range weapon," he said to Qrysta, with a grin. "Just what you said we could do with!"

Grell couldn't resist the jewel-hilted great sword. He slung it over his shoulder, next to Fugg. We didn't blame him. We're warriors. We appreciate weapons. We don't leave the good ones behind.

Qrysta found a small, light buckler, which she poked with the end of her short sword. Its niblun point didn't leave a dent in the buckler's surface, nor even a scratch. Interesting. Qrysta was happy to fight sword-and-board, if necessary. This little thing looked useful. Light, maneuverable, impervious. She slung it on her back.

It wasn't much further to the end of the tunnel—where, waiting for us, in his ancient black robe, with his inkwell, and his quill, at his upright desk, perched in an alcove in the tunnel's wall, was the old, bent clerk.

We stopped.

He said, "tickets."

Oller handed his to the clerk, who stamped it and waited while we searched ourselves for ours.

We couldn't find them. They must have fluttered loose during the battle.

The clerk said, "You'll just have to stay here then."

I said, "Not going to happen."

He said, "Well, you're not going to get out without them."

Grell unslung Fugg. "Are you going to stop me, mate?" he said.

The wrinkled old clerk peered at him mildly. "No."

"Very wise," Grell growled, and marched on past.

For about a foot.

"*That* is going to stop you," the clerk pointed out, as Grell rebounded from the invisible blockage.

"I know!" Oller said brightly, reaching into one of his many inner pockets. "How much?" He held out a fistful of gold coins. "Or," he said, opening his other hand, revealing jeweled rings and necklaces, "these ought to be enough, eh, mate?"

The clerk glanced at them, uninterested. "Tickets only."

Oller's face fell. "Oh," he said, tucking his loot back into his pockets, and turning to us, ruefully, "Well, I suppose this is goodbye then.

It's been very nice knowing you, I must say. Lot o' fun, you chaps have been. Look me up if you ever get out of here, okay?"

We were still searching ourselves frantically, again and again, for our damn tickets. We'd been sure to put them away carefully, as we knew that we'd need them.

Shocked, I looked up. "Oller—wait, what?"

Grell said, "You can't just leave us here!"

Oller said, with an apologetic shrug, "I've got to get back to Little Guy. He'll be hungry."

It was Qrysta who twigged first. As Oller passed her, on his way out, she grabbed him in a bear hug and said, "Grell, hold the little shit upside down and shake him." Oller wriggled, and protested, and the laughter he'd been suppressing welled up and burst out of him, and Grell and I realized what had happened.

"Oh, so you think this is funny, eh?" Grell growled, and the next moment Oller was hanging by his heels from Grell's huge paws. Qrysta and I searched him and found our tickets soon enough. Oller was still hiccuping with laughter while protesting, until Grell dropped him without warning, and he landed awkwardly with an *oof.*

We handed our tickets to the clerk.

He stamped them, one after the other, morosely, carefully, and handed me another, multipage, red-ribbon-bound form.

He said, "You need to sign these out."

I looked at the papers. It was a list of everything we had looted from the hoard.

Reversive Mirror, one (1).
Loot, miscellaneous, see attached.

I turned the page.

Every item that we were carrying was listed—and, interestingly, described.

There were a lot of pages. I wanted to study them later, at leisure, so I said, "Can I have a copy of this?"

The clerk nodded at it, and said, "The bottom copy's yours." He placed our tickets in his out tray. "Have a nice day."

We said goodbye and moved on.

Keep going forwards.

Before long the tunnel sloped upwards, and turned, and ended in another portal. We stepped through and found ourselves on a ledge just inside the cave's mouth. We hadn't noticed it when we came in, tucked away and hidden high above us as it had been.

We peered over. There were no handholds.

There was no way up that we could see, so even if we'd spotted this opening, we could never have climbed up here, not even Oller. Well, perhaps, if he'd had his stickies, but he didn't. They'd gone down with the rest of our gear on the ghost ship.

It also meant that there was only one way down.

It wasn't too far; we shouldn't hurt ourselves.

I popped Shields on us all, and, one at a time, we jumped and rolled.

We picked ourselves up and dusted ourselves off. I cast Area Heal All on us, to take care of any bruises, and we left the cave behind the skull in the cliffside.

It was long after dark when we made it back to Sallen's tavern. Jess was delighted to see us. Her face lit up in a big smile as we trooped in from yet more rain, and she ran over and hugged Qrysta.

"Where have you *been?!*" she demanded. "I've been so worried!"

"Tell you all about it over dinner, Jessie," Qrysta said, ruffling her hair.

"Coming right up," Sallen said, and ducked back into the kitchen.

Jess sat down with us. "Can you see how clean it is?" she said, indicating the warm little room. "Me and Sallen and the others gave the whole place a good spring clean. Patty said sorry about putting me in the stocks. I don't think she was—she enjoyed it all right. But she makes me laugh, all of us—she's very sharp. And it was nice of her to pretend that she was."

"Smart girl," Grell muttered. "Knows what's good for her."

"And guess what?" Jess went on. "A man came by with a big basket of crabs, all *alive, alive-oh,* and Sallen said, 'These'll be dinner for your friends when they come back.' Sallen says her crab stew is the best on the island. Crab stew and mashed potatoes with butter, and spiced cabbage, and green beans and leeks!"

Her little face was shining with happiness. She would recall the misery she'd been through soon enough, of course. How could it not

131

keep coming back to her, wave after wave of it, again and again, for as long as it took to fade? But at least she now had a rest from it, for a little while. Sallen returned with a jug of ale and five tankards and smiled when she saw Jess chatting with us. Jess had, clearly, lifted her spirits.

"She's a good girl, your Jess," she told me quietly, as she poured. "Worked as hard as she said she would, and never a moan."

I thought, *Our Jess.*

Qrysta said, "I'm sorry we'll be taking her off your hands, Sallen."

Sallen pushed her bright red hair out of her eyes, and replied, "And I'll be sorry she's leaving. You'll be welcome here anytime, any and all of you will." She reached over and pinched Jess's cheek, with a motherly smile, before heading off back to her cooking.

Oller stopped her by saying "Got something for you, Sallen."

She looked at him, surprised.

He held out his hand. In it was a small, silver brooch, shaped like a leaping fish.

Sallen's mouth dropped open in awe. The little piece was probably worth a month's takings to her. "No, I can't possibly …"

"For taking care of young Jess while we was away? *'Course* you can!" Oller said.

"It's beautiful," she was saying, "thank you, sir; thank you kindly! I'll treasure this, that I will."

She pinned the brooch on the front of her dress and smiled. She bobbed a curtsey, and pushed back her unruly red hair again, and hurried back to her kitchen, from which wonderful, rich smells were coming.

I was leaning back in my wooden armchair, my feet up by the fire and my boots steaming, thinking: A few hours ago, we were in the hardest combat we've faced on this rock. And now, everything is cheerily, busily, comfortably normal.

There's nothing like a fight for your life for working up an appetite. When Sallen's crab stew—with all the trimmings—arrived, we fell on it, mooing. Best on the island? Best I'd ever eaten. We shoveled. Jess and Sallen and the other staff and customers watched. Some of the other customers got the scent of it and ordered a bowl for themselves. It was companionable, comfortable. I had an odd sense of *this is what we're fighting for.* I didn't know fighting *what,* any more than I knew who these strangers were. But this normality *mattered*—whether they knew it or not. And why should they? They were living their lives, doing what they did—being peasants, farmers, craftspeople—and we were doing ours. Questing. Even though we didn't know *What the Fuck This Quest Was.*

As I ate, and recharged, my anxieties lessened, but only, I think, because I just told them to go away and give me a break for a while. *You don't have the answers? Then don't beat yourself up looking for them. You probably don't even have the questions. Later, okay? Meanwhile, today: We fought, we won, let's eat. And we learned things. Even if we're not entirely sure what they are. The picture is emerging. Don't bang your head against it. Give it time, stand back, consider. Life is lived forwards but understood backwards.* Keep going forwards. We'll see what we see.

A night of blessed sleep; too many roosters too soon; breakfast; our goodbyes to one and all, and an early start on a bright morning to our destination.

First, though, Jess had something she wanted to show us. She was a bit guilty about it but insisted. We saw why soon enough. She led us to a spot just outside the village and started uncovering a pile of leaves by a big beech tree.

From under it, she pulled out a bundle wrapped in oiled cloth. She unrolled it. It contained a small bow and a quiver full of arrows.

Looking up at us shyly, us four large grown-ups, she explained that she had omitted a detail in her story. Yes, she'd run back into her cottage as the raiders rowed ashore, but not just to bolt the door to delay them. She'd wanted her bow and arrows.

"My brother taught me," she said. "He went off for a soldier, the day he turned fourteen. We used to shoot together, since I was about six. He was mad about weapons and training and drills and such. He wasn't very good with bow and arrow. He'll never make an archer, but he's a big lad, he's strong, more like a pikeman we all thought. And he was a good teacher. I don't usually miss."

She didn't. Even with a homemade bow strung with a damp string and her rough arrows. We needed a target. Qrysta said, "How about this?" and unslung the little buckler that she'd found in the helldragon's hoard. Oller, of course, had string in one of his pockets. "Useful stuff, string," he often said. "I always keep plenty about my person. You never know when you might need it."

Recently he'd "needed" it for attaching dead rats to his belt. It had taken Sallen a long while to make him trade them all in for a sealed earthenware jar of her mutton stew. "Come on, Oller," I'd said. "Little Guy may have lived on rat half his life, but given the choice, which d'you think he'd rather have: Raw rat or mutton stew?"

Oller had seen my point. The stew had won, and the rats had gone onto Sallen's compost heap.

He strung Qrysta's buckler up to a branch on a tree, and we all stepped back to give Jess room, so that she could show us what she was made of. She wasn't as good as any of the rest of us, but we'd been trained by Serjeant Bastard. Even so, tongue stuck between her teeth, she hit the buckler more often than not, from twenty paces. And her stance was good, weight just right, elbow up …

Qrysta said, "Oller?"

Oller saw what she meant and unslung the little whitewood bow from his back. "Try this 'un, Jess," he said, offering it to the girl.

She looked at it in awe. Took it. Hefted it, raised it, tested its string.

We watched, all seeing how it fitted.

Something changed.

We all saw it and exchanged glances. We knew what it meant, even if Jess didn't.

She reached for an arrow, without looking, from the doeskin quiver that Oller was holding for her.

She nocked it on her bowstring. Sighed. It was the sigh of someone coming home.

Jess drew and loosed. The arrow missed the target completely. She giggled.

She turned to us, her eyes shining.

"I'm not good enough for this!" she said—not in a defeated tone, but in an excited one.

Grell glowered at her and said, fiercely, "How do you know?!"

Jess was taken aback, her happiness evaporating. "I, I … don't," she stammered.

"Good!" Grell said. "You don't. 'Cos I say you are! You're good enough for anything you put your mind to. And you don't want to argue with *me*, do you?!"

"N-nn-no," Jess managed, cowed.

"And d'you know how I know that?" Grell went on, forcefully, and I was thinking, *Hang on, Grello, this is a bit much—*

Jess whispered, "No?"

"I saw what happened. We all did. When you held it. It had found you, just like this found me."

He unslung Fugg from his back and showed it to her.

An enormous Orc, with an enormous battle-axe, towering over a little orphan girl with a small, whitewood bow.

Jess looked at Fugg.

And then, her expression changed as she studied it. She saw the whorls in the layers of steel that had been folded into Fugg's blades, again and again and again.

"She's beautiful," she breathed at last.

"Isn't she just?!" Grell agreed. "Her name's Fugg. That's the name of the Orc Goddess of War. So, she's special. Now," he said, slinging Fugg back over his shoulder, "you try again."

Jess returned to her mark. Nodded. Nocked another arrow, and loosed, and missed again.

She looked at Grell, puzzled.

The rest of us might just as well not have been there.

"What am I doing wrong?" she asked.

Grell said, "Let *her* do the work."

Jess frowned.

"You're getting in her way," Grell said. "When we fight, Fugg and me, I let her lead. She knows what she's up to. She's an extension of my arms, and I'm an extension of her. I'm just the horse, she's the rider."

I felt Shift in my hand laugh at that. *What have I been telling you?*

The truth, I agreed.

"It's the same with me and my staff," I said, showing her Shift—who quivered with interest when Jess touched her.

Jess thought about what we had said. "Oh."

"You said it yourself," Grell pointed out. "*I'm not good enough for this.* So, let the one that *is* 'good enough for this' take over. You just get out of her way."

Jess, unsure, nocked another arrow. She took her time. Relaxed.

She drew, bringing the flight back tight to her ear as she held, and aimed.

She inhaled, to the point of stillness that every true shot needs. She smiled and closed her eyes.

And then, deliberately, she started waving the bow around and about, eyes tight shut so that she lost her bearings on the target.

She slowed her waving and zigzagging to a gentle, rhythmic motion, breathing normally, waiting. She exhaled, and in the depth of that outbreath, in the heart of all her quiet movement, her arm froze, locked on target.

Her fingers opened of their own accord.

The arrow flew.

Instead of the clang of arrowhead on buckler, which we were all expecting, there was a dull chop and a thud.

Jess opened her eyes to see what we all saw.

Her arrow had cut Oller's string exactly in the middle, and Qrysta's little buckler had dropped to the ground.

We all let what we had just seen sink in.

Grell reanimated first. "I'd think that just about sums it up," he said. He stomped over to fetch buckler and arrows.

Jess handed the whitewood bow back to Qrysta.

Who didn't take it. "It's yours now, Jess," she said.

Jess said, "But I can't possibly ..."

Qrysta smiled, and said, "It's not up to you. She's made her choice. That's why we found her. That's why she made us bring her to you. She's yours, you're hers. And if you treat each other right, you'll look after each other."

Jess seemed lost for words. She looked at her bow, at Qrysta, at all of us, back at her bow again. "I will," she said at last, "I promise. Thank you."

"Here," Grell said, handing her the arrows he'd fetched from the tree, and passing Qrysta her buckler.

Jess took them to put in her doeskin quiver.

She couldn't. It was full.

"*Well*, now!" Qrysta said.

Oller said, "Fire off some more."

Jess did, loosing six arrows in succession.

We all watched the doeskin quiver. We couldn't see how the arrows got there, but it was always full.

The whitewood bow had its own self-loading quiver.

"That's some weapon you've got there, lass!" Oller said.

Jess was lost for words.

"She'll be needing a name," Grell said, with a grin, ruffling Jess's untidy brown hair. "Better make it a good one, a fine bow like her!"

"Mm," Jess nodded, and studied the bow, thinking.

We set off. Jess knew where we were going—in general, if not in detail. Qrysta had told her what we were: Fighters. Who had a job to do. Jess could stay with Sallen if she wanted. She'd be looked after; she'd be fed, and housed, and safe. Jess was quite firm that she was coming with us. Which was, I think, why the first thing she had done was to lead us to her hidden bow and arrows. It was her way of saying *I can fight too. I'm one of you.*

There was no question about that. Little Guy was one of us, and Oller had found him on the road north of The Wheatsheaf, quite by chance.

"Quite by chance"?

Really?

I wondered what, if anything, ever happened to us in this world 'quite by chance.' Oller could have not noticed a small stray dog. We could, easily, have walked on past the little soaked girl in the stocks. We ourselves had been hungry, cold, anxious, on a mission, *eager to do what was needed.* We had things to do. We hadn't needed to spot something out of the corner of an eye, and think *hullo,* and give enough of a damn to take a diversion, across the muddy square, and talk to her. But we had, and we did: And … here we were.

Diversion, I thought?

Where we came from, we called those side quests.

Hmm. Where might this Jess side quest lead, I wondered. Time, no doubt, would tell.

Meanwhile, we had a friend to get out of jail. And a challenge to answer.

Oh, I'd worked that out all right.

It was, as no-face had said, very simple when you thought about it.

11

Face Off

Jess had certainly been telling the truth about one thing. She was stronger than she looked. She showed no signs of flagging as we reached the top of the hill where we'd emerged into the rain only two days before. She hesitated at the mouth of the entry to the underground, but Qrysta held out her hand and said, "Come on, it's okay." Jess took it and we went on down.

There were no giant spiders in our way this time. Well, only the corpses of the ones we'd killed on our way up.

Jess looked at them, alarmed.

"Any more attack us, we'll let you shoot 'em," Grell said. She saw that we were all calm and confident, and drew strength from that.

"Sorry," she said, "I've just never seen anything like them before."

"Stick with us, lass," Oller chuckled, "and you'll see all sorts, I guarantee you!"

She gulped. And then pulled herself together, and said, "I won't be a burden to you, I promise."

"Course you won't," Oller said. "Come in useful, you will, I've no doubt. You can go places where Grell can't, eh? Listen in marketplaces, with those sharp little ears. Talk to other kids. Kids always know things grown-ups don't think they know. And they always want to tell other kids, but never grown-ups, especially strangers. And I bet you know some songs we can sing around the campfire."

Jess frowned, thinking. "Only nursery songs," she said. And then added, "And sea songs, that Da taught me, I know 'Sailaway' and 'Barrel o' Rum,' and 'The Wreck of the Seagull,' and 'Jack and the Mermaid.'"

"Never heard any of those!" Oller said, pleased. "It'll be nice to have some new ones. You ever have hoolies here?"

Jess, walking along between him and Qrysta, frowned, and said, "What are they?"

"Sing-songs. Everyone gathering to sing and play, maybe at a place like Sallen's?"

Jess shook her head. "I don't think so," she said. "There aren't many people on the island. Ma used to sing to us, at bedtime …" She tailed off, and her face grew sad.

We left her to her thoughts.

Before we entered the cavern where we'd parted from Little Guy, we stopped and explained to Jess what we were going to do. She was to wait there, out of sight. *And don't worry, you'll be able to hear us, we won't be far, and we'll come and get you as soon as we can.*

She was nervous, but we stressed how important it was that she do exactly as we said. She had her whitewood bow and her razor-sharp arrows, so she should be safe enough for a little while, all right? *Yell for us if you have to, but otherwise keep dead quiet. It won't be for long.* She nodded and promised that she would wait where we said. Qrysta patted her shoulder and smiled encouragingly, and the four of us left her in the shadows where she couldn't be seen.

As our footsteps rang out on the cavern floor, shapes appeared in the distance: Bubblehead, his imp, and Little Guy, who ran towards us, barking with excitement, his tail wagging furiously. He made no sound, of course, in the silence imposed behind the no-face man's invisible prison wall.

When they stopped, we stopped.

"Welcome back," the no-face man said.

I said, "Not exactly."

His no-face stopped shifting, and his body went still. "You ran away?"

I said, "Grell?"

Grell held out the horn he'd hacked off the helldragon's head. "She's dead."

Bubblehead said, "So what is this 'not exactly'? You didn't find it?"

"Oh, we found it," I said. "*Not exactly* means we're not coming in there."

He considered. "Let me see it," he said.

"All in good time," I said. "First, we need to come to an arrangement."

"I don't think you're in a position to make demands," he said. But he didn't sound quite as sure of himself as he had before.

I said, "I'm not going to. I said 'arrangement'; nothing about demands. And we *are* in a position to make demands, should we wish, as it happens. All you can do is kill our dog. And where would that get you?"

He didn't reply.

"Exactly," I continued. "You can hardly pretend you don't want something from us. Or why go to all the bother of bringing us here and staging that shipwreck? We've proved our worth. I have no idea if we're who you think we are, and quite honestly, I don't care if we are or we aren't, because that's your problem. You want something from us. So, let's come to an arrangement, and then we'll decide if we're going to cooperate."

This, clearly, hadn't been what he'd been expecting. He no longer held the whip hand. We could simply walk away. And where would that leave him?

In his prison.

Where—if we really were who he hoped we were—no one would ever again come to help him. Because that was what *we* were for. We were his only hope. And he now knew that we knew that.

He also knew that we weren't going to do anything without the information.

"Very well," he said, at last, "tell me what it is you want."

"The answers to two questions," I said. "One of which I will ask you now and one after you've answered the first one."

"Go on ..."

I said, "What do *you* want?"

I could see him thinking. "You've worked it out, I suppose?" he said, eventually. "The answer to the question you asked, before you left here—'Where do my enemies come into this?'"

I said, "Of course I have."

"Well?"

"As you said, it's very simple. The answer is that you're obviously not the only one who knows that verse."

Once again, he went still. That seemed to be his body language for "yes." Eventually, he agreed. "Correct."

"So, who else does, and what do they want, and how does that affect what *you* want?"

"Well done. It affects you too, of course. When they learn about you—which, because it took you over a month to set sail from Mayport, they no doubt already have—they will want to make sure that you are who they fear you might be; and when they are sure that you are, they will hunt you down and kill you. To prevent you from doing what you are here to do."

"Which is to free you."

"Indeed."

Seems straightforward enough, I thought. In general terms. Now I needed to hear the specifics. "Okay," I said, "from the beginning."

"That verse refers to their only failure," he said. "They won. Here I am. Locked away on an island under an island where they put me, apparently forever. But they are also about to lose, because also apparently, according to that verse, if we're reading it right, a group of four will appear and undo all their careful work, so it's not 'forever.' I will, one day, get out. And we all think that we're reading it right.

"As you say, it's hardly a puzzle. So, for many years, we've all been keeping an eye out for that Four. For you four. They think it's you. I now *know* it is you. As proof of which, having killed the helldragon, you will, I have no doubt, have the 'small, ordinary-looking object' that I sent you to bring me?"

I said, "I do."

"May I see it?"

"When you've finished answering my question," I said.

He grunted. He didn't like that. "Very well," he said, understanding that he had no choice in the matter, "I'll be brief. The verse appeared in an unusual, and very noticeable, way. Outside their headquarters, staring them in the face, so to speak. One night it wasn't there, the next morning it was. A large, black monolith with those words carved on it. Which they immediately tried to destroy, of course, but they can't get within two feet of it. They tried putting big drapes over it, but they all just melted. They built a high fence around it, but it collapsed in the night. It disturbs them. It challenges them. It gives me hope. Hope that one day I will indeed get out of here and become again what I once was."

I said, "Who put it there?"

That surprised him. "I'm sorry?"

"The monolith?" I said. "Things like that don't happen at random."

"No, you're right," he agreed. "No one in this realm knows. But I believe I can take an educated guess—someone, on the higher planes, who favors my side rather than my enemy's. I could name some names, but they wouldn't mean anything to you. Gods, demons, this side, that. Perhaps, one day, all will be revealed. Who knows? Meanwhile, there is much to be done."

I considered that. I couldn't see how it helped, but maybe I would later. "Who are these 'they' that you keep mentioning?"

His tone changed to a sneer. "The Devoted Children of Mercy, they call themselves. A more pious, well-meaning, contemptible rabble of smug, indoctrinated do-gooders you could never hope to meet. And you might well hope that you will never meet them, because they will haul you up before their oh-so-holy, oh-so-sorrowful tribunal and, after an interminable trial, will, with awe and respectfulness, bless you with the honor of martyrdom. Which they will do by burning you at the stake. While singing hymns of joy and praise of the gift of suffering."

His voice dripped with contempt. "Well, forget that hope, you're going to have to meet them; that's your first job. But I can make sure you do so under our terms rather than theirs."

He saw my frown and continued. "I understand your confusion. They are, indeed, sincere, pious people. I, as you will have come to see by now, am not. They will kill you, be in no doubt about that. I won't. So, you're working for me now, whether you like it or not."

I said, "We don't have to."

"I think you're missing the point," he said.

"Which is?"

"I'm your only chance."

"Because?"

"Because if you choose to stay here, on this island, and try to find a way off, you'll walk straight into their arms."

I said, "How do you know this?"

"It is known that the Four will come from overseas," he said. "As you four have done. It is also known that no one born in this realm can enter the places where you must go, to bring me what you must find. What is not known, to anyone but me, is where those places are. Which I will tell you when you agree to take on the tasks.

"There is therefore a complete ban on foreigners entering the realm—which is one reason it is underpopulated and mostly empty. Foreigners may come here to trade, but only in the free ports. Any who venture beyond them do so in peril of their lives. So none do. The only ships that come to this island sail from ports where the Devoted are powerful, and their eyes and ears are everywhere. At any port on the mainland you would be noticed and arrested."

He looked us over. "You four? You'd stand out like four sore thumbs. No matter whether you take passage on a legal ship or a smuggler vessel. All captains, smuggler or legitimate, know that they're looking for you. They will shop you without a second's hesitation. They don't want to cross the Devoted. They would burn with you. I, and only I, have a way to prevent that happening to you."

I said, "Explain."

"Simple. They are looking for four. They know that the ghost ship suddenly set sail, after riding at anchor for over two hundred years, under its dark shadow, in the harbor at Seacastle, where no one could board it. Their spies in Mayport will have reported that it collected you four. They will have been on high alert for a month, waiting for your arrival. But your ship won't arrive where they can scoop you up and arrest you, because it foundered and sank.

"You will wash ashore at night, and separate. They will only capture one of you. That one will convince them that the other three drowned. I'm thinking that will be your role, caster. You seem to be the one who is good with challenges. You're certainly capable in an argument; you should be able to handle yourself in your tribunal. The others will not be noticed, because they will go their separate ways and no longer be a group of four. They will each have their own errands to complete before you all meet up again, should you survive your tribunal. And if you don't, well, they'll just have to do the job without you."

I said, "How could they, if they're not four?"

"It doesn't say that all four get to survive. It could be that all it needs is for there to be one of you standing at the end. That's what you're going to find out, isn't it?"

Well. *Plenty to think about there,* I thought. *Working for the bad guy, hunted by the good guys …*

Did we have a choice?

"And what happens to me?" I said.

"You convince them that you are of no interest to them, now that there aren't four of you, and that therefore the verse doesn't apply. You tell them that you are bringing them great news and that they should be happy. The thing that they have feared most will now never happen, so they won't have to worry about it anymore."

"Sounds iffy," I said.

"Very," he agreed.

"So how do I do that?" I asked.

He snorted. "That's up to you. You either pull it off or fry."

I thought it over. "Can't I just disappear like the others, help them with their tasks? I don't see why I have to walk into their arms and risk my neck like that."

"Because," he said, "you need to set bait."

I considered the implications of that statement for a moment. "What?"

"I'll be happy to explain once you've finished with your questions. I'll tell you all you need to know, in great detail, and provide you with everything you will need to help you on your separate ways."

I pretended to consider. I knew perfectly well that we'd have to fall in with his plan, but I wanted to make it look as if I was unhappy with the idea.

I said, "Right, here's my other question."

"Ask away."

"Can I trust you?"

"Yes."

"How do I know that?"

"Because our interests are aligned," he replied. "As I said, you are working for me now."

"Then I want your promise that every member of our party will be transported ashore, safe and sound, the way you are suggesting."

"You have it."

"In gold bubbles, I assume? Like how you rescued us?"

"Indeed."

"Each of us, safe and protected by your powers, until we wash up on shore?"

"You have my guarantee," he said. "Why do you keep asking this?"

"You'll see," I said. I looked at Qrysta and nodded.

She turned and walked back the way we'd come. She disappeared, briefly, around the corner of the tunnel that led out of the cavern.

When she reappeared, she was holding Jess by the hand. They joined us.

The no-face man was silent for a long while. Eventually, he said, sounding dubious, "A serving girl?"

"She's with us," I said, "and she's coming with us."

He said, "Interesting." He appeared to study Jess. Who, naturally, was clinging to Qrysta.

I waited.

He said, "May I see it?"

I produced the little handheld mirror.

He held out his hand for it.

I passed it through the invisible barrier.

He took it and gazed into it. "Ah," he said, "there I am!"

He reached into the reversive mirror and retrieved his face. He replaced it, on the blank where his head had been, and said, "That's better!"

He looked at us and smiled. It was a strange smile, in a strange face, with its deep-set, dark eyes under a high forehead, and a small mouth surrounded by a black beard. Not particularly threatening, not particularly anything, really. It didn't look much more than middle-aged, but it somehow seemed ancient. It was a full face indeed, fully animated, but somehow still fluid, as if mounted on that blank bubble rather than on solid bones.

And then, he said, "Well, what are you waiting for? Your little friend wants his dinner."

We stepped across the invisible barrier. The small man with his old face back in place was all hospitality now. We could talk and move of our own volition, and Little Guy could bark and leap and lick, which he did frenziedly, until Oller opened the earthenware jar of Sallen's mutton stew. Then it was Little Guy's growling and eating noises, and Oller stroking him and us all watching, taking pleasure in his pleasure, his bogbrush tail wagging happily.

And then I noticed the imp watching. It was taking no pleasure at all in what it was seeing. It noticed me noticing it and looked up with its hooded, dark red eyes.

And locked on.

Gods it was frightening. And only a foot and a half tall. I nodded at it, warily, respectfully. It did not acknowledge. I knew we'd be seeing it again. And I knew that it knew that I knew that. I held its eyes as long as I could. Which seemed forever. I was determined that I wouldn't look away.

The little man with his old face back in place said, "You won't win."

I looked at him.

He said, his new-old face shifting at the edges, "No one does."

I glanced back at the imp. Who was still staring at me.

His guardian said, "Shall we be on our way?"

I nodded, and we moved off. I was relieved to be no longer on the end of that invasive stare. What in all hells *was* that little thing?!

I exhaled, hard, and wiped the sweat off my forehead.

We settled back in our seats at the long library table, and the imp padded along it, handing us marked maps and a sheet of parchment each. In addition, it gave me a small, cloth-bound booklet. I read the title on its cover. *The lands, places, customs, and histories of Mourvania.* So, I thought. That's where we're going.

No, I realized, as I compared the rough map on its frontispiece with the far more detailed maps we'd all been given: This is where we already *are*, here, on this island off to the north and west of the mainland, Wester Isle.

"The last thing I remember," Oldface said, and we all turned our attention back to him, "was the incantation. I alone heard it, in my head. He did not chant it aloud, for his followers to hear. This was to be our secret, between victor and vanquished. He thought that would be its strength. None but the two of us would know what he had done to doom me. No one who wanted to free me would know where to look or what to look for. In a way, he was right, for no living person has uncovered our secret. In another way, he was wrong. The secret is its weakness, not its strength. For *I* know what he did. And I know how to undo it.

"And that is what I brought you here to do."

He paused, then continued. "He won. I was helpless, unable to move, lying on the sand floor of what had been my home—my stronghold, in the heart of the burning desert, where I had held my power and wielded it as I pleased. I couldn't understand it; couldn't believe it. And then, that voice, echoing in my head, his arms raised to the heavens:

North and South and West and East
Lock the gates and cage the Beast
Seal so none shall ever find
Head and Heart and Soul and Mind.

He let that hang in the silence that followed.

"He divided me," Oldface took up his tale again. "Quartered my essence. Scattered, and separated, I am nothing—just as a quartered body cannot function. I must be whole again. That is your task.

"Who was he? An incarnation of my enemy. Who has now left this mortal plane, having handed his authority here down to his disciples. Well, that was his move, breaking me apart, and sealing me away. Now, all these long years later, it is time for mine."

He let that sink in while he gathered his thoughts.

"Outside my cage, as I told you, I am weak. I can travel beyond it, in my spheres, within limits, but out there I am defenseless. It is my belief that he left me the power of travel to torment me, so that I can see the world beyond my prison, now at peace and prospering, and know that I am at its mercy, where before it had been at mine. Which it will be again, should you succeed in your tasks. You've already succeeded in the first. You broke the north seal and brought me my face back. Now you must find my Power, my Nature—heart and soul, the fool called them, but what did he know?—and my Mind. At least he got that one right.

"Each is protected by its opposite. Its counterpart; its nemesis, which will do everything it can to keep that which it guards imprisoned. My face, trapped in that reversive mirror, looking *at* me instead of *from* me. As to the others: Who knows how he defends them? The places that you need to break into are sealed by magic, both high and dark. No living person knows about them or where they are.

"Even so, we can't risk you going from one place to another in a group, because the four of you will attract attention. No, you need to reach them and clear them all at the same time, more or less. Which means one task for each of the rest of you, while our caster here pleads for his life at his tribunal and tries not to be burned alive. It seems obvious to me which of you is suited best to each task, but see what you think. It's up to you whether you agree with me. You can change them between you if you prefer."

We studied our maps. On each were four crosses in red circles. Only one of them was near a town—a place called Cressen. We read about the tasks that lay at three of them. We consulted. We discussed.

It didn't take long.

We agreed.

"Good," he said, as his imp handed each of us a small, brown stone. They looked like flint cobbles that had been cut in half. They were vaguely arrow-shaped, somewhat resembling the spade symbols on playing cards. Their gleaming black tops were flat. Their dull brown undersides bellied out into smooth, fat curves. "These are lodestones," he said. "Set them on your map, on the point where you want to go, and leave them to absorb the location. After a few moments, they will turn to point the way."

Wow, I thought.

To me, he said, "You need to give yours and your map to one of the others. We can't have the Devoted finding them on you."

I nodded and handed them across the table to Jess.

"Me?" she said.

"The others all have one; you don't," I said.

"I'll look after them," she promised, and started studying the map.

"When you have what I need, I will meet you"—he pointed at our maps—"here."

We looked at the spot where his finger was pointing. It wasn't a town, or even anywhere near one, nor on any road that I could see. It was just a small, black dot, in the middle of nowhere, next to the words, *High Rock*. "It is a sanctuary, so once you reach it, you'll be safe until the rest of us arrive.

"You," he turned to me, "will have to find your own way there. The map in your guidebook is crude, but that's the one I want them to see." I opened the book to the map. The only circled X on it was the one far to the South, in the Great Waste. That one did not have a task associated with it. Its X was laid over a miniature symbol of Old Birdbeak. "They will see that and be alarmed. You will tell them that that was where the Four were to complete their task. They know about that place. It is where I was defeated and bound. You will tell them that it is where my enemy, in his turn, now lies bound and defeated, awaiting my revenge. He has been relinquished to this mortal plane again by those loyal to me in the higher spheres. That news will send them into a panic. Delivering it is your job, whether you fry or not."

I said, "Bait ..."

He nodded. "I believe they will take it."

"And send their armies there?"

He smiled. "Right into my trap. Like I said, it's time for a little payback. We will allow you one month to join us at High Rock," he continued. "I hope we see you there, as we would probably benefit from your skills, but if we don't, we'll go on without you. I'll leave a sign there for you, to show that we've gone on ahead, and a map and lodestone. If you don't see them, wait for us."

I said, "What sort of sign?"

He tossed something into the air from his empty hand. "That," he said.

There was nothing up there. I pointed Shift and cast Reveals.

Above him, glowing red, the familiar symbol hung in the air.

Old Birdbeak.

12

Enemy Territory

We stared up at the ominous sign floating above our heads.

"If you see that, you'll know that we will have gone on south, to my stronghold," he said, "to turn the tables on my enemy."

Interesting, I thought.

He said *enemy,* not *enemies* …

It seemed like this was personal.

And what lay ahead of us seemed straightforward enough. Three Fetch Quests, for the others, and a try not to fry quest for me.

I said, "And then what?"

"Then you will have your reward."

The others looked at him sharply, with interest. They liked the idea of *reward.*

I said, "And what will that be?"

"I won't kill you."

Qrysta, frowning, said, "That's it?"

Oldface looked at her, his eyebrows raised. "Sounds pretty good to me," he said, "compared to the alternative. Die here, now, screaming. And when I say now, I mean very slowly. Drown in the storm. Burn at the stake. Fail to survive your separate challenges. Come out of this still standing? I'd call that a result."

I turned it over in my head. Normally there's some prize at the end of a quest. But, as we were learning in our time on this rock, what we used to think of as "normal" no longer applied.

As if reading my mind—which he no doubt had been doing—Oldface turned to me, with a disconcerting smile, and said, "Oh, and as an added bonus? I'll let you keep everything you took from the helldragon's hoard."

I saw the others' faces fall.

Oldface chuckled. "No, I'm not letting you leave here with it. But it's yours, should you come to claim it." He pointed at the four of us, one by one, first Grell, then Oller, then Qrysta, then me, as he continued. "Don't worry, I'll keep it safe for you. A pretty good reward, I'd say? And so, I think, would you, now that you've seen it for yourselves." As he spoke, the packs and bags that we'd loaded with loot left us and settled on the table in front of him. The various objects rose out of our deeper-than-they-looked niblun backpacks and flowed off in a stream of gold and silver and glittering colors. The chests we'd taken bumped out onto the tabletop. We stared at our treasures, wondering if we'd ever see them again. Oldface, knowing that Jess hadn't been through the portal with us, didn't include her, so her whitewood bow and doeskin quiver full of arrows stayed with her.

He upended one of Oller's capacious loot bags, and inspected it, while Oller's belongings scattered everywhere. "Mm," he grunted. "This'll do. You, caster," he turned to me. "Can you make this lightproof? Completely opaque, so that no light can get in, or out?"

I thought about it. Yes, Blackout should do.

I cast it on Oller's bag and said, "How's that?"

Oldface opened it and put it over his head. He grunted. He took it off, and laid it on the tabletop, and motioned to his imp to lie inside it, which it did. Then he rolled it tight. He went still. He was, presumably, communicating telepathically with the imp. We waited. There was a muffled *whoompf*, like gas catching fire, and a sizzle, and a sound like a series of short circuits, crackling one after another. The bag writhed and puffed and went still.

"Mm," Oldface said again, apparently satisfied.

He, like us, had seen no light leak from the bag.

He unrolled his imp, who stepped out of the bag amid a cloud of smoke as little zips of lightning flashed off it, sizzling. It looked at us with its usual baleful stare.

"When you have found my Power, under no circumstances expose it to the daylight. Use this to contain it," Oldface said, handing Oller back his loot bag. "So, let's be on our way."

"We'll need gold," I said, "for supplies and such. Horses don't come cheap, for example."

He nodded. "Fair enough," he said. "A hundred each. Not you, I think," Oldface looked at Jess as the coins stacked themselves in front of the rest of us. "You're not one of the Four."

She looked like she didn't know what to say.

"If you succeed," he said, with a smile, waving at the mounds of treasure beside him, "you'll share in all the rest of this eventually, no doubt."

Qrysta turned to her, and said, "That's a promise."

Jess couldn't help glancing at the loot piled up around Oldface. She'd clearly never before seen so much wealth.

"There's one other thing," he continued. "You won't be going back the way you came in, once you're through the seals. You'll be going on, to High Rock. So, don't leave anything behind that you'll need later on." He looked around, from face to face. "Any questions?"

"One," Qrysta said. "How did you know my name?"

Oldface smiled. "I don't. But I now know that you were the one who found the letter. I made it self-addressing. Whoever found it would also find their name on it." He rose to his feet. "Right then. Off we go."

He got up from the table and led us out into the ruins of the temple, where our bubbles formed around us, and we were off, floating above the ground, in the dark, above the little pools of gold light that they cast, to the shore, and down into the water, all the way to the sea floor. After a while, we stopped in a line. Oldface and his imp in their bubble passed along in front of us, inspecting us all. Clearly, he would be coming no further.

He waved. I nodded in reply. Our bubbles moved on. His didn't. They gazed at us until we disappeared into the gloom ahead of them.

Up we went through the tunnel, and down again into the ocean itself. We traveled among the slow, deep fishes, over the bleached bones of the whale, and past the wreck of the ghost ship. And on, many miles on, until the seabed began to rise upwards towards the land. We rose with it, our bubbles rocking as the water began to churn. The sound of rollers, pounding, resonated from above, and we burst up among them as our bubbles burst, and the wind howled, and rain slashed, and cold seawater flung us ashore, where we heaved each other out of the water and staggered up a stony beach to dry land.

Grell had the hardest time of it. If his armor hadn't been light, niblun plate I don't think that, even with the four of us all hauling, he'd have made it. He dropped to his hands and knees when he reached the beach, head down, heaving for breath. I hit him with Heals, but even so, it took him several minutes to regain the strength even to get off his hands and kneel upright. Eventually, he nodded and, with Oller's help, stood up. "I'll be fine," he gasped, at last, above the shrieking gale. He didn't sound it. But we needed to get away from there *ASAP.*

No Glows, I thought. Not until we knew if anyone was around who might see them.

We stumbled past spars and barrels and planks—flotsam from the wreckage of the ghost ship. The scene was set clearly for anyone to read it.

I couldn't tell how long it was until morning. It was the new moon that night, so the sky was pitch black. *The empty moon,* Marnie had called it. Good, we thought. The less light the better. And the weather was filthy. No one would willingly be out in this. So, with luck, we wouldn't be spotted until daybreak. A few hours, then, in which to do what was needed.

We set off inland, then turned south and west along the coast, downwind, hurrying, trying to get some warmth into our bodies while the gale tried to freeze us. At last we were on the top of a low line of cliffs, with the sea booming and crashing below us. There were few trees on the ridgeline, those that were were small and stunted, bent by the prevailing wind in the direction that we were heading. Jess was fine, she assured us. She was a tough little thing indeed.

We must have been marching for an hour in driving rain before we found shelter, right where Oldface had said it would be. It wasn't much shelter at all, nothing but a crude animal pen roofed with turf. But at least it was covered, and we were dry. We wouldn't make a fire, much though we longed for one. The fewer traces we left the better. With our casts, Shift and I dried us out, as best we could, and we passed around

New Rock New Realm

food from our rations. Oller slipped out into the driving wind and rain to scout the area. He came back ten minutes later and told us that there were no other buildings nearby. We assumed that this pen, out here all by itself, was for sheltering beasts during the summer, when they might be grazed in this remote spot. It didn't smell as if it had been inhabited recently.

We wrapped ourselves in our cloaks and dozed off, fitfully, waking when the wind blew harder or the rain increased. Jess had no cloak, so Grell lent her his. "Orcs don't mind cold," he told her. It was not the most comfortable of nights.

We knew that we didn't, of course, have to go our separate ways immediately. What difference would it make if I were to be found tomorrow or next week? Just so long as I was found near the shore, by the flotsam from the ghost ship. But we also knew that the longer we stayed together, as a group, the more chance there was of us, the Four, being noticed together—and captured together. We couldn't risk that. This jaunt would be over before it had begun.

As dawn broke, we discussed what "they" might possibly know about us. If there had indeed been spies on the dock at Mayport. they might have sent descriptions of us. That could be a problem, for Grell at least. Were there Orcs in this realm? Grell recalled Klurra saying, "There are no Orcs overseas," when we first encountered her. He'd replied that of course there were, she was looking at one—but that was just Grell bullshitting his made-up story. He didn't actually know. Klurra might be right. He might stand out here like a sore thumb.

I could lay a Glamour on him, which would deceive most eyes. But suppose he did manage to find some Orcs here? Orcs tend to be hostile to strangers. Fight first, ask questions later. He had his papers from Chief Elbrig of Stonefields, but if he didn't look like an Orc when he presented them, those would only land him in trouble.

The others should be all right. Jess, or rather Rosie, would be safe with her big sister, Kate. The Devoted might know our names as well as our descriptions, so we needed aliases. No more Oller and Little Guy for the time being, it would be Davy and Jim. Grell decided he'd take his chances as he was. He'd be avoiding anywhere with people in it. He didn't mind sleeping rough. If anyone asked, and he felt like telling them, he'd be Bugrov of Stonefields, on a private mission for his chief—and yes, here's the paperwork from his chief, so stand aside. He liked the idea of telling people who asked him his name and business, "Bugrov."

It was a hard parting. We didn't know if we'd see each other again. They had their missions, which Oldface had laid out for them, in detail, with maps. I gave most of my money to Qrysta, keeping back a little—a few golds, some silvers and coppers, not too much, as everything I had would no doubt be confiscated by those who were going to arrest me. I only needed enough to buy food and shelter for a few days.

We said our goodbyes, and hugged, and told each other that we were the best. The more I thought about it all, the weirder it seemed. Especially, now that I'd had time to reflect, because I had come to see that I had no way of knowing if Oldface had been straight with me. Had he been telling the truth? All of it?

Somehow, I was pretty sure he'd only told me what he wanted me to hear. I didn't discuss this with the others. They had enough on their plates and three long roads and three hard tasks ahead of them. They didn't need my worries on top of the challenges they already had.

They set off, Grell one way, Davy and Jim another, and Kate and Rosie a third.

I watched them go with a heavy heart.

I turned and headed back towards the cove where we'd been blown ashore by the gale. The rough grassland was still wet from a week of storms. The weather was still foul. Gray skies, wet winds. I wrapped myself in my cloak and trudged on towards my arrest.

When I got to the cliffs above the cove, I crouched, making myself invisible on the skyline. There was no one down there. No one on the horizon. I was soaked enough from the rain, so I didn't have to roll around in the sea as if I'd just washed up.

Nor, I thought, did I have to hang around there till they found me. What would an innocent person do? Anyone who survived a shipwreck would, if he wasn't injured, look for food and fire and shelter. Which would be easier to find here than it had been when I'd first landed in Jarnland. There were people here. There were roads, and towns, and I had a map.

I thought about my options. If Oldface hadn't told me all that he had told me, I wouldn't know that I was a wanted person, would I? An innocent person would head for safety—without the knowledge that I had: Which was that, in my case, it would be anything *but* safe.

155

But what if they didn't find me right away? I could learn things. I wouldn't have to reveal myself until I chose to. Which I would do, "in all innocence," because, if they caught me lying, they'd immediately wonder what else I was lying about. And then my story that the others were all dead would be suspect.

Inland, then.

I'd studied the maps that Oldface had given us and knew which way to go. There would be a path soon enough. There was. West to the fishing village of Endcott, or east, inland towards the nearest town? There probably wouldn't be squads of these Devoted Children of Mercy looking for me in out-of-the-way places like Endcott, but strangers are rarer in villages and always stand out.

In a town I might be able to pass unnoticed for a while. And in that while, I would watch, and listen, and learn. There would be stalls, inns, crafters. I could find a room, and lie low, and take my time deciding when to walk "innocently" into trouble.

Huntsbroke, the town's name was. Which seemed worryingly appropriate, as I was the quarry in this particular hunt. The sound of the ocean faded away behind me.

They'll find you, Oldface had said.

No, I had decided: I'll find them. And I will take a good look around before they bust me.

The path led away from the crest of the hills that we'd emerged onto when we'd dragged ourselves out of the sea and up onto the cliffs. The land sloped, up and down, and up again, gently. The trees that grew in this harsh land became sturdier, and taller, and more plentiful the further I got from the prevailing onshore wind. The day was dull, and gray, and cold, and windy, but at least it was no longer raining. I tried to anticipate what lay ahead but had little to go on.

As I walked, I studied the small book of lore about this realm, Mourvania—I say *book*, but it wasn't much more than a pamphlet, really. While it was quite a lot bigger than Jarnland, more than half of Mourvania was uninhabited. It stretched hundreds of leagues south from the Northern Ocean to a semi-desert known as The Great Waste. What lay beyond that, the small book could not say.

To the east, forests—hardwood and evergreen in the north, some tracts of it mountainous, falling away to become bog and marsh in the lower ground to the south, finally meeting the sea in mangrove swamps along the eastern coast. To the west, farmland, then open plains, and hills and mountains; where, once again, my book's knowledge ended.

Two factions, the Ostvar and the Ældvar, had been fighting over the throne here since time immemorial, led by various noble families, of which cadet branches occasionally rose to power, causing schisms and feuds. Many had lasted centuries. Some were still ongoing.

Confusingly, the Ostvar came from, or at least controlled, the lands to the south and west, while the Ældvar seemed to be relative newcomers, who had pushed in from over the eastern seas, and displaced the Ostvar, who had fallen back south and west before them. The Ældvar regarded themselves as superior, because they were the oldest and most powerful clan in the realm they'd come from, while the Ostvar regarded themselves as superior because they were the only true Mourvanians. Which, my book told me, wasn't true. They had simply conquered the indigenous Mourvanians and either enslaved them or driven them off into and beyond the Sunset Mountains to the west.

The further their castles were from Kingsworth, the capital city, the more independent and disloyal the nobles who owned them became. It had been that way for a long time, I read, as I trudged on towards Huntsbroke.

The path, as I knew it would, eventually joined a road, which curved west to my left and east to my right. I watched from the cover of trees for a while, to see what sort of travelers were using it. In the half hour I watched, there weren't many on the road. A few in wagons or on horses, most on foot. One knight on his destrier, trailed by his squire on a pony, leading a pack-mule.

And then I saw them for the first time: A group of eight, in brown habits, the men with their heads shaved in tonsures, the women with their hair bound up in coif and veil and wimple. All wore sandals, some carried staves. They walked briskly, contemplatively, in silence, apart from the one at the head of their group, muttering. Something holy, no doubt.

I studied them carefully as they passed. They looked harmless enough—decent, pious, godsfearing folk. Purposeful, though. Businesslike. I wondered if they worshipped one particular god, or goddess, or many. No doubt they would tell me soon enough. Humble though they appeared, they carried authority, and looked grim. I was glad they were going west, in the opposite direction from me. I believed

I'd be having more than enough to do with the Devoted Children of Mercy before much longer.

Time for a disguise, I thought, as I watched them dwindle into the distance. I chose Elderly Scholar again, as I had for our rendezvous at The Wheatsheaf. I wanted to look like someone who might have friends in high places and who belonged on foot, on the open road. Someone who knew the letter of the law and would face down nosy guards. Someone poor—not worth robbing or harassing.

I laid the Glamour on me and closed Shift's eye. I stepped out from the trees and turned east onto the road to Huntsbroke, an ordinary traveler with his ordinary wooden staff.

The walls of Huntsbroke appeared over the brow of a low hill a few hours later. It was well into the afternoon, and I was looking forward to putting my feet under a table and getting some hot food inside me. There were guards at the gates, as I'd expected. They didn't seem on any state of alert, high or low. They seemed bored and uninterested in the travelers passing in and out of the town.

There were two women ahead of me, young and happy, with baskets. Obviously old friends, they hadn't stopped chatting since I'd caught up with them. I'd kept back a dozen paces behind them and listened, but it had been a nonstop stream of gossip, and chuckles, and the occasional ribald comment. They walked in cheerily, smiling and waving at the guards, who obviously knew them—and who, as I'd thought they might, followed them with their eyes.

I trudged in, deliberately stooped and tired, limping, unthreatening, my thoughts miles away, as if I hadn't even noticed the guards. In return, they didn't notice me. I kept walking through the narrow, cobbled streets that led to the town square.

Well, so far, I thought, *so good.*

It was, I was pleased to see, market day. There were stalls everywhere, selling everything from arms and armor to pies, from toys and trinkets to medicines and clothes. Merchants were calling their wares; housewives were bargaining and arguing; children scampered; two bards played on opposite sides of the square, their hats laid down for coins. A man in bright, zigzag clothes was putting his performing dogs through their paces. One walked on its hind legs while another somersaulted in the air, and a third jumped through hoops. A fourth dog burst in from nowhere with a string of sausages in his mouth, pursued by an angry butcher's boy, who was led a merry dance in and out of the crowd, to roars of laughter and cheers.

The butcher's boy slipped and fell into a puddle. The crowd loved it. The thief dog sat, panting, and his master took the sausages, cut four off, and gave the dogs one each, which they wolfed down. Dogs and trainer and "butcher's boy," the trainer's son, took their bows to great applause. Coins were thrown. More was demanded. The encore was a frenetic loop-the-loop of dogs weaving in and out of each other, and walking on their forepaws, and rolling over and jumping each other, and catching balls in midair, and finally leaping into their owners' arms, where they gave three "cheers," barking after their master's *hip hip— woof!*—wagging their tails enthusiastically. More coins, more bows.

No one, in all this noise and hustle and bustle and color, was going to notice me in my travel-stained cloak. I could observe, unobserved, and overhear. There was an inn set back from the square, but I didn't head for it. I could always come back, or there might be other inns. I didn't want to take the weight off my feet until I'd explored the town. I knew that, if I sat down now, I wouldn't want to make myself get up again, after all the long hours I'd been walking. And in an inn I'd be talking to people, even if only to the servers, and they'd maybe notice that I wasn't from around there.

I wandered down a broad side street, chosen at random, studying the neat houses, with their overhanging upper floors, their steep-gabled roofs, and diamond-paned windows. All looked orderly, some prosperous. Rounding a corner, I came to a smithy, where half a dozen men and boys, stripped to the waist behind leathern aprons, were hard at work, sweating and hammering, and fetching and carrying, and working the bellows, while their forges flamed, and their customers, and the town's idlers, watched. Some samples of their work hung on the back wall. Fine-looking work it was too.

Beyond the forge lay a stable. Presumably I was nearing another edge of the town. Stables are usually located near to gates. I turned again and stopped.

The large, rather featureless building opposite me, standing back from the street behind its own bushes and flowerbeds, was not immediately impressive. Indeed, if anything, it tried not to draw attention to itself—even though it was four stories high, with a tall tower at one end of its roof. It was a plain, uninteresting structure, dressed in drab, brown stone. One thing about it, though, caught my eye at once. By its open front doors, to one side, small and modest but plain enough to those who knew what to look for, was the staff-and-stone symbol of the Guild of the Arcane Arts.

Well now.

I hadn't expected that.

I was a member, of course, having been initiated into the GAA by the Conclave at the Guildhall in Mayport. But that didn't mean that I should just walk in there. People were looking for me here. Enemies. I couldn't give a false name at the GAA. That would beg all sorts of searching questions.

I walked on, before anyone might see me staring at the building and wonder why.

Interesting discovery, though.

Useful?

Could be. If I could think how.

There was a sudden clattering noise behind me and running feet. Startled, I turned—perhaps too quickly, I thought, and made myself slow down. *Innocent people don't look anxious. Don't draw attention to yourself.* A girl ran past, bowling a hoop with a stick, laughing, overtaking her younger brother who was whacking away at his hoop ineptly. She certainly had the technique, and the legs, as she was several years older than him, around Jess's age.

Jess, I thought. One of the crew now. Just because we'd kept our eyes open and not passed her by.

What else was there here to *keep my eyes open* for and see, that I wasn't seeing?

I *kept going forwards*, seeing, by the way the street ahead curved, that it would lead me back to the market square. At the corner there was a beggar. He was dressed in rags, standing on his one leg, leaning on his crutch, his cap held out. I studied him as I drew near. Had he been put there on purpose, for me to talk to? What had I missed, since I came into this town?

As I passed him, I veered towards him as if just noticing him, and dropped a silver and a couple of coppers into his cap.

He jumped.

It was as if he hadn't been expecting something like that. He glanced at me. His face was lean, and taut, and healthy, and his eyes were alert, and shifty, under his mass of stringy black hair. He didn't, somehow, *look*, or should that be *feel*, like someone who needed help.

He mumbled, eventually, "Thank'ee, sir."

I said, "I hope it helps a little. I'd give more if I had more."

He grunted, shifting on his leg and crutch. It was clear he wanted me to go away.

Odd. Beggars are usually keen to collar any possible sucker. I'd deliberately given him a nice score, a silver and change. I thought that I might get more out of him than if I'd given him just a copper, and I'd also thought, *Maybe he'll have noticed stuff. Let's ask …*

I said, in a sympathetic tone, "How did you lose your leg?"

He was looking around beyond me. Then he glared back at me and muttered, "Fuck off."

Startled, I said, "I'm sorry?"

"You fucking will be if you don't fuck off!" he growled.

I stared at him. "*What* did you say?"

He saw something behind me, said, "Oh, shit," dropped his perfectly good second leg to the ground from where it had been tucked up under his coat, and jumped into the street as a man ran past, chased by another man. The "beggar" expertly tripped him with his crutch, leaned down, and slit his throat. His accomplice frisked the corpse, found what he was looking for, and they took off in opposite directions. I—making sure not to call attention to myself—backed carefully away, back the way I'd come. Nobody seemed to notice anything until I got to the corner by the GAA, when the girl and boy returned, running, and bowling their hoops, the boy protesting, the girl laughing.

And then they stopped upon seeing the pool of blood spreading around the corpse, and shrieked.

I melted into the GAA's bushes, and worked my way around behind the building in the shadows.

Its back door was open.

I could tell, by the sounds and smells coming out of it, that it led to the kitchens.

I thought, *Well, why not?*

I cleansed the Glamour from myself, as I wanted to look like a caster, who belonged in the GAA, rather than a mendicant scholar, who did not.

I straightened up, opened Shift's eye, and walked in.

13

The Guild at Huntsbroke

Nobody, to my relief, paid me any attention. I got a mumbled, "Afternoon, sir," from a large-eared, red-faced boy peeling potatoes, who knew from my staff that I was a caster.

I replied, trying to sound just the right amount of jovial-condescending-tired-after-a-long-day-pompous, "Hullo, laddie, the masters keeping you busy, hey?"

He grinned. "That they are, sir!" he said, and went back to his peeling.

I moved on, through the bustling kitchen, where everyone was far too busy to bother about me, and through the green baize door into the central hallway of the Guild of the Arcane Arts. All was quiet and orderly. I looked around and didn't see what I wanted to see—the library. I mounted the central staircase and found what I was looking for.

People don't bother people who are studying in libraries. There were long tables, with benches, and sloping desktops for writing on, complete with inkwells and quills and penknives, and sealing wax of all colors, and an assortment of GAA seals.

I sat down and got to work, cutting myself a new quill and then writing two messages.

The first was to Marnie. I so badly wanted her advice, but knew that we were far too far apart for her Thinking Into powers to be able to find me.

The second was to myself, care of Eydie.

It was quite possible that I wouldn't survive my tribunal, so I wanted to take this opportunity to set down everything I could think of in my report to Marnie. She'd know who to share the information with. She'd also know what, if anything, to do about it if we failed. Send in the next lot, maybe? Well, wish them good luck from us.

My message to Marnie was much the longer of the two and was in proper, formal prose, for the record. It took the best part of half an hour to write. She, and the Conclave, would want to know every detail.

My note to myself was brief.

It was just one sentence that consisted of two connected questions.

I ended both with, *Reply requested.*

I didn't really need a reply from Marnie, although her insights might well be useful.

I would, though, be interested in a reply from myself. Not that I even knew if it was *possible* to hear back … I knew that I had a pigeonhole aboard Eydie. I'd received a very messed-up pigeon through it, but—would it work without me there to receive the message? Might I be just sending a pigeon out into the void, where I wasn't, and where no one would hear, and no one would answer …? Would the pigeon realize that I really wanted the letter to be delivered to Eydie herself?

Well, I thought, who knew? I'd just have to hope for the best.

I left the library, walked downstairs to the front desk, and introduced myself to the porter. His eyes grew round in surprise as I told him my name, Daxx of Pytte.

He said, "I don't believe I saw you come in, sir."

I said, casually, "I came in through the tower." I thought, *might as well keep up appearances.*

I could see him thinking, *Yes, wizard trick all right, flying in up there …*

He put my two messages into separate pigeonholes.

Turning back to me, he enquired, nicely enough, "Dining with us this evening, sir?"

And, also nicely enough, I said, "Yes indeed, most sharp-set I am!"

He chuckled.

I smiled and sauntered back into the guildhall.

Right, I thought, let's get some food inside me before my arrest. There was no doubt about it: He'd made me. Daxx of Pytte. One of the Four that "they" were looking for.

Unlike the guildhall's library, with its studious quietness, the dining hall was bustling with noise and jollity. And it was only just dusk. These wizards, and sorcs, and mages certainly knew how to indulge themselves. All were seated at long benches, and more were arriving every minute. I leaned Shift up against a wall and sat down on a bench beside her. I looked around, at the High Table on its raised dais at the end of the hall, which was filling up with the local Conclave, as servers hurried everywhere with jugs of wine and ale and trays of steaming food.

And *gods* it was good. A bowl of rich mushroom broth was set in front of me by none other than the large-eared, red-faced boy, who gave me a grin on recognizing me. I helped myself to lumps of soft, brown bread from a basket he'd also slapped down, and tucked in.

My tankard was filled with ale. Both ale and soup were excellent. The old geezer next to me was slurping away, happily and noisily. Opposite me a learned-looking, serious, thin girl dressed all in black was arguing some esoteric point with a grumpy, old fat woman, also dressed all in black, who didn't like what she was hearing but didn't have a good answer however much she objected.

I felt a nudge under the table. *Little Guy,* I thought.

I looked.

No dog.

The nudge had come from the knee of the old geezer beside me.

I looked at him. He was still slurping his mushroom soup.

Between mouthfuls, without looking at me, he said, quietly, "I wish—*slurp*—I'd been as receptive as you, at your age."

I said, "Excuse me?"

"It's a great advantage—*slurp*—to be able—*slurp*—to be open—*slurp*—to suggestion."

I couldn't make sense of that. I said, "Surely it's better to make your own mind up?"

"Oh yes, about the things you're concerned with, indeed—*slurp*. But—*slurp*—when someone needs *you*, and needs to attract your attention, confidentially, and you don't know it—*slurp*—well, you sit where you're meant to, because you've been so 'open.' *Slurp*."

I wasn't quite following, but said, eventually, "I'm listening."

"Good—*slurp*. And keep eating, and keep your head down, and don't look at me, and don't move your lips any more than absolutely necessary, because they're watching." He paused, slurping a lot more, then continued. "No, I don't know *who* here is watching, at this exact moment, any more than I know whom they are watching, which is probably everybody. It might be us; it might be those nice ladies the other side of the table; it might be all sorts of other people with their own agendas. It's not a comfortable time. You have about four hours, at most. They haven't noticed you yet, but they will soon enough. Did you send any pigeons?"

Could I trust this character?

"Yes, you can," he said, as if reading my mind.

I started, then tried to hide my reaction. "Can you read my mind?"

"Not necessary. What sane person wouldn't ask himself that question?' Yes, you can. Why on earth do you think I'm here?"

I said, "I've no idea."

"To talk with you, while we still have the chance. So, did you send any pigeons?"

I answered, "Yes, two."

"Replies requested?"

"Yes."

"Mm. You won't get them before they arrest you. Not to worry, I'll field them and you can pick them up later. My name, by the way, is Avildor. My official title is Keeper of the Light. This amuses them, as it shows how unimportant I am. And how out-of-the-way and provincial." He slurped some more, clearly enjoying his soup, so I did the same. "Well, of course, they don't know *everything*. Give me your little book and I'll show you where to find me." Then he tensed a little. "No. *Under* the table, not on top. This town is infested with spies. The whole blasted realm is. Not to worry."

I passed my *Guide to Mourvania* across to him and put it on his thigh.

He took it and glanced at it between slurps. He turned to the page he wanted. He reached down with a stick of charcoal and drew a dot on it.

"There," he said. "Meet me there, as soon as you can. It's my home. Out of the way—no one goes there normally. We have things to talk about, you and I."

Under the table, he passed the book back to me. I checked where he'd put the dot. It was on the northernmost point of the mainland, well east of Huntsbroke.

I said, "How will I know which is your house?"

He chuckled, as he mopped up the remains of his soup with a hunk of bread. "You'll know," he said. "Well. You are in a pickle, aren't you?"

I said, "I believe I might be."

"Just remember," he said, "that everyone is lying to you. Except me, of course, but I can hardly expect you to believe that, seeing as we don't know each other. Yet I will just say this: I made sure the back door was open. You found it. You came in. You had time to send your pigeons. I induced you to sit here in this exact seat so that we could have this little chat. I very much hope," he said, sounding anything but hopeful, "that it won't be our last."

I didn't know what to think, or what to make of this strange, bumbling old geezer. But thinking isn't the thing we go on, is it? What we go on is how we *feel.* And I don't know about you, but most of the time I feel confused, or inadequate, or frightened, or just plain stupid. And then I just do the stupid things that those feelings make me do. And here I was, in a strange town, sitting next to a strange old stranger …

"Thank you, Avildor," I said. "My name is—"

He jabbed my leg sharply. I looked down. A name was written in charcoal on a scrap of paper.

I got the idea and read it aloud. "Kel of Arnstead."

"Nice little place. How are things there, since Beadle Velmott departed this world?"

I said, eventually, "You probably know better than I do."

He chuckled. "I certainly do, you never having been there in your life. I do not wish to know your name," he added, in a lower voice. "That way, they cannot get it out of me, even under torture. Kel, I will truthfully say, is the name you gave me."

Torture. I didn't like the sound of that.

Hold on, I thought. "I'm more likely to be tortured than you."

"Almost certain to be. But if you reveal my name, so what? It's not me they're looking for."

Our soup bowls were removed and replaced with wooden tren-chers. Large dishes of roasted meats, and baked fishes, and vegetables and pies of all shapes and sizes and colors were placed at intervals along the tables, and we all helped ourselves.

I said, "Is it always this busy? Must be a lot of casters in this town …"

"Only about half the people here are GAA." Avildor said. "The others are guests, family, and friends. No one refuses an invitation to eat here; we have the best cooks in town. No, it's not always this crowded—we had a Summoning. To hear our instructions from the Devoted." He paused, seemingly for significance. "The number four was mentioned, frequently. Curious, that, no? Every guildfellow from many leagues around had to attend, by order, as did our Coven friends." He nodded at the two women across the table, who were still arguing earnestly between mouthfuls. "Which is a good thing," he said. "The more strangers in town the better for you to blend in with, eh?"

I saw his point.

"I would fill up," he said, "if I were you. Not too much ale or wine, though; you'll want to keep your wits about you. But you won't eat anything this well at the Orphanage."

"The what?"

"Orphanage. Headquarters of the Devoted Children of Mercy. No, you probably won't eat very much at all while you're their 'honored guest.' Which you will be before they name you penitent. After that: Well, good luck."

"Is there anything else you should tell me?" I asked.

He considered, while chewing. "A great deal," he said, "that's why I sought you out. It will have to wait until we meet again, though. What you don't know you can't tell them, can you? Even if they tear out your toenails. All I'd say is, while you're their, um … 'honored guest,' be as truthful as you can. A lie is always best hidden behind the truth."

I nodded, thinking, *torture …*

"A shame your friends all drowned," Avildor added. "Must've been something you cast that kept you alive, eh?"

I "agreed"lying, "Indeed it was."

"And then your staff was swept away. Terrible misfortune for a caster."

I said, alarmed, "What?!"

He said, calmly, "Well, you wouldn't want her to fall into the wrong hands, would you?"

With a small turn of his head, he nodded at Shift, leaning against the wall, and added "A lovely piece of rowan like that," pronouncing it to rhyme with *cow* and *now* and *how*. "With luck you'll be needing her again."

I understood what he meant. If I survived my tribunal, I wouldn't want to be without Shift. I definitely didn't like the idea of the Devoted keeping her—or, worse, destroying her.

"Eye closed, I see," he said. "Very wise. What's her stone?"

"Tourmaline."

He turned and looked at me directly for the first time. "Really?" he said, impressed.

"Really. Red on top, green below."

"Goodness me. I bet they pack a punch together! I've never found a moonstone heart for my black willow, and she yearns for one. I make do with a jasper—a fine one—but it's not what she deserves. Do keep an eye out for one, would you?"

"Of course," I said.

"How did you find yours?" he asked.

I told him. Perhaps I shouldn't have. For all his friendliness, he could have been an enemy spy. But I didn't think so. He'd wanted to meet me, and warn me, and tell me what he had told me. So, I told him how Oller had found my tourmaline heartstone and given it to me despite him being a professional thief, and how Marnie had sent me to choose a stave, in the dark in her woodshed, and how Shift and I had chosen each other. By the time I'd finished, and he'd finished his questions, supper was being cleared away, and I had eaten my second large slice of plum tart and downed my third mug of ale.

"Most interesting," Avildor said, looking at me and nodding. "And even more interesting are all the things you aren't telling me. I look forward to hearing them when we meet again. Which will be your first priority."

Would it? I said "Why?"

He said, "Because you have no idea what's going on. Well, you have *some* idea, but it's far from being the *whole* idea. What little you know, shall we say, is just one side of the story. And, well, I don't know about you, but in your position I'd be inclined to wonder how reliable the information I'd been given is. Actually," he reconsidered, "getting my help will be your *second* priority. Your first will be to get out of the

Orphanage alive. The which I very much hope you do. For many more sakes than just your own.

"And when we meet again," he added, mopping his mouth with his sleeve, "I shall return you your beautiful staff. Not too much ale while you're waiting, now," he advised, still not looking directly at me. "And certainly not in front of them, when they come for you. They don't approve. You'll be drinking their water from now on and eating their dry bread and gruel. Rather you than me, young Kel of Arnstead!"

He swiveled on our bench and heaved himself to his feet. He was tall, and stout, and dressed in excellent wizard's robes, of fine black cloth, with silver and white stars, and moons, and planets, and arcane symbols embroidered onto it. He retrieved his pointed hat from its hook on the wall and placed it on his head. He picked up Shift and brought her over, as if to show me for the first time. "Rowan and tourmaline," he said, as if confirming what he'd already told me.

I reached for her and stroked her. "She's beautiful."

"Isn't she just?" he agreed, and stood there, as if happy to let me admire her.

I knew what he was doing. He was, after all, a wizard himself. He'd have his own staff, with their own, private relationship.

I felt a reassuring warmth from Shift flow up my arm. There was no fear, no sense of alarm. The longer I held her, the more I felt something else underneath her calm. What? She was trying to hide it. That wasn't like her. We had no secrets. She didn't want me to know. Why not?

As soon as I worked it out, I gave her my silent thanks and let go.

She was worried about me. She had done her best to shield that from me.

Avildor slung her over his shoulder and left. I noticed that he hadn't brought his own staff with him. Presumably, I thought, he didn't want to be seen leaving with two, which might raise eyebrows.

Well, I thought, what's the difference? Lose her to my captors or to this old geezer. One of them had indicated that he'd give her back. The others—less likely. And Shift had gone with him quietly.

I emptied my mug and called for a refill.

Water, and gruel, and dry bread?

Screw that. This GAA ale was too good to miss out on. Especially if, as seemed probable, it'd be the last I'd be tasting for a while.

Maybe the last I'd ever taste.

I thought, *Might as well make the most of however much, or little, freedom remained to me.*

I drained my tankard, and held it out to the large-eared, red-faced boy, who refilled it, with his usual cheery grin. I worked my way through it slowly, thinking about all that Avildor had told me; and about Oldface; and the others, and our tasks; and then headed back to the library.

Forewarned is forearmed, I decided, so I wanted to read up as much as I could on the Devoted Children of Mercy before they came to take me away. I learned that they were devotees of Valmynia, goddess of Mercy and Suffering. The sect had been founded hundreds of years ago by a charismatic young mendicant named Chidian, who had come from overseas, no one knew quite where, and had, by the force of his zeal, united the rulers of the various realms where the Cult of Varamaxes held sway. He had led their armies against their foe's stronghold, far to the south in The Great Waste, and defeated his hordes.

Varamaxes had been overthrown and bound; shortly after which Chidian had disappeared, leaving the first of a long succession of Abbotts as his deputies in this world, to guide the Children from then on. It was a practical faith, in that it was the principal power in the realm, of which the king was little more than a figurehead; but it was also a mystic one.

This was particularly noticeable in its approach to astronomy and astrology. The first—a science, where I came from—seemed in their eyes to be conflated with the second, which IRL astrophysicists consider anything but. So, for example, a treatise on navigation would combine detailed observations and readings and mathematical calculations based on their cosmic calendar, with mythology, and factoids about constellations and the heavenly, or hellish, beings that were believed to inhabit them.

There were lots of Reasons for Everything, in their study of the stars. Their maps of the heavens were beautiful, intricate, and detailed. Their zodiac had twelve houses, with names like The Swallow, The Thief, The Urn, and The Fisher. They, and the many other named constellations, all had strange properties and stories attached to them. Reading about them made me want to study the skies so that I could identify them. One, The Demon, was composed of thirteen stars around which a familiar shape had been drawn: Old Birdbeak. So, he was up there in the sky as well as down here on his island under the island, it seemed.

180 degrees across from The Demon was The Protectress: The bust and head of a woman in a flowing headdress, her right hand raised in blessing. Everything, in this belief system, seemed to revolve around opposites. For every heaven, there was a corresponding hell; for every god, a demon. Valmynia and Varamaxes.

I would be in need of her protection soon enough, I thought. Let's hope that it's mercy in my future rather than suffering.

I was absorbed in the legend of the Fisher and the Whale, and trying to puzzle out the riddles they asked each other in turn, when a young under-porter came to fetch me. I was needed at once, he told me. I feigned surprise. I asked who by.

"Emissaries of the Devoted!" he urged, nervously, as if that was going to galvanize me into action.

"You may tell them I will be down in a few minutes, if you wish," I said, absently.

He didn't like that at all. He wasn't going back to *them* without me. "Th-they," he stuttered. "I ... I've been looking everywhere for you, master ..."

Well, I didn't want to get the lad into trouble, so I closed the book and replaced it on its shelf. The underporter was holding the door for me, positively hopping with anxiety.

"After you, if you please, sir," he said, in a tone that meant *hurry*. I walked down the wide staircase to the lobby, not hurrying, and saw my reception committee, all of them in brown habits, like the travelers I'd seen on the road. I also saw that the porter was as nervous as his underling.

"Good evening, ladies, gentlemen," I said, with a friendly smile, "I understand that you wish to see me?"

Not one of them smiled in return.

A plump, sour man said, "You are the caster known as Daxx of Pytte?"

"I am," I said, still smiling pleasantly. I didn't feel pleasant inside. I knew what was coming. But I didn't want them to know that I knew. "And you are?"

"Brother Marten of the Children of Mercy. You will come with us."

I allowed my surprise to show. "I beg your pardon?"

He repeated, in more of a bark than a normal voice, "You will come with us!"

Clearly, he wasn't used to being crossed.

"Why in the world would I want to do that?" I said. "I've had a long day, and a long walk, and I'm tired, and I have a bed here at my guild, and—"

That was as far as I got. A hard-faced brother took my right elbow and a hard-faced sister my left, and they began marching me out of the guild, Brother Marten leading the way.

"Hey!" I protested, "Let me go! What do you think you're doing?!"

"Placing you under arrest, by order of Mother Abbott."

"What? You're not watchmen, you're not guards!"

Brother Marten stopped. He turned around. He glared at me. And slapped me across the face, hard.

"Ow!"

"And I'll tell you what *you're* not," he said. "You're not to speak. Understand?"

I stared at him, shocked, and nodded. Message received. I looked, I knew, suitably cowed. It was a lot easier to look than the "cheerful and confident" I'd been putting on had been—because *suitably cowed* was how I indeed felt. And scared. These bastards would burn me alive if I didn't play my cards right. And I was holding a pretty weak hand. I'd have to make sure they didn't find that out and would buy my bluff. They just might, if I could make it worth their while to do so. And if they didn't—well, I had no Shift to protect me.

He grunted, turned, and our merry little band left the warmth and comfort of the GAA guildhall, hurrying out into the cold night.

I was hustled along the side street, past where I'd witnessed the "beggar" and his accomplice murder and rob their victim, and around the corner into the town square. It was almost deserted. What few people there were in it disappeared the moment they saw us. Nobody wanted anything to do with this lot. There was an enclosed wagon waiting for us, drawn by four horses. I was bundled inside and locked in with only Brother Marten for company. He reached over and bound my hands.

The wagon jolted off, and we lurched across the cobbled square.

I said, "Can I ask you a question?"

He slapped me across the mouth again.

He reached to his belt, from which he detached a flail. I took in the leather thongs, studded with iron, attached to a wooden handle. I looked back up at him, my mouth dry.

"Next time you speak when not spoken to," he said, "you get this."

I nodded, and sat back, and avoided eye-contact.

14

The Orphanage

It was a long journey. I slept deeply that night—hardly surprising, as I was wiped out after all I'd been through—and woke up when a boot kicked me in the ribs. It was soon after dawn. I was pushed outside and allowed to take a leak. Which was not easy, with bound hands, but I managed.

I tried to play "completely beaten" as best I could. It wasn't hard. I was frightened, and lost, and more than a little confused. People who are answerable to a "higher power," and who have no interest in our common humanity? Scary. Stupid. Stupid people are scarier than intelligent people. They do what they are told, and believe what they believe, without question. And, even more unfortunately, take a grim pleasure in doing so. It's easier that way. It's less of a challenge for their tiny, closed minds. They don't want to think. Thinking confuses them. They just want to be told that they're right and obey orders.

I got some small comfort from telling myself that, one day, I would kill the lot of them. Would I, though? Even if I had the chance? How pathetic these mean-spirited sheep were. How glad I was not to be one of them.

I didn't think about them much after I'd realized that. Screw them. Nasty, smug, bitter, glum sheep.

I thought of Oller and Qrysta and Grell. Their largeness of spirit. Their loyalty, and humor, and inventiveness, and lively humanity. These poor fools would never be able to think outside their tiny little, sad little box. And if their god or goddess ever appeared and showered them with love and glory? I couldn't imagine this lot dancing for joy and singing praises and laughing. No. They were living examples of the expression "misery loves company."

Which was informative in itself.

If that was the tone of what lay ahead, I would have to play to it, and not expect sweetness and light. I reminded myself that I was, to a very small degree, ahead of them. I knew more than they knew. I had a strategy. I had a fighting chance. Whereas, if Oldface hadn't wrecked us and rescued us, I'd be here with the others now, and we'd all be heading to our martyrdom.

I thought, looking at these sour, cold, busy people, *Children of Mercy?*

The ironically ill-fitting name reminded me of the old joke: "You know that two positives can never make a negative?"

Yeah, right.

We'll see, I thought. We'll see.

Dogma. Thinking inside box. Every answer ordained.

Okay. I can work with that.

And on we jolted. Mile after mile, hour after hour. Day after day.

We only stopped at sundown, for prayers.

I was made to attend. I was jabbed in the ribs when I didn't respond correctly and was cued the words. It was usually *amen*, or, *so be it*, or, *praise be to our Divine Mother.* They stopped jabbing me on the third evening when I got everything right. On the fourth day the jolting stopped, and the cart turned, and its wheels were crunching on gravel.

We're here, I thought.

The back doors opened, and I was led out. I made sure to look back, in the direction we'd come from. And there it was, beyond the gates that were now closing behind us and being locked by guards.

The black monolith on which the message that unnerved them was carved.

So, you still can't get rid of it, I thought.

The knowledge encouraged me. My captors were no more competent than I was.

My next thought bothered me. These are "the good guys." And I'm pleased that they can't ""the bad guy from their lives, even when he is locked up in a prison on an island under an island, which they don't even know about?

I shook thoughts of Oldface and his malevolent imp away, and how my unpleasant captors were the "good guys."

No. That would be me, and Qrysta, and Oller, and Grell.

Thinking of my crew gave me heart. I was, after all, doing this for them. For *us*. Not for the "good guys" or the "bad guys" of this realm. For my team. My friends.

I held my head up and followed my captors into The Orphanage. It was a big, solid stone building, with windows that seemed too small and walls that seemed too high. The whole place felt like a prison. Which it was going to be for me, I knew.

There were lawns all around it, neatly mown, but with only a few scant flowerbeds and just one tree, an old, shadowy yew. *These people needed a little design help,* I thought. *This place is as dreary as their brown habits.* The doors were opened—swung back, I saw as I walked in among my captors, by young novices in white robes, who kept their heads bowed and avoided eye contact. Poor kids, I thought, growing up here. Talk about oppressive.

Not everyone in the wide, high hallway that we entered was in one of those uniforms. There were servants, in drab but regular clothes, going about their business. No one talked. On we walked, past a tall statue of a robed woman looking piously down at us, her right hand raised in blessing. The Divine Mother herself, no doubt. Valmynia.

My escort touched the fingers of their right hands to their foreheads as they passed and muttered their cantrip, *Praise be to our Divine Mother.* I was among the devout, and they cared nothing for me, only for their own creed. *Humility,* I thought. *Respect. Flattery.* I needed to show an awareness of, and a growing shame about, my own lack of understanding.

I needed to "see the light."

Out of the hall, through a chapel, and into an antechamber we went, out, and downstairs, and down more stairs, and more and more, until we reached the lowest level. The cells.

I was signed in, and handed over to the Brother Jailer, and searched. He found my purse and my little guidebook to Mourvania, both of which he removed. He prodded me towards a cell the size of a table, untied my hands, pushed me in and locked the door.

The only light came from a high shaft in one corner. I leaned over and looked up it. All that I could see was a small circle of gray sky, far above me. There was a bed of slabs, a pallet of straw, a bucket for my ablutions, a three-legged stool, on which stood a jug of water and a plate of, indeed, dry bread. *Not now, thanks,* I thought. There was also a little book on it. I picked it up and held it out into the last of the weak afternoon light and looked at its title.

The Devotions of Chidian.

So. They wanted me to improve my mind.

I was too tired to read. I lay down and went straight to sleep, trying not to think of dying on the martyr's pyre.

I had two days to myself in that cell. Two days of water and dry bread, and shitting on my bucket, and each evening the treat of a bowl of gruel, which was nothing but warmish onion water, with bits of carrot and spinach floating in it. I was made to say grace before I was allowed to eat. *Praise be to the Divine Mother for sparing her child the suffering of hunger, and the joy of her mercy.* I tried not to think back to my supper with Avildor at the Huntsbroke GAA.

On the third morning I was stripped, and scrubbed with harsh soap and harsher brushes, and had buckets of cold water doused over me. Brother Jailer threw a "towel" at me so that I could dry myself. It was the size of a handkerchief and the texture of sandpaper. So far, so mortifying.

I was handed a rough brown shift to wear. My niblun clothes had disappeared. Then the bastard sat me down in a chair and hacked off my hair. I protested. Daxx's long, flowing, blond Viking locks were my trademark.

I was hit, and held, and hacked at; and then, in one final, creepy indignity, Brother Jailer brushed and combed my hair neatly, slowly, carefully; setting it in place with some sickly smelling unction. Or, as he'd no doubt put it, "anointing my head with holy oil." *Yeah, yeah, creep.*

Whatever. Let them play their game. Go with the flow. Two thoughts wrestled with each other. One: These people were hardly a Church Militant, so I doubted I'd ever face Brother Jailer in combat. Oh well, I'd just have to find another way of getting my own back, should the chance arise. And Two: Grell and Qrysta would be giving me grief for a long time when they saw my new haircut.

Thinking of them made me smile. I hid it as soon as I felt it on my face. Luckily, I was facing away from Brother Jailer.

What a circus it was. I was frog-marched up all those stairs and into the entrance hallway, which was lined with people. Servants, cooks, gardeners, boot boys, scullery maids, porters, all standing along both walls, the men bareheaded and holding their caps and hats in their hands, the women in headscarves. They watched me pass with my escort, in silence.

I see. Everyone has to bear witness.

I could hear chanting coming from ahead. I was marched into the Great Chapel. Every Child of Mercy in the community was there, all standing in their pews. The chanting was coming from a choir that was ranged on steps at the back of the stage ahead, behind a long, empty table. Above and behind the choir reared another enormous stature of the same goddess, with the same robes, and veil, and raised-hand pose, and the same mournful expression as the statue in the entrance hall. I was led to a small table below the stage and ordered to stand. The chanting continued. I stood. I tried to make out the words. Mercy. Judgment. Suffering. Right and Light, Ire and Fire. And a name, Valmynia. Divine Mother of Mercy and Suffering.

Well, wish me luck, Val, I thought.

After an interminable while, doors opened at the sides of the stage. Children of Mercy filed in, men from one side, women from another. My jury? Seniors of the cult, certainly. They sat at their high-backed chairs, not passing each other, the men stage right, the women stage left. The central seat was more of a throne than a chair. It was the only colorful object in the room. The congregation in brown, the novices among them in white, the senior brothers and sisters at the High Table in black, white walls, dark wooden pews—and this throne glowing like the tabard of a Royal Herald, its cushioned back embroidered with designs in red and blue and green, and threaded with cloth of gold. *So, that is where the head honcho goes,* I thought. *Well, bring him on.*

The chanting stopped.

Silence fell.

From stage left a large woman entered. And all at the High Table rose as she strode to her throne. She was as colorful as it was, all in a brilliant blue, which shimmered as she moved. It must be interwoven with some other hue, I thought, to give it that texture and depth and life. Blue over silver, I decided. She stood at her throne and intoned the phrase I was already sick of hearing, "Praise be to our Divine Mother."

All echoed her in response.

Including me.

She reached for the gavel that was beside her and rapped the wooden block next to it.

"In the name of Valmynia, Divine Mother, I declare this tribunal in session."

She sat.

Everyone sat.

Excluding me. I'd been told to stand, so stand I did.

She looked at me. It was not a kind face. A heavy face, it was, with sagging jowls, and a sharp chin, and dark eyes sunk in mottled pouches, and skin that was nearer gray than pink. She looked both strong and unhealthy.

"You will tell the truth," she addressed me.

"Yes," I responded.

"Yes, Mother Abbott," she corrected me.

"Yes, Mother Abbott," I echoed.

"Where are the rest of you?"

"My friends?" I asked. I knew perfectly well who she meant, but I had a role to play. The less intelligent she thought me, the better.

"My friends, *Mother Abbott*," she snapped. "Yes, if that's what they are. There are meant to be four of you. Why aren't they here?"

"They drowned, Mother Abbott."

I heard murmurs of consternation in the congregation all around me. Mother Abbott rapped her gavel for silence.

It fell instantly.

"You will tell me how."

So, I did, leaving out everything about Oldface. I emphasized, indeed embellished, the storm. They all remembered it battering the area for days. I'd been in light clothes, so had floated. Grell had been in plate armor—he'd never stood a chance. Qrysta's leathers were soon waterlogged, no doubt, and Oller was a country lad who'd never seen the sea and had told me during the storm that he didn't know how to swim and was terrified. I didn't mention the island under the island, or Jess, or Little Guy. I told Mother Abbott that I hadn't seen any of them since the hull burst. It was all I could do to stay afloat, and I'm a strong swimmer.

Spars and barrels banged into me in the dark, and I managed to grab them among the heaving waves. And that is what I did, and clung on for dear life, and let the wind and the waves take me where they willed through the black, rain-lashed night.

Eventually, long after I'd given up hope, and was slowing up from the cold, and could hardly move my exhausted limbs, I heard rollers pounding on a shore. The gods in their mercy drove me that way. At last, I was flung onto a beach of hard pebbles. I barely managed to drag myself away from the waterline. There was a cliff, but I didn't have the strength to climb the path that led up it. Die of cold ashore, or die of cold afloat. I had lost my staff, so could neither heal nor heat myself. It was raining, hard, and blowing, hard. I was sure that I was finished.

But I woke the next morning, more dead than alive, and realized that I must have been spared for a reason. It took me all day, and all my strength, to cover a few miles. I slept under a bush. Another day and I came to a road. There were some travelers, but not many. I was a stranger there, so I didn't dare talk to anyone.

I turned east, and walked, keeping my head down and myself to myself, all the way to Huntsbroke. I had a little money, so could buy food. It was market day. I was still scared, still lost. I decided to explore the town before finding an inn and found instead the local Guildhall of the Arcane Arts, of which I am a member. I was welcomed, and fed, sumptuously. And then I was called to the porter's lodge, where your escort was waiting for me.

They arrested me, I still don't understand on what authority (shocked murmurs in the congregation, another bang of the gavel). I had intended to stay the night in one of the GAA guest bedrooms, and have my clothes laundered, and begin to see if I could find out what had happened. I still did not know why the ghost ship had been sent for us. Did she?

She didn't answer.

I hadn't expected her to.

Instead, she began her questions.

Where was this beach?

I gave its location as accurately as I could. A nod at her neighbor, who stood and hurried out. Search party on the way. The others had had nearly a week to make themselves scarce. *Oh, and guys? If you want to arrest Qrysta or Grell, you'll need a bigger party than the one you sent for me.*

Blinkered, I thought. Used to being obeyed. Well, those poor innocents had probably never faced a truculent Orc with a battle-axe. Or a sweet-faced, mild-mannered, deadly sword-dancer.

"You examined the message?" Mother Abbott demanded.

Ah, I thought. They know about that. Well, we'd seen no reason not to talk about it. We'd told Esmeralda, in court. Dozens of ears would have heard. We'd discussed it at the College of Lore and Learning and the GAA in Mayport. We'd asked around. We'd wanted to find out what it meant.

I frowned, acting puzzled, and said, "Message?"

She glared.

"I mean: Message, Mother Abbott?"

"Addressed, we are told, to the one called Qrysta," she said.

"Oh, the verse—yes, of course we examined it, Mother Abbott."

"And?"

"It seemed straightforward enough. Someone needed our help," I replied. And quickly added, as she stiffened and glared at me again, "*Mother Abbott.* We didn't recognize the seal, though, so asked around."

"Who did you ask about it?" she said.

"The College of Lore and Learning, the GAA, a senior Coven Guildsister. No one liked the seal. The Guildsister remembered it from an old map, in a little guidebook to this realm, which she gave me, in case we should find ourselves here—as we have. Or rather, *I* have." I hoped my slipup wasn't noticed. "I assume you've seen it, as the book was taken from me?"

She didn't answer, so I continued, "That was just about the only information we managed to gather. It's the seal of the Archon of Varamaxes, we gathered (rumbles of disapproval at the name, another bang of the gavel). But no one seemed to know what or who or where that was. Is it you?"

Gasps of shock and outrage.

Frantic banging of gavel.

When order resumed, I said, "I'm sorry, I mean is that you, Mother Abbott?"

Pandemonium.

Gavel hammering.

The Seniors at the High Table were on their feet, yelling for order, yelling at me, their faces bulging with fury. I did my best to look scared and confused. Inside, I was pleased. I'd just dragged a nice, fat red herring across their paths.

When the din subsided, I said, "I'm sorry if I don't understand everything, Mother Abbott. *Anything*, really. Did you send for us? And use a seal that you're implying isn't yours? I think you owe me an explanation, because if you did, my friends are dead because of you, and your message, and your seal—"

The gavel banged to quell the uproar.

"You will answer *my* questions. That is all!" she said. "I do not owe you anything."

"I disagree, you owe me three lives, Madam Secretary."

She gasped. *"What* did you call me?"

"I beg your pardon, Mother Abbott, I was getting confused. I expect you'll explain everything you want me to know when you see fit."

Silence. Everyone was wondering what I could possibly mean by that: *I* wanted *her* to explain? But, what, wait—*I* was the one who should be doing the explaining …

"Three lives," she said, eventually. "Soon to be four."

I frowned. "What? You sent for us just to kill us?"

"We did not send for you," Mother Frogface said.

"Well who did?"

"You will stop asking questions!" she ordered.

I ignored her and kept going. "It makes no sense. Why all the rigmarole, a ghost ship? That can't be easy to organize. I'm sorry, but this really is ridiculous."

More uproar. More gavel banging.

"Your life," Mother Abbott stated, when silence had at last fallen again, "is already forfeit. Before you lose it, you will receive any chastisement that you earn through your conduct in this most holy and solemn tribunal. This is my only warning. In her mercy at our weakness, our Divine Mother blesses us with the gift of suffering, in her name, and at the hands of her servants, so that we may purge our bodies and purify our souls."

I said, humbly, "Thank you for the instruction, Mother Abbott. I will heed it."

"Finally you say something sensible. I cannot believe that any of the Four we have been awaiting can be quite so stupid as you clearly are. Perhaps we have built you up, over the years, to be more than you could possibly be. Whatever the case, you are most unimpressive. Do you really think yourself capable of defying us, and undoing decades, hundreds of years of our work?"

I had no answer to that.

She waited, while I gathered my thoughts.

I took my time. I can string out a pause. "How in the world can I know, Mother Abbott? We came here to find out what we were wanted for. We came with good intentions, intending to help whoever had sent for us. We had just saved our kingdom and were heroes of the realm. No doubt that's how you heard of us. Well, since I've been here, no one has told me anything. And my friends are dead. So, Mother Abbott, it would seem that we have failed to do—whatever it was we were meant to do. That *you* presumably wanted us to do. We didn't even get to find out what that is, and to get started before that horrendous storm wrecked us. And now you want to kill me. May I ask why, Mother Abbott?"

She said, harshly, "To end the threat."

"You think I'm a threat?" I said, spreading my arms wide, in a gesture of defeat. "Look at me. I'm unarmed, alone, completely in the dark about what is going on, scared out of my wits, and the owner of a horrible new haircut thanks to your blasted jailer, Madam Bishop. And all when I came in here in all good faith to help!" I paused, as if seriously judging their actions, finding them wanting. "I still would help, if I could, despite the rotten treatment you've given me. Where I come from, we have laws of hospitality. Where I come from, it is *presumed innocent until proven guilty*. If this is justice, Mrs. Archimandrite, or whatever you call yourself, I am a potato!!"

Yes, there was yelling coming at me now, but I was yelling louder. I was determined to have my say.

Gavel gavel gavel ...

Eventually the racket subsided.

"You have just earned yourself a scourging, Daxx of Pytte."

I bowed my head and waited for the silence.

When it came, I raised it, and looked her in the eye, and said, "And you, Mother Abbott, have now missed the opportunity that I intended to offer you."

That surprised her. She was about to gavel the tribunal closed but hesitated. "And what is that?"

I said, "I will tell you in private."

She glared at me.

I added, "I believe you'll like it."

She considered. She warned, "If I don't, your punishment will be severe."

I smiled. "And if you do, Madam Abbott, your reward will be as welcome as it is unexpected."

She frowned, and said, warily, "My reward?"

"The reward that you will gain from what I tell you."

I deliberately didn't say *Mother Abbott*. That was my way of letting her know that we were equals in this negotiation.

She didn't know what to think. One moment I'd been a frightened ignoramus, and now, suddenly, I was bargaining, with confidence.

I couldn't see how she could resist hearing what I had to say.

She continued staring. She made up her mind. "You will burn," she said, adding, "Scourge him!" as she banged her gavel to close the tribunal.

I was seized, stripped, stretched over the table, and scourged. By, of course, Brother Marten—who, I could see by the fierce grin on his face as he pulled the flail from his belt, couldn't wait to lay into me. The iron studs in their leather thongs tore into my back. My right hand jolted open wide in shock, instinctively reaching. I longed to close it around Shift. After the third blow, I fainted.

15

The Information

I came to when a bucket of cold water was thrown over my back. The sting of it in my whip wounds jerked me awake, shocked and gasping. I was hauled to my feet and dragged off back down to my cell, unable to stand or walk.

Everyone was happy to strike at me on the way. I kept my head down, and my bleeding shoulders up, and ignored their kicks and blows and insults. I was thrown onto my cell's thin mattress, face down. I lay there, exhausted from lack of food as much as from exertion. The pain in my back was excruciating. I couldn't heal myself without a staff. *Well*, I thought, *Oldface had not been lying when he told me that life would be grim here at the Orphanage.* I just hoped that the others wouldn't be having such a bad time of things on their quests.

I'd probably never know. Apparently I'd be fuel for the flames soon enough. I'd played my weak hand as best I could. I'd thrown out my bait. She thought she was cleverer than me. I hoped to all hells that she indeed was cleverer than the dullard I'd presented myself as in my tribunal. If she was a closed-minded, by-the-numbers idiot, I was as good as fried.

We'll see, I thought, as I wrapped myself in my cloak on my pallet. It was cold in my cell, deep belowground. I lay awake, fretting and turning instead of sleeping. My head thought that I'd done okay, but my heart felt that I was hanging by a thread. Tomorrow would tell.

It didn't.

Nor did the next day.

The longer they deliberated the truth of my words, I thought, the more chance the others have.

Gods, how I missed them. In what fitful sleep I got, I dreamed of battles, lined up with Grell, and Qrysta, and Oller and Little Guy, against these sanctimonious jackasses. Sometimes Jess was shooting her whitewood bow beside me, while I unleashed fire and fury at Mother Misery and her acolytes, and Grell and Qrysta and Oller did their butcher's work while Little Guy fizzed in and out, bothering everyone. It felt good, even though I knew I was sleeping.

I woke always dulled and tired and confused. Why the delay in deciding my fate? All I could think of was that she was waiting for her search party to report back. And every day was another day for my crew to do what they needed to.

Every morning I grew more confident. Not confident that I would live, but rather that they would prevail, and get what had to be done, done. I wondered what they would do if I perished.

I could imagine myself telling them, *Okay, so when I'm gone, Jess takes my place. You guys all train her up. You'll need a healer, she needs healing—it's a perfect fit. Swap out that whitewood bow for a staff. Maybe that weird black one that we found in the hoard—the twisted one with the claw head, and the heartstone that I couldn't identify. Why not? Put that in her hands, see how she gets on with it. Studying is all very well, but the best way to learn is on the job. Start her out as a noob; help her level up. Wish I could do that with you.*

Oh, how I longed to be out there with them, not cooped up in this dismal, damp, cold cell, with my back on fire from the pain of my scourging and the rest of me shivering.

But that was my reality, so all that I could do was plan ahead. The more days that passed without them burning me alive, the more that I knew I'd piqued Madam Abbott's interest. Better get my pitch together, then. There'll only be one shot at this.

They came for me on the third day. I was woken by sudden footsteps, and clinking, and jangling, and voices, and what little light there was blocked by bodies looming outside my cell. I was escorted back up. I had no gauntlet to run this time. I was just shoved into a side passage, out of sight, and hurried along, around, and up some steps. A door. A knock, from Brother Jailer. "Enter." We did. Just Brother Jailer and me. He was dismissed with some kind of blessing. And there she was, sitting behind a desk, waiting for me.

So, respectfully, I waited for her. I knew that I was going to have to obfuscate and bamboozle. I needed to have her looking every way but the right one, and not give her enough time to think clearly. This wasn't going to be a straightforward, logical march to a consensus. I'd have to hit her from all sides, then let her off the hook, smooth her down, and get her to have the idea that I needed her to have. If I failed, I would be burned at the stake. So, I needed to have my wits about me. I was pretty confident that I did. I'd been preparing for this since Huntsbroke.

She said, "Sit."

I lowered myself into the chair opposite her. I looked up at her.

She studied me, then said, "Speak."

I realized that the search party must have returned empty-handed, or she'd have immediately drawn attention to my lies.

I said, "You have a problem."

Her eyebrows rose.

"Which I can take care of."

She said, a little too quickly, "Alone?"

I bowed. "Alone."

Her eyes narrowed. "Define the problem."

"Your enemy. He will destroy you, or you will destroy him. I am willing to do that for you."

She frowned. She said, "Gods cannot be killed."

I said, "We killed one in Jarnland."

That adjusted her attitude. "Tell me."

I told her about Grell and Klurra killing the winged monster in the underground, far to the north, below the Western Mountains.

"Demigod," she said. "Immortal, in that they will live forever, but mortal in that they can be killed. Which comes from having human blood in their veins. Or giantess blood, in that case. Our enemy is no demigod."

I said, "Your turn."

Offended, she glared at me. "I beg your pardon?!"

"To explain. About your enemy."

"He is a demon."

I had guessed that much. I thought, *So?* I said, "And?"

"And he's been waiting many long years for the Four to appear and free him from his prison. Our founder, Blessed Father Abbott Chidian, condemned him to eternal confinement, many long years ago. Only the Four can unbind him, it is believed. They must not be given the chance to do so."

I couldn't help but feel unease at mention of the Four, even though I'd known it had to be coming. "Do you know how they would do that?"

The question unsettled her. She fidgeted with scrolls and papers on her desk and did not answer. Eventually, she admitted, "No. No one does. Neither us, nor his followers. Of whom there are still some, though we hunt them down without—despite our name—mercy. That was our Blessed Father's intention, that he be lost forever."

"Thought not." I said, nodding at her, "But I do."

She went still. "How?"

"By going to places that I alone can go."

This was where it was going to get tricky. I needed to hide my lie behind truth that she would swallow. Until Oldface had told us about Head and Heart and Soul and Mind, no one but he and Chidian, his enemy since time immemorial, knew about them.

"What places?"

I leaned forward and lowered my voice—not just because I was taking her into my confidence, but also because what I was about to say was disturbing.

"Hidden places. Which no person born in this realm can access. You know that, of course. Which is, as you also know, the reason that foreigners are forbidden from entering this land."

I let that sink it. So far, all that I had said rang true.

She nodded for me to continue. So far, so good.

I returned her nod with one of my own, to signal that we were making progress.

"I am relieved that you saw through my act at the tribunal, Mother Abbott. I was confident that you would, as it was a pretty thin act, just put on for show, for your followers, as what I have to discuss with you is for your ears only. You were right to not believe that any of the Four could be *quite so stupid as I clearly was,*" I quoted her own words back at her. "The moment you said that, I gained heart. I knew that I was dealing with someone intelligent. It was a relief, I can tell you. Living with the prospect of being burned alive has not been pleasant." I moved right on, not giving her time to respond. "You have questions. I know because I planted them in my responses to you at the tribunal, and you have clearly had time to work them out. I have answers."

I waited for her permission to proceed.

"Go on."

"The Arch Historian of our Faiths has seen our purpose. She consulted the stars, and the old writings. The Confluence, she called it. It has been revealed to her that the wheels of time have turned, and the tables with them. What has lasted, until now, is coming undone. Your founder, Chidian, will be returned to this mortal plane by those who are loyal to Varamaxes in the realms above and below. He, as you know, lies helpless in that temple under the sands that your faith holds accursed. When released he will become again what he was, only greater. Chidian will be bound and sealed in his stead, and you and your Children will be scattered and broken."

And that was the bullshit hidden behind the screen of truth. No one had told me any of that, least of all Eldress Quen. I had put two and two together and made a nice, fat, juicy seven. I was laying bait, and I needed her to seize it.

She was staring at me aghast, eyes round, mouth open.

Okay, I thought. So far, so good.

She swallowed, and said, *"Chidian?* He ... ascended many ages ago!"

"The war in the heavens has delivered him to the one he bound," I said. *Time for a little Shakespeare,* I thought, and continued, "The whirligig of time brings in his revenges. You can leave him to your enemy's mercy; or, with my help, rescue him."

I could see that this was all too much for her. She was fiddling with the pendant hanging from her neck—a large, jeweled crescent, I saw. In the shape of a C. The insignia of the Abbacy? C for Chidian?

I leaned forward, and said, "Here's what I suggest, Mother Abbott. You let me try to do just that. If I succeed, you'll be the first Abbott of this Order—the *only* Abbott in its entire history—to have destroyed the Devoted Children of Mercy's archenemy. And if I fail, well. Who cares about me? I would have died here if you hadn't been wise enough to give me this chance to lay my case before you. What," I added, "do you have to lose? Some washed-up caster from another land? What *I* have to lose is my life. Burned at the stake. I'd rather live and give it a go. Even if it seems an impossible task."

I could see that she was intrigued. Tempted, even.

I pushed my case. "Also, of course, you have your founder's fate in your hands," I observed. "I assume you'd rather rescue him than not. This is what I *do*, Mother Abbott," I continued. "I solve problems. Do you want me to solve yours? And by yours, I mean *yours alone*, not the Devoted's."

That surprised her. "Mine?"

"The Four appeared on *your watch as Abbott*," I explained. "That has never happened to any Abbott before. History is in the making. The game has changed. You, Mother Abbott, can win it. With," I added, "my help."

I didn't need to say, *And your name will be revered for ever after. Why, you might even get a "Blessed" before it, like Father Abbott Chidian. How about that, huh? Sainthood! How does that sound?*

She was already thinking all of that.

While I was thinking, *Forget Mercy and Suffering, let's work on Pride.*

She studied me while she gathered her scattered thoughts. She dropped her gaze, and fiddled with the papers on her desk, while she tried to think.

She found a page. She looked it over.

Okay, I thought, *this is what you wanted to show me. Let's have it, then, and see where we're heading.*

But she decided not to show it to me after all. She grunted and knitted her fingers on the desk in front of her.

"You're alone," she said. "A caster, not even a warrior. And you don't have your staff."

I said, "So burn me."

She watched me. Closely. Her eyes flicked from side to side as they studied mine. She couldn't read me; I was confident of that. How? Because she wasn't actually trying. She was trying to hide her own inner conflict, which I could read as clear as day. On the one hand, her obvious duty. *Burn the last of the threat.* That's what any other Father or Mother Abbott would do. Yes, but they're not here now, and they're not her. And wasn't her higher duty to her founder? Burn me, and Chidian could remain lost, bound in place of his archenemy for all time?

Not only that: Her pride and potential glory would go up in smoke along with me.

I could tell that she didn't know what to think. Which is exactly what I'd been aiming for. I said, quietly, "Look, you may think it's a risk, but even a long shot is not a hundred to *nothing*. It's a hundred to one. Every now and again, that one will happen. And I'm anything *but* a long shot, Mother Abbott, although you have no way of knowing the truth of that. You'll just have to trust me."

I let her weigh her options. She didn't like the spot she was in. The uncertainty.

Okay, time to help her out of it. "Set me off, and I'll do this or die trying. How does that sound?"

She said, "You're not one of us. Why would you do this?"

"What?" I laughed. "For my reward, of course!"

She froze. "Your *what?!*" she demanded, astonished.

"My reward. This is what I *do*, like I said. And like any job, it pays. In my case, it pays well, because I happen to be very good at it. Ask Queen Esmeralda. Ask the people of Jarnland. She'd be dead, and they'd all be thralls to an Undead king by now, if it weren't for me. I have promised you *your* reward, which is high honor as the savior of the Devoted and the destruction of your enemy. *And* the eternal glory of your name. It seems only fair that you should promise me mine."

She didn't like this, but I could see that my professed greed made my proposition much more understandable to her—if less palatable.

"We of the Devoted give our lives and possessions to the service of our Divine Mother," she said, sanctimoniously. "We have no use for worldly goods."

"Then you must have a nice, whole heap of them in a nice, secure vault," I said, leaning back in my chair and trying to sound all cynical and mercenary. "If all these people, and all who came before them, gave all that they owned to the Devoted, then the Devoted have got to be rolling in it. You may not have any use for it, but I most definitely do."

She considered. "How much?" she asked, eventually.

"Fifty thousand gold."

"What?!"

She was outraged at the figure. I held up my hand and went on, "*If* I succeed. I trust you to pay me when I do. Well, I'll need it in writing, of course, just in case you drop dead while I'm away and I need to bother your successor for it. For now I only need five hundred, for supplies and equipment and so on. As you've pointed out, I lost my staff. I'll need a new one, and they don't come cheap. A horse, clothes, armor, and so on."

She was glaring at me, her eyes dark with anger. She had been confused by all that I had thrown at her, but now she had something concrete to focus on. A negotiation.

"If I agree," she said, "I will advance you twenty. "I'm not having you taking ship back to Jarnland. We will supply everything you need. Those who have abjured the Arcane Arts, and become gathered into our Devoted fold, surrender their staves before entering novitiate. You will have many to choose among. You may find other items that are useful in your line. Brother Collector Urdwyne will help you."

She glanced at the paper in her hand again.

I waited. I'd challenged her enough. Time to let her lead. She was going to have to make the decision, and to do that she'd need her authority back. I waited, politely, while she considered her options.

She was thinking, what should she do with me? Another exemplary execution, at the stake? To glorify the Devoted, and cow all her followers, and keep them on the straight and narrow?

Do that and she might just also be burning her one shot at fame and glory. Not to mention failing her founder and Divine Mother.

Well, I wasn't going to come around again, was I? What did she have to lose?

I saw her shoulders soften and knew that I would not burn at the stake quite yet.

She challenged, "And just how are you going to do all this?"

Now was the moment to answer her earlier question. "By finding those things you mentioned."

She looked at me, puzzled, trying to remember.

It would be a gamble—a gamble with my life—but now was the time to play my trump card.

I leaned forward again and played it.

North and South and West and East
Lock the gates and cage the Beast
Seal so none shall ever find
Head and Heart and Soul and Mind.

I held her eyes.

She was staring at me, open-mouthed.

I let her turn it over in her mind. *The Four. Four directions. Four things, hidden and sealed. Where none should ever find.* She could see the links clearly enough. There was much that she couldn't see.

She closed her mouth and swallowed. "Explain."

"You have no way of ascertaining the truth of this, Mother Abbott, but I need to say that we came into this with no bad intentions. We wanted to see who needed our help. Our Arch Historian of the Faiths believes that that is none other than your revered founder, Chidian. You are of the opinion that it is his enemy, Varamaxes. Until we received that riddle, delivered by the ghost ship, we'd never heard of either of them. We had no idea that we were part of some age-old ... well, problem. I solve problems. I will solve this one, if you'll permit me."

"How?"

"By entering the forbidden places and carrying out the tasks that lie within them."

"What tasks?"

"The Enemy was broken and scattered. Chidian secured his Head and Nature and Power and Mind behind seals that none born in this realm can enter. Without them, he is powerless. If I give them to you, he will remain that way. And, for fifty thousand gold, that is what I will do."

"Where are these places?"

"North and South and West and East," I quoted. "Our advice is that they will be well guarded. Maybe it would need the four of us to get the jobs done," I shrugged. "Well, I'll just have to do my best on my own."

I sat back.

It was up to her now.

Her attention returned once again to the piece of paper she was holding.

"The verse that was sent you as a message is widely known," she said. "It taunts us, daily, from that accursed monolith, for all to see.

192

This," she raised the scrap of paper, "is not. Only a few of us are aware of it—our Chief Archivist; one or two of the Synod. It is from the strophes of Blessed Sister Gortha. A truly devout, truly holy woman, she was offered the Abbacy three times, more than two hundred years ago, but always refused, preferring to spend her time in meditation and prayer. In return for her eyes the Divine Mother granted her the gift of scrying. She saw through the mists of time, and many events that she foretold have come to pass. Others wait in the years to come, we believe, and will be fulfilled in due course. Some are impossible to pin down, being vague to the point of maddening. Indeed, they have cracked the minds of many of our scholars over the years. Some, though, are very specific."

She turned the paper around and handed it to me. "Such as this one."

At the top, the familiar verse. *The Four will come across the sea,* etcetera. Below it, in a different, careful hand, were these words:

A Caster, a Dancer, a Monster, a Thief
Come from the North to bring havoc and grief
To scatter the Children, defile our belief
To the Mother, destruction, the Demon, relief

*BSG, 24.xi.9   Dictated in the eighty-sixth year of her age to me,
Scribe Odit.*

I felt the skin crawl on the back of my neck. *Gods above and below!* If I hadn't just recited Oldface's verse for her—wow, I could have been for the pyre. But thank all those gods that I had. Because it must have confirmed to her that I was telling the truth. I made myself not move my hands, as I could feel them shaking. I just sat there, staring at the paper as if studying it.

Okay, how to respond? I read the verse again, trying to find something in it I could work with.

I looked up at her. "Interesting that it says 'Mother,' don't you think?" I indicated the bottom line of the verse. "I'm guessing that the Abbott is not always female?"

She pursed her lips in disapproval. "Mothers have, indeed, been in a minority in the history of our Abbacy," she admitted sourly.

She seemed to have fallen for it. "Mother" could equally well, perhaps better, have been a reference to their divine mother, Valmynia. Good. She wasn't thinking clearly.

I nodded. "So that's you, and those four are us," I pointed at the first line, "the Caster being me. But why would we want to do what it says?"

"It is generally assumed that it is in your interests to do so."

I said, respectfully, "Mother Abbott. I have nothing against you and your Devoted Children. I believe that, if they were still alive, my friends would also assure you of that."

And with that, I rested my case.

She looked down at her hands on the tabletop. She had much to consider. I let her take her time.

Eventually she looked up at me. "I believe," she said, "that we could work together."

I needed to present her another face of the prism. I didn't want her owning me or trusting me. I wanted her to know exactly what she was dealing with. "For fifty thousand?" I said, with a laugh. "I could work with Varamaxes for that!"

That didn't go down well. At least, not at first. She sat back in shock and glared at me.

Then it went down better, as she thought, *mercenary.*

She could see that all I cared about was money. Good. She "knew me for what I was" now. In her mind, I no longer had an ulterior motive, cause, or hidden mission. I just wanted the biggest payout. All she had to do was just hire me for *her* specific purpose.

"No doubt," she said, primly. "Well, we'll just have to make sure that that doesn't happen, won't we?"

I leaned forward towards her. "Mother Abbott," I said. "I will bring you his head on a plate. And I will present it to you in congregation. And I will tell all your Children how I could never possibly have done it without you. And that we did this for the greater glory of the Devoted Children of Mercy."

She shifted on her seat. She clearly wasn't used to that level of flattery.

I said, "Not bad for twenty gold down, right?"

She glared at me in disdain. Then she found another piece of parchment, turned it around, and showed it to me.

It was a map, and not a very detailed one.

On it, far to the South of the Orphanage, a shaky, hand-drawn circle enclosed a rough cross.

Below it were the words, *Drawn in her sleep by B.S.G. and found by me when I woke her, Scribe Odit. B.S.G. 33.xxii.13.*

As I was studying it, she slid my guide to Mourvania into place beside it, open at its simple map, with its circled X on the same exact spot. Right where Oldface had said it would be assumed we'd be going. His stronghold.

I looked up at her. I nodded. "I will see you there, with your entire army at your back. I look forward to it."

I got to my feet, and added, "Just be sure to bring my reward."

Sister Clare of the seamstresses brought me my niblun-tailored clothes, laundered and pressed, and a couple of blankets as well. It felt good to be dressed in my own outfit again—with my little guidebook, which Mother Abbott had returned to me, tucked into the inner pocket of my jerkin, next to Marnie's Infinite Notebook.

Brother Collector Urdwyne gave me free rein of his treasury. There was some fine stuff in there. None of the staves were *mine*, the way that Shift was mine, but there were some powerful beasts among them, things that could hit hard and heal forever. There were drawers and chests full of rings, and amulets, and bracelets imbued with powers. I spent a morning in there, Divining, as best I could, what they held. It was hard without Shift, but absorbing.

It was clear that I would gain degrees of Protection, Attack and Trickery, if I could get the balance right. Back and forth I went, from staves to jewelry, seeking the deep truths of these pieces that were eluding me. I felt sadly incompetent. I should be able to *know*, I thought. But there was no readout, no table of contents, nothing to help me. Different staffs gave me different *indications* of the pieces they cast Divination on. All, in sequence, confused me.

What was I looking for? Specifically, I didn't know. Generally, for "the best." By what definition *best?* It was maddening. And tiring. Would I ever know? Would I, by some fluke, hit a hundred percent? Probably unlikely. Make your choice. Live with it. *But supposing ...*

Yeah. That's the thing, isn't it? You're never going to have the chance to come back and start over.

195

Rings. Torcs and pendants and necklaces. Bracelets. Brooches. Staves. Choices.

At last, I decided, *Well, the only thing I really know about is staffs, so let's start there.*

After much to-ing and fro-ing, I whittled my choices down to three. One of them, the lightest in color, was clearly a powerful healer. I cast my best Heals on my back, and the pain that I'd been living with since my scourging disappeared at once. Brother Collector Urdwyne reported, with astonishment, that there was not even a trace of scarring, where before my back had been crisscrossed with welts and ridges. That staff was *definitely* coming with me.

The other two promised equally powerful Damages, from what little I'd been able to learn of them in an enclosed space full of valuable objects. I knew nothing about woods, so I couldn't tell what they were made of. I knew even less about stones, so I didn't know what their heartstones were either.

Using those three staves, in turn, I studied the jewelry and, eventually, made my choices. It took a while, because some combinations of rings or necklaces or brooches seemed to hate each other, and I'd feel hostile bursts of their energies fighting between themselves, along my fingers, or into my chest, or at my throat. In the end, there was some kind of consensus from the three staves and the items of jewelry themselves; I made my choices. One ring of silver, set with three blue stones. One of gold, set with a large green gem. A torc of gold links. A copper brooch shaped like a stag. A gold bracelet set with red stones. They all seemed to harmonize with each other. It felt as if they were, together, more than the sum of their parts.

I, myself, had no idea why I'd chosen these pieces. I simply assumed that I hadn't and that they had chosen me. I didn't know what they'd bring me. Protection? Power? Evasion? All that I had to go on is what I felt and what these three staves that I'd selected had helped me feel.

At midnight, when the Children were asleep, I presented myself again to Mother Abbott. She didn't want me to leave in full view of her flock. I was, after all, the enemy. I thanked her, and she wished me good luck.

I knelt, and she placed her hands on my head, and gave me her blessing. *In the name of the Divine Mother.*

I was sworn, and shriven, and sanctified, and named Knight Errant of the Faith. *Sir Daxx,* I thought. I couldn't wait to tell the others. I kissed her Ring of Abbacy. "I won't let you down, Mother Abbott."

Brother Jailer led me to the stables. Sister of the Stables Molleen had a sleek bay mare for me, saddled and loaded with provisions. She led me to the gate, at the end of the Orphanage's long carriageway. I stared up at the moonlit monolith, on which was carved a familiar figure, standing out in relief.

Mouth open, a broken body in each claw, striding, his dragon tail curved behind him.

Old Birdbeak.

Below his shape were the words that Oldface had told me I would see carved into the stone:

The Four will come
Across the sea
To break my chains
And set me free

Yes, I thought, *we may come to do that—but will we succeed? And what if we do? And what if we don't?* Questions, questions. Puzzle. Problem to be solved.

I turned south.

Followed, as I had expected, by my escort.

I wasn't surprised that Mother Frogface didn't trust me an inch.

16

The Tower of Light

The escort was irritating, but they weren't going to be a problem for long. They accompanied me quietly enough. None of them wanted to talk. Not even dear old Brother Marten, to whom I owed two slaps in the mouth. We rode slowly, at a walk most of the time. I made sure of that. Didn't we want to hurry, they asked? I said that we didn't, giving no further explanation.

The first night we slept rough at the side of the road, wrapped in our cloaks. The second we spent in a village inn. Brother Marten had the other travelers thrown out of its bedrooms and made to fend for themselves in the parlor downstairs. He told them that they could sleep by the fire—once we'd left our chairs around it, after our supper. Charming fellow. I was looking forward to pissing him off hugely before much longer.

People like him need their comeuppances. They didn't pay for room or board. All they offered was their blessing. The innkeeper expected no less. Clearly, they'd been this way before. The other customers kept as far away from us as possible. Six thugs from the Devoted, and a caster with three staves? Trouble. No one enquired about our business, or our destination. They knew better than to ask questions of the Devoted.

As to where I was going, it wasn't where we were heading at all. Brother Marten had been shown the map, with its *X marks the spot,* drawn in her sleep all those many years ago by the blind scryer, Blessed Sister Gortha. The circled X was indeed where I'd eventually be heading. I just wouldn't be going there with these fools. And I wasn't taking the direct route. I was going the long way around. My first priority was to put a few days between us and the Orphanage before I dropped this lot and turned to my real destination. The trouble was, I was heading away from it, so every mile luring them along with me was a mile that I'd have to go back again.

After an early, and excellent—and, once again, free—breakfast, we remounted and continued on our way. One more night, I thought. I can't afford to wait any longer before ditching B.M. and company and getting going on my real journey. That third night we slept rough again, under trees by the roadside. The next morning, I Rooted the lot of them in Ice Traps, relieved them of all their food and money and weapons, shackled their hands with ropes and magic, and tied their horses behind mine.

Brother Marten fulminated, furious. Until I belted him in the mouth.

"You have one more of those coming," I told him. "I don't forget my debts, and I've owed you two since Huntsbroke. I'll happily give you more, though, if you give me a good excuse."

He glowered at me. An angry, stupid, small-minded man. A bully, used to getting his own way. This was a "child of mercy?" I didn't think so.

"You won't get away with this," he challenged. "The Devoted have eyes and ears everywhere!"

"Really?" I said, mildly, "as well as arseholes?"

Brother Marten turned purple with fury.

I held up my hand to stop him talking. "Listen," I said. "You tell Mother Frogface this, from me: I'll be back for my reward. Having done everything she wants. She can count on it. Okay? I don't need you cluttering up this operation and getting in the way. I know what I am doing. And you, and these other clowns, are superfluous to requirements.

"I know what you're going to say, *I'm a fugitive from justice from now on,* blah blah blah. Not bothered. All right? I'm doing this my way. Not your way. And I *am* going to do it. Mother Frogface can send more of you after me if she wants, but if I see anyone in brown habits heading my way, I'll kill them. Without hesitation. The only reason that I am letting you all live is because I need you to deliver her that message. Got it?"

He glowered at me. "I'll see you burn!"

I backhanded him across the mouth again. Hard. "Next one's free."

Blood ran from his busted mouth, and he wiped it away with the back of his tied hands. And looked at me, trying to scare me, but looking scared himself. "I. Will. See. You. Burn," he repeated.

I snorted. "No, you won't. I won't burn, because if I ever see your miserable Orphanage again, I will have succeeded in my job and will be coming for the reward that Mother Frogface has promised me. In writing. And it will be cheap at the price. You do what you do for your reasons, Brother Marten, I do what I do for mine. And there are fifty thousand golden reasons why I'm going to succeed at this, all right?"

His eyes grew round in astonishment at the figure.

To rub it in, I unrolled the contract that Mother Abbott had written and signed and held it up in front of him. He stared at it. He read it, frowning.

I'd thought, *let's sow a little disharmony here among the Devoted. Get the gossip mill churning. Mother Abbott has promised him fifty thousand gold!* Brother Marten was the mean-spirited, snitch type. He'd tell everyone who'd listen. They wouldn't like that. *I saw it, in writing, signed by her!* They all gave up their worldly goods when they joined the Devoted, *and now Mother Abbott is bribing a mercenary? Unacceptable! Shame on her!*

"And if I die doing what I'm going to do," I went on, "well, then it'll be too late for you to drag me back to the Orphanage for a nice fire show, won't it?"

Ooh, he didn't like that.

"So," I said, mounting my mare, "this is goodbye, Brother Marten. Give my regards to Mother Frogface and tell her I look forward to seeing her again."

I cast every possible Time Snare and Lock and Auto Refresh on my Ice Traps, turned back onto the road, heading in the direction we'd all been going for the last three days, and put my heels into my bay mare's sides. I could run her as long as I wanted now that I had six spare mounts. When she got tired, I'd swap her out for one of them, and then the next.

My escort were all Rooted for a couple of hours at the least. As soon as they were out of sight, I cut off west in the direction I really wanted to go. Yes, they might possibly follow me, to see if I'd done anything clever like that, but I didn't think they were that type. They had all struck me as neither suspicious enough nor bright enough.

They'd hurry back to the Orphanage to report and for orders. Maybe four days on foot, maybe less if they commandeered horses. And, knowing the muscle that the Devoted had around these parts, I doubted that anyone would put up much of a fight if their horses were requisitioned. So, I needed to get a move on.

Soon enough the entire realm would be on the lookout for me. I wanted to be well away from there before then. Most of all, I longed to be with my crew again, doing what we were meant to be doing. Taking the fight to the enemy.

First, though, there was someone I needed to see.

I wheeled around and headed north, back the way we'd come— only now, I was not using the road, of course. I stuck to the open country, the more wooded the better. After two days of hard riding, as fast as my string could carry me, I circled well to the west of Kingsworth and kept going North, all the way to the sea. Avildor had marked his location on my map, and it was a straightforward job getting there.

By the evening of the third day, I was far to the north and west of the Orphanage, and I very much doubted that they'd even started looking for me yet. I also very much doubted that, when they did, they would think of looking way up here, in this remote spot in completely the wrong direction, with nothing connected to my quest in it.

I'd been puzzled as to how I'd know Avildor's house, but it couldn't have been easier. *Keeper of the Light,* they called him, "in mockery at his lowly status," he'd said. Low his status among his guildies may have been, but his house was as tall as anything I'd seen on this rock. A veritable tower of light it was indeed.

It stood on a bare promontory that jutted out into the sea, the light at its top turning slowly, beaming brightly out across the ocean in the last of the twilight.

I smiled when I saw it.

I knew I'd liked Avildor when I'd met him, and we'd talked out of the corners of our mouths at that supper in a dining hall which might have been full of spies. Now, seeing his home, I understood *why* I'd liked him. He had a sense of humor: *Tower of Light*.

I'd been expecting something wizardly and arcane. Nope. Nothing but a big, solid, stone lighthouse, standing on a remote cliff top, and the rollers thumping onto the shore below.

I was riding up towards it, out of the shadows, when the tower's front door opened and a figure appeared in it, waiting.

I waved upon seeing him, and he waved back. I dismounted and walked my mare towards him, thinking that I'd have to find out how he did all that. He'd opened the back door of the Huntsbroke GAA for me, somehow. He'd guided me to take my seat beside him at supper, somehow. *How?* He'd known that I'd be coming that way, to Huntsbroke, and now he'd known that I was arriving exactly then at his house out there on the cliffs, far beyond the middle of nowhere.

He knew things.

That was a skill I would *love* to have. What was it? Awareness of the future? Of the surroundings? Something, in his skill set, was very finely attuned to a knowledge that I'd never even heard of. I could sense a whole new field of training opening up in front of me, like those I'd learned from Serjeant Bastard, and later from Marnie.

"Hello," he said, not in the least surprised to see me, "looking for this?" He was carrying Shift.

"I am indeed," I said, dismounting. "Thank you."

I took her in my hand. I could feel the warmth of her welcome jittering into my arm, lively and playful. She, I could tell, was as relieved to see me as I was to see her.

Avildor said, "What took you so long?"

"You don't know?"

"No idea," he replied, "but I expect I'll hear all about it. I also expect you're hungry?"

"Famished."

"Good, me too!" he said, energetically shaking my hand. "What nice horses. All yours?"

"They are now. They were the Devoted's."

He chuckled. "Much too good for that lot!" he said. "Follow me, the stables are round the back."

A groom took the horses when we reached the stables. I slung my bags over my shoulders, and Avildor helped me with my load by taking the three staffs I'd chosen. He inspected them with professional interest as we walked to his home. "Interesting," he said, studying the darkest of the three. "Not sure about this one, I'd be careful with her …"

"I agree," I said, "and I certainly will. But I have a feeling she packs a punch."

"Mm," he grunted, "no question about that."

We reached the front door. "Welcome," he said, "to my humble home."

"Tower of Light," I said.

"Thought you'd like that," he chuckled. "Let's get out of this cold and into the warmth, and answer each other's questions, shall we?"

"Sounds good to me."

"First, though," he said, as he ushered me inside, "you'll be wanting your mail."

I said, "I have answers?"

"You do," he said, leading me up the iron stairs embedded in the walls that circled the room. They ended at a small landing, and a door to the next floor. He opened it, and we emerged into a laboratory. Alchemical flasks bubbled over naked flames, and glass tanks held scenes that I could only think of as "works in progress." These varied from snail farms to entire miniature landscapes to empty vistas of nothing but patches of mold.

There was a pigeonhole in the central workbench. Two pigeons were lying outside it, dozing. "I'll leave you to it," Avildor said, and went on up the iron stairs to the next room. "Join me for supper when you're ready."

I went over to the pigeons and looked at them. They were fast asleep. I cleared my throat. The nearest one opened a bleary eye.

It groaned, and said, "Gawds, finally!"

I said, "You have my answer?"

"Yur," it said. It levered itself to its feet, and stood there, swaying, the way that birds do. *Hrum, hrum,* It cleared its throat. "Reply from Marnie to Daxx. *Your report most concerning. All here putting heads together, maximum priority. Avildor and Elun are vouched for, will help in any way they can. Even so, tell no one anything. A secret shared is no longer a secret.* Ends."

The pigeon looked at me and then hiccupped.

I said, "Thank you."

"No probs," it said, and pecked its neighbor before squatting back down.

"Oy!" The other pigeon objected. "Watch your bloody beak!" It roused itself and saw me. "Urhh. There you are. Reply from Eydie. *Not compatible, sorry. You'll have to make your own way home. Have a nice day.*"

Damn, I thought. So much for her dropping out of the sky and getting us out of here.

Oh well, it had been worth a try.

Both pigeons waited, watching me.

"Thanks," I said. "No replies."

"Looks like that's it," one said, eventually.

"Yur," the other agreed. "Come on, then." They waddled over to the pigeonhole, and squeezed into it, and lay down, closed their eyes, and slowly faded away.

The late autumn evening closed in over the sea that stretched to the horizon below us in every direction. This Tower of Light was situated at the top of a promontory where the east and north coasts met. Avildor and I sat at a table in a circular room not far below the light chamber, and ate, and drank, and relaxed, and got to know each other.

I'd climbed through several rooms on the iron stairs that encircled the walls of his tower. Each floor above the cellars, which were much wider than the tower itself, was just one room. The storerooms and staff quarters were belowground. Above them were entry hall, laboratory, bedchamber, guest room, library, kitchen, parlor. We ate in the latter, the food brought up by perfectly normal staff—no otherworldly minions, no floating trays carried by nothing.

Avildor spoke first, being host. "We all knew the game was afoot when the ghost ship left Seacastle," he said. "And by 'we all,' I mean about eight or nine people. We had been watching the northern lands for many long years. When it sailed into Mayport, *well* now! And when we heard it was for you four—*Four*—we found out everything we could about you. And soon heard what you'd done in Jarnland. Clearly a very capable four, we realized.

We knew we weren't the only ones watching. The Devoted were all buzzing about all over the realm in a sudden state of high alert. *Oho,* we thought. *Here we go, at last!*

"Now. First of all, you need to know about the Devoted. They are diametrically opposed to the Cult of Varamaxes. Whether that makes them any better than it, who can say? Belief is belief. You make your decisions and pick your side." He held out his hands. "Devoted," he said, indicating his right hand, and then turning to his left, "Cult. What do I know? Just about nothing. Except that they are locked in eternal combat, and that affects everyone else here. So, we needed to be aware of what is going on, whether we are involved ourselves or not.

"If you were to ask me my opinion," he continued, "I'd say we could do just fine without both of them. But that's not a decision that I get to make. We're in a war here. The Devoted are making everyone's life miserable, yet things are so much better now than they were when the Cult held sway over this realm and made everyone's lives far *more* miserable.

"And, by the way, it held sway over many other realms, at the height of its power. People were subjugated. Brutalized. Preyed on, sacrificed, fed to demons. Things were much worse then than they are now under the Devoted. And, well, what this all means is: No one hereabouts has any kind of idea of how to stand up to either of them; how to resist, how to ... change things. Improve things. And they're decent folks here, believe me—good people. They know right from wrong. They want better. For things to be better. Better opportunities for their children." He sighed. "Which they won't have until this interminable Unholy War is over."

He poured me another cup of wine, and said, "And this is where you come in."

"Thank you." I took a sip. Nice stuff, rough and ready, but rich and rewarding. I waited.

But he wasn't going to go on.

I said, "So the ghost ship sails from Mayport, with us onboard. And you're all suddenly thinking, *Whoa, it's happening at last?*"

He nodded.

"And what did you, and these maybe eight or nine other people, expect?"

"That it would bring you, the Four, here. And that we'd like to talk to you before you did anything ... *unwise.*"

I said, frowning, "So who sent it for us? Where did it come from in the first place?"

He said, "We just don't know. The Devoted might, of course." He looked up at me sharply. "Do you?"

"Me?" I protested, all innocence. "How should I? We never made it to anywhere, to find out." Friendly he might be, but that didn't make him a friend. My friends were away on their quests—about which no one else must know.

"Hm," he said, in a tone that didn't convince me that he'd bought my lie.

I waited.

"What was it like, onboard?" he asked.

"Confusing," I replied. "Everything looked rotten and worn out, but she sailed beautifully, and even though her sails were rags full of holes, they held the wind. There were some ghosts, downstairs, or whatever sailors call it."

"Belowdecks."

"They didn't do anything, though—just floated in place."

Avildor said, "Hm," again. He thought for a while, nodding. "And then it sank and your companions all drowned, but you didn't."

Relief flooded through me. So that's the way he saw it. Good. "Yes."

He frowned. "Seems odd, don't you think? Magic ship, hundreds of years old, powered by strong magic, but not protected by it?"

"It was a hell of a storm. Days of it. Amazing that we lasted that long, really."

He grunted. "Yes," he said, sounding dubious, "I suppose that could sink anything. 'We,' by the way, being the Conclave of our local GAA. We knew there'd be a caster among the Four. The Devoted don't have very good security. We'd learned of Sister Gortha's scrying, and her verse, long ago—which was why we'd made sure to have eyes and ears in the realms to the north. *Caster, dancer, monster, thief.* And here you are. One of you, anyway. It all seems to me quite straightforward."

"Does it?"

He nodded, smiling. "On the one hand, the Devoted. On the other, their archenemy and his Cult. On the third hand, that eight or nine of us. Our Conclave, and other Guild leaders. Hoping for better times." He leaned forward, and his voice grew urgent. "You see, Daxx: We believe that their time is over. A new age is emerging. The battle royal between those old foes will decide much. And we, who live here, will have to put up with the consequences. You must see how that old dynamic needs to change. We can't just leave the field to them. Wars can end, can't they? There should be another way."

"Which is?"

"Where you come in. Good, bad; this side, that side: It's all back to front. The powers that be hand down their decrees, and order us all about, and tax us and exploit us and keep us all down. It shouldn't be like that. No one needs instruction from above. We, at the GAA, may indeed be alarming to ordinary folk, but we believe that we exist for their benefit as much as for our own. We use our powers on their behalf, to benefit the realm, for the common good. Well, those of us who haven't gone rogue do, anyway.

"And, similarly, we believe that the powers that be exist for our benefit as well as theirs, the priests, and nobles, and judges, and kings. How important and powerful and splendid they think they all are. Well, they're not. They don't own us: They *work* for us. Their jobs are to protect and govern and guide and see that justice is done. It's not about them. It's about *us*. All of us. Cooperating, at our different levels, with our different skills."

I smiled at the thought. Oldface and Mother Abbott were not *about us*. They were about themselves.

I said, "So what do you suggest, Avildor?"

"I suggest it's your turn to talk."

Which I did.

I told him about everything that we'd done in Jarnland. And how we'd boarded the ghost ship, with open minds and free hearts. And—skipping over Oldface—how I'd washed ashore here in Mourvania.

I stopped.

Eventually he said, unsatisfied, "Really?"

"Really," I said.

He grunted. "Well, that's only partly believable," he said. "Not to worry. I'm sure you'll tell me all in good time. When you're ready to. Meanwhile, we have a problem."

I said, "We do indeed."

"So?" he said. "What do you intend to do about it?"

"What I always do with a problem. Solve it."

His eyebrows rose, and he chuckled.

"And my first step in doing that," I went on, "will be to pick your brains and get your advice. Which is why, I believe, you took the trouble of contacting me in the first place."

He nodded.

I waited.

"Blind Sister Gortha spoke of relief, for the demon," he said. "We know he was defeated and bound. One immortal overthrows another, and seals him away, no mortal knows where, apparently forever. And then the monolith appears, with its inscription. The game, it seems, is not over. Sister Gortha's scrying underlines this suspicion. Well, we thought: If it's not over, what happens next?

"Rather than simply waiting and seeing, we decided to work backwards from an ending that, obviously, has yet to happen. Presumably, we realized, the rematch of Varamaxes versus Valmynia was coming our way, eventually. Who would win this time? The holder, the goddess? The challenger, the demon?"

He looked at me, waiting.

I said, "How should I know?"

He leaned forwards, and said, with a smile, "How about neither?"

I said, "You mean, like a tie?"

He shook his head. "Then the question was turned around. It was asked, who would *lose* this time? How about both?"

I remembered what he'd said earlier. *I'd say we could do just fine without both of them.* Clearly, that was the future that he, and his allies, wanted.

"Okay," I said, "and how are you going to bring that about?"

"We're not," he said. "You are."

I thought, *whoa* ... "I am? How?"

"That's up to you. Yes, I know, highly unsatisfactory. I told you, we're working backwards from the ending, but as to how we get there? Well, we'll just have to see. What I can tell you is that we will help. Which," he added, wryly, "seeing as you're all alone, now that your friends are dead, you're most definitely going to need. I would expect that Mother Abbott gave you your instructions."

I nodded. I reached inside my jerkin and brought out the map she'd given me.

I handed it to him. He opened it and smoothed it out.

He studied it.

"Hm," he said. "X marks the spot. It seems that she knows no more than we do. Yes, that is where this matter will be settled, we believe. A long, difficult, dangerous way from where we are now, safely up here in the north. And you won't be going straight there, will you? Not if you have all your dead friends' tasks to accomplish."

208

He waited for me to react.

I was so tempted to level with him. But I couldn't. My friends' lives might depend on my silence.

He saw that I wasn't going to say anything, so continued. "You're the only survivor of the Four, so you're going to have to do them all by yourself, it seems," he continued. "But we can help get you there. If," he added, "you'll let us?"

"My motto in life is 'we all need all the help we can get.' So, yes please."

"Good. We can help with supplies and skills. My good lady wife will provide everything you need, much of which you have no idea about. I will teach you Light Magic. I believe you have no knowledge of it?"

I said, "I can cast Glows. Static ones or ones that travel along with us, overhead. But I've never actually heard of Light Magic. As a craft. Fire, Storm, Ice: Those are my combat skills. And I have a range of Heals, and Wards, and Shields and so on."

"Mm," he grunted. "As I thought." He pushed against the tabletop and got to his feet. "Come with me," he said.

Once again, we took to the wrought-iron staircase that started to one side of the window, beyond which there was nothing but darkness now, with the beam of light from above slowly sweeping the sea. We walked up, circling the room, to the small landing with its door into the next level—a storeroom, filled with barrels, and boxes, and scattered mounds of equipment. The stairway continued on and up to another small landing, and another door into the light chamber itself.

Where I joined him.

"Well now," he said, "how would you explain that?"

In the center of the chamber, hanging suspended by nothing that I could see, was a rotating, pulsing ball of light. Pure, yellow light. I stared at it, trying to think what it was. All I could come up with was, *small sun*. A black shadow slid around it in a continual, smooth motion. I'd been expecting a blazing fire, banked up against a wall, rotating in a huge pit, and mirrors—something mechanical, and comprehensible. This was like nothing I'd ever seen.

It was mesmerizing. I felt as if I never wanted to look at anything else ever again. The shadow turned. The light from the sunball moved its beam across the sea. I gazed at it in silence, scarcely daring to breathe. And then, I realized that both sunball and shadow were entirely silent themselves. Something burning as fiercely as that should be fizzing and crackling. It was almost as if we were standing on a wooden platform in the vacuum of space, where no sound carries. We were within feet of a star. And no heat was coming from it. I wanted to reach out and touch it.

I thought, *Light Magic.*

I had a thousand questions, but none of them mattered. All that mattered was gazing at the beautiful, wondrous sunball. I felt that all I wanted to do was search out the glints of orange and red that were shimmering deep within its blazing yellow, and study them, feast my eyes on them forever.

Avildor, beside me, was also gazing at it.

He said, "Lovely, isn't it?"

I nodded. "Amazing," I whispered. "How …?" I couldn't even figure out the right question to ask.

"All who live are light," he said, quietly, "mortals as well as gods— though no mortal shines with the pure white light of the divine. Our lights are not all the same. Some lights are gray and weak, some harsh and redder than blood. The great in soul radiate blue or green. Only those of us who follow the Light become gold. He shines brightly now, but one day will fade, as we all must. And I will take his place."

I turned to him sharply. He was smiling at the sunball.

"He?" I said.

"My predecessor. My mentor. I've been looking for a pupil to train up for years but haven't found a suitable candidate. Just as I haven't found a moonstone heart for my black willow. But perhaps the time will come."

I stared at the slowly rotating light that had been his mentor.

"Doesn't it … bother you?" I said, eventually. "Becoming that?"

His eyebrows rose in surprise. "I look forward to it," he said. "It will be a nice rest. Plenty of time to be the Light. Pure light, pure thought. But not the sort of thought that bothers our little heads in this day-to-day existence." He tapped his temple with a finger, smiling. "There's far too much going on *in here* all the time, getting in the way.

"Yes, that is how I found you. I sought your light, brought you to our table in the GAA. I'll teach you what I can of the first steps of Light Magic, in the little time that you'll be here. It'll be useful, where you're going. So, we have a long day ahead of us tomorrow— ah, there she is."

I looked up, as a door that I hadn't noticed in a landing above us opened. I'd assumed that this was the topmost level of the Tower of Light. Clearly, it wasn't.

No light came in from above.

Nor any person.

"She's waiting," Avildor said, calmly, "for her eyes to adjust."

I said, "What's up there?"

"My wife's observatory. You will be studying the stars with her, tonight and tomorrow night."

I felt a surge of interest. That had been what I'd wanted to do in the GAA library in Huntsbroke. A new field of learning, opening up before me. Just like Avildor's Light Magic.

I knew, then, that I had come here for more than just to reclaim Shift.

A figure emerged from the darkness above and began to descend the stairs.

"Good evening, dear," Avildor said. "Our young visitor has arrived. My wife, Elun," he said to me, as she came down towards us, followed by her yellow-eyed black cat. Black robes, pointy black hat, broomstick. And a gaze, when she met my eyes, that was as piercing as Marnie's. I felt that she'd learned all about me in a couple of seconds.

"So, this is Marnie's caster, is it?" Elun said. "Hmh! Well, she said he was a handsome lad, and she wasn't wrong. Shame about the haircut, though—is that the latest style in Jarnland, young feller-me-lad? You look like you've been chewed on by squirrels."

"Sheep," I said.

"Eh??" she frowned at me.

"My barber was the Brother Jailer of the Devoted," I said.

"Ah," she said, nodding. "They do like to shrive. Free you of your worldly vanity, and all that. Well, come along, let's get downstairs to that nice fire I expect you've got going; it's a cold night out there."

She led the way, one hand on her broomstick and the other on the rail that was set into the wall, her black cat trotting at her heels.

17

The Warrior's Apprentice

They'd washed ashore on the northwest coast of this realm, and Oldface had shown them where they needed to go. One goes *here*, another goes *here*, the third *there*. And then, it will begin. Get those tasks done, and the way ahead will be clear. Follow it, and, all being well, we'll meet up again.

Qrysta and Grell and Oller knew that they had to disappear, to melt into the background. They stood more chance of doing that if they split up. So, the tasks that Oldface had laid out for them made sense. If the eyes and the ears of this realm would soon enough be watching out and listening for them: Well, lone, normal-looking travelers would be less noteworthy than a group.

Grell's way lay south, along the coast, into the wild lands, and would then curve westward to the Sunset Mountains. Oller and Little Guy would head pretty much straight east, where there were farms and villages, and towns and cities. Oller was a city boy. He knew how to work the streets. He'd learn what he could learn, and find what he could find, before attempting the job at Cressen.

Qrysta knew Oller was looking forward to it. A raid on a Lord's estate? *Now* you're talking! And Oldface just wanted the one thing? "Ooh, nice, all the rest for me, then," he'd said. "No," Oldface had replied, sharply.

"Leave no trace. No sign of thief! No one must know you've been in and out. No mortal knows that it is concealed there—but if word of a robbery gets out, my enemy will hear. We cannot risk that. Take nothing else."

Qrysta and Jess would have much the longest march ahead of them. Their way would take them at first south and east through wilderness and woodland, and eventually to a road. Once they hit that, they would turn due south, and in a day or two come to a town, Lindfirth, where they would learn what they could learn, and buy what they needed. From there, they would head south on the road again, until striking out east for the climb over the Heartline Mountains.

If all went well, they would all meet again at High Rock, where they hoped Daxx would join them. If he didn't, they'd just have to take on the task themselves. If the Devoted had burned Daxx, then their decision would be easy. In revenge for Daxx, they would do what Oldface wanted, or they would die trying. If Daxx caught up with them, well, then he'd have the information, wouldn't he? And they would all put their heads together and make their choice based on what they had all learned.

Jess proved remarkably hardy on their walk. She never complained, never wanted a rest, was content with whatever food they had. She was happy to sleep rough. Qrysta's feet ached after a couple of days, but Jess's feet had soles like leather. She didn't really need shoes at all, she said. She took them off and walked for an hour barefoot to prove it. "We run about on the beach without shoes all the time," she said. "And it's a stony beach, not a sandy one."

She told Qrysta pretty much everything about herself. She'd been born in the coastal cottage that had been her home. Her father fished, her mother grew vegetables, bred ducks and chickens, sewed, and wove, and baked, and raised the four children. Her older brother went off for a soldier at fourteen. Dillan, his name had been, but everyone always called him Coppy, on account of his copper-colored hair. They'd not heard from him since, in three years.

Jess and her mother would head off to market every week or two, with her mother's baskets full of her mother's pies and her mother's embroidered aprons and kerchiefs, or some chickens and ducks and eggs, which they would sell. And they would buy provisions at the market, with the money they made, and afterwards they would walk home, the five or fifteen miles, singing. Other coast families might fall in with them.

The roads were safe. There were no highwaymen on the island. Some villains, yes, but everyone knew who they were, and they were no threat. There's no future in robbing people who know where to find you. Each village had its stocks, and each villain spent enough time in them to learn not to do *that* again. Jess hadn't been surprised when Patty had caught her by the ear, and sat her in the stocks, in the cold rain, for thieving a crust.

The paths were grass and mud, rather than stone. They led up through groves of trees, some evergreens, others bare of leaves now that it was winter. It was still mild, and the world seemed peaceful. The air was full of birdsong, and the voices of bright streams chattering out of the high lands to their north, as they worked their long way east and south to their destination. After a while, they didn't need to talk any more. Jess had asked plenty of questions, and Qrysta had told her what she could—anything that would make sense to the child. And she'd seemed satisfied. She'd never asked the obvious question: *Why are you doing this?*

Qrysta had wondered why not. And then she had seen why not. It was no different than asking the pirates who had stolen her siblings and killed her parents why they did that. People did what they did. She was a practical little thing, Qrysta thought. She trusts me. Wow. How does she know to do that? *I* know that I won't let her down, but how does she know?

On the third day of their long trek, the weather turned from mild to chilly. Deep winter had begun. They were looking forward to getting to the town. Each night spent in the open was less comfortable than the one before. They were only a few hours walk from the road, by Qrysta's reading of the map that Oldface had given her, when the bandits strolled out of the trees, seven of them, calm and confident, and took up their positions ahead of the two girls coming towards them. Qrysta quietly motioned Jess to hang back, which she did, whitewood bow in hand, arrow on the string. The bandits smiled. A child, with a child's bow. Nothing to see there.

Qrysta kept walking up to them, calm and confident. She stopped, by the four men who blocked her way, ignoring the three others in the trees around them. *Yes, right,* she thought, as the two flankers moved round to hem her and Jess in. She smiled at them, eyebrows raised, unthreatening. They smiled back, with different, harder smiles. Smiles of owning.

"Good morning, gentlemen," she said, politely.

They chuckled.

"No gents here, girlie," the man in front of her said.

They didn't look it, Qrysta had to agree. Ruffians the lot of them.

She looked at him, with a smile just for him. "Nor here," she agreed.

"No," he said, grinning, "we can see that."

She waited. Calm and confident. The man in front of her didn't quite know what to make of that. He drew himself up. "First," he said, "we'll take your weapons. And your purses."

Qrysta said, "And then?"

"And then," he said, "we'll take you."

Qrysta's smile broadened. "I see."

And then it was his move.

He shifted. He didn't want to draw his sword. On a slight, almost delicate young woman? That would have been an admission of his own weakness, his lack of authority.

"Right," he said, "take them."

The man to his left headed for Jess while the two to his right made towards Qrysta.

The two on his right died before the one on his left had gone five paces. A blur of steel, from swords that a moment before had been in her belt, two hard stopping blows punched into their chests, and killing touches completed in passing. They fell, dead before they knew it.

The man who was heading for Jess yelped, "Ow, shit!" and dropped his sword. He could no longer hold it, with Jess's arrow sticking through his shoulder.

Qrysta said, "Shall we stop this now?"

The man in front of her drew his sword and hefted his shield. His companion sank to his knees, whimpering, "She *shot* me!" The three in the trees raised their bows. Qrysta said, "We can talk about this, or you can all die. Your choice."

The leader hesitated. The others waited, bowstrings strained, as they waited for word.

A nervous hand loosed an arrow by mistake, which Qrysta sliced out of the air. "Look," she said, "I don't want to have to kill you, but you're becoming annoying. I suggest you drop your weapons, now."

She waited.

They didn't. "Last chance," she said. "I'd rather talk with you than kill you."

The leader, humiliated, charged. He stumbled, Jess's arrow slammed into his arm, and Qrysta's backhand took off his head. It thumped to the ground behind his corpse. The others backed away.

"I'd still like to talk to you," Qrysta said.

They lowered their weapons. Silence.

The shorter of the archers, a bearded man, said, "Sorry, miss. We …"

Qrysta said, "No apology necessary. You made a mistake. We all do. Now—shall we talk about this like civilized people?"

A pause. His gruff, awkward voice replied, "Yes, miss, by all means."

The wounded man was still whimpering.

Qrysta said, "Hold him." They did. Before they knew what she was doing, she had sliced the back of the arrow's shaft off, an inch from his skin. "You, with the gloves," she said. "Pull it out, forwards. Mind the head, they're sharp."

The bandit did as he was told.

"Staunch the wound and bind him up," Qrysta said. "He'll live. I'll take that arrowhead," she added. He handed it to her, and she tucked it in her belt. She and the others had all marveled at how sharp the arrows in the doeskin quiver were. Imbued, perhaps, with some trait? It seemed that way. They hit harder than regular arrows and would slide through the toughest target with ease.

"Now," she said, "there is probably no need for introductions, seeing as we'll all be lying, but my name is Kate. My sister here is Rosie. We're heading for Lindfirth. If you are robbers, you no doubt prey on travelers passing through your turf. Well, not us. However, in return for your lives, I'd like a little information. If you would be so kind?"

The new leader, uncertain of his position in all of this, said, "Yes, miss."

Qrysta unrolled her map. She pointed to a spot on it. "What do you know about this place?" she said.

She could tell by the way they stiffened that they didn't like it.

Another, a thin, sharp-faced man with long, limp hair, said, "You going there?"

She wasn't, but Grell was. "We're thinking about it," she said. "Why?"

He grunted. "Rather you than me!"

Qrysta waited. When he didn't elaborate, she repeated, "Why?"

He glanced at her, and away again. "Them as goes up in them mountains, don't come back down," he said.

"Any idea why not?" she asked.

They all looked at each other. Warily, but also as if she was an idiot.

"Er ..." the new leader said, "no. No one ever comes back down, to tell, anyone, why ... no one ever comes down."

Qrysta nodded. *So.*

The third archer said, "Cursed, they say they are—them mountains."

"Ah," Qrysta said. "I see." She pointed at another spot on her map, in the wilderness far to the east: The Forest of Secrets. "Any idea what's over here?" she asked.

They peered. "Never been that way, miss," the new leader said. The others shook their heads. "Bit of a ways from here. And ..." he hesitated and glanced at his crew.

Qrysta said, "And?"

"You want to avoid them woods, miss," he said.

"Because?"

"Them as lives there don't take kindly to outsiders."

"People?" she enquired.

"In a manner o' speaking," he said. "Not people like you and me, miss. *Wood* Folk."

"Ah," she said. "I see. Well, thank you for your advice, it's appreciated. Now," she continued, taking a cloth from her pack, and carefully cleaning her curved blades, "technically speaking, the possessions of those I killed belong to me."

She looked at the new leader for confirmation.

He nodded.

"I don't need them," she said. "Any more than I needed to kill them. They're yours. You'll bury your dead?"

"That we will, miss. Yes."

"Then we'll be on our way," she said, sheathing her swords in her belt. "Your arrows," she said. "I don't want you shooting us in the back."

They unslung their quivers and held them out.

Jess collected them.

Qrysta said, "Good day to you, gentlemen."

They understood that the parlay was over and went to deal with the corpses of their companions. Qrysta and Jess continued on their way.

Jess couldn't help turning around, to make sure no one was following them or had spare arrows to train on them. When they were safely
out of range, she said, "Can you teach me, Qrysta?"

"The sword dance?" Qrysta said.

Jess said, "Is that what it's called?"

Qrysta nodded and said, "I can try."

Jess frowned. "I'll study hard, I promise, anything you tell me,"
she said. "I want to be able to do that. If I'd been able to do that
when … I could've …"

Qrysta tousled Jess's mop of brown hair. "No, you couldn't have,"
she said. "It takes more than a child's strength to dance the sword
dance against grown men. But if you start learning as a child—why,
you'll have all the steps and moves ready for when you grow into your
body. Yes, I can teach you. But only *you* can make yourself a master."

Jess looked at her, puzzled. "I don't know anything about swords."

"That's the easy part," Qrysta said. "That's the technique. The moves,
and the steps, and the forms, and the feints, and the counters. The hard
part," she stopped, and tapped on Jess's forehead, "is *in there*. If you
haven't got what it takes in there, you'll never be a master."

Jess turned that over in her mind. "How will I know?" she said. "If
I've got what it takes?"

"Ah, well, that's not the question," Qrysta replied. "The question is,
when will you know. And, for most who learn the steps and the moves,
the answer is never. Because they never get there. You'll know when
you know." She could see the girl's confusion, and added, "Can you see
any reason why you couldn't?"

Jess tried to think what to say.

"I couldn't see any," Qrysta said, to help her, "when I started out. I
trained. I learned. I practiced. I got all kinds of bumps and bruises and
cuts in the course of it. But I did it. I got there. I can teach you everything I know. If I could do it, why can't you?"

"I don't know," Jess said, sounding uncertain.

Qrysta smiled. "And *there you have it*. When you get there, your
swords will feel more a part of you than you are. Remember what
Grell said, about your bow? *It knows what it's doing.* I've been in many
a fight with Grell, and he never puts a foot wrong, never makes a
bad move. I've seen him backed up in a corner, wounded, heaving for
breath, barely able to lift his battle-axe, almost out on his feet, and still

everything he does is *right*. He has no idea how, or why. He's just that good. He sees things before his foes even think of doing them.

"Does he always win? No. He's had the fight beaten out of him. We all have. Especially when the numbers against him are too big to handle. I've seen him knocked cold and throwing down his weapon in surrender. And that's all part of the learning. But that's where you can get to, if you put," she tapped Jess's forehead again, "*this* to it. Or Oller and his knives. He could probably throw them blindfolded and hit his targets. And I expect you've never picked up a sword in your life."

"No," Jess admitted.

"Well then," Qrysta smiled down at her. "Long way to go, right?"

She walked on, Jess falling in beside her.

"But you will teach me, won't you?" Jess pleaded.

"I will," Qrysta promised. "I will teach you until the point where you quit."

"I won't!" Jess protested. "Never ever!"

Qrysta added, "Or, until the point where you're better than me."

"I … don't think that's possible, is it?" Jess said.

Qrysta smiled at her. "To be better than me? Of course that's possible. Not that I've met anyone in a long while who is, but it has to be possible. Every day, I strive to get better, all the time. No, what is impossible for me, or anyone, is to teach someone skills they don't themselves have."

Jess said, seeing the sense in that, "I suppose not."

"Meanwhile," Qrysta said, stopping, "I think we can dump those here." Jess handed her the bandits' quivers, and Qrysta threw them into a thorn bush. "And …" she continued, checking the ground for sticks, "yes. These should do."

She picked up four sticks of unequal length and cut them to size. Two long, two short.

"Right," she said. "Stick these in your belt. Like the way I have my swords. See? We'll start with them tomorrow. Today, you need to get used to the feel of having them there, at your side. For whenever you need them. So that they're a part of you, all the time, for the rest of your life, whether they are asleep in your belt or awake in your hands."

Jess did as she was told.

Qrysta ran her eyes over the child, and the stick swords poking out of her belt. "Mm," she said. "They suit you."

By midday they had come to the road and turned south on it. They left it for the woods again a couple of hours before sunset and made camp—which meant little more than putting down their packs. From then until dusk, Qrysta gave Jess her first lesson. Jess was surprised at how slow everything was, at first.

"We start with forms," Qrysta explained. "You need to know those before anything. You're not in combat yet. You're learning shapes. How to draw and sheathe your swords. How to step. How to move your weapons in and out of and around each other. Main hand first, off-hand second. Then the other way around. One at a time, both together. First, bow to your opponent."

They bowed to each other, stick swords crossed over their chests.

"Bow, pause, move, draw, step, shuffle, stroke. Overhead strike, slowly down onto the target's head. Off-hand strike, backhand across into target's side. Again, and again, and again."

"What about all the other strokes?" Jess asked.

"Get these two right first," Qrysta said. "You can't learn everything at once. But you can learn everything in the right order." They got the chill of the night out of their bones the next morning with another hour of forms. By the end of it, Jess's thin arms were aching. But she never complained, never asked for a rest.

"Right, we won't overdo it," Qrysta said, as they hefted their packs and set off. "Little and often, that's the way."

"We'll do some more tonight?" Jess urged. "I want to get good."

"With that attitude, you probably will."

"And then," Jess said, "I want to get swords!"

Qrysta smiled at her. "We'll just have to see if we can find you a pair, then."

There were travelers enough on the road so that two more were not a curiosity. Nobody paid them any mind. Most were on foot, some on carts, a few on horses or mules. The gates of Lindfirth were open, the guards bored and uninterested in the last of the day's stragglers coming into the town. They were looking forward to lockup, and the warmth of the guardhouse, ale, and an evening meal.

It was a lively little town. The market was still doing a busy trade, with some stallholders lighting lanterns—obviously in the hope of more customers after night fell, which it did early this late in the year. Two boys ran past, stick-fighting and laughing. Jess stared, taking a

220

professional interest in their moves. She was not impressed. One boy noticed and stuck his tongue out at her. Jess stuck hers out in return.

The first order of business was to get Jess kitted out. She had been hesitant, when they'd talked about what she'd need, knowing how expensive cloth was; but once Qrysta had persuaded her not to think about the money, she made her wishes clear.

"You'll need it," Qrysta had told her. "Die of cold, or save a little coin? You can't spend it when you're dead."

"Leather," Jess said, firmly. "Like yours."

She'd questioned Qrysta about her clothes, as they walked. Did women *really* wear clothes like that, where she came from? Trousers, rather than skirts?

"They do if they're warriors," Qrysta had replied. "You try fighting in a skirt!"

"Then that's what I want."

Qrysta, smiling at her determined little face, had thought, *Hmm, seems that I have an apprentice …*

The tailor was a shortsighted, tiny, bent old man, sitting on a stool at the back of his stall, patiently sewing. His clothes were simple, rustic. He looked like a pile of autumn leaves raked up against a hedge. But everything about his palette, from matt green through orange and red to brown, and the cut of his simple garments, and the fall of their hems, was *right.*

Qrysta watched him, in the light of his lanterns, as he plied his needle. She approved of his steady, calm, rhythmic movements, and the faraway, almost dreamy look of knowledge on his face. She wondered exactly *what* he was. Smaller than Jess. Something like Nyrik and Horm, maybe? They'd looked in at other stalls, where the tailors had been more outgoing, more persuasive. They'd moved on.

Here, she thought. She said, "Good evening, master."

The old man stopped his sewing and peered up at her. His lined face opened in a gentle smile. "And a good evening to you, miss," he said, in a soft, high voice.

Qrysta stepped into the lighted stall, followed by Jess. "My sister is in need of a suit of clothes," she said, "growing as she is."

"Ah," the tailor said.

"Leathern," Qrysta said, "as you see mine."

"Ah?" the tailor inquired, intrigued.

"Might that be something you could make for her?"

The tailor looked at Jess. Then at Qrysta. Then at Jess again. "It might," he allowed.

"Then could you show us your wares?" she asked.

The tailor considered. Frowned. Contemplated Jess. Nodded, and got down from his stool.

He shuffled across to a chest of drawers and opened one. He rummaged inside it, and eventually brought out some squares of hide. He stroked them, contemplating them. He nodded and brought them over to Jess.

"Oxhide," he said, offering her a red-brown square. "It's the strongest, but too heavy for you, I'm thinking." Jess felt it. "This is calf leather," he said, showing her another. "Lighter, might suit you. Or there's this." Jess took the third hide, which was lighter still.

"What is it?" she asked.

"Akin to your sister's fur-elk, like but not like. Buckskin. And not a young buck, mind: A full-grown stag, as big as this stall. Fold them," he said. Jess did. The oxhide took effort, the calf leather less, the buckskin none at all.

"Imagine moving in each of those," the tailor said.

Jess's attention kept returning to the buckskin.

The tailor noticed and smiled. "You have an eye for quality, young lady," he said. "This buckskin is my finest. It's not as tough as oxhide, so it won't protect you as well, but it won't tire you out either. So: Keep moving and try not to be hit, eh?"

Jess's eyes lit up, and a smile grew on her face. "Can I really have it?" she asked Qrysta.

"If I can afford it," Qrysta said.

"Ten for calf, twelve for oxhide, twenty for buckskin," the tailor said.

Qrysta nodded, and said, "Buckskin it is then, master."

He bobbed his head, and shuffled back to his stool, saying, "It won't look like yours."

Qrysta couldn't think how to reply to that. Eventually, she said, "As long as it looks like hers."

He looked up at her sharply. Held her eyes. Smiled.

Clearly, he liked that answer. "That it will," he said. "Hers, and no one else's."

He turned to Jess. "Now, young lady," he said, getting his lengths of knotted string from his desk, "I'm going to measure you. Inside and out. Outside is the easy part, that's just shapes. Inside, well now. Who knows what's in that young head of yours? Whatever it is, we need to make a suit of clothes to fit it. Clothing isn't just protection against weapons and weather. It's who you are. Why would anyone wear anything that they aren't? But, sadly, people do," he sighed, "all the time. Let's not make that mistake, eh? You, miss," he said, over his shoulder to Qrysta, "if you would be so kind as to leave me with my customer?"

Qrysta said, "Of course," and left, saying, "I have gold—"

"I know," the old tailor cut her off.

Qrysta had taken a gold piece out of her pocket.

She did not know whether to place it on his desk, as a token of earnest, or whether to replace it in her purse, to avoid insulting him.

She stopped. "Master," she said, "we'll need a full suit for my sister, as well as two winter cloaks, a blanket each, boots for her and a pack like mine if you have one, under- and overgarments against the cold. Any of those you cannot make—"

"Won't be worth having," the tailor interrupted, chuckling. His old, shrewd eyes looked up at Qrysta. "Step outside, miss, if you'd be so good."

Qrysta put the gold coin down on his table and left, drawing the flap of the stall behind her. She looked around the busy market square and wandered into it. Anything that she could need was there, from arms and armor to every kind of provision. People chatted, and bargained, and argued. Food turned on spits as cooks called out their wares. Potions for every ailment, real or imagined. She'd lost hers when the ghost ship went down, so consulted with the apothecary, and bought some jars of Vigor, which would, he assured her, enhance her endurance, and some Quickwork "for speed of thought and limb."

Sounded good, she thought. She'd just have to hope he wasn't a quack, and that they'd do what he said they would. She was paying for them when Jess ran up to her and took her hand.

"It'll all be ready in the morning!" she said. Qrysta frowned, thinking, *that's hardly likely*. The order that they'd put in would surely take days. Surprised, she said "Really?"

"First thing," Jess said, nodding and smiling, "I can't wait! I'll look like a proper sword-dancer too, now!"

"Talking of which," Qrysta said, "the armorer thinks he has the very things for you."

Jess's eyes grew round in surprise. "Really? Where?"

"This way," Qrysta said, nodding at a nearby stall.

Instead of hurrying eagerly ahead, Jess hesitated.

"What is it?" Qrysta said.

"I ... I don't know how to thank you," Jess said. "I can never repay you."

Qrysta smiled and took her hand. "You don't have to, Jess," she said. "All you have to do is keep your eyes and ears open. And one day, you'll come across someone who needs *your* help. And then, you'll know what to do, won't you?"

Jess thought about that and, eventually, nodded.

"Yes," she said. "Yes, I will."

18

The Trouble With Dogs

"I do believe," Oller muttered, chewing on the last of his lamb chop, and passing the bone under the table to Little Guy, "that you are the cleverest of the lot of us." Little Guy's happy eating noises came back by way of reply. *Umf wumf snarf.* "I do believe," Oller continued, "that if I told you to think of a way of dealing with them bloody great guard hounds of His Lordship of Cressen, you'd trot up to 'em and say, 'Oy, lads, you'll never guess what I found round the back! You should come and see, *stone me!* Come and look at this, it's incredible!' And they'd pad round after you all agog and trusting, and you'd keep them there as long as needed while I sneaked in past them and did the business."

He nodded. Yes, it was always the blasted dogs that were the problem. *In* is easy, *sneaking and hiding and finding* is easy, once you know how, and *out* is easy. Usually the hard part was picking the locks, but with his silver key on its chain around his neck under his jerkin—well, there might just as well *be* no locks. If only there were a silver key for guard hounds. Big, lean, hungry brutes they were too, at least four of them.

Their handler kept them on leashes while he quartered the grounds with them. The hounds gave tongue at every new smell they came across. Oller had watched, from his perch up a tree beyond the back wall of His Lordship of Cressen's estate. Hounds and handler, passing on their rounds—and then the handler's boys, with their sacks of shoes and clothes running out from the kitchens, giggling, and dragging a shoe or a cote or a kirtle across the way the handler would soon be coming.

And when he did, leaning back against the eager, straining hounds, the hounds caught the new scent, and howled, and tugged at their leashes to track down the "intruders." And then the handler unleashing them, and the brutes galloping around every which way, barking fit to wake the dead, attacking each other in their excitement, the handler whipping them in …

And that was in the daytime.

At night, they roamed the grounds *off the leash.*

Free to come and go, and sniff, and attack as they pleased.

They'd get wind of him long before he got to the mansion. And no, he couldn't outrun them.

So, yes. Problem.

There was no way across to the mansion that he could see that didn't involve a lot of ground level. No outhouses, not enough trees, and the few trees there were spaced far too well apart. His Lordship's demesne was more of a park than a true woodland. Pleasure gardens, to one side, not at their best this late in the year. There was some kind of lake, over beyond the pleasure gardens, but … could he what, row to the house? He'd need a boat, and he couldn't see one. He didn't know how to swim to it. Even if he did, and didn't freeze to death, he'd leave a lot of wet footprints inside the house, which wouldn't go unnoticed.

To the other side there was a walled kitchen garden, with hothouses. It was a nice high wall, but it only enclosed the square of the kitchen garden. It didn't connect onto anything. And he knew better than to think about walking along the roof of a glass-paneled hothouse.

He was going to have to find another way in.

Normally, in a strange town, he'd make his number with the Receiver at the Thieves Guild. But not here. This entire realm was on the lookout for him, and the others. And you don't give false names to the Receiver. Besides, who knew who the Receivers here in this realm were taking kickbacks from?

With the Devoted all-powerful hereabouts … TG never liked to upset the authorities. They made sure to cooperate with the powers that be. *You scratch my back, I'll scratch yours. Yes, my lord, here's your cut of this quarter's takings, and if we happen to see your ancestral chalice what mysteriously disappeared last week, we'll drop it by next Tuesday.*

Besides, they were all thieves, right? *What's in it for me?* To any TG Receiver, the upside of shopping some wanted stranger to the Devoted was far greater than the downside of protecting a fellow guildie, only to have the Devoted cracking down on his entire operation. Sacrifice one to save the many? Or earn the thanks of the Devoted .... *Of course we will! Here he is, Brother Constable. Our respects to Mother Abbott, and if you would be so good as to pass on this little offering, from our guild, for the Devoted Children's coffers ...*

Especially when the one you're sacrificing was some nobody from nowhere, and a bloody foreigner to boot.

Oller knew the risk was too great. So, he couldn't ask around in the Cressen TG, and find out if there were any underground tunnels, or suchlike, into His Lordship's estate.

Hm. What to do?

Little Guy's head appeared between his knees.

Oller looked into his shining, brown eyes, and pulled his scruffy ears. "Bet you'd know what to do," he said.

Little Guy's tail thumped against the table leg. Oller scratched Little Guy's nose, the way he liked it.

Little Guy sniffed Oller's fingers. Licked the lamb grease off them. Looked up at Oller, adoringly, hoping for another bone.

Oller stopped scratching and sat bolt upright. *Well that's it!* he thought.

He chuckled. He said, "Love you best, Little Guy!"

Little Guy's tail thumped the table leg harder.

Oller ordered two more lamb chops and another mug of ale, and sat back and sighed, happily.

Of course, he thought.

One lamb chop went straight under the table for Little Guy, as his reward, not even a bite taken out of it, and all the fat left on. The little feller could have the whole thing. He'd earned it. He'd solved not the one problem, but two. Oller had been so bothered by the second problem that he couldn't properly puzzle out the first. And Little Guy—who basically *was* the second problem, had cracked them both at once. Oller chewed on the other chop thoughtfully, between sips of ale. Good ale it was too. A nice inn. Not too crowded, so that he'd have had to share a table with strangers who might strike up a conversation; not too empty, so that a lone traveler like himself would be the only customer—and, inevitably, noticed.

Tonight, then.

He was looking forward to setting about a bit of thieving again. It had been far too long. It was all very well being a Hero of the Realm—not this realm, of course, but back in Jarn. Just as it was all very well being an adventurer on this quest with Daxx and Qrysta and Grell. He could never have imagined the like of it, back in his old life, before being impressed into His Lordship of Brigstowe's army.

There was no question: It was a far better life that he was living now than the one he'd had before. He and his crew had a whole world to explore, and who knew what new lands to discover, and all the necessary skills to discover them, and to face down any challenges that were daft enough to confront them. And above all, he had *them*. Friends. For whom he would do anything, die if needed. Us Four against the world. *Yeah, bring it on.*

Oh yes, he was a soldier now, no doubt about it—not a regular rank and filer, but a fighter, that was for certain. A warrior. Not one of Serjeant Bastard's by-the-numbers squaddies. No: He and Grell and Daxx had graduated with honors, and, since deserting from My Lord of Brigstowe's army, had progressed way beyond that level.

With a crew like ours, he thought, we can take on anything. He'd back the four of them against any ten. He'd seen Grell in action, like a bloody whirlwind of steel, never tiring, swinging that damn great Fugg of his around his head and roaring. Qrysta flying like a bird and striking like a snake. And the miseries that poured out of that staff of Daxxie's, *well*. Yeah. We took down a helldragon! Not many people can say they've done that.

But even so. Thieving was what he *did*.

Okay, yeah, "did" when *that was back then*, while *this is now*, but it's nice to revisit the old ways occasionally, isn't it? The old, familiar skills. They say you can never go back. But, well, just for one night, he was about to.

He sipped his ale and smiled.

Thinking it over, it wasn't hard to see why they'd split the tasks up the way they had.

Imagine Grell having to do this. Slip into His Lordship of Cressen's mansion, and retrieve the necessary? *Grell?* As if. Well, he'd kill half the people who tried to stop him, and all the damn dogs, but he wouldn't know a hidey-hole if one bit him in the arse.

Oller chuckled.

Can't wait to see that big hairy bugger again. Wonder how he's getting along on his leg of this triangle.

A pestle and mortar, painted on a board, weather-beaten and fading, was the sign of the apothecary, same at Cressen as anywhere. It was tucked away down a quiet alley, some streets away from the market-place at the town's center. Cressen wasn't big but it was busy, which suited Oller fine—there were plenty of crowds to blend into. And plenty of back alleys to explore. Like this one.

Oller opened the door and poked his head inside, and when the apothecary looked up from behind her counter, he asked, "All right if I bring my dog in, ma'am? He's been sickly, and I was hoping you'd have something as could help."

"Might be as I might," she said, and Little Guy made his entrance, his tail wagging gently. "Aah, isn't he sweet?" the apothecary said, with a smile. "Lift him up here, then, and I'll take a look. Now then, little chap, let's see what we can see."

Little Guy sat patiently, and was poked, and prodded, and squeezed, and had every opening inspected, while Oller made up a list of symptoms to keep the apothecary interested. "Mainly just vomiting, though," he ended, when he'd seen what he'd needed to see. The various phials and bottles on display were of no interest to him. But there it was, on the floor, behind the counter: The safe cabinet. He believed she'd have some of what he wanted in there.

Back in his soldiering days, in My Lord of Brigstowe's army, he'd had many an interesting chat with Watkyn of Lorton, former apprentice alchemist, who'd signed up for a soldier rather than serve time in His Lordship's dungeons—as who in their right mind wouldn't? Very popular with the ladies, Wat had been, and very keen on them in turn; but porking his master's wife in her very own broom cupboard had not been a wise move on his part. Watkyn had told Oller that the lines between alchemists and apothecaries were blurred—even though both

229

sides fiercely defended their turf. Alchemists worked more with the unknown, and the arcane, Wat had said, exploring new lines of enquiry, while apothecaries did what they knew, what had been tested by time, and preserved the lore and tradition of healing.

The sense was that apothecaries were stuffy old fuddy-duddies, while alchemists were the daring innovators, the adventurers, the experimenters. But, in reality, they often worked the same ground. The difference was that the alchemists knew everything that the apothecaries were doing, in their traditional ways, while the apothecaries had no idea what weird new things the alchemists were up to.

Wat had told Oller all the juicy stuff about the apothecary trade. It was very strictly regulated by their guild, as all crafts and trades were. The Chymical Guild of Apothecaries was the most old-fashioned, by-the-book guild in the land. Anything on *The List* had to be kept under lock and key, at all times, no matter the inconvenience of having to unlock the safe place and lock it back up all the time.

They *really* didn't want the Guild Inspector walking in while they were serving customers, and he sees the safe place open behind their counter. The reason for this, Wat had told him, was because anything on *The List* was deadly—some of it even in very small quantities. Too much of certain sleeping draughts, for example, could make the sleep they induced permanent.

Oller had been intrigued. How did they know how much was too much? You do it by body weight, Watkyn had explained. So many grains, or drops, of such-and-such powder or tincture per pound of patient. It doesn't have to be exact. With most of them you just use a rule of thumb. *She looks about a hundred pounds, a grain to every ten pounds should sort her out. Five would knock her out for a couple of days. Ten and she'd never wake up.*

Oller remembered the names of the ingredients that went into the potions, things he'd never heard of, such as night moss, and bile cherry, and bluebark. Not that he'd be looking for those. He wasn't going to have to mix his own potions. No, he was going to get his ready-made, by a proper apothecary. He learned a lot from Little Guy's new friend, who was a chatty soul, as she examined him, and had much to tell him about the goings-on in town.

Nothing he heard alerted him to anyone looking for four strangers. Good. He paid for the two phials she gave him for Little Guy's nonexistent ailment, thanked her, and wished her a good day. And—but this was unsaid—a good night. She looked the deep sleeper type: Healthy, hardworking, a little on the plump side, and walking with a bit of a limp. Arthritis? She might be taking something for that. Something to help her sleep.

She'd talked about everyone and everything except a husband. Children, yes, who'd moved on and had families of their own, and given her five lovely grandchildren to spoil. A widow, then, by the sound of it. Oller and Little Guy made their way back to the inn where he'd taken a tiny room, and settled down on their bed for a good, long nap.

He'd be working tonight, rather than sleeping. He smiled at the thought, and at being back at his old trade again, in his old routine again: Sleep by day, work by night. With his catlike ability to nod off seemingly at will, he was asleep before Little Guy, who curled up beside him, under Oller's armpit just where he liked it, sighed contentedly, shoved his nose up into his bottom so that he could dream while inhaling his own magnificence, and closed his eyes.

They slept through what was left of the afternoon, through the evening, and deep into the night. The noise from downstairs grew, as the evening wore on, and the travelers and traders and locals gathered for their ale and their suppers, and voices became louder, as all spoke above each other. Laughter, song. The evening slipping into night, and the customers slipping away, to their homes, to their rooms upstairs; the public room calming down, the staff mopping up and cleaning floor and tables.

It was the quiet that woke Oller, the quiet that he'd been waiting for: The heart of the night. He prepped his equipment, patted Little Guy, saying, "See you in a bit, matey, you just stay here, all right?" and opened his room's small window. Not a good idea to walk downstairs and out, at this hour. That would have made anyone who saw him curious—and remember that he'd gone out.

Leave no trace, that was always the best way. Out of the window; along the ledge below; down the wall—easy. Tuck the dark rope back up out of sight, where he could find it by touch later. And off, about his business, keeping to the shadows. His Lordship's estate lay, he knew, to the south and east of town. First though, through the dark streets to the back alley where the apothecary had her shop. Up the wall, on the new stickies he'd made for himself, over the roof, hang there and take a dekko … yup. Window open, for the fresh air.

Sticklers for their health, apothecaries. She'd sleep with her window open all right. Down the wall, carefully, stickies holding him to the wall like a spider as he came to her window. In. *Oops.* Two yellow eyes gleaming at him in the dark. Cat. Curled up next to its mistress. Oller thought, *just have to hope it's not the hissing kind . . .*

It wasn't.

The yellow eyes followed him as he let himself out of the bedroom door, and *almost closed* it behind him. No point in making a noise shutting it, or when opening it on his way back. Down to the ground floor, and into the parlor. Good: Just as he'd hoped, she'd had a fire going. The embers were still glowing. A few puffs, and he had enough flame to light the stub of candle he held into it. Then to the shop. Out with the silver key, and the safe cupboard opens as if by—indeed, *actually* by—magic. He held his candle up and shone its light on the treasures within.

There they were, labeled just the way Wat had told him. Just the way that the sticklers on the Committee of the Chymical Guild of Apothecaries insisted.

Light Sleep. Sleep. Deep Sleep.

He poured off enough of the Deep Sleep to render several dozen large people comatose into the phial he'd brought with him—a phial that had, earlier, been filled by the apothecary herself with the potion that Little Guy had never needed.

Oller let himself out again by the way he'd come in. Followed to the open window by two staring, yellow eyes.

Back to the inn, back up the rope and through his window. Little Guy woke up as he entered, and Oller picked him up and popped him into his Blackout bag. Little Guy didn't mind. He was happy as long as he was with Oller.

Oller ruffled his ears, and said, "Quiet now, matey. Job o' work to do," and slung the bag on his back. He settled his knife belts around him, crisscrossed over his chest for swift access, and shouldered his niblun pack. He left a couple of coppers on the bedside table for the maids—he'd had to pay in advance for the room, of course. Innkeepers always want their money up front. Then out of the window again, and down, coiling and stowing his rope, as he wouldn't be coming back this way.

He set off south and east through the back streets. The town was locked up for the night, but his stickies soon had him over a dark part of its walls. And then he was off to his target, Little Guy trotting beside him.

Oller perched in his tree outside His Lordship of Cressen's high walls and considered his options. Yes, he could make sure he wasn't attacked by the guard hounds by the simple expedient of overdosing them. But Oller liked dogs. Okay, so, yes, these dogs would like nothing more than to catch him and tear him to shreds. They wouldn't hesitate for a second. They'd love to kill him. But he wasn't a dog. He was better than that; he was a higher being. And he didn't like the idea of killing them.

Dogs just did their job, right? He didn't have to *kill* them in order to do his. He just had to knock them cold, for long enough to get in and out again. Which shouldn't take more than an hour or two. Double that, to be on the safe side. Add two more ... it'd be coming on daylight.

And kennel keepers are always early risers, aren't they? To get the hounds up and fed and ready for the day. So, he'd need to be in and gone inside four hours, then—and he was wasting time, sitting up in his tree, calculating dosages, *just have to kill the poor brutes, I suppose ...*

Whoa, he thought.

That's the fly in the ointment, isn't it?

If I kill these dogs down there, what'll their handler find in the morning, eh?

Four of his prize hounds dead. And if that don't arouse his suspicions, I don't know what will.

Four dogs, all dead at once, well that's a hell of a coincidence!

There'd be uproar. Any thicko could put that two and two together. Guard hounds all poisoned? Why? Who'd want that?

Thief!!!

Oho, they'd realize. *We've had a visitor in the night, haven't we?*

He recalled what Oldface had told him. *Leave no trace. No sign of thief. No one must know you've been in and out.*

Because that would alert the hell out of them. The word would spread soon enough. And then, should word get to the wrong ears, Oldface's enemy, he'd know the game was afoot.

And if his followers, the Devoted, still held Daxxie ... between them, they might connect the dots. And maybe they wouldn't then be so ready to believe that Daxx was the only one of the Four to have survived.

Wouldn't give much for his chances then, Oller thought.

Three of the Four dead, you're telling us? We have evidence to the contrary.

That decided him. To his relief. The hounds don't die. Indeed, they *mustn't* die. Just let's give them a nice, long snooze, after eating all these lovely lumps of fresh meat from the butcher in Cressen.

Right. How big were those buggers, then?

Far too bloody big. Eighty, a hundred pounds? Two drops of Deep Sleep per ten-pound weight, Wat had said. Sixteen each. And a couple for luck. Okay. Easy enough.

Hold on.

Suppose one dog eats two lumps of meat? Two might kill it …

Okay, just have to feed them one at a time, then.

Blimey, that could take all night. Wonder how quickly this stuff works? Can't have Bruiser down there looking around for another nice lump of meat for hours, while he fails to fall asleep, and Gnasher is wondering where the hell this lovely meat suddenly came from, and where's his piece?!

Only one thing for it. Try tonight, see how it goes, and if it gets messy, come back again tomorrow.

Oller got to work. Lumps of meat; phial of Deep Sleep; eighteen drops onto each. And then, listening. Night noises. Wind in the tree around him. Owls, one near, one distant, hooting at each other in doleful conversation. The squeaking of bats, hunting insects. And then, below, beyond the wall, the rustle of leaves as something large pushed through the undergrowth and emerged, panting.

The dark shape of the guard hound, black outlined in faint silver from the moonlight. A soft thump as Oller's treat landed at his feet. Shuffling over, sniffing, eating. Sniffing around for more. *Wait here, good doggy, might be more coming in a bit, you never know …*

Paws trotting around as it searched. Paws stopping. A low grunt of surprise, more like a sigh, really, like all the air going out of him at once. The thump of eighty-plus pounds of guard hound hitting the ground.

Blimey, this stuff works fast …

Oller emitted a low whistle, to alert any other nearby dog.

Then yips like a fox.

Fox?! Here? Where, I'll have the bastard—!

A rustle through the undergrowth of guard dog number two looking for the damn fox—sniff, *whoa, meat??*

Gulp … search for second helping … thump.

Repeat. Twice more.

Oller eased himself out of his tree and knelt by Little Guy where he'd tethered him to the trunk. "Got something for you, matey!" he said, and got out another lump of meat. He contemplated Little Guy. Twenty-five pounds? Thirty at most. Six drops. Little Guy *snarfed* and bolted the meat and looked up at Oller eagerly for more.

Half a minute later he was blacked out in the Blackout bag on Oller's back, and Oller was scaling the wall that surrounded His Lordship of Cressen's demesne.

No guard hounds bayed as he dropped from the wall. The only sounds they made were deep, slow snores. No one saw him as he slipped from shadow to shadow across the park. All was quiet, just the way he liked it. He could have done without the bright, three-quarter moon, but it was sinking towards the horizon, where the sky was cloudy. It would soon be hidden. Even so, he chose a wall of the house in the moon's shadow, where its light wouldn't shine on him as he made his way up on his stickies.

And along. Peering in, to see what he could see. Finding a spot he liked the look of: It would let him in at the end of a corridor. Not too high up, that'll be where the servants sleep, up topside, and there are always a lot of them, crowded in their garrets. And bare corridors outside their doors, not carpeted like this one, and rotten old floorboards up in those attics, like as not to creak. Servants are more likely to be up and about than His Lordship, and his family and household and guests, after their fine supper and fine wines.

The window opened easily enough, thanks to a little encouragement from his knife. He climbed in, as silent as the apothecary's cat, and closed the window behind him. *Leave no trace.* He crouched in the shadow of the windowsill, to let his eyes grow accustomed to the darkness. And then on, along the corridor.

In his inspection of the estate during the day he'd pretty much figured out where his destination must be. Funny that it would be another chapel, just like where he'd found Daxx's tourmaline heartstone.

That had turned out well. So, let's make sure this one does too. If it doesn't, it's game over.

Game Over. A phrase the others used, and that he'd picked up. He'd wondered what it had meant, at first. It certainly seemed to mean something to them. He supposed this was all a game, really, this thieving lark. Playing the sleeping nobs for suckers. Pinching their stuff. *Bet there's some good pickings here too,* he thought—somewhat ruefully, as he knew he couldn't lift anything, however small. *No sign of thief.*

He made his way along the corridor. Down the stairs, keeping to the shadows. It felt good to be back in the old life again. He was enjoying himself. *First time I've ever done a job carrying an unconscious mongrel in a bag,* he thought—and felt a grin spreading on his face, and a chuckle rising in his chest, which he quickly squashed. *Don't want no one hearing a mysterious laugh ...*

Across the wide entrance hall into some sort of assembly room. Through that and out into another short, carpeted corridor. Carpet, good: Footsteps won't make a sound. Open the door at the end of it, and into His Lordship's private chapel. Close the door behind him. Listen. Nothing. Look everywhere, all the way into the corners. No movement. On, then, to the altar. Round the back of it. Lift the heavy, embroidered altar cloth, and peer in underneath.

There was not much light, but the chancel window behind the altar faced the setting moon. Weak moonlight filtered in through the window's stained glass, dropping blobs of ghostly colors onto the floor around him. Better than nothing.

He looked up at the window. It was an intricate portrayal of some woman, her hand raised in blessing. Nice workmanship, that, Oller thought. As was that big gold salver on the altar, *ooh ....* No, don't even think about it, chum. *In the floor,* Oldface had said. Warded and bound and triple-locked, sealed by Blessed Abbott Chidian himself, with his most powerful magic. Unbreakable seals, Oldface said. Hidden locks. Traps as well, no doubt. *And how are you going to deal with all those, Thief?*

Oller hadn't told him about the silver key, hanging on its chain around his neck, under his jerkin—the magical one that could open many a door or chest. None of the old sod's business. Threatened to kill Little Guy, he had; he won't get no favors from me. Let him stew while he waits.

Have to see, won't we? he'd replied.

Oller crouched and lifted the heavy altar cloth that reached down to the floor. He slipped inside and lowered the drapes behind him. He withdrew the silver key from its hiding place and moved it around over the marble floor within the altar. And then there it was, glowing into life, so brightly that it lit up his hiding place: A silver keyhole, responding to his silver key.

Which, in turn, itself began to glow. Well now, that was new! He'd never seen his silver key light up before. Didn't even know it could. Very helpful—he now had enough light to work by. The silver key grew to fit the keyhole. There was no click when he turned it—just a slab of marble loosening, and opening as he pulled up on the key. It was a bigger slab than he'd expected and took a deal of lifting. It opened past the vertical, on hinges, and stopped. So far, he thought, so good.

He looked in.

Well now. He hadn't expected this. Stone steps, leading down into the vaults.

Oh well. Nothing for it. In we go. *Keep going forwards.*

He lowered himself in, his feet finding the top step easily enough, and then closed the lid of the trapdoor behind him. And locked it again. Not that he expected anyone to stumble across it, while he was down there doing what he'd come to do. But you can never be too careful. *Leave no trace.*

The silver key continued to glow as he descended the stone steps. Probably in response to all the magic down here, Oller thought—the seal, and such. Its light wasn't as good as Daxx's Glows, but a damn sight better than creeping down in the dark, feeling his way, worrying about those traps that Oldface had mentioned.

He tested every step as he went. The fourth one down swung open with a thud that made him jump. He peered in. A long drop, sheer sides, taller than he was, and nasty iron spikes for him to fall onto. He'd never have made it back up out of there. Not a nice place to end his days. Nor a nice way, impaled, in the dark. Don't want to do that to Little Guy.

He found two more false steps before he reached the floor of the vault, both of which would have dropped him into deep, spike-filled pits. He didn't trust the floor itself either. With good reason. Two of the slabs he tested were also booby traps above more spiked pits. Inching forward on his stomach, holding a knife out in front of him, waving it up and down, before crabbing ahead on his elbows—and there it was. Just as he knew there would be: Tripwire, at ankle height.

He reached out as far as he could and cut it. Missiles whirred over his head—he couldn't see what type—and clattered off the walls that they struck all around him. They'd come from every direction too. *Thorough*, he thought. *Would've got someone less savvy than me.* But so far, all so mechanical. Nothing he couldn't deal with.

As he negotiated his way into and along a twisting passageway, he soon saw a white-blue glow ahead. When he rounded a corner into the catacomb itself, he saw what was causing it. First, though, in the soft light that it was throwing around the chamber, he checked its walls. Symbols, paintings, carvings, statuary. Nothing moving.

He turned his attention to the source of the light.

Well, there it is, then, he thought.

The portal.

He approached it cautiously. There might be one last trap here, one last trip wire. He tested the floor with his daggers, feeling for anything suspect. There was nothing. That alarmed him more than if he'd found something. There's always something, at the end, protecting the big prize, just when it's caught your eye and you want to grab for it.

He dropped onto his belly again and inched forward. The portal was just ahead of him, no more than a couple of paces, all serene and tempting, and glowing blue-white. *No*, he thought. *You can't fool me.* He backed off, and slid, on his stomach, to his right. With his left hand, he kept tapping a dagger point at the floor. He was about to give up, thinking, well, even *I've* found nothing, when he realized: *Yup, that's just what they want you to think.*

He was beside the portal now. He could stand up, and step through it. He knew that that would be the last thing he'd ever do. He stayed flat on his belly, and his daggers, one in front of and one behind the portal, found the release catches. He smiled. *Yeah, nice try*, he thought. They were so small he could hardly see them, and so light he'd never have felt them with his foot.

He tripped the one in front of the portal first. A blast of flame blew up from the floor while another shot downwards, incinerating anything that was between them. Nothing was. Oller's arm was safely back at his side. He repeated the process with the release catch behind the portal. Two more flame blasts. He let the furnaces die away. Then silence. *Got you, old son,* Oller thought, smugly. He stood up and entered the portal.

Sky-blue ribbon-path. Starflakes, humming in disharmony above him. Orange and yellow and green ribbon-paths, weaving in and out of each other, going from nowhere to nowhere, in every direction, over and under and around. Red and blue and white paths twisting through those. Peace, and almost quiet. Just strange paths, and strange sounds, and an infinite, indigo distance, dotted with stars.

He felt a movement behind his back.

So, Deep Sleep was wearing off, then. He set his bag down and rolled Little Guy out of it. Little Guy snuffled, and twitched, and grunted happily.

Oller waited, and watched, while Little Guy returned from his land of dreams.

Abruptly, he reanimated, and lurched to his feet. He looked around with interest at his strange surroundings. Then up at Oller and wagged his tail.

"Okay," Oller said, "let's go."

They moved on, up the sky-blue ribbon-path, around and down, and in and out of the other paths, always upright, even when, looking back, it made no sense, and they were clearly upside-down. On and up, into the field of starflakes suspended around them, waiting. Humming. Expecting. There was no threat here, now. Only ... completion. They came up onto a large, circular platform. At its center, a red ball of light hung from nothing above nothing.

Oller stared at the living, writhing ball, suspended in the air, like a miniature, dying sun.

It shimmered, turning slowly, with darker reds and purples and specks of orange glinting deep within it.

It burned, and turned, making no sound.

It was beautiful, yes, in a somewhat unnerving way. And definitely unusual. Oller had never seen anything like it before.

Power indeed, he thought.

He approached it, and held his hand out to it, as close as he dared.

The slowly rotating sphere of dark red fire emitted no heat, just as it gave off no sound.

Right, he thought. Let's be having you.

He lowered his Blackout-suffused loot bag over the glowing red ball.

He scooped it up, and as he did so the starflakes around him changed their singing, from that calm, disharmonious hum to a high, swelling chorus.

Oller looked around at the sudden change in pitch and volume, and saw lines of starflakes circling in towards him from every direction, three-dimensional spirals of white light whirling into the Blackout bag.

He stood there, Little Guy beside him, watching in wonder, knowing what he should do but not knowing why. He closed the neck of his bag, slowly, as the whirlpools of stars rushed into it, faster and faster, surrounding the red glow, joining it but not merging with it. As the last of the starflakes settled in, and the last of their singing ceased, Oller closed the bag and tied it off. He exhaled, shivering at what he'd just seen.

Well now, he thought, in the sudden, empty silence. *Wonder what that's all about. Time will tell, no doubt.*

He slung the bag over his shoulder. It felt no heavier than it had when it was empty.

That's that done, then. Now what?

Keep going forwards.

He looked at the choices facing him. There were so many ribbon-paths, of all colors, and so many platforms, and connections, leading off into the indigo distance in all directions, that it was impossible to know where to start. *Need to find the way,* he thought.

He wasn't concerned. He was good at finding. He looked around, and thought about the problem, and found the solution soon enough. Up paths they walked, and across platforms, and down paths, and around and through, and back and forth. After more twists and turns than he could count, he saw ahead of him a familiar shape on the orange path that led towards his destination.

The clerk was waiting for him, perched at his high desk.

They signed the Power out, Oller with an X, and Little Guy with a paw print, and walked on, down a final ribbon-path to the exit portal.

19

Murruk

Grell was in a foul mood. His feet ached, from hour after hour of day after day of walking, through these endless trees, up hill and down dale, across marshlands and grasslands, miles from anywhere. He hadn't seen a settlement in a week. His bones ached from nights of sleeping rough, on hard ground, under dripping trees. Nothing but the howling of wolves, and the hooting of owls, and the yipping of foxes and the ruffling of the wind in the branches for company.

Sod this for a laugh, he thought every night, as he wrapped himself in his cloak and tried to sleep.

And he thought it again every morning, when he woke up, and hauled himself upright, and ate some hardtack and dried meat and stale cheese and a withered apple, and drank water from the last stream he'd filled his flask in. Then climbing into his plate armor, which Old-face had said he'd definitely be needing.

Thank the gods it was niblun-made and a lot lighter than it looked. Strong as stone, light as leather, the niblun smiths had boasted. The *light as leather* part was nearly true, too, if they had been talking hell-dragon hide. At least he had his comfortable niblun leather boots on, under their plate sabotons. It was easier to march in his armor than to carry it. On him, it fitted snugly. Bundled up on his back, it shifted around, and clanked, and poked into him, however carefully he'd tried to settle it in place.

Well, it was not too much farther now, by his reckoning; maybe only two or three more days, but meanwhile—here we are, on another gray morning, with thin, cold rain, and no one to moan to.

Don't you hate it when you have nothing to complain about, Grell? Qrysta had once teased him, when he was in one of his grumps.

He'd fallen straight into her trap, with his, "Too bloody right, Qrys!"

They'd all laughed at him. *Yeah, yeah,* he'd agreed, sheepishly. There was no need to be a grouch.

Was there something Orcish about it, he wondered? Being sour? Orcs seemed to be pissed off a lot of the time. Well, when they weren't partying. His kind of people. He didn't actually like it, in himself. It was just—who he was now. Grumpy bloody Orc.

I could work a little on my self-improvement on this trek, Grell thought. My geniality, my lovability, my sweetness and light. Meanwhile: Just keep going forwards.

Forwards, through these leafless trees, on these little slippery paths, past these damp banks of dead ferns and brown bracken, and the occasional pond or stream, and up slopes and down slopes, and on, and on, and on …

And now there's this little fuck standing in my way.

It was the first living soul Grell had seen in days. *Here's me, just trudging along, minding my own business, head down against the rain, and I look up and see him, standing there up ahead, in the middle of this muddy path, arms crossed, eyeing me thoughtfully, waiting for me to stop and talk to him.*

Grell unslung Fugg and held her at the ready.

Get the message, shrimp?

The shrimp's eyebrows rose. An odd little fellow, he looked to Grell more like Horm and Nyrik than Oller. Kind of like one, kind of like the other. Nothing resembling a big nasty Orc. In a category of his own, then.

Long, mud-colored hair flowed out from under his pointed cap, tied up at the back with a strip of leather. *He had to be forty at the very least,* Grell thought. *Fifty, more like, on a closer look.* He was in travel-stained clothes—jerkin, leggings; some kind of half-sleeved, raggedy cote over the top of it all. Everything he wore was brown and dark green and splattered with mud. He was leaning on a stained old hand-axe. It looked more like a woodman's tool than a proper weapon. He had a knife in his belt, a sword at his hip, and a small, round board on his back, beneath a full, sealed quiver and what looked to Grell like a hunting bow, unstrung because of the rain. He was small, far smaller than Grell. Also more relaxed than Grell was. He didn't seem to have gotten the message that Fugg in Grell's hands was meant to be sending him. *Stand aside, or you get some of this.*

His eyes went from Fugg to Grell's face, and back again.

"Mm," the little—whatever he was—said, nodding, "pretty, that."

"Pretty," Grell grunted. "Yeah, and pretty fucking sharp. It's niblun steel, this is, so back off, you little twat, before I cut you in half with it."

"Ooh," the reply came, "someone's in a bad mood."

"Yeah, someone is," Grell agreed, "and *someone's* on his way, which you're blocking, granddad. So if I were you, I'd take *someone's* advice and stand aside!"

The—*person*—stopped his contemplation of Fugg and looked up at Grell. Not with fear, or hostility, but with amusement. He folded his arms. His smile widened. His eyes narrowed, and he shook his head, chuckling.

"Niblun," he said. "Really? You seriously use that crap?"

Grell was shocked. This little old geezer, mocking his gear?! "Best there is, mate," he snarled, "and you're welcome to a taste of it!"

The "little old geezer" peered at Grell, baffled. Then he chuckled and shook his head.

"We gonna fight or what?!" Grell said, towering over him, confused.

"Nah, mate. We need to talk."

"What about?"

"Your manners."

"The fuck's wrong with my manners?!"

"They'll get you killed, that's what. If you're going to ponce about like some terrifying bloody warrior, you'd better be able to back it up."

"I fucking can," Grell barked, "you just see if I can't!"

"What??" the other frowned at him in disbelief. "With *niblun* shit? You'd be dead by now if you'd bumped into anyone else 'round these parts and talked that rudely to them, instead of someone nice and kind and reasonable like me."

Grell was, by now, beyond enraged. "I'm five times your size and armed to the fucking teeth!" Grell roared.

The frown turned to a smile and another bemused shake of the head. "Yeah, well—that's your problem mate, innit? You're armed with niblun crap and dressed in niblun crap."

"This stuff is impregnable!"

The little creature's smile faded. He stared at Grell in amazement. Eventually, he said, "You're not from around here, are you?"

Grell shot back, "So what?"

"So, you don't know shit about nothing, that's so what."

Grell had had enough talk. Time to put up or shut up. "Look, just shut the fuck up and fight, all right?!"

The person shook his head. "I'm not the murdering kind," he said. "I'm not going to kill some poor innocent foreign fuckwit just for being a rude ignorant tosser. *Grandad*," he muttered, as if he almost couldn't believe he'd heard it. "Dear oh dear."

That was more than Grell could stand. He charged, bellowing, whirling Fugg at lightning speed around himself like a tornado of razor-sharp steel.

The little person watched him come, sighing.

Then he moved. Fast. His stained old hand-axe took Fugg's shaft in midair and chopped it in half, while his off-hand sword speared through Grell's plate-armored foot like a skewer through butter, nailing him to the ground. Grell jerked to a halt, from full tilt to immobilized, gasping, holding what remained of Fugg's shaft in his grip.

"What I suggest," the person said, "is you stop being a silly boy."

Grell managed, by way of reply, *"Aaah …!!"*

"And if you agree that you will do that," the person continued, "I will remove my sword from your foot, and perhaps we can calm down and talk about this. How does that sound? From where I'm standing, it would seem you could use a little friendly advice."

"Aah," Grell whimpered again.

"Would that be a yes?"

Grell gasped, nodding, "Yes."

"Jolly good," the little, oldish person said. "Allow me to introduce myself. My name is Murruk of the Woodlake. And you are?"

"Grell. Of Stonefields." No more Ozgaroos nonsense now that he had papers from Chief Elbrig.

"Pleased to meet you, Grell of Stonefields," Murruk said. "We don't get many strangers around these parts, so I'll be most interested to hear what brings you this way. I'm going to remove my sword from your foot now, all right?"

"Urhh," Grell said again, and then, faintly, "Yes, please."

With a gentle pull, Murruk slid his scruffy old sword out from Grell's finest niblun sabaton.

"Aaaaahh!!" Grell said, tottering. "Oof. *Whoa* … Thank youhhh …" He stood on his good leg, his recently skewered one dangling in the air, far too damaged for him to stand on.

"My pleasure," Murruk said, sheathing his sword, and settling his hand-axe on his belt. "Now, I don't know what you're doing in this neck of the woods, but you seem like a nice chap, so perhaps I can help?"

"Nnnggg—yes …"

"My clan lives not far from here. An hour's walk. Even with a bit of a limp. Our healer is excellent, she'll sort that foot out for you. Come and meet the folks, have a night under shelter, and a nice hot meal, and you'll be on your way in no time with a spring in your step. Sound good?"

Grell's thoughts were a whirl. *Who was this person? Why should I trust him? Why is he being friendly? I need to get this foot sorted; I've got a delve to clear—can't fight on one leg …*

Hot food, shelter.

Information.

Gods, how did this *happen … ?!"*

He gasped, "Yes. Please. Thank you. And, I apologize for my attitude, earlier. I …"

"Don't worry about it, we all make mistakes." Murruk took Grell's arm and bent it before settling the top of his head under Grell's elbow. "Yep, that'll work," he said. Grell didn't have to lean over much for Murruk to support him, taking the weight that Grell couldn't put onto his skewered foot. "Think you can manage?"

"Yes, thanks," Grell muttered, still shocked from his wound. "I'll need my axe-head," he said, seeing Fugg's top half lying in the mud.

"Nah, we'll get you better than that rubbish, mate," Murruk said. "Our smith's the best in the land, and you want him to take you seriously, eh? You can't be seen carrying a piece of junk like that. You all right in all that armor?"

"Yes, fine …"

"You sure? You could just dump it here; Smithy will get you kitted out proper. Or he could use the steel, I expect, melt it down

245

and make hinges or something with it. Nails—you can never have enough nails, eh?"

Grell's mind was racing, between his confusion and the agony in his foot. *His niblun plate, no better than nails??*

"I … she's … she's a *part* of me," Grell said, as they shuffled past the forlorn double-bladed axe-head that he loved so dearly.

"Oh well, if you insist." Murruk bent down and picked up Fugg's severed head. "I do understand. We warriors get sentimental about our kit, eh?" He patted his old hand-axe, and said, "If Willy could talk, he'd tell you a tale or two!"

Grell said, "Who's Willy?"

"Not who, what," Murruk said. "Willy," he paused, and lifted his hand-axe to where Grell could see it. "My little chopper."

He grinned, waiting for Grell to get it.

Grell chuckled at the lame dick joke. "Nice one," he said.

"Thank you, Grell. Yes, he is. He may not look much, my Willy, but he's made a lot of people sorry they laughed at him."

"Including me," Grell said.

"Including you. Well," Murruk said, as they shuffled on towards the Woodlake, "now you know not to do that again, eh?"

"I do indeed."

"Size isn't everything, right?" Murruk teased.

"Hehe. Clearly not," Grell agreed.

They hobbled on. In great pain though he was, Grell found that it was nice to be talking to someone again. A friendly face. With a breezy sense of humor.

"You all right on that foot of yours?" Murruk said.

"I'll be fine."

"Tough bugger, I'll say that for you. Orc, right?"

"Right."

"We've never had any down our way before. Be most interested to meet you, folks will."

"I'll … be interested … to meet them," Grell panted, as they walked on—or rather, as he limped on, and Murruk staggered on, his head jammed under Grell's elbow. "Who are you all, by the way? Your … people?" Grell asked.

"Eh?" Murruk seemed confused by the question.

"I'm an Orc," Grell said, "and you're a—what?"

"Oh, I see what you mean. Kinfolk, we call ourselves. And other folk are just ... *folk*. Wood Folk in the forests, Little Folk in the hills and valleys, Big Folk in the towns and villages, Stone Folk in the undergrounds. Lost Folk in the pits and tombs and such."

"Like Woods Kin?" Grell suggested.

"Like and not like," Murruk demurred. "Distant cousins, you might say. Like you lot and Ogres."

"Eh?" Grell said, sharply. "We're not fucking Ogres!"

"That's not what I said, is it? But somebody was, once. According to the tale, anyway."

Grell didn't understand. "What tale?"

"Of how the world was born, and how all that live on her came into being. And how they lived, and died, and some faded away and disappeared, and some changed, over the ages. And in the Ice Time, it is said, which was long, long ago, when things were harsh and bitter cold, and many kinds of folk disappeared forever, there was a tribe of Big Folk and a tribe of Ogres who put aside their differences and banded together. Thanks to pooling their varied skills, they survived the long years of the Ice Time in the stronghold they built and provisioned.

"They lived by hunting seals in the Ice Seas, and walrus, and such, and reindeer when the herds migrated. Grew what they could, in their hothouses, above hot springs that bubbled up from deep in the earth. Brewed ales of sugar beets and honey, and salted meats, and pickled vegetables. Long winter nights in the longhouse, they had, with the big fire in its pit below the smoke hole all that was keeping any of them alive, and got to know each other."

Murruk paused, as if to let the picture grow in Grell's imagination. "Sang each other's songs, they did. Heard each other's stories and learned each other's natures. Saw what they had in common, and what they didn't.

"It was many generations later that the sun warmed the world again, as he had done before, and by then the children of the two tribes were neither the one nor t'other. Orcs, they had become. Best of both, some say. Others beg to differ. And that is how your folk began, if the tale tells it true. So, back then, your Big Folk ancestors were indeed fucking Ogres, and you lot came of the couplings in those long, cold nights."

Blimey, Grell thought. *I'm a product of unnatural selection.* "Are there any Ogres around here?" he asked.

"Nah, they all died out long ago," Murruk said. "You lot are all that's left of them."

"There are some in Jarnland," Grell said.

"Really?" Murruk was surprised. "And where's that, then?"

"Where I come from. Across the seas to the north. Long way. We still have ogres there, although I've never met one. Woods Kin friend told us a cousin of his had married one."

"Who's 'us?'" Murruk asked. He asked it innocently enough, but Grell was instantly on the alert. He wasn't going to mention the others. Not in this realm, where the Four were wanted, dead or alive.

"Us Orcs," he said. And, by way of changing the subject, continued, "We have giants too, up in the Western Mountains. Me and my lady friend met some. Very hospitable, they were, but you never can tell with giants, she warned. One moment all peaceable, next moment they're stomping on you or whacking at you with their stone clubs."

"Blimey," Murruk said. "Glad we don't have none o' them hereabouts, Grell. Giants!" He shook his head. "Who'd 'a thought it? I thought they was just inventions, out of the old wives' tales. How much bigger than you, Grell, are they then? I mean, you're bloody big enough."

"Me and my Orc lady friend sitting on a horse with her perched on my shoulders," Grell said, "is about the size of a big one."

"Gawds," Murruk said, impressed. "Poor bloody horse …! So, what you doing all this way from home then, Grell?"

"I'm on a mission," Grell replied.

"What kind of mission?"

"Confidential one, I'm afraid, Murruk. From my chief, Elbrig of the Stonefields. I'll show you my papers when we get to your—village?"

"Island," Murruk said. "Yes, we'll be needing to see those. Not that we're sticklers for protocol much, with few coming and going through this way; but it's good to know who's legit and who ain't. I 'spect you'll be hungry by the time we get there, eh?"

Grell grunted. He was.

After nearly two hours, rather than just one, of hopping, and slithering, and putting his wounded foot down by mistake, and *ouching*, Grell was just about out on his feet. Conversation had long since dried up. At least the rain had dried up as well.

After a long silence of panting, and grunting, and lurching, Murruk said, at last, "Well, here we are then!"

Grell looked up. Through the trees, ahead of him, water. The Woodlake.

Grell might, if he'd had two good feet, have managed to squeeze one buttock into the canoe that was drawn up among the reeds at the water's edge, but not both.

"Hm," Murruk said. "Tell you what, Grell—you wait here, I'll pop over and come back with the raft. The which we use for supplies and such, or deer when we shoot 'em. No big autumn stag's going to fit into this little thing, any more than you are."

The island didn't seem far, not more than three hundred yards away.

"You'll be all right here," Murruk said, climbing into the canoe, "I'll be back in a jiffy."

Grell slumped to the ground. "Thanks, mate," he gasped.

"For what, giving you that foot injury? No no, I done that to you, the least I can do is undo it. Won't be long."

He wasn't. He was back within twenty minutes with three companions, who assisted Grell onto the raft. He didn't register their names, even though they all introduced themselves, and asked how he was doing, and gave each other orders about how to look after him, and carried him onto the raft, with a lot of *oofing* and *carefuls*.

The last thing Grell thought was, *I don't think I can take much more of this.*

He couldn't.

He woke up as the sun was setting. He was lying on a bed, looking up at the underneath of a thatched roof, above smoke-blackened rafters. The bed felt wonderful. Comfortable. Warm and safe. He inched his head around and took in the rest of the room. Wattle-and-daub walls, a chest, a cupboard, some shelves filled with bottles and flasks. Quiet. Peace.

He rolled his head back and shut his eyes again. A hand lifted his wrist and took his pulse. He opened his eyes and found himself looking at a tiny old woman, her eyes shut, her mouth moving as she counted.

She placed his hand, gently, back onto the bed and looked at him. Her eyes were the brightest blue he had ever seen, so light they were almost white.

"Well now," she said, "we've seen to your foot. All mending nicely! You'll be as right as rain in the morning. Only a few bones cut through, easy fixin's. So now, what you want to do, I suggest, is sit up, and see if you can't stand."

Grell hauled himself upright, as instructed. Gingerly, he lowered his wounded foot to the ground. It was in some sort of casing.

"Up you get."

He did. To his surprise, he could stand. On both feet.

He looked down at the tiny old woman, who came up to the level of his hips.

"Just the one leg—the one Murruk skewered," she instructed him.

Grell wasn't sure about that. He lifted his good leg warily off the ground. The other leg held him up just fine.

"Hop," she said.

He stared at her.

She nodded, smiling.

He hopped. His foot felt as if it had never been hurt. "Thank you."

"You're welcome, young fellow. Keep that cast on it tonight and tomorrow, and you'd never know our Murruk had touched you. Now. Everyone is agog to meet you, and the cooks have been busy as bees. We don't get many excuses for a feast, and if you're not one I don't know what is. Pop this under your arm," she said, handing him a crutch. "Foot's mended, but it needs time and rest."

The healer's sanctuary was part of the longhouse. It led through into another bedchamber—hers, presumably—and, from there, along a short corridor with doors on either side into the main hall.

It was full of Kinfolk, all sitting at long, communal tables, drinking and chatting with their neighbors. A noisy, cheerful room. And smells of cooking coming from the adjacent kitchens. All heads turned to Grell as he limped in, on his crutch, and then Murruk was at his side, and the other rescuers he recognized from the raft before he'd passed out, and they all clapped him on the back and made him welcome and said how well he was looking.

He sat at a bench next to Murruk. A stoneware mug was pressed into his hand. He drank. Oh, *gods,* was it good. A thick, brown ale, with a foam head, bitter and sharp and sweet and refreshing. He looked around, seeing the faces all looking at him, interested and open. He felt tears come to his eyes. He wiped them away with the back of his hand.

His companions all suddenly looked worried.

"I'm fine," he said. "I just … didn't expect this."

"Oh," Murruk said, relieved, "We thought you was upset. Well, *we* were expecting *you*. Been looking forward to meeting you, we have. None more so than Smithy here."

A bearded face grinned at him from along the bench beyond Murruk.

The smith hauled himself to his feet and came over to size Grell up. Literally. He was only an inch or so taller than Murruk, but twice as wide. "Pleased to meet you, Grell," he said, as he and his two apprentices measured Grell every which way with lengths of knotted string. "Name's Derwyn, but everyone calls me Smithy. Don't mind my 'prentices here. We've a deal o' work ahead of us tonight. If you could give us tomorrow as well, why, that would be all the time we need, if you're not in a hurry?"

"No, that would be fine," Grell said, thinking, *Well, what's one more day?*

"Good to hear!" Smithy beamed. "Can't have you going where you're going in anything but the best. And I've never had the pleasure of kitting an Orc before. Come and see me in the morning, all right?" He leaned closer, a broad grin growing inside his bushy beard. "I've got something for you. I think you'll like it!"

"Oh," Grell said. "Thank you, Smithy."

"My pleasure, old son!" Smithy said, thumping Grell on the back surprisingly hard. Strong little bugger. "My very great pleasure indeed! See you bright and early, eh? Come on then, lads, we've a busy night ahead of us!"

Smithy hustled out, followed by his apprentice boys, who were already talking forge talk to each other.

"Well, that leaves us time to eat, drink, and be merry, eh?" Murruk said. He refilled Grell's ale and raised his own mug. "Cheers, Grell, and welcome to the Woodlake!"

"Cheers," Grell replied, "and thank you for having me."

They clinked their mugs and drank.

20

The Quest Request

It was a night that Grell had been needing. Good food, warmth, shelter, companionship, and a chance to recharge his drained batteries. It was a welcome break from the mission he was on. He was knackered, so it wasn't going to be a long night—he'd be hitting the hay early—but it turned out to be an informative one.

Grell learned two things: One, they'd been expecting him, and two, he could trust them. How did he know that? It was pretty obvious once he'd worked it out. If they'd been expecting him, and had wanted to shop him to the Devoted, they could simply have done that, on the road. They could have set a trap for him, tied him up and carted him off. No need for all this rigmarole, bringing him here, filling him with their excellent food and ale, and answering all his questions without a hint of demur.

Kinfolk, it became clear, minded their own business, and didn't share it with outsiders. Grell *was* their business, so he could ask away. But no Big Folk would be hearing of the Orc they'd invited back to the Woodlake, any more than they would hear of what they discussed with him, or of where he was going, or which way he'd gone when he left, because there'd never been an Orc here, had there?

Kinfolk were wary of Big Folk and kept their distance. They visited Big Folk villages and farms, occasionally, to trade, and sometimes, but rarely, their towns—where they kept themselves to themselves, and minded their own business, and were polite, and cheerful, and unobtrusive, and respectful, and never a hint of trouble.

Even the Devoted didn't bother them. The Kinfolk had no time for the Devoted, but never let that show. They treated the brothers and sisters they met with courtesy, and gave generous donations when collections were made, with a smile; but Valmynia wasn't their goddess—due respect though they paid her. There were few Kinfolk in the places where there were many of the Devoted, and none of the Devoted within many dozens of leagues of the Woodlake. The two groups left each other alone. It was a big, mostly empty realm, with plenty of room for all to live in, in peace.

Which did not mean that the Kinfolk were ignorant of what the Devoted were up to. In the farmsteads, and in the markets and taverns of the towns and villages, Kinfolk kept their eyes and ears open, and their mouths shut. They listened. They learned. They'd heard soon enough when the ghost ship sailed from Seacastle, and knew that they would be about to have their part to play.

They saw that the Devoted were now in a frenzy, with envoys fanning out all over the realm from the Orphanage, on urgent Devoted business. When the news came that the ghost ship had foundered, and sunk, with only one survivor, washed up on a northern shore, they had a good think about it. They were as unconvinced as Avildor. Hundreds of years, just to sink? They didn't think so. So, Caster's whereabouts known: What about Dancer and Monster and Thief?

Well, they would be coming this way sooner or later, wouldn't they? Or how could they get the job done?

And Grell, alone, had duly appeared. That evening, over their food and ale, Murruk wasn't going to ask directly about the other two, because Grell would pretend ignorance about the whole subject. All he would say was that he was on a secret errand for Chief Elbrig of Stonefields.

"Must be important, for your Chief to send you all this way, over that big Northern Ocean?" Murruk observed, with a solemn face, but secretly enjoying himself.

"It is, mate. Very," Grell replied, in all seriousness, mopping up the remains of yet another plateful with a hunk of bread.

Murruk laughed inside. Not the world's best liar, this Orc. Lovely fellow, though. Hope he makes it back this way.

"Wish I could tell you about it, Murruk," Grell clumsily embroidered his lie, "I really do, but. Chief's orders. Orcs only. You understand."

Murruk nodded. " 'Course I do, Grell. None o' no one else's business, eh? Well, I expect you'd like to hear why we've been on the lookout for you?"

This was what Grell definitely wanted to know. "I would, yes."

"Obviously you've been stared at, from time to time, right?" Murruk began. "Since you landed here, in—wherever it was, up there on the north coast? Like I said, we don't get many Orcs 'round here. Well, you was noticed, and word spread, and soon enough us Kinfolk heard you was in the realm: Bloody great Orc, and heading this way."

"Who told you?"

"Little Folk. What you call Woods Kin. Like I told you, they're kind of our distant cousins. They've been keeping tabs on you." Grell was startled. "Nothing to worry about, Grell. You said you had woody mates, up in your country? Well, then you'll know you won't see them if they don't want to be seen, right?"

Grell remembered Nyrik and Horm stepping out of thin air to capture them, appearing in front of them where they'd been invisible before, even though they'd been talking to him and Daxx and Qrysta for several minutes.

"Too right about that," he agreed.

"So, they knew we'd be interested to hear about you, when it was clear you'd be coming through our turf. And we were, and we are, and here's why—and don't worry, it's nothing to do with your chief's secret errand. We don't need to know anything about that.

"A couple of days from here, three at the most, is a place where we can't go, but you can."

Grell said, "Why not?"

"It's closed to us. *Magic* closed. To all as were born in this realm. The which," Murruk pointed out with a smile, "you were not, were you?"

"No," Grell agreed.

"And that makes you eligible. You can do this, no one else we know of can. So," Murruk leaned forwards, and Grell realized that conversation all around them had ceased, and everyone was listening, "this is our opportunity to get you to do a very important job for us. Well worth it, it'll be, I should point out. For starters, you just see what Smithy and his lads are knocking together for you! It'll be yours to keep. You may be the richest Orc in Stonefields, Grell mate, but you could never afford the gear they're going to kit you out with. The reason for that being that Kinfolk don't craft for outsiders. Unless they happen to want to.

"Smithy's turned down thousands and thousands of gold; not interested. Told the king's armorer to bugger off with his chests of coins. That's one reason why no one bothers us out here. They know what we're wearing, see, and what we're wielding, and they know that they don't have anything that could match up and compete. Not even the king's army wants to be rowing across to the island into a storm of Fletchy's warheads, shot from Chips's warbows. They know they'll come off second best if it comes to blows."

A thought struck him. "Come to think of it," Murruk added, "Chips'll make you a bow, if you like? You ever use bow?"

"Yes, plenty," Grell said. "Not as much as I used to, though. I'm usually the tank."

That baffled Murruk. "The what-now?"

"I, er, charge in, and challenge the enemy, and everyone attacks me," Grell explained, "and I cut them up, and my mates get in among them and cut them down again."

"Oh. Right. Sounds like a strategy. You have a good team, then?"

"Yes," Grell said, "the best," and then remembered his cover story, and quickly added, "they're all back in Jarn, of course. Solo mission, this one. Chief was very specific about that."

"I expect he was. So, no bow?"

Grell thought. Could come in handy, a good bow. Might be useful, to have a range weapon, now that he didn't have Daxx with him, and his Area of Effects attacks, nor Oller or Qrysta with their bows. Which had, of course, gone down with the ghost ship, along with the rest of their gear. Yes. Why not?

"Well," he said, "if he wouldn't mind ..."

"Mind? He'd love the challenge! Longbow, for a lad your size, I expect?"

"Yes. Please."

"I'll get him on it." He turned and waved at another Kinfolk across the room. "Oy, Chipsy, over here mate a moment!"

Chipsy stood up from his bench at another table and joined them. He listened. Nodded. "Right you are," he said, looking Grell over. "Got some lovely yew heartwood been waiting for something like this; six hundred years old the tree was if it was a day. It'll be the biggest bloody bow *I've* ever made, I can tell you that! Most powerful too, probably, a great big feller like you hauling on the string. Could put one o' Fletch's bodkins through a tree, I'd reckon. Not that I'd recommend doing that!" he added hastily, his hands up, "the trees wouldn't like it, and you don't want to be out in the middle of a lot of angry, trees that don't like what you're doing to them."

"I won't, I promise," Grell said, and, "thank you."

"Don't mention it, my pleasure," Chipsy said. "So, what do you think: Fire, Frost, Fever, or Fury?"

Grell said, "Huh?"

"For the Imbuing. Set 'em alight, slow 'em with cold, weaken them with sickness, or stab 'em with lightning?"

Grell thought, *wow*. They all sounded good.

"Can I get all four?" he said.

Chipsy's eyebrows rose. "Blimey," he said. "Never thought of that …. You tend to want it to hit as hard as it can, with just the one. That would mean having only a quarter of the power in each. Better to max out the one."

Grell thought it over. Foes on fire usually means them out of the way. Or, of course, running around madly and setting your team on fire, which is annoying. Ice, immobilized. Qrysta and Oller can take their time finishing them off. Fever sounds … contagious. Fury, lightning? Yeah, that would be bad for anyone trying to get cast attacks off at you, it would short-circuit them. But that's not everyone.

"Frost," he said.

"Right you are!" Chipsy said. "See you tomorrow. I shall be interested to see you trying her out."

"I look forward to it," Grell said, and Chips hurried off to get to work, taking his apprentice with him. He thought, *New bow, new arms and armor: This must be some important task they'd like me to do. Side quest, eh? Well, I expect I'll have time for a quick one. I'd be happy to help these friendly folks out. It'll be the least I can do, for all this fine food and strong ale, and a couple of nights in a warm bed rather than under dripping trees. And besides, who knows what I might find on a side quest that I can keep for myself?*

"So," Murruk said, "you on, then?"

"Don't see why not," Grell said, which, while being noncommittal, basically meant *yes.*

This was what he did, wasn't it? Quests. Adventures. *Yeah,* he thought, suddenly interested. You never know where the next one is coming from.

"Splendid," Murruk said. He reached into an inside pocket and got out a linen pouch. From within that, he withdrew a scroll of parchment.

He unrolled it on the table in front of them.

It was a map. A beautiful, detailed one. It reminded Grell of the map that Esmeralda had liberated from her father's library. Mountains outlined in white and light blue; forests in greens and browns; fields among tiny farms; towns as little cartouches, castles within their walls; wildernesses dotted with picturesque dragons and unicorns and sheep. Krakens and monster fish in the seas.

"So," Murruk said, jabbing his finger at a point on the map, "we're here. Not marked, of course, just the way we like it. This island, in this lake. Which isn't drawn in on this map. Nothing to see here, right? Just trees. Okay. So, on we go, pretty much due west, and eventually arrive … here."

Grell froze. There could be no mistake about it.

Murruk's finger was standing on exactly the spot he was already heading for.

All his alarms went off at once. He didn't know what to think. Coincidence? Almost certainly not. He didn't know what to say. So, he grunted.

"What's there, then?" he said, as offhandedly as possible.

Murruk said, "The job we need you to do."

"And what's that?"

"Get in, get it, get out again," Murruk said.

" 'It' being what, exactly?"

"The most important thing in the world to us Kinfolk." Murruk sounded suddenly both sad and serious.

"Go on."

Murruk looked down at the tabletop and nodded and gathered his thoughts. "You do understand, Grell, mate," he said, quietly, "that we don't usually talk about this? And never with outsiders?"

Grell considered. "Thank you for trusting me with it," he said, eventually.

That seemed to reassure Murruk. "Gods, where to start?" he wondered. "At the end, mayhaps. We only have one shot at this. That one shot is you. So. Now you know. Everything we have, and are, and want, is riding on your big hairy shoulders. As to what that everything is ..."

He took a deep breath and began. "We were the first here. In this land. The land knew us, and raised us, and liked us. All to ourselves, we had it, many long ages.

"Until we didn't. First the Little Folk came and settled, as did the Stone Folk, and the Wood Folk, and the Big Folk, and there's room enough for all, and pits enough for the Lost Folk, and we all rub along with the usual spits and spats. By staying out of each other's way, mostly. There's few of us, and not too many of them, not even the Bigs. So, no, we don't need what they've got, and they know better than to bother us and try to take what we've got.

"Well, that was the way it was. And then this other lot appeared. Gods knew where they'd come from, we'd none of us ever seen the like. Made everyone's lives miserable, for hundreds of years, they did. They called themselves the Cult of Varamaxes."

Murruk glanced at Grell to see if the name meant anything to him.

Grell kept his face as still and empty as possible.

"It's a religion, of some sort, Grell—and not a nice sort at that. And it wasn't just a Big Folk religion. There was all sorts in it—alive and undead, and shape-shifters and *Weres*. It brought dark times, and for a long time. Far too long."

He shook his head and lowered his voice. "Folk disappearing. Fed to some kind of demon, rumor had it, but who can trust the tales Rumor tells? Mind you, she's the only one who can come and go as she pleases. No living being ever made it out of their stronghold, having once gone in, whether willing or unwilling.

"Its leader, the Archon, was the power behind the throne, and other thrones in other realms beyond our bounds that we know little of. Under his iron rule, we all were.

There was no standing against such a power. They took what, and who, they wanted; but mainly, they stayed down in their retreats, as they called them. We paid our tributes, every half year, in goods and cattle, and boys and girls, and thanked the gods they didn't come upground for more.

"The which, as time went on, they did. And the realm grew poorer for it, and weaker for it, and sadder for it. Until a day came when a stranger presented himself to the king as was on the throne at the time. A scholar, he was, in the brown habit of a man of religion, young but wise beyond his years. He had walked the length and breadth of all the realms where the Cult held sway and had consulted with their kings and queens. And the upshot of it was, a pact was made. An accord, between realms that had been allies and enemies by turns, on and off, since time immemorial. And that was when the tide began to turn.

"How he did it, this young Chidian, was to reveal to Their various Majesties what had been revealed to him. The eternal war between the gods and demons was being waged in our world. We were living on what was now their battlefield. And not all gods are the same, just as not all Folk are. There are gods of joy and gods of anguish, gods of light and dark, and heat and cold—and them being gods, well, it's all beyond us and complicated. This Chidian was an acolyte of the goddess of Mercy and Suffering, Valmynia. And how are Mercy and Suffering related and woven together, we might ask?"

Murruk shrugged. "That's god business, and not ours. The war was here, like it or not, Chidian said, and those caught in the middle must needs choose a side. Choose hers, and Valmynia would show us the grace of her mercy. Choose her enemy, and we would suffer for eternity along with him. 'Suppose her enemy won?' it was asked. 'Then things will continue as they are in the world, but will worsen, until he has consumed all that live on it,' he said. 'And then, at the end of his time, he too will perish, having taken every living soul with him. He is the demon of hunger and despair. Hunger, which consumes the body, and despair which consumes the soul.'

"So, there's our choice, he said. Mercy, or despair. Which was to be our future?

"Put like that, the powers in the lands made their decision. The Accord was sworn, and the war taken to the Cult, which after much strife and bloodshed was defeated. Varamaxes was no more, and no longer did his Archon hold sway over the kings and queens. Who, by the by, were soon back at their old squabblings, but what can you do? Royalty, eh?

Murruk shook his head, and allowed himself a brief smile at the foolishness of mortals. "But the realms were freed at last of the shadow, and free for them to squabble in, and free for the rest of us to live in, in whatever peace we could find for ourselves and protect from each other.

"But there was a price. There is always a price."

He paused. Grell waited. *Here it comes,* he thought.

Murruk reached out for the ale jug. He refilled Grell's mug, then his own.

"Thank you," Grell said, and took a draught.

"Thirsty work, talking," Murruk said.

He still didn't seem quite ready for what he wanted to say.

The other Kinfolk were watching, in silence, listening. Grell sensed that they had been waiting a long while for this moment.

Murruk took a deep breath, and exhaled, and nodded. "You ever wonder, Grell," he said, "*how* geese go south in the winter, and come back north in the spring? They probably wouldn't be able to tell you. They just *know*. Which direction to go in, and how to come back. Well, we can't navigate like they can. There's all sorts of things we two-legged folk can't do, that other creatures can. But there was one thing that only us Kinfolk, of all the living beings in this world, could do, or be.

"And that was the price we had to pay. Chidian told all us Folks that the only hope we had was for each kind to give up that which was most precious to them. The more precious our gift, the more we stood a chance. That seemed a difficult choice. We don't know what the Big Folk or Little Folk or Wood Folk or Stone Folk offered, or whether the Lost Folk were even asked.

"But we know what we gave.

"Our council put their heads together and offered this. It was something Chidian had never heard of. *Beyond price,* he said. *This might just make all the difference.*

"So, we gave it."

Murruk paused. Cleared his throat and continued. "When I said we were here first, Grell, I didn't say we *came* here first. We *grew* here. Out of the land. Out of the streams, and the trees, and the mountains and dells. This land *is* us, and we are it. Both good and bad. The malevolent took up with the Lost Folk and went underground. The benevolent: Well, we gave up our most precious possession, for the cause, for the war. And now we're shadows of what we were, and we yearn to be our true selves again.

"We yearn to have our Natures back."

Murruk let that sink in. Grell didn't know what he meant, but he could tell that this was of great importance to his hosts.

"If you don't succeed, Grell, we're finished. Which may be how it's supposed to be, we don't know. Like I told you: Folk come, and Folk go, over the years, and not all last the test of time. Maybe our time is coming to an end too. Maybe not. Well, we'd like to know, one way or t'other, and see what we see—and see what, if anything, we can do about it.

"But back to Chidian. We should have smelled a rat, of course. Turns out there was more to Blessed Father Abbott Chidian, as he is now known, than met the eye. Pious, earnest, mystical young man, he seemed. Not long out of his teens. And how does a youngster visit all those realms, and counsel with all those kings and queens, and know so much—which none in the land had heard before—and have had so many revelations? People hung on his every word, they did. And he persuaded one and all with his righteousness, and his learning, and his insights.

"Well, he'd given the clue, right at the start. *The war of the gods and demons was being fought on the mortal plane, and in our realms.* And how did he know this? Well, who should know better than one of them, eh? In all the tales, of all the beliefs, there are gods turning up in the world as ram or rainbow, as lightning or eagle, as siren or serpent—so why not as a young brother of this new group of Devoted Children? In the service of a goddess that all knew. But no one was looking at him as the divinity; he was just the man of the moment.

"He told us the price. *All must offer what most they value.* The greater the value, the more it would weigh in the balance, and the greater the chance of overcoming the foe.

"What we offered, Grell—*sacrificed*—tipped the scales. The power on our side overcame the power on the enemy's. The war was won. The foe was overthrown and sealed up in his doom. Being immortal, they say, he cannot be killed. But, in the long years since, many have wondered: Did Chidian say that just because he was immortal himself? And because he didn't want to let on to us mortals down here that he, too, could die? Who is to say? All that is believed is that all things must end, mortal or divine. As to when, and how: That remains to be seen, and maybe there'll be none left here to see it but Time himself.

"But one curious thing did come out of it. When Chidian had cast his seals, and Varamaxes was pent up forever, Chidian himself faded. 'I am not dying,' he said. 'I am leaving this mortal frame, as our enemy has left his. For the one cannot live without the other, any more than the one can die without the other. Thus the balance is maintained, both in this fleeting world of you mortals, and in the eternal one of us gods.'

"*Us gods*, eh? So, which one was he? There was never no god named *Chidian*.

"Whatever the answer to that may be, it was through his workings that the foe was vanquished, and his power replaced by the power of the Devoted; and while things are better now than they were, and better now than they would have been if we hadn't all worked together and acted—they are still out of balance.

"And maybe they never will be aright again, for one and all; but as far as we Kinfolk are concerned, we can't consider those higher things. We can only consider the here and now. How it has affected us. What we have lost. We may be mortal, like other Folk, but we are mortal in a different way. Less mortal than other Folk, more mortal than the gods.

"Or we *were*, until we lost our Nature. We want it back. We yearn to be in the trees and rivers again, in the high places and the wind and the weather. To be the wheat as it grows under the summer sun; to be the gleam that wanders the marshes at night. The ice that guards the fish through the winter. The flowers that feed the spring bees, and the fruit that falls in autumn. The world may still be here, thanks to what we and others gave up for it. But it is a poorer place for the *lack* of what we gave for it. And we of the Kin are the poorer for it.

"Imagine, Grell, if you were a harper, and one day lost your music. Or a warrior, who wakes up as weak as a babe. It is still in us, we know that. Look how Healer Ria set your bones and closed your skin. You'll know, when you see what Smithy crafts for you, and Chips's longbow, and Fletch's shafts. You'll never have seen the like! It's still in us but we can no longer be in *it*."

He stopped and looked at Grell again.

Grell shook his head. "I'm not following, Murruk mate. You ... have this—thing, but you don't?"

"We have what we have, our skills, our gifts, they are in our Natures. But we cannot be in *our* Nature. We are locked out of it. We cannot be as we *were*, Grell, and yearn to be again."

He could see that Grell was still struggling.

"Think of it as our magical essence, Grell. That we lived not just in these Kinfolk bodies, but in our land itself, lake and stream and field and forest, tree and flower, root and leaf, and all those that walk or swim or fly or burrow."

"You … become them?"

"Join them. Live in them and through them."

He waited while Grell thought about that. "I … can't imagine."

There was a rustling in the room. He glanced up, to see that people were shifting on their seats, their faces worried, fretful.

"No, Grell," Murruk said. "Neither can we. None of us, these many generations, has known the peace and wonder of that. And we long to. Because it's where we belong. Where we should be. We should be everywhere, and not just in these forms, as you see us now, here, in the Isle of the Woodlake."

He stopped. No one said a word.

All eyes in the hall were on Grell.

He frowned. Something was bothering him about this.

He saw what it was. Oldface had said that no one knew about these hidden places. He looked up at Murruk, and said, "How d'you know that's where it is?"

Murruk grunted. "You might as well ask how we know where *we* are. That's a part of *us*, in there, Grell! We know where we are, same as anyone, same as you."

Grell nodded, satisfied. "Sounds like my kind of a job," he said, and all watching him relaxed. Smiles broke out on their anxious faces.

"So, what's this *it*, then," Grell said, "and how do I know what to look for?"

"An iron chest," Murruk said.

The smiles around him vanished. Clearly, the Kinfolk didn't like to think about that iron chest.

"Anything … particular about it?"

Murruk said, "Imagine the last place you'd want to be cooped up in, forever. When you're used to running with the wind, or drifting with the snow, or growing with root and leaf, and fruit and flower.

"And instead, you're stuck in an iron box."

Grell grunted. It didn't sound good at all. "So, your … Nature is in an iron box …"

"And outside another box, that has another Nature held inside it, thanks to us, and Chidian's sealing. We'd very much appreciate it if you'd be so kind as to find it and open it."

"Does it matter where? Or when?"

"No. Whenever you're ready to deal with the other Nature that ours is guarding, only *then* release it—and we'll be off and away, and free again!" Murruk's eyes brightened in anticipation, then he grimaced. "Him too, by the way. Without us there, he'll be out and about soon enough."

Grell said "He?"

Murruk nodded. "And he'll be your problem from then on," he said, "and no longer ours."

21

Arms and Armor

Grell woke late the next morning, gradually, as if still in a dream. No hard stones were poking into him. No discomfort jerked him into the new day. He drifted into consciousness with a smile on his face. Healer Ria was at his side, as he lay there, comfortable. *You have to have been through days and nights of misery to appreciate how good this feels,* he thought. She felt his pulse; lifted his eyelids and peered into his eyes; poked and prodded. She gave him a draught of something warm and smoky tasting. "Knitbone," she said.

Grell drank it, slowly.

"You'll do!" she said. "Just keep the cast on that foot till tomorrow."

He had no difficulty walking to the forge. Smithy and his apprentices were hopping up and down with excitement, waiting for him. They led him to a bench, on which pieces of armor were laid out.

"Right," Smithy said, "put it on."

Grell had been expecting them to arm him. He looked at them, puzzled. They looked at him, grinning. They weren't going to. He turned to the armor and wondered where to begin.

Legs, he thought, and reached for his greaves. He clapped them around his waist and buckled them in place. Sabotons on his feet next. He could hardly feel them. Then the skirted cuirass. When he set that on his chest and back, the two pieces locked together by themselves. *What?* That was new. Sleeves, shoulder pieces, neck, helm, gauntlets: Everything molded together, seamlessly. Also, the entire assemblage weighed next to nothing. He bent his knees, flexed, jumped. It was as if he was naked. When he looked at Smithy, he said, "Wow, mate. This is …"

Smithy chuckled.

He nodded at his two 'prentices. Who charged at unarmed Grell with forge hammers and started pummeling him, as hard as they could.

Their blows felt like soft taps, as if they were politely trying to get his attention. Smithy signaled them to stop.

Grell had just taken a beating … by two flies.

"Now," Smithy said, "I told you that I've got something for you, didn't I?"

"You did," Grell said.

"And I saw that battle-axe you brought in—nice piece of work, but not up to what you'll be needing—so I know you're a two-hander. The which I would be myself, if I were your size. You recognize that lot over there?"

He indicated a target dummy standing nearby.

It was dressed head to toe in Grell's old niblun plate armor.

"Yes."

"Best where you come from, right?"

"Yes," Grell agreed.

"What d'you think, eh?" Smithy said. "Nothing can damage that?"

Grell hesitated. "Not as far as I know …"

Smithy chuckled. He walked over to his bench and picked up a long, lumpy object.

Grell looked at it. A maul.

He thought, *What? Blunt instrument?! I use precision, and blades—*

Smithy held it out to him. "See what you can do with this," he said.

Grell took it.

Gods it was light! It looked like the heaviest damn two-handed weapon you'd ever seen in your life. It felt like a toy.

It was no longer than Fugg and had the same comfortable grip in the handle that he was used to when wielding Fugg, that fitted his hands so perfectly. Instead of a blade at its tip, the shaft thickened into a long, solid head that was ribbed with sharp goose bumps. He touched one with his fingertip. His skin parted, dripping blood. And he'd thought

Fugg was razor-sharp …! He flicked the maul around with his wrists. It was as light as a twig. He'd never get tired wielding this.

Smithy nodded at the target dummy.

Grell walked over and hefted the maul.

He whirled, and whacked—but not with his full strength, because that was niblun armor, and he didn't want to break his wrists.

The maul didn't bounce back as he'd expected, wrenching his arms. Instead, the niblun armor on the dummy crumpled like paper.

Grell hardly even felt the impact.

He stepped back, stunned. He looked at the target dummy in disbelief. The best gear in Jarnland, reduced to tinfoil.

"How about that?" Smithy said.

Grell said, "Gods …"

He took a closer look at the maul. A brutal, unsubtle weapon … but so light, and so maneuverable …

Smithy said, "Suits you."

Grell grunted in agreement, staring at his new weapon. He could see that it was, in its own way, as beautiful as Fugg, but made with far superior craftsmanship. Eventually, he said, "This is amazing."

"Crush 'em," Smithy said. "Bones break, armor splits. Warhammer, great sword, battle-axe: They're all well and good, in their own way. But if you wield two-handed, best of the lot is maul. Nothing can stand against it, if you know what you're doing.

"The which you, Grell," he added, with a grin, "clearly do."

"I can't believe how light this is," Grell said.

"You shouldn't," Smithy said. "She's much heavier than she feels. Mauls need weight, that's what gives them their punch. And maulers need lightness, so their arms don't drop off from exhaustion. So, we balance 'em out. She feels light, so you feel you can keep going all day, twirling her around like a toothpick. But she's no lightweight. Easily twice the weight of that old battle-axe of yours, even if she feels a quarter of it. And that," he said, with a chuckle, "is worth remembering. Because you will not believe how every muscle in your body will ache the next day. You'll be barely able to move. But everyone and everything that you've flattened with her won't be able to move ever again, so you'll be ahead there, eh?"

Grell considered all he'd said and shook his head. "How do you do that?"

Smithy grinned. "Craft secret. Now. We're going to do a little spar-ring, so's I can see if we need any adjustments, and then we'll see what Chipsy and Fletch have for you."

Smithy led the way outside, Grell following in his new suit of armor. This was armor? It felt like a light shirt and leggings, not even leather but summer linen. Smithy and his two apprentices had long poles. The boys were bursting with excitement, eager to get started. There was quite a crowd of Kinfolk in the adjacent field, waiting for the show.

Murruk caught Grell's eye and waved.

Smithy said, "Visor down, Grell, we'll be going for your face." Grell lowered his visor. Stopped. Raised it again. Lowered it. There was no difference in visibility. Normally, in his experience, a visor restricted his field of vision to about a quarter. This one did ... nothing.

Smithy said, "Ready?"

"Ready."

They attacked. Full on, full contact, full speed ahead, shrieking and slashing and jabbing and whacking. Grell took a few seconds to get going. A dozen blows had rained in on him in those few seconds. He felt almost nothing. Then he got to work. Smash those poles, was his first thought. He couldn't. He could hit them easily enough, but in-stead of splintering, they merely bounced away. He was soon in full battle mode, busy, concentrating, working on instinct while seeing ev-erything around him.

Right. Change of tactic. One of the 'prentice boys was getting a lit-tle too cocky. Grell pretended to be occupied with his other two assail-ants, then whirled around and counter-attacked, adding a savage Orc war-bellow for good measure. The ferocity of his onslaught surprised the lad, who backed off, blocking Grell's attacks ineptly. His pole stuck in the ground, Grell shattered it, the lad slipped and fell, and Grell shoved a foot down onto his chest, ignoring the blows from the other two behind him. "You're dead," he said, and kicked the lad away, who rolled, and wriggled to his feet, panting.

He turned and faced Smithy and his other apprentice.

They stopped hitting him.

He said, "Well?"

Smithy, breathing heavily, said, "Never seen that before."

"Never seen what before?" Grell said.

"One of my pikestaffs broken."

"Eh?" Grell said. "It's only a bit of wood."

"Not wood," Smithy said. "Same as what you're wearing and wielding."

"That's steel?"

"*Kin*steel. Kinblades, and kinskin. Best there is."

"I'll say!" So. This maul of his had just splintered a kinsteel pole. *Well* now.

"So," Smithy said, "what do you think?"

"I think," Grell said, hefting the maul in his hands, and contemplating it, "that this beauty needs a name. And seeing as everything hereabouts is kin-this, and kin-that, I believe I know what her name is."

"And what's that?" Smithy asked.

Grell said, "Kinell."

It was a choice that met with universal approval.

"Perfect!" Smithy roared, laughing. His apprentices and Murruk cackled, and Smithy thumped Grell on the back once again. "Ouch!" he said. He'd forgotten that Grell was kitted out head to toe in kinskin plate. "*Gawds* …. Remind me not to do that again!"

In a nearby field, Chips and Fletch were waiting. Grell and the crowd he had gathered trooped up to join them.

"Here you go, then," Chips said, thrusting a longbow towards him.

It was indeed, as Chips had promised, massive. It felt almost too thick to be comfortable, even in Grell's large hands. But then, when he settled his left hand around its grip and lifted it, everything seemed to coordinate. The bowstring was so strong that it felt like piano wire; but, clearly, it wasn't. He ran his fingers over it and could feel that it was fibrous, rather than metallic. And the fiber felt, somehow, alive. The ancient yew heartwood was lighter on the outside than the inside, which was so dark it was almost purple. He knew why this was, from his conversations with His Lordship of Brigstowe's bowyer. The best yew for a bow was where the heartwood merged with the outer wood. Heartwood for strength, outer wood for flexibility.

He felt like saying that he wasn't the world's greatest archer, but made himself not. *Don't tell them what you aren't,* he thought, *show them what you are.*

He took an arrow from the quiver that Fletch held for him. It was armed with a target head, not a warhead.

And there was the target, no more than fifty yards away.

Well, with luck he might be able to hit that. He drew.

It had been effortless to wield the maul. Drawing this massive bow took every ounce of his strength. He brought the flight back to his ear, settled, inhaled, held, waited between heartbeats, and loosed.

To his relief, the arrow hit the target. Nowhere near the bullseye, where he'd been aiming, but a good two or three inches in from the one o'clock edge. Phew. Not a total embarrassment, then. He looked again.

The arrow had slammed almost entirely through the thick, straw-stuffed target.

And that was an arrow armed with nothing but a practice, target head. *Wow,* Grell thought. *This thing packs a punch, all right …*

He looked up, hearing the murmurs and chuckles.

Fletch was shaking his head, Chips was grinning. The spectators were buzzing quietly.

Chips said, "Fletch bet you'd never be able to draw that! He and I tried together, him left me right, and we couldn't, not even the two of us—but I knew you could. You stick to your trade, old son," he teased Fletch, "and I'll stick to mine!"

"It took all I had," Grell said.

Chips snorted. "I should damn well think so too! You think I'd make you a bow that wouldn't get everything you have out of you? Right, want to try a bodkin?"

"Sure," Grell said.

Fletch held out a bodkin. Rather than a conventional slim arrow-head, a fat, rounded bolt tipped the shaft, a good eight inches long. Bodkins are for punching through armor. Or for taking down horses. *Pity the poor animal that had this brute shot into him,* Grell thought. He took the bodkin, thinking, *that head looks far too heavy for the shaft, it'll never fly true.*

But, to his surprise, the arrow felt scarcely heavier than the target arrow he'd just shot. He balanced it on one finger, and the center of gravity was in the shaft where it would be on a normal warhead, not partway along the bodkin tip itself. He shook his head in surprise, thinking, *amazing work, this kincraft.* He didn't need to feel the bodkin's tip to know that it was as sharp as the points on Kinell's head.

He nocked. He drew.

He aimed. Inhaled. Held. And, between heartbeats, loosed.

Again, the arrow struck nowhere near the bullseye where he'd been aiming; but again, at least he hit the target.

He could hear the crowd murmuring with shock.

The bodkin had punched a hole the size of his fist through the thick, straw target.

Bleeding hells, he thought.

Chips strolled over, and said, "Been a while, right?"

Grell nodded. He knew how out of practice he was.

Chips said, "Couple of things …"

They got to work.

It was a couple of *hours,* more like, and in them Chips had many more than a couple of things to help Grell with. By the time they broke for a midday meal, Grell's arrows were grouping tightly in and around the bullseye, both on the fifty-yard and hundred-yard targets. Chips complimented him on his technique, and Grell silently thanked Serjeant Bastard for all those long, cold days in the Brigstowe butts.

Chips relieved him of the bow, to make his final adjustments, while Grell sparred with volunteers, armed with every kind of weapon. Then he shot again with Chips, while Smithy fine-tuned his armor. Fletch balanced every arrow in his three quivers—two of razor-sharp warheads, sixty in each, one holding forty of the thicker bodkins. The 'prentice boys took care of his arms and armor, polishing and cleaning, and sealing up the quivers against the rain.

Grell was pouring with sweat by the end of the afternoon. The master craftsmen, with several of the crowd tagging along, took him down a path through the woods to a secluded glade by the water's edge. At its center was a large pool, from which steam was rising. They all stripped off and jumped into the lake, which was as cold as you'd expect so close to the winter solstice. The Kinfolk got that bit out of the way as soon as they could, and scuttled shivering for the hot-spring-fed pool in the glade. Grell, being an Orc, didn't mind the cold, and swam around lazily for a while, numbing his aching muscles. And then lumbered into the hot pool.

Children appeared with trays of herbal elixir. Grell sipped, and simmered, and felt all his stresses and strains melting away.

I could get used to this, he thought.

That evening they shared another meal, the friendly Kinfolk telling him everything they could think of, and Grell replying with as much as he dared. After supper, in her sanctum, Healer Ria inspected his foot and gave him a sleeping draught. Early the next morning, Grell donned his self-sealing kinskin armor, settled his weapons and packs about himself, and followed Murruk and the three master craftsmen onto the raft.

The Kinfolk had provisioned him with everything they said he'd need, including two light, thin kincloth blankets rolled up on top of his pack. They didn't look as if they'd be much protection against the winter cold that he'd be trekking into, as he climbed the Sunset Mountains, but he wouldn't be surprised if kinfolk tailoring was as advanced as the rest of their crafting. At the mainland shore they said their goodbyes. He could see, by their anxious expressions, how much they hoped that he would succeed.

"I'll give it my best shot," Grell said. "Wish me luck!"

They did.

They waved him off down the woodland path, and watched him go, as he trudged on towards the task that lay ahead and disappeared into the trees.

Now that he was alone, Grell had time to think. No, it almost certainly wasn't a coincidence that this side quest for the Kinfolk was going to take him precisely zero miles out of his way. They'd known he was going there. That's why Murruk had been waiting for him—but did they know why?

They probably had some idea, passed down the generations in their kinlore. It seemed that they didn't want to stop him doing whatever else he was going into the forbidden place to do. Grell wondered, *How does this extra piece of the puzzle fit?*

Oldface had sent him to get his Nature back for him. Which is what he was now also going to attempt to do for the Kinfolk. So, presumably, the two errands weren't incompatible. It seemed odd, though. Wasn't it their sacrifice that had made the binding of Varamaxes possible? Clearly, he didn't have the whole picture yet. And that bothered him.

The further he walked the wilder the country became—and the wilder the creatures that lived in it. That night he heard wolves, several of them, moving across his path ahead of him. He was confident he could see off a few wolves. It would be an unlucky wolf that tried to bite through his kinskin plate, he thought, as he drifted off to sleep in the warm cocoon of his kincloth blankets.

The next morning dawned gray and misty. Grell almost walked into her before he saw the bear ahead of him. The bear, clearly, knew that Grell was approaching, as she was sniffing the air, and was down-wind of him. She saw him and reared up above him on her hind legs. That was when Grell saw the cubs behind her. *Not good.* He unslung Kinell and waited. He had no wish to harm mother or cubs.

The mother snarled at him. It wasn't a battle cry before an attack, more a warning, *Come no closer!* Grell backed away until she was lost in the mist in front of him. That took only a few paces. Visibility was no more than twenty yards. He kept backing, not turning, in case she came charging out of the blankness that he was staring into, straining to hear. He started moving sideways, to his right, as well as backwards. He heard nothing, saw nothing. Best to take a big circle around her, he decided, and hope she wouldn't come after him.

His detour took him well out of his journey path, but he never saw the bear and her cubs again. He was climbing, now, up into the foothills of the Sunset Mountains, so even as the winter day grew milder, the mists never completely cleared, and eventually merged into low-lying clouds. It was a long, damp, tense, tiring day. But it ended well. He found a cave, under an overhanging wall in the hilltop. It was unoccupied. And dry. He'd be warm enough in his kincloth blankets; even so, a fire would be nice, he thought. But although there was plen-ty of wood nearby, for he was still well below the tree line, it was all sodden. He had tinder and flints, but was no magician with fires, like Oller. Or, indeed, like Daxx, who could put a Flameball into a wet pile of logs and have them blazing in no time.

Not for the first time, Grell wondered how the others were getting on. He'd done plenty of soloing, in all his adventures and on all his explorations, but that had always been by choice, by way of a rest from running with a crew. Here, soloing was anything but restful. It brought with it the added anxiety of worrying about the others—never mind worrying about what he was going to find when he reached his desti-nation—and, would he let the team down?

He slept in his armor, wrapped in his cloak and blankets, dry and warm. Sleeping in his old niblun armor, on the way down to the Floor of the World, had been awkward, but bearable. And it had been better to wake up stiff and sore than to be attacked in the night without it.

This kinskin, though—this was something else. It almost seemed to flex with him, as he shifted around on the dirt floor of the cave. He even tried pulling at it, and twisting it, to see if that was what it was indeed doing, but he might just as well have tried to twist a tree. Solid on the outside, no question. But from where he was standing—or rather, lying—it felt fluid. He'd never known anything like it. And when he woke, to another gray, misty dawn, he didn't have an ache anywhere in his body—least of all in the foot that Murruk had skewered.

Interesting lot, the Kinfolk, he thought, as he loaded himself up with his gear. *There's much I'd like to ask them. As would the others. Daxxie would love to talk Heals with Ria.* He hadn't, Grell suddenly realized, seen any casters among the Kinfolk. At least, none that he could identify, with heartstone-set staffs. But there was clearly magic there, in the healing, and the tailoring, and in the crafting of armor and bow, and Fletch's arrows. And this maul. Kinell was no ordinary maul indeed.

The one problem with her, that he'd found so far, was how to carry her on his back. If any diamond-sharp bump on her head touched his skin, it cut, hard and deep. Mounting her so high that his head would never accidentally rub up against hers threw him off-balance, with the bulk of her weight leaning way above his shoulder and rocking with each stride. He tried rigging up a sling, using his backpack, but that didn't work.

Eventually he just decided to carry her over his shoulder. She nestled up against the deflecting strike-plates on the pauldron on his shoulder, her head well back and away from his. She was no trouble to carry like that, and was ready to hand, should it come to blows. Which, no doubt it would, soon enough. He wondered what against.

The snow began to fall late that afternoon. It was gentle enough, and there didn't seem to be a storm coming, but it was cold. Very cold, well below freezing. By his calculation, and going on what Oldface had told him, the entrance to the seal wasn't too much further. He should reach it the next morning. He'd need to be fresh and well rested, for whatever lay within it.

So, an early night, he decided. He kept his eyes open for shelter, but it didn't seem that he was going to be lucky three nights in a row. He trudged on, and up, and thought, *Looks like I'm in for another night out in the open—in this snow, in this cold: And a long, winter night at that.* Not the coziest of prospects, even with his remarkable kincloth blankets.

There were rocks, plenty of them, as he made his slow way on. He supposed he'd have to pick one, soon, and hunker down in the lee of the wind behind it, and wrap up and settle in. He was resigning himself to the idea, and telling himself, *Well, at least I've got plenty of food, and that nice, warming tincture that Healer Ria gave me, and my kincloth blankets …. And it's only one night, I'll just have to lump it,* when he saw the orange gleam in the mist ahead.

He stopped. Peered ahead through the drifting snow. Moved closer.

It was, indeed, what he'd thought it could only be.

Firelight.

Grell unsloped Kinell from his shoulder and held her at the ready as he slowly moved forwards. Mist, cloud, cold and swirling snow. The suffused glow of firelight. The wind moaning. He looked down and saw his footprints, big fat Orc marks pitted deep into the snow. There'd be no pretending he'd never been here, then. But there was no sign of anyone else. No other prints. And yet, yards ahead, a fire. In this weather? Out in the open?

The closer he got, the brighter and warmer the glow of the fire became.

And, as the night closed in on him, the more enticing it looked.

He didn't trust anything about it—much though he'd like to get close to a nice warm fire.

The air around him was dark as he edged towards the firelight. The snow was growing heavier, and thicker, as the night wind whipped up, and whined in his ears.

He stepped into the pool of light around the fire.

There was no one there.

There was no *fire* there.

No burning sticks and logs.

Just flames.

22

A Little Light Magic

Light Magic, I learned, is, another form of seeing, but one that doesn't involve the eyes. It seemed to me, as Avildor explained the basics to me the next morning, to be somehow akin to Marnie's Awareness skill of Thinking Into other people—which is, in a similar way, another form of hearing.

He was showing me around his study, which was filled with more than just books and papers. As well as bookshelves, there were high chests of drawers, topped by glass domes containing living colors that shone, and faded, and cycled through the spectrum. One cabinet contained dark, polished spheres, neatly arranged in padded sections. Their surfaces seemed to be brown glass, with bands of copper encircling them around poles and equator, but they reflected no light.

Avildor noticed me staring at them, wondering what they might be.

"Orbs of Remembrance," he explained. "From those who have come before me, so that their memories may refresh mine. I shall leave my own beside them, when it is time for me to join the Light."

He led me past strange contraptions of wooden wheels and cogs and leathern belts, which stopped, and started, and clanked, seemingly at random. It was a busy, bustling room that felt like a workshop full of artisans going about their business.

There was nobody in it—as far as I could tell—but us.

He sat behind his desk and motioned for me to take the chair opposite him.

"I was able to see you by finding your Light, when you came ashore," he explained. "I had been seeking it ever since the ghost ship sailed from Mayport."

How in all hells, I thought, could he do that? The stony beach where I had washed ashore was two days' walk from this tower, where we were now.

Avildor smiled, and answered the question that he knew I was asking myself.

"The 'sight' that Light Magic endows me with can see through obstacles, as well as over long distances. There is much that it cannot do. I couldn't see the details in such a faraway scene, such as the waves, or the rocks, or the cliffs above them. In essence, you might say that I could only focus on *your* essence; which I saw, very clearly, as light. Green light, in your case, weaving in and out of red light."

Of course, I thought. Just like Shift's green-and-red tourmaline heartstone. I felt my staff quiver in my hand as she thought the same thing.

"It confirmed something about you," he said, "when you told me about your stick and stone. *Green light good, red light bad,* is the general opinion we who practice Light Magic hold. Those whose reds are deep and dark are to be avoided. Your reds are bright; but for someone to have both red and green is a conundrum."

"What about other sorcs?" I asked. "Battlemages, and so on? The harder they hit, the redder their Light?"

"Perhaps," Avildor agreed. "But there's a lot more orange than red in those of us who have those powers. And they are few and far between these days. The Cult of Varamaxes hated them, and killed all that it came across. The Devoted Children hold that they alone should have power in this realm. So, the Arcane Arts that are permitted here do not include skills such as yours. Marnie has told us about your Ice and Fire and Storm, and so on. Suchlike have been long forgotten here, if they ever were known.

"Well, that's the official line anyway. We're an independent lot, and who knows what my guildfellows get up to in their spare time, eh? And Coven, as my good lady wife will no doubt tell you, come and go and do as they please. Which irks the Devoted, but, as Co-ven steer clear of Devoted and do nothing to upset them, they don't give grounds for offense. What they, and we, do behind the scenes: Well, I wouldn't tell you even if I knew more than a hundredth of it. Suffice it to say that, from our point of view, we are all on the same side. And it's not the side of the Cult, any more than it is the side of the Devoted."

He stopped and held my eyes. "There's a long game being played here, young Daxx. We know what they're up to, more or less. They don't know we're even *in* the game. In a nutshell, as I hope I made clear last night, our time has come. All that remains is to ensure that their time has gone. Which," he added, "is where you come in."

I blinked, surprised. "It is? How?"

"That remains to be seen. It will depend on the choices you make. You've promised Mother Abbott that you're going to put an end to the threat once and for all. Are you?"

"I'm going to try."

"Are you? Why?"

"Fifty thousand gold?" I suggested.

He nodded. "A considerable sum, I'll grant you that. I don't believe, though, that you are motivated by money."

He was right about that. Money was just about the last thing on my mind. But I wasn't going to change my story.

"Isn't everyone?" I said. "It's easy to sneer at money when you've got it, but when you have to survive, it's just about all you can think about."

"Money didn't bring you here," he pointed out.

I wasn't going to tell him about Oldface. So, I gave him the answer I'd given Mother Abbott.

"We thought we were sailing off to answer some kind of plea for help. We didn't know about any of this. So, no. I won't say no to any reward that comes my way, as who would? But now, I just want to get out of here alive."

He grunted. "Well, there's only one way to do that."

"Which is?"

"Avoid being captured by the Devoted again. They won't let you get away twice, not after what you did to get rid of your escort. As far as they're concerned you've made your guilt plain."

I nodded. It was hard to disagree with that.

When he saw that I wasn't going to volunteer any more information, he spoke again. "I suppose," he mused, "if Thief had been the one to survive your shipwreck, he might have made for the nearest branch of the Thieves Guild? Which would have been a bad idea, as those scoundrels would have shopped him to the Devoted as soon as he made his number. Or Monster: I wonder where he'd have gone. If he'd had any sense, he'd have headed off into the wilderness. We have many of those in this realm, sparsely populated as it is.

"What numbers there are of us here tend to concentrate in a few unneighborly patches up here in the north. Below which … well, even our maps disagree about where the realm ends, east and south. West there are the Sunset Mountains, and no one in their right mind goes far into them. Dancer? Well, she was a surprise to us. We'd never heard of a swordswoman like her. I'd have liked to have met her. Where would you have gone, if you'd been her and washed up ashore here?"

I shrugged, trying to show a calm I didn't feel. I was pretty sure he was playing with me. I'd already asked myself the obvious question: If he could "see" my light, why couldn't he see those of the others as we came ashore? And I'd assumed that the obvious answer was that he could and had.

I wondered if he could still "see" them. How far might the range of this Light Sight stretch? Much though I'd like to ask him, and much though I longed to know where the others all were now, I wasn't going to. Because I wasn't going to change my story. The risk of being wrong about him, however small, was too great to take. As he'd said, a long game was being played here. I knew better than to play it unwisely. *Keep my cards to my chest; don't lay them on the table.*

"How should I know?" I said. "I don't know this realm."

"No," he agreed, eventually, letting me off the hook. I tried to stifle a sigh of relief. "Of course you don't. Well, if I'd been her, I'd have steered clear of the Mercs Guild, because they're even worse scoundrels than TG, and I'd have kept my eyes and ears open for job opportunities. Those she was suited for wouldn't be strictly legitimate jobs, not with her skill set. Reavers, down south towards the Great Waste, I'm thinking. They can always use good swords. They lose many to the guards of the caravans they prey on. Or the ports to the east, beyond the Heartline Mountains, far from Kingsworth and the king's law. They're a law unto themselves there, more or less. And offshore, the Morning

Isles? Well, those that sail there don't fear His Majesty's navy, is the kindest one can say about them. So, if I were her, I'd be long gone by now, beyond the reach of the Devoted.

"Which leaves just you. To do what was meant for the four of you." He leaned forward and fixed me with his shrewd gaze. "Or, of course," he continued, "something else entirely."

He held my eyes, smiling, and waited for a response.

I didn't have one.

Abruptly, he leaned back, and spoke again. "You have outwitted Mother Abbott. I won't ask what it is, but I find it hard to believe that you don't have a plan. And I'm not about to interrogate you. My good lady wife gave you much more of a grilling last night, even though you didn't notice it. She took a good long look at you, much the way Marnie did. But no," he chuckled, seeing my shudder at the memory of Marnie's huge, red eye burning into me, "you didn't feel a thing.

"Don't worry, I'm here to help, we both are. I shall tell you what we believe you should do, should there be four of you, which as we know there aren't. And I'll initiate you in Light Magic, and get you started on learning the art. And then we'll see you on your way. How does that sound?"

I said, "That sounds very useful. It's very kind of you."

"It will be my pleasure," he said. "You're doing this for us, as well as for you, you know, so it's the least we can do. 'Kind?' Yes, well, indeed it is kinder than what the Devoted would do to you, or the Cult, should that side win their war. So, for the Light, you need a flame. You saw my predecessor's, in the light chamber up above. Bright as day, and strong as steel, and good as gold, eh? And all," he said, reaching down and opening a small drawer below the table near his right hand, "growing out of this. Or one like it."

In his hand was a ring. A simple gold band set with an oval-shaped, orange gem.

"It's beautiful," I said. "What is it?"

"Fire opal." He offered it to me.

I took it and turned it over in my hand. It was a pretty thing indeed. It made me smile just to look at it.

"What do you think it means?" he asked.

I considered. My answer, I thought, was going to tell him more than I realized.

"Well," I said, "you've told me a bit about fire, and about light, and about your predecessor upstairs, spreading his light across the night seas; and about Light Magic, and how that means another way of seeing." I paused, to pick my words. "I would think," I guessed, "that this is a light."

Presumably this ring, when I knew how to wield it, would emit a beam of light, to illuminate a path, or a room. I looked up at him, confident that I'd got the right answer. An immediate thump on my back from Shift told me that I hadn't, even before Avildor frowned at me in surprise.

"A *light?*"

"Or, er—a flame," I moved on quickly. A fire opal that, um, fires fire."

Shift, on my back was now quivering. She was laughing at me.

"It's not a weapon, Daxx," Avildor said. "I didn't ask you what it does—and, needless to say, it does none of those things. I asked you what it *means.*"

"Oh. Right." Embarrassed, I returned my attention to the fire opal ring and studied it again. I couldn't think clearly. I reached out to Shift but got nothing—presumably because I wasn't holding her in my hand. I turned the ring over and over, losing myself in its beauty. I became absorbed into the dancing flecks of fire-colors in the opal. Tiny glints, as of pent-up power, waiting to emerge, to grow …

"I think," I said, speaking before I'd thought it through, "that this is a seed. And what grows out of it is what it finds in you. As if," my thoughts clarified, "I am the soil. So, what this makes of me, it would never make from, or for, anyone else. It will tune itself to me, you might say. Grow out of me. No, wait—*outgrow* me. This will become— or, rather, *I* will become, because of this—more than I can now know. Together. The two of us. Greater." I stopped, turning the thoughts over in my mind as they presented themselves to me.

I looked up at Avildor, and gave my answer. "Power. Light needs power to shine."

Avildor's eyebrows rose. He nodded, slowly. "Your intuition for the Arcane Arts is profound, Daxx. It is buried deep within you. Open your mind, as you have just done, and it will reveal itself."

I nodded. "I will, Avildor. Thank you."

He held out his hand for the ring and studied it. "The fire opal," he said, "is a stone of power, as you divined, but also of protection. Power for those who wish to walk their own path. Protection on that path. No soldier, be he ranker or lord, needs one. Their power is in numbers. It is obvious, for all to see.

"Those of us who walk alone are different. Our power is hidden—until it is revealed and shines out in its truth." He held out his right hand. "My predecessor, my mentor, gave me mine when I came to him as apprentice." On his ring finger, his ring: A simple gold band, set with a single, glowing fire opal.

"This one," he said, holding it up, "I made for you. Ring finger, right hand," he said, noticing that it was already occupied.

I removed the silver ring and put it down on the workbench between us. Avildor looked at it with interest.

"Where did you get this?" he asked.

"I was given free run of the treasury at the Orphanage, to equip myself."

"Interesting," he said. "We'll need to take a look at that later."

He handed me the fire opal ring he'd made for me, and I slipped it on.

It fit perfectly. I looked at it on my hand. It belonged. Not only that, it *mattered*. I could feel a warmth in its simple gold band. A potential. Time slowed as I gazed at it. A thought bubbled up in my mind: *From here, to where … ?*

I closed my newly ringed hand around Shift, so that she could get to know our new ally. I sensed her interest in it. Silently, I spoke to my Lightfire ring.

Where will you take me? What will we do together? Between now and … wherever we end?

I hadn't expected an answer and didn't get one. The answer lay ahead. We'd seek it out together.

I looked up at Avildor, and said, "Thank you."

I knew he'd seen something settling within me. That was all he needed. He was all conviviality again. "My pleasure," he said, nodding. "Now you need to learn how to use it. Eventually, you won't even need it, except for real challenges, such as seeking over a long distance. So you will be able to remove it and still use the power it has taught you, should you wish to equip yourself with some other magic item, for example. To start with, it is your teacher. It's quite possible that you won't even get a glimpse today. Don't be downhearted if you don't.

"Remember, always, that this is not 'power' so much as *your* power. You. Yourself. On *your* path. Which, whether we have companions or not—such as my good lady wife, or your sadly drowned friends—for the most part we always walk alone. Just as we are born alone and die alone. You walk it alone, with your individual passion, your energy, your drive, your desire.

"Your fire."

As he spoke, I felt that no one had ever told me so much about myself, in so few words, and so accurately, so deeply. I felt overwhelmed. Something, here, was beginning. And, probably because I was staring at it, I imagined that I felt the warmth of the fire within the opal ring seeping into my finger.

Avildor pushed back his chair and rose to his feet. I stood too.

"Ready for her to give you your first lesson?"

Light Magic, thankfully, came easily to me. Within an hour, I could close my eyes, and concentrate on the fire opal on my finger—*putting my mind into it,* Avildor called it—and through it cast Lightseek, and within moments locate the dim, gold glow that was my mentor.

It would fade after a second or two, at first, but was soon stable for five seconds, then seven or eight, by which time I could also track his movements. By afternoon the secrets that he shared had given me the basis of a whole new skill line. I sought him, and found him, in other rooms, on other floors of his Tower of Light.

The tests became more and more challenging. I was to count, slowly, to a hundred, while he went outside and hid. I Sought about for him, and found him, eventually, crouched behind the stables, a faint blob of gold, visible in my mind from forty feet above him, through several walls. The glow faded within seconds, but by then I was on my way to where I'd seen him. I had to stop to make two more casts, and then I was at his side. It was, I thought, like using heat sensors in a game.

It was a curious, stop-start variation on hide-and-seek, in which moving interrupted the process. It would be a while, he told me, before I could walk and seek at the same time.

"You'll get better as you work at it," he said. "Nothing comes without study, and practice. You've done better than I'd feared. Learning a magic skill line—well, learning *anything,* really—is all about aptitude and attitude. Clearly, you're open to this, to Light Magic. You have the aptitude. Work at it, and who knows where you'll get to? Mayhaps, you'll come back here one day and be my apprentice, and take my place in the chamber when my light fails." He chuckled. "Although I think that not likely. You're more of a wanderer than a settler, in my view."

Yes, I thought. You're right about that. I have a universe to explore.

"Will you be able to see me?" I said. "Where I'm going?"

"For a while," he replied, "until you fade into the distance."

Mastery of this Lightseek skill would be great of course, I could see that—but how about this basic ability for a start? I'd have comms with the others, even if they only worked one way and they couldn't reciprocate. I'd be able to find them, whether they knew I was Seeking them or not. That was so surely going to be useful. I couldn't help thinking ahead, and wondering when any of them would be within range.

Avildor explained that, to start with, I'd only be able to Lightseek for those I knew. Later, as my ability developed, I might be able to find others, if I had information about them that would help my "aim," as he called it.

Elun was my next target. She proved harder to find than Avildor—which was, he said, because I hardly knew her. Her color was purple. She was sneaky. It took me a long time to pin her down even once. Next try, nothing. The one after, she fooled me and was somewhere entirely different from where I was looking.

Slippery skill, this, I thought. Shift was easy to find: Bright red and rich green, shining where she stood propped up in our bedchamber. I could see her from two hundred yards away, through walls. Which was not surprising, Avildor said, seeing that I knew her best of all.

It was a long workout. Towards evening, as we headed back to the tower, he told me that I'd done well. "The more you practice, the easier it will become, and the further you can Seek. Light Magic will also give you Insight," he added. "For when you can't see what you're meant to be looking at. Or for when you want to look for yourself."

I said, "Why would I want to do that? I know where I am."

He turned to me and raised an eyebrow. "Do you?" he asked, with a smile. "Always?"

I didn't know how to answer.

"Put your mind to it," he said. "When you're more skilled, you'll see what I mean."

Back in his laboratory, Avildor wanted to find out about the jewelry that I'd chosen in the Orphanage treasury. He was interested that I'd chosen these particular pieces without knowing quite why, just relying on instinct. He cast Lightseek on each piece, and, as their colors glowed, he gave me his readings of what they were. The bracelet of red stones was a boost to Shift's firepower. The copper stag brooch was, in essence, a battery, which would increase her reserves before she became drained—very useful in combat. The gold ring with its large green jewel would strengthen my casts of Healing and Protection. The gold torc, which I was wearing around my neck, would increase my own reserves of health and stamina.

The silver ring set with blue stones, that had caught his eye when I'd taken it off, gave him pause for thought. "This," he said, "is a ring of evasion." He studied it, and then chose his words carefully. "I wouldn't have thought this would be for you," he said. He paused, then, handing it to me, and looking me in the eye, added, "but what do I know? Everyone would rather evade damage than take it, I suppose."

Once again, I felt busted. He surely knew that the others had survived the shipwreck, and that, without knowing it, I'd picked this ring for one of them. I wondered which one. Oller? Evasive enough already, you might think. Qrysta? Grell? Well, who couldn't do with avoiding damage? The moment would present itself, I thought, in which the choice would become clear.

We ate an early supper. Avildor had warned me that I had a long night ahead of me. He looked out as the sun set beyond the Northern Ocean, where his mentor's light was already slowly panning its long beam over the darkening sea. "Better than last night, eh?" he said to his wife. "Not a cloud in the sky. You'll be able to show him everything."

"Fifty years of reading the stars?" Elun retorted. "All in one night."

He chuckled. She knew what he meant.

"How did he do?" she asked.

"Better than I'd feared," he said, "considering what Marnie said about how he couldn't grasp her *In* Magic."

She wiped her lips with a napkin, pushed her chair back from the table, and stood up. "Well then, young 'un," she said, "come with me."

I followed her up the stairs, through the storeroom and the light chamber, and up and out onto the floor of her observatory. We'd been up there the previous night, but thick clouds had made stargazing impossible, so we'd gone back down to the library, where she'd set my curiosity on fire. The first impression of this knowledge that I'd gained in the library of the Huntsbroke GAA had been confirmed by everything she'd said, as she showed me her books, and star charts, and astrolabes. Here, in Mourvania, study of the night sky was indeed a conflation of science and magic. An amalgam, I'd decided. Just like Ken. This realization felt, somehow, comforting—as if I was on the right track.

On this second night, by contrast, the sky was ablaze with stars.

There was no light pollution. The beam tracking rhythmically across the Northern Ocean was aimed downwards, in a tight focus, and little of it leaked up in the direction we were looking. The walls of the observatory were topped by a collar that sloped outwards, blocking light from below. It made the space we were standing on feel protected, and private, and aimed upwards towards the stars. I knew that I was there to learn, to listen—but all I wanted to do was look, wherever my eyes led me, and to wonder.

Elun said nothing, for a long while, letting me drink in the glory of the heavens. I was both on edge with excitement, and lost in awe, as if dreaming. I turned, slowly, in all directions, studying the layout above me, recognizing constellations from my lessons the night before. All was silent, but for the distant murmur of the waves far below.

"When we look to the stars," Elun said, after a long while of contemplation, "we are always reminded of how small we are. We cannot go there. We cannot despoil them, as we harm our own world. We do not even influence them. But we are not nothing to them. They influence us. Why would they do that, if we were nothing to them?"

She let the question hang between us.

"One disappointing answer, of course, might be that they cannot help it. They just do what they do. Their influence spreads, and affects us as it passes, and they may not even know that we exist down here. But I do not believe that. For that would be to believe that we do not matter. Do you, Daxx, believe we do not matter?"

"To us? Or to the stars?"

"Don't answer a question with a question. You know what is happening here. The war between the gods and demons. On our mortal plane. Consider why they are doing that. Why here? Why them, those two? Would they be doing that if we did not matter?"

I thought it through. "Yes, quite possibly."

She averted her gaze from the starscape above us and looked at me. "Why do you say that?"

"It's obvious. They might not care about trampling all over us, and wreaking havoc, while all we want is just to get on with our little, humdrum lives. Why do they have to think about us? Isn't that just—human arrogance?"

She considered what I'd said. "Interesting. It is generally assumed that they *do* care about us. That what we think of them is … important to them."

"Well," I said, "that's only because *we* think we're important. And that we must somehow matter in this game of theirs."

She said, sharply, "Game?"

"War," I said, correcting myself. "Struggle. Which, well, maybe we don't come into? Maybe we're just—innocent bystanders? Collateral damage?"

She studied me. "Aren't you forgetting something?"

"Almost certainly."

"What are they gods *of*? Mercy and Suffering; against Hunger and Despair. States that we mortals undergo."

"So?" I replied. "If they really cared about us, wouldn't they stop all that? We don't need any of it. Wouldn't we be better off without those in the first place?"

She inhaled and sighed. "You're talking about what 'would' be. What matters to me, is what *is*."

She stopped.

I waited.

"Yes," she said. "In an ideal world, of course. We would all live happily ever after. This world, sadly, is not that world. So, let us move on from what we don't know about to what we do." She lifted her gaze to the heavens again, as did I. Above us, a million diamonds scattered on black glittered, enticing the eye so that it was impossible to know where best to look.

She pointed to a group of stars above us. "Do you recognize that cluster?"

I studied it. A dozen or so points of light, in an awkward, angular arrangement … I knew that I'd seen it before, both in the Huntsbroke GAA and in her own library the previous night—where she had shown me so many constellations that I struggled to recollect any of them.

Then I recalled the outline of the figure that had been drawn around it and recognized it.

"The Demon," I said.

"Indeed. Now, what do you notice about it?"

I studied it. It didn't, to me, look much like the seal, or the mural that I'd seen in the temple of Varamaxes. As to *noticing* anything about it—what did that question mean?

I said, eventually, "What am I looking for?"

She seemed to like that question. "Well now, it appears that it is my turn to answer a question with a question. Which is: What are you looking *at*?"

I studied the star cluster. "Thirteen stars."

She said nothing.

I wondered if I was meant to add more.

I couldn't think what. I didn't want to bring my vague knowledge of modern astrophysics into the discussion. *Thirteen gaseous flaming suns of various sizes and ages, all at various distances from both each other and us, which only appear to have a relationship to each other because we're looking at them at this angle, from this spot in space. Who knows how many tens, or thousands, of light-years away they actually are from each other?*

I didn't think any of that would help. I wanted to listen, and to learn, from an expert in her field, not to give some kind of half-baked lecture that she wouldn't comprehend.

"Yes," she said, at last, quietly. "And that is the problem."

I waited.

"You don't see it?" she said.

"No," I admitted.

"When we studied the maps of the heavens, last night?" she hinted.

"I'm sorry," I admitted, "I must have missed something."

She chuckled. "Missed, indeed," she agreed. "Something that is *missing*."

Ah. A hint. I studied the constellation again, comparing it with my recollections of the old engravings in her star charts.

And then I saw it.

I closed my eyes, to review my memory. I wasn't sure, but her talk of something missing made me think it was more than just a stab in the dark. "There should be fourteen," I said.

"Yes," she said, "there should. The charts that I showed you are old, hundreds of years old. In all of them there are fourteen stars in The Demon. Then, only two or three centuries ago, the star-readers saw, and recorded, no more than thirteen.

"The question that has been occupying us, since then—and by 'us', I mean those who study these mysteries—is: *Why?* What happened?"

Well, again, I could have unloaded my little learning on her, and said, *Well maybe one of them went supernova. It happens, stars explode and die.*

I didn't.

Elun continued. "By our calculations, this happened around the time that young Chidian overthrew the Cult of Varamaxes. Now, you can't see her, because she is below the horizon at this time of year, but if you could, and if you were observant, you would see that The Protectress also now has one light missing. She who is diametrically opposed to The Demon up there, across The Axle, our pole star. And she lost that light, according to the record, around the same time. Coincidence?"

Well, possibly. Two stars many millions of light-years away from each other die; that doesn't mean they have anything to do with each other. But things were different here. I remembered what Jewelwright Neva had said: *I don't trust Mr. Coincidence further than I can throw him.* So, I wasn't going to say anything. I needed to hear what Elun was getting at.

"So, what's the answer?" I said.

"We believe that the two are connected." She waited.

Eventually, I said "Is that … significant?"

"Extremely."

I couldn't see why. But I didn't want to come across like an idiot. "Because?"

"They have both lost something. Some part of themselves."

Okay, I thought. I was having a hard time thinking of a couple of dozen supermassive balls of superheated gases millions of light-years apart having anything to do with each other. We just happened to be in the middle, and the people here looked up at them, and saw what they thought they saw, and made up their own stories, and … came to their own, not necessarily very well-informed, conclusions. And one of those supermassive balls died, and another. Why do we read something into that? Something portentous about us? Knowing what we know, how can we think that we are anything to an exploding sun millions of light-years away?

And yet … I was all too aware that I didn't know what I was talking about, nor what I was thinking. Elun knew far more than I did.

"Do you know what they've lost?" I asked.

"No. But I'm fairly sure I know where they lost it."

She waited for me to pick up the thread.

"Down here?" I suggested.

"Down here," she agreed. She listened to the silence of the night sky, looking up and away at the stars overhead, and came to the point.

"We know they are enemies," she said. "We know a god and demon are in a war. We know they have been waging it *here*, on *our* mortal plane, for centuries. There is nothing we can do about that, you'd think. Us being mere mortals. But ask yourself: What are they fighting over? Us? Possibly. But I'm inclined to agree with you, that we are hardly their first concern. What do people usually fight over? Principles. Ideas.

"Mercy and Suffering," she continued, after a pause. "Hunger and Despair. What reconciliation is ever possible between those opposites? If none, then what is the answer? Their war will go on forever. Or until one of them wins." She stopped, thoughtful.

"What are you trying to tell me, Elun?"

She turned her gaze from the heavens and looked at me. "I don't know," she admitted. "Fifty years of struggling with this study, these questions, this knowledge …. Sometimes, I feel as if everything that I have ever learned has got me nowhere. *What are they fighting over; what have they lost; must the war go on forever? I* know all the questions, and none of the answers. But the answers are out there, including the ones we have been seeking tonight."

Staring up at the infinite space above us, in that star-filled darkness, I felt both awed, at the beauty of the night sky, and insignificant.

What was I, to all that majesty?

"I also," Elun said, turning to me and laying a hand on my arm, "believe that you will find those answers. And to do that, you will need this."

She handed me a small book. It felt familiar, even though I couldn't read its title. I popped up a Glow and smiled.

Of Gods and Demons
A Guide to the Known Heavens and Hells
With Star Maps

The next morning I saddled up and we said our goodbyes. Avildor and Elun filled my packs with provisions, which included a bewildering number of Elun's potions. "It may be that you won't need all of them," she said, "but better to be safe than sorry, eh? You'll be a long way from anywhere if you ever have sudden need of my scorpion salve, the which you'll need to slather on double-quick if you hope to live after a sting. I've labeled them all, and there's my notes in there about each of them; you'll want to study those."

I was thrilled to have them. I'd told her that we'd lost all our buffs in the shipwreck, and she'd had no idea what a "buff" was. I'd said, "Potions, like these." I thanked her, and her husband, mounted my bay mare, and rode off, leading my three spare rides behind me. I left the other horses I'd taken from the Devoted with Avildor, to do with as he wished.

I was taking another long way around. I would first be heading south, traveling mostly by night, and avoiding towns or settlements. And then, where the Last Bay stretched west again, I'd circle below Lastharbor and strike out west for the Sunset Mountains.

On the way, well away from prying eyes, I experimented with the three staves I'd picked out at the Orphanage. I didn't know what woods they were. One was the color of sand and mud, a sort of ochre. The other two were black, and blacker. Ochre had no offense at all that I could find. She could, though, cast Heals to a level that Shift and I were nowhere near reaching. The Wards that poured from her would bloom around me as green as her peridot heartstone.

Nothing that I threw at them from the other two staves could make a dent in them. It was impossible to damage myself with my own magic, so I cast some sharp attacks at the horses, and then stood back to see what she could do to heal the damage. She was seriously good. She could also calm them, to allay their fears.

I have to say I got a bit loopy trying to see how much damage I could do to them, knowing she'd save them. The answer was: A ridiculous amount. Ochre was a deep wellspring of care and healing indeed.

Black was a tricksy beast. It took me a while to figure out what he was trying to show me. Every time I raised him, to cast, he'd drag my arm down, and point his sullen, mulberry-purple amethyst the wrong way. Eventually I stopped fighting him and left myself open to learning what he intended. When I gave him his head, he positively heaved on my arm, aiming downwards. One by one, I discovered that his unique attacks were subterranean. His amethyst eye would brighten, and its mauve beams would pockmark the ground with pits, which I could never see, or with quicksands, or hot, bubbling mud pools. His traps were ferocious—not just Ice Traps, which were my go-to cast, but the ground itself, grabbing at my targets with rock teeth, or coils of clay. And he had range.

We startled many a deer and fox and badger and bear, on our way. All they could do was struggle and protest. And those traps lasted way longer than Shift's had ever done. I healed them with Ochre, who soothed their spirits, as I had no wish to ruin their days. When she cleansed Black's traps, and released them all, unharmed, they calmly went back about their business, as if nothing had happened.

Blacker was the unsubtlest of the lot. She didn't like me. I don't think she liked anyone, or anything. After a while, I decided that she probably hadn't liked her caster either. But, *gods,* could she hit! She hit with all the spite of her infinite disliking.

I knew better than to aim her bloodstone at a tree. Nyrik and Horm, back in Jarnland, had told me that I didn't want to anger the trees, and I most definitely did not want to anger them out there in the wilderness, with nothing but them all around me. Rocks, though, I thought. Would I anger the rocks, if I tried Blacker out on one of them? Perhaps. But perhaps they wouldn't be able to catch me, the way the trees would.

I tried out a simple Boltbomb at a boulder on an open stretch of moorland, well away from any trees that might take collateral damage. Boltbomb uses the electricity of lightning to permeate the target, where it builds up, rapidly, swelling within its victim, and then, as the bomb part of its name indicates, explodes. It's a base-level attack, nothing too advanced, not fancy but effective—good for spamming into enemy mobs. Decent defenses will stand against it, and just deflect it away, not allowing it in among them to do its work.

That boulder, old and huge and solid as it was, did not have decent defenses. It would have taken me a week with a lump-hammer and wedges to do serious damage to it. Blacker blew it apart in seconds. A sizzle, a hum going from low to high to hypersonic, as the boulder swelled, and a bang of thunder as it burst apart.

Fragments of granite whizzed past me. I reminded myself not to do that again. My horses, back where I'd tethered them a hundred yards away, were panicking. I calmed them with Ochre as I hurried back to them. All I could think of was, *I need to get the hell away from here. That rock's friends are not going to like me.*

Well. I could fight with these three and heal. I wasn't at all sure how to swap staffs around in combat, but I supposed I'd just have to learn.

As I rode south I tried my Lightseek all the time, on the way to our rendezvous, for two reasons: First, to improve my ability. Second, to find my friends. So, I'd Lightseek animals that I found nearby using Reveals. Reveal weasel, Lightseek into it, find its light, lose it deliberately, wait, cast Lightseek, try to track it. I got steadily better. These were simple targets, of course, and nearby. But the skill came to me, I was pleased to find, steadily if slowly.

I wasn't much better after four days than I had been at the Tower of Light, but I was improving. I stopped to cast Lightseek regularly, as I rode, but never found a trace of my friends. I hoped that this was a good sign. If I'd found any of them, I'd have changed course and headed for them, so that we could join forces on their missions. But I didn't. So, either they were all still beyond the range of my lowly skill with Light Magic—or they were no longer on a plane where I could find them.

Which would mean that they had found, and entered, their portals.

23

Fire on the Mountain

Grell stared at the writhing flames, taller than he was, dancing above the snow, orange and yellow above red—but fed by nothing. He, in turn, had nothing in his head. *Right,* he decided. *Puzzle.*

Is this important? Relevant, even? Could he just walk on by? Leaving behind … what?

An unsolved puzzle. Fire. On the mountain. Burning above the snow.

He stood Kinell head down on the snow-covered ground and leaned on her. And contemplated the flames. So now what? Whack them with Kinell? Yeah, right: Big thick Orc, all he can do is whack things. Is that my go-to move? Can't think what to do, so just whack? Why do I have to make the obvious "Orc" move?

Hit Problem With Big Thing. No. Surely not.

Not every Orc has to behave in the obvious Orc way. Klurra wouldn't. Smart, that girl. She'd think things through. She'd work this out.

Well, if she could, so could he.

Fire. Mountain. Snow.

No, wait: This wasn't a fire. This was just flames. Fed by no fuel source that he could see. They were growing out of nothing.

What did that mean?

They were real flames all right; he could feel their heat. It was love-ly, in this bitter cold dusk. Fiercely hot, if he got too close.

So … what were they coming from?

He thought, *heat rises.*

Grell hefted Kinell and held her at the ready.

No, he wasn't going to whack the flames. He wanted to find out about them, not just make them go away. Gently, he poked Kinell's lumpy head into the space between the flames and the snow that they were burning above.

His maul didn't poke up against an invisible pile of wood. But above her, the flames shrank, shriveled, and died.

In the sudden gloom, Grell looked around, expecting attack.

What just happened?!

His nerves were stretched taut, jangling.

This has to mean something. There's no way this fire on this mountain that holds my quest isn't something to do with it. What in all hells?

He was looking this way, that way, turning and listening and star-ing into the darkling gloom, at the ready, in full combat mode.

Nothing but shadows, and drifting snowflakes, settling on and around him, and cold.

Until, turning, he saw a new soft, orange light shining through the mists ahead.

He trudged towards it, onward, upward, into the gusting, snow-filled wind.

It was the light of, he saw as he neared it, another stack of flames.

Orange and yellow above red, writhing and hot and living, and taller than he was, and fed by nothing.

He stared at them.

Were these flames, he wondered, here for him? Orc he may be, and tolerant of cold, but their warmth was so lovely. He could settle by these flames, in his blankets, and wake up warm and fine when the night ended. But, then: Who would have done this? Wasn't he head-ing for a challenge, deep below these mountains? One that might well involve a fight to the death?

So, why would anyone bother to keep him alive, out here, only to kill him later? He couldn't think of an answer. And if the flames were nothing to do with him, specifically—well, what *were* they to do with?

Why were they here? Not to mention *how* were they here, hot and bright above nonexistent bonfires?

He didn't know how to think about this. The valley, far below and behind him, lay shrouded in gloom below the tree line. Bitter wind was whipping snow into his face, and night was already upon him. *These warm flames, way up here* …. It didn't compute. They had to be burning here for a reason. But what? It was hard to believe that there was some other purpose up here, which didn't involve him, and that he just happened to be a lucky traveler passing through and getting the benefit of their warmth. No.

And it didn't feel like a benefit. It felt like threat and warning. Flames don't grow out of thin air above snow. The whole scene said *unnatural*. Grell was wary of the unnatural. *Unnatural* usually meant danger. And the more unnatural, the more likely it would be that the danger involved magic. He didn't have Daxx with him, to help him out with counter-magic. He had no magic skills himself, so he wouldn't be able to fight …

…*fire with fire*.

He thought about that.

He held Kinell towards the flames.

Instead of using her to cut the root of the flames off from their non-existent bonfire, as he had done before, and instead of whacking the flames, obvious Orc style, he put the head of his maul into them.

At their top, their hottest part.

The diamond-sharp edges of Kinell's business end began to glow.

Soon, she was a thousand points of light.

He removed her from the flames.

The flames came with her.

Kinell was now both weapon and torch.

As if they had now transferred into Kinell, the flames that had lit her died back down into the snow and vanished.

Kinell burned on, bright and strong.

Again, unnatural. Torches burn wood; they don't flame around kinsteel, which they aren't feeding on for fuel.

Nice, though. Comforting.

Grell held her in front of him and walked on up the mountain.

Well now, he thought. *I wonder how that happened. And, again, why.*

Fire with fire.

His spirits lifted. Using the flames, to his benefit, made him feel that he was, somehow, getting on top of this puzzle.

On, and up. The walls of the high cliffs on either side closed in around him. He was walking, now, through wind-driven snow, into a narrowing cleft between them. He stopped and looked up. The cliffs disappeared into the night sky. He didn't think he'd be able to climb up either side. Only one thing for it, then. Keep going forwards.

He set off again, on, and up. Looking ahead, with his eyes narrowed against the snow that was now whipping around him, he saw another light emerging, faint against the gloom. A small point of red, dark red below yellow and orange, that seemed to swallow the blackness of the night. He approached it, his flaming maul aloft. Another pile of flames, yes, once again not fed by any natural fuel; but this pile of flames wasn't standing in the open. Behind it was a massive boulder that blocked the way ahead. He could see where the two cliffs met behind it. They had merged into an impassable, impossibly high wall. He looked at the boulder, and thought, *Well, there's no way I can move that.*

He didn't have to.

The boulder moved itself.

As he watched, fiery Kinell at the ready, the boulder unfolded itself, with a sound like a landslide, stretching, expanding, straightening. Standing. Rearing high on two huge legs. Towering over Grell and staring down at him.

Grell saw eyes of red fire within a head made of stone, it seemed, but it was a liquid stone, in a halo of deep red flames. Its hands were holding a great stone club nearly as tall as Grell; its limbs were of molten rock. It reached out, and pushed its club into the flames, and held it there.

Grell stared at his gigantic opponent. He knew what would happen. The club would catch fire, as Kinell had done. And then: Well, he didn't think this lava giant was going to stand aside and let him pass. He was going to have to go through it.

His mind raced. He had, he knew, only seconds before the attack. The stone club was already beginning to glow. *So, how do I do this?!*

He did not have the advantage of size, nor the advantage of reach. Nor the advantage of being made out of molten rock.

What advantage did he have, if any?

All he could think was, *Well, looks like I'm the little guy here ...*

As he thought that, the memory of Little Guy in Niblunhaem came to him. Dressed in his niblun battle leathers, streaking across the cavern to catch the stick that he'd hurled for him …

Speed.

He reached into his pack for the flasks that Healer Ria had put there for him. Knitbone, Goodnight, Moonview. He found the one he was looking for. Fastbreak. He uncorked it and drained the flask. *Let's go,* he thought.

The lava giant removed its burning stone club from the flames and started towards him. Grell hefted Kinell and charged. He was through the giant's legs and pulverizing its feet from behind with Kinell before it had even noticed. The lava giant roared, and flamed, and turned. Grell sped around inside its reach, slamming Kinell into its knees and thighs and crotch, at hyperspeed, screaming.

Kinell hardly made a dent on the giant's skin. But sparks leaped off it, wherever she struck, and lines that leaked hot, black lava scratched across it wherever she hit. Under the influence of Fastbreak, Grell had all the time in the world to avoid the giant's blows. He shot in and out, feeling as if he were Qrysta, dancing—*Wow, this is what she does!*—while hammering Kinell into any part of the giant he could reach.

It got better and better, and he got surer, and more confident, until the first thump of the lava giant's club caught him. He didn't understand. He was flying, dazed. He'd been in the right place, doing the right move. He ploughed through the snow, only still alive because of his kinskin armor, sliding to a halt, spluttering. Everything was, suddenly, awkward, out of tempo, wrong. *Slow.*

Fastbreak had worn off.

He rolled aside as the flaming stone club slammed into the ground where he'd just been. He jumped to his feet, breathless, and turned to face his foe. He stared at those burning red eyes, eyes that held no common humanity. He was dead, he knew, unless he won this fight. And he was slowing and weakening.

Achilles tendons, he thought, and raked Kinell across them. The blows made little impact. A few blooms of black, steaming lava blood. The giant's burning club smashed the ground around him. The brute was no more tired than it had been before this battle had begun. Grell knew that he couldn't outlast it. He needed the kill, and soon. Another couple of minutes, and he'd be out on his feet. The giant lifted its club in one hand, distracting Grell, and backhanded him with the other. Grell felt his kinskin plate buckle around him, as he flew across the snowfield. *Gods*, he thought. I'm out of my depth here. Had he done any damage at all?

Yes, he saw, as he struggled upright, shaking the snow out of his face. Clearly the lava giant was lurching, awkwardly, rather than striding with confidence. The blows that Kinell had rained into its feet had eventually, cumulatively, had an effect. Grell saw, *right rather than left.* He focused on the right foot. He skipped in and out, with whatever strength still remained to him, and pulverized. The giant slowed under his relentless assault. It stopped. It could no longer support its weight on its right foot. Grell, at the end of his tether, his stamina drained, got a final boost of energy when he saw that.

I can move, you can't. Time to die. With his last reserves of energy, he charged, all systems go, beating the lava giant's left foot until it was also immobilized, and then smashing at heels and calves and ankles, until his foe toppled and fell. He stood over the prone body, gathering his last ounces of strength. The lava giant lay there, face down. Grell stepped around it, walked up to its head, and swung Kinell down into the back of its skull, again, and again, and again. At last, the stone skull broke; the maul bit; the giant juddered and died.

Grell dropped to his knees, exhausted, his lungs heaving.

I'm not even in there yet, he thought. *Was this the guardian? Or just the first boss I have to fight my way through?*

And then, the molten stone corpse beside him began to move. Grell wrenched himself to his feet, alarmed, maul at the ready. He watched, as, with a noise of crackling and crunching, the giant's arms and legs and head shrank inward, and its torso swelled, and rose out of the snow-covered ground, and merged, and settled into place, and stopped, and cooled.

He was looking, once again, at a boulder—one that might have been lying there, on this mountain, for as long as the mountain had existed. Snow began to settle on it.

There was one difference, though, between this boulder and the one that the lava giant had risen from.

It was no longer blocking his way.

And that way, as he could see by the light of the fireless flames ahead of him, led into a dark hole in the mountainside.

299

Okay, then. Keep going forwards.

Grell refreshed Kinell's flames in the hovering fire and held her up high above his head. Her light threw red shapes and black shadows ahead of him. He took a deep breath and entered the cave.

The snow stopped abruptly. The wind died, its noise fading as he walked on. And down, and along. He was on a hard, dirt floor, sloping ever downwards, along a tunnel that was neither wide nor claustrophobic. His spirits lifted. Hadn't he done this before, a hundred times? *Down into the delve, to see what we shall see.* Alert, armed and armored, capable. On edge, yes, of course, but not scared.

Hardened to combat as he was, Grell didn't think about fear. He thought about the task. Every now and then he stopped and listened. He peered ahead, as far as the light of Kinell's flames would let him see. He heard nothing, saw nothing. Felt nothing.

On, then. Down, and down, into the heart of the mountain. He'd often thought, on his long march from the shore where the storm had thrown them, why it was these three particular things they were questing for. Nature, Power, Mind. Why not, say, heart, as in the heart of this mountain? Spirit? Strength? Blood?

The things that they were to find and recover were all, he decided, nonspecific. *Go and get my stolen sword.* Straightforward. But what *is* a nature, or a power, or a mind? Trudging on down the long, shadow-filled tunnel, he asked himself that question again. He wondered what a "Nature" might look like. He had no idea. But he wasn't going to have to search for something he might not recognize. Thanks to Murruk, he knew where it was—trapped inside an iron chest.

He stopped.

Something was nagging at him, trying to get him to see what was right in front of his eyes but that he hadn't understood yet. He frowned, puzzling.

Grell shook his head in frustration. *I'm onto something, I just know it ...!*

Right. Take as long as you want. Follow every thread, until you're sure they lead nowhere. From the beginning.

Recap: I left the Woodlake. Trekked into these mountains, days and nights. Up into the clouds. Fire. No, check that: Flames without a fire source. Boulder coming to life as a giant of molten stone and attacking me.

What aren't I seeing here?

Gods know. I don't even know what I'm looking for.

Well, no, wait a minute—I do know that. I'm looking for the Nature. In fact I now have two quests to find Natures.

Grell felt himself hanging suspended on the threshold of a discovery, holding his breath …

The pieces, one after another, clicked into place.

He exhaled, slowly, and smiled.

He shook his head. *I saw the answer long ago,* he thought. *Only I just didn't realize it.*

Flames with no bonfire.

Boulder coming to life.

And what did I think?

Unnatural.

He recalled what Oldface had told them. *Each is protected by its opposite. Its counterpart, its nemesis, which will do everything it can to keep that which it guards imprisoned.*

The Nature. Imprisoned by the Unnatural.

Grell nodded. That, at last, made sense.

Whether it was right or not, he thought: *Well, we'll soon know.*

But it would explain the unnatural flames, and the cold boulder that became a giant made of red-hot lava, and his flaming kinsteel maul. Stones don't come to life; flames don't exist without fire; torches don't burn steel. *Unnatural.*

He walked on. Down, and down.

After a while he heard running water. Underground stream? Well, possibly. Why not? Here, at the heart of the mountain, it might not be freezing, and water could flow. He could see, beyond the light of Kinell's flames, an opening into a chamber ahead. It was filled with its own light—a soft, rich blue, the blue of an early dawn. He approached the end of the tunnel cautiously, and peered in.

On various ledges and mounds, some close and some far away, plants and trees were growing. Moss, vegetation. The air was warm, and damp. Odd. All this, without sunlight? But there was light here, that mild, blue light, suffusing the cavern. No doubt that fed the plant life down here. Grell looked up, and around.

On the edges of the cavern's walls, trees grew in all directions. Down, towards him, as well as up beyond him. Normal trees don't do that. No, wait—*natural* trees. These were growing at unnatural angles, inward, outward, downward, backward. In the middle of the cavern there was a waterfall, fed by a river. The waterfall rose from the floor, and plunged upwards to the cavern's ceiling, where it churned along in a fast-flowing stream until it disappeared into a fern-fringed chasm above.

Unnatural.

This, he felt, was where he would find what he was looking for. The Nature, held in check and guarded by the Unnatural.

He walked into the cavern, looking around in all directions. Right, so where is it, then? Kinell's flames made the trees and rocks and circular ledges nearby gleam red and gold. He heard no sound above the roaring of the wrong-way-falling waterfall. He saw nothing moving beyond the cascade tumbling up to and along and into the roof above. His feet sank into moss and mud. He waded towards the cavern's center, coming out at last onto a dry bank of stones and dirt. All around him, trees and vegetation leaned in at absurd angles. To either side, paths led who knew where. Ahead was a high, smooth, dark gray wall, granite, rearing up to the cavern's roof. Something, he saw, was gleaming up there, between the wall and the chasm into which the stream plunged upwards. He peered.

Yes, he thought. There it is.

A portal.

Hanging from—or should that be standing, upside down on—the ceiling.

That portal was what he had to go through, but there was no way that he could see of reaching it.

Everything upside down.

Maybe, he wondered, that included him?

He didn't feel upside down. His feet were solidly planted on the ground.

Only one way to find out, he decided.

He crouched, and put his head on the ground, and set his hands down to make a triangle; then, unsteadily, levered himself into a headstand.

He wobbled there, upside down, long enough to realize that that wasn't the answer. He hadn't dropped up to the ceiling. So, not that then. He got back to his feet, and brushed the dirt off his hands while he looked around.

He studied the waterfall, and the rushing river above—a torrent, disappearing into the chasm. He did not like his next thought. *Am I* going to have to jump into the river? Let it carry me up the waterfall there, and along, and then—I'd have to grab the ceiling and haul myself out, before I'm swept away and flushed up off into gods know where.

Grell grimaced. I'd have one shot at it. In my armor, carrying all my gear, because Oldface warned us not to leave anything we'd need behind.

He looked at the cavern's ceiling. The churning current was swift. And the ground up there, he thought, that looks slippery, with all that water spraying around. And moss, which would be slick. No, I don't like my chances with that idea.

He stared at the glowing, upside-down portal standing downwards from the ceiling—what, sixty feet above him?—and thought, how the hell could he climb up there, without a ladder?

He answered his own question. He couldn't.

So, what? He was screwed?

Yeah, clearly. Gods ...

What was it Daxx always said? "When you can't find the solution to a problem, turn it around and peer up its backside until you see daylight."

Grell had got the general idea, but still didn't really know what Daxx meant.

Turn it around, peer up its backside. Okay, let's give it a try.

Slowly, he recited the problem. Backwards. Ladder a without, air the in feet sixty, there up climb he could hell the how.

Fat lot of help. Help of lot fat.

What don't I see?

He sighed, and took a deep breath, and tried again. Ladder a without—

He stopped. He didn't have a ladder? So, make one.

The next realization was almost instantaneous. Almost before he'd started thinking about cutting down trees and lashing them together, Kinell and his pack were down, his bow was unslung, and he'd nocked the first of Fletch's bodkin-tipped arrows to the string.

He hauled back on the string, aiming a couple of feet above the ground, and loosed.

The bodkin punched into the granite wall, and stuck.

Grell walked over to it and tested it. It was immovable. Not only that, but frost was spreading from it. The Kinfolk bow's imbuing, Frost.

He stepped up on it and rocked up and down. It didn't budge.

Yes, he thought. Instant piton.

He walked back to his gear, and, thirty bodkins later, he had his ladder.

He worked his way up it, carefully, one rung at a time. He could feel the sharp cold of the bodkins through his kinsteel gauntlets. Frost that severe would slow any foe to a halt, he thought. He looked forward to trying his bow out in combat. She'd need a name too, he decided. *Kincold*. Perfect.

His Orc feet were almost too wide for the rungs that the bodkins had become, but he'd be okay, he thought. He would manage.

As he neared the ceiling, the thunder of the torrent funneling into the chasm was almost deafening, its spray splattering in his face. Now for the tricky part, he thought. He hoped it wouldn't matter which way up he was, relative to it, when he entered the portal. Anyway, he didn't have enough room on his makeshift rungs to try to maneuver himself around and stand on the ceiling. There was no sense of gravity suddenly reversing itself up there. He was pretty sure he'd simply plummet straight back down to the cavern floor.

He looked down, to see where he'd land. His head swam, and he immediately wished that he hadn't. He looked back up again, clinging onto his narrow ladder, letting his dizziness subside.

Woof, he thought. *That had been unwise.* His head cleared, and he decided *the sooner this is over the better.* He stepped one foot into the white-blue sheen of light that was the portal and pushed hard with the other. Once through it, he fell, with a thump, onto a blue patch a couple of feet below his head, twisting just in time to take the impact on his back and shoulders. In his kinskin armor, he felt only the slightest of bumps. He rolled to his feet and stood up.

Below him, a ribbon-path of sky-blue light led off into the indigo distance, weaving in and out of and around paths of other colors.

Behind him, the portal.

Well, he wasn't going back that way and falling to the cavern's floor.

Onward, then, and up along his ribbon-path.

Ahead, a platform.

At its center, in a pool of light, was a small iron chest.

Grell walked over to it and picked it up. It was about twice the weight that he would have expected from looking at it.

Good, he thought. Had to be a box within a box—just as he'd been told to expect. The Nature, held in thrall by the Kinfolk's most precious possession.

He stowed it in his pack and moved on. He wondered where he'd be coming out of this portalscape. He was pretty certain it wouldn't be an exit like in the helldragon's cave, one which had looped back to a point above where they had entered the delve. Yet again, he thought about the others, where they were, what had happened to them. He hoped that, now that he'd completed his task, he'd be seeing them again soon.

He weaved around other rainbow threads, wondering where all the starflakes had gone. It was eerily still without their glassy, discordant humming. Another long, twisting path looped the loop around itself as it rose and led him up onto another platform.

At its center, perched behind his high desk, was a familiar, black-robed figure, scratching away at a piece of parchment with a quill.

The clerk looked up as Grell approached. He said, "Hello again."

Grell said "Hello." And then, "Do I need a ticket, or something?"

"No," the clerk said, dipping his quill into his inkwell and then offering it to Grell, "I just need you to sign for that." He nodded at Grell's backpack.

Grell read the words on the parchment.

Nature, 1 (one)
Natures, Kinfolk
Iron chests, 2 (two)

Below them was a dotted line. Grell signed.

The clerk dusted it dry with fine sand and blew on it. "Thank you," he said, putting it in his out tray.

Grell said, "Can I ask you a question?"

The clerk contemplated him. "By all means."

"What is this place? How does it work?"

"It is a connection system of shortcuts. *How* it works is by exploiting both science and magic; but it's easiest to think of *what* it does in terms of mathematics. It subtracts you from out there and adds you to wherever you leave. Obviously, you cannot subtract from a vacuum. Even using magic. The helldragon, for example, knew her way all over the place, and became perfectly used to popping in and out, and then flying long distances when *out* to find another way back *in*. With her ever-growing hoard of treasures."

Grell was surprised by the completeness and detail of the answer. He'd expected something mysterious and confusing. That explanation could hardly be clearer.

"Who are you?" he said. "And why are you here?"

The clerk said, "Oil and water don't mix."

"I'm sorry?"

"It's the same with science and magic. They dislike each other. Magic could be thought of as science that hasn't been understood yet. We know that such-and-such a spell unleashes a Flameball, but we don't know how it does it. You've seen Flameballs?"

"I have."

"Can you explain them?"

"No."

"Well then. My job is to keep an eye on things. Make sure that everything runs smoothly. When you mix science and magic you tend to get unstable results. As you can see from the paths. One of which you will need to take to get out of here."

He waved an arm, and Grell looked around. Everything, it seemed, was down from there. The platform where he'd found the iron box was far below them, a pool of light at its center. The colored ribbon-paths led on, and away, in all directions but up.

Grell said, "Which one?"

The clerk shrugged. "Any of them. They all lead out."

"But to different places, right? Which aren't near each other?"

"Correct."

"So, how do I find the one that takes me where I want to go?"

The clerk's eyebrows rose in surprise. "You know how to read a map, don't you?"

"Yes ..."

"Well then."

Grell frowned. He walked on and stopped at the far edge of the platform. He gazed at the indigo horizon ahead. Ribbon-paths disappeared towards it, bright nearby and fading off into the gloom. Glowing in the distance, standing out against the inky backdrop, were more lights. Some were mere points, as if faint constellations. Others were larger balls of light. He studied them. There was something familiar about the arrangement of them. He couldn't think what.

He wondered, yet again, where he was, and where he was going.

And that was when he saw the pattern. He got out his map and studied it. He held it up in front of him to compare with the distant lights ahead.

He wasn't looking at constellations. He was looking at a map of Mourvania, made of stars. He could see where they had been washed ashore, and the towns and cities and rivers and roads marked on the paper map he was holding. Well, he knew where he wanted to go next: High Rock. He spread his map on the ground, got out his lodestone, and placed it on it at his destination.

He looked up at the star map.

Slowly, the point of light in it that corresponded to High Rock grew in brightness as the lodestone turned towards it. Something orange emerged from beneath it. Grell watched as a ribbon of orange light began to flow towards him. It suffused the space between them, the orange of the path that he needed to take outshining all the other ribbons.

He turned to smile back at the clerk, and to give him a thumbs-up *thank you.*

The clerk, and his desk, had gone.

Grell stepped onto the orange ribbon-path and made his way along it, through the empty indigo depths no longer filled with discordant, humming starflakes to its other end.

24

The Last Town

Qrysta and Jess sparred every day, morning and evening, on their trek through the Heartlines from Lindfirth to the last town. Sometimes they used the sticks, knowing they were of the same length as each other's. Sometimes Qrysta let Jess use the weapons the armorer in Lindfirth had found for her. Poniards, he'd called them: Short swords with long, slender blades like daggers. They weren't of the quality of Qrysta's niblun blades but were light and maneuverable enough for Jess's young arms and wrists.

Jess had been unable to believe they were actually hers. On the first day back on the road, heading south, she kept drawing them and admiring them, and practicing moves with them—skipping and twirling beside Qrysta as they walked. That night Qrysta added another move to Jess's repertoire. Jess saw how it blended with the ones that she already knew.

The next morning, Qrysta opened her eyes to see that Jess was on her feet, practicing her forms. The same moves, again, and again, and again. Qrysta watched. The girl's feet were still awkward, her rhythm ungainly, her paces unequal, jerky. There was no flow in her steps yet. They breakfasted, and then Qrysta made Jess put her blades back in her belt.

They crouched, on their heels, and started moving around, low to the ground, Jess copying Qrysta's every move. She took slow steps, fast hops, long slides, sideways shuffles, her backside always as close to the ground as she could get it. Jess found it almost impossible.

"You have strong legs. We've seen that with all the walking we've done," Qrysta said, hauling the girl upright after yet another tumble. "But it's not the right kind of strength yet. It'll take a while, but keep working at it—you'll get there."

Late that afternoon they made camp, and then it was an hour of crouching and forms, and half an hour of archery until dusk and supper. The next morning Jess couldn't stand up. Her legs had seized up like iron. But she refused to complain.

"I'll walk it off," she said, as Qrysta helped her to her feet. But she couldn't walk either.

Qrysta lowered her down to the ground again, face down, and went to work on her leg muscles, banging her knuckles into Jess's thighs and calves and kneading the lumps out of them.

Not much muscle there at all, really, Qrysta thought. *All skin and bone, this girl.* But hard skin and hard bone, and a hard, determined mind, no doubt about that.

"I've been pushing you too hard," Qrysta said with a grin as they took to the road again.

Jess said, "I don't mind." She walked the cramps out of her legs soon enough.

That afternoon, they headed east, away from the road, towards the last town. Woods, and hills, and streams, and eventually the spine of the Heartline Mountains, for five days, more up than down. At least their nights were more comfortable now, in the layers of clothing and the cloaks and blankets that the little Lindfirth tailor had made for them.

On the fifth afternoon they came down to the eastern ridge of the Heartline foothills and looked at the landscape spread below. Most of it was a carpet of deep green dusted with white; a forest of evergreens, stretching towards mountains on the far horizon. Nearer, though, at the foot of the pass that they had climbed over, was a darker patch. The town. And the castle that loomed above it, across the bridge that spanned the silver glint of a river.

They studied the wide vista before them, taking in the lay of the land. The air was cold. Snowflakes fluttered past, the wind in their faces, their cloaks whipping around them. Above, the sky was the color of lead. The sun, hidden by heavy clouds, was already settling towards the mountains behind them. There were no more than a couple of hours of daylight left; but that would be enough time for them to reach the town before the gates were closed for the night. Not much more walking now, after days of it.

"How are you doing?" Qrysta asked.

"I'm fine," Jess said.

She didn't sound it. But she sounded determined to sound it. *I'm not tired, I can keep going.*

"Hot food," Qrysta said. "A fire, dry clothes, warm beds. How does that sound?"

Jess managed a smile. "Sounds good."

"On we go, then!" Qrysta said.

She wasn't feeling too good herself. She'd argued, with the others, about whether this was really the task best suited to her. *I'm no good with puzzles,* she'd pointed out. But Daxx, who was good with puzzles, had to go for his tribunal before the Devoted. Oller was to find the Power, and that job involved sneaking and stealing. So, no question about that. Grell's task was to recover the Nature.

Why couldn't she do that? Anything Grell could kill, she could kill better. But Grell needed to stay well away from watching eyes. The Devoted would be on the lookout for them, and an Orc would stand out around the more populated areas. Best if he headed into the wilderness, where he wouldn't be seen. On the road, she and Jess would look like two ordinary travelers. Clearly, the Mind had to be her task.

It was a task that would take her many leagues beyond the little town that lay below them, on the edge of the Forest of Secrets. Whiteholme, it was marked on her map. It seemed a cold name, an unwelcoming one. *You won't be noticed there. Grell would be,* she reminded herself.

The eyes and ears of the Devoted would be everywhere that there were people.

None of these jobs will be easy, the others had pointed out. *Okay, so yours is the vaguest of them all, and you'll have to work it out when you get there. So, do that. No good at puzzles? Then get good, Qrys! Fast. Or we're finished.*

Qrysta hadn't liked it. She liked knowing what she had to do, and how to get there, and then she was fine. Put her in combat, and she was in her comfort zone. But now, without the information, knowing that she'd have to figure out what needed to be done and how to do it—she hated the spot she was in. She hated that she might let the others down. She hated that she was taking Jess into, *argh,* the unknown.

Well, tough, Daxx had said. *Get your head around it and solve the problem!*

Easy for him to say. She had no idea what the problem even was yet.

Only where it lay. Down there, between the last town and the horizon, hidden in that carpet of dark green dusted with white. *Forest of Secrets.* Qrysta didn't like secrets. She liked to know what was what.

She and Jess tramped and slithered down the steep, snow-covered path. There were no footprints on it. No one had passed this way all day. Or—for how many days? Down there, that little town, Qrysta felt, was a place apart. Few went to it, buried as it was in this endless forest, lost to time.

The path joined a rough, muddy road from the North, White-holme's only real connection with the rest of the realm, which skirted the mountains they had just crossed. The road was deserted. The snow swirled and thickened, and the light faded behind them beyond towering trees that leaned in above their heads. They tramped on in silence, through the falling snow, passing no travelers, falling in with no one.

Qrysta's thoughts chased each other around in her mind as the town walls rose ahead of them. Usually she liked to keep a low profile. Stay out of people's way. Bother nobody. Especially anyone important. Sometimes they would bother her, as My Lord of Hartwell had done, in which case, she had to put a stop to the bothering. But she never picked fights. What was the point? She didn't need to prove herself. She didn't need to kill people for their goods, or their money. Qrysta only fought if she had to. This, though …

In this, she had to take the *lead.*

So, forget the keep-a-low-profile thing. She needed the information. And that would mean talking to folks.

Night was falling as they reached the town gates. No one was coming out, and they were the only travelers going in. The two shivering guards seemed startled to see them. They stood aside, without a challenge, without a word, watching them as they passed. She and Jess turned along the narrow street towards the town center.

There were few people abroad, even though it was still, just, daylight. The whole town had a vacant, furtive air. The marketplace in the town square was empty, its few stalls shuttered. The doors to the surrounding houses were closed. Well, Qrysta thought, there's always a tavern.

There was, but it wasn't much of one. The Holly Bush. A wintry name. It had a good fire going in the hearth, but that was about the only welcoming thing in the place. The few customers in the parlor stopped what they were doing—drinking, or muttering to each other—and stared at them as they entered. Qrysta was used to being stared at, by now, and was unconcerned. Jess instinctively shrank closer to her.

A large, yellow dog, lying by the fire, got up and slunk off into the kitchen, its tail between its legs. Not what tavern dogs usually did—they made friends with people and hoped for scraps. A bald, stooped man wearing an apron was the only person standing. Obviously the innkeeper. Staring at them, just like his customers.

"Good evening, mine host," Qrysta said.

The man animated. "Er, evening, m-miss," he stammered.

"Ale, and a meal, and a room for the night, if you please?"

"Yes, of course, certainly, miss." He seemed flustered by the request. "I'll have my lass make the beds up. Please, take a seat by the fire. We've bread, and cheese, and some offcuts o' ham, and winter pickles, is all—"

"And chickens," Qrysta said. On their way in she and Jess had noticed them, scratching in their run beside the inn.

She held up a gold coin.

Every eye in the room turned to it. The innkeeper was lost for words.

"This should suffice?" she suggested.

"Yes, miss, a pullet, with pleasure, potted up with herbs and roots, all nice and rich." He shuffled closer, wiping his hands on his apron, before daring to reach out for the gold piece. "Make yourselves at home, ladies, the fire is yours, and I trust you'll like our black ale, the first brew of which I've made this winter!"

He hurried off through the open door to the kitchen, calling for Robin and Elyse and wife. Elyse ran through and up the stairs, a girl not much older than Jess, looking at them in awe as she passed. Younger Robin brought in two earthenware mugs, which he filled from a pitcher.

The ale, as he poured it, was black indeed. They raised their mugs silently to the company, who nodded, or looked away, and drank. It was, to Qrysta's surprise, excellent: A fine balance of sweet and sharp, bitterness and brightness. She swallowed, put down her mug, inhaled, and sighed, feeling the miles draining from her aching legs.

She smiled at Jess, who smiled back. *Better than another night in the open,* was the unspoken agreement between them. The fire spat and crackled, warming them. Urgent voices could be heard in the kitchen as innkeeper and wife got to work. There were chopping sounds, one of which interrupted a squawk.

The last town. Which meant the last inn. And the last night in any sort of comfort.

Jess was nodding off when their supper eventually arrived, and they moved from the fireside to a nearby table to eat. It was a welcome spread: A loaf of crusty bread, baked fresh that morning, with a mound of butter, and a tureen of chicken stewed with vegetables—leeks, carrots, turnips, onions, parsnips, white beans, and winter greens. The innkeeper's wife ladled it out into bowls for them. *All nice and rich* it was indeed, in its broth, as her husband had promised. She stood back, while they ate, smiling nervously.

Jess attacked it with gusto.

"She's got an appetite, your lass!" the cook said.

"My sister, goodwife," Qrysta said.

"Ah. Of course. I can see the family resemblance."

"Not surprising she's hungry," Qrysta said, "it's been a long walk."

"Yes. Well. We're a long way from anywhere. What brings you all the way out here, if I might ask, miss?"

Qrysta had her answer ready, which is why she'd dangled bait. *"Sister?"* she echoed, as if the cook should have already understood the message. She knew that every ear in the room was listening. "Guild business," she added.

She saw the thoughts flicker across the cook's face. *Guild. Sisters. Coven?*

The cook's puzzled face opened wide as she realized and thought *better not pry.*

"Ah," she said.

"I'll be sure to mention this excellent meal and your hospitality when I make my report," Qrysta said, with a smile.

"Ah," the innkeeper's wife said again. "That would be most appreciated, miss."

"As is this stew," Qrysta said.

"Very glad you like it, miss. Kind of you to say so." She bobbed a curtsey and left them to their meal.

Well, Qrysta thought, as she ate, *we've been made now.* Wonder if anything will come of it. There's no reason anything should, is there? People go to inns all the time. Their visits don't have to be eventful. Things don't *have* to happen, as they had happened that evening at the White Hart in Hartwell. Ale, a meal, a bed for the night. *Nothing to see here, folks. We'll be on our way in the morning. Coven business. Ask me no questions, I'll tell you no lies.*

Their room was small but warm, being above the parlor. The chimney from the fireplace below bulged out of the wall between their two beds, radiating a gentle heat. Before she blew out the candle that the landlady had given them, Qrysta said, "Are you sure you don't want to stay here?"

Jess was startled. "You heard what he said about not being able to come back! I'd be stuck here forever, I don't know anyone here; I'd rather die with you."

"I'm going to try *not* to do that," Qrysta said. "I'd just … rather not take you into danger."

Jess said, quietly, "I know."

That, somehow, seemed to be that. Qrysta couldn't think what to say.

Jess, too, was thinking. Eventually, she said, "I'd *rather not* have lost Ma and Da, and the babes."

Qrysta considered that. "Mm," she grunted. "Seems we often have what we'd rather not."

Jess nodded. "Keep going forwards," she said. "Isn't that what you four always say?"

"It is indeed," Qrysta agreed. " 'Night, Jess," She blew out the candle. " 'Night."

Qrysta didn't feel safe until they were well away from Whiteholme. She'd been on edge the whole time they'd been there. Strangers are noticed. Anyone might ask questions, cause trouble, send for the reeve. Now, out in the deep forest, she could relax.

Only she couldn't, of course: The forest was full of its own dangers, to which she needed to be alert. Bears, wolves, sabercats—perhaps outlaws. Not that there were any signs of people out here. People might not be the worst of it. Tree-sprites, wargs—possibly even pit elves, or their forest equivalents. All best avoided.

Before too long they'd be where they were heading. And the business would begin. They'd filled up with supplies at The Holly Bush. They weren't going to die of starvation. They might well be going to die from other causes. If not natural causes, then unnatural ones.

Oldface had told them about their tasks.

It had taken him many long years to work out what Blessed Father Abbott Chidian had put in place, to seal him in his confinement. He knew that he'd taken his Head, and his Mind, and his Power, and his Nature—but what had he done with them?

Over time, and after much study, he had reached his conclusions.

Each was guarded by its nemesis, he said. Its opposite.

His Head, trapped in his own reversive mirror, guarded by the helldragon.

His Power, hidden under the sanctified floor of Valmynia's chapel at Cressen.

His Nature, entombed as far as possible from where it belonged, in the cold depths beneath the Sunset Mountains.

His Mind, though. What was the opposite of that? Oldface hadn't known. He'd told her she'd just have to find out. *Mind*. It puzzled her. Oldface was able to think, still—and how could he do that, without a mind? The word must mean something else. But what?

It was only after much wrestling with the question that she thought she might have an answer. What he must have lost—because he could not remember it—was what had once been *stored* in that mind.

His knowledge. His secrets.

Strange that she was going deep into the Forest of Secrets to find them—to find that which, combined with his other essentials, had made him what he was. His divine self, all powerful. Yes, he was still immortal, but a prisoner, confined to the cage in which he'd been sealed, his powers limited.

It was a puzzle. She was going to have to solve it.

They saw no one on their journey into the forest. Whether anyone saw them …. Well, how could they know? All they knew was that they hadn't been stopped or challenged.

They spent the first night wrapped around each other under their cloaks and blankets at the foot of a fir tree. Their exposed faces were chilled by the time the sky began to lighten, but the rest of them was warm enough. Not for the first time, they thanked the little master tailor of Lindfirth. Not twenty gold he'd charged them but thirty, for all that he'd made for them. It had seemed steep at the time; but now, out in the frozen depths of the Forest of Secrets, they knew that it had been a bargain.

The second night they found shelter under an outcrop—not much shelter, but enough to keep the snow off them, and enough room to light a fire. There were plenty of sticks lying around, some of which must have been seasoned for years, drying out in the summers, and soaking up the wet in the winters, becoming as frail as honeycombs.

A few were dry enough to catch. Qrysta had tinder and flint, but it was Jess who knew how to use them. After watching Qrysta try and fail, she'd taken over, and, by patiently blowing on the tongue of flame that she coaxed to life in the tinder, lit the stub of a candle, and then another from that, to be on the safe side. She stuck one candle into the ground and stacked up a neat pyramid of twigs over it, which soon caught.

Other sticks and logs dried out around it as she fed the flames, blowing out the spare candle to save it when she was confident that the fire was going to hold. Yes, it was a risk, Qrysta knew; but they'd left a trail of footprints that anyone could find and follow, so they'd just have to hope for the best. Jess kept feeding the fire until they fell asleep. They both added logs to it anytime either of them woke up. They slept close and warm against the winter night.

They woke in much better shape the next morning, and, after an hour of training, got going, breaking their fast as they walked. The trees loomed over them, oppressive. It was hard going. They had to clamber over fallen tree trunks, or skirt thickets of undergrowth, and cross frozen streams. As far as Qrysta could tell, from the sun hidden behind the clouds above them, they were going east and north. All that she could do was trust her lodestone and follow where it led.

In the middle of the morning of the fourth day, after no more than three hours of walking, they came to their destination. Ahead of them, light. A clearing. They approached it cautiously, keeping to the shadows of the trees.

After the gloom of the forest, the daylight they peered into was startling. Once her eyes had adjusted, Qrysta saw that it was really no more than another dull winter day, but they hadn't seen open space for so long that it was almost dazzling at first.

It was not, after all, a clearing. There was no sign of trees having been felled, just as they hadn't seen signs of forestry—no cut limbs or tree stumps—on their walk from Whiteholme. The ground was uneven, with thick clumps of grass, snow-covered, on a long, steep slope leading down away from them, from all sides, before rising up again far below them in a small tor at the round glade's center.

On the top of that little hill hidden below the forest rose a tower.

It was slight, and black, and at its top had an uneven, forked crown.

Qrysta looked down from her height and studied it. *If only we could glide down from here to its roof, and start at the top. It's always easier to fight your way down than up.*

Not possible; so what was?

There was a path at the tower's base, winding down to the foot of the buried hill.

So, presumably, there would be a door, or gate, or some kind of entry at the top of that path. Which, of course, might be guarded.

Any other way in, perhaps?

There was only one way to find out. They descended the slope on the opposite side to the path. In places it was so steep that they slid down on their backsides. They climbed the sunken tor and scouted left and right. They found no rear or side doors.

Just the one way in, then: The front door. They stepped onto the path that led up the tor and followed it up.

The black tower above them seemed to have no windows, not even arrow slits. It was tall enough, and wide enough, for many people to live in, but it felt more like a monument than a dwelling. And there were no signs of people. No sign of life. Qrysta didn't think that "life" would be the problem in there. She suspected that they weren't going to be dealing with anything living.

Well, she thought as they approached the arched doorway that led into the tower, *We'll soon know.*

It was not long after midday that they stopped by the entrance, but the light was weak, and the interior ahead of them dim. There were no guards, which was good; but Qrysta knew that what they were looking for would be guarded.

"You okay?" she said, turning to Jess.

Bow in hand, an arrow on its string, Jess said, "I'm fine."

Qrysta drew her twin blades. "Good girl," she said.

They entered the tower.

Their feet rasped on the loose stones of the courtyard. Empty, the place felt; but not in a good way. A stone staircase curved upwards around the tower's wall to their right. So, up then. They mounted, Qrysta first, swords at the ready, Jess holding her bow. They crept, stopped; listened, waited. Nothing. The stone flags of the staircase were old and worn. Edges crumbled beneath their feet, and dropped, rattling. They froze. Waited.

Relaxed, if only a hair. Nothing had been alerted by the sounds, or disturbed. Which was a relief, but only up to a point. Something was there, they knew. Sleeping. Or waiting.

They came to a landing. Below them, to their left, the circular courtyard. Above them, the undersides of the stairs, winding up, and other landings, and then the ceiling. Above which, presumably, would be the interior. The tower was no longer a shell, up there, but a keep. They moved up, as silently as possible. Another circuit, and through the ceiling to another landing, walled in on all sides. Ahead of them, a doorway.

The door was closed.

Qrysta took hold of the knob in its center and pulled on it. It would not open. The knob did not turn, in either direction.

Well, why would it? If it controlled a latch, it would be at the edge of the door, not in its middle.

So, she thought. Problem. How to solve it? There was no keyhole. Not that she had a key, but still.

Now what?! She crossed her arms and thought.

Beside her, after a while, Jess stirred. She moved past Qrysta, put her hand on the doorknob, and pushed. It sank into the door.

It clicked, and the door swung open inwards.

Jess glanced up at her.

Qrysta thought, as she always did, *Argh, why didn't I think of that?! It's so obvious! Am I a complete moron??*

What she said, was, with a nod of appreciation, "Smart girl!"

Beyond the door was a dry, dusty room. It was empty, apart from cobwebs. There were more steps going up, nothing more than slabs of stone standing out from the walls now, with gaps between them, rather than a complete staircase. On and up them they went, making another full circuit of the tower. A platform landing. Another door, another knob. Qrysta stepped back and let Jess the expert open it.

A red glow greeted them as they entered the chamber. It emanated from something hanging in midair in front of them. Something, they saw as they approached it, that was staring at them, from empty eyes.

Hanging in the air in front of them, suspended by nothing, was a silver skull, polished to a high sheen and encrusted with red and purple jewels, garnet and spinel and ruby and amethyst, lit from within by that deep, red glow.

The floor around and below it was a charnel house.

A mass of bones, whitened by age, some with shreds of rag and skin still clinging to them, lay scattered across the room. Among them were weapons of all kinds: Swords, and spears, and pikes, and axes; most pitted, many rusted almost completely away.

Qrysta and Jess surveyed the scene.

Qrysta thought, this is obviously *it*, but—why?

An empty skull isn't a "Mind." It's just a container, made of bone. Or, in the case of this one, mirror-bright silver covered with red and purple gems.

She knew better than to walk up to something like that and take hold of it. That was, presumably, what the owners of all those bones had done. Result: All those bones. Was she going to have to fight—whatever it was that had taken all those fighters down? If so, how likely was it that she would fare any better? And there was Jess to think of.

Puzzle, she thought. *And not one that I can duck out of. I'm going to have to solve this without us ending up dead on the floor here and rotting away until we're just bones ourselves.*

She considered the skull. Taking hold could trigger traps or defenses. Yes, something as rare and valuable as this jeweled skull could set a thief up for life. Or, as those who had come here before her had found out the hard way, for death.

She drew her swords and moved them above and below the hanging skull in all directions as she circled it.

Nothing happened.

Nothing changed, but for the shifting light within the red glow coming from the skull as she moved around it.

She stopped by Jess. They both stared at the problem. Oldface wanted his Mind back. Was the red glow inside the skull, his Mind? How could she get that for him without taking the skull itself?

Which she knew that she didn't want to touch.

She thought and thought. Oldface had warned them that their objectives were well hidden and well guarded. This was about as open and obvious as you could get, as if to say, *Come on in. Help yourself.*

So, there's no way I'm doing that. Things will happen when I do. There will be fireworks.

Qrysta crossed her arms, and studied the problem hanging in the air in front of her.

Mind. Skull. Unprotected.

She looked up, and all around. The stairs continued up the walls, she saw, disappearing into the roof. Odd. Qrysta peered up, in the dim, red half light. *Ah,* she saw: At the top of the steps there was a trapdoor into the ceiling. Now, what might be up *there?*

She wondered if any of the corpses around them had noticed the trapdoor and gone up the steps to explore. Quite possibly they hadn't. After all, they'd come into this room, and seen this rich prize hanging before them, ripe for the stealing. And glowing. Attracting their eyes, which might not have looked anywhere else before their hands reached for the unprotected treasure …

Unprotected. That word again. Something clicked in her mind.

What do skulls do? They protect the brain. Where the mind resides.

Maybe this isn't so much *unprotected* as the protection.

And there was another thing. Who were these dead treasure hunters? She would never know; but, quite possibly, they were no more than explorers, adventurers who had found their way here and decided to take a look around this hidden black tower. They very well might all have come there with no knowledge of what the tower held.

Unlike her. She knew what she was looking for. She now knew that this wasn't it.

A decoy. And a deadly one, at that.

"Come on," she said, quietly, to Jess, "we're going up." She led the way up the stone steps around the chamber's walls to the trapdoor in its ceiling.

Around, and up.

They paused, watched, seeing nothing—stopping halfway, listening, hearing only the sounds of their own soft footsteps. Cautiously mounting again.

Qrysta heaved open the trapdoor at the top of the steps, slowly, on high alert.

As she pushed, the trapdoor passed the vertical above her head and wanted to drop.

She didn't let it. She wanted it to make no sound. She lowered it, carefully, to the ground.

She raised her head and looked in. Another chamber. Circular, like the chambers in the other levels below. It was dry, and old, and dusty, and appeared to be empty. She stepped up, and moved in, crouching by the trapdoor. Jess followed, arrow nocked. They were both as taut as Jess's bowstring.

The chamber was lit by a low, pale light. They could not see where it was coming from. They could, however, see what it was lighting: A wood floor, on which two dark, crumpled shapes lay.

As they watched, the shapes began to move.

They bulged, and grew, and solidified, and stood.

And turned to face them.

It was like looking into a mirror: A new Qrysta, in her black leathers, and another Jess, in her brown buckskin, stood in front of them.

Four twin blades. Two whitewood bows.

Qrysta thought, *I'm going to have to fight myself?*

She was never going to make the first move, of course. She was a counter-attacker. She'd wait. *Show us what you're made of.*

The other Qrysta walked forward. Bowed. Drew her swords in a blur of shapes and glittering steel, and found her stance.

Qrysta recognized the message. It was the message in any challenge she'd ever made to any opponent.

You or me.

Behind her, to one side, the other Jess unslung her whitewood bow, and nocked an arrow to the string, ready to draw.

Against any other opponent, Qrysta would have accepted the challenge. Plainly, that was what was expected. But this needed thought. A lot of thought, ranging from, *Why me?* to, *Can I beat myself?*

The true puzzle was: *Why am I standing there, opposite me, ready to take me on?*

The obvious answer: *To fight me, presumably to the death? And Jess?*

That's not what we came here for. If we have to go through "ourselves" to complete the task, so be it. But who says it has to be that way?

Qrysta considered the alternatives. *What are the outcomes? This, presumably, is how our goal is guarded. The Mind. His mind, which we have to go through our own minds to get to.* Qrysta paused, considered. *And anyway, where is it? What does a "Mind" look like?*

She looked around the bare chamber. Nothing.

Just another Jess and herself, facing them, ready to fight.

25

Graycote

I rode, as hard as I could and as cautiously as I could, avoiding all roads and settlements, mainly by night, towards our rendezvous. The others had more than a head start on me. I'd been in my cell at the Orphanage for over a week while they'd been on their way south and west and east. Yes, they were all going the long way around, but any who had managed to pass through their portals would be safe and sound at High Rock by now. All they'd have to do was wait for me there. I didn't want to hold them up. The realm was a hornet's nest of alarm and activity, with patrols of the Devoted searching for us everywhere. If I were captured: Well, I was dead. We'd agreed, the day that we parted after coming ashore, that we would allow each other a month, a moon's full turn, to make the rendezvous. After which, any who survived would attempt the task that Oldface had said awaited us.

As I thought about it all, riding south and, eventually, west, I came to a conclusion.

If I were captured, I was dead. Yes, but what if I was stopped by a squadron of the Devoted, but *not* captured?

Suppose, in other words, I were able to talk my way out of trouble?

That made sense. I needed to give myself every chance I could. They were looking for a caster with three staves. Tall, fair-haired, and with a terrible haircut. Well, I could easily lay a Glamour on me that would make me look different, to all eyes but ones as penetrating as Marnie's. I had four staves now, not three, but they were bound to attract attention—and three of them would no doubt have been described in detail to every search party. I should get rid of them—never Shift—but not before I'd had a chance to explore them, to learn their secrets.

I wasn't sure how I'd accomplish that, as I'd never tried anything quite like it before. But that was no reason not to try. If I could get all the knowledge that was stored in Ochre, Black, and Blacker into Shift, I could discard them. I would then no longer be a caster with multiple staves. I'd be, under my Glamour, whatever seemed best for the situation at hand. Also, if I could pull it off, I'd be giving Shift one hell of an upgrade. Her Heals would be a lot more powerful once I could get her to Ochre's level. And Black and Blacker contained Damage skills that she and I didn't even know existed. I would love to learn them. All it would take was … me in the middle figuring out how to do the transfusion.

Heals first, I thought.

Heals are less likely to backfire if you don't know how to handle them. Heals are benign. If I couldn't transfuse those into Shift, I wasn't going to try the other staves' Damages. That would be playing with fire. Or, worse than fire, which I knew a bit about. I'd be playing with Damages I wasn't even aware of, and so probably wasn't competent enough to handle.

I stood, on a damp winter morning, in a glade in the forest that stretched for leagues in all directions, and put Ochre through her paces. I cast her Shield on myself, and her calm, glimmering green sphere settled around me. I then swapped her out for Shift and used Absorb Magic on the shield. I could feel Shift's confusion up my arm. *What is this?* she was wondering. I kept repeating Absorb Magic, and she kept fighting back, *no, I can't.* I wasn't taking no for an answer. I added Reveals, and that made a difference. Ochre's green sphere hung around me, holding effortlessly, and Shift studied it, now curious, anticipatory. Its essence, the Shield's life gradually revealed itself to her. I could sense Shift changing. Becoming interested. As if she was saying. *Oh. That's new. Hm. Yes, I get it.*

And she did. She opened up to my casts of Absorb Magic and inhaled the secrets of Ochre's Shield.

I cleansed it off me.

I raised Shift, hoped for the best, and through her cast Ochre's Shield again.

A rich, green sphere formed around me.

I smiled.

Shift preened in my mind, and I praised her, feeling her responding warmth radiate up my arm to my heart. She had got it indeed.

I fired off a few attacks at myself: Cloudburst and Fragbomb and Iceshards.

They wouldn't have hurt me, of course, because your own magic can't hit you—it can only affect your targets—but they would have smashed our shields fast enough if they could.

They couldn't. *Nothing* got through.

Shift's sparkling new green Shields were as strong as anything that Ochre had cast—and a lot stronger than her own had ever been.

Excellent.

Okay, I thought. All I have to do is take this slowly. Not compel Shift. Let her discover everything for herself.

I could feel her interest, jittering up my arm.

Yes, I thought. *You can do this, my friend. Go for it.*

Her tourmaline heartstone glowed bright and eager, red above green.

One by one, I leached Ochre's Heals out of her, and Shift and I learned them. There were a lot of them, in branches of healing and protection that I'd never heard of. I transfused them all into Shift, where they settled and became ours.

Black, despite his name, seemed quite pleased to show me all the power he'd got. It wasn't a quick process, because he kept needing to do the same things again and again, as if I hadn't understood. I had. I got the impression that he was a somewhat denser staff than my quick-witted Shift. Down-to-earth, solid, simple. Sly, in his own smug way. But, basically, as thick as mud.

Powerful, though. If he were a person, he'd be some farmer's lad, as strong as an ox; mischievous, unsubtle. The sort who would set up a practical joke for you to walk into, and then stare at you, grinning, so that you knew something was up, and were on your guard.

Blacker fought me like a cornered wildcat, spitting, and snarling, and slashing at me while I worked her to my will. She wasn't letting me in on any of her secrets. I had to battle her for every inch of ground

I made. In the end, we were both exhausted. I was sweating, and panting, and she was seething with fury.

As far as I could tell, I'd forced everything out of her.

Again, as with Ochre and Black, she knew a lot, in fields that were completely new to me. There was no question that Shift was nettled about the whole process when I urged them into her. She felt reluctant, offended—maybe even felt a little sullied. I told her to stop being so prim and proper. *Get yourself some nasty here,* I thought at her. *Think how hard you could hit with that lot!*

She gave me the silent treatment, but she heard me. I suppose it must be confusing, being a stave that has always had a split personality. She could hit like a ton of bricks and heal like a saint. Those two contradictory halves of her had to coexist, in the best truce that they could manage. I found it interesting that she was less than keen to take on the brute force of Blacker's vicious Damages.

I told her, *You're an old softie.*

I felt her growl, wearily, through my wrist and up my arm.

Yes, I agreed. *That was tough.*

What I felt from her, in return, I can best translate as, *I need to lie down.*

You got it? I asked. *All of it?*

She resonated in the affirmative. She had. Everything.

Good, I told her. *You are going to like what you can do in combat now.*

She didn't answer. She was already comatose. I slung her on my back and left her to sleep. She'd earned it.

I dug the heartstone eyes out of the other staves. They didn't like it. Hell, *I* didn't like it. When you form such a close bond with your own staff, you don't see others as just inanimate objects to destroy. But they knew that I had won and that there wasn't anything that they could do about it. Each of them were potential future threats to me if I didn't disable them and they fell into any Arcane hands.

I thanked them, each in turn, before I blinded them. Ochre and Black responded quietly, resigned. I could feel them wishing me well. Not Blacker, though. She struggled, and swore, and only yielded her bloodstone eye after a fight, in which I had to lean over her and wrap her under my elbow before I could dig in enough to get purchase on the stone.

I apologized, of course, before I put the blade in. She told me to go fuck myself—without words, but the meaning was clear. She shuddered in my grip, and screamed in my head, as the point of my dagger took her eye. *I curse you*, was her message. I set her down on the ground, blinded, impotent, seething, and contemplated her. I thanked her again. She was mute now, and I heard nothing in return.

I will take your rage, I said, silently, in tribute, in appreciation of what I had learned from her, *and use it well.*

I built a fire, out there in the winter wilderness in the middle of nowhere, and put the three staves on it.

They caught, like the three ordinary sticks of wood that they now were, and began to burn. I wished I hadn't had to murder them, but I couldn't risk them falling into the wrong hands, however remote that possibility might be. They were just too dangerous. Especially Blacker. As Avildor's introduction to Light Magic had shown me, some casters have powers that others of us know nothing about. They're not called the *arcane* arts for nothing. The study is full of secrets, well hidden and jealously guarded. Who knew what abilities experts in, for example, Divination might possess? An artifact as powerful as Blacker might radiate a signal for a hundred leagues around, to be picked up by any with the art to hear it. And who might well be interested enough to track down such an unusual distress call, thinking, *Hullo, let's see what's sending that …*

If she were found, and fitted with a new eye, and by some chance came face-to-face with me, in combat—wielded, perhaps, by a caster as advanced with her Damages as Avildor was with Light Magic, which would mean they'd be way better than me and Shift—well, I would be dead.

And not before suffering. Blacker would not have forgotten, nor would she forgive. She would pour every ounce of her spite and cruelty into wreaking her revenge. Remote though the possibility might be, it was a scenario that I had to avoid.

The sticks burned and I smelled their history, their age. I watched, as they glowed, and shrank, and cracked, and separated into red hot embers. I tucked their heartstones into my niblun backpack, mounted my mare, and moved on.

I followed forest and hill paths south, curving around east and then back west, always avoiding both highways and byways. I was even reluctant to take sheep tracks along the bleak, wintry hills that loomed out of the trees. I struck out across open country whenever I could, and made my way through uplands, and moorlands until I plunged again into woodlands. The days were dark, and cold. The nights were long, and colder. The emptiness of the land was oppressive, somehow threatening. I felt on edge, most of the time, as I rode.

I could sense that the horses felt it too. There was plenty for them to eat, but I knew that they needed to be tended to. They wanted grooming, and warm, dry stalls, and a blanket, and a nose bag full of oats each. They deserved it.

I did not see the chance of anything like that on my long way south. If I saw a village—which I only did once, from a hilltop, far away to the east across a remote valley—well, I wasn't going anywhere near it. I also came to think that there was something not quite right about this environment. I saw no people, and was relieved—and, at the same time, concerned. Where was everyone? Why were they avoiding this wilderness that I was making my way through? The open country. Pleasant nature, at one with itself and me?

No, this was not that. This was the wild—the hostile, predatory wild, where I was an intruder. I was some townie, thinking that I knew what it was like out there. The further I rode, the more I saw that I didn't. The longer my journey went on, the more I realized how different this life was from "a game."

In a game, things happen relatively quickly. You might ride, for a few minutes, across what looks like wilderness, before you and your group reach your target—maybe with your chosen music blaring in your ears. That was just shorthand, teasing you towards your next action. All of us were safe behind our keyboards or consoles, watching the vista unfolding around us, chatting, joking, forming strategy as our mounts carried us towards our goal. We were living vicariously, at secondhand.

Yes, we loved the idea of it. *How great it would be to be doing that for real*, we would think, *instead of my dull, everyday life.*

Well, let me tell you: When it's at firsthand, for real, it is much different. A ride takes days, not minutes. You're cold, and tired, and hungry. Your thighs ache from long hours in the saddle. You're on constant alert, and anxious. A ride along a range of hills takes as long as horses need. You can't hurry it. We had come from the triumph of our championship, Qrysta and Grell and I, from the comfort of our own homes, into this. This unknown, confusing mess. Just as any life is, really; but here it was bigger, more unsettling, less safe. Yes, we fit in here.

Yes, this was so much better, and richer, and more exciting than the lives we'd lived before. But it was also much more demanding. Much more immediate, up-front, firsthand, in your face.

Much more *real*.

And, in a way, much more boring. You're strung out, and edgy, and it's hour after hour and league after league of riding across terrain—eyes and ears open, nerves jangling, the horses thumping along—all of us just wanting to *get there*. Roof, stables, fireside, bed. And instead, having to settle down night after night, out in the cold, and crowd in together, and listen to the wind and the night noises, which included wolves.

Bats, squeaking. Clouds scudding across the moon. Shadows moving below the trees, around us. Who? What? Foxes yipping, owls in mournful conversation. One night, a monstrous roaring, of, what? Sabercats attacking a mastodon? The howling and bellowing echoed down the wind from, gods be thanked, leagues away. It faded, at last. Sleep did not come easily after that. The moon hung high in the sky above us, behind shreds of cloud, its pale light throwing shadows around us under the trees.

It would be full tomorrow night. Half the month gone. I'd had the longest journey, apart maybe from Qrysta and Jess's, but the others were all on foot, and I had mounts. The others could cover, what, twenty-odd miles a day? I could ride double that and more with my spare horses. I was in good time, I believed. I might even be there before some of them, if all went well. That night, wrapped up in my cloak and blanket, I remembered the words that Avildor had said.

It's a long game being played here, young Daxx.

No kidding, I thought. Long game? Every day was longer than the one before. Here I am, on this planet I've been landed in, and there are no shortcuts. Day after day. Night after night. This wasn't "what it was like, in those days." This was what it really *is*. For me. Now. And, unless I was mistaken, forever. *Oh well,* I thought: *Warm and safe though it was, I don't miss my bungalow.*

Every dawn meant another long, cold trek down another endless range of hills. The sky to the west, my right, as the sun passed its zenith, looked ominously dark. Within hours, light snow was falling, wind pushing it in from the horizon.

As twilight fell, the full moon was already bright in the sky off to the east. It was snowing, hard. The moon would be covered by clouds before much longer. No point going on in this, I thought. Find what shelter I can, among these trees, and hunker down for the night.

Dusk was on us now, and I was peering ahead, looking for a nice thick grove of evergreens that might give us at least some protection from the driving snow, when I saw movement. Something was coming towards us through the trees, with an unsteady, unnatural motion. I felt a jolt of alarm, and the hairs on the back of my neck stood up, my skin crawling. What in all hells *was* that thing?

A black, shuffling, awkward shape … a beast, of some kind, on all fours—but *what* kind?

A halting shadow, limned by silver from the full moon.

I dismounted, Shift at the ready, and tethered my mare to a tree branch in case of fireworks. The rest of the string were hitched to her, so none of them could escape if spooked. I removed my backpack and stowed it carefully under a bush. I didn't want it obstructing my movements. I stepped away from the horses, to give them breathing space, and moved towards the approaching creature.

Which stopped, and snuffled, and, to my horror, stood up on its hind legs.

I froze. It was looking around, swaying. It lurched on, towards me. And that was when I saw the silhouette of an arrow sticking out of its back. It turned, this way and that, weak, uncertain. It kept looking behind it more than ahead, in my direction. It? No, I saw. Not it—*him*. That was a human being. Badly injured. At the end of his tether. Frightened too.

As I walked towards him, he dropped abruptly to his knees. He knelt there, panting, his chest heaving for breath. He forced himself upright, to his feet, but couldn't manage it, and collapsed down onto hands and knees.

He was, obviously, exhausted. If he fell into the snow, that would be the end of him. The cold would take him, and his agony would be over. Shift was already pouring Heals into him as I reached him, including new skills that I had transfused into her from Ochre—Revival, Bloodboost, Allsalve. Ochre's green Shield bloomed around him, protecting him from wind and snow and warming his chilled skin. I

330

leached Warmth into it, and zapped little shocks into his chest, to invigorate him.

He coughed, and stirred, and stared around in confusion through his sudden green surroundings, eyes blank. And then, hearing my approach, looked up, startled, both at me and the Shield that was now keeping the snow and wind off him and warming him—and mending him, although he could not yet have known that.

He backed away, feebly, and I was kneeling by him, arm around his shoulders, saying, "It's okay, hold on," things like that.

There was more than one arrow in him, I saw. Four, in all—back, shoulder, right arm, left thigh. Gods, how had he even been able to *move?!* Tough old bugger, that's for sure. Old? Well, middle-aged: Fifty-ish, dark hair turning gray, dressed in sturdy brown and gray field clothes under a long, ragged cote of gray-black fur. The fur looked familiar, I thought, as Shift and I worked on him frantically. It reminded me of the pelt of the wolf that I'd skinned, my first day in this world.

A long time ago, that now seemed. Well, no doubt wolf fur made excellent winter clothing. Hunter, maybe, I thought, looking at him—although I saw no bow, no knives. Odd. The only weapons I could see were the arrows sticking out of him. Those needed to come out, *ASAP*, and with as little bleeding as possible.

I cast Soften on their shafts and Numb on the wounds. When I was sure that he couldn't feel anything, by tapping on its shaft gently,and seeing him not wince in pain, I cut the arrow out of his shoulder. A short, thick ash shaft it was, with a razor-sharp, but also fat, gleaming warhead. Brutal. Built to inflict maximum damage on its quarry's internal organs. He was too delirious to notice what was going on. I worried that I might be going to lose him. I was so absorbed with working to keep him alive, to get my Heals doing their job, to dig out the arrows as quickly and carefully as I could, that I didn't really pay them much attention, apart from—*arrows, need to get those out.* I hit him with Close Wounds, and Mend, and Staunch Bleeding, and then unhooked the Restore Health potion I kept at my belt, unsealed it, and held it to his lips. His eyes were closed, but he half opened them on smelling the potion and peered at me vacantly, eyeballs wavering.

"Drink," I said, "it will restore you."

He strained, feebly, to do so much as take even a mouthful. Slowly, painfully, he swallowed. Tasted. Looked at me with the last of his strength ebbing from his eyes. Even in the fading dusk I could see that they were an unusual, amber color.

This is still touch and go, I thought. He was as weak as a kitten. I could lose him at any moment. I smiled, calmly, to reassure him, and nodded. "Go on." He drank again, and again, falteringly, until the flask was empty.

I thought, *Yes. He might just make it.*

He looked at me. Summoned some strength. Opened his mouth to speak, but no sound came.

He swallowed, gathered himself, and tried again. He said, his weak, puzzled voice a croak, "Why?"

That took me by surprise. I said, trying to make light of his peril, "Looked like you needed it, friend."

His eyes wavered uncertainly, from side to side, as he tried to get a read on me, frowning.

"Friend," he echoed.

He coughed.

It was, I realized, almost a laugh.

I waited for his response.

He shifted, uneasily, found a shred of strength, and muttered, "Then they will kill you too, 'friend.'"

I didn't like the sound of that. "Who will?"

His head slumped forward onto his chest.

Then, with difficulty, he turned and groped on the ground until he found what he was looking for, where I'd laid them after extracting them from his body.

His hand closed around an arrow.

He picked it up and showed it to me so that I could see its head clearly.

Its point glittered in the light of the full moon.

The arrowhead was not made of steel, but of silver.

"Night ..." he mumbled, turning his face up to the moon. "Need the night. She will restore my strength; our mother ..."

Gods, I thought. *What have I done?!*

And then, as I heard the baying of a hound catching his trail, I thought *what now?*

The man coughed, another weak laugh deep in his chest. "They have brought more dogs," he rasped. "I killed the others, last night. *Night.* How long, do you think?"

More hounds joined their voices to the lone cry of the one who had found the man's scent.

"Minutes," I said, still racking my brains as to what in all hells I was going to do. He took hold of my arm with his hand. "Hold them," he implored, in his feeble croak. "Until the night."

The belling of the hounds grew into a chorus, louder and louder by the minute. They were running, this way, towards us. And behind them, a horn blared.

Another, off to the east.

Another to the west.

Hounds answered to west and east as well.

I stood up and walked towards them, to put myself between them and their quarry. There were too many voices in that eager chorus to count. Ten hounds? Twenty? Some high, some low, some long and hollering, some answering with short, eager yelps of excitement.

And then, rustling in the undergrowth.

Bushes parting.

Dark, charging shapes running towards us, their backs silvered by moonlight.

I pointed Shift at the ground between us and cast into it the traps that we had learned from Black, and some of my own for good measure.

The hounds slammed to a halt, fixed in clay coils and ice traps and puddles of glue-like tar. They stopped, but their chorus did not—although it changed, abruptly, to squeals of alarm and fear. In reply, the horns sounded again, urgently, a different tune, one of warning, responded to by horns to left and right.

I fired up a bright Glow above the anchored dogs, so that anyone approaching would see what had happened. And would stop, I hoped, and have a good long think about what they were seeing: Their hounds, immobile from the legs down, complaining, scared. Then I heard the thumping of hooves, heading my way from front and sides, and voices, and the baying of the flanking hounds.

Well, I'd make my choice, without even really thinking about it.

I started thinking about it as I waited for the hunters to appear.

333

Mainly what I thought was, *What in all hells do I know about werewolves?!*

Just about nothing.

Except, don't mess with them.

The man I'd rescued had seemed normal enough. Nice enough, grateful.

Yes, but that was the *man* part of him. What about the other part? The *were* part?

And what about the hunters who were appearing on their horses through the trees, and reining in, and dismounting, and wondering in very salty, angry language what in all hells had happened to their hounds?!

And there was me, in the middle, out in the open, with nowhere to hide—and nowhere to run to. I'd never make it back to the horses on foot; and anyway, the hunters had mounts too.

Pandemonium, all around me. Barking, howling, whimpering; neighing, whipping; cursing and shouting. Yes, they saw me all right. They saw their trapped hounds under the Glow I'd raised above them. Some stamped around on their alarmed horses, trying to bring them under control. Others dismounted and headed for their dogs, or for me. There were a lot of them, flanking me as well as ahead of me.

I needed to take control. I threw some Barkers up into the air above them, and sent some shrieking Airghouls over their heads, to chase them hither and yon, and shut them up. I added a Thunderclap and drew a curtain of lightning across the air between us while pitting the intervening ground with traps.

The hunters reacted, startled, regathered, and got the message.

Warning.

They stood, opposite and encircling me, itching for a fight.

But they were wary now.

One of them stepped forward. A big, solid, bearded man. Dark hair hung down his back, surrounding a black beard frosted by the full moon's silver.

"Who are you?!" he demanded.

"Kel of Arnstead," I replied, as calmly as I could. "And you?"

He ignored the question. "Where is he?"

"Where is who?" I said.

"Graycote," he spat the name.

"Never heard of him."

334

He stared at me. Hard. "The gray," he said. "The Packfather."

The lightning wall between us had faded. The Glows above them were dying. I needed to keep up appearances. I threw three more Glows above them and sent another Barker overhead past them, and popped a green shield around me, just for the theatrical effect.

Almost fully dark now. I needed to buy time. I didn't know why I was playing it this way; I just was. I was following the lead that I'd somehow given myself. Protecting the wounded man that I'd tended. Seeing my decision through.

Perhaps, if I'd been alert enough, or smart enough, I might have thought, *Hullo,* I started this on the wrong foot, I need to change tack here. I might have stepped aside and said, to the hunters, *Here he is, dying werewolf. He's all yours, gents, don't mind me.*

I didn't. Because, like most of us, I'm slow to reconsider. Stubborn, I suppose you could say. I'll admit to that. Don't we all hate to admit we're wrong? Even when we *are* wrong?

Well, wrong or right, whichever I was, I couldn't have, at that moment, for one second justified that what I was doing was "right." So, no, I had no idea what I was doing. I was just ... *keeping going forwards. You've saved this guy, so—keep on saving him. Serial killer or saint? How am I meant to know?*

The hunt master, though, had a very clear idea of what he was doing.

"We know he's here," he said, his voice harsh. "We shot him full of arrows last night. And come the daylight this morn, he'll have Turned. With silver in him he can't Turn back again, full moon or no. We owe him many deaths. Men, and half my hounds. We'll kill you if we have to. So now, step out of our way."

I didn't like being talked to like that. Even when I was in the wrong, and they were in the right. "No."

More murmurs, and angry growls—not all of them coming from the hounds.

And a dozen arrows pointed at me from a dozen drawn bows.

Without moving her, because I didn't want any movement to cause those arrows to fly at me, I got Shift to strengthen the green Shield that she'd learned from Ochre. Once it was glowing around me, I added Reflect Attacks and Armor. I felt them settle onto me and knew that those arrows would not be able to get through my defenses and harm me, at least for the couple of minutes while the casts held.

I said, "Turn around and go back to your homes."

The hunt master said, "Kill him."

I unleashed a variety of traps and a Shockfield as they loosed their arrows at me.

They were overmatched. Shockfield would mess with them, severely, but not kill them the way a Flamefield would. I hoped it would make them see sense and go away. It didn't. There were a dozen of them, and twice as many hounds, and only one of me between them and their prey. They could swat me out of their path easily enough, right?

Wrong.

Their arrows bounced off my shield. Their hounds struggled, yelping, in their traps. All the shouting and threatening in the world did not bring the hunters any closer to me, on their trapped legs, to where their blades could have an effect.

I held up my hand.

The commotion subsided.

I said, "Final warning. Go."

And then, I—and they—heard the howl behind me.

Long, and deep, and filled with infinite malice, the sound made the hair stand up on my head.

Heavy paws padded up behind me and stopped.

I turned and looked up at the great head of the werewolf hanging above me, drool oozing from its open jaws.

He stared at the men, and hounds, and horses—no longer wounded but bursting with power, his long, taloned arms curved towards them at his sides.

He snarled, deep, and long, and loud.

My blood turned to ice. I was standing within inches of him. One swat of those claws, and nothing that I or Shift could do would protect me. There was power there, far greater than anything I knew of, or possessed.

I pointed Shift at the ground where the hounds were held. They were no longer struggling but cowering in fear. I released them, and they scuttled away immediately, tails between their legs, whimpering.

The men around them backed away too. Some shot silver arrows at us, but they did not get through our Shields—the one I had thrown around Graycote, and my own, which I had refreshed—and dropped to the ground.

The hunt master, last to leave, looked at me. "I know you," he said. "You're the one they're looking for."

Damn. I realized I hadn't thought to lay a Glamour on myself. *Idiot.*

"Caster, tall, cropped fair hair, stag brooch on his cloak."

He nodded, as the dismay on my face confirmed his discovery, and smiled. "You cost me my reward for that monster," he said, "but they'll pay me ten times that for you!"

He turned and ran. I fired what attacks I could after them, but Shift was drained, and there were too many of them, and they were too far away for her to hit them with what little firepower she had left. The last, faint light in her heartstone dulled.

And—so what if the hunt master died? The other hunters knew me too, now.

I lowered Shift, wondering what in all hells I'd got myself into.

A mess, I felt her respond up my arm. She wasn't teasing. She was as apprehensive as I was.

I looked up at the werewolf, towering above me.

I thought, *Packfather?*

He threw back his head and howled at the full moon. The roar in his chest vibrated down into the ground and then up again through my feet and legs into me, like an earthquake. I had never felt so vulnerable in my life.

He turned and stared down at me. There was no humanity that I could see in those eyes—eyes that were no longer amber but yellow and burning.

I glanced at Shift's heartstone, to see if she'd recouped any power yet, in case I had to fight him. It was all the time he needed. I turned back towards him just in time to see the back of his paw hurtling towards me before it struck the side of my head, lifting me off my feet. I dropped to the ground. The last thing I felt, before I blacked out, was his hot breath in my face, and his growl rumbling through me, and his teeth ripping out my throat.

And my lifeblood draining into the snow-covered forest floor.

26

The Oak Grove

I woke, struggling to scramble away from those jaws. I blinked my eyes open, looking around, gasping for breath, trying to work out where I was, what had happened ...

The blow to my head had knocked me cold. My nightmare had seemed to follow that moment immediately: My death from his tearing teeth. But it was hours later, and I was alive. I was not lying on snow, but on something soft, under my cloak, surrounded by trees. I could see the sun in the sky beyond them. It was just about where it should be at a midwinter midday. There were shapes, high up in the bare branches above me: Round balls of darkness against the sky—darknesses that resolved themselves into clusters of deep green leaves, with pearls of white in their midst.

Mistletoe.

I turned my head and immediately wished I hadn't. My death might have been imaginary; the headache was all too real. As was the pain in my jaw, where he had backhanded me into oblivion.

Where was I?

Where were my packs, Shift, the horses ...?

I levered myself up onto an elbow and tried to take in my surroundings.

I was at the base of a great oak, the tallest and widest and most central of several dozen oaks grouped around it. I could feel moss under my hand. It was warm—whether from the heat of my body lying on it, or from some other source, I could not tell. There was hardly any wind. Birds flew in and out of the trees, settling at will. All seemed calm—eerily calm, after the chaos of the night before. The only sounds were the occasional chirps of birdson, and the gentle whispering of the breeze in the leafless branches.

I sat up, still groggy from my headache, and felt my cheek where the blow from his paw had struck. It was sore and swollen. I needed Shift, and Heals, and a flask of Elun's Restore Health potion. Where were my packs …?

Looking around for them, I saw him.

He was sitting on the ground with his back against one of the oaks, his arms around his knees; so still that, in his grays and browns, he blended into the trunk that was supporting him. He was watching me, from hooded eyes under a dark brow surrounded by graying brown hair. Even in human form, as he now was again, there was no mistaking the wolf in him.

He uncoiled from the ground and got to his feet, strode over to me, and stood above me, looking down. He said, eventually, in a low, rumbling voice, "Hello … *friend*."

The way he said *friend* didn't sound at all friendly.

"Hello," I replied.

He continued to contemplate me. Offering nothing.

Okay, I thought, my turn.

I said, or rather gasped, my mouth dry, "How are you feeling?"

"Probably better than you are. You'll have a fine bruise on that cheek for a few days."

I was shaking. I felt weak. I tried not to show it.

"I can fix that," I said, "if you give me my staff."

"Don't have it," he said.

"What?!"

Where was Shift? I'd be lost without her, wouldn't be able to defend myself—I already missed her.

"Didn't need it," he said, dismissively, crouching slowly down beside me; which made me feel even more uncomfortable, and vulnerable.

He stared at me with his strange, amber eyes, a disconcerting blend of brown and yellow. "What I needed," he said, "was to talk to you."

I was scared, confused, defenseless. "Of course," I croaked, trying to sound cooperative. "My pack ..."

He frowned, as if insulted, and snapped, "Your *pack?!*"

"I have more potions in it," I said. "Like the one I gave you."

He was puzzled.

"Last night?" I reminded him. "After I got the arrows out of you?"

"Ah," he said, shaking his head. "Is that what happened?"

"Restore Health potion," I said. "I could really use some of that now, I feel—terrible."

"Ah," he grunted, dismissive. "That kind of pack. No, *friend*, I don't have your 'pack.' What I have is a question."

He studied me, hunkered down as he was beside me, on his haunches, his face too close for comfort. Like a wolf, I thought: Sitting like one, staring like one, his amber eyes searching mine. I wanted to back away but made myself hold still.

He didn't ask his question for a long while. His eyes bored into mine as he studied me. Gleams came and went in them, now yellow, now brown, as if his thoughts were conflicting, and changing. Or rather, his mind .... Not "him changing his mind," but his mind itself altering.

I didn't like that idea. *Man-mind; wolf-mind.* He—what had the hunt master called him? *Graycote*—must have brought me there, for his own reasons, rather than killing me. But—what had happened, after he'd poleaxed me? Where were the horses? I doubted they'd have willingly followed an eight-foot-tall werewolf. I shuddered at the memory of that monstrous head glaring down at me, those long teeth inches from my face.

He was looking down at me again now, but in his other form.

Considering me.

"Why?" he said, at last.

I knew what he meant. It was the same *why* as the one he'd asked me the night before, when he'd drunk the Restore Health potion that I'd given him.

"You needed help," I said.

He didn't take his eyes off me.

Eventually, he said, "Your kind doesn't help our kind."

No doubt that was true, in his experience. But it wasn't in mine. IRL, in some games I'd played, I'd run with werewolves, on raids. Tough fighters, the best of them were, and fast. We'd be all sorts, in a group: Ghouls, vamps, zombies, humans, and near-humans of all sizes, from elfin to demi-giant, mounted on ostriches or unicorns or lizards—whatever took our fancy. So, truthfully, I said, "We do where I come from."

He frowned in surprise. He didn't want to believe me. But—I'd helped him, hadn't I? Saved his life, indeed. Shot through with silver arrows, the silver in his flesh preventing him from Turning into his wolf form: He'd been as good as dead, when I found him and tended him, from cold if not from the teeth of the hounds and the blades of the hunters who would soon catch up with him. I'd dug the silver out of him. I'd bought him the few minutes he'd needed. And at nightfall, under the full moon, he'd Turned, into the creature that had sent his pursuers running—with a little help from his, well, "friend." Me.

Whom he had then savagely coldcocked, out of the blue, and brought to … wherever we were now.

"Where?" he growled.

"A land to the north of here," I said. "Across the seas."

He searched my eyes for the truth. He didn't know what to think any more than I did, each of us feeling the other out.

"Your home," he said. It was more of a statement than a question.

"Yes."

"Why are you here?" he challenged. "In this land, now?"

"I have a job to do," I told him.

"Tell me," he said.

I had to improvise, fast. I didn't want to lie to him. He was staring at me closely, scanning me for signs of evasion or dishonesty.

"I'm a hunter too," I said, to throw him. It worked. I saw the sudden wariness in his eyes, his suspicion. "A treasure hunter. I've learned of a trove of rare value, down in the Great Waste, far to the south. I intend to find it."

His eyes darkened. "We do not go there."

"Why not?"

"It is guarded."

"What is? The whole Waste?"

"Yes."

"What by?"

"Creatures of the sand. They hate us. We hate them. We keep our distance. They do not like the wilderness, the wet. They are sun. Hot, dry. We are moon."

I was interested. The others and I were, after all, going there. Couldn't avoid it. "What can you tell me about them?"

"Only that they will hunt you and kill you. With heat, and dryness. Beyond that, we do not know. We do not go into their lands, any more than we allow them into ours. Just know that they hate you, and will hunt you, as surely as your kind hates and hunts us. As we, in turn, hate and hunt them."

"Why?" I said. "Can't you … leave each other alone, if you don't get along?"

His eyes narrowed. I saw the loathing in his face. "They kill us. We kill them. We kill them, and their sheep, and their cattle, and their dogs, and their horses, and eat them. They kill us for our skins, and our bodies, which they sell for their silver to those who use them for …" he paused, and said, with contempt, "their *potions*." He nodded, making sure I got the point. "Silver to kill us, silver to buy our skins and bones."

His voice was filled with anger.

"How much for?" I asked. I thought I had to try to keep him uncertain, off-balance.

He glared. "You crave their silver?"

"Me? I have no idea who 'they' are," I said. "I just wondered how much they thought you were worth. And no, I don't need their silver—theirs or anyone's. I have silver aplenty, and enough gold for my needs. Soon I will have a fortune. I am no threat to you."

"I know that," he said, dismissively, and the way he said it worried me. Cold, calm. I suddenly realized, *whoa*, wait a minute: This isn't a get-to-know-you meet and greet. This is an interrogation. He is pumping me for information.

Why? What does he want to know?

He answered that question almost as soon as I thought it.

"I'm trying to decide what to do with you," he said, unfolding himself to his feet.

"You don't have to do anything with me, I can be on my way in—"

"Quiet!" he barked.

Normally, when humans bark, it isn't much of a bark, it's more of a whiny yap. This was ferocious, lung-filled, bass-deep, resonant, impatient—and, above all, feral. I reminded myself that what I was dealing with only looked human. He was also that slavering beast looming above me in last night's moonlight. We weren't equals here.

He wanted something. I'd better find out what and give it to him.

I heard the warning rumble deep in his chest as he stood above me, head down, thinking.

He raised his chin and looked at me. "You gave me my *life!*" he said.

It sounded like an accusation. As if he'd said, *You took my most precious possession, you bastard!* Rather than "gave."

Take, give.

Opposites.

I couldn't think how to reply. So, I didn't. I just looked up at this tall, brooding, dark gray man, who was staring down at me, wondering whether I should live or die.

As it turned out, it was both.

"Which is what I shall do to you," he decided.

I nodded, relieved, and said, "Well, there's really no need to kill me, I'm just some traveler passing through, and—"

I stopped at his growl. Which rose, impatient, threatening. "I did not say that!" he snapped. "I will give you my greatest gift. The gift you gave me. My life."

That made no sense, I thought, staring up at him, trying to think—

In an instant, his hands had reached down and grabbed the back of my head, their nails digging into my flesh, so that all I could do was stare up at him. And watch him grow, and swell, and change into the beast he had been in the night, his great eyes now yellow rather than amber. And then, with a snarl, his fangs were sinking into my shoulder.

The pain was horrific. I hung helpless in his grip, unable to resist, as his talons dug deeper and deeper into my neck. His saliva ran into my bloodstream, and he chewed, slow and deep, his jaws working on the muscle and tissues below my chin. I knew what he was doing, and that there was nothing I could do about it.

Wolfbite.

No, I thought; *no, I don't want this …!*

At last, after a long minute of his wolf-nature leaching into mine, he yanked my head back, my hair still in his claws, and stared down at me with those wild, yellow eyes. My blood dripped with his saliva from his jaws. His long tongue licked his lips, as his face shrank and settled back into his human form.

"So, *friend*," he said.

And studied me with his once-again-amber eyes.

I felt myself shivering, aching, bleeding from his wolfbite.

He lowered his face to within inches of mine. "They killed my pack," he said. "They hunted me down and filled me with the curse of silver. They had me, weak and exhausted, cornered. You saved me. I ask you again, *why?*"

I saw what he meant. "I'm a healer," I said, "that's what I do. I saw a wounded man, who needed help. I didn't even think about it. I just did what I could do."

He watched me closely, to see if I was lying.

Concealing some other motive from him.

"If you'd known?" he said, eventually.

I understood what he meant. *If I'd known what he was, would I still have saved him?*

"No one is ever told what would have happened," I said. It was a quote from somewhere, I couldn't remember where. I'd always liked it, and often used it when people made pointless speculations, such as *"that's what you would have done if ..."* Waste of time those were, more often than not.

It seemed to work. He grunted, and nodded, and let go of my hair. I dropped onto my back as he pulled away from me and straightened up.

Phew, I thought, at the same time as, *I'm going to become that??*

"Tonight," he said, "our mother will show you her gift. Use it well."

He turned away.

"Wait," I said.

He stopped.

"Where are we?"

"The Oak Grove. It is hidden. Our sanctuary. This is where I was making for last night, when we met. Only those of the blood can come here. With," he added, and I didn't like the implication, "those we bring."

There was a lot unsaid, under those words. Bring for what purpose?

His words echoed in my mind. *We kill them. We eat them.*

"But—why hit me, bring me here, why not just—thank you, and goodbye, and we go our separate ways?"

His eyes gleamed. He chuckled, deep in his chest. "You will see," he said.

That didn't seem to help.

He saw my confusion, came back, knelt down beside me again, and stared into my eyes.

"It is not easy to *think,* when in the form," he explained. "We feel. We smell, we hear, we hunt, we kill. We kill men. You were man, your scent, your blood calling to me, within inches, overwhelming. The hunger was on me. I was torn. Before I Turned, as the night fell, I told myself, *If I live, I must not kill this man. I must talk with this man. Learn. Learn why. Spare him.*

"Some memory of that stopped me. That memory saved your life, as you had saved mine. I was maddened with the blood-calling, the hunger. You will see for yourself, tonight. The last Moon Night. There are three: The night before, the full, the night after. Those nights are yours, now and forever. On other nights, on other days, you can choose the form. On the Moon Nights, the form chooses you. One Moon Night, if the mother so desires, we will meet again, you and I."

Gods, I thought.

He was watching me, intently. "It is a gift that I have given you," he said.

He waited for my answer.

I thought, *what if I don't want it?* But what I said was, "Thank you."

His eyebrows rose a fraction. He nodded. "Yes," he said, "a thank you gift. Thank you for my life, *friend.* And for your little black horse. He was delicious."

He smiled—yes, *wolfishly*—turned on his heel, and walked away, through the trees and out of the oak grove, never once looking back.

I lay back, exhausted.

I thought about all that had happened, and all that he'd said.

And worried about the coming night.

When I woke it was dusk. I blinked my eyes open and looked up at the moon above the bare trees. I sat up, gingerly, my head spinning. I was still weak. I'd lost blood. I'd been beaten senseless and interrogated by an inquisitor who was half man, half monster. I was not ready for this.

I was not …

Wait a minute …

I stood up, and got to my feet, and felt myself growing, as the last of the twilight faded, and night fell on the oak grove. I looked down, at long, hairy arms that hung from my shoulders. I raised my hands to examine them. They were no longer hands, but paws, the black claws they ended in sharp and long. I swayed, unsteady, on wolf legs that were equal in length to my arms—or rather, my forelegs. My spine was much longer than legs or arms. My body was hound-shaped, huge chest, stomach curving in towards powerful hips. I heard the heaving of my breath in my ears, inside and out, and felt the hunger on my tongue, lolling between my long, fang-filled jaws. I felt awkward on my two hind legs, as if I'd rather be running on four. I could smell scents that I had never in my life encountered, from the winter sap deep in the oaks to the blood coursing through the veins of the birds that were sleeping high overhead in the branches, their heads under their wings.

I could smell the snow on the air.

The clouds in the wind.

The old mulch of dead, fallen leaves, rotting at the end of the year, and the worms and insects burrowing among them. The world, as I inhaled it, was a kaleidoscope of aromas; clouds of smells, of ten thousand flavors, wafting in and out of each other. What I could see was clear enough, much sharper than anything I could see with human eyes on a night even as moonlit as this, but all was dull by comparison with what I could smell. Which was, all of it, glorious. Delicious. Demanding.

Deer, shrew, squirrel, rat. I longed for all of them. *Bloodlust,* I thought, as I tasted their potential on the wind, in my nostrils. It was a term I'd never understood before. Who, I'd always thought, ever lusted after blood? Good grief—what kind of a sick fool would that be?

I now had the answer.

Me.

I ached to hunt, to wear down my prey, to kill, to sink my teeth into its throat and drink its life.

I dropped onto all fours and ran out into the forest that spread beyond the Oak Grove. It was, I saw, enclosed within a circle of high cliffs. Hidden indeed. I followed the way that Graycote had gone and found the tunnel. Through and out, galloping, following the scent trails in the

346

wind and on the ground, zigging this way, zagging that; excited, alert, waiting for the moment. Locking on, knowing, hunting down, killing.

Deer. A young doe. Her blood delicious on my tongue, her flesh sweet, lean—oh so rewarding to chew. Her bones cracked between my jaws, yielding their marrow. Her organs, greasy and slippery, full of bile and blood and mess. I shoved my nose into her still-warm intestines. I bit, pulled, chomped, ate. Her liver, when I chewed my way up to it and found it at last, was bursting with oil and flavor. I had never felt so driven, so present.

The next day, when the fog of my transformation had cleared and I was back in my *me* form, I would think: *Well, it's never like that at a restaurant. Everything nice and civilized.* This was not that. Far from it. This was life, and death, and die, and diet, in the raw. I crunched the doe's bones. Spat out her hide. Sniffed around her hooves, her nose, and teeth. Prized her jaw open and took her tongue. Tore it out of her. Chewed, and tasted the fat and the richness of it, and swallowed.

I was humming with satisfaction, deep in my chest.

I leaned back in towards her frail corpse, took her throat between my jaws, picked her up, and shook.

Her crumpled remains flapped against the sides of my head.

I let go and flung her into the sky. Caught her as she fell. Chewed, until there was nothing left to swallow.

Sat down and licked my lips.

Licked my paws.

Pawed my ears.

Recovered from the feeding frenzy.

Sat back, replete, on my haunches, and stared, satiated, at the moon.

My moon. Our mother, he had called her.

I felt, staring at her, that I knew why.

I studied her pearl-white face, breathing deeper, and deeper until my lungs were full, and aching.

The howl rose in my chest before I knew it. I threw my head back to let it out. It sang from deep within me, for as long as the long breath lasted.

In the silence that followed, I listened to its last echoes dying away, always gazing up at the moon.

From far in the distance, Graycote answered.

Shreds of cloud drifted across the mother's face.

I listened to the night noises.

I inhaled the night air and sifted through the riot of smells that poured into me from all directions. I studied them, one by one, noting location, direction, freshness, species; whether alive or dead, growing or rotting. The hunger had left me. Again, thinking back over it the next day, in my *me* form, I would decide that this was something like looking at an entrancing view: A landscape, full of forms and details, all alive—sunlight playing on leaves, or birds landing on a river, everything animated. This, though, was a landscape I could taste. Badger, owl, ivy, mouse, leaf-mold, fox, toadstool, pine needles, bullrushes in the mud of a pond's edge, wildcat—

Horse.

I could feel my ears twitching as my head turned in the direction that the horse scent was coming from.

Faint. Far.

Dead.

I ran on all fours, galloping through the trees, leaping fallen boughs, clearing streams, homing in on that irresistible, tantalizing smell, getting closer, ever closer.

The rats were at it when I arrived at the corpse of the little black cob. On seeing me they scuttled off into the undergrowth.

There wasn't much left of him. His head, a shoulder and foreleg, some ribs, and guts. There wasn't much left of "me," either—just enough to know that this was where I needed to be, when day came, and I could Turn into "me" again.

While I was here, I thought: *Waste not, want not.*

I began to eat.

27

Hue and Cry

I lay stretched out on the ground, comfortable, dozing on and off, watching the eastern horizon through the darkest hours of the night. The black sky softened. The stars faded. First one bird stirred and chirped, in the boughs above, and then another, then more, until the trees were alive with the dawn chorus. Day broke, and at last the winter sun emerged beyond the distant hills. I got to my feet and watched it rise, and wondered what it meant for me; and before I knew it, I was standing up again, on two legs not four.

You can choose the form, Graycote had said. *Except on the Moon Nights, when the Form chooses you.*

It was no longer a Moon Night.

I thought, *Should I choose were-me again, just to see, to check how it was done?*

Better not, I decided. There might be a minimum time limit. Maybe I wouldn't be able to Turn back again for—well, who knew how long? An hour? A day? I'd have to look into all that later. I certainly had enough to think about already. Meanwhile, there were other priorities to deal with, for which I needed to be human and have a mind that was capable of clear thought.

I looked around, in the growing morning light, and saw that no, I didn't recognize my surroundings. Therefore, presumably, Graycote had brought the cob here, to eat it. I imagined the scene: Him seizing it in his jaws, slashing his claws at the leading rein that tied it to the other horses, them maddened with fear, rearing and kicking, him bounding off with his prey. It would be too much to hope, I thought, that they'd still be tethered to the branch where I'd left them. It hadn't been a particularly thick branch, just something low and nearby. In their panic they'd probably have broken free and scattered. It would be inconvenient if that were indeed the case—a blow; but I could manage without horses.

I couldn't manage without Shift.

I settled myself, as Avildor had taught me, and cast Lightseek.

I held my breath as I concentrated.

I found nothing.

I couldn't "see" Shift.

I made myself calm down, and try again, and pour every ounce of my being into it. I was dead without her.

Don't think about it. Don't lose focus. Stop interrupting yourself! Get out of your own way. Concentrate. Empty your mind. Fill it only with her.

Now. *Seek.*

I found the calm, the silence.

My breathing slowed.

I cast.

Again. Again. Again.

I opened my eyes.

I'd moved. I hadn't noticed. I couldn't yet—what was it Avildor had said? *Walk and seek at the same time.* So why had I been walking? I was fifty paces from the remains of the cob.

Why this way?

Don't ask why; just *keep going forwards.*

I walked another fifty paces in the direction that my legs had carried me without my knowledge. I stopped. Closed my eyes. Waited. Slowed my breathing.

Cast Lightseek.

Emptied my mind to everything but Shift.

Cast again.

Waited …

Behind my closed eyelids, something tiny glinted, for a microsecond, and was gone.

Something that just might have been green.

I hurried towards it, another hundred paces. I stopped and closed my eyes. I emptied my thoughts and cast again.

And there she was. A speck of green swirling within red; distinct, unmistakable, fading away almost immediately.

I ran towards her, thanking all the gods in my relief.

She was further than I'd thought. It was a good five minutes of hurrying, and stopping to recast Lightseek, before I found her.

She was lying on the ground, in the snow and mud, where I must have dropped her when Graycote knocked me senseless.

I picked her up and felt her comforting, friendly warmth jittering up my arm. *There you are! Where have you been?*

I breathed a sigh of relief.

I raised her and cast Close Wounds and Heal All on myself.

I felt the pain in my shoulder from Graycote's bite fade to nothing. The ache in my jaw where he'd backhanded me melted away.

So much better.

As long as I have Shift, I thought, I'll be fine. Werewolf or no.

Gods! Werewolf? I felt her seeking warmth as she seemed to study me.

I didn't have time to think about that now. What could I do about it anyway—wallow in confusion? Feel sorry for myself? If there was anything that I could do about it, I didn't know what that might be. I'd have to find out later. It would take research, and resources. At least I had another month, before ...

There's no answers of that nature out here in the wilds. What should be out here, though, if I could just get my bearings, was my pack. I looked this way and that, into the trees surrounding me, trying to orient myself to the scene of the night before. There were no paths. Fresh snow had dusted the forest floor. But it couldn't obscure everything. The ground where my traps had immobilized the hounds and the hunters was churned up and plain to see. I worked out which way I'd come and walked back to where I thought I'd put my pack down. It was an anxious few minutes, in which I thought, *Why in all hells did I put it under a bush?* before I found it.

I checked inside. Nothing had been disturbed. It was full of Elun's potions and my supplies.

I sighed with relief.

All in all, I thought, this could all have worked out worse. I had no horses, true, but did I need them any longer? I had a feeling that I could outrun, and outlast, any horse. I wasn't dead, either from the hunters' arrows or Graycote's teeth. On the other hand, the Devoted would be learning of my sighting from the hunters soon enough and flooding this part of the realm with search parties. I had to get beyond the reach of any net that they might try to cast around the place where the hunters had seen me.

Yes, I had Graycote's "gift" to worry about, but that would just have to wait. Meanwhile I could put it to good use and get as many miles as possible, as fast as possible, between myself and here. If there were horses to outrun, they would surely be those of the mounted squadrons of the Devoted. I did not want to come across any of those. I had a head start on them. I needed to make the most of that. Time to get going.

I strapped on my backpack and slung Shift beside it and Turned. And ran.

In wolf form, as Graycote had told me, and as I'd seen for myself the previous night, it is hard to think at all, let alone clearly. But some small human part of me remained, at the back of my mind, while the front of it was reveling in a saturated world of smells and feelings—enough for me to know that I was indeed running faster than I'd ever ridden a horse. I didn't tire. I didn't stop. I crossed moorlands, woodlands, hills and dales, jumping all obstacles in my way. One wide river I sprang over, thirty feet across or more, without breaking stride.

The miles fell behind me as the sun fell towards the west, away to my right as I ran south. Only when night fell did I slow down. I knew that no one would be hunting for me after dark. Not out there, deep in the wilderness, far from anywhere. *My turf, not theirs.* If they found my trail, way back behind me, they would follow by day—but not by night. Night was my kingdom, and they would be all too aware of that. They weren't stupid.

On the other hand, they were fanatics. They would hunt me down. They would not give up. Neither, though, if I could help it, would they catch me up.

I felt the hunger again. Hardly surprising, considering the fuel I'd been burning. I killed again, a buck this time, and ate my fill. I slaked my thirst at a stream, one that was ice-free and running swiftly, and less biting cold than I had expected. Yes, it was winter still, but a milder winter here farther south, in the lowlands below the hill forests.

Refreshed, I headed on, at first in the wolf-trot that ate up miles upon miles and used no stamina, while I digested my meal. After an hour I was cantering again, an easy, loping pace as fast as a galloping horse. Far off, down to my left, the east, in a valley below the ridge of hills that I was traversing, I saw a distant light, glinting yellow-orange between trees.

Men. The hackles rose along my back. I slid back behind the ridgeline, even though no one that far away could possibly see me. But, somehow, I knew that I didn't want to be the silhouette of a wolf, running along against the moonlit sky. Thinking about that, the next day, when I was in human form, I realized that I had *felt* "man," rather than thought "campfire."

Long after midnight, in the dark hours after the moon had set, I stopped at another stream and drank. I was on the west side of the hills that I had run down now and could see the faint lights of Last-harbor below me. From there, I knew, the land stretched west, rising into the Sunset Mountains. I followed the stream down and looped around well east and south of the town, then struck out into the hills that would take me to my destination. I found another stream, went into it, and turned back south and ran down along it, for a mile or two, as it descended into the wooded valley ahead, so that its water would cover the scent of my trail. For all I knew, the Devoted could be hunting me with hounds.

I padded onto a gravel shore on its western bank, treading lightly to leave no paw prints. And there, I Turned. Or, should that be, I thought, as my mind cleared and my *me*-self came to the fore again: *Re*-Turned. Returned from that world of smells and sounds and feelings to the world of thoughts.

It wasn't much later that I learned, in a somewhat dramatic fashion, that, from the outside, a Turning is an alarming spectacle. From the inside, it feels like nothing so much as *settling* into another, natural state, like falling asleep, or waking up. And there I was, on my own two human feet, on gravel, which I swept carefully, all the way from the running water to the bank, to erase any sign of wolf prints. Then, I stepped up onto the bank and walked a couple of hundred yards away from the stream into the woods. There was no light, but I didn't need light.

What I needed was to learn.

First, I cast every kind of Divination spell that I knew on myself. I was not surprised at the results, but I was disappointed. My Divination skills were weak, and it is a very demanding discipline. I had hoped to learn what my *were*-nature was capable of. Did it have particular abilities of its own? Wielding Shift, my Heals and Shields were many and varied. My Damage skills ran from overhead to underground now, thanks to everything that I'd learned from Black and Blacker. Qrysta could attack in dozens of different ways. Grell could soak up more Damages than he could deal—and he could deal plenty of those, enough to carve through mobs single-handed.

I Divined nothing about my *were*-self. There was no indication that particular attacks that I might do in *were*-form would have particular results. Oh well. My *were*-form was ferocious, and terrifying, and fast, and very, very tough, with a stamina reserve that never seemed to deplete. I wondered who'd drop first in a fight between him and Grell. But then, even if the weapons they were wielding were equally matched—claws and teeth against battle-axe—Grell would have armor, which I'd have to think would be tougher than even werewolf-hide. Of course, the problem might be simply this: I'd learned nothing about myself from casting Shift's low-level Divination on me, because I wasn't in that form. I'd cast my Divination on *human*-me.

What could *human*-me reveal about *were*-me?

And equally: If I were in the Form, would *were*-me have even the vaguest clue how to cast a Divination spell, on my *were*-self?

I doubted it. I doubted that *were*-me would even think to pick Shift up, let alone know what to do with her. If he even noticed her, he'd probably just rip her in half.

So, nothing there, then.

A thought struck me.

Being in the Form gave huge buffs to my strength, stamina, weapon attacks and speed. I could probably scatter a sizable mob, I thought, as long as they weren't armed with silver. My howl alone would paralyze them with fear. Then I could leap in among them, slashing and biting and rending. A kick from one of my hind legs would send an armored man flying.

And that's just vanilla *were*-me.

Maybe I could juice that a little …

I unslung my pack and opened it, and popped up a Glow above me so that I could see what I might find.

There were far more of Elun's potions in my niblun backpack than would seem possible—but that's nibluns for you. Layer after layer of them there were, down and down, under all my other gear. It took a while to unpack them and check them all out. Some, as she'd said, I might never need, but it was better to have them than not, just in case. Among those, as well as her Scorpion Salve, were:

Waterbreath (one mouthful = 5 minutes)
Deathmask (2 hours no pulse; never take more than once per week!
   Use Easelife on revival)
Carnage (emergencies only)
Leadweight (renders immovable. DO NOT USE WHILE SWIMMING)
Thunderfart (for clearing rooms. Allergens: Cabbage, fishpaste, garlic)
Horrorfog
Distortion (head will alter to ghoul form, and alarm foes. Lie down
   within 20 minutes of using)
Stoneskin
Sleepdeep (use with caution. Addictive)
Arcanaboost
Mindstun (secrete 5 to 10 drops into target's drink. Do not consume)
Springheels

Well, I thought: Much to look into there, when I get the chance. Among those various flasks there were also plenty of Restore Health potions, and Mending potions, and Stamina Wells, and Stavecharges. All of which, I anticipated, would come in useful. We were, after all, going to be contesting with gods and demons, so we'd need all the help we could get. None of those potions, though, seemed to be anything that would be needed by a werewolf—except, perhaps, one that was wounded.

There was one potion, though, that I thought might buff my *were*-me: *Longstreak*, which enhanced speed and endurance.

Only one way to find out. I unsealed the flask and took a mouthful.

I sealed it back up, replaced it in my pack; felt the warmth of the tincture suffusing my blood, and decided to go for a little run. I was a hundred yards away before I knew it.

Whoa, I thought, as the world swam back into focus and time slowed back down to normal. That's just *human*-me. What about *were*-me …?

Yes, well, okay, let's try the other guy …

I took another mouthful, and Turned—again without effort, without any wrenching, or gasping, or roaring, or histrionics. This was just *me,* after all. Another face of my prism. Another aspect of my personality. Like when, on occasion, you might be with your bank manager, or your parents, or your boss, or your friends, or your lover, or a police officer, or whoever, and you adjust accordingly, without even thinking about it. All those adjustments are still *you*; you're not being untrue to yourself, or untruthful to others. Are you just one simple, simplistic, one-dimensional being? I'm not. I've never met anyone who is.

I dropped onto all fours and ran.

I ran so fast that I outran my ability to adjust, to react. I caromed off the trees that surrounded me like some demented, hairy pinball. I bounced back and staggered—and my staggers were so fast and blind-sided that I ricocheted from one tree to another, and twirled off in the direction they all threw me towards the next one. I was moving faster than I could think. And was being hit harder, because of the speed I was going, than anything had ever hit me before. Except Graycote's backhand. It was the barrage of thumping into trees that stopped me, eventually, battered, and panting, and confused—and two miles away from where I'd left Shift and my pack a few seconds earlier. *Gods above and below,* I thought. What in all hells was *that?!*

I tottered, and then slumped onto the ground, my chest heaving.

When, some long, baffled minutes later, I eventually recovered, I realized something.

I was bruised and breathless from the beating the stationary trees had given me—but not from the exertion of running under the influence of Elun's Longstreak.

I got back up on my paws, and wolf-trotted back to Shift and my backpack, thinking, *well now. If I can get the hang of that* …. What I'd done, in those crazy, few hyperfast seconds was the equivalent of jumping onto a gunsled having never ridden even a tricycle. *Now that could be useful*, I thought. If I could learn how to ride that in *were*-form, using Elun's super-fuel: I'd be the fastest thing on four legs or forty.

I examined the potions that I'd laid out on the ground around my pack.

There were only two flasks of Longstreak.

My first thought was, well, that should put some distance between me and my pursuers, wherever they come from.

My second was, *No, hold up, wait; using that up that might be a waste. You might need it later ...*

I wasn't even in a fight here. I was just on the road. A road that I could run fast enough in my *were-*form.

I still had half a month to catch up with the others. After which, we might well be needing buffs like Longstreak.

Think what Grell, Qrysta or Oller could do with that boost. Or Little Guy, who was already as fast as fury in his speed-imbued niblun battle leathers. He'd be like brown lightning with a gulp of this in him. He'd be an uncatchable, unavoidable nuisance. Some damn vicious little thing you couldn't even spot down there, biting you in the leg or the nuts, and then fifty yards away before you even feel it? If that doesn't distract you long enough for Oller to slip a knife into your neck, I don't know what would.

No, I shouldn't squander this. I should hoard it.

Maybe one more mouthful, though ...

I swallowed, and resealed the flask, and replaced it in my pack, and slung it and Shift on my back, and Turned: And, driven by Longstreak, streaked long and fast into the night.

All the way to dawn. And into the morning that followed, and then to noon, before the boost wore off, when eventually I slowed, forty leagues from where I'd started.

I only managed, at an ever-dwindling pace, another ten leagues before the next night fell; when I slowed and found a scrape under a bush where I could sleep.

Which, once I'd Turned back into human form, I almost instantly did—sleeping until daybreak, when I was woken by distant horns, and the baying of hounds.

And then answering horns, from another direction entirely.

And then more.

I was, I could hear, surrounded on three sides.

357

I had no doubt that I was the quarry.

I sat up. Listened.

They don't know, I thought. They're just guessing. There are probably dozens of these patrols out here, coursing this way and that, on the off chance of finding me.

Can't let that happen.

There was only one way to go, and that was away from the horns that I had heard—and soon heard again, as they called to each other.

Keep going forwards.

Which is what I did, right into their trap. I decided to stay in human form, as I didn't want the smell of wolf to carry on the breeze, and I'd rather be able to think clearly and wield Shift in a fight—and besides, what if they had silver arrows? So I made my way, as silently as possible, away from the sounds of the hunters. They didn't seem to know I was nearby. There was nothing urgent about the calls of their horns, no *tallyho* or *view halloo* alerts. This was probably, I thought, just one search party out of many. Yes: I should be okay here, if I can just work my way around to get downwind of them, then I can Turn and run like hell.

It was going well, until, one moment I was sneaking, carefully, into a narrow gap between thick undergrowth on one side and a cliff on the other, straining to hear sounds of pursuit, and the next, I was tumbling through artfully laid, leaf-and-mud-covered branches into a pit three times as deep as I was tall.

28

The Pit

I bumped down as the branches broke under my weight into a deep, sheer-sided pit, where I landed with a thump, lurched forwards, the breath knocked out of me, and bounced off the opposite wall. It all happened so fast that I hardly had time to react, just managing at the last moment to hold Shift in my crossed arms out in front of me to take the impact. It was soft and wet underfoot, and I could feel cold mud splattering my face. Incoherent thoughts chased themselves through my mind in my panic. They cleared fast when I heard the horns again.

The hunters. *They mustn't catch me here. I have to get out. There is no way out. There has to be, or I'm dead. I can't hide, they'll see the trap has been sprung; they're bound to look in. And the hounds, they'll smell me, they'll give tongue. Wolf form? No, they might have silver! And if they don't, they'll just wait up there, while I snarl up at them, knowing what I am, and send for silver. And then they'll just use me as target-practice, until I'm dead. But they're looking for me, the tall caster with the cropped fair hair, copper stag brooch. If they see me that'll be even worse …!*

I could hear voices. They weren't alerted yet, and not too close yet, but they were coming this way, no question. They would have to pass through the narrow bottleneck between the cliff and the thickets.

That's why they had laid their trap here. *Take off the brooch? So what, I'm still a caster with a terrible haircut—*

No, wait …

I remembered what I'd thought, when the huntsman had known me—and I berated myself for taking so long to think it again now. *Idiot!* I was not going to make the same mistake twice. The voices changed, now nearer, louder, more urgent—they'd spotted something. My footprints, perhaps. My scent. A hound bayed, then others.

"Over here, this way, come on!"

A horn sounded a signal. Shouts, footsteps, shadows against the tree-filled sky above me, heads and tongues and ears, excited, jumping, barking.

Then men hurrying up, pushing through the frantic dogs and peering down.

Stopping, confused, not believing what they were seeing.

And me, staring up at them frostily, impatient, annoyed.

I made myself breathe calmly and keep my pulse from racing.

I assumed an affronted authority that I certainly wasn't feeling.

"I suppose," I snapped, in my new cracked, old voice, "you're the fools that dug this pit?!"

I let that challenge hang in the air and crossed my spindly old arms and glared at them, waiting to see who would reply.

It was a small, leathery man who answered, nervously, "Er, and who are you, ma'am, if I might ask?"

So. Him, then.

I knew what I was looking at: A man of the woods. A man who knew the wilds and the dangers they contained. I also knew what he was seeing: An angry, malevolent, warty old hag in black clothes and black hat, holding a staff. Out here. Alone. What kind of crone walks the wildwood by herself, with only a staff to protect her …?

I withered him with my witchiest scowl.

"Why?" I threatened. "You want to know me, do you, laddie?"

"No, no, ma'am," he said, quickly, and was going to say something else, but I cut him off.

"Well, I know *you*, now!" I croaked, jabbing a bony finger at him. "And it'll be *turn and turn about* between you and me now, boy! Remember what they say: *One bad deed deserves another.*"

I could see the fear growing in his face.

"No, ma'am, it wasn't, we wasn't—"

"It is!" I cut him off. "What is done, is *done*. What is to be done about it," I nodded, slowly, not taking my eyes off him, "will be seen. Oh yes! You can be sure of *that*."

One of his hounds bayed suddenly, nervous. I fired a Flameball at it, knocking it six feet into the air, sizzling and squealing.

"Now, are you going to help me out of here," I said, "or are you going to make me wait until night?" I held my staff up, as if to say, *this will be a broomstick after dark.*

"I will rise out, and fly to join my sisters at our gathering, and tell them what *you* did to make me late for it. Quite a tumble I've taken, thanks to you, and a shock to my poor old heart. Well, two can play at that game, my lad, if it's shocks you want! One bad deed deserves another. Two bad deeds deserve *worse*. My sisters will take umbrage,when I tell them what you've done—great offence. We'll come looking for you. Oh yes, that we will. We always do. All of us. For all of *you!*"

I nodded, slowly, scanning the anxious faces above me, and passed my staff in front of me, turning round to include them all, dipping it meaningfully at them, one at a time. "And we'll find you. Have no doubt about that. I've marked you all, now. Marked you well. There's no hiding from a Marking!"

I smiled a mirthless, toothless smile. I raised my arms, and chanted, *"One by one, each by each, turn by turn, lessons teach!"*

A rope dropped into the pit in front of me.

Another fell beside it. Two men shimmied down them and tied a knot in the end of their ropes.

"Here, ma'am, if it please you," they said, and, "our apologies for the inconvenience; we'll have you out of here in a jiffy," and, as they joined their hands to form a seat for me, "take a hold on the ropes, sit back."

I sat on their hands. They stood on their knots, arms around the ropes, gripping them with armpits and knees. Their companions hauled us up. Not without difficulty—I was, after all, heavier than I looked. They set me down carefully on the ground, and all backed away from me, warily. I turned my scowl from one face to another, taking them all in, step by step on my creaking old hips. I raised Shift, and they all quickly moved back another pace or two. I Feared their hounds, who ran off in all directions, whining.

I nodded at the small, leathery man.

"Name?" I said.

He didn't want to tell me. He shifted from foot to foot. I stared, and waited, letting my impatience show, my eyebrows rising into my gray old hairline.

"Hubb," he said, at last.

"Hubb," I repeated, nodding, making a note of the name. "Hubb, eh?"

"Yes'm," he said, miserably.

I pointed a bony forefinger at him. "We'll meet again, Hubb, you and I."

He ducked his head, and shuffled awkwardly, and touched his cap, and managed not to whimper.

"And when we do," I said, "you'd best remember your manners. Or it might not go so well for you as this day."

"Yes, ma'am," he mumbled. "Certainly, ma'am. Sorry, ma'am, no offense meant."

I snorted. "You dig any more traps on *my* paths, in *my* woods, Hubb, offense will most *definitely* be taken!" I promised.

"We won't, ma'am. You have my word on it."

"Mm," I grunted, and gave him one last, hard stare. "And a wise word it is." I could see his relief. He thought I'd let him off the hook. I hadn't. I wanted to dig my hook deep into him, and into all the rest of them. I'd Feared the hounds. Now to put the fear of their lives into these men.

"Best not be out and about after dark tonight, on this night of all nights, is my advice," I said. "The winter solstice, it is, the longest night, when the old year dies, and we gather, and *do*. And we don't hold with those as interrupt our gatherings."

I turned away, without waiting for an answer, and stumped off down the forest path, hauling my bent old body along, hanging from the thumb notch in my staff.

They didn't even think of following.

I went my way, slowly.

They went theirs, as fast as they could.

When I could no longer hear them, or their horses and hounds, I was able to lower my guard, and I hurried along. *Craft,* I thought. *Coven.* I knew little more than the hunters did about it. I was not, after all, a member. But what I did know what this: You do not want to mess with Coven. I'd chosen my Glamour well, as a cantankerous old crone. And they'd bought it, hook, line, and sinker.

It was telling, I thought, that a lame old woman could scare the crap out of so many men. They had hounds, and teeth, and knives, and bows, and blades, and muscles, and numbers. And a more than healthy respect for the hag they'd dropped into their pit. They had wanted to be anywhere else rather than out in the wildwood, messing with her.

Marnie, I thought.

I could so have done with her swooping out of the sky and setting my head straight, knocking some sense into it. She'd know what I wasn't seeing. She'd know what I should do.

Just the thought of her gave me strength and made me smile. I felt her backing me. And I looked forward to talking it through with her when this was all over.

Which, of course, it was still a long way from being. As I was still a long way from meeting up with the others at our rendezvous at High Rock. I just hoped I'd be in time and would get there before they moved on. I had many leagues to cover yet—and, who knew, maybe many dangers to face. I cleansed my "spiteful crone" Glamour from me, and settled into *were*-form, and began to run, in the easy, loping wolf-strides that ate up the leagues.

My mind fogged, as it always did in *were*-form, but I could still think, if slowly, about whatever I had at the forefront of my mind. My thoughts didn't dart here and there, as they tended to do in *me*-form. They didn't jump to conclusions or have sudden revelations. They also didn't have distractions. League after league I hunted in my mind, all my concentration on that one question: *What to do?* Sometimes, IRL, I had needed to go back to bed to think, to sink into that alpha state where I was completely open to whatever needed to come in. No screens. No phone. No interruptions. Just me, drifting off, considering the question, listening, waiting. Waiting for the answer, open to it, hoping it would present itself.

Being in *were*-form was like that. The world coming to me, through my nostrils, through my paws, through the wind in my pelt and the speed of my running. My mind empty, receptive. My blood, pumping in my ears, my tongue hanging. Yes, I was far stupider in *were*-form. I couldn't have strung two words together, even if my wolf lips and tongue had been able to form them. But I was more alert, more *alive*.

What to do? What to do?

The rhythm of that question loped along with my feet. And, just as if I was lucky when drifting off into an alpha state IRL, and something would suggest itself to me, I found the beginnings of an idea, in the quietness, the alertness, as memories of voices that I had heard on this quest echoed in my mind.

God.

Demon.

Back the winner.

Both lose.

It wasn't the answer itself. Not yet, far from it. But, somehow, it seemed that something in there made sense, as if I'd distilled the problem to its essence. I tried to work it out, but my fogged *were*-mind couldn't cope with it. I let the knowledge settle into the part of me where it belonged: My instinct. I *knew*. I couldn't say exactly what I knew. I couldn't verbalize it to anyone. I couldn't explain. All I could do was feel. I felt the growl of contentment in my chest as that slow conclusion came to me. *Enough,* I shook the thought off. *We have the end of a thread. We'll pull it later and see what's all the way at the other end of it.* I saw a low rock outlined against the night sky above me and jumped up onto it.

I crouched, threw my head back, and howled at the moon.

Sleeping was easier in *were*-form. It came more naturally, just as running did. All I needed to do was curl up in my own warmth, on whatever dry patch I might find, and, day or night, I would drop off, and wake refreshed an hour, or several hours, later. It was so simple, just doing what came naturally, obeying the dictates of my own body. If I was tired, I slept, long and deep. If I needed a rest, I dozed, light and short. If I was hungry, I killed.

I was hungry less often than I would be in *me*-form. A kill, a meal, and I would be fueled for days. My senses were also sharper. I could smell human on the wind and avoid them—although, in the wilderness of that sparsely populated realm, people were few and far between. No other creatures showed any interest in confronting me. I crossed paths with bears, and sabercats, and a mother wyvern with her five pups. Sweet little things they were—no bigger than chickens, tottering along behind her. Their baby wings poked out of their backs like the fins of seahorses. They wouldn't be flying for months, until they were properly fledged. She was half my size, but I wasn't going to tangle with her. She was all teeth and claws and scales, and her eyes were hard. She opened her beak in warning, and I saw the glow of fire in her throat. I waited, respectfully, for her to go about her business. Among my sharpened senses was my sense of danger. Few of the wildlife that I encountered alerted it. We knew not to bother each other.

The further west I went, the further I got from any human presence. I sensed other presences, though—people who weren't quite human, but near enough for me to steer clear of them. *Folk*, the word came to me. They felt as if they belonged there, in those deep woods, among its ancient trees. My memory was also fogged, in *were*-form. The longer I stayed in it, the less human I was becoming, I felt. It was all feeling, in *were*-form, and little thinking. I made sure to Turn back from time to time and walk as myself on two legs. That gave my mind time to recover, and the chance to consider more deeply.

Folk. Yes, my cleared mind thought—as in Wood Folk. Nyrik and Horm. Friends, they had become, but I remembered their archers. Archers who might shoot first and ask questions later if they saw *were*-me. I steered clear of the few that I sensed. There were none after several days of hard running, as the land began to slope upwards into the foothills of the Sunset Mountains.

Every dawn, and every dusk, I cast Lightseek for my companions. I never found the slightest trace of them. I considered that a good sign. Oller and Qrysta should be far away to the east, on their quests. Grell would only be showing up if he'd failed in his. I honed my Lightseek skill by leaving Shift behind me and casting it to find her. She always showed up bright and strong, her red and green lights intermingling. I could leave her five miles behind me, then ten, and find her without difficulty. I didn't have time to keep going back for her, as I needed to press on; but I was confident that I could find my other targets over such distances now.

All in all, I felt pretty good about things. I had a grasp of the problem, I thought, and some ideas about how to solve it. Which I would only be able to do, of course, once I'd found the others and learned what they had learned. I still couldn't quite see how I was going to get there, but I was thinking like Avildor now about it all.

Decide on the result and work backwards from that.

The first snow I'd seen for a while fell one morning before I'd left the tree line. The cold didn't bother me. If anything, it made running in *were*-form more comfortable. I didn't overheat so quickly, nor did I need to rest so often. I saw tracks, of deer and hare and fox, and caught drifts of their scent on the wind. By evening I was out of the trees and heading up bare, snow-covered hills that merged into the Sunset Mountains. I slept in *were*-form when I tired, warm in a hollow between boulders.

The next morning, I re-Turned, and walked upright for some hours, to refresh my thoughts. It seemed important to establish that I, Daxx, was the dominant partner in this relationship, not my *were*-alter ego. I wondered how long I'd have to search these mountains for the entry to the portal. Grell had had his lodestone and map. I would have to make do with trial and error—which was why I had aimed for a point well to the north of where I thought the portal should be. I remembered the mark that Oldface had put on Grell's map as being pretty much in the middle of the range. Around noon, as the nearest mountains reared above me, I changed again and began to run on all fours.

I found nothing that day. I wasn't going to keep running at night, because I might miss a cave entrance in the dark, even with my sharp wolf eyes. Once again, I curled up around myself in the shelter of some rocks and slept until daybreak. I was warm, and comfortable. I didn't even feel the snow when it began in the night. I woke up before dawn to find myself covered in it. I rose to my paws and shook the snow off my pelt. Once again I began to run, always upward. The air grew colder. The wind drove snow into my face from the mountains ahead. Late the next morning it brought a strange, new scent to me: A strong, musky odor of some big, powerful creature. Definitely not human, but similar. If I had known then what I learned later, when Grell told me Murruk's story of how Orcs had originated, I'd have put two and two together right away. But I was in *were*-form, tasting that distinctive, perplexing smell in my nostrils, puzzling at it as it teased me—and in *were*-form, it's hard to think.

The odor grew stronger as the wall of the mountain to my right grew higher and steeper, becoming a cliff. I cantered along it until another cliff loomed up ahead of me on my left. The unfamiliar smell seemed to be everywhere now. It was not just coming to me on the wind: It was a distinct trail on the ground, leaching up through the snow. The odor trail led to the mouth of a cave, where the two cliffs converged. A large, snow-covered boulder sat beside it. There were signs of fire everywhere, on the cliffs, on the underside of the boulder below its cape of snow. The ground reeked with the creature's scent. I stopped.

My wolf brain couldn't think, so I changed to *me*-form.

My thoughts cleared.

A strange—almost certainly large and powerful, going by the smell of it—creature.

Cave. Which could be its home.

Have to check it out, though. This could be the place I'm looking for.

I buffed up for combat. I cast a green Shield around myself, and Muffle on my feet, so that the large and powerful creature wouldn't hear me coming. I threw a Glow above my head and entered the mouth of the tunnel.

It was a relief to be out of the wind. I'd only been in *me*-form for a few minutes out in the open; but that had been long enough for my skin to wish it still had a thick wolf pelt covering it. The tunnel sloped down. Every Reveal that I cast showed only rats and mice ahead of me. No *large and powerful* creature. I was wondering what rats and mice lived on, up there, where there was no plant life. Worms, maybe. Insects. Then, ahead of me, I saw a faint blue light. I approached it with caution. I had no way of making myself invisible. I might, I believed, be able to sneak past whatever *large and powerful* creature it was, that lived down there. I'd try to do that before risking combat. I could hear the faint sound of running water coming from ahead. I flattened myself against the tunnel's wall and peered round it into the cavern.

Well.

I saw at once that I'd been wrong about there being no plant life up there. The place was lush with growth. Trees, leaning in from all angles—even, I saw, as I looked around, from the ceiling.

And then, finally, I put that two and two together.

Unnatural.

Its nemesis and opposite guarding the Nature.

I was amused at the thought of telling Grell what he smelled like.

This was the place all right. And he'd been here, no doubt about that. I cast Reveals, in case he was still there and I could creep up on him and scare the crap out of him. No blurry red outline of Grell was revealed. I knew now that the cavern was uninhabited, so I walked on into it. The sound of running water grew louder and louder as I neared an upside-down waterfall. I stared in it in disbelief, watching as it thundered up into the cavern's ceiling. Unnatural indeed. My eye followed the torrent that poured along over my head and emptied itself up and away through the hole in the cavern's roof by the far wall.

Where something white-blue hung, suspended from the cavern's ceiling.

The portal.

I thought, *How in all hells had Grell managed to get up there?*

I walked over to the granite wall, and saw the ladder of bodkins, frozen into it. I smiled. So. The big guy had done it.

I started up the bodkin ladder, thinking, *There has to be a story behind this. Wonder where Grell got hold of these things. And the bow to fire them with.*

It had to be a hell of a weapon, to drive cold steel—*very* cold steel—into granite.

I stopped and examined an arrowhead closely. Definitely steel, I decided, but not like any steel I'd ever seen before. It was freezing under my hands, as if infused with ice. I didn't want to touch it for long, in case my skin froze onto it.

Weird, I thought.

I climbed on and reached the top, where, tentatively, I stretched out one foot into the portal. It disappeared through the blue-white sheen. I cast another Shield around me, just in case I was about to plummet to the cavern's floor, and, hoping for the best, pushed off and jumped through—plummeting instead, in the direction that had until recently been "up," onto my back beyond the portal. The Shield cushioned my landing. I righted myself, stood up, and set off along the sky-blue ribbon-path that stretched off and away in front of me.

As in the portalscape that had been home to the helldragon, the path twisted around and about, weaving in and out of dozens of other ribbon-paths, leading off into the indigo distance in all directions.

Directions that were soon to present me with a problem.

It was a problem that I saw as I came up my ribbon-path onto a platform.

Paths of all colors, twisting this way and that, led off from it. Some led to other platforms, above and below, and to either side, from which yet more colored paths led off, to yet more platforms, all the way every way into the far distance wherever I turned to look, left or right, up or down. I could see thirty, forty, or more platforms, interconnected by twisting ribbon-paths that led off everywhere—almost certainly, I felt, to innumerable other platforms. It would take forever to try them all. I would run out of food long before I'd explored a hundredth of them.

I could die of starvation in there, chasing shadows, before I found the right one.

Yes, I might be able to try exit portal after exit portal, but supposing I tried one that was hanging from a ceiling, like in the cavern? I'd go through it and fall to the floor, from gods knew what height, and might never be able to get back up to reach it again.

Could I stick my head through, to take a look around—like I'd stuck my foot through back there, before pushing off from the frosted bodkin ladder?

There'd be only one way to see: I'd have to try. But if the rest of me was pulled through, I'd be trapped out there—wherever "out there" was—if there was no way back in here. And then I'd be separated from the others, and in some other place with some other problem, while they had to solve ours without me.

I tried to think the situation through.

I was in the right place; I was sure of that. Grell had come through after building his bodkin ladder. He must have completed his task and found the Nature, because I hadn't seen anything within the portal. There was no sign of him. Therefore, he must have gone on out, to the rendezvous at High Rock.

Yes, I thought.

Easy for him; he'd had a map and a lodestone. I had neither.

I was stumped. I had no idea which way to go, which direction even to start running in. I thought, glumly, *I wish he'd left a trail.*

But Grell had had no way of knowing that I'd be following him, so he wouldn't have thought of marking any of these paths.

I stood there, deep in thought, for a long while, wondering what on earth to do. Just start running, as fast as I could, and hope to get lucky before I starved to death?

Did I have a choice?

I couldn't see an alternative.

Around and around in my head the same thoughts kept going, getting me absolutely nowhere—until two of them collided.

Trail.

Running.

I took a deep breath, and exhaled, and smiled.

Of course.

I Turned—and the odor of "large and powerful creature" immediately poured into my werewolf nostrils. I ran along it, as it led me through the portalscape.

I'd never have found the way in a million years. Grell's scent trail led me to platform after platform, from where it branched off on ribbon-paths of different colors, often doubling back on itself, curling around and then back in the opposite direction. Eventually, I could see the end of it, in an indigo wall ahead patterned with stars. I cantered towards it, on an orange ribbon-path, and stopped, and sniffed.

No question. Grell had gone out this way.

As I neared the exit portal, I saw a familiar shape on a platform ahead of me.

I stopped by the clerk at his high desk and looked down at him.

"No animals allowed," he said.

I re-Turned back to *me*-form.

I was worried. I didn't have an exit ticket. I'd seen what he'd done before, when Grell had walked past him and thumped into an invisible barrier.

"You may proceed," he said.

"Don't I have to sign out?"

"Sign out what?" he said. "You haven't removed anything from in here, have you?"

I shook my head, and said, "No."

"Well, then," he said, dismissively.

"Thank you," I said.

"You're welcome. Have a nice day."

I walked past him and stepped through the portal.

I landed, to my relief, not upside down but the right way up, on the dry, sandy floor of a cave. Ahead of me, coming around a corner, I could see light. I walked towards it, wondering if anyone else had got there before me. I turned the corner, cautiously, looking around, listening …. I didn't think Oldface was to be trusted. He might have lured us here, into … what? I moved forwards, slowly, towards the bright blue sky that I could see at the cave's end, no more than fifty yards away. I hadn't crossed more than twenty of those yards before the silence was broken by a familiar voice.

Not Grell, or Qrysta, or Oller—but Little Guy.

I'd recognize that sound anywhere.

I smiled, and settled Shift on my back, straightened up, and walked to the end of the cave. I couldn't *wait* to see Oller and Little Guy again! But, as I emerged, coming down to a wide expanse of sand under a clear, blue sky, I had already sensed that something was wrong. Little Guy's barking had grown into a frenzied yammering, becoming an alarm that was a mixture of warning and terror. There was a large pool ahead of me, surrounded by palm trees. It was a peaceful enough looking place, but it was in anything but a peaceful state as I came into it. It was in a state of high alert. Oller was in his crouch, a knife in each hand, tensed to throw, and Grell had a monstrous bow trained on the cave's entrance.

I stopped, and held my arms wide, and grinned at my friends. They relaxed, and stood up, downing their weapons. "Daxxie!" Grell roared, and Oller said, "Daxx! You made it!" They were all smiles. Little Guy was still all warning and terror. Naturally, because of the racket Little Guy was making, they'd been expecting trouble. I walked down, and they hurried up, and we whooped and chortled— Grell stopped and stared in horror at me, and said, "What the fuck's with that haircut, mate?"

"Long story."

It would have to wait, because Little Guy's panic had grown ever the louder the closer I got to him. Oller started shushing him, while trying to greet me, but couldn't. The nearer I came to them, the more frantic Little Guy became, his lips drawn back in a terrified snarl, his barking a desperate volley of fear and fury.

"Oy, stop that, you little bleeder!" Oller was saying. "It's *Daxxie*, for gawds' sakes. What's wrong with you?"

By this time, Grell had me in a bear hug, and I was rocking him in my arms—and taking a surreptitious sniff of the air around him, to see if I could get any hint of that large-and-powerful-creature smell. In *me*-form, I couldn't.

"Bleeding hells, mate," Grell said, "is it good to see you! I've been pissing myself with worry they'd burned you alive."

"Unburnt," I said, grinning. "Talked my way out of it."

"You silver-tongued bastard!" Grell's face was one huge smile.

Oller was still trying to calm Little Guy. He wanted to greet me, but he had a problem on his hands.

"What the fuck, Little Guy?" he was shouting. "What's got into you?!"

The little dog was making the most desperate racket, shivering under Oller's armpit where he was trapped, his feet scrabbling at Oller's jerkin in an attempt to get away.

Ah, I thought. *I know what's got into him.*

I said, above the incessant, crazed barking, "It's okay, Ols."

"No, it isn't; the little sod needs to mind his manners!"

"It's not his fault," I said.

Oller said, "Eh?"

"It isn't his fault," I repeated, louder. "It's mine."

He looked at me, puzzled.

I said, "Stand back, okay?"

Oller said, "Eh?' again.

"Stand back," I repeated, "and put him down when he stops yapping,"

Oller backed off, as did Grell.

I Turned.

Oller staggered backwards, gasping. Little Guy exploded in a volley of barking. Grell picked up some weird-looking blunt instrument and sank into his combat crouch. They were both shouting; but in my *were*-form I couldn't make out the words, and Little Guy was barking even more madly than before.

I stood there, as still as I could manage, while they jabbered at me and each other in alarm. I couldn't speak, of course, but had a pretty good idea of what they were saying. Which was the obvious—what anyone would say if their friend turned into an eight-foot-tall werewolf. Their scents hit me at once—*gods* they smelled good! It was like standing outside a kitchen where a feast is being prepared, after a long day's walk and nothing to eat. *Oh*, how I longed to sink my teeth into them ... Little Guy smelled especially tasty. But I'd told my *were*-self what I needed to do, and eating my friends wasn't part of the plan. As carefully as I could, I dropped to all fours, and crouched, low, and slunk up to Oller's feet, my belly to the ground. He was still gibbering at me and holding hysterical Little Guy up and away from me above his head.

Little Guy's fear and fury subsided. His barking was punctuated by growling, and snarls, and then replaced by them altogether. I lowered my head, meekly, and glanced up at him, trying for a "please don't hit me" expression. His growling lessened and ceased. He sniffed the air, interested. His fear and fury had clearly been replaced by curiosity. I saw his tail wag, beyond Oller's arms. Oller felt it, and looked up at Little Guy, who was looking down at me, ears pricked. Oller brought him down, from high above his head, and stroked him, and said something to Little Guy, in an encouraging tone, and lowered him to the ground.

Little Guy looked at me, and then did what I'd hoped he'd do.

He trotted round and shoved his wet little nose up against my butthole.

I'd raised my tail so that he could do just that. He took several good, long sniffs.

I rolled over onto my back.

Little Guy checked me out thoroughly, all over, then stood over me, wagging his tail.

I rolled back onto all fours, and repaid him the compliment, by checking him out doggy style. *Wow,* I thought. What a *fantastic* smelling butt he has! I *like* this dog! We're going to be friends, right?! Ohmigod—and his little dick??! Sweet! I have to check that butthole out again …

Little Guy's fantastic-smelling backside detached itself from my nose as he headed off down my body, which was three times as long as he was, for another inspection of mine. I let him take his time. Then, when I felt nothing but happy dog vibes coming from him, I trotted off and took a leak against a palm tree. Little Guy followed, sniffed my mark, and laid his over it.

I turned, and sat, and looked down at him.

He sat opposite me.

I pricked my ears.

He responded in kind.

I could *feel* him grinning. His tail was sweeping the ground behind him.

Okay, I thought, wagging my own tail in response, let's go for it! I shot off around the pool. Little Guy, in his niblun-imbued speed leathers, easily caught up with me in seconds. Together, we tested our limits. Around and around the oasis pool we sped. *Well, if I ever had to leave the others behind and make a break for it, Little Guy would easily keep up with me.* His short legs were a blur of motion. He bounced along beside me, ears streaming in the wind, yapping occasionally in excitement. Every few seconds we'd pass the others, who were loving the spectacle. I was at full gallop, straining every muscle in my body to lose him in my wake, when he turned on the afterburners and streaked ahead of me. In less than four more circuits he had caught up with me, and was cruising along at my side again, turning his head at me in mockery, his ears flying. I'd thought I was the fastest damn thing on four legs, but I'd been lapped by a thirty-pound mongrel.

Yeah? I thought.

Okay, you have the speed, little feller, let's see who has the stamina.

I put my head down and ran. Little Guy ran with me. *As fast as we can, as long as we can.*

Little Guy broke first. He slowed to a trot, then shuffled over to Oller, who leaned down and pulled his ears, the way he liked it. He sat, panting hard, and they watched as I ran a few more laps around the pool, at the same, relentless speed, just to show that I could keep going, and going, and going. I pulled up by them, and reared up, and stood, all eight feet of me looking down at them. I spread my arms wide, and threw my head back, and unleashed my most terrifying howl. Oller and Grell jumped back, their faces slack with horror. Only Little Guy stayed where he was, enjoying the show, wagging his tail happily. I re-Turned to *me*-form, and Little Guy padded over and stood up on his hind legs, his forepaws on my thigh.

"Hey there," I said, ruffling his head.

He licked my hand.

Grell, lowering his weapon, said, "Fuck, mate!?"

"Yeah," I said, "tell me about it."

Oller said, "Blimey, Daxx. It's good to see you, but …"

Words failed him.

I said, "We have some catching up to do, right?"

29

Her Own Worst Enemy

It was the first thought Qrysta had, staring at "herself." *I'm my own enemy?* And then—*my own worst enemy. I'm the last person I want to fight. She'll know all the moves I know, all the counters. She has the same swords I have, and I don't want to be on the sharp end of those. Just like that Other Jess behind her has a whitewood bow. Where did they get those? Two niblun swords made for me alone, and a bow like Jess's? Out of thin air?*

So, what are they, then, these two echoes of us? Growing out of shapes on the floor. They may look human, same as Jess and I do, but they probably aren't. In which case, they might not tire; they might be stronger and faster and better than us.

She's ready to rock, clearly. Standing there, challenge laid down, waiting for me to respond. Well, I'm not ready. Let her wait. I need to think this through. If I have to fight her—well, so be it. I'll do my best and win or die trying. But … maybe I don't have to? Maybe there's another way.

Puzzle. Solve the problem. That's me over there. How do I beat me?

Qrysta didn't know where to start.

Okay, just forget that it's me for a moment. How do I beat anyone? I dance with them and find their weaknesses. Which I then exploit. What are my weaknesses?

Well, she thought, *I don't need to dance with "me" to find that out. I've known my weaknesses as long as I've been alive. Hidden away they may be, from the rest of the world, deep down inside this Qrysta that I now am, but they're still there. My sorrows, my failings. The things that I'm hopeless at. All that baggage that never goes away. Those wounds, those disappointments. You compensate for them, you work on them, you do your best to play the hand that life dealt you. But you don't deny their existence.*

There are so many things I'm not good at. Just about the only thing that I am good at, meaning expert at, is being Qrysta, in combat. No doubt she's expert too—that Other Qrysta facing me. So, let's not play to her strengths. Let's exploit her weaknesses.

Which would be my weaknesses.

She lowered her swords, slowly, and then sheathed them in her belt.

Other Qrysta opposite her shifted slightly, swords still raised at the ready, her eyebrows also raised now a fraction, in surprise.

Qrysta said, "Jess, what were your brother's and sister's names?"

Jess said, "Joey and Am. Short for Amila."

At those words, Other Jess jerked her bow up and drew the string back to her ear, its arrow pointed at Jess. She held it, at full stretch, her left arm trembling.

Jess didn't respond in kind. She stared at Other Jess, holding her eyes.

Other Qrysta turned and nodded at her Jess.

Slowly, Other Jess lowered her bow, easing off on the string.

So, Qrysta thought. *Standoff.* Which is better than fighting. As long as it holds. As to how long that might be, she had no idea. *Why me? Of all the foes I have to face here, why me?*

Something nagged at her, as she thought that.

What am I missing?

She re-ran the sentence in her head.

Of all the foes I have to face here, why me?

The words rearranged themselves.

Why me, here? Why not me some other place? Why here?

The pieces of the puzzle fell into place.

It's all in the mind.

His Mind; bound captive here in this sunken tower by its nemesis, its opposite. The one thing that will do everything it can to keep him under lock and key.

And should anyone come to free it for him: *Their* nemesis; *their* opposite.

Qrysta's own strengths turned against her. Her own weaknesses exposed.

So, if I'm reading this right …

Looking at Other Qrysta, standing there opposite herself, Qrysta felt a wash of understanding. She longed to tell her who she was—that she had built her, crafted her. Much as she had longed to live in a world such as the ones that she, and Grell, and Daxx had run together in so well. Even more so, she longed to be Qrysta. For real. She knew it was impossible, of course: "Qrysta" was just an avatar. But oh, it would have been *lovely*. Just *imagine* …

And now, she had been Qrysta for real, for over a year.

She didn't want to fight her. She wanted to thank her.

She undid her belt and dropped her swords to the floor.

She stepped over to Other Qrysta, standing there, with her swords raised in the stance she knew so well. In a heartbeat she'd be dead, if Other Qrysta wanted. So be it. She, her own Qrysta, smiled. Other Qrysta stared, impassive, hostile.

"I am so grateful that you came into my life." Qrysta held her double's gaze.

She could feel the smile on her own face. And then, the tears filling her eyes.

The other Qrysta faltered.

"Any moment that I wasn't being you, I was so much less," Qrysta continued. "Every chance I got, we'd be running, you and I, together, and life was fine. I knew you weren't real, just as I know you're not real now. But you meant more to me than just about anything that *was* real. I knew that if I ever met you, I would have done anything for you, Qrysta. Just as I knew that was impossible. But now I have met you. And I'd do anything for you now."

The other Qrysta's eyes darkened. She didn't like the way this was going.

Qrysta reached out her hand for hers. "Don't leave me," she said, "now that I've found you."

She stared at her. Herself. All that she could ever want to be.

In a sudden blur, Other Qrysta snapped her swords across her neck in scissor form. She flinched, but then understood, and agreed. It was the same shape that she herself had used on His Lordship of Hartwell, when he'd been bothering her.

Good for you, she thought.

A half-inch further, with either blade, and she was dead.

Qrysta, said, quietly, "I don't mind if you kill me. If you did, I'd know that I deserved it."

Behind her, she could vaguely hear Jess saying, "What do I do?"

She smiled. "Nothing."

The other Qrysta stared at her.

Let her take all the time in the world, she thought. She waited. *Accept me or reject me. Your choice.*

Other Qrysta did not move. Qrysta could feel the tension in her through the blades scissored across her neck. She didn't mind. Whatever happened would be fine by her.

Other Qrysta frowned. And, for the first time, spoke. "Fight."

Qrysta—gently, so as not to cut herself—shook her head. "No."

She held her arms wide, her chest open to attack, and said, "I could not bear to hurt you. You win."

Other Qrysta frowned. "You yield?"

She closed her eyes, smiled, and opened them again. "I yield."

Other Qrysta stared. Nodded, at last, in acceptance, and lowered her swords.

They held each other's eyes, wondering what they would find there.

And then all hells broke loose.

There was a loud blast as if a bomb had detonated below. The floor under them bucked. Fire and smoke blew up through the open trapdoor, accompanied by a bellow of fury. Footsteps stomped beneath them, at first on the wooden floor of the chamber, and then thudding up the stone steps towards them. Both Jesses backed away from the trapdoor, hurrying to take their positions left and right on the steps that circled up to the tower's roof. Both Qrystas waited, swords drawn, as the red, roaring creature emerged through the trapdoor, its horned head splintering the floor around it

It opened its mouth and bellowed flame at them. Its shoulders and massive torso rose towards them, saled and red and burning, rearing up almost to the ceiling until it was three times their height. It had claws at the end of its arms, and talons for feet. Wings unfurled behind it. Everything about it was on fire.

The jeweled skull, transformed into this.

Arrows punched into it time and time again from both Jesses' whitewood bows as they shot as fast as they could. The arrows stabbed deep into its red hide, enraging it. Both Qrystas danced into, and around, and through, and beyond it, carving and slicing, neither ever getting in the other's way, both always a step ahead of the Guardian. One of them, alone, would have stood no chance. Together, they toyed with it. Rolling, crouching, jumping, springing off hands and feet, they knew what they had to do. Wear it down, tire it out. The death of a thousand cuts.

It wouldn't be quick, but the outcome was never in doubt. Bristling with whitewood arrows, howling, hamstrung, blinded, kneecapped, bleeding from a hundred wounds, the Guardian staggered, and stopped, and swayed. It toppled, and, slowly, fell.

It hit the floor not with the crash of the monster it had been, but with the small, metallic clatter of the red-jewel-encrusted silver skull that it now was once again. Which rolled, and stopped, staring up at them with empty eyes, as the steaming blood which had covered their swords and clothes evaporated, and whitewood arrows fell out of the air around them.

Qrysta turned to face Other Qrysta.

Both were sweating, drained, heaving for breath.

They crossed their swords, points down towards the floor, and bowed to each other.

Qrysta retrieved her sword belt from where she had dropped it and wrapped it around her waist. She sheathed her blades, walked over to the skull, and picked it up.

She studied it. She held it out to Other Qrysta, who shook her head. She put the skull into her backpack.

Other Qrysta turned away and led the way up the last stone staircase to the trapdoor in the ceiling.

They followed, emerging into daylight and onto the roof of the tower, with its strange, black turrets.

Other Qrysta stopped. She turned, and said, "You were wrong."

Qrysta blinked, surprised. "I was?"

"You said 'you win.' You were wrong. *You* did." She sounded sad.

Qrysta said, "Didn't we all win?"

Other Qrysta studied her. She said, at last, "I liked being you. I wish I could go on."

"Can't you?" Qrysta said. "We could use another me."

Other Qrysta shook her head. "No." She waved a hand. "I'm not really you," she said. "You know that. I wish I were. You must have a very interesting life."

Something glowing appeared in the air between them.

Qrysta recognized it.

A portal.

She turned to her Other. She knew that she would never see her again. Except, perhaps, the image of her, if she were ever again to look into Oldface's reversive mirror.

"Who are you, then?" she asked.

Other Qrysta took her hand. "Not who," she said. "What."

"And what is that?" Qrysta asked.

Other Qrysta smiled, a sad smile, and said, "It's all in the mind."

For a moment, they held each other's eyes.

Other Qrysta, and Other Jess, deflated, crumpling into small, black shapes on the floor of the tower's roof.

The sight of them ceasing to be filled her with sadness—as if, she thought, she and Jess had just witnessed their own deaths.

She turned to Jess. "You okay?"

"I think so," Jess said.

"Good girl."

"That wasn't really me, was it?"

"No," Qrysta put her hand on Jess's shoulder. "*This* is really you. And I could never have done what we just did without you. I'm proud of you."

Jess blushed. "Thanks."

"Thank *you*, Jess." She smiled. "Not bad, for a first fight, right?"

"It was all so fast. I didn't really know what to do."

"And that," Qrysta said, "is why you did so well. Don't overthink. Do your work beforehand, be ready: And then, when it's action time, let your skills lead."

Jess thought about that and nodded. "I see."

"Yes," Qrysta said, "I think you do. So. Ready to get out of here?"

"Yes."

She took Jess's hand, and they stepped into the curtain of white-blue light and entered the portalscape.

Ribbon-paths, blue and orange and yellow and green, twisting in and out of each other into the indigo distance.

Qrysta felt Jess's hand trembling in hers. She squeezed it.

Jess said, "Where are we?"

"I don't know," Qrysta said, "but I've been here before, if that's any help."

Jess's eyebrows rose. "You have?"

"This is where we came when we left you at Sallen's tavern. And we came back from that all right, didn't we? So, no reason we can't do that again, right?"

Jess, sounding dubious, said, "I suppose not …"

"Good. Just keep supposing, Jess. And—"

Jess interrupted her, before she could say it: "—keep going forwards."

"That," Qrysta agreed.

Forwards, this time, didn't keep trying to challenge them. The ribbon path that they were on—sky-blue once again—did not divide every now and then, asking them to choose which fork to take.

They felt in no rush to go on. Sometimes, Qrysta thought, it's nice not to be running from one task to the next. Yes, they still had a to-do list. It could wait. Meanwhile, *to be*—just to be in the midst of this and take the time to drink it all in—felt amazing. Almost therapeutic. They walked, suspended, on a ribbon of sky-blue light, in an endless field of other light paths of all other colors. It would be a shame to hurry through, head down, seeing nothing, not witnessing this.

The old saying occurred to her. *It's not the destination, it's the journey.*

It's both, she knew. They'd decided that before, she and Grell and Daxx, when they'd talked it all over. The two weren't mutually exclusive. Destination and journey were a part of each other. Without the one, the other would not exist.

So, why not appreciate both?

"What happens in the end?" Yes, everyone always wants to know that. She herself would love to know where this journey that they were on was taking them.

On one hand, she'd say that she couldn't wait to find out.

On the other, she was now seeing that, actually, she *could* wait.

Because first, before finding out what happens in the end, she wanted to discover what happened along the way.

And she saw that she wanted to miss none of it. Look up, and around, and notice. Take it all in. Consider the journey, while on it. *Lived forwards, understood backwards? Fair enough. Maybe I'll understand later. But I won't be here, then, will I? This moment, this lovely moment, will have gone.*

They walked on, and around, always, it seemed, up, on the spiraling sky-blue ribbon, their eyes darting around in all directions, absorbing the wonder of it. Qrysta could tell that Jess no longer felt alarmed at that strange environment. She was, instead, fascinated. As was she. It was hypnotic, beautiful. And so peaceful. It made a welcome change from the long trek, and the cold, and the constant sense of danger.

Eventually, they came up onto a platform. Other paths led down from it, in seven other directions, spaced equally apart—with their path making the eighth point of the compass. A small ball of white light hovered at its center.

"Ah," a muffled voice said. "At last."

It was coming, she realized, from behind her.

She retrieved the jeweled skull from her backpack and walked towards the ball of light.

She held it out.

The little ball of white light drifted into the skull.

"Ah," the skull said, *"now* I remember!"

It made her jump. She felt it vibrating in her hands with a sudden energy.

It said, "Shall we be going?"

"Yes," she said, recovering her equilibrium. "Which way?"

"Follow me," the skull said.

It lifted off from her hand and drifted on ahead of them.

Could she trust it? She had no way of knowing. It didn't seem trustworthy—but at least it seemed to know where it was going. *Might as well follow,* she thought, drawing her swords.

They walked after it, stepping onto an orange path that headed towards a distant wall punctuated with stars. On another platform, halfway along it, they came to the clerk sitting at his high desk.

"You need to sign me out," the skull said.

Qrysta did.

The clerk said, "Thank you," and filed the form in his out tray.

They moved on behind the floating skull.

When they came, at last, to the end of the orange path, they saw another portal. The skull stopped in front of it.

It turned to face them. "You'll be pleased to see your friends again, no doubt."

"We will," Qrysta said.

"And I'll be pleased to see what they've brought me. I'll need you to take me through."

Qrysta held out her hands. It floated back to her and settled onto them.

She put the skull in her backpack, took Jess's hand, and stepped through the portal.

30

The Oasis in the Sky

We knew that we'd have to do our catching up all over again when Qrysta and Jess reappeared, but that wasn't going to stop us telling each other everything that we'd been through. Above all, Grell and Oller wanted to know about my interesting new alter ego. So, I told them about how I'd met Graycote, and saved him from the huntsmen, and how, in the Oak Grove, he'd "rewarded" me.

"So, what you're saying," Grell said, "is, you can take it or leave it, except for the three nights round the full moon?"

"Apparently," I said.

"Whooh," he said. "We'd better make sure you're well away from prying eyes on *those* days, then."

"That's for sure."

"What's it like?" Oller asked. "Being … that?"

"Different. Very, *very* different. I hardly know I'm there. I'm all feeling, rather than thought. Thinking is *hard*—almost impossible. But I can run forever, and fast."

"Must be how you got here so quickly," Grell said.

"Yes. I'd still be days away, on foot. And it's not just me that's different. The world is different. The colors are different; there are fewer of them, there are no reds or oranges or greens, and there are so many different grays in the middle, between yellow and blue. *Were*-me has a far wider field of vision than I do. I can almost see behind me—and I can see a lot better in poor light.

"And the *smells!* Everything comes in through my nose, on the air. I can sort through them without thinking about it: Hare over there, owl up that tree, marsh to the east, snow on the wind; it's easy. You have no idea how rich everything smells. You, Grello, for example. You're about ninety different ingredients. Like, I don't know—a complicated recipe. Or—you know the way people talk about wine? 'Blackberries, and gravel, overtones of charcoal, elderflower, and orange peel'—that kind of thing? I'd always thought that was just pretentious nonsense, but I *get* it now. I can tell one tree from another with my eyes closed as easily as you can tell night from day. You smelled like a water buffalo smeared with old cheese."

Grell frowned. "Yeah?!" He wasn't sure about that.

"Yes indeed," I confirmed, "plus a whole lot of other things. Feet, lemons, bonfires, garlic, steel, I could go on."

"Um, well …. Thanks, mate."

We were sitting cross-legged at the edge of the oasis pool, under the palm trees, in the bright winter light. I reached out and patted Grell on his enormous, rock hard, hairy shoulder.

"You smelled excellent," I said. "Really. *Wonderful.* Just …" I searched for the word. I found it. *Perfect.* "Overpowering."

Grell shifted on the sand beside me. He grunted.

I said, "That's what you do, isn't it? You overpower."

He settled down a bit. "Yeah, but …"

"But what?" I said.

He said "I dunno. It sounds like you're criticizing my personal hygiene."

I understood what he meant. "When did you last take a shower? Or a bath?"

"Not recently."

"Nor me. We're not living like that anymore. Who you are, your essence, isn't masked by soap or deodorants. I hate to think what those things would smell like in *were*-form—harsh, if you ask me. Chemicals."

Grell thought about that. Relaxed a little more.

"You know when people say, '*I saw through you?*' " I said. "I *smelled* you. All the way through you. It was *good*, Grello. Rich, and

385

strong, and strange, and—all right, no, not what we're used to as humans, but: Excellent."

There was a silence.

Grell reached out his massive paw and took my hand. Neither of us said anything.

"What's that little bastard smell like, then?" Grell said, nodding at Oller.

"Next time I change, I'll let you know. What do you think? Dishrags and stable straw?"

"Fish," Grell said. "Fishy little bugger."

"Cobwebs."

"Drains."

"Damp leaves."

We ran out of feeble ideas and looked up at Oller, the awkwardness gone.

"Finished?" Oller said.

I said, "Yes."

"Lucky for you he did," Oller said.

Grell and I didn't understand.

I said, "Did what?"

"Stink."

"It is?" I said. "It was like an assault up my nose. How is that lucky? I was wary at first, I thought there was some damned great monster up ahead. Then I figured it out, when I saw the ladder he'd made."

"You wouldn't be here now," Oller pointed out, "if he didn't stink."

I thought about how I'd followed Grell's trail into the cavern, and through the portalscape. Oller was right.

"True," I agreed.

"Seeing as you didn't have a map," Oller continued.

He was smirking at us.

Uh-oh. I knew that look. He'd found something.

"What have you found, Ols?" I said.

He turned to Grell. "You used the map and the lodestone, right, Grell?" he said. "To find your way here?"

Grell grunted. "Thanks to the old clerk, I did. Doubt if I'd ever have thought of it by myself."

Oller rose to his feet, grinning at me. "Come with me," he said. "You need to see this. You too, Grell."

We followed him into the cave, and to the end of it, and stepped through the portal. Oller, with Little Guy at his heels, trotted on ahead of us, along the orange ribbon-path to the nearest floating platform.

We stopped and turned around.

He pointed at the star-wall we'd just come through. "What do you see, Daxxie?"

"A wall of stars."

"Which one did we come out of, then?"

I pointed to the exit that led to High Rock, the oasis in the sky.

He nodded. He said, "Take a look at the others."

I did. I studied the layout carefully. I couldn't see what he was talking about. Grell knew the answer, so was also amused by my bafflement.

Oller said, "You don't see anything?"

"Just … stars," I said.

That clearly wasn't it.

"Umm …" Oller said, letting me know that I still needed to work it out.

"Lights," I said, trying again, "against the background?"

"Nothing you recognize, matey? No pattern, of any kind?"

"No …"

"Keep looking," Oller said, enjoying my confusion, as I heard the rustle of paper behind me.

"Now," his voice came again, from lower down, as if he was crouching. "Name a place, here in Mourvania."

"Huntsbroke."

I kept my eyes on the star-wall.

Eventually, a star towards the top of it, to the left of center, began to glow brighter.

"Another," Oller said, when I didn't say anything.

"That island of Jess's—Wester Isle," I said.

The brighter star soon began to fade, and, after a while, another star brightened, the one highest and furthest to the left on the star-wall.

I understood.

"Whoa …!" I breathed.

"Now you see it, eh?" Oller chuckled. "That's how we got through here. So, keep looking. You too, Grell." There was another rustle of paper behind me. I kept my eyes on the star-wall—which was not hard to do, it was so beautiful.

387

And then, like a slow cross-fade in a film, the vista altered. The stars that I'd been looking at dimmed out, and a whole new pattern of stars grew out of nowhere to replace them.

One of them, left of center and three-quarters of the way up, began to glow brighter than the others.

Again, I didn't know what I was looking at. "What aren't I seeing, Oller?"

"We was halfway along the path to get here, me and Little Guy, when I had this thought. I wondered where *else* there is. So, up on one of them platforms, I stopped. And found *that*."

He waited, while we tried to work it out. We couldn't.

"Picked my hometown, o' course, Brigstowe …?" Oller hinted.

I heard Grell whistle beside me in astonishment, as I said, "That's *Jarnland?*"

"Yep," Oller said happily.

Grell said, "Wow."

Suddenly I saw it. I gazed at the familiar layout shining against the darkness ahead of me. My mind was racing. This portalscape was a way between? Well, how useful might *that* be?! And—what other realms might it show that we knew nothing of? Of course, we didn't have any other maps of those other realms, so there was no way of finding out …

As I watched, a red ribbon-path began to stretch out from the Brigstowe star-point towards us.

"Yup," Oller said, happily. "I put my map of Jarn down, and set the lodestone on Brig, and look what happened!"

I said, "Did you try it?"

"To get back to Brig?" He said, his eyebrows raised in surprise. "No, 'course not!" A thought struck him. "What, d'you want to? I'm up for that! Wonder where it would pop us out. Not in the middle of the market square, eh? Somewhere no one will be watching, I hope …"

When the red path attached itself to our platform, we set off along it.

"You do realize what this could mean, don't you?" Grell said, as we followed Oller towards his hometown.

"Yes," I said, "we could get the hell out of Dodge."

"Eh?" Oller said, looking back at us, "what's 'Dodge'?"

"Foreigner talk," I said. "It just means, erm, 'dodge away, and leave this place behind.'" Which would be a damn good thing, I thought. This entire realm was on the alert for us, armed fanatics searching for us everywhere, and a huge problem waiting for us under the desert. This would be a *get out of jail free* card.

"Not without Qrysta and Jess," Grell said.

"No," I agreed. "Of course not. This is just a recce mission."

It stopped when we reached the end of the red ribbon-path.

There was no blue-white portal out to Brigstowe in the indigo wall ahead of us.

We looked around, but this was clearly a dead end.

"Um," Oller muttered. "Pity, that. Must be something we still have to learn about how this place works."

"Still," I said, "it was worth a try."

"Maybe one day?" Grell suggested. "When we have the know-how?"

"Could be," I said. I was disappointed. So much for a shortcut to safety. I had been worrying for days about our odds. On the one hand, the entire Devoted army. On the other hand, ranged against them, the host of undead that Commandant Bastard had told us about. Both led by immortals, a god and a demon. All converging on the place where this whole thing was leading up to. And the four of us, plus Little Guy and Jess, caught in the middle.

Whichever side we chose, we'd have the masses of the opposing horde to deal with. Survival would be no small challenge. And if, by some miracle, we all did survive, as fighters on the winning side we'd picked, how would they treat us? I'd betrayed Mother Abbott. She was going to be no friend of ours, even if I'd be able to point out that we'd destroyed her nemesis.

Fifty thousand gold? That had to be a long shot, even with the signed agreement we had. How could I enforce that, if she decided to withhold payment? Us, against her whole army? I'd have to think that her letting us leave with our lives—no doubt after a thorough scourging—would be a good, and not very likely, result.

As for the other side: Oldface hardly struck me as the trustworthy type. Why would he care what happened to us? All he wanted was to be his old self again; and when he was that, we'd be rag dolls by comparison to his divine power, and he could do with us as he liked. The problem had been going around and around in my head, and I was no nearer to solving it than I'd been when I left the Tower of Light. And then, out of the blue, Oller's discovery about how maps worked within this portalscape had given me hope. Which had now been dashed.

Another dead end. Damn it, there *had* to be a way out of this. I just couldn't see it. I couldn't think where to start, other than with what I already knew.

Which was: We were screwed if we did, and screwed if we didn't.

Okay, I told myself, for the umpteenth time. *What I told Qrysta,* before she set out on her quest with Jess. *Solve the problem.* I was the one who was meant to be good with problems.

I had no idea how to solve this one.

Qrysta and Jess joined us the next day. Oller and Grell and I had talked long and late, under the high desert stars, and slept well, knowing that we were safe up there in our eyrie. Which is how I'd begun to think of the place, after we'd explored it the next morning. There wasn't much to see; just a few hundred yards of sandy shelf running back along the cliff to either side. Two ribbons of water fell from the great height of the snow-capped peak behind us and meandered into the pool at the heart of the oasis. Otherwise, that was pretty much it.

At one end of the shelf, they showed me an enormous nest, the size of a shed. Bones were scattered around it, old, and white, and dried by age, and all far too big for Little Guy to carry, even the smallest of them. Among the bones were long, curved teeth. Incisors. Whatever had nested there—long ago, thank the gods—had carried *sabercats* up here to eat?? Oller set about extracting the incisors. "Worth a ton, saber fangs," he explained. "Sea captains sell 'em to merchants overseas. There's tribes which use these as handles for their daggers, which they tuck into their belts. Worth their weight in gold even in Jarn, so they must sell for ten times that at the end of the trade chain."

We stood at the top of the cliff that dropped for a mile or more below us and looked down at the Great Waste. Brown, and blurred, and featureless it looked, and, even though it was winter, parched. Dry and cold now, dry and hot most of the rest of the year. That was where we were going. We didn't like the prospect.

I didn't tell the others about the "creatures of the sand" that Graycote had said infested the place. They had enough to worry about. We gazed off into the southern distance, where the brown haze above it merged into the horizon. How we were going to get down from there none of us knew, not even Oller. He'd looked for a way and found nothing. And Oller was good at finding.

We were trapped.

Safe, yes. But waiting. And wondering what was coming.

So it was a welcome relief when Qrysta and Jess ran out of the cave, and we were all suddenly laughing and hugging, and filling each other in on everything that we'd done.

That night, as we settled down to sleep in our cloaks and blankets around the pool in the oasis in the sky, the thought struck me: *What aren't I seeing?*

I lay back, frowning up at the glittering desert stars, wrestling with our problem—and at the same time trying to make it go away, so that I could *please* get a break from banging my head against it. I tried to identify some of the constellations I'd learned about. I found The Fisher, with his rod and line, and, rising towards him, half of The Whale. And off on the southern horizon, by some unsettling coincidence pretty much right above our destination in the Great Waste, his temple stronghold: Old Birdbeak. The Demon. I didn't like looking that way and kept trying to search other parts of the sky, but my eyes kept being drawn back towards him.

And then it hit me.

I could swear that I felt an actual, physical *clunk* in my head as I finally saw the answer. Or, at least, what I hoped it would be.

I sat up, slowly, so as not to wake the others, and rose to my feet.

Little Guy opened an eye, just to let me know that he was on guard all right. His tail thumped the sand sleepily a couple of times, and his eye closed again.

I picked up my pack and tiptoed towards the cave.

31

The Lost Star

I stepped through the portal and hurried along the orange ribbon-path towards the nearest platform, a dozen conflicting thoughts interfering with each other in my head as I ran. They seemed to be coming at me from everywhere. I knew that it could all be just wishful thinking, but I felt sure that something had been unlocked in my mind. I thought, *Why does the Boss Fight always have to come at the end?* And then, *Well, that's just a game convention, isn't it? End of dungeon, everything leads up to climax, end of problem.* Think outside the box. Suppose this jaunt of ours *doesn't* end in a Boss Fight?

Or, if there is one, does it have to come at the end?

Only if we're being conventional.

If it doesn't—then what does?

Something that doesn't involve us being caught in the middle between two huge armies led by two hostile—whats?

Basically, bosses.

We do not want to be in that situation.

So, don't be.

Which means …

Does it have *to be a Boss Fight?*

Answer: *Not necessarily.*

Or more to the point: *Not necessarily one involving us* .... There might indeed be a Boss Fight—while we might be miles away, and out of the firing line ...

I reached the platform and turned around to look at the wall of stars I'd just come through.

I held my breath as I brought my *Guide to the Known Heavens and Hells* out of the inner pocket of my jerkin, above my heart.

I put it down, on the platform, open at its star map.

I closed my eyes for a moment and prayed, to every single god I could think of. *Please let this work.*

I knelt by the star map and studied it.

So many possibilities, but really only two choices.

I put my lodestone down on The Protectress, and stood up, and waited, watching the star-wall against the indigo background ahead of me.

For what seemed like an age, nothing happened.

Then, and I found myself exhaling with relief as I watched it, the lights that represented Mourvania faded out, and the lights of all the heavens and hells faded in to take their place.

I stood there, drinking in the scene.

I was right!

We weren't "in" Jarnland, so its map wouldn't work for us here. We couldn't use it to get out any more than I could use Eydie. We weren't "in" any other realms that there might be in this world, so we couldn't access them either. We didn't even know anything about them. But the heavens are all around us wherever we are. They encircle every realm, above and below and all around—and, as I watched, an orange ribbon-path was reaching out towards me from the center of The Protectress.

Orange, not red.

Orange worked, we'd found.

I watched the ribbon as it approached and attached itself to my platform.

I stepped onto it.

I couldn't wait. I Turned and galloped along it as fast as I could run. Around and about it twisted, over and under all the other green and yellow and blue and red paths. I kept straining my wolf eyes ahead, scanning the distant star wall for the light that I hoped would be at

393

the end of it, sniffing the wind for danger. And there, at last, it was: An unmistakable, white-blue dot at the path's end, which became, as I neared it, a screen, glowing in the dark center of the constellation that was The Protectress.

I re-Turned into *me*-form and studied the scene ahead.

The portal was not, I was glad to see, positioned in front of a light representing a star in *this* constellation. I didn't want to jump through it into the heart of a sun and incinerate. So, what was there, I wondered, ahead of me, beyond it?

There was only one way to find out.

I stepped through the portal.

The blue-white sheen faded into mist.

No—into *cloud* ...

I couldn't see my feet, let alone what I was standing on, but it was solid enough. I edged forwards, wondering if I'd fall off the side of ... wherever I was. The mist thinned around my feet as I walked on. Ahead of me, shapes loomed into view in the darkness. They resolved themselves, as I neared them, into two tall, closed, iridescent gates. At another high desk, in front of them, was perched another old, white-haired man, in a white robe, writing in another large book with another quill pen. I thought, *really?* I remembered what Qrysta had said, in the portalscape beneath Wester Isle: *Environment's certainly dicking with us.*

Pearly gates.

Riiight.

As I approached, the gatekeeper looked up at me. His eyebrows rose.

He said, "You don't look dead."

"I'm not."

He grunted. "Well, that's easily fixed," he said, reaching under his desk and bringing out an actual blunderbuss, which he leveled at me.

"I don't want to stay," I said, quickly.

He stopped fiddling with the blunderbuss, and looked up at me, and frowned.

"Oh?" he said, sourly. "You just want to take a look at the accommodations, before you check out the alternative?"

"No, I have business here. I have business in *the alternative* as well," I added.

"What kind of business?"

"I need to speak to whoever's in charge."

He peered at me. "Are they expecting you?"

"If they are all-seeing and all-knowing, yes. In which case, they will also know why I would like to see them. And if they aren't," I added, "I have information they will want to hear."

He grunted. He levered himself to his feet and fumbled among the keys at his belt. "Nothing personal," he said, shuffling over and unlocking the pearly gates. "It's my job to keep the riffraff out."

The gates swung inwards, and I walked through into a moonlit courtyard enclosed by cloisters. I was, I realized, in the Orphanage. Or, at least, something very much like it.

Ahead of me I saw a familiar figure. Standing in her robe of shifting blue and white.

Mother Abbott.

I walked up to her and stopped to look at her.

She was looking in my direction, but not at me. *Through* me. She didn't, I decided, even see me. Or her surroundings.

A voice behind me said, "She is sleeping."

I turned, and saw a thin, pale, earnest young man in a simple brown habit. He looked no more than twenty-five years old.

"She is my representative on the mortal plane," he explained. "Frail, and human, and imperfect. But she was appointed as his successor, for her qualities, by the last of those who have followed after me."

I said, "Brother Chidian, I presume?"

He inclined his head. "At the moment," he agreed. "I believe you understand the concept of an avatar?"

That I did indeed. "Yes," I said, as the truth of who I was talking to dawned on me.

"We assume them because they are kinder on mortal eyes. What we are made of is ..." he hesitated. "Let us say if you were to cast your Lightseek on me, it would be too much for you to take in. It would, at the very least, blind you, if only temporarily."

I knew that I was in the presence of something far greater than I was. I didn't have any clever answers. Or any answers at all. Only later, thinking back on it, did I come up with the phrase *starstruck*. Yes, I thought. By an actual star. I found that my mouth was reluctant to work, and that I could hardly speak. It was as if I was having an out-of-body experience while still in my body, standing in front of the experience itself. It was unsettling, comforting, fascinating. Being pretty much incapable of speech didn't bother me. I wanted to listen, to hang on his every word.

Divine Wisdom ...

Chidian walked over to Mother Abbott. His steps made no sound.

"She is not here in person," he said, studying her, "but her essence is. Being mortal, she is limited, of course. But she will witness. She will hear. And she will understand this dream that she is having. And she will, when she awakens, act accordingly on what she will have seen."

He turned to me.

"So," he said, "the time has come. Have you made your decision?"

I found my tongue, and said, "I think so."

"Only 'think'?"

"This is a little out of my comfort zone," I explained, uneasily. "I feel like ..." I didn't know how to put it. We were in a negotiation, I knew that. I had just one small bargaining chip. What I *felt like* was that I'd brought a pop gun to a firefight. It didn't seem a good idea to tell him that. In a negotiation, it helps to appear to have a position of strength, rather than to admit you're as weak as a child.

Chidian, avatar of Valmynia, goddess of Mercy and Suffering, saw that I was suffering, and took pity on me.

"Go on," he said, "tell me what you feel like."

"I just want to run away," I said. "I don't want anything to do with any of this."

"Then why don't you?" he asked.

"Because this needs to end."

His eyebrows rose as he looked at me. "You think you can end it?"

I shook my head. "No," I said, "as far as I can see, that's impossible. How can I end a war between gods and demons? I don't have the first clue as to what you're doing, why you're here instead of—where you came from. All I know is—"

I stopped.

Chidian raised an eyebrow. "All you know is what?"

"I have something that you want."

He nodded. "True," he acknowledged.

"And that if I give it to you—down there, on our mortal plane—we'll be at your, well ... mercy."

I'd used the word deliberately.

He was about to reply, when I interrupted to say, "The mercy of *both* of you. You might want to grant it to me—but would your enemy?"

"Ah," he said. "You see the problem."

"I do," I said. "Once I return you your power, and your enemy his power, we're lost. And I don't just mean me and my friends. I mean everyone down there. All of us mortals."

"So, you understand how it is, then."

"Yes. You gave up your Power to contain his. Just as the Kinfolk gave up their Natures to contain his. And just as you scattered the knowledge of his Mind beyond his reach."

"And why," he asked, after a pause, "do you think I did that?"

"Mercy," I said, "and suffering."

He studied me for a long time and finally nodded. "And will you," he said, "now show me the same?"

I looked him squarely in the eye. "No," I said. "That's not my job, that's yours. How could I? You're a god. You're always going to be that. I'm never going to be. Are you suddenly going to stop being one? Of course not. Even if there were no more of the likes of Varamaxes to oppose you. You're immortal, aren't you?" I noticed his eyes fixed on me, with a strange look in them. "Which means forever and ever," I went on. "Eternal mercy, eternal suffering. An endless cycle."

I stopped talking.

I watched him.

Slowly, his shoulders slumped, and his eyes dropped.

In the long silence that followed, I said, "That's what you do, right?"

He raised his head and looked me in the eyes. "Yes," he said, "that's what I do."

Another silence fell between us. I tried to imagine what that was like. Eternal suffering ...

I said, "Forever and ever."

He nodded.

I said, "Are you all right with that?"

He smiled, a thin smile. "It is, as you say, what I do."

I saw that a chord had been struck. "And the other guy?"

He grunted, a hollow laugh. "He does what he does too."

"Hunger and Despair."

"Indeed."

I felt the hairs on the back of my neck rise. I'd discovered something .... What? I went over what we'd said again, in my mind.

Then I saw it. Realized it.

One of them wanted to do what he did, the other didn't.

Hunger and Despair. Varamaxes couldn't get enough of it. Mercy
and Suffering. Valmynia was prepared to take all of it.

And Valmynia stood between him and us.

It was what she did.

I said, "And you keep on his case and limit the damage."

"As best I can," Chidian acknowledged.

Mentally, I crossed my fingers and played my one, small bargaining chip. "I have a proposition for you."

His eyebrows rose as he looked at me. He hadn't expected that.
"Which is?"

"I give you *both* what you want."

He went still.

So did I. I wasn't going to help him. I had nothing to help him
with. I had played my one, small bargaining chip. I had nothing else in
my armory, so I just stared him down.

"How is that possible?" he asked.

"Simple," I said. "I have your Power in my power. I return it to you.
To both of you."

"But then," he hesitated, "the war between us will recommence."

I shrugged. "Entirely possible," I acknowledged. "As you say,
it's eternal."

He frowned. "I stopped it," he said. "I caged him."

"For the time being," I said. "Yes, he is caged. But where does that leave
us? Us mortals? At your mercy. In which you specialize. And which you
handed on to your followers; who, being fallible humans, have let your
power go to their heads. And who tell everyone how it *has to be* this way
forever, and that *we have to* get in line, and *do as we are told*. So, we're
stuck. Stagnant. No change possible, no progress. Ever.

"I've seen them in action, your people," I continued. "They are not
among our finest citizens. They use your authority to push us around,
and make themselves important, and keep us in our place. Well, that
place is no longer acceptable, and we're not staying there any longer.
You liberated us from your enemy's yoke, and we're grateful for that.
Now, we need to throw off yours."

He stared at me. "Yoke?" he said, affronted.

"Suffering," I pointed out.

He didn't like the consequences of his actions being reflected back at him.

I said, "It's what you do, right?"

"Yes!" he shot back, "I suffer! For *you*."

I said, "And we do likewise."

"For me? You do nothing of the sort! I showed you mercy, I released you from your oppressor!"

"And are you happy you did that?"

"Of course!"

"Fine," I said. "So, do it again."

I could see the anger crossing his face, mixed with confusion, and something else. Uncertainty? Fear?

"Are you," he said, "accusing me ..." He tailed off.

I waited. I could see him trying to follow my argument. "Accusing you of what?"

"Of being like ... *him?!*"

I shrugged. "Yes. Not to the same degree, of course."

"Well, thank you for that, at least!" he muttered.

"And our next oppressor will, with luck, be even milder," I continued. "And, eventually, we won't need any oppressors at all. No overlords, no tyrants, no authorities, no gods, no demons. And no doubt we'll make a mess of it—we're only human, after all. But honestly, we'd rather it was all *our* problem, and we'll handle it ourselves, thanks all the same.

"So, if you could just go away? Both of you? And—well, come back in a millennium. Why not check us out, see how we've done? You might be pleasantly surprised. Or you might just think, *Poor fools, never stood a chance, weren't up to it. See? Knew they'd be lost without us.*"

I waited, but he had nothing to say. He'd never before considered the idea of not being essential to us.

So, I said, "in which case, I would suggest you rephrase your question."

He was puzzled. "Which question?"

"You asked, 'How is that possible?' That I give you *both* what you want. I can answer that easily, if you change the *how* to *where*. *Where* is that possible?"

He asked, eventually, "Do you know?"

"Not exactly," I admitted. "That's kind of up to you. But I do know one thing for sure."

"Which is?"

"Anywhere but here."

Surprised, Chidian said, "Excuse me?"

"Take your eternal war, Blessed Abbott Chidian, and leave. Leave this mortal plane. Go back to where you came from. Or go on to where you're going next. The wheel of the sky turns, this little world turns with it. Up there in the heavens you are all going where you're going. Which is fine with us. Just leave us down here out of it. *Go.*

"Maybe you'll end up somewhere you can find peace with each other. I dunno, sit down and have a beer. Why not? Did you ever try that, the two of you? Look, you hate each other, you couldn't be more different, but—opposites attract, right? Or why do you bother with each other? Okay—foolish, ignorant mortal perspective, what do I know, but—what can I say? Where's all this cosmic strife getting you?"

He shook his head.

"I am glad," he said, "for your sake, as well as mine, that you came to me first. He does not listen to reason."

I'd gotten that impression already, from my dealings with Old-face—and from watching his terrifying imp. It hadn't been a difficult decision, given the choice. The good guy or the bad guy? Forget the fact that the good guy's army wanted me dead, and that the bad guy wanted me alive.

"I agree," he said, abruptly. "Your proposal is accepted. The trouble is that my enemy won't agree, so you need to convince him. If you succeed, we will both take our quarrel elsewhere, and no one on this mortal plane will ever see either of us again. If you fail, well ..." He smiled a thin smile. "In the end, doesn't every mortal fail?"

"In the end, yes," I agreed. "But this isn't the end."

"No," he said. "Perhaps not. You should know, though, that while we may leave, there will always be hunger, and despair, and mercy, and suffering."

"I'm sure there will. And we'll try to deal with them as best we can."

Chidian grunted. "Good luck with that," he said, in a voice that sounded weary with experience.

I turned to look at Mother Abbott again. I asked, "She will remember my part in this?"

Chidian nodded. "To an extent. She will know that you are responsible for events taking a turn she would by no means have wanted."

I thought about the reward she had promised me. As if reading my thoughts, Chidian said, "She will be no friend of yours. She will consider you a traitor. You betrayed her trust, turned on her followers. You did not deliver what you had promised her."

That was going to be a problem, I thought.

She had the entire realm searching for me. Spies, squadrons, armies …. And now I had the others with me. Caster, Monster, Dancer, Thief. *Plus* orphan and dog. We would attract much more attention as a group than any of us had done while traveling alone. We could hardly hope to sneak through the entire realm of Mourvania, attempting to get out, without being noticed. And what about Jess? We hadn't rescued her from the stocks just to have her burned at the stake.

So, forget the fifty thousand gold that Mother Abbott had promised me. What about Oldface? The loot he'd confiscated from us could well be worth more than that, perhaps even a lot more. But what would he care about us once he was his old self again? He might just kill us for the fun of it. Even if he didn't, he'd cast us aside, with or without our loot, and we'd have to fend for ourselves. Our highly noticeable little group, wandering a land full of enemies, in search of an escape route, possibly weighed down by a haul of valuable treasure?

I didn't like our chances.

But that was a problem I'd have to deal with later.

I turned back to Chidian. "Any ideas about how I might be able to convince him?" I asked.

"None."

Great, I thought.

I could feel myself struggling with the problem. Oldface wouldn't trust me an inch. He'd have his agenda, and whatever I suggested that didn't fit with it he'd find suspicious. Besides, he hadn't struck me as the trusting type. How in all hells was I going to get him to come with me?

Well, I'd just have to figure that out.

"So," I said to Chidian, at last, "where do you want me to bring him?"

32

Beneath the Sands

I galloped back through the portalscape in *were*-form, as fast as I could. I presumed that Oldface must have some way down from our oasis in the sky, or why would he have wanted us to gather there? I'd seen that vast desert below us, stretching to the horizon. It did not look a welcoming place. And I didn't believe for a minute that there'd be a welcome for us at the end of our journey across it. I remembered what Commandant Bastard had told us, in his recounting of his youthful expedition into that hell. A buried temple; a horde of undead rising out of the ground; the *Fearing*, men running for their lives—even *him* ...

I re-Turned into *me*-form and spread my map of Mourvania on the platform. I placed my lodestone on the spot on it that marked High Rock. Within minutes, I was stepping through into the shallow cave and coming quietly back to take my place beside the pool among my sleeping friends.

I pulled Shift close, seeking her comfort—realizing I was an idiot for leaving her, my source of power, behind—and she agreed, her warmth spreading through me as I wrapped myself in my blankets and looked up at the stars. As before, my gaze kept returning to The Demon, now low in the southern sky.

I thought about what I'd just been through, with Chidian, and Mother Abbott witnessing in her sleep-trance. Obviously, I hadn't been in an actual constellation. There had been no flaming balls of gas hanging in space. There had been nothing cosmic about where I'd found myself. I'd asked Chidian about that. We had met in a simulacrum, as best I could understand his explanation—a representation, which stood in for everything that those stars in the sky, themselves, represented. I'd been somewhere that was a constellation, but wasn't.

How small we are, I thought. How unimportant.

And how understandable that we feel the need for gods and demons to explain things. The wonder, the majesty of the night sky. It was hardly surprising that we'd invented them, to try to make sense of it all ...

Except that I'd just met one.

He hadn't been some idea, some abstract. He'd been right there. Talking to me.

Really there.

So, not some human invention, after all.

I wondered where that left me, as a ... what? Sceptic? Atheist? Unbeliever?

It left me having to reconsider my views, that was for certain.

I mean, what would a "god" be anyway? A Superior Being. Which could mean any number of things. It could mean a member of an unimaginably advanced alien race. Who looks down and sees us as not much more than bacteria, really. Or it could mean something a bit nearer to us. Superior, in many ways, but more relatable. Like, how we relate to other creatures that we consider lesser beings than our fine human selves.

Pets, for example. We love our pets; they love us back.

Or pests. With which we are at constant war.

Whichever thread I pulled at, I found nothing at the end of it.

I couldn't get anywhere with any of it.

I was exhausted. The last thing I remember thinking, before I fell asleep, was: *Well, do they need us, or do we need them?*

The sound of Little Guy barking urgently woke us. We scrambled awake from our cloaks and blankets and grabbed our weapons, Shift already in my grasp. The waning moon was low on the horizon, throwing deep shadows across the sand of our oasis. It was long past midnight, and long before dawn, the air cold on our faces.

Qrysta was the first onto her feet, blades drawn, looking in the direction that Little Guy was facing, the hackles on his back standing up as he snarled, teeth bared, wide-eyed, tense. Grell snapped on his kinsteel armor in seconds and stalked up to take his place ahead of Qrysta, on point as tank, Kinell at the ready. I hefted Shift, cast Shields on all of us, and threw some Flares overhead to flood the area with light. Oller crouched by Little Guy, a throwing knife in each hand. Jess, behind them, had an arrow stretched on the string of her whitewood bow, trained on the mouth of the cave.

Out of which light was coming, growing steadily brighter. Throwing shadows ahead. Bobbing up and down, as if being carried.

Yellow light. A lantern.

The silhouette of a figure appeared in the cave's mouth.

Grell ordered, "Stop right there!"

The figure halted. A smaller figure appeared beside it, one that reached barely to the top of its legs.

Grell relaxed.

Oldface and his imp.

"There's no need to shoot, young lady," Oldface said, calmly.

Jess lowered her bow.

He walked towards us, lantern in hand, his imp padding along beside him. "Well done," he said, again in that calm voice. Calm, but not pleasant. "You did it, all of you! Congratulations." He looked at us, one after the other. "Right, let's get started, then. You too," he added, with a sly smile, when he noticed me. "Excellent! We could use your skills where we're going."

I said, "And where is that?"

"Down there." He nodded towards the south, and we understood what he meant. The desert, far below us, and the long march to his temple beneath it. "It's hard going," he said. "We'll need protection, and healing. It's winter, thank goodness, but it will still be hot and dry and dusty by day, and by night, freezing. There'll be inferno winds, whipping up whenever they feel like it. And, of course, the denizens. Creatures of the sand. We'll do our best to avoid them, but it won't be good enough. We will inevitably bump into some of them. Let's hope it's not too many of the things, eh?

"It shouldn't take us more than a week, all being well. All not being well: Well, we won't make it, so all this will have been for nothing, and our bones will bleach under the desert sun. Still, worth a try, right?" He chuckled. He was clearly in a very good mood. Which was understandable. He had been waiting a very long time for this.

None of the others knew what to say. And I wasn't going to say anything, because I had my own plan in mind. I wanted to wait before I put it into action. It's always a good idea to let your opponents make the first move. If they don't hear you talking, they think you have nothing to say, and that lulls them into a false sense of security.

Oldface continued, "I expect this is all a bit confusing for you, so let me make it simple. One of us will win. You're on my side, others are on my enemy's. And when this is over, the winner will then destroy those who helped his foe. So, for your own sakes, you'd better hope that the winner will be me."

Yes, I thought. So far, so good. Time for a little rope-a-dope. First, distract; second, get them to underestimate; third, hit hard.

I said, "Where's our loot?"

He looked at me in surprise. And then smiled his sly smile again. "Where I left it," he said, "waiting for you to claim it."

The others reacted as I'd hoped they would, with indignation. He'd cheated us? They instinctively dropped into aggressive stances, facing Oldface.

"Well, I couldn't carry all that lot with me, could I?" he said. "Don't worry, no one else is going to find their way into my former prison and scoop it up. The island is almost deserted—the island under it, where they sealed me, completely so. You can stop by for it on your way home. Meanwhile, I did bring you a small token of my integrity."

From the bag that was slung over his shoulder he brought out a little chest. "It's as much as I could carry," he said, "but it should suffice, I think?"

It was the chest full of heartstones—the ones that had glowed when I'd cast my Divination on the helldragon's hoard.

He opened the lid so that we could see the treasures within.

Jewels of all kinds and colors, all large, some almost as big as my fist. Even though he'd seen them before, Oller couldn't help himself. He whistled.

"Pretty, aren't they?" Oldface agreed.

They were indeed.

I glanced at Oller. He nodded quickly, and turned his eyes back to the sparkling gemstones, drinking in their beauty, calculating their value.

Oldface closed the lid of the casket and tucked it back into his bag. "So," he said, pleased at our reactions, "I believe you have some things of mine?"

He looked from face to face. I was going to let the others lead here. They'd done the quests he'd set them. I hadn't.

"We do," Grell agreed.

Oldface held out his hand, smiling.

Grell shook his head.

Oldface's smile faded. "We had an agreement," he said.

Grell said, "We still do. What's yours is yours. We'll give it to you, you can be sure of that. Just not quite yet."

"May I ask why not?"

Grell gestured at the oasis in the sky. "We can't see a way out of here. We're not going to risk you just swanning off with everything we got for you and leaving us up here when you no longer need us."

"Well, I'm not going to do that," Oldface said, "I most definitely still need you."

Qrysta grew suspicious. "For what?"

"Protection. I told you; I have no power out here. Not beyond the prison that my enemy caged me in. Out here, I'm weaker than your nice little dog, remember? I need you to escort me to our destination. Make sure that I get there safely, return to me what was mine, and I'll be able to become again what I once was. At which point, I will be more than capable of looking after myself. And you will have your reward. Which is, as we agreed, your loot and your lives. And then, we go our separate ways. How does that sound?"

I watched the others. I could see that none of them liked it. I could almost read Oller's mind. *Kill the little sod, get the chest of gems, and scarper back through the portal, take our chances, find a way out of this realm ....* They kept turning their glances towards me, looking for guidance. They didn't, of course, know where I'd been earlier that night, or anything about the plan I'd formulated.

It was time to put it into action. "You can let him have it, Qrysta." I said.

She frowned at me, uncertain. "You're sure?"

I just nodded.

"Okay," she said, "if you say so."

"I do."

Qrysta had been with me in enough scrapes to know when I felt I was on sure ground. She sensed my confidence, and, even though she didn't have the first clue as to what I was up to, could tell that I had a plan. *Daxxie, the Puzzle King.* A look passed between us, hers saying, *I hope you know what you're doing,* and mine saying, *I've got this.*

She took the jewel-studded skull out of her backpack. It shone, red and silver, in her hands, reflecting the light from the Flares hovering above us.

"Ah," Oldface said. "That'll do nicely."

Qrysta held it out to him, and he took it. He gazed at it for a while, smiling. "Yes," he said. "Lovely. At last!"

He reached behind himself and inserted the skull into the back of the fluid bubble that was his head, on which his face was floating. As he did so, his features solidified, settling into shape on their foundation.

He inhaled, deeply, through his nose, and closed his eyes.

"Oh, yes," he murmured, exhaling. "Oh, that's good. *Now* I remember. *Oh,* do I remember!"

He turned to Qrysta, and his eyes were moist with tears. "Thank you, young lady," he said, bowing slightly. "I have spent far too many years wondering if I'd ever be ... back together again."

"You're welcome," Qrysta said. "And I couldn't have done it without my apprentice."

Oldface gave Jess a bow.

"Thank you too, child," he said.

Jess, nervously, bobbed her head in reply.

"I expect it was protected?" he said to Qrysta.

"It was."

"I look forward to hearing all about it."

Oldface turned to Grell. "And yours?"

Grell looked at me.

I nodded.

He reached into his pack and brought out the small, iron box.

Oldface stared at it.

"This was the worst one," he said. "To be unable to be true to one-self. Perhaps you cannot imagine that."

Actually, I thought, *nothing could be easier*. I'd let myself down hundreds of times in my life. Who hasn't? But then, I saw that he did have a point. I'd never been *unable* to be true to myself. I'd just, with depressing predictability, so often failed to do so—out of cowardice, or laziness or fear. I straightened up and told myself to get a grip—forget about all that, concentrate on the matter at hand.

Grell was looking at me, enquiringly.

"You can open it," I told him.

He nodded. Slowly, he lifted the lid of the little iron chest. As he did, golden vapors, like steam, wafted out of it, inch by inch. It was like watching something beautiful releasing its essence, very, very slowly. Gold flecks emerged. They seemed to hesitate, as if they weren't sure where they were, or what was happening. They waited, at the chest's rim, and revolved, as if looking around to work out where they were. I didn't understand, right away, until I remembered that they'd been sealed in that iron box for hundreds of years. And then, as if they re-alized what had happened, at long, long last, they got a second wind. They rose, one after another, spiraling around each other, golden specks, hundreds after dozens, and lifted, above us, faster and faster, as if cel-ebrating their freedom, and faded into the night sky above my Flares, all of us in utter, spellbound silence.

We looked up, straining to see where they were going.

North, and west, like a flock of golden birds in the night, or a gentle whirlwind, accelerating off, and up, and away, and vanishing from sight.

I looked at Grell. He was gazing upwards, smiling. He knew where they were going.

Home, to the Woodlake.

It was an odd moment when our hearing returned. The silent, swirling gold points of light had left us with silence. Now, we heard the sighing of the wind in the palm trees above us again and reanimat-ed from our trances.

Oldface said, to Grell, "And now mine."

Grell reached for the smaller box inside the iron chest but stopped when I said, "No."

Oldface turned to me sharply. "No?"

I ducked my head, submissively, and said, "Not *no*, I mean not yet. Not here."

"Excuse me?" Oldface said, annoyed.

I said, to my team, "Guys? Take them."

There was a moment's hesitation on both sides. Qrysta and Grell were used to taking their leads from me, from our thousands of hours running together. Oller had taken that onboard. He knew what to do. Jess and Little Guy were on our wavelength. We were a team, we work together, no question.

Oldface and his imp were a step behind us. Grell was flat on top of Oldface within seconds, bearing him to the ground with his far superior weight. Oldface was trussed and out of action before he could think.

The imp, though, was a different proposition. Tiny though he was, he fought like a dozen cornered cats. He was all teeth and claws and anger and, above all, speed. The little bastard shot among us, biting and slashing, faster than we could even see, inflicting wounds on all of us, so that we were soon all bleeding profusely. All of us, that is, except Little Guy. Jess shot, as best she could, and Qrysta danced, and Grell jabbed, and I cast, but for some reason it was immune to my Traps. Only Little Guy had a handle on it. In his niblun battle leathers, he tracked the speeding imp effortlessly, sinking his teeth into the imp's legs between strides. It was, we saw, as the fight slowed, a beautiful tactic. Stay out of the imp's range, his teeth and claws, and pop back in when you get the chance.

The two of them slowed. Little Guy was clearly in control. The imp staggered, and slashed and bit at the rest of us, but dropped from exhaustion and the damage that Little Guy had dealt to his legs. Grell sat on him, and Oller bound his arms and legs behind him with lengths of the string he always kept about his person, and we had them both where we wanted them. Oldface jabbered and threatened throughout, but I couldn't be bothered to listen, so I cast Mute on him, and on the seething, snarling imp.

Grell tucked Oldface under one arm, and his imp under the other, and they all looked at me, heaving for breath, and unsure of what was happening.

"You do have a plan, right, Daxx?" Qrysta said.

"I have a plan."

I could see their uncertainty.

"Want to tell us about it?" Grell said.

"No need," I said, and slung Shift over my back. "I'll show you."

When we'd collected all our gear, I led them back into the cave towards the portal. I stopped, before stepping through it. "We have one shot at this."

They didn't ask what *this* was.

I led the way through into the portalscape.

"Anything we need to know?" was the only thing anyone said, once we were all inside. It was Qrysta who had asked.

"No," I said, "just be ready for anything."

Once we were on the first platform, I got out my celestial guide and laid it down. We watched the star map ahead of us change. I set my lodestone on our destination, and studied Oldface, as we waited for the orange ribbon-path that was curling out towards us. He went still, and his eyes grew round as he realized where we would be taking him. His eyes met mine, and they were filled with hate.

I nodded, to confirm what he now already knew. "Okay," I said, when the orange path attached itself to our platform. "Let's go."

We set off across the void, Oller on point ahead as always, Little Guy at his heels, then Grell with our captives under each arm. I followed under the Glows that I had thrown up to travel along above us, with Jess and Qrysta behind me. Around and about, and up and through, we twisted and turned with our path as it climbed, and fell, until we were standing at the end of it, in front of the blue-white sheen of the portal that led into the heart of The Demon.

We exchanged glances.

I said, "Better buff up."

I passed around Elun's potions, and Grell offered Healer Ria's to any who wanted them. Not to be left out, Qrysta passed around the Quickwork she'd bought at the market in Lindfirth, and we all took a mouthful. I cast the strongest Shields I could muster on each of us. Oldface had stopped struggling and hung limp under Grell's huge arm. The imp continued to writhe, and twist, and kick, even though its legs were pinioned by Oller's string.

"Ready?" I asked, not really sure if I even was.

"What's in there?" Grell said.

"Let's find out."

This was my idea, so I should take the lead. If there was trouble ahead—well, it was only right that I should be the one to face it first. Maybe I could do something about it while the others came through after me.

I walked past Oller and stepped through the portal.

33

In the Belly of the Beast

I recognized where I was at once. Not because I'd ever been there before, but from what Commandant Bastard had told us—his memories of that place, deep beneath the Great Waste. We were standing at the top of what must once have been a wall that had long ago collapsed. Below us, under a tumbledown clutter of old masonry, lay a wide, sandy floor, out of which rose the columns and walls of an ancient temple.

In the center of that floor, on a dais at the top of several steps that led up to it from all sides, stood an altar. I tried not to think about the stains on it. Behind it was a stone statue of Varamaxes, rearing up toward the ceiling of the cavern that was lost in shadow far overhead. His feathered head was thrown back, his beak of a mouth open in a roar of rage. Each taloned hand held a human body. His scaled tail curved around itself in a circle, its end an arrowhead.

The air was hot, musty, stifling, but not still. It was, somehow, trembling, as if waiting to move, to come to life. I remembered Commandant Bastard's tale, of how they had arrived down here, where it had at first been empty, and how hordes of undead had poured out of the ground, and the walls, and every nook and cranny .... I was as on edge as he had been, I felt, waiting for the eruption of that army.

412

Qrysta was beside me, now, on my right, Jess next to her, and then on my left Oller, and Little Guy, and finally Grell with his captives tucked under his arms.

We stood, in line, in silence, taking in the scene. We all knew where we were. We all knew what had happened here before. I looked around, for the way out. Which way had he run? Young Jack Blunt, with his fellow soldiers, when the demon had Feared them? I could see a sandy path off to our left, leading up and away, into the dark distance. *That way.* Up to the chasm of molten rock, and the bridges that their sappers had laid across it, and over them to safety. But those bridges wouldn't be there now, I knew. There was no escape that way for us.

Beside me, Qrysta whispered, "Gods, Daxxie ..."

"I know," I said.

"Is this where I think it is?"

"Yes and no," I said.

She frowned. "What does that mean?"

An explanation would take time. We didn't have time. I needed to act, and fast. Nor did I want to confuse my friends and give them more to worry about. "It's complicated. I'll explain later."

"If there *is* a later," she muttered.

We looked around, all as taut as bowstrings.

"Now what?" Oller said.

I looked at Grell and the burdens he was carrying.

The imp had gone still. His head was lifted, and he was staring ahead, at the statue.

Looking at him, I felt my blood turn to water. I had never felt so frightened. It wasn't terror, or panic—something that hits you in an emergency. It was the knowledge of what he was. His nature.

Which we were about to return to him.

I had worked it out. It was the imp who had been quartered, and scattered, and imprisoned—not, as he had led us to believe, Oldface. Who was merely his mouthpiece. His chief disciple. His Archon.

I nodded at Grell and said—and I had to clear my dry throat in order to say it—"You can put it down now."

Grell set the imp down on his feet.

I knelt in front of it and locked onto the imp's implacable gaze. I felt it boring into me, merciless, hostile.

I said, "I'll need a knife," and held out my hand to Oller. Who put a throwing knife into it. Not breaking eye contact with the imp, I slowly, deliberately, cut the cords that bound it.

Its red eyes burned into mine. I knew I wouldn't win. *No one ever does,* Oldface had told me, back in his prison under the island.

I nodded, in acknowledgment, closed my eyes, and rose to my feet.

The imp raised his chin before releasing me from his stare, and I got the message. *I'll deal with you later.* It padded off past me, and clambered its way down the fallen masonry, down to the sand floor, and towards the altar.

We watched as it mounted the steps, up onto the altar, where it stood, its back to us, staring up at the towering statue in front of it. It looked little more than a tiny, dark doll. Quite insignificant, if you didn't know what it was. Well, I knew what it was, and what it was, was terrifying.

It crouched and sprang, grabbing onto the folds that had been carved into the stone. Like a spider, it began to climb, slowly, handhold to handhold, foothold to foothold. Gathering speed, it flowed up the rock face that was the statue, knee to thigh, to pelvis, to stomach, until it turned, inwards, and away from us, and slithered into a cavity at the statue's core. Its navel.

A voice behind me said, "It is time."

We turned as Chidian came towards us from the portal.

He stopped beside me. His young face was a mask, but a mask that looked a thousand years old. He held my eyes for a moment.

He said nothing. He inclined his head, in understanding, and walked past us—but not down the fallen wall. He stepped onto the air and drifted down towards the altar.

I nodded at Grell. He put Oldface down and reached into his pack. He brought out the small, iron box and opened it.

At first, nothing happened. Then, in contrast to the light that had emanated from the outer chest that had held it before it was opened, and the golden Natures of the Kinfolk that had risen to their release, a darkness emerged. A shadow that flowed densely out of the little box, down the tumbled blocks of masonry, across the desert floor, and over the altar, and up the statue of Varamaxes, feet to legs, to stomach, to heart, to head, until the yellow stone in which the Demon had been carved was as dark and gray as the imp that was now concealed within

414

it. When it had all been flooded with that dark tide, the statue came to life, and moved.

The Demon.

Grell set Oldface on the ground, where he tottered and slumped down onto his backside.

I pointed Shift at him and Unmuted him, feeling her nervous energy dance up my arm at the decisions I had made.

Oldface was gasping for breath, and looking at the ground, and shaking.

"I tried," he said. "I tried …"

I said, quietly, "You can come with us."

He turned his head and looked at me. His eyes were vacant. Lost. He whispered, "He won't let me."

I said, "Stay with him, or come with us. It's your choice."

His eyes searched mine, for understanding. "No," he said. "It isn't. It's his."

He struggled to his feet. He stood there, swaying. He found my eyes, and said "When … *afterwards* …. You know he'll need another?"

I looked into his helpless face and understood the warning.

Another Archon. That would be me.

My blood chilled at the thought. Centuries, in thrall to that monster, serving it, *feeding* it …

The Archon turned away and stumbled down the ruined masonry towards his master. He tottered across the sand floor of the temple, as if drawn, both reluctant and accepting. He mounted the steps to the altar, and dropped to his knees, his head bowed.

I heard Chidian's quiet voice in my head. "Now," he said.

I looked at Oller and nodded.

He unslung his Blackout-infused loot bag from his back and put it down on the ground.

He looked at me and said, uncertain, "You sure?"

"I'm sure."

Oller untied the neck of his loot bag and opened it. He tilted it forwards, holding it by its base, and, gently, shook its contents out. The ball of white lights that spiraled around the little red sun that they were holding within themselves floated out, and away, and downwards, rotating as they all drifted towards the figures far below.

Oldface, kneeling. Chidian, waiting. Varamaxes, towering above them both.

"Be ready, guys," I said.

Grell said, "Maybe we should go now …"

"No. We need to know."

We watched the scene below, our eyes following the white sphere. We could see glimpses of the red deep within it, held there by all that Chidian had done, long centuries ago. When the ball of lights reached Chidian, it stopped. He looked so small, down there; so frail, compared with the beast that loomed above him, waiting.

Chidian reached out his hand. He touched the white ball, and its shape altered. It flowed into him, along his arm, returning his power to where it belonged. As the enveloping white shield lessened, the red sun inside it grew stronger, until it broke free from the last wisps of white. Gathering speed, it rushed towards the living thing that the statue had become and buried itself into it. A glow spread on the gray-black of the creature's skin, as if heating it, until it was burning a fiery red. Varamaxes threw back his head, and roared, a roar that boomed off the walls and ceiling of the temple and echoed around the cavern.

Suddenly, where it had been ponderous, and slow, the demon was agile and moving at speed. Its arms slashed down and seized Oldface, and tore him in half, before shoving the pieces of his corpse into his beak, chewing and swallowing one after the other.

All around him the ground erupted. Long-dead creatures poured out from their resting places. Lights, off to our left, swam down towards us—flaming torches borne, we saw, by the massed army of the Devoted Children of Mercy. Brother Chidian was now surrounded by an aura of bright white light, his arms held high. He faced the Demon, as they had faced each other so manytimes before. The armies clashed. Above them, their leaders unleashed fire and fury at each other. The thunderous sounds of battle roiled up towards us, as the old war that would never end resumed once more.

It was a war we wanted no part of.

We needed to leave them to it, before whoever came out on top turned his attention to us.

I looked at the others and nodded. Time to be going. I hurried back to, and through, the portal.

I Turned, into *were*-form, before all of them were even through it to join me, and galloped to the nearest platform, where I Turned back, and laid my map of Mourvania down, and put my lodestone on it. The others ran up to join me as the star-wall changed behind them. I'd asked Chidian if portals could be destroyed, and he'd said they couldn't be by any mortal means. So all I could do, I thought, was make them lead somewhere else.

I had no way of knowing what might happen, after the battle that we'd just avoided had ended. Could they come back this way, Varamaxes and Valmynia, and bring their eternal war to this mortal plane again? Maybe. How could we mere mortals know? And how would they do that, through that maze within the portalscape, with its myriad of ribbon-paths and platforms? There were all the worlds in the universe for them to use as their theater of war. What were the chances of them alighting on this one again?

I explained to the others, as best I could, what Chidian had explained to me. We'd been in a simulacrum of the stronghold beneath the Great Waste. Wherever it was, it wasn't here, and the armies that were now locked in battle down there weren't of the world we were returning to. Which led to our next problem. The army that *was* of this world, the Devoted Children of Mercy, would be searching high and low for us. I told them about the sleeping Mother Abbott, witnessing Chidian and me in her dream, and how she would know that I'd betrayed her.

They saw the problem. We needed an exit strategy if we didn't want to burn. Which we didn't.

As to what we had just done: I didn't know if I was right about this, but I hoped that they would be fighting it out from then on in a simulacrum of The Demon—just as I'd made my bargain with Chidian in a simulacrum of The Protectress. And that they would never be bothering anyone in any world with their eternal war ever again. I would never know, of course. But I preferred to think that I'd made the whole problem go away, for all people, everywhere.

As I stood up, and we studied the star-wall ahead of us, which was once again a map of Mourvania, Qrysta said, "So, now what?"

Grell suggested, "Wester Isle? There are no Devoted there, right Jess?"

Jess nodded.

"And we can pick up our loot," Grell added.

"Yeah, but then what?" Qrysta said. "You heard Oldface. There are no ships from there that wouldn't turn us in for the reward. We'd be stuck there forever. Or until word made its way to the mainland, and then they'd come looking for us."

So, where on the mainland, then?

We talked it over. The Last Town, maybe, Qrysta suggested, Whiteholme? Head off into the Forest of Secrets, trek for a week or two until we reached—what? The edge of the map, basically. The Eastern Mountains, and, if we could find a way over them, into whatever realm lay beyond. Where, of course, the authorities might be no more welcoming than they'd be in Mourvania. We could disappear into the swamps that lurked at the southeast of the map, and try to get through them to the south, skirting the Great Waste. Somehow, that didn't appeal. Grell didn't think that we could cross the Sunset Mountains in the far West. "Very high," he said. "Very steep. Very cold."

So—where?

"Cressen was nice and quiet," Oller suggested. "We could hide out there, till the hue and cry dies down."

I considered it. "Five of us?" I said. I didn't need to point out that, being an Orc, Grell would attract attention anywhere. And a group, with him in it, and the rest of us, all strangers: I doubted we'd pass unnoticed. Yes, I could cast Glamours on us all, but they don't last forever. Besides, they don't fool everyone, only the unsuspecting. Anyone even a tenth as perceptive as Marnie would see through them. Reeves would be notified. Guards would be summoned. Arrests would follow.

"The Kinfolk will take us in," Grell said. "We've done what they wanted. They'll be grateful. And they don't have any love for the people who are looking for us, the Big Folk. They'd hide us, for sure."

A good suggestion, I thought.

But there was a problem with it. "Well, that's just it, isn't it?" I said. "*Hide* us. We don't want to have to hide out forever, do we? We want to leave this realm *ASAP*."

"What about your guys?" Qrysta asked. "Avildor and Elun. They won't turn us in."

"No," I agreed. "But they won't get us out either.

Oller said, "A ship's what we need. Get out, stop off on Wester Isle on the way home, pick up our loot before anyone else gets at it." He thought about that. "Any of you know how to sail?"

We didn't.

"Ship, *and* a crew, then," Oller said.

We all fell silent.

"Yes, well," I said. "Any ideas how to find those? Seeing as every ship, and every crew, will sell us to the Devoted in a heartbeat?"

It wasn't Grell, or Oller, or Qrysta who had an answer to that, as we considered the problem.

It was Jess.

"There," she said.

We looked at where she was pointing. The easternmost edge of the map on the star-wall.

"There's ships there," she said. "And those that sail them do what they want, not what they're told."

We were all looking at her.

"They don't pay mind to the authorities," she explained, her eyes shining. "They pay mind to those who pay them." She looked from face to face. "Well? You've got that chest of jewels. They're worth a pretty penny. You can buy passage with them!"

Qrysta said, "How do you know this, Jess?"

She shrugged. "We get traders of all sorts on the Isle. Some proper merchantmen. Law-abiding. Others, well …. The sort that don't like paying the king's excise, thanks very much, or having to present manifests to nosy harbormasters who'll send in the revenue men to poke about their cargo holds … they like to make their living the way they want, without any prying."

Interesting, I thought. *Smugglers.*

"They're our best traders," Jess went on. "We deal with them rather than with the merchantmen. Better prices; cash on the barrelhead; no questions asked. Suits us, suits them."

I studied her. I said, "Are you sure your father was a fisherman, Jess?"

"Oh, yes," she said, a butter-wouldn't-melt-in-my-mouth expression on her young face.

Which turned into a grin, as I held her eyes. "Among other things," she admitted, with a giggle.

"Ah," I said.

"What do you know about those islands, Jess?" Qrysta asked. "The Morning Isles?"

"They're run by the free fleets." Jess replied. "Biggest port is Freehaven. That's where all the trading happens. Mostly the captains avoid each other. They're always quarrelling, among themselves, lording it over each other. One of the top ones was a woman—like you, Captain Qrysta. She commanded *The Red Rose*, until she had her throat cut. By her mate, according to her parrot."

Qrysta said, "According to her *parrot?*"

"Yes," Jess said. "Talking parrot, obviously. It witnessed the whole thing and told everyone who'd listen; but no one was prepared to take the word of a parrot, so the mate was never tried for it. And he's now the captain. He's not the biggest captain out there, that's Bartle."

I saw Qrysta look sharply at Jess.

Interesting, I thought. I wondered what the name meant to her.

Qrysta asked, quietly, "And who's that?"

"He's been the top captain forever," Jess said. "People call him the Admiral sometimes, even though they don't have ranks, in the free fleets, like a proper navy. Captain, mate, and crew, that's all. They say there's something about him, though. That he's … different."

I kept my eyes on Qrysta as she considered her reply. "In what way, Jess?"

Jess frowned. "People say he's … not just powerful. He's got *power.* The way they say it …" she hesitated. Then went on, "They don't like to talk about it. They sound—well, frightened."

"Any idea why?"

We waited as Jess thought back over what she'd heard.

"Well, they say his fleet sails all over the world. Which is why he's rich, and powerful. But also, he brought someone back. From the ends of the earth. Someone who turned him into what he is."

Turned him into, I thought. I didn't like the sound of that.

Qrysta's eyes grew more calculating. "And what is that?"

Jess didn't know, shrugged. "Something they're 'fraid of."

There was a silence. An ominous one.

Oller said, "What's this town like, then? Freehaven? Big?"

"I think so."

"Reeve and watch, that kind of thing? Guards?"

Jess consulted her memories, of what she'd heard. "I don't know."

Oller seemed to like that answer. He looked at me with a smile and winked. I knew what he was thinking. *Sounds like the sort of place thieves like. No lords, no authorities. Maybe even a TG there. Wouldn't surprise me; we're an organized lot.*

I remembered what Avildor had told me about the Morning Isles. *Them as sail there don't pay much mind to the king's laws.*

I had no way of knowing if we'd be safe there, but at least we'd be beyond the long arm of the Devoted Children's law.

I placed my lodestone on the Morning Isles, on my map of Mourvania, and we all stood back to watch the ribbon-path unfurl itself from the star-wall and weave its way towards us.

Not exactly orange, I noticed. A bright, coral pink.

It attached itself to our platform.

"Right," I said. "We need to take this carefully."

Grell said, "Duhh, obviously!"

We all looked at him.

"Well, we're not going to just swan in there, are we?"

Which was more or less what I'd meant. I didn't have an actual plan, so I asked, "Suggestions?"

Oller said, "Jess is from hereabouts. I can blend in. Grell can't. You lot hold back, me and Jess'll take a look around and see what's what."

That sounded good. I said, to Jess, "Are you okay with that?"

She grinned. "They won't be looking at me, will they? They'll only want to talk to Little Guy!"

We set off along the coral-pink ribbon-path, wondering what we'd find at the end of it.

Qrysta said, as we walked, "So how do you think that works, Daxxie? Portals, and maps, and access, and so on?"

I said, "According to the rules."

She grunted acknowledgment. She had no more idea what "the rules" were than I did. But she knew that at least we'd escaped with our lives. *Out of the frying pan,* I thought. Into … well, what?

"Yeah," she said.

"I expect we'll find out, one day."

Qrysta looked at me and smiled. I knew what she was thinking, just as I was. *Ken.*

"If we live that long, right?"

"If we live that long," I agreed.

We reached the blue-white sheen of the portal at the end of the ribbon-path. I cast my strongest Shields on all of us.

"Okay," I said. "Usual order."

Oller pushed through the portal, followed by Little Guy.

And then the rest of us.

34

The Confluence

I stepped through the portal into the back of another cave. In turn the others joined me, Qrysta, Jess, Grell. Cautiously, we followed Oller along a dark tunnel, with dim, blue light emerging at the far end of it. Evening light. More intense than that soft light, though, was the smell, which was strong, and immediate. Salt air. Sea winds. Out there, ahead of us, was the ocean. The Morning Isles. Quite *where* we would be in them—well, that we'd have to find out.

We made our way onward, making as little sound as possible with our footsteps on the cave's sandy floor. Soon we heard the sounds of waves—small waves, breaking gently and rhythmically on a nearby shore. There were no people in the cave, but they obviously came here. It was filled with supplies. Large, wooden cargo chests, some of them nearly as tall as I was. Barrels. Boxes and sacks and baskets, wrapped up in netting. This cave was a storage depot.

I held up my hand, and we all stopped.

I thought, *This makes no sense.*

Grell saw that I was puzzled, and said, "What?"

I said, "You think the people who put all these crates here wouldn't notice the portal?"

We looked back at it, glowing blue and white behind us in the wall where the cave ended.

They all understood what I meant.

And we all thought the same questions. *So, why hadn't they tried to go through it?* Or, *why weren't they guarding it?*

I needed to know how this worked.

I went over, in my mind, how we'd navigated our way here through the portalscape; and, once I'd made my decision, said, "Hang on."

I got out my map of Mourvania and my lodestone.

The last spot on the map that I'd placed it on had been right here, where we were now.

I thought, so maybe there's some relation between the lodestones and the portals. Some connection, which we need to understand.

I put the map on the ground, and the lodestone on Kingsworth, the capital of this realm.

I let the lodestone orient itself to that destination, for a minute or so.

I picked it up, settling its brown, curved back on the palm of my hand.

After a moment, it turned, towards the west.

Towards Kingsworth.

As it turned, the portal at the cave's end faded and disappeared.

So. There was the answer. No map with a lodestone on it, pointing here: No portal. To close a portal, use the map and lodestone again to direct it elsewhere.

This, I realized, meant that whoever might be ahead of us wouldn't know that we were coming out from behind them. They wouldn't even know that there was—or had recently been—a portal back here, which people could emerge through. As far as they knew, all that there was at the back of this cave was a blank wall. They wouldn't be expecting anyone who hadn't gone in, past them, to come back out of it.

Good. We would have the element of surprise on our side. And stealth. If people aren't expecting you, they won't be on alert.

I nodded, and we moved on, Oller on point ahead. He made no sound, as always, and, behind him, we trod cautiously. Supplies, we all knew, were always guarded. There would be sentries. We'd need hiding places, if any of them came our way. Kill a sentry, and it's not long before the alarm goes off. Avoid them, and you buy yourself time. And there were only five of us, and a dog—and who knew how many of them? The supplies stacked up in this cave suggested numbers, as we passed more barrels, more crates, more sacks and bags and bundles.

All of which meant more people.

I stopped again, and motioned for everyone to draw close, so we could confer.

"We have no idea how many of them there are," I whispered, "so we don't want to alert them. Ols, can you scout the place out? We'll wait here."

Oller grunted, "Right you are," and looked down at Little Guy. "Stay," he ordered. Little Guy sat obediently, and Jess ruffled his ears. Oller trotted off towards the dim blue evening light ahead of us, making no sound.

We sat on the cave's sand floor and waited.

He was back within five minutes.

"Two guards at the cave mouth," he said. "Both dozy as all bollocks, not expecting any kind of trouble. Just sitting out their shift, looking out at the rain and grumbling about pay. Not even bothering to patrol."

Qrysta said, "So things must be nice and quiet around here."

"Would seem so."

Grell said, "We want to keep it that way."

I concurred. We could start a firefight, but where would that get us? Killing the two guards that Oller had seen would make our presence known, sooner or later. Kill them, get out and away—fine; but when the bodies are discovered, who would people be looking for? Strangers.

That would be us.

Better to keep things nice and peaceful. No deaths, no bodies, no alarm—and no one, with luck, bothering much about strangers.

I said, "Did you see any ships?"

"Several. Riding at anchor. There's a bay out there, nice and sheltered, with a natural harbor."

"People?"

"Didn't see any. It's raining, like I said. Not hard, but steady, like. So, all's nice and quiet."

Good, I thought. *Nice and quiet.* Let's not make it *nasty and loud.*

I considered our options.

It was quite possible that we could capture a ship. That might not be too hard. Run in, while it's at dock, unleash our Damages, kill crew, cast off. But then what? None of us had any idea how to sail an ocean-going vessel. I imagined us overpowering a crew and then blundering around the ship we'd just captured, trying to figure out how the sails worked, and to make our way out to sea, while other ships calmly, expertly, intercepted us. And their crews boarded us. It wouldn't be long before we'd be dead, or prisoners. Not a good prospect. Nor was the prospect of trying to get ourselves a crew a good one. Once out to sea, they'd realize that we were complete incompetents, and would simply take over, and there'd be nothing we could do about it.

I was out of ideas.

Well, I thought, we can't go back. Just—*keep going forwards.*

Okay, so how to do that? We have a chest full of jewels. Yeah, right: Let any pirate captain know about that and it'll be, *Thank'ee kindly, mate, we'll take those.* I didn't think we could buy our passage home from pirates. Especially not via the route we wanted to go. We didn't want a crew of lawless pillagers taking us to Wester Isle, only to watch them help themselves to all our hard-won loot. We needed to be in charge; to be the owners, the masters, rather than paying passengers at the mercy of some unscrupulous scoundrel and his merry men. Yes, we had firepower, and we could fight, but against numbers of hardened fighters—well, I didn't like our odds.

So, I didn't think force would get us anywhere. Nor did I think bribery would work. Which left guile, and subterfuge.

I said, "Ols, what's out there? Port? Town?"

"Couldn't see, but I'd think so," he said. "Ships at anchor. Harbor. Cave full of stores like this? Guards?"

That made sense. "Okay," I said. "You and Jess need to scout it out. With Little Guy. Wander around, as if you belong. Which," I said, turning to Jess, "you do. You're a local, act like one. Don't ask questions, don't answer questions. Just listen and learn. Work with Oller, he knows the ropes. You okay with that?"

Jess nodded. "They won't notice me."

Qrysta said, "The guards will. When you go out of here, and they hadn't seen you come in?"

Oller, with a grin, said, "No they won't."

We looked at him.

He jerked his head at the supplies stacked floor to ceiling. "You haven't noticed what they're guarding?"

We hadn't.

"Come on," he said, clearly enjoying himself, "you can't all be that thick!"

We looked around.

Crates, boxes, sacks, bags, bundles—and barrels.

I walked over to a row of barrels.

Rum.

"Yep," Oller chuckled, "sailor's delight. There'd be a steady stream of them sneaking in here all hours of the day and night and helping themselves if it weren't guarded. Well now: Who's to say the guards themselves ain't partial to a tot every now and then?"

Very possible, I thought.

But that would help us—how? If they came back for a crafty slug?

Oller said, "Remember how I told you I dealt with them guard-hounds, at Cressen? Well, I still have a measure o' that. Couple of drops of Deep Sleep in a cup of rum, and we could march a bloody army past them. Daxxie: You cast one of your traps on them and mute them, so they can't cry out, I'll pour enough spiked rum down their throats to knock 'em out for the night. And when the next shift comes to relieve them, they'll be flat-out and snoring and reeking of rum. And who's going to believe them saying some bloke comes out of nowhere and forces fine rum down their throats while they can't move, eh? *Oh yes, a likely tale, my lads—clap 'em in irons!* They won't see the rest of you, so there won't be no talk of a gang of strangers."

Excellent, I thought.

"Okay, good plan, go for it," I said.

Oller said, "Come on, Grello, I need one o' them barrels on its side, bung up so I can tap it." Grell obliged, tipping an upright barrel over into the position Oller wanted. Oller filled a flask and added a few drops of Deep Sleep to it. Grell resealed the barrel, knocking the bung back into place, and then hauled it upright. It would have taken six of not-*Were*-me to have done that, but then, Grell was strong.

"Right," Oller said, "this shouldn't take long."

I said, "I'll cast a Glamour on you, just so they can't describe you."

Oller nodded. "Yeah, good thinking."

And then, after I'd cast it, and he saw us all suddenly grinning at him, challenged me, "What?"

I said, "Take a look at yourself."

427

He looked down at his ample, low-cut, lace-edged bosom, and the green dress below it, and then noticed the long, red tresses as his hair fell forwards around him.

"Whoa!" he said.

"Off you go then, gorgeous," Grell said.

"Gorgeous, eh?" Oller said.

Grell said, "*Oh, yes.*"

Oller chuckled. "Yeah," he said, "nice one, Daxxie," and he said it in a sultry, teasing voice that made us chuckle too. "Gorgeous girl appears from nowhere and offers them rum—*love* it! Wish I could see the looks on their officers' faces when they babble that story at their superiors tomorrow. Hells, this might even give them some naughty dreams." He grinned, which somehow managed to look sultry. "Right then. Come with me, you lot stay here."

I followed him as quietly as I could.

It wasn't long before he stopped and pointed at the two figures silhouetted against the sky, sitting cross-legged on the ground at the cave's mouth, staring out through the drizzle at the evening seascape. I hefted Shift, and Muted them, while casting one of the underground traps we'd learned from Black. Sandy coils rose out of the ground and wrapped around them. They struggled, startled, but couldn't even rise, let alone escape. I didn't want to Inert them. Oller needed them movable rather than rigid. He sashayed up to them, and stood over them, and smiled and actually said, or rather purred, in a voice even sexier than Qrysta's, *"Hello, sailor,"* before pouring spiked rum down their throats, one after the other.

It wasn't long before their shoulders stopped struggling, and relaxed, and went still, and their heads dropped. I Cleansed the coil-traps off them, and they slumped to the ground. Oller splashed rum all over them. I went back to get the others, thinking, *Well, they'll have a hard time talking their way out of that.*

When we rejoined Oller, he said, "Coast's clear. Literally, this is the coast. Not a soul about."

I said, "What do you think, Ols? Stay like that? You and Jess, two girls …?"

Qrysta shook her head. *"Way* too hot," she said. "Every head's going to turn to look at that. You're one sexy beast, you know that, Oller?"

"Yeah," Oller said, "I've always thought that." He added, wistfully, "No one else has, though,"

He caught Jess's eyes, and she giggled.

"No," Qrysta said, "they need to blend in."

She was right. I Cleansed the Glamour off Oller, and he was his scruffy self again. Someone you wouldn't want to look at twice.

"Come on, lass," Oller said. "Time to use them sharp little ears, eh? You too, mate." Jess and Little Guy joined him, one on either side, and they left the cave.

They set off towards the dwindling light ahead of us. Grell and Qrysta and I watched them go. Our three new companions, who we'd found in this world. A thief, a mongrel, and an orphan. All three of them, now, as much a part of our team as we were.

We looked at each other and settled down to wait.

"Time to put our heads together, eh?" Grell said.

"That it is," I agreed.

Qrysta said, "So what do you think?"

I said, "I think we're better off here than we were back there just now."

"No argument," Grell agreed. "That was a shitstorm."

"A no-win situation," Qrysta said. "Glad we got the hell away from it. Nice work, Daxxie." She gave me a big smile.

I felt it all the way down into Shift, who echoed her own smile back. "Thanks."

Grell said, "Yeah, I wouldn't have fancied being in the middle of that bloody mess."

I said, "Nor me."

Silence fell among us as we thought about what we'd been through.

We'd lived to fight another day. Why should we care about what we'd left behind? The Cult. The Devoted. The war between gods and demons. Leave them to it. Number one priority was, as always, to look after number one. Solve our own problems. That was, after all, our quest, as far as Ken had explained it. *Deal with what's in front of you.* Which, so far, we had. Now we had the next problem to deal with. How to get out of there.

Qrysta said, eventually, "I need to tell you guys something."

We looked at her.

"Yeah?" Grell said. "What?"

We were sitting cross-legged on the sandy floor of the cave, by the snoring, comatose guards. We knew that we had a while before Oller and Little Guy and Jess would return. The sounds of the sea echoed down the tunnel towards us, slow and gentle. It was relaxing after the turmoil we'd just left behind us. We were by no means home free yet, but we felt that we were out of the woods, and that the worst was behind us.

"Well," Qrysta said. "While you guys were otherwise occupied with your, ah *rewards*, I was riding off to Westwich. Through the rain—worse than this, it was bucketing down—at the head of the useless waterlogged palace guards, and four hundred Orcs singing their war songs, alongside Commandant Bastard. And he and I fell talking."

She paused, and took a deep breath, and told us of the conversation she'd had with Jack Blunt: The conversation in which he'd told her of the abduction of his wife.

We all noticed the name when she said it.

It was the name that Jess had mentioned.

Bartle.

Our eyes met. This was a convergence.

"We picked up Jess," Qrysta said, "sitting in the stocks, in the rain, outside Sallen's inn. We didn't need to do that, but we did. *Why?* I rode to Westwich, and Commandant Bastard unloaded his story on me. *Why?*"

She stopped.

Grell looked at me, and I shrugged. I didn't know either.

Grell said, "Does there have to be a reason?"

Qrysta looked him in the eye, and said, "It's just interesting that there's a connection, don't you think?"

Grell grunted. Nodded. And, eventually, said, "Yeah. Interesting, indeed."

I knew what he was thinking. On the one hand, Jess's story. On the other hand, Commandant Bastard's. Neither of them, on the face of it, our problem.

But we'd taken them both onboard.

Jess, an orphan from a remote, empty island off the coast of nowhere.

Commandant Bastard, a soldier from another realm, hundreds of leagues from where Jess lived. Also, our mentor.

They had nothing in common—except a name in their stories.

Bartle.

This was more than a coincidence, I thought. And just like Neva, I *don't trust Mr. Coincidence.*

Qrysta said, "No, Grello. You're right. There doesn't *have* to be a reason. But wouldn't you say there's a smell?"

Grell nodded, slowly. "Yeah," he said, "I would. A nasty one."

We'd been through things like this manytimes, the three of us. It was always the unknown that alerted us; the unusual. It was, in a way, a riff on the old line: *If it walks like a duck, and quacks like a duck, it is a duck.* We'd learned, over our many adventures together, that *if we don't know why it is, and we don't know what it is, it might well be a duck.*

If you happened to be alert and happened to know enough to listen to that little prickle in the back of your mind when you spot something unusual but innocuous—why, you might just think to go over and take a second look. And one of those second looks might just uncover some secret quest that no one was aware of, that no one even knew existed. And you'd be the first team to go through the hidden quest gate, and tackle it, and clear it. And at the end of it, because you were the first and only people in there, there would always be some unique, and valuable, prize. A prize that no one else would ever have the chance to win again. We'd done that, before, Qrysta and Grell and I, time and time again.

I could see them coming to the same conclusion that I was reaching.

Does this place think it's dealing with amateurs?

So, they were both right, we all knew that. There didn't have to be "a reason." But that didn't mean that one might not reveal itself.

Jess. Commandant Bastard. Bartle—the boss of the Morning Isles. Confluence.

431

35

Freehaven

Oller, Jess, and Little Guy made their way along the shore to the town that they could see ahead of them. No one paid them any attention. They blended in among the beached boats, where fisherfolk were gathering in their nets after the day's catch and carrying them out of the rain.

It wasn't much of a rain, just a thin drizzle, getting thinner. To the west, behind the low hills at the center of the island, the sun was sinking, red against a pale sky. The clouds overhead were lighter than the ones that had been driven onshore earlier. To island folk such as these, this was no kind of bad weather, just a passing shower. Children ran and played on the stony shore, ignoring the rain. Seabirds hung above the fishing boats, squawking, hoping for scraps. From time to time a curious dog came over to inspect Little Guy.

Jess and Oller knew how to act. Keep walking; stay about your business; respond to smiles and waves cheerily enough, but don't stop; keep seeming tired, and poor, and downtrodden. They knew how to be uninteresting—a couple of scruffs and a mongrel, heading into town for the night.

Steady, small waves rustled as they broke on the stony shore. All felt calm, remote, unbothered. There were no patrols clumping hither

432

and yon, pushing everyone around. There was no sense of high alert, like there had been on the mainland. The rain had stopped by the time they left the shore and walked up a sloping ramp built of stone blocks, which led into the town itself. It wasn't walled or guarded.

Oller stopped before they went into the town. He wanted to get a sense of the place.

It felt, he thought, like somewhere he could like. There was an ease about the citizens there, as they emerged from where they'd been sheltering. None of them looked particularly important, or lordly. Yes, some men wore swords at their hips, or had knives on their belts, but there was no sense of them strutting around, looking for offense, for insults, for a fight. He'd seen tense places, where everyone was always moving fast, always raising their chins in defiance, moving on ... this was different. He knew how this town would have been, half an hour earlier: People gathered under awnings, in stalls, chatting and waiting for the shower to pass.

Now they had emerged and were strolling among each other, calm, and peaceful. They stopped, and exchanged greetings, and took their time, and spoke, and listened, and laughed. And there were people of all kinds. Some were taller even than Grell, others a head shorter than Jess; some were elegant, others grotesque, and the rest all shades of everything in between. Huge, hairy blue ones—not Orcs, exactly, but not far off, either. Thin, wiry little folk, like Nyrik and Horm, but also not like. Sea Kin rather than Woods Kin? Copper-colored, weather-beaten men and women, with babies in bright, many-hued slings of woven string on their backs. Children of all kinds, running everywhere.

Oller and Jess exchanged glances. No, they'd never before seen anyone like the half of them. But it felt fine. Relaxed. They thought: If all these folks, of all these various strangenesses, didn't feel uneasy with each other—well, then, why should we?

"Not everyone from these parts, eh?" Oller muttered.

"No," Jess agreed. She was gazing at the scene, round-eyed.

Oller asked, "Recognize 'em?"

Jess shook her head.

"Nor me," Oller agreed. "Right," he said, leading off; and they walked on, into the town. Voices filled the air all around them. The smells of cooking wafted from the market square ahead. The light was fading in the sky, even as it cleared of clouds, but torches were burning, their flames illuminating the movement of the many, very different people wandering around. It felt both relaxed and lively. It felt as if the night was young.

Many types that they saw were familiar. There were plenty of sailors, with their easy, rolling gait—most of them locals, by the look of them, but a number of whom must have come from far away, in strange clothing, with complexions of different colors, and different styles of beard and hair. A party of tall, black-skinned women, with bows slung on their backs alongside filled quivers, sauntered through the square, gathering at a food stall that they obviously knew well, where they swapped greetings with its owner, who was clearly pleased to see them again, and remembered what they liked, and bustled about getting their delicacies ready.

We'll be all right here, Oller thought. *They're not going to bother us. Everyone's different, so we're not going to stand out.*

He bent down, although not very far, as Jess was only an inch or two shorter than he was, and said, "You go left, see what you can see, hear what you can hear. Move around, listen; ask if it seems right, don't answer. I'll go right. Meet back here in ten minutes. Little Guy?" He switched his attention to his dog and gestured. "You go with Jess and look after her. Anyone messes with her, use them teeth of yours, all right?"

Jess, on Little Guy's behalf as well as her own, said, "All right."

Little Guy wagged his bogbrush tail, and when Oller went one way, he went the other, trotting at Jess's heel, head up, alert.

They met, ten minutes later, and told each other what they'd learned. Which, so far, was not much.

On, then. *Keep going forwards.* They were hungry, so they headed out of the square into a side alley, where they found a backstreet tavern. *Nothing to see here,* they thought, as they supped a thin, poor ale each. *No point in eating here, let's move on.* The next tavern seemed even less promising. Its ale was weaker and sourer. They took their time, and learned nothing, and left, and wondered where next. All part of the job, they thought. Have to go from one place to another, eyes open, ears open.

Outside, in the quiet, dark back alley, Oller halted. He fidgeted, trying to understand what he'd learned. "I think we're doing this wrong, Jess," he said.

"In what way?"

"Lookit," Oller said. "Dozens of folks, from all over the world, milling about all over the place here. And what do we do, eh? We head for the dives. The places where the likes of us nobodies feel at home. You and me, eh?" He shook his head and grinned at her. "So, what does our raising tell us to do? *Hide away. We don't belong rubbing shoulders with the nobs.* Well, that's not going to get this job done, is it, girl? We're not going to learn nothing from the nobodies."

Jess saw what he meant. "We need to see who's in charge."

Oller clapped her on the shoulder. "That we do, lass!"

Jess said, "So, we need to go to the nob places."

"Yup." Oller nodded. "Up for this?"

"Yes."

"Right. Let's join the somebodies."

They walked out of the back alley, Little Guy trotting at their heels, and headed back to the market square. It was still bustling. And they were still hungry. They hadn't wanted to eat anything that was on offer in the two taverns they'd visited, and now the aromas of cooking on the evening air were tantalizing.

"Come on, then," Oller said. "Where's the place you'd never in a million years think of going into? You little scruff from nowhere, like me, where the likes of us don't belong?"

Jess looked around, and eventually pointed at a tall building. "There."

Oller looked up at a high roof, above four floors of lit windows, and then down at the base of it, where tables were laid out at the edge of the town square.

"Yur," Oller said, "nor me. Hungry?"

"Starving."

"Good. Now remember: We're two travelers in need of a meal. All of which is true. And we've plenty o' gold in our cly, so hold your head up, and walk in as if you own the place!"

Jess squared her shoulders and straightened up beside him.

Oller didn't set off right away. He looked down at Jess, and looked her over, and chuckled. "You ever want to learn thieving, young Jess, you just let me know," he said. "You're a natural, you are."

She grinned.

They set off across the market square, past its outdoor tables, and entered the large, well-lit tavern.

It was busy. Serving wenches and pot boys were hurrying about, bringing food and drink to its customers. Oller pushed through the crowd that was gathered around the bar and headed towards an empty table in the shadows beyond the wide hearth, in which a fire burned. He sat, with his back to the wall, so that he could observe everyone and everything. Jess automatically sat opposite him. Oller caught her eyes and shook his head.

He patted the bench beside him. Jess joined him. "Listen, look, and learn," Oller muttered, below the hubbub of voices. "Can't look with your back to the room, eh?" Jess nodded, and started to look around with interest. Little Guy settled in under the table between them and lay down with a contented groan.

He knew that food would be coming soon enough. Oller scanned the scene that they'd just passed through. At the front, by the door, there was a rudimentary counter, where the drinkers gathered, some of them standing, others perched on stools. Behind it were barrels and earthenware jars, and the tavern keeper, red-faced and bald and plump, bustling hither and yon in his ale-stained apron. At the center of the room was the fireplace and the best tables, for the best customers, well lit with candles. Along the back walls, where they were sitting, there were other small tables like theirs in the shadows.

They took everything in, making sure not to stare when anyone glanced their way.

Listen, look, and learn.

A girl not much older than Jess appeared at their table. She wore an off-white apron over a brown skirt. She smiled, and said, "Evening sir, and miss, and what's your pleasure?"

"A mug of ale each," Oller said, "and supper, if you please, we're sharp-set!"

"We've shore soup," the girl said, "the which is samphire and sea-weeds and barley in broth, with garlic bread, to start; then fish stew, with ramps and roots, and leaves, and onions and all."

Oller glanced at Jess, who nodded. "Thank'ee, lass, that sounds fine; and you'll keep them ales coming, if you know what's good for you."

The girl smiled at the promise of a nice tip, and said, "We've two, brewed here, and I won't bring you the one that I don't drink."

"That's what I like to hear," Oller said, returning her smile.

The girl walked away, and Oller and Jess made eye contact again.

436

"Better here than sitting on our arses in a damp cave like the others, eh?" he said.

Jess giggled. "Not half!"

"They'll be fine," Oller said. "They've got food, got water, they ain't gonna starve." He paused. "Now. What *we've* got is a job. While we wait for our supper, I'm going to be looking round. And so are you. Put them sharp little ears to work. All right?"

Jess nodded.

"You're nobody, remember?"

Jess went still.

Oops, Oller thought. He sensed her discomfort. *No family. Nobody. Thief in the stocks, in the rain.*

He said, quietly, "I'm nobody too, lass. Never have been. Not until I met Grell and Daxx and Qrysta. I was a little back-alley thief. A better one than you were, mind; I'd never have been caught for a crust o' bread and stuck in them stocks. You know that, o' course, but you don't know more than that."

Jess looked up at him.

"Don't know much more than that myself," Oller said. "There's a lot more to this than I know, all this that we're in, you and me, and the others: But one thing do I know is, I'm here now." He held her eyes. "You too. You and me, doing what we're doing. And what I'm good at doing is finding. So. That's what we do, now. Find what we need to find."

Jess said, "I'll do what I can."

Oller leaned across the table, and said, "And what you can do is what the rest of us can't."

Jess said, "What's that?"

"Talk to the young 'uns."

Jess nodded. She looked around the room. There were people of all ages there, she saw. Families, locals, visitors. She ignored the adults, and checked out the children of her own age, or thereabouts.

He was sitting at the edge of the fireplace. A boy, maybe no more than a year older than her. Flaxen-haired, empty faced, tired-looking, wrapped in a travel-stained cloak, nursing a mug of something, staring into the flames.

He felt her looking at him and glanced over.

She looked away quickly, as did he. "I've not done this before," she said, unsure of herself.

"Done what?"

"Gone up to folks and started talking."

"It's easy," Oller said. "You don't. You start *listening*."

Jess looked at him.

"If they've got something to say, they'll say it. If not, they won't."

Jess thought about that, and said, "Oh." She glanced across again at the lad by the fire. She saw the last twitch of his head as he turned away, as if he hadn't been looking over at her at all, really.

"You said, '*talk* to the kids,'" she said.

"Yep. And that starts by listening. Look, lass, it's simple. If you show someone you need them, they're on their guard. We're here to listen, right? To learn. So: Let folks as want to talk and tell, talk and tell. Give them the chance to do that. If no one takes the bait—move on."

He let that sink in.

Jess nodded, understanding.

"That lad," Oller said. "The one who likes you." He felt Jess bristling beside him, and chuckled. "Nothing wrong with that, lass, hey? People like people, every now and then. It happens. You may marry him or never see him again. Who knows? No one. He may have nothing to offer you. He may have something. Even a tiny little something you may not even notice, let alone understand, it'll sink in, and days later pop out and you'll go, *Whoa, that was exactly the information we needed!* And there's your answer. And if he doesn't have anything to offer, well then, what do you do?"

She thought it over, and eventually nodded, and said, "Move on."

"*Right* you are, young Jess! On to the next one. And the next. And you keep …?"

He waited for her to fill in the missing words.

"…Listening, and looking, and learning."

"Got it in one!" Oller said, punching her gently on the shoulder. "Off you go now. Food'll be here soon. A few minutes, that's all it can take, sometimes, to learn what's to be learned. Cold, isn't it? And that rain?"

Jess frowned, puzzled.

"You must be soaked," Oller suggested. "So, you might want to dry out by that *nice big fire* …?"

Jess understood. She looked at the fire in the hearth at the center of the room and hesitated.

Oller could see that she was worried that she would fail. "It'd be all too easy if everywhere we went there was the answer right in front of us," he said. "Wouldn't that be nice, eh? If it is. If it isn't …?"

Jess nodded, and straightened up, and said, "Move on."

"There you go." Oller grinned his lopsided smile at her and stood up to go about his business.

Jess looked over at the fire and the boy sitting at the end of the bench beside it. *Soaked*, she thought. *Tired.* She shrank within herself, feeling the cold and damp in her clothes, in her bones. She got up and walked, hunched, over to the hearth.

Where she stood, rubbing her hands, holding them out to the fire, shivering, her wet clothes steaming.

She stared into the dancing flames, thinking *I haven't even noticed him. He's nothing to me. All I want to do is dry out, warm up. The last thing I want to do is talk to anyone else, because I'm exhausted. Ooh, this steam rising from my clothes! How lovely is that?! This warmth, filling me in, from skin all the way into bones. This poor kid, I know he's watching me, and pretending that he isn't. Poor? Why do I think that? Oh, well, who knows? Who cares?*

She turned around, putting her back to the fire, and felt the steam rising from behind her, and sighed.

She relaxed and smiled. She saw what Oller had meant. *It doesn't matter. If it happens, it happens.*

In that moment of freedom, that smile, she turned, and, as if for the first time, noticed the boy sitting on the bench. She raised her eyebrows and smiled about the happiness of her warmth. *Hey, traveler, isn't this nice?*

He smiled back. And then looked away.

He doesn't know how to do this any more than I do, she thought.

And then, a moment later, she realized: No, he has *far less* idea than I do. *I'm in charge here.*

All her doubts dropped from her shoulders. She knew what to do.

She sank to her haunches, her back to the fire, and put her hands over her head.

She felt the heat working into her clothes, and the steam rising from them.

Who wouldn't want to do that? Cold, and soaked? *Oh, to be dry, and warm …*

439

She swiveled on her heels to dry her front.

On the way, she "noticed" the boy again, and briefly smiled at him again. The smile wasn't about him, but about how good it felt not to be cold and wet any more. He understood, she could tell, because this time he grinned back. She gazed into the fire, and held her hands out towards the flames, and settled. In her mind, gradually, she lost herself, until she was a long way from there. And she knew that the lad was, often, looking at her.

She had his attention and it didn't matter.

All that mattered was the heart of the fire. Let him see someone enjoying the warmth. A cold, wet kid, someone his age, just drying out. He could relate to that, right? And if nothing is said, and if nothing is listened to and learned, well: At least we made someone else's evening warmer as well as our own.

Marry him? she thought. She couldn't help the grunt of laughter that welled up inside her, as she recalled what Oller had said. *Yes,* she thought. *Maybe I will.* The idea was so absurd that she shook her head and realized why Oller had said it. *It doesn't matter. If it happens, it happens.*

She now knew what to do. She turned, away from the boy, and said to the woman opposite him, nearest the fire, "I hope I'm not in your way, ma'am? I got caught out in the rain."

The woman said, "No, no, that's all right, lass."

Jess turned and looked at the others facing the fire. All agreed. "I'm drier now," she said, looking from one face to the next, with a smile, "thanks."

She unfolded herself from her crouch and stood.

Her smile ended on the boy.

He shifted on his seat, making space for her next to the fire.

"Are you sure?" Jess said.

"Yes," he said. "You're still steaming."

"Am I?"

He nodded.

"I promise not to steam all over you," Jess said.

He smiled, shyly, and Jess sat next to him.

"Thanks," she said. "I won't bother you for long."

"It's no bother," he said, quickly. "I'm keeping a place for my Da. It's better to have someone sitting in it. People won't ask if they can have it."

Jess thought of her own Da, and her smile faded. The boy noticed.

"Someone else might move," he said, thinking that she thought she'd have to go when his father returned. "So, you can stay, when he gets back."

Jess knew, then, what to do. Use her story.

She sighed. "Thanks," she said, in a small voice.

The boy sensed her discomfort, and said, "What's wrong?"

"Mine won't," Jess said. "Come back. My Da's dead."

The boy looked over at Oller, who was talking to someone on the other side of the room, and then back at Jess.

"No," she said. "He's … family."

The boy said, "I'm sorry."

Jess looked at him with a grin. "Why? Was it your fault?"

The boy was flustered, confused. "No," he said, "I meant …"

"Killed by pirates, he was," Jess said, by way of explanation. "You don't look like a pirate to me."

The boy settled, and, eventually, returned her grin with another shy smile.

They both turned their attention back to the fire. The boy took a sip from his mug. He noticed that Jess didn't have a drink.

He held the mug out to her.

"Are you sure?" she said.

"Go on," he said. "It's not very nice."

Jess took a sip. It wasn't.

She grimaced and caught the eye of the serving girl. A shake of the head, a point to her own table, two fingers held up and a sharp nod, and the girl understood. She grinned. Jess saw that she'd got the message. *No more of the bad stuff, and right away.*

"Thanks," Jess said to the lad beside her, and not with enthusiasm. She passed his mug back to him.

"You're welcome," he said, and took the mug, also not with enthusiasm.

Eventually, Jess said, "What's your name?"

"Evall."

"Hello, Evall. I'm Jess."

"Hello, Jess."

With a grin, Jess said, "You're not from around here, are you?"

"How d'you know?"

"'Cos there's two ales here, in this tavern, and they gave you the one they don't drink themselves. This," she said, as the serving girl handed them two full mugs, "is the one they do."

She passed the unfinished mug of poor ale back to the girl, who chuckled, and winked at the lad before leaving. Jess and he clinked mugs, and drank, and his face changed.

"Better, right?" Jess said.

"Much better," he agreed. "Back home, where I come from, we brew ales as fine as you'll find the world over. Small beers, for your breakfast, which are as pure as snow, because no one wants to drink the water from the rivers and such, all mud and sickness as it is. Safe, the small beers are, and weak; they don't make you merry and stop the day before it's started. Fruit ales, summer ales, ales of wheat and oat and barley, and birch and elm bark—those are the ones we sup of an evening, when the day's work is done. This," he said, nodding at his mug, "is proper."

Jess said, "So, where's home?"

"Normark."

Jess had never heard of it. "Where's that?"

"North," Evall said. "And also east of here, I think. Those as sail around these parts don't seem to go there."

"Why not?"

Evall shrugged. "Da says it's trade. The richer markets are down south. We've not got much up there. Except forests, and reindeer, and Ogres, and such. And the Ice Lands, and no one goes into them."

"Why not?"

" 'Cos of those that live there. Although *live* isn't always the right word, Da says. Some of them up there not being *alive*, the way we are. The old wives say they reach all the way to the crown of the world, where the moon sleeps when she's not lighting the sky; but I reckon that's just childer tales."

"Sounds awful," Jess said.

"Where we live's nice enough, though," Evall said. "Farms, and towns, and the like, but we're down the southern end of the realm, where the warm current comes in from the South Sea."

He sighed. "I wish I was back there, back home."

"So why aren't you?"

"Da's a merchant. Well, no, that's too grand a word; he's not one of the rich ones who sit in their godowns at the docks and send everyone scurrying. He's one of the scurriers. He's been clerk to one all his working life. Does what he's told—and suddenly he's told to

442

go overseas and see if he could make the step up. Which would be the making of him. Why, he could end up a Master himself! He never expected he'd get the chance of that. 'Go off and do this,' he was told. And he scarce knows how, not at this end, out here, in the … well, where it's all done, the wide world.

"Back there, in his books, why, it all makes sense to him. That's what he's good at. Numbers, and records, and such. But it's different when you have to go out and do it yourself. He knows what needs to be done, which is come back with contracts, for this and that, and letters of marque, and samples, and such. So, he's been all over, doing that, but …"

He tailed off.

"But?"

"He's not had much luck. Just one tavern after another, in one port after another, and one merchant after the other, or his snooty chief clerk more usually, showing us the door. We've been all over, lands down the south, and east, strange places I can tell you. And now we're here, and we have to get home, because our year is up, and we've little to show for it, and we can't find ship. No one here sails to Normark, as far as we can find. Been here weeks, me and Da have, trying to buy passage. The which he's off doing now."

"And why are you with him?"

Evall looked at her and frowned. "I'm his 'prentice. I'll be following after him, in the trade. It's time I learned the ropes, Da said. Even though … well, from what I've seen, he don't know them himself, all that well. He's fine back home, working for our Master, but out here …. Learning on the job, we are, the both of us. He's said that more than once."

"Doesn't the merchant have introductions? The man who employs him?"

"Yes, but Da don't need those. He don't need people our Master already does business with. He needs to find new contacts. New markets. New goods."

Jess turned her attention back to the fire.

She thought about what Evall had said. And saw something.

"What are your *old* goods?" she asked.

"Timber, hides; metals, iron and copper and such; salt fish and meat, fyrkvasr."

"What's that?"

"Strong drink. Means *fire juice,* in our language. We jar the autumn fruits in it, and they flavor it. Special, it is. And Ice Balm, but we already sell all we can get of that, which is little, to the Southrealms. They pay handsomely for it."

"What's Ice Balm?"

"Cools you in the heat."

"Oh."

Jess compared what Evall had said with what she knew of Wester Isle trading.

"So, what do your folk want, in return?"

"Gold. Gems and jewelry. Craft pieces. Arms and armor. Learning. Scrolls, and books, and recipes, and ingredients for the vandfolk—the seers and scryers and soothers. Herbs and roots and spices, and such."

Jess said, "What's a soother?"

Evall shrugged. "Them who you go to when you're sick. Or when you need to know the truth of things. Wise men and women. Them's the ones who keep us safe, it's said. Although I never met one I felt comfortable with."

"Safe from what?"

Evall looked at her. "You ask a lot of questions," he said, suddenly wary.

"What you're saying is interesting," Jess replied. "You don't have to answer if you don't want. You can ask me anything, if you'd rather."

She smiled at him. Evall's shoulders relaxed.

"Safe from the Ice Lands," he said, "and them as is in it."

Jess knew that another question would be a bad idea. "I'd like to go to your realm," she said.

Evall smiled at her. "Yes," he said, "me too. And if you do, come and say hello, all right?"

"I will," Jess said.

She looked up and caught Oller's eye across the room. He nodded at her.

"Where d'you live?" she said.

"Sondehafn. Our main port. Although it's smaller even than this one, let alone the big ones in the Southrealms. Ask for me, Evall Evallsson. They all know us there."

"Will do," Jess said, standing up. "Thanks for the seat by the fire, Evall Evallsson. It's good to be dry and warm again!"

444

They exchanged grins, and Jess made her way back to the table where Oller was sitting and her bowl of shore soup was slowly cooling.

"What you got, then?" Oller muttered.

"Things," Jess said, "but I don't see how they'll help."

"What sort of things?"

Jess recounted her conversation with Evall.

"That's more'n I got, girl!" Oller said, with a smile.

"It is?"

"Much more. You did well. Nice job, Jess. Very good work. So, want to know what I learned?"

"What?"

He nodded at her bowl of shore soup. "Eat up, and I'll tell you," he said. "We've a busy night ahead of us."

36

What Oller Learned

Night had fallen when Oller and Jess arrived back at our cave. Oller, of course, couldn't resist the chance to prank Grell, so crept up on him and tapped him on the back. Grell's startled, "Shit, Ols! You scared the crap out of me!" had Qrysta and I reaching for our weapons instinctively. We hadn't seen him coming either.

"Dozy bugger!" Oller chuckled. He let out his low whistle.

Jess and Little Guy joined the others, stepping around the unconscious guards.

The five of us sat on the cave's sand floor as they told us what they'd learned. Jess didn't quite understand why Oller wanted her to go first, telling of her conversation with Evall Evallsson. She thought that it didn't seem nearly as important as what he'd told her, while they ate their supper in the tavern—which they'd done in a hurry, before leaving a nice tip on their table for the serving girl.

Qrysta, and Grell, and I, of course, understood the implication of her information at once. *Normark. Another realm.* We'd cleared Jarnland; and, if we got off these Morning Isles, we'd have cleared Mourvania. Next up: Where? Normark? The Ice Lands? Or those richer markets to the south, that Evall had spoken of? Time, no doubt, would tell. This world was expanding all around us, revealing itself. *Finish up here,*

446

we felt, *and that would be far from the end of it. All indications were that there was plenty more to come for us on this rock.*

"So, then," Oller said, when Jess had finished and all eyes turned to him. He was no more than a silhouette against the night sky beyond the cave's mouth. I wasn't going to risk throwing a Glow up above us so that we could see each other. Someone, out there on the water, might notice it, from the deck of one of those ships riding at anchor in the bay, and think, *Hullo, who's got a bloody great light lit in my supply cave ...?!* We didn't want a crew of sailors, or pirates, or smugglers coming our way to take a look.

I felt my eyebrows rise at Oller's, "So, then?"

I knew that tone of voice. He had something.

"While Jess was off chatting up her new boyfriend," Oller began— but broke off when Jess punched him in the shoulder, and said, "Shut up!"

Grell and Qrysta and I made sure not to laugh, because we wouldn't want Jess to think we were laughing at her, and Qrysta said, "You're such a *dick*, Oller!"

In the silence that followed, Oller saw that his "friendly banter" had fallen flat and cleared his throat. "Yes, well, no," he said. "Sorry, Jess, lass, that didn't ... wasn't. Um. I just meant ..." We all let him struggle to dig himself out of the hole he'd dug himself into.

Eventually, he said, "I want you to have friends. Fun, and that. I mean, you've got us—we're your friends, no question, but .... You know. Kids your own age. Er." He realized that no one was going to help him, and shut up.

When he'd got the message, I prompted, "So, then .... What did you find?"

Find. Oller's favorite word. He immediately perked up. "Only a way out of here," he said, sounding smug. He was back on safe ground.

That was what we wanted to hear.

"Mind you," he said, sounding less smug, "it could be a bit of a barney. Chances are we'll have to knock a few heads together. But when has that ever stopped us lot, eh?" He paused and shifted closer. "Spotted him right off, I did. Roomful of people. When Jessie and I met back at our table, for our supper, after she'd gone her way and I'd gone mine, I pointed him out, subtle like, and she took a look at him, and soon got it. Got good eyes and ears, our Jess has, and knows how to play a fish.

447

"So, I goes over, while Jess is … otherwise occupied, and *bingo bongo, dingo dongo, a* couple of phrases and we both know what's what, him and me. Just as I thought by looking at him: *TG if ever I seen one.* I also thought, from the way he was sitting, moping over his ale, staring over at the fire: *This poor sod thinks he's almighty buggered and has no idea which way to turn.* So, end of the day: Uncle Oller turns out to be the answer to his prayers.

"Gelbert, his name is. Bloody odd one, if you ask me, but he says it's normal where he comes from. Which is up Eastbay way. Never been there meself, but that's all he can think about, is getting back home there. Not much older'n me, he is, but a sight dafter, in my not-so-bloody-humble opinion, doing what he did. Which was only to sign up aboard a pirate ship! Right? Had this notion that pirates were like thieves, he did, and he was a thief, so, they were just like thieves on the water. *Pff!* Not by a million bloody leagues.

"He learned *that* the hard way, soon enough. *Whoof,* brutal, it was, what he's been through, by the sound of it. I mean, the poor lad. He was just a wharf rat, a back-alley boy like me; and now he's out there, in the gales, standing soaked and cold on a wet rope, forty feet above a heaving deck, clinging onto the spars, hauling the sheets in, with the rain lashing his face? He didn't know what had hit him.

"And d'you know what? He plays the reed pipe! He thought it would be all plunder, and gold to spend in the ports beyond the law, and the rum and the ladies, and hornpipes, and yo-ho-ho, and feasts in the firelight under the palm trees—the daft twat. I dunno. Some people, eh?"

He chuckled. I reminded him, "We set off without much of a clue, Oller. You and me, and Grell and Qrysta, aboard the ghost ship."

Oller grunted. He saw what I meant. "Yeah," he said. "Might not want to do that again. Anyway, where was I? Oh, yes. Well, he signs on with this crew, aboard *The Red Rose,* and he knows right off it was a mistake. Not cut out for it, he wasn't, but he also knew not to let on, not to stand out. TG, see? We teach 'em well. *Never complain, never refuse, blend into the background, do what's wanted, nip in when no one's looking and pinch the prize.* Well. Gelbert didn't know which way was up from down, for weeks, months—three years of it now. Just storms, and orders, and *do this, do that* all day and night, and hardly a moment to sleep, let alone think.

"But in it all, from listening, and looking, he learned a thing or two. He weren't aboard the only Rose ship. There was *The Dog Rose*, and *The Briar Rose*, and *The Rambling Rose*, and others, and they was all under the sway of *The Rose Revived*."

He paused. "And this is where it gets interesting," he said. "All of the smugglers, in all them other Roses, are in mortal fear of *The Rose Revived*. The which is where their Captain lives. Only, it seems *'lives'* ain't exactly it, necessarily. *Dwells*, let's say. And he don't sail no more, this Captain Bartle. Though he longs to, 'cause that's what he does, being a pirate, see? Sail the seas, take ships. Not no more, though. *Torn*, he is.

"Seems he lurks in his ship, moored up in his holdfast, hunkered down, waiting for something. Or someone. None of them knows what. Anytime any of their own captains is called onboard *The Rose Revived*, they're scared as kittens, near wetting themselves. When they come back aboard their own ship—*if* they come back aboard—it's a treble tot o' rum waiting for them at the top of the rope ladder, and no questions asked. Shaking, they are. And if they don't come back—well, some first mate takes their place, after going over to *The Rose Revived* for his promotion, and he comes back white as a sheet.

"It's a fleet that rules the oceans, Gelbert says. They can go anywhere, and no one gives them any trouble; no one dares. But within the fleet, it's like there's a drain at their center. They all feel they will get pulled off down it, any moment, and disappear. And it's holding them in—they can't get away."

Oller stopped and fished in his pack for a flask of water.

Grell said, "So, what do they do?"

"They don't," Oller said, after taking a sip. "It's like they're waiting."

Qrysta said, "For?"

"It to unjam."

We thought about that. I said, "And this helps us, how?"

"Well, listening to him, Gelbert, I got this idea. At the moment, they're a fleet, right? United under this Captain Bartle. But only because they're all scared of him. *Beyond* scared—scared out of their wits, the lot of them. Not so much of what he makes them do, but of what he *is* and what they fear they might become—what *he* might make them become, which is like him. Like what his sorcerer has made him—the sorc he brought back from the ends of the earth. Which is more dead than alive, Gelbert says the rumor is, but a lot more powerful as a result.

I couldn't help but interject when I heard that someone skilled in the arcane arts was involved. "Do you have any details on this sorc?"

"Name of Malamyr. Sounds a bad lot, from what Gelbert told me. Smells like necromancer, if you ask me. And with *foreign* magic?" Oller paused. "I don't know as how I like the sound of it.

"And I wouldn't even think of going anywhere near any o' that if we didn't have Daxx onboard. If he thinks he can handle it," he said, looking at me.

He waited for a reply. I didn't have one. I said, "Go on."

"Thing is," Oller said, his tone changing from apprehensive to intrigued, "he's terrified too, for his life, this more-dead-than-alive Captain Bartle. Has been for years, and no one knows why. Sees enemies everywhere. And he keeps his crews close about him, for protection. And they can't see no way out.

"Well," Oller said, shifting on the sand, "my idea was: Supposing he *wasn't* captaining *The Rose Revived*? Keeping all them other Roses in his thrall?"

The question hung in the air.

"They'd all go their separate ways, wouldn't they?" Oller said. "They don't owe no loyalty to each other. They're effing *pirates*! Take out that linchpin, what's holding them all together: They'll all be off and away, thank'ee very much, and about their own trade. And I got this feeling that there's many more'n some of them that would very much like to do exactly that, and as soon as you like. Get out from under his sway while the going's good. Well, how about we take the opportunity to get out along o' them? With Gelbert, and those he can trust?"

Get out, we all thought. Exactly what we wanted to do.

The questions were obvious.

Where was this Captain, and *The Rose Revived*, and the other Roses in his fleet?

I put them to Oller, and he leaned forward and set his map of Mourvania on the cave floor.

"Pop us up a Glow, Daxxie," he said.

I said, "Grell, shove over." He did, until his huge back blocked the cave entrance.

"Be quick," I told Oller, and cast the lowest, softest Glow I could manage, a foot above his hands and the map.

"There," he said, pointing to the most easterly of the islands off Freehaven.

Dawn Isle.

I killed the Glow, and darkness returned to our cave.

Qrysta said, "And how do we get there?"

"All sorted!" Oller said. "Gelbert, and his mates aboard *The Red Rose*, will do everything. All we have to do is overpower the rest of the crew—which, by the way, is most of them. He says the crew's muster is summat like sixty, and he thinks maybe a dozen or so will fight with us. That should be plenty, yeah?"

I said, "Depends what they're armed with."

"Cutlasses, bows, same as us, but they're sea wolves, Daxx. They might be good in a boarding, swinging in on ropes and that, but in a proper land fight? Each of us is worth ten o' them. Besides which, they don't have no caster to heal them. I mean, you know how good we are. And we'd have the element of surprise on our side. Then they'll bring us in to the Cove. They'd be enough for a skeleton crew, he says, they ought to be able to sail her a short distance, to where we can pick up the numbers we need."

"We can't strike out for home with twelve?" I asked.

"No way. In the Isles here, it's sheltered; out on the open sea, no one in their right mind would chance a crossing without a full crew. You saw the weather coming over to Wester Isle, Daxx. This time o' year? Forget it! It's days and nights of foul weather and hard sailing. They'd need watches of twenty in good weather, and when it blows, it's all hands on deck. I asked Gelbert; he said we'd need three watches, that's sixty minimum. He says that the Northern Ocean is not to be taken lightly. He's thought *The Red Rose* was about to sink any number of times out there, full crew and all, everyone battling for their lives."

Well, I knew nothing about sailing. So, I'd have to assume that Gelbert knew what he was talking about.

"What's this Cove?" I said.

"Their base," Oller said. "Big cavern, where they hole up, nice and hidden. Plenty of room for their ships. Bartle's holdfast is at the end of a lagoon, up a narrow approach way at the back of it. We get him there, and Gelbert will go out and about, and gather enough lads from those he knows from the different crews to slip aboard *The Red Rose* and sail us home. There's enough of 'em, he says. He's been listening and looking and learning, proper TG-style. He's picked out those who can't wait to sneak away, all quiet like, and would like nothing more than to put Bartle as far behind them as possible.

"If we can get out, and away, Bartle might not notice for long enough for us to disappear. And when we've done that …. Well, if he's terrified for his life, like Gelbert says, then he might want to keep his other ships close about him. So, he might not send them out to hunt all over after one little ship, to bring us back in, if he don't like the idea of being unprotected from whatever it is he's scared of."

Well now, I thought; that is indeed plausible. A ship. A crew. Just what we needed.

Would it be easy to put the two together?

Almost certainly not. But what choice did we have? We didn't have a better plan. We didn't have *any* plan. And now Oller had come up with one.

We needed to get out of there.

Others, it seemed, wanted to get away too. *Win-win,* I thought. *If we could pull it off.*

There was a lot to think about there. For a start: If this Bartle was so powerful—powerful enough to keep his fractious fleet under his sway—well, he could easily be more than we could handle.

Did we have to go *through* him, or could we go *around*?

We'd gone around the firefight between Varamaxes and Valmynia.

I had the distinct feeling that we weren't going to be able to pull that trick off again.

So, I thought. *How do we approach this?*

I didn't have an answer to those questions, but I instantly realized what "this" was.

"This" was what we thought we'd sneaked away from, back there, behind us, in the temple under the sands.

The Boss Fight.

I closed my eyes, and inhaled, and hoped to all the gods that I was wrong.

Qrysta broke the silence. "Ols, you remember Commandant Bastard?"

Oller chuckled, wryly. "As if I could ever forget that sod! Why, what's he got to do with anything?"

"He was their serjeant, Jess," Qrysta explained, turning to her young apprentice. "That was his nickname; his real name is Jack Blunt.

That's how these three met, Daxx and Grell and Oller—in Blunt's army, when they were raw recruits. It was he who trained them up to be as good as they are."

"Couldn't have had a better master-at-arms," Grell said. "Master of all of them, he is, every weapon you can think of. You should've seen the scrap between him and Qrysta! Fought each other to a standstill, they did. It was only a tourney fight, mind. They were using blunts, but still. They both moved so fast and fierce you couldn't hardly follow."

Jess said, "Who won?"

"Neither of us; we both quit at the same moment," Qrysta said. "Any other weapons, he'd have had me, no problem, but dual-wield: I managed to hang on." She turned back to Oller. "The Commandant and I went on an expedition, at Their Majesties' command, to sort out a problem for them. He and I were leading it, so we rode together at the head of the army. And I learned his story along the way."

She told Oller and Jess what she'd told Grell and me earlier.

They, too, made the connection as soon as they heard the name.

Bartle.

When she finished speaking, Oller whistled. "Sounds like we've got a job to do," he said.

"I promised him that I'd settle the matter on his behalf," Qrysta said, "if I ever ran across this guy. He hated the idea, I could tell. Almost panicked he was, when I made the offer. I could see how he yearns to finish the job himself. That's what's been driving him, half his life. I can't blame him. But he's not here, and there's no way to get word to him, and no way for him to get here, that I know of; and anyway, that could take months. We don't have months. We probably only have days. We need to get out of this realm before someone shops us to the Devoted for a nice, fat reward. So, we've two things to do now, not just one: Get ourselves a ship, and keep my promise."

"Blimey," Oller said. "The first is going to be sketchy enough, Qrys. As for the second ..."

"True," Qrysta agreed, "but I'm not going to let the Commandant down, any more than I'd let any of you down."

Instinctively, I reached over and patted Qrysta on the back. "Nor me, Qrysta," I said.

"I know that."

"I'm in!" Grell said. "And when we see Commandant Bastard again, I'm gonna challenge him to a one-on-one, fighting two-handed. And I'm going to knock his fucking brains in for all the bruises he gave me in training!"

Oller grunted. "Yeah, well, no way that's going to happen. He'll have you flat on your big hairy arse in seconds."

"You think?" Grell challenged.

"Ten o' gold on it," Oller said, "to your eight, you great lump. You'd be out of your league. In the square, you against Blunt? Forget it!"

Grell growled. "Right," he said, "now we *definitely* need to live through this! And when I've got your ten gold, mate, I'm going to buy a barrel of ale with it and shove you down in it face-first and hold you there till you drown, you cheeky little fuck!"

Oller chuckled. "Can't think of a better way to go!" he said. "Right, enough of that. Gelbert and his crew are on shore leave. They have been for days, just waiting here for provisioning. There's nothing doing out there on the water at the moment, he says—no nice fat merchantmen to capture. Which is part of the problem: Bartle and his crews have scoured the seas clean hereabouts, so no traders in their right minds come this way. None making for Normark, so Evall could get home. Which is also why the captains are getting restless. No prizes, no paydays. And no permission from Bartle to be off and away and hunting, on pain of their souls.

"Like I said, scared and bored they are. And nervous. Have to hunker down, is the order from above. He needs everyone around him, on the alert. Expecting trouble, he is, they all believe—but who could bring trouble to the fleet that rules the waves?"

"*We* could!" Grell said.

I could tell, from the tone of his voice, that he was still irked at the challenge that Oller had thrown at him.

Oller said, "Yeah, well. I wasn't expecting none of this, not knowing what Qrysta just told us. So," he turned to me, "up to you, Daxxie. You're the thinker. I've got Gelbert on standby, and that's about it. What's your thinking?"

I didn't have enough to go on to make a reply, so said, "You have an arrangement?"

"Him and his mates, the ones he trusts, will be by the end of the ramp at midnight. Eight bells, we'll hear it from all over, from the watches on the ships anchored in the bay here. They'll have a tender, the one they used to come ashore. They'll be expected back on *The Red Rose* at eight bells; no one will pay them any mind. Two-thirds of the crew will be asleep in their hammocks. We can take out the duty watch, then go down and deal with the others."

I said, "Okay, just to back up for a moment: Do *you* trust him?"

"No! Are you joking?" Oller laughed. "What? *'Course* not. I don't trust no one, Daxx—you know that. Well, you chaps, o' course, but only 'cos you earned it. What I go on is someone's story. If it makes sense, if it seems this is in his best interests as well as mine, well—I didn't tell Gelbert nothing about me, mate. I just let him ramble on. He wants to get out of here, is all. Get home, that's all he can think about. I dropped the odd word, like, *Devoted,* and *reward.* He didn't pick up on any of them. Yeah, he's pretty much broke, has a few coppers in his cly, but that's about it. Would he shop us for a bag of gold? *'Course* he bloody would. He's just not thinking like that. He don't know that me and my mates are valuable fugitives. He thinks it's just me and my young cousin, Jess, as is out here. And I didn't give no hint of me being desperate—I know better'n that! *He's* the one with the worries, not me. I'm the one with the answers. And he don't know about you lot. I said *we'd* meet him at midnight. I didn't say how many of us 'we' was."

I said, "You think he'll be there?"

"I know he will."

"How?"

"Like I said, Daxxie: He's down to his last few coppers. I told him to look under the table. I opened my hand, and there was golds in it. You should have seen his eyes; went as round as saucers! He'll be there all right. And if he's there because him and his mates are thinking of knocking me and Jess on the head and taking my golds—well, he'll think different when he sees you lot at my back, eh?"

I thought it over. A dozen, nervous, soon-to-be-mutinying pirates, anxious to get out and away, not knowing who to trust, or what to hope for, on the shore at midnight. Just wanting to be anywhere but where they were, with only some vague information given to them by one young and, by the sound of it, not very expert recruit: They'd definitely be on edge …

And out of the dark appears Grell, with a huge maul on his back? Yes. I didn't think they'd mess with us. They'd be well advised not to.

What about an ambush? A hundred of them, concealed—where? Under upturned fishing boats? Easy. I'd be casting Reveals, and if a hundred fuzzy red outlines showed up, we'd simply melt back into the night and leave them there to argue among themselves.

Yes. At the very least, we needed to check this possibility out.

Who knew; it might be our ticket home.

We saw them long before they saw us. They were standing, and we were flat on the ground. We'd crawled our way to the rendezvous over the stony beach, slowly, silently. They were silhouetted against the night sky. We blended into the ground. They were muttering, nervously, among themselves, grumbling as the midnight hour came and went. We were silent, except for one low growl from Little Guy, and a sharp *shush* from Oller. And, of course, I was casting Reveals. Shift showed me a clump of red outlines, gathered together. No outliers. No point men, front and sides. No one was going to jump us.

So far, Gelbert and his cronies seemed legit. And they'd be panicking while trying to hide it from themselves and from each other. They were, or soon would be, mutineers. They probably had some backup story ready to tell the officer of the watch when they went back onboard, such as, *Rafe got drunk and we had to carry him home,* or *Dannl got robbed by this floozy, and we found him in an alley, butt-naked and with his skull cracked.*

We waited. They fretted. We could hear their muttered arguments. We hung them out to dry for a while, listening to them getting more and more agitated and fractious. I tapped Oller on the shoulder. He got to his feet and trotted out to them, Little Guy at his heels. He had his story, and his reassurance, and his gold. I could sense the group relax. I couldn't hear the words, exactly, but I could guess what they were saying. *Where's Jess? What 'others?'* The obvious questions. Oller answered them. His answers soothed them.

He whistled, and Jess and Qrysta and Grell and I rose out of the shadows and walked down to join them. I could sense the intakes of breath as they saw Grell looming above us as he approached, his maul slung above his back. He didn't say anything. He didn't need to. We got into the tender, and the mutineers rowed us out to *The Red Rose*. I sat in the stern and studied their faces as they pulled us across the bay. They kept glancing at Grell beside me, with a mixture of fear and hope. I knew what they were thinking. *Glad he's on our side.*

We took *The Red Rose* in less than ten minutes. Gelbert gave the password to the watch as he went aboard. We shimmied up the rope ladder. Gelbert's cronies distracted the watch while Oller, followed by me, then Qrysta, and finally Jess and Grell, joined them. The watch were stuck in Shift's Traps and Muted before they knew what had hit them. Our mutineers trussed and gagged them. They led us belowdecks, where we overpowered the sleepers in their hammocks. Their officers knew nothing about any of it, asleep as they were in their berths. They, and those that Gelbert didn't trust, were soon locked up in the brig, and *The Red Rose* was sailing east before a steady wind. It could hardly have been a smoother operation.

37

The Cove

The Red Rose laid up off Spider Island the next day, riding at anchor in a wooded inlet that, we hoped, would shelter us from prying eyes. She was in a bay that curved within the narrow mouth of an estuary, which no one could see into from the open sea, Gelbert said. He also told us that no one came this way if they didn't have to. There was nothing on Spider Island except trouble, most of it in the form of spiders—some huge and horrible, some tiny and worse—and the things that they ate, and the things that ate them, all of them vicious, hungry, and poisonous.

Some of those things flew over on the breeze to torment us. We battened down the hatches and holed up belowdecks but still spent the day being chewed on by mites we couldn't see and stung by hornets the size of rats. Gods know how they got in to torture us, but they kept on coming. I hadn't had to do as much frantic Healing since the battle for Niblunhaem. Shift was exhausted by the end of it.

Bartle, we were told, condemned those who displeased him to be marooned on Spider Island. No one bothered to come back for them. There was no point. The first of his landing parties that had explored the place had hardly stepped ashore before they were swarmed and bloated with bites and stings, and bleeding, and flailing their arms madly around while they leaped into the water and waded back to the tender. All hands pulled away back to their ship as hard as they could while chased by ravenous bugs.

Our navigator, Dirk, and helmsman, Ernsten, had brought us into the inlet before dawn so that we'd be hidden there, where no ships came, until night fell, and we could sail on. A good, stiff breeze sprang up towards sunset, which blew the damn bugs away, and Gelbert was eager to head on. But before we heaved anchor, I called a muster of the crew. Our dozen mutineers stood alongside us. The other forty-odd faced us, sullen and wary. I gave them a choice. Me or Bartle. If you're loyal to him, or more scared of him than you are of me, speak up. They looked at each other, wondering which way to jump. I then played my ace in the hole.

And if you choose him, we'll put you ashore now.

No one picked Bartle.

I told them they'd remain in shackles for the time being, but that they'd also remain alive.

They were trooped belowdecks, and Ernsten sailed us out to sea on the evening tide.

We'd learned that it would not be a good idea to sail into the Cove in daylight. This plan of ours called for stealth. *Get in, crew up, sneak out.* Well, that was "the plan" as far as Gelbert and our mutineers knew it. They knew nothing about the rest of it, which was to take this Bartle out and settle the debt that he had long owed Commandant Bastard. I suspected that our new recruits would have been unhappy to hear about anything other than running like hell away from there—and with good reason; so I kept them in the dark. We needed them onside and doing their job.

They did it well. It was clear that they knew their work. It was also clear that I didn't have the first clue about it, their work being sailing, but that seemed not to matter. I was the captain now, it seemed. My word was law, and whatever I wanted would be what this skeleton crew would do, without question.

Skeleton crew. I didn't like the term, nor its association with what this Captain Bartle might now be. The undead can be killed. Grell and Qrysta and I had learned that in our raids together. But it was usually a lot harder to kill the undead than the living. The undead tend to be tenacious, untiring, and utterly without fear—or the slightest thought for their own preservation.

The Red Rose ran before a stiff breeze until the following afternoon, when it died, and we drifted for hours in the sudden calm. Dawn Isle lay ahead of us, small on the eastern horizon. We had no way of knowing when we'd get there. We gathered in my captain's cabin and formulated our plan of action. I cast Muffle over us, so that no one outside could hear a thing; I knew they'd be listening. That's what I'd have been doing in their place.

We had detailed charts of the Cove, and the island that it lay within. Various crewmen had helped us when we interrogated them about the locations of its guard posts, and resources, and tunnels, and waterways, and wharves. They told us that half of the interior of Dawn Isle lay underground, half aboveground. The aboveground part was, like Spider Island, a volcanic jungle, with high peaks, and waterfalls, and clearings, and at least one swamp teeming with crocodiles. Belowground, it seemed, it was safer, and more habitable. A big place, this Cove was, we were beginning to understand. A harbor lay within the cavern, a lively town along its wharves. Beyond it, a narrow inlet led deeper into the interior, its shoreline dotted with guard posts. Everything that came in along it was watched. A lagoon lay at the end it, where *The Rose Revived* lay at anchor above a wide beach. *The holdfast,* Gelbert had named it.

Not that way, I told the others. There'd never be wind in there that we could sail in on, even if a tempest were howling out to sea. It was a dead end. Pulling in, in a tender? We'd be under surveillance from the moment we left *The Red Rose.*

This way, I said, pointing at the charts.

Dozens of passageways led off from the harbor in different directions into the island; some up to the surface, some down into the network of tunnels that linked the various guard posts, and depots, and barracks, and settlements. All, in turn, led back to the holdfast—where Bartle dwelled, protected by his gates, and his guards, aboard *The Rose Revived.* It was a long way to there from the wharves through the island. No one among our informants had ever thought of taking it. They had all made sure to stay well away.

The only one who had ever been inside the holdfast was our captured captain, who was more than eager to tell us everything he knew, trussed and scared as he was, with Grell glowering down at him. He'd been rowed into the lagoon to receive his promotion aboard *The*

Rose Revived, after Bartle had "dismissed" his former captain, whom no one had ever seen again. All he could tell us was that the cavern ended in a dark beach, where *The Rose Revived* lay at anchor and hadn't moved in years.

Well, we knew one other thing. We'd be going in there.

We were all agreed about that, especially Jess. We told her that we thought she should stay aboard *The Red Rose—for her own safety; this was going to be dangerous.* She replied, in no uncertain terms—in, indeed, very unladylike language—with what she thought of that. She was short, and sharp, and adamant; and we understood. She'd lost her family to the likes of Bartle. She was coming with us. She glared at us, each in turn, challenging us to forbid her to do so.

I wasn't going to. Grell, I could see, was trying to hide a grin. Oller was perplexed, but too shrewd, or too wary from his last misstep with Jess, to say a word. He kept glancing at me, expecting a firm order for her to stay here and do as she was told.

Qrysta reached over, and took her hand, and patted it. "That's my girl," she said, and that was that.

We'd be working by night. We had more chance of succeeding with our plan when all but a few watchmen were asleep than we would in daylight hours, when the Cove would be busy. A proper port town it was, by all accounts, and its rum shops and bars stayed open till the midnight curfew.

Sailing into the Cove, on the night tide, would be easy enough. But we needed not to get boarded, nor be bothered by anyone—friends, officials, or anyone in between. How were we to make sure of that, when Gelbert had said the place was "easy come, easy go"; where everyone came and went as they pleased, and visited their mates aboard the other Roses? They'd be immediately suspicious if they were denied entry to our ship.

It was Grell who cracked the problem.

"Yellowjack," he said.

Qrysta said "What's that?"

"Quarantine. Yellow flag. Fly that at the masthead, everyone will keep well away. It'll send a message to everyone, harbormaster and other ships, saying, *sickness aboard.* We keep our distance, lay up at anchor, wait until dark, and get Gelbert and his lads to row us ashore to do our scouting. Well, when I say *us*, I mean Oller. Job for you, eh, Ols?

Look, listen, learn. Report back, and we figure out a plan. I'd stand out, you'll blend in."

We all looked at him, impressed.

Qrysta said, "Good thinking, Grell."

I agreed. "That'll get us in. Next step is to get eyes on the prize. That would be you, Ols, obviously enough, but also Qrysta. Gelbert says there are lots of women there, from captains to crew to cooks; all sorts."

"Can I go too?" Jess jumped in before Qrysta could answer.

We all looked at her, instinctively thinking, *No.*

She saw that, and said, "I did all right in Freehaven!"

When no one contradicted that, because we all knew that indeed she had, she pressed her case.

"If there's kids there, and why wouldn't there be, I can talk to them. You can't."

I hated to send Jess into danger. But she was right. Being protective of her was only natural, but she was crew now. One of us. She wanted to pull her weight. So, let her. She could do what I couldn't— what Grell *certainly* couldn't. If we set down a bloody great Orc in the middle of that peaceful town, everyone would know something was up.

They wouldn't notice a scrap of a girl like Jess.

But she would notice them and learn what they were up to.

Thinking that over gave me an idea.

They'd notice Grell for sure, and that would set off the alarms. I'd attract plenty of second looks myself: A tall caster, with a staff at his back? Where had *he* come from …?!

But, what if … "And you won't be the only one going, Jess," I said.

She frowned at me, and said, "Huh?"

I raised Shift, smiled at her anticipatory excitement, and laid a Glamour on Grell.

"Your older brother," I said.

Jess looked at him. He was Grell no longer, but a big lad a year or two her senior.

"And if any kid gives you grief," I said, "he'll sort them out."

Jess laughed.

Grell said, "What are you laughing at?!"

Jess said, "You!"

Grell, human, fourteen, awkward, plagued with acne, frowned.

I explained that I'd glamoured him, and he got the point.

462

He chuckled, and said, "Nice one!"

"And I think that I," I said, casting a Glamour on myself, "will go full pirate."

I did. Even to the extent of an eyepatch, a striped shirt, flare-topped seaboots, a wide-brimmed hat, and a rolling gait.

"How's this?" I said.

Qrysta said, *"Har harrr."*

The wind picked up. *The Red Rose* sailed into the Cove, yellowjack pennant hoisted, the sunset orange behind us. We struck sheets and anchored. No one rowed over to us, warned off as all were by the quarantine flag at our masthead. After dark Gelbert's mutineers pulled us ashore in the tender. I checked out the lay of the land with Reveals. The place was busy. Good. The more people there were moving about to blend in with, the better. Ernsten berthed the tender at a slip ladder, and we climbed up to the wharf, Little Guy tucked under Oller's arm.

The mood in the little harbor town was calm, if somewhat muted. There were no riotous celebrations going on, as there might be if a crew had taken a prize. The feeling was a sense of boredom—safety, yes, but also wariness. That suited us fine. People didn't want to mingle, to talk with each other. They just wanted to eat, drink, and be, if not exactly merry, then at least comfortable. We were aware, from what Gelbert had told us, that no one knew what they were all waiting for. No one knew what might happen, nor when.

Meanwhile there was food to be eaten and drink to be supped. And there was music, in the inns and taverns, although it seemed … thin. There was singing, and piping, and harping—all nice enough; but it was languid, desultory, as if the players, and singers, were just going through the motions. There was a *truth* missing, it felt. Until Qrysta tensed and stopped.

We waited, watching her.

She was listening.

We listened too.

And heard the song that had frozen her in her tracks.

A voice, rising clear and aching.

A woman. A melody. A tale.

Beside me, Qrysta was staring towards the source of it, her eyes wide but vacant.

I did not want to interrupt, neither her thoughts nor the song.

Listening, I let my mind wander, to imagine the tapestry that the singer was weaving us into. She was singing unaccompanied. Pure, and high, and heartbreaking. I felt that any accompaniment would have been an intrusion. Had a harp, or a drum, or a pipe struck up to join in, I'd have wanted to *shush* it. However skilled the player, it would have been a distraction—a barrier between me, the listener, and her, the teller, which I did not need to help me drink in her tale. That pained, sweet voice wanted for nothing. It sang its story, its people, its tune, itself. It was—even before we could hear the words that she was singing—wondrous, both simple and profound, painting a picture in music.

I felt tears forming in my eyes. When Qrysta moved towards the tavern where the song was coming from we all stirred out of our private reveries and followed her. Its door was open. We gathered on the threshold, holding back, not wanting to make a sound, as that gentle, aching voice held us all in its thrall. No one moved in that crowded room. All were spellbound, listening, as the song and its story reached its end.

She asked not for money
She minded not poor:
She'd lived so, she'd die so,
The maid of the moor

The maid of the moorland
Alone with her grief:
She'd live so, she'd die so,
In her love's belief.

The singer let her song fade. Its ending was followed by absolute stillness. The room waited, enraptured. Then began the rustle of movement, stirring, as her audience reawakened from the heartbreaking scene that she'd sung us all into. The low murmur of voices began around us. And then, applause. Surprised, it felt, at first—as if no one had realized that the singer should be complimented, because we were all so lost in the vision that her singing had conjured up in our minds.

We stood in the doorway, unmoving. A young woman, standing on a table, her head bowed after singing her story, the room coming to life around her, quiet, respectful, all coming to terms with what they had heard, hardly daring to speak. A hand reached up, and, eventually, she took it, as if awakening from her own trance. She stepped down from the table, from where she'd been holding this room in her thrall with her song, a tale that spoke to us all so profoundly. No more than twenty or twenty-five years old, she looked, but she walked with the burdens of one of twice those years.

Qrysta watched her go, intently.

She glanced at me, for a moment, to confirm what I had realized.

She knew who the singer was. And her song.

The Maid of the Moorland.

Jenny Blunt.

The singer walked away, slowly, into another room, her back turned to her applauding audience, flanked by two tall, armed men. Jenny's head was bowed, her shoulders hunched. The room returned to life around us. Voices called for ale, and rum, and vittles. A spell had been lifted. All the folk in the tavern felt better for what they'd just heard, and didn't quite know why, and needed to talk to their companions, to share what they'd felt. We found a table and sat. When a serving lad arrived, Qrysta asked him for four tots of rum. No one needed to speak.

So Jenny Blunt was alive, then.

And was the same age she'd been when Bartle had abducted her.

That wasn't natural. No more than, from what we'd heard, Bartle himself was "natural."

The lad returned with our rums and set them down in front of us.

Qrysta raised hers to us, and said, quietly, "Three jobs, not two."

We raised our cups and drank.

"One at a time," she said.

We understood.

Qrysta rose and headed out after Jenny Blunt.

It was only then that I noticed that Oller was no longer with us.

I was confused, for a moment, until I thought, *Well, no one else in this room would have noticed him leave, either.*

He'd slipped out ahead of her.

I nodded at Jess and Grell, and quietly they made their way to the back door that led out of there.

465

I called the serving lad over, a silver in my hand.

"I need the head," I said. "Is it yon way?"

"More of a privy than a head, and it'll be stinking by this time o' night," the lad said, grinning, and then said, "Thank'ee, matey!" when I dropped the coin on the table.

Calmly, attracting no attention to myself with my rolling seaman's gait, I followed in Jenny Blunt's footsteps. I knew how to proceed: As if I had every right to go where I pleased and just needed to relieve myself. No one challenged me. I went through the door to the back room, where Jenny and her escort had gone. It was empty. I could smell the privy off to one side. I crossed the back room and, cautiously, opened the door into a corridor. I heard footsteps, fading into the distance; steady footsteps, which suddenly changed, and suddenly stopped. *Oller,* I thought. I hurried on. The corridor became a tunnel, its walls rock rather than plaster. Its floor was sand, not stone. On it lay two lumps; Jenny Blunt's guards. Each had a throwing knife in his neck. Jenny Blunt was staring at her dead escorts, her jailers, her hands to her mouth, and then up at us.

Qrysta stepped forward, and said, "Mrs. Blunt, we're friends of your husband."

Jenny Blunt didn't move. Her eyes darted around us, confused. Eventually, her eyes settled on Qrysta.

Qrysta waited, letting know Jenny that it was her turn to speak.

Jenny Blunt said, "I …" She stopped and gathered herself. After an effort, she said, "He …" She looked behind herself, in the direction that her guards had been escorting her.

Qrysta understood. One simple gesture, telling everything.

Jenny met Qrysta's eyes again, and we could see that she was frightened.

Qrysta shook her head. "No," she said. "Your husband is Jack Blunt. Not Bartle. You know that."

We saw the flicker of recognition in Jenny's face.

"You don't know me," Qrysta said, "but we have come for you. We will take you home. Away from here. That is what you want, more than anything."

Jenny Blunt's face fell. Her eyes had filled with a sudden hope, which immediately faded, and her head drooped. What she had heard was not possible.

"We have a ship," Qrysta told her. "We have a crew. We will kill the man who stole you from your husband."

She waited.

Jenny Blunt said nothing and didn't raise her head.

"I heard you sing," Qrysta said. "It was the song your husband, our friend, told me you sang, when you judged the contest. 'He was good, but he didn't make them cry,' you told the goodwife. And then, sighing, because it had been a long day and you were tired, you got up on the table, in The Mermaid's Arms in Westwich, and showed them what you meant. You sang 'The Maid of the Moorland.' And everyone wept."

Jenny Blunt lifted her head and was staring at her.

"Every year, when his job allows," Qrysta said, "your husband searches the wide world for you. Every realm in it, that he can reach. He is a good man, as you know. As good as any we have met. So, you know he'd do that, don't you? Without a doubt."

She waited again.

Jenny Blunt was wringing her hands, uncertain, her body stiff.

I could see Qrysta thinking, *She doesn't know whether to trust me or not.*

There wasn't much that she could do about that. Except not push.

She waited. Not for the first time, I thought, *What a cool customer this girl is.*

At last, Jenny Blunt nodded, as if against her will.

She's terrified, we all knew.

It was hardly surprising. She'd been held hostage for half her life—by a captor who, judging by what we'd heard, was not exactly *human* anymore. What hope could she have left? And wouldn't that little hope have been torturing her, rather than comforting her, for the last twenty-odd years?

Qrysta reached out and took Jenny Blunt's hands in hers. "All you need to do," she said, "is tell us what's ahead."

Jenny stared at her. Tears glinted in the corners of her eyes.

Qrysta gave her a smile of reassurance, and said, "You can do that, can't you?"

Jenny Blunt swallowed, then nodded again.

"Good," Qrysta said. "You can leave the rest to us."

Jenny Blunt was looking at us uncertainly, from face to face.

She said, hesitantly, "A girl, with two swords? And a little man, with only knives. And a sailor, and a couple of children, and a dog …"

She tailed off.

Qrysta turned to me. "Daxx?"

I was about to cleanse the Glamours off Grell and myself when Qrysta held up her hand.

"I should warn you," she said, to Jenny Blunt, "one of us looks a little alarming."

Jenny Blunt frowned.

I cleansed our Glamours, and Grell was all too visible, even in the low light of the corridor: A mountain of brown-gray muscle, bristling with arms and armor.

Jenny Blunt took a couple of paces backwards.

Grell grinned, which is a sight almost as alarming as his glare.

"You're safe with me, Mrs. Blunt," he growled. "Your Jack taught me everything I know. The best, he is, and I'm his best student; so you be sure to watch and tell him everything you see!"

She swallowed, then managed to say, "All right."

"Good," he said, "you tell us where to go, and we'll do the rest, you just see if we don't!"

Jenny Blunt nodded.

Qrysta said, "Now: Is there somewhere we can hide these bodies?"

"The storeroom, there," Jenny said, her voice firming, as if now be-ginning to believe she really could be rescued. She pointed at a door in the side of the tunnel. "No one will be using it this time of night."

"That'll do," Qrysta said. "Daxxie? Take a good look at them. Think you can Glamour those on us?"

I studied the dead guards briefly, raised Shift, and Glamoured her and Grell.

Jenny Blunt's hand flew to her mouth as she looked at her two "guards."

"Okay, get these two in there." Oller grabbed one of the corpses by the heels and pulled it towards the storeroom. Grell took hold of the other. They dragged them inside and closed the door on them.

Qrysta said, "Mrs. Blunt, I promise you that you will be away from here tonight. And I'll tell you how I know this. Because I promised your husband that if I ever heard of you, or Captain Bartle, and where you were, I would go there, and I would kill him, and bring you home. And I always keep my promises."

Jenny Blunt's mouth tightened. She was trying not to weep.

Qrysta leaned in and embraced the long-lost wife of the only man who had ever equaled her in combat.

468

We all knew what she was thinking. We were thinking it too. *He'd do this for me, if things were the other way around.*

We also knew that Jenny Blunt was under some kind of spell. She looked twenty-something but was nearer fifty. Add that knowledge to what we'd heard—of Malamyr, a sorcerer from the end of the world, who had made Bartle something more than human …

There was magic here, and of a foul kind.

Well, I had magic of our own. *So, we'll see.* And I could sense the confidence the others had in me and Shift's eagerness jittering up my arm.

Sorcerer from the end of the world? You have no idea what's coming, mate.

Well, I'd back Grell against anyone, two-handed; and Qrysta at dual-wield; and Oller with his knives and speed; and Little Guy distracting his targets. But me? Against this Malamyr, about whom I knew little—and that little sounding really bad …?

Strange, I thought, how we doubt ourselves when others don't.

I don't doubt you, Shift leached her thought into me. I knew it was a challenge. *Do you doubt me?*

I pulled myself upright, and thought, *Well, let's see.*

We followed the tunnel past the storeroom and headed on, and down, and around, as it curved its way into the middle of the island. It was quiet now, the only sounds our footsteps on the sandy ground. We couldn't hear the sea behind us. I kept the Glows above us dim, so as not to alert anyone of our approach. Oller led the way, as always, on point, but now with Jenny Blunt beside him, guiding him.

They stopped as the tunnel led out into the open. We'd reached a deep basin, surrounded by cliffs and filled with vegetation, ferns and palms and damp bushes above muddy pools. I looked up at the night sky, the stars blazing overhead—and recognized the constellation above us at once. The Demon. I was struck by the coincidence—no, the *confluence*—and the sight of it held my eyes. Fourteen glittering stars. It took me a moment to realize. *Wait, what—whoa! Fourteen, not thirteen.* The lost star, found and returned. I felt a moment of truth, of hope. It was, perhaps, no more than *so far, so good;* but it felt bigger.

Job done.

We did that. *Us.*

So, maybe, we can do what's next.

"Hold up," Oller muttered.

Little Guy, he had seen, was suddenly alert, ears pricked, staring at the way ahead.

"Guard post," Jenny whispered, "and kennels for the hounds." I cast Reveals and counted twenty or thirty fuzzy red outlines. Qrysta told Jenny to stay back, with Jess, and we went in. I didn't want to throw up Glows or cast luminous green Shields around my crew. I limited myself to Traps and Mutes so that what was going to happen would happen in darkness and silence.

Oller, Qrysta, and Grell slipped in, and a few minutes later out again. All taken care of. I cast Heal All over them, but they didn't really need it. Reveals showed no life remaining in the barracks or the kennels. Jenny Blunt, I could feel, even though I could not see, was gaining encouragement. This had started, for her, in despair—the despair she'd been imprisoned inside for half her life. Out of nowhere, we had appeared. We'd killed more than twenty men and dogs in complete silence, without breaking a sweat.

She was beginning to see that, maybe, she finally had a chance.

The same tactic worked for us as we made our way into the heart of the island. Sneak up, Traps, Mutes, kill. At a bend in the path, between a cliff and a swamp, Jenny told us that the path led up to the main barracks. It held more than a hundred men, a third of them always on watch, on Bartle's orders.

Best, we decided, to go around.

We couldn't scale the cliff, so "around" meant through the swamp. Grell took the lead there rather than Oller. Striding waist-deep through the brackish water, in his Kinfolk armor, he cleared a path for us through crocodile after unfortunate crocodile as we waded along the shoreline behind him. The crocs felt his presence, through the water, and homed in on him, hungry. They lost their teeth on his armor, and Kinell crushed their skulls. We only had a couple of hundred yards of swamp to negotiate. Mud sucked at our feet, and there were low-hanging trees to duck under, and mosquitoes and needle-toothed flying things swarming us; but Shift and I spammed Heals, so their bites melted away, while Grell grunted as he brained crocodiles.

Once we'd clambered out of the swamp, beyond the barracks, we gathered in to listen to what Jenny Blunt could tell us about what lay ahead.

"There's a door in the cliff," she said. "It's the only way in. From here, it's ringed with magic. He'll know we're coming. He'll also know it's me, and I'm expected. But …" She tailed off. "He allows me to sing," she explained. "He knows that it, well, keeps me from dying inside. And keeps his crews happy. I come home, every eve, so …"

Again, she stopped. "No," she said, "not home." And she straightened up as she said it.

"Jenny," I said, "what's going to be facing us in there?"

38

The Holdfast

"A door," she said. "A guard." She hesitated. "And ..."

She stopped.

We waited.

Qrysta said, gently, "And?'

Jenny Blunt said, "My son."

That we hadn't expected.

Jenny looked at us, from face to face, wringing her hands. "He thinks Bartle's his father," she said, at last. "What could I tell him? I was pregnant when I was taken. I never saw my Jack to tell him; he'd have been so happy ..." The smile at her memory lit her face, and then faded. She dropped her eyes. "And then ..." She tailed off.

She didn't need to explain further.

I said, "We won't hurt him."

She said, when she could find the words, "I wouldn't be too sure of that."

Qrysta said, "Why, Jenny?"

"He'll fight. Him, and his boys. Trusted, they're called, and proud of it. Sworn to protect him with their lives, they are: Bartle. Hand-picked. My Jack chooses them himself, the best of the best, trains them up. He has more than just his name in common with his dad,

472

though he doesn't know it. It's not just sworn, they are," she added. "It's *fastened*. By Malamyr." We could hear the drop in her voice as she said the name. *Dread,* I thought. "The one he brought back, from the distant land. What he's done, that one," she said, and shuddered. "He's *changed* them. Changed them all. Changed Bartle most of all. They say he can't be killed. When he spars with his lads, Malamyr pours his black light into him from his staff, and he grows, to twice his size, and becomes …" She shook her head and closed her eyes. After a deep breath, she continued "…something horrible. And then he's sparring with his lads, six or eight at once, and taking cut after cut, and blow after blow. And he just stops, and stares at them, and his wounds heal themselves."

I could feel the others turning to me in the darkness.

They didn't like what they were hearing. I didn't blame them. I was about to ask Jenny a question when she spoke again.

"And sometimes, if he's displeased, and thinks one of them didn't fight hard enough, he'll strike," she said. "Out of nowhere, so fast you don't see the blow, and the lad's dead. And the next day, another one's taken his place, like it or no. They don't have a choice, once they've been chosen. And Malamyr works on them, bends them to his will. They're no more than slaves. They don't think for themselves anymore. I don't think they can."

She stopped, and I asked my question.

"What's he afraid of, Jenny?"

Jenny Blunt lowered her voice, and answered, "Of what I've told him. Over the years, night after night, when he sleeps. *My Jack will come for you. He will kill you. You will never have peace.* Over and over, I whisper it, again and again, those fifteen words, in his ear, in the dark, twenty years and more. And he tosses, and turns, and groans. He hears, of that I'm sure. He hears, and he fears. And that has been my consolation, all these years, knowing that he suffers too. That, and my son."

I said, "What else can you tell us, about where we're going and what we'll be facing?"

"There's a door, set into the rock wall. There's no other way in, bar by water, up the inlet. The guard will open a grille, when we knock, and he'll see it's me. I'll get close, I'll pretend to be feeling faint, and will drop my head against the grille, so he won't see there's no escort, and he will hurry to help me inside."

"There's no need for that," I said. I indicated Qrysta and Grell, under their Glamours. "I told you," I said, "your husband trained us."

"Best of the best, eh?" The "guard" who was really Grell winked down at her.

I could see her shoulders relax a little.

She said, "Once inside, there's a tunnel, down past the guard rooms, that leads to the beach. The ship's moored at the dock on it. A big, open beach it is, and the barracks all surround it, up against the cavern wall. So's the Trusted can muster as soon as called."

Grell said, "How many? Of these Trusted?"

"Thirty."

Gods, I thought. Four of us against thirty brainwashed, elite fighters? No, not four, I reminded myself, don't forget Jess and Little Guy.

"Doesn't sound like we can go around, to board the ship," I said. "We're going to have to go through. Or," I turned to Jenny Blunt, "back."

She knew what I was suggesting.

"Not without my son," she said.

"No," I agreed.

I didn't see how this could be anything but a mob fight. Kill the boss, kill his sorc/healer, then maybe whoever was left of his thirty guards would surrender. They wouldn't until then—they'd be too scared of their boss. Also, we were to take her son alive. Which would probably not be easy. If he had anything of Commandant Bastard in him, he wouldn't go down without a fight.

I said, "ITA, FTB."

Qrysta and Grell grunted their agreement.

Ignore the adds, focus the boss.

"But not until we have to," I added. "First, we'll try to take out the barrack dorms, one by one. Probably won't get too many of them. When they come off the ship, usual formation: Grell on point as tank, goad this Bartle, keep him from hitting the others. Beat the crap out of him, or anyone else who comes at you. Qrysta and Ols: Pick your targets when they present themselves, cut down the numbers. Jess, shoot at anything you don't like the look of. Little Guy, speed and teeth. I'll spam Heals on all of us and will also try to take out this Malamyr. We don't know what they've got, any more than they know what's coming to get them. Bottom line, kill them all except young Jack. What does your son look like, Mrs. Blunt?"

474

"His father."

"Equipment?"

"Sword, shield, and captain's markings."

"What are they?"

"Red blazons on his armor, red plume on his helm."

I glanced at the others. "Take him down, as soon as you can, but not *out*. Jess, shoot at his men, kill any of them you can, but not him. We want him alive."

Jess nodded.

I turned to Oller, and said, "Got string?"

"O' course."

"Truss him and get him out of harm's way when he's down. Okay," I said, "let's do this. Before we do, though," I fished a flask of Elun's Longstreak out of my pack, and uncorked it, "take a mouthful of this each."

Oller said, "What is it?"

I said, "You think Little Guy is fast? Wait till you see what this stuff does to you. And it'll keep you going forever."

"Ooh," he said. "I like the sound o' that!"

They drank. As we all buffed up with our other potions, I remembered the ring of evasion that Avildor had identified for me, and gave it to Qrysta, who slipped it onto her finger when I told her what it was. Then we walked to the small, iron door in the rock wall ahead of us.

Jenny knocked on it, between "her returning escort," *a.k.a* Qrysta and Grell under their Glamours.

We heard the grille opening and the short conversation. The bolts slid back. The door swung inwards.

Jenny walked over the threshold, and the guard dropped, gasping, Qrysta's blade through his neck. I cast Muffle, to mask the sound of his body hitting the floor, and then put glowing green Shields over all of us as we slipped inside the tunnel. Grell closed the iron door behind us and rammed the big steel bars home. There would be no reinforcements coming from outside. Which was some relief. We were going to have enough numbers inside the holdfast to deal with, from what Jenny had told us.

Thirty Trusted.

A sorc, of unknown power, with unknown skills.

And our quarry, with his crew.

There were four guards in the duty rooms, who died before they knew what had hit them. They were not Trusteds, Jenny said when I enquired, just duty guards. So. There were still thirty of Bartle's finest ahead of us.

"Let's get to work," I said, and Grell led off. With Longstreak working its magic inside him, he was out of the tunnel and onto the shore in a couple of seconds. Oller, Little Guy, and Qrysta slipped in and took up their stations to left and right, while I held back, in the shadows. Jess and Jenny joined us.

"Stay right behind me," I told Jenny. "If you get hurt, tap me on the shoulder and I'll heal you. Jess, are you ready?"

"Ready," Jess said, an arrow drawn.

I turned back to Jenny Blunt and whispered, "You might want to put your fingers in your ears. It's going to get loud."

Frowning, because she didn't quite understand, Jenny did.

"Jess," I said, "take down anyone who comes for her, okay? They probably won't, because they are going to be occupied with everything we'll be throwing at them. But we are going to keep Jenny safe."

Jess nodded. "Will do."

I boosted the Shields on my crew to the max.

Party time. I felt Shift's excitement as she quivered in my hand. She was straining like a hound, eager to be unleashed.

"Right," I said. *"Shit, fan.* Go! Cell by cell." We sprinted along the cavern wall to clear the barrack dorms.

It wasn't, as we knew it wouldn't be, a clear run. We got the first dorm room cleared quickly, but not quietly, and the alarm sounded before we'd finished. As we made it back outside, Trusted were pouring out of the other dorms, armed, armored and angry. *Twenty-odd to go,* I thought, as I filled the beach with Traps and Grips, and threw a Thunderstorm overhead, and then sent Barkers and Ghouls over the Trusted, to harass and Fear them.

Shift was singing her joy of battle up my arm, reveling in the symphony of destruction that we were unleashing. And she was also switching seamlessly, as was her nature, to her *con*-struction: Her Heals, which kept our crew alive and rocking.

The Trusted attacked, and fought, and died. I rooted them to the ground with Earthcoils and Ice Traps, and blew Flameballs and Iceshards into them. We were about halfway through them, I thought, when their reinforcements arrived—and there were, I saw to my dismay, a *lot* of them. From *The Rose Revived*, moored at the wharf, a light bloomed. Her crew poured out. A dark figure, in a dark robe, with a dark staff floated after them.

Floated.

Across the air, above the walkway, over the water, his staff in his hand and a dark red glow around his head. I didn't like the look of him one bit. And then, Bartle walked out. Malamyr raised his staff, and indeed, just as Jenny Blunt had said, a jagged stream of black light arced from it into Bartle, who grew as he advanced, looming above his crew.

Grew, and changed.

Twice as tall as Grell, he was, as he strode ashore, a black shadow surrounding him, a gigantic cutlass in each hand. He came towards us, and I felt my heart fail. A dozen Trusted were still opposing us. Another hundred crew were streaming towards us—and, yes, they were a skeleton crew indeed: Skeletons, in boots and belts and leathers, armed with cutlass and pike and bow and dagger. Towering over them was that huge, shadowed brute striding towards us, his hovering sorc Malamyr throwing everything he knew our way.

Time to unleash.

Okay, I thought. *What have you got, pal?*

I poured fire and ice and lightning at the mage from the end of the world, and saw him turn his head towards me, and raise his stave.

A moment later, I was flat on my back, fifty feet behind where I'd been standing, gasping.

What in all hells had hit me?!

I rolled to my feet, and instinctively dodged to one side as a blast erupted at the spot I'd just landed on. Also instinctively, Shift was replying in kind, refreshing our Shields with strong new ones, and firing one of our specials at Malamyr with all the fury I knew she was feeling.

She flung a Meteor. *Good choice, my friend,* I thought, as it slammed down out of the sky onto him and blew him off his feet, ten feet into the air and thirty back into the water. *Back at you, chum,* I thought, and turned my attention to the mayhem ahead of us.

Time seemed to slow as I took it all in. The brown streak of nuisance that was Little Guy was everywhere at once, startling his targets up out of their defensive crouches and distracting them, while Oller's knives and Jess's arrows picked them off, one by one by one. Qrysta was dancing, but, thanks to Longstreak, to some superspeed tune. It was hard to keep track of her, and impossible to see her bladework. Not that I needed to, because I was busy enough, but one by one our foes dropped, not knowing what had hit them.

"There," I heard Jenny shout, behind me, above the chaos of the battle. I didn't have time to look, as I Feared the mob that was crowding in on Grell to overwhelm him, in the microsecond that I could take out from spamming Heals at my team and keeping our Shields up. Pirates and Trusted broke and ran, in all directions, scared. Bartle kept raining blows on Grell—or rather, on where Grell *had* been before zipping away, untouched, and thumping his maul into Bartle's legs, or feet, or hips. I could hear Grell roaring his challenges, and then a sweep of Kinell would send three or four bodies flying into the air, some crumpled, some in pieces.

Then I saw where Jenny was pointing and cast Inert at her son. He froze, solid as a statue, and I popped a Shield around him, so that he wouldn't take any friendly fire.

Shift's tourmaline eye was dimming, I saw, so I downed another of Elun's Arcanaboost potions. Instantly, Shift's heartstone blazed up again, brighter than ever; and, with a joyous burst of new energy, she hit the mobs with half a dozen Area of Effect attacks at once, so that the shore became a field of Earthcoils, rained in on by Sheet Lightning, and Iceshards, and filled with Landmines. They were rooted, sizzled, and blown to pieces.

They had no leader. They could see young Jack, immobile, and Shielded. He was a captive, they realized. They lost discipline. They were hesitating, we could see. Oller and Qrysta and Jess finished them off, while Grell swatted at Bartle, and taunted him, to hold his attention, and tried to avoid his blows. He couldn't. Every now and then, Grell was caught and knocked like a bowling pin across the sand. I did what I could to help the others, but I had problems enough of my own. Malamyr was focusing everything he had on me.

And everything he had was more than I had.

He wasn't going to underestimate me again, that was clear.

He had surrounded himself in a Shield of his own, a thick, dark sphere that nothing I threw at could penetrate. And he had some kind of Light weapon that I'd never encountered before. It was an offensive version of the buff that he'd cast at Bartle. He would raise his staff, and black lightning would slash out of it, forking around his forces without touching them but hitting all of us at the same time—*hard*. Each attack that jolted into us was more intense than the last. The pain was brutal. The shock of it drained me, sapping, disorienting, disheartening.

What was this?! I could barely keep up my Heals to repair us. The tide had turned against us, I realized. There were still dozens of his forces out there, struggling in their traps for the time being, but those traps wouldn't hold much longer. Once they were free, and on the attack again, I didn't like our chances. Bartle seemed to be unharmed, despite the punishment Grell had been giving him. Oller and Qrysta were, as per our plan, ignoring the rooted adds and focusing the boss, but nothing they did to Bartle damaged him. And the black lightning strikes knocked them off their feet, and staggered them, while Malamyr calmly boosted his damages on me.

Shit, I thought—and could hardly hear myself think over the cacophony that was enveloping us—*this bastard is good*.

And then, a moment later, as I picked myself up once more, fifty feet from where I'd just been standing, my Shield blown apart, I thought, *Too damn good*. I quickly cast another Shield on myself, just in time for it to repel another of his black lightning attacks. But it was a weak Shield, because Shift was drained.

It was impossible to think calmly in the firestorm that we were all unleashing on each other. I barely had time to spam Heals on my team and refresh my traps and Area of Effect attacks. But one thought loomed large in the spaces between my actions.

I'm in trouble here.

Nothing that I threw at Malamyr seemed to work. He was my focus, not Bartle, because I knew that, to bring Bartle down, I had to destroy his dark protector. And I couldn't think how: Malamyr's Shields were impenetrable. They were much stronger than mine, clearly, because his attacks blew chunks out of the green bubbles that Shift had cast around my crew. Jess's arrows did nothing to him. She'd caught my eye and understood, and shot a couple at him, but they bounced off the black sphere that enveloped him. It was the same with Oller's knives. Qrysta was busy distracting and attacking Bartle. She knew better than to waste time on Shields that I couldn't bring down. Her job was to help our tank, Grell, who was being battered.

Our damages were doing no damage. We had whittled down their advantage of numbers, but Bartle and Malamyr still had the advantage of power. Whatever we did to them seemed to make no difference. Whatever they did to us hurt like all hells.

Shift and I were getting drained again, quicker and quicker. I chugged Elun's Arcanaboost potions, but each one restored less, and I was now out of them. If I were out of power, we were finished. If we had no Heals, Kinfolk armor or no, Grell would die. Then Bartle would be free to take out Qrysta and Oller. And me, and Jess, and Little Guy.

Well, maybe Little Guy knew that. Who knows, with dogs? Some instinct made him break away from the brawl raging around Bartle and streak over to Malamyr. The sorc from the end of the world was hovering over the beach, glowing black and red and powerful beyond Bartle in the glare of the battle, and calmly searing his black bolts into us. His staff was raised to unleash another volley of anguish at us when something small and brown attached itself to his foot and savaged it. Malamyr looked down, missing his attack, and Little Guy was already a hundred yards away, bothering skeleton pirate after Trusted, and weaving among them at such speed that Malamyr could not get a lock on him. His staff was raised, pointing at Little Guy as he flew all over the place, but he was never sure enough of his aim to unleash his black lighting attack, in case he killed his own troops—

It hit me.

Black Lightning?

There's no such thing!

Light isn't black. It can never be. Black is the absence of light. Its opposite.

Little Guy kept running, in and out of everyone's legs. Malamyr was intent on him, wanting to punish him for daring to jump in through his black sphere and bite him.

Yes, I thought.

Thank you, Little Guy. I couldn't get anything through that Shield, but you just showed me the way.

The realizations kept coming as I poured every ounce of my power into the fray, healing and hitting as hard as I could.

Black light?

Riiiight.

I gave our Shields one last boost, hoping they'd hold up for a few seconds, for long enough for me to do what I needed to do.

I closed my eyes, and turned inward, and remembered the lessons that Avildor had given me.

Now or never, I thought.

I cast Lightseek at Malamyr.

I could hear the battle that was raging in front of me, as I waited, my eyes closed, but it all seemed far away. Everything that I had was going into one of my weakest, newest skills.

Nothing happened.

I "saw" nothing.

But I knew that, if I opened my eyes, my chance would be gone. Our Shields would be down. I would be out of power, and we'd be lost.

I went down, and down, further, into the heart of what I had learned in the Tower of Light, and the sounds of the combat around me faded to nothing.

Nothing was revealed.

I had to be right. Or we were finished.

And then I saw it.

A tiny glow, ahead of me.

I let myself open up to it, and let it grow. Until I could see it clearly.

Hanging there, exactly where Malamyr would be: A black ball of light, turning, radiating—but *inwards.* Bringing everything into it, inexorably. Not a small, yellow sun, as I'd seen in the Tower of Light; nor a harsh red one, which had been Varamaxes, but a black one. Black light. Hanging there, against the fire and fury of the struggle in the cavern, drinking everything in.

The opposite.

I'd think about that later, I knew, as I heard the word in my head. So many opposites in this journey. But for now, there was a job to be done.

I had my answer.

Nothing escapes a black hole, not even light.

I raised my head, and opened my eyes, and hefted Shift, and blasted Malamyr with as much Negation as I had. *The opposite.* The opposite of his dark well of gravity, from which nothing could escape. Knowing that nothing could escape, I hit him with as much Nothing as I'd got.

*Nothing gets through your Shields, right? Okay, buster: Have a bellyful of
Nothing. Eat it. Eat it all. Have a taste of your own dark medicine.*

His black shield blew apart. He staggered, wondering what had hit
him. He'd never find the answer. *Nothing* had hit him.

I Turned into *were*-form and charged. Little Guy was on him a
moment before I was, biting chunks out of his feet, and then I body-
slammed him, all eight-foot-tall teeth and claws and fury of me,
knocking him flat on his back on the sand, rending, tearing, savaging.
Malamyr screamed, and flailed, and curled up, and wriggled, and died.

There you go, pal, I thought, as I tore out his throat with my teeth.
Two negatives making a very satisfactory positive. I spat it out and looked
down at the shriveled corpse below me, and saw the pallor, and the dry,
ancient skin, and the long, yellow teeth below his upper lip.

Vamp.

I threw my bloodstained head back and howled. Bartle turned at
the sound and saw me. He hesitated. Oller slipped in behind him and
stabbed about eight knives into him in a second. That got his attention. Bartle jerked upright. I charged, Little Guy racing ahead of me.
Qrysta drove in, blades whirling. Jess poured arrows into him from her
self-refilling quiver, and Little Guy jumped six feet into the air and
sank his teeth into Bartle's wrist. He hung there, growling and shaking furiously, while the others danced, and slipped, and bellowed, and
I flailed my claws and chewed nine kinds of hell out of the man who
had stolen my friend's wife. It didn't take long. Without Malamyr's
protection, Bartle was defenseless. He shrank, and shuddered, wondering, and swayed, and fell on his back.

I re-Turned, and healed us all with what little energy Shift had left,
We all stood and heaved for breath. Grell strode up to Bartle, kicking
his giant cutlasses aside.

Grell sneered down at the pathetic excuse for a pirate and raised
Kinell for the killing blow.

"Goodbye, arsehole," he said.

I said, "No, Grell, stop."

He held back, his brutal maul above his head.

We waited, in the sudden silence.

Jenny Blunt walked over to the man who had stolen her.

He lay there, rooted by my Earthcoil, looking up at her blankly.

"I told you," she said, and then lowered her voice to the whisper she'd filled his ear with, night after night after night. "*My Jack will come for you. He will kill you. You will never have peace.*"

Bartle looked at us, from face to face, wondering which of us was Jack Blunt.

"He sent us," Grell said, "and said to say hello."

Bartle stared, knowing that he was about to die.

Grell, even though he was itching to thump Kinell into Bartle's skull, said to Jenny Blunt, "After you,"

Jenny Blunt looked at Qrysta, inquiringly, who handed her one of her blades.

Jenny took it and set it on her abuser's throat.

They held each other's eyes. Jenny Blunt lifted her chin. "You had no right," she said.

She waited for a response.

Bartle had none. He spluttered, and gasped. We knew that he knew. She was right, and he was wrong.

And justice would be done.

Jenny Blunt slid Qrysta's niblun blade, slowly, into his throat, holding his eyes as she did.

"My Jack will come for you," she said. "He will kill you. You will never have peace."

39

The Rose Revived

We gathered around Jenny Bartle and her son.

This is between them, I thought. *Not much that we can contribute, except support.*

He was immobile, staring vacantly, sword raised for an attack that he'd never managed to complete.

"Can he hear?" she asked me, searching his eyes.

"Yes."

Her son was, indeed, the spitting image of Commandant Bastard, only younger, and leaner, and somewhat more handsome.

"These people," she told him, quietly, "were sent by your father, to bring you and me home."

He couldn't move, but he could take that in.

Jenny Blunt, turning to the corpse on the beach behind us, and then back to her son, said, "No, not him. Your *true* father."

"And a better one than that fuckwit," Grell said, glowering. "A better man than any of us. Better than any I've ever met. You have a problem with that, you take it up with him, face-to-face. And good luck to you." He flexed his muscles, leaning in. "Meanwhile, you behave, all right? Or you'll have me to deal with. You got that?"

We let that sink in.

I thought, simultaneously, *dangerous warrior,* and *poor bastard.*

Jenny turned to us and thanked us all, in turn.

We told her that there was nothing we wouldn't do for her, and her husband. Then we walked off and left the two of them to it. When we were a suitable distance away, I cleansed the Inert off her son, and saw him reanimate, and totter, and sink to his knees, head bowed, chest heaving as he gasped for breath. His mother knelt beside him, her hand on his shoulder. *Up to them, now,* I thought.

Right. Let's take a look at our new ship.

The Rose Revived was twice the size of *The Red Rose,* and ten times as unpleasant. She looked sound, as we walked up the gangplank at her midships. All was in good order, her lines neatly stowed, her decks holystoned and scrubbed.

It was a different tale below. It was not nice down there. Aft, the captain's quarters were pleasant enough: A large bed below the wide stern window, chests, chairs, a table. Oller immediately began hunting through Bartle's possessions. *Pirate captain, got to have some loot worth looking through, eh?*

It was not the sort of place I'd like to be imprisoned, I thought, *with one such as Bartle.*

The further for'ard we went, the nastier it got. The poor, naked, chained creature we found in Malamyr's cabin was beyond my help. His neck was crisscrossed with bite marks. He was as thin as a reed and as pale as ice. I sat on the floor beside him and gave him a mouthful of Elun's Sleepease. He stopped shivering and looked up at me as I cradled him in my arms. The others had hurried out of the room, aghast at the sight of him.

"You're safe now," I said. His throat moved as he swallowed. "He's dead," I said. His vacant eyes searched mine, uncertain. "There will be no more pain," I told him. I felt him soften in my arms. I held him, and waited, while his breathing slowed. "Another mouthful?" I offered, holding the flask to his lips. Our eyes met again, and I could see that he knew what I meant, for I sensed his relief as he nodded.

He drank deep, and inhaled, and closed his eyes.

Elun's magic did its work. The ruined man sighed, long and low, and died.

I lowered him to the floor, and covered his drained body with a shroud from Malamyr's nest. I just wanted to get out of there, but the sight of a vampire's nest on a sailor's bunk gave me pause. *Not so fast*, I thought. I looked around the small cabin. A desk, chests, scrolls, jars, flasks, powders, phials, tubes, books …

I'd never seen Grell scared before, but when I told him what I needed him to do, his eyes grew wide with fear. He understood, and nodded, and turned to young Jack Blunt, and said, "Right, make yourself useful, son, come with me." Jack followed him into Malamyr's cabin, and they packed up everything they could find, which I intended to study later, with Marnie and the Conclave of the GAA.

I left them to it. I had realized that there was something else I should do before we left. I went ashore, to Malamyr's corpse, and picked up his staff. I needed to learn all about it, as I had learned about Ochre, and Black, and Blacker. I thought that there would be lore in it that I could use, if I could get at it. It was a dull, dark brown thing, curiously shaped. It wasn't twisted, exactly, but it seemed fluid, as if it was, somehow, moving. Which it wasn't; I could see that. It was immobile in my hand. I wondered what sort of wood it was. Knowing little about wood, I didn't attempt to put a name to it—I was just looking at it, warily, not liking anything about it, when I felt the hairs on the back on my neck rise.

It wasn't wood. It was a long, brown snake. I threw it away from me. It didn't move. It was a staff. But a staff that had once been a living creature, and had been trapped in sinuous motion, its life bent to Malamyr's purpose. I stared at it, down on the sand before me. The snake's mouth held a huge, dark red heartstone. Everything about this staff and stone scared me. I imagined slinging it on my back, and it coming alive and sinking its fangs into my shoulder …

I acted without thinking. Even the possibility of that nightmare was not to be contemplated—and I could tell from the shocks jumping up my arm that Shift felt the same. I backed away and she blasted fire attacks at it—probably far more than were needed. When the smoke cleared, there was nothing left of it but ashes and the blood-red heartstone.

Glaring up at me from the sand.

I didn't want to but made myself pick it up and stow it in my pack. The GAA should know about it, I knew—and Marnie, and Coven. The sooner I gave the damned thing to them, the better.

We all met on the quarterdeck of *The Rose Revived* when we'd done what we needed.

It was a simple question: Power, or practicality?

A big brute of a ship like this, which would be a terror in a sea battle: Or something we could actually use?

What was it Gelbert had said? We'd need sixty crew for *The Red Rose*. Well, we knew nothing about sailing, but we all thought that meant we'd need at least twice that number to crew a ship the size of this.

Besides, the damn thing stank of evil.

No. We didn't want any part of it.

After much confusion, and arguing about ropes and pulleys, we managed to lower a tender over the side, the right way up. Well, *we* didn't: Young Jack Blunt did. Humiliated as he was, and grim with anger, and clearly loathing the lot of us, he had enough sense to see what needed to be done. He took charge, and the tender was in the water in no time. He and Grell took the oars, and we pulled away from the benighted flagship of Bartle's Rose fleet.

When we were a hundred yards off I made them stop rowing. I stood up. I raised Shift, and she blew Flameballs into *The Rose Revived*, until she was an inferno, its flames throwing mad shadows up onto the rock ceiling of the cavern. We watched her burn, and slowly sink, as we pulled away, around the inlet and into the hidden harbor.

We kept our eyes on the cliffsides as we rowed. We knew that the nest holes in them would be full of guards, which would mean archers, so we were ready for trouble. But the guards had melted into the night. Word had spread. The center of gravity that had been holding them all in its orbit, whether they wanted it or not, had been removed. Without fear of retribution from above, all were free to think for themselves. And when that happens, the number one priority is, well, Number One.

We relaxed as we passed empty guardhouse after deserted checkpoint. We knew what they were thinking: *Run. Duck and cover. Plunder. Hoard.* As we came to the harbor town we saw movement on its wharves. Furtive, shadowy figures, hurrying about in ones and twos and small groups. Looting, no doubt. We pulled across to *The Red Rose* and whistled. The rope ladder dropped. We climbed aboard. Under the lanterns that our men were holding up around us, casting dim light on their strained, taut faces, I told them what had happened, and what we were going to do, and that we should get going *now*.

I saw their anxiety turn to relief and their stares to smiles. Orders were given. Men hurried to their stations with a will and we weighed anchor. Two longboats were lowered, filled with men eager to pull us out of the Cove and into the wind. They were back aboard within the hour, laughing and excited. Once out of the sheltered bay, a sharp easterly breeze caught our sails, and we ran before it.

Our first task was to put as many sea leagues as we could between us and the Cove. We hoped that the Rose fleet was now scattered and had other priorities, but we were well aware that we would stand no chance if they all came after us. *Sail,* we thought, as far and fast as we could.

Our second task was to ensure that we *could* do that.

The Red Rose, Gelbert told us, was low on everything. She had been riding at anchor in Freehaven while waiting to revictual. The port chandler was expecting to fill her hold with everything she needed. Instead, she'd slipped anchor and left. We had to take the risk of calling in there. We'd never survive the voyage to Eastbay without supplies.

It wouldn't take long, Gelbert said. The orders had been put in before we'd hijacked *The Red Rose.* All had been paid for and would still be in the godowns. He went ashore with Jess, the local girl, and Oller, who would learn what he could. Two days later the chandler's barge was alongside by midmorning, unloading our supplies.

We took on more than just supplies.

Jess had brought Evall with her.

She knew we wouldn't mind, when she'd explained what had happened; and, when we heard his story, we didn't. His father had been robbed and killed. Evall had been stuck in Freehaven, running out of money, with no friends and no way home. He had jumped at the chance of coming with us. Eastbay ships often came to Sondehafn, the main port in Normark, where he and his father worked for its most prominent merchant. He thought he'd stand a good chance of finding passage home from there.

A steady southeaster filled *The Red Rose*'s sails and stood us fair for our destination: North and west, back beyond the Morning Isles, and then into the Northern Ocean for home.

With two stops on the way.

After a week of hard sailing, broken by sudden calms, the crew were all ours. They knew where their best interests lay. No Bartle meant no reason to worry about him. We'd destroyed him and the dark magician who had held them all in his thrall. So, perhaps it would not be a good idea to mess with us?

The officers were harder to persuade, because they had more to lose. Status and face. I visited them in the brig, where they glared at me. "Look," I said, "you're not who you think you are anymore. Imagine you are a king who was captured, and dragged behind a chariot in a triumphal march, and is now a slave. That's you. Your situation has altered."

Most of them didn't get it. I could see them all trying to come up with a way out, how to turn the tables on us.

Not going to happen.

Well, that was their problem. Ours? Yes, there's always a problem. You solve one, and then there's another waiting for you. Life's like that. Relentless, implacable, always challenging—and would you rather be experiencing the alternative? Boredom? Not me. I'll take what comes. Terror. Delight. Confusion. Pain. Laughter. Despair. Betrayal. Bereavement. Ecstasy. Whatever the world throws our way.

I think I'd never felt more alive than I did aboard *The Red Rose* as we beat westward through the wild seas off the north coast of Mourvania. Great gods, it was horrible out there. I felt small, and weak, and cold, and inept, and sick, and immensely grateful. To be there, in that battle of the elements, storm raging above, mountainous swells below, clinging onto the rails, sharp rain stinging my face, and the deck heaving beneath my feet, and my stomach dropping and lurching—*aah*, I thought. *Live, or die!*

It was painful, and frightening, and I did not belong out there on that damn cockleshell—but, I thought: I'll take *live.*

Which is what we did; although, with the wild winds, and high seas, it often felt as if we were about to founder. But our crew was good, and our navigator and helmsman, Dirk and Ernsten, knew their business. We stood well out to sea once we were off the north coast. We didn't want any of His Majesty of Mourvania's fleet taking an interest in us and giving chase. Not that our crew seemed too worried by them. *Not enough ships, not enough men, in the Royal Navy,* was the impression I got.

One clear, gray, relatively calm morning, I called all hands on deck. Minus the officers, and those we didn't trust, there were fifty-four of them. They mustered, wondering what was coming. Some kind of speech, they probably expected. A bunch of orders from us inept, but dangerous, landlubbers. I didn't say a word. I nodded down from the quarterdeck at Oller, and Grell, and Qrysta, who stood on the main deck below me, yards apart.

"Form three lines!" Grell barked. "One in front of each of us."

They hurried to comply. Nobody wanted to disobey the big Orc. They'd all heard of how he'd fought in the Battle of the Holdfast.

"Step forward, one at a time!"

The man at the head of each line hesitated.

Each was wondering *what was going to happen …*

"Quick now!" Grell ordered, "or you don't get your pay!"

Pay?

They hadn't expected that.

The first three stepped up, tentatively, to Grell, Qrysta, and Oller, who gave them each a gold piece.

"Don't spend it all at once," Grell ordered. "Now bugger off about your duty!"

"Aye aye, sir!" the man said, and hurried off past him, biting his gold coin to make sure it was real. It was. We knew that. And we knew that we had a lot more of them waiting for us on Wester Isle. The crew was all ours after that. *Gold. Pirates. More where that came from.*

Our first stop came two days later. On the afternoon of the ninth day out of the Cove we saw the light, sweeping slowly across the seas from the headland. We were within the reach of its beam by nightfall. That dependable light was a familiar sight to these sailors. What was an unfamiliar sight to them was a black dot in the sky, heading our way, growing quickly larger until it landed, sending them running.

Elun looked around at the crew as she dismounted from her broomstick, and waited. They touched their foreheads in reply and ducked their heads. Elun nodded at them, and then climbed the stairway to the quarterdeck, and joined us.

"Avildor found your light two days ago," she told me. "He's been tracking you since. He knew you'd pass this way."

"We were going to stop by," I said.

"Were you now?" she wondered.

"Yes," I said. "I have something for him."

"And what would that be?" she asked.

"Something he's been looking for," I told her. "For a long time."

Her eyebrows rose.

From a pocket inside my jerkin, I brought out one of the gems from the casket that Oldface had brought us, and given us in the oasis in the sky, as a "token of his integrity."

I opened my hand, and she stared at the large, ghost-pale stone.

"Pretty," she said.

"Watch."

I raised Shift, and cast Divination on it, and it began to glow, radiating a pale silver that illuminated all our faces.

"Well," she said, as it slowly faded, "that's unusual. Not that I know what it is—sticks and stones not being my craft."

"A moonstone heart for his black willow," I said. Oller had identified what it was. Knowing about gemstones was an important skill in his line of work.

Her eyes looked up from the gleaming gem to mine.

She smiled. "He'll like that," she said.

"I don't have anything for you," I said, "but I do have a task. And a request."

Elun said, "Oh, ah?"

"We'd have died without your help, Elun," I told her. "Your potions made all the difference. My request is to ask you to teach me how to make them."

Elun stared up at me, studying me.

"And the task?" she asked.

I turned, and said, "Jenny?"

Jenny Blunt stepped forward and joined us.

"Elun, this is my friend, Jenny Blunt. I believe you will be able to help her."

Elun held Jenny's eyes for a few moments. She grunted. "You poor girl," she said. "Come with me."

She took Jenny Blunt's hand and led her down the companionway, and then belowdecks.

"We'll ride at anchor here," I told Ernsten. "Anywhere you like. We may be a while."

Elun left late the next morning. "She's sleeping," she said, as she joined us on deck. "She'll sleep for days. I've done what I can to show her the way. Erase, calm, focus forward, regather." I understood what she meant. I had no idea if any of the others who were grouped around us did. This was shop talk. Elun and I knew the language. GAA talk,

491

Coven talk, healer talk. She was telling me how to treat Jenny Blunt. "Let him see her as she is now, which is as she was then, when he lost her," she advised. "You'll know what to do after that."

I said, "Thank you, Elun. And please thank your husband too. I'm very grateful, to him, and to you. We all are."

She said, to my surprise, "It's us as should be thanking you, young lad."

"Me?"

"We can put things to rights in this realm now. Move on. We're not caught in the middle of that stupid old war any longer. It'll take time, but time heals. Marnie was right about you."

I couldn't resist it. I smiled at the name, and said, "In what way?"

"She said you'd solve the problem. She couldn't see how, any more than we could, but you did."

My heart warmed. "I wouldn't be anywhere if it weren't for Marnie."

Elun said, putting me in my place, "She told us that too."

That sounded like her all right. Marnie, my ferocious old mentor, who had restored my arts to me.

I wondered. "Can you send her a pigeon?"

"Of course."

"Tell her everything." I waited, and Elun nodded, understanding. "And that we'll be home soon. Eastbay, our navigator says, which is closer than Mayport. A week, maybe two, depending on winds and tides."

Elun nodded.

She reached inside her black robe and brought out a small, black book.

"It's all in here," she said, "what you need to know. It's not hard. The hard part was the discovering. Once you know what works, all you have to do is make another brew. My notes are in there too, about the learning. Page ninety-four," she said, handing it to me. "Nearly the death of me, learning that one was."

I said, "You just happened to have it on you?"

"I popped back for it in the night, once Jenny was settled into a healing sleep."

"Thank you," I said, taking the book.

She grunted, then raised her voice.

"Good people can do bad things," she announced, knowing that all were listening. "For the wrong reasons, which seem right to them. You have enemies aboard, but you know that. Some won't change, some will.

492

That's up to them, and up to you. Things are going to change here, in this realm, and we'll be working to make sure they change for the better."

She turned towards us. "We wouldn't have had this chance to do so if you hadn't done what you've done. For which we thank you. I can't give you anything equal to what you've given us, but I can give you this."

She held up her hands, palms towards us, and moved them in two slow, opposite circles.

We all felt it.

Something had happened. Something was different. What it was, we had no idea, we just felt … better. *Way* better. Stronger, brighter; more awake and aware and capable.

Elun mounted her broomstick and looked us over again.

"Mm," she said, satisfied. She rose into the sky and flew towards the distant Tower of Light.

We watched her dwindle into a tiny speck in the sky.

Grell broke the silence. "Whoof!" he said. "I feel …"

He shook his huge head, which was wreathed in a daffy smile. Oller was chuckling beside him. Jess was grinning, wide-eyed, and Little Guy was wagging his bogbrush tail.

"Me too, Grello!" Qrysta said, laughing aloud.

"…*fabulous,*" Grell chortled.

"The very word, mate," Qrysta agreed. "*Fabulous.*"

"Yes," I said, looking from her to Grell, "to a—whole new level, wouldn't you say?"

There was a fine, following wind filling our sails. We ran before it. We believed we would reach Wester Isle in a day or two. As we indeed did, without mishap, but with one curious occurrence along the way.

We'd become accustomed to seabirds following us. Some landed on our spars, even on our decks, from time to time, where they strutted about, and checked us out, and amused the crew as they accepted scraps. Frigate birds, drifting high above; puffins and terns beating alongside; gulls of all shapes and sizes—and, the afternoon of the morning that Elun left us, an albatross. It glided in on wide, unmoving wings, and watched us, for a while, from above our mainmast. Then, it descended, effortless, folded its long wings, and settled on the quarterdeck.

We all knew that something unusual was happening.

The albatross waddled, awkwardly but calmly, over to Grell.

It looked up at him and raised its right leg.

There were five gold rings on it.

Grell nodded and smiled.

He crouched down and gently removed the rings, sliding them over the bird's webbed foot while he stroked its head with his other hand.

"Thank you," he said. "And all my friends of the Woodlake."

The albatross shuffled away, turned into the wind, and opened its wings. It stood there, looking as ungainly as anything does that is not in its element. It trotted forward, awkwardly, then the wind took it, and lifted it, and it was back where it belonged, soaring above us, motionless, before veering away towards the open sea.

"I do believe," Grell said, "that I know what these are."

Qrysta said "What?"

He looked the five rings over, and chuckled, seeing the letters engraved within each of them.

O, and K, and J, and D, and G.

"Our Natures," he said, handing them to each of us in turn.

We all put them on.

They shrank, or expanded, to fit our fingers.

We all felt that we had, somehow, doubled.

The gold coins we'd given them, we told our crew, came from our buried treasure. We'd discussed the problem in private, and thought, *pirates, right? They'll get that.* It had been Oller's idea, him knowing a thing or two about scoundrels, and it sent a ripple of excitement through our crew. We saw them conferring in whispers. We knew what was going on. They were all thinking, *How much more would we give them?*

What they didn't see, because we'd dazzled them with the lure of "promised gold," was that gold wasn't the point. The point was, how to make these men of uncertain trustworthiness wait at anchor, aboard our ship, while we went to fetch the loot we'd taken from the helldragon's hoard? How to stop them sailing off, and fetching the entire army of the Devoted from the mainland, and taking the no-doubt-considerable reward while we were trooped off in chains? We couldn't have them thinking about any of that. We just needed them to sit tight and wait, for a few hours. So, while being sure not to say anything, but being unable to help ourselves giving the occasional secret smile, and wink, we kept them on tenterhooks.

One of them had apprenticed as a jeweler before running away to sea. I asked his opinion, casually, of a large sapphire that had been in the chest of heartstones. He'd been speechless at the sight of it. From what I *didn't* say, he inferred that we were going ashore to "get the rest." They'd wait, I hoped. They might wait just in order to try to kill us and steal everything, but they'd wait.

The one thing that we did *not* want was to be marooned on Wester Isle. The one thing that they did not want was for us *not* to come back aboard with the rest of our treasure. which, they anticipated, we would share with them.

Gelbert and a crew rowed us ashore early one misty morning. We'd brought everything with us, not just our arms and armor but also the chest of heartstones, just in case they did maroon us there. We told them to wait and trudged uphill, into the cold clouds that settled around us, soaking us as we headed for the cave that led down to the island under the island.

We reached it that afternoon and were glad of the shelter it gave us from the rain that had been driving into us for hours. It had been a hard climb. Once we were out of the foul weather I popped up some Glows. In the light of them, Oller scanned the floor. He grunted, satisfied. No recent footprints. We headed on down. Through the spider cave; past their corpses; down into the neck of the tunnel that led us into the underground.

We remembered the last time we'd come this way. *Jess sitting back and waiting here, out of sight. Us heading in to report back to Oldface, and rescue Little Guy.* The air was easier now, less oppressive. We passed the point where Oldface's invisible barrier had been, across which we'd bargained our way in, and entered the buried temple. It was still lit with its eerie, ectoplasmic blue light. Motes of white dust drifted in the silence, the only sounds our footsteps on the white marble floor as we passed through the chapel and the antechambers and entered the library.

Ahead of us, on the far wall, reared the familiar mural: Old Birdbeak. Between us and that was the long, pale table at which we'd sat and made our bargain with Oldface. Heaped behind it, where Oldface

had set them, were the piles of our treasure. All exactly as we'd expected and hoped.

With one difference.

Between our loot and us, at the end of the table, a figure was seated,
looking in our direction, waiting.

Yet another elderly clerk, surrounded by his papers and quill
and inkwell.

We stopped.

We all looked at each other.

We shrugged, and hefted our weapons, and walked towards him.

"Do sit down," the old clerk said, in a dry, sawdusty voice, motion-
ing towards the chairs to either side of him.

We sat. He fossicked around in the pile of papers in front of him
and found what he was looking for: A large bundle bound together
with red ribbon. He handed it to me.

"Your manifest. You need to read it carefully."

I opened it. An extravagant, large letter **A**, illuminated in reds and
blues and gold leaf, began the following:

*An accurate accounting of items removed by me this day as wit-
nessed and subscribed thereunto by the appointed Archivist on Duty,
Senior Clerk of the Honorable and Ancient Compagnie of Knowledgers
Esotericists Recorders and Scribes, attested to under oath by myself the
signatory hereunder.*

I read that sentence twice. It didn't take long to spot the acronym.
If the Guild of the Arcane Arts was GAA, and the Thieves Guild was
TG, then ... *HACKERS*?

I was pretty sure who I was dealing with.

I looked up at him, imagining the Amalgam Ken behind that
Glamour as Elderly Ink-Stained Pen-Pusher. He knew that Oller and
Jess would not be able to comprehend him as he really looked—but
Elderly Clerk they would understand.

"Before I can sign you out I need to ask you some questions," he
said, in his reedy old voice.

"Go ahead."

He pointed at the long list of items that we had looted from the
helldragon's hoard. "Why these?" he said.

A simple question, but a hard one to answer. "We only really needed the mirror," I said. "The other things just … interested us."

His eyebrows rose. "Ah." He dipped his quill in his inkwell and scratched some words on his notepad.

"Some are very valuable, obviously," I went on. "The jewel-hilted great sword, for example. The goblets and chalices and gold and gems."

"And others … ?"

"May have hidden qualities?"

He nodded and pointed at my red-tape-bound manifest. "As you will see," he said. "All are detailed there." He looked up at me. "Those were interesting choices that you made, when you picked through her hoard. I must say, many wouldn't have spotted what you did. Whether you know it or not, those items will lead you in new directions. I would tell you what those will be if I knew, but, as you can probably guess, sad to say: I have not been given that information. You're on your own. So. Just—keep going forwards, eh?"

I said, "We can do that."

He studied me. I could almost see his invisible antennae waving. He was enjoying this as much as I was. I could read the unspoken message perfectly. *You've won this round. Well done. Job done—quest cleared. Next.*

His voice as dull as ever, he said, "One more question. For the record."

"Ask away."

"You didn't want to see who won?"

It took me a moment to realize what he was talking about. *God or demon.*

Their war, their problem.

My answer was simple. "No."

"If you had to pick a side?"

I smiled. "I'd pick us."

His eyebrows rose.

"Leave us out of it," I said. "Let us get on with our own lives."

A ghost of a smile almost appeared on his wrinkled old lips.

"Wouldn't that be nice?" he said. He dipped his quill in his inkwell again and started writing in his notebook. "You're free to leave."

I looked at the others. We got to our feet.

Oller, frowning, said, "What was all that about?"

"I'll know when I read this." I tucked Ken's manifest inside my jerkin. "Let's load up and get out of here."

It was more than another week to Eastbay. Every day Qrysta and Jess trained on the main deck, hour after hour, and we all watched. Some of our crew wanted to dance with Qrysta, and she was happy to oblige. Jess sparred with cabin boys, and midshipmen, and then other sailors. They had size, and brawn, and speed, and stamina—but she had technique. Towards the end I noticed her working with the younger lads, showing them what was what, helping them with grip, and stance, and steps.

Teacher, to pupil, to the next pupil, I thought.

That thought stayed with me as I worked on healing Jenny Blunt, following the guidelines that Elun had given me. I was nowhere near as skilled at Curing as Elun was, but I did what I could for Jenny—and though she responded well, I knew that it wasn't going to be instant. How could it possibly be, after all that she'd been through, for twenty and more years? What I could do, though, was shield her from her past. I worked it all as best as I could, from the front of her mind to the back, easing her past into the section marked "bad memories," which we all have, though few of us have them to the extent of hers. I found a strength in her, underneath it all—a small, hard, precious rock. And I saw what it was, and where it came from. Her son. She had kept going, through all the hardships, for him. And, in return, the fact of his presence had kept her going. I knew that she would need help more skilled than mine; but I felt hopeful that she would, in time, recover.

Because I knew that that help would be waiting for us at Eastbay and that Jenny Blunt would be in good hands.

40

The Challenge

"Thank'ee, lass," Jack Blunt said, as Eva refilled his mug with The Wheatsheaf's best ale. "A fine brew, this, one of his best—my compliments to Jan Brewer."

Eva smiled at him.

"Anything you want, Jack Blunt," she said, "you just let me know!"

She winked, and turned away, and swished off to her other customers.

Commandant Blunt, sitting on a wall bench inside the wide hearth of The Wheatsheaf's parlor, supped his ale and turned his attention back to the fire. He inhaled, deep, and shook his head, and lost his thoughts in the flames, and sighed.

He heard the chuckle from the opposite bench, and looked up across the firelight that was dancing above the logs.

Nyrik grinned at him.

"I've told her you're spoken for, Jack Blunt," he said, "but she has a sweet spot for you, our Eva. When I told her you was coming she perked up something lovely. Set her hair up nice and all. You know Eva has a twinkle in her eye for a man when she does that."

Jack Blunt said, "She's a good lass, is Eva. He's a lucky man she settles on."

He returned his gaze to the fire.

After a silence, Horm said, "No luck your end neither, then?"

Blunt shook his head.

Horm grunted. "Asked high and low, me and Nyrik did," he said. "Niblunhaem, and the buried towns, and up across into the moorlands. Giants had nothing, the Orcs said, no more than they had themselves. Nothing from the forests."

"We won't stop, Jack," Nyrik said. "This year, next year, who knows. Someone will hear. And when they do, we'll hear, you can be sure o' that. And we'll find you and tell you."

Silence fell.

The logs crackled between them.

Jack Blunt sighed and took another mouthful of ale. He looked across again at Nyrik and Horm, his dark eyes brooding. "I know you will," he said. "You have my thanks, friends."

They watched the flames and thought their thoughts.

Eventually, Nyrik asked, "Which way this time, then?"

Jack Blunt said, "North, I'm thinking. North, as far as my horse can carry me. And then west. I've heard as there might be a passage, over the ice, into the land where the east begins."

Nyrik blew out his cheeks. "*Woof!* Rather you than me," he said, and took a long pull from his mug of ale.

They all contemplated that hard journey over the ice seas of the frozen north to who knew where.

"What's in the land where the east begins?" Horm asked.

Jack Blunt shrugged. "That's what I'm going there to find out."

"No news from there?" Nyrik asked.

Commandant Blunt shook his head and looked across the dancing flames at them. "No news from anywhere, young Nyrik. It's a fool's errand I'm on, more like than not, I'll admit to that," he admitted. "But any man as wants to call me fool for following it to its end is a bigger fool than I am."

Nyrik chuckled. "You won't find me nor Horm naming you fool, Jack Blunt! We like our heads just where they are, thank'ee very much."

Blunt looked over at them, and a small smile cracked his hard old face. "You're good lads, you two," he said. "For slavers, that is. Saved me a deal o' time, over the years, you two have." He thought about that. "Twenty-four years. A deal o' time indeed. Looking hither and yon."

He tailed off and contemplated the fire. "Well," he said, "it's not as if I have anything better to do."

"Us neither," Horm grunted, "now that this young queen has outlawed our trade. Deprived us of our livelihood, she has! I've half a mind to go down to Mayport, and—"

"And what, mate?" Nyrik interrupted. "Lose the other half of your mind, when she chops your thick head off, for cheeking her? Get used to it! Them days are gone."

"Yur," Horm said, unhappily, and lapsed into silence.

Jack Blunt felt the word echo in his head. The word that had been haunting him for nearly half his life.

Gone.

Not for the first time he felt the worm of doubt at the back of his mind. It did its usual work. *Would he ever see her again?* became *he'd never see her again.* He dismissed the worm, the way he always did. *It doesn't matter. I'm not going to stop looking.*

He took another swallow of his ale and stared into the flames.

A thought struck him.

It was so unexpected, so peculiar, that it made him grunt a sour laugh.

If I do see her again, and bring her home, will I miss this? This ranging the wide world, searching for her?

The thought was absurd. Considering it, though, he saw that it revealed something to him, something fundamental about himself.

This was what he *did.*

The illusion faded.

He didn't miss soldiering, which had also once been what he did. He didn't need to look back and contemplate past glories. Yes, he'd won battles, and done his duty, and risen through the ranks: But, as far as Jack Blunt was concerned, soldiering was nothing to do with glory. It was a matter of survival. No, he wouldn't miss this either, this searching.

What he missed was his Jenny. That was all there was to it. And he wanted her back, and would keep seeking for her the wide world over, until he found her, or died.

Lost in his thoughts, he didn't notice the door open, and the old woman enter. Everyone else did. And everyone else noticed the black robes, and the pointed black hat that she was removing, and the broomstick that she nonchalantly parked by the door, knowing full well that no one in the room would dream of touching it—let alone stealing it. She hobbled across the parlor, which fell silent around her, and lowered herself onto the bench by Jack Blunt, inside the hearth. He looked up, feeling her presence, and turned to her with a frown.

"Good evening, Commandant," she said, and then glanced across at Nyrik and Horm, who had gone still. "And you lads too. Been a while, eh? How are you keeping?"

"Very well, thank you, Marnie," Nyrik said quickly, on his best behavior. "Yourself?"

"Aches and pains, and moans and bones, and more of them each year. I'll take a glass of your damson wine, Eva, if you'd be so kind, and a plate of bread and cheese and pickles."

Eva, who had hurried up to serve Marnie, bobbed and hurried off.

Marnie turned to Jack Blunt. "It's a week's ride to Eastbay," she said. "You'd best set out first thing in the morning."

Surprised, Blunt stared at her.

"Yes," Marnie said, "that's good. Keep your eyes on me. There's things you need to know."

As she finished talking, Blunt could not look away, could not turn his head or avert his eyes.

"This won't hurt," Marnie said. "Well, not once it's over." She raised her eyepatch. Her huge, red eye burned into Jack Blunt.

Across the fire, Nyrik and Horm were statues. They watched and saw something they'd never in their lives have thought they'd see: Jack Blunt terrified.

"There," Marnie said, at last, lowering her eyepatch into place. Jack Blunt jerked back to life, and bent forwards, and then recovered himself, gasping, and automatically reached for the knife at his belt.

Marnie looked at him mildly. "You have suffered enough," she said.

As she sat back, the room around them reanimated.

"I'll see you in Eastbay, Jack Blunt," Marnie said, and then, smiling across at Nyrik and Horm, "You too, lads?"

Eva hurried up with her food and drink.

"Ah, thank you, Eva," Marnie said. "And how is Tom the Barner's chest, after this wet winter?"

They were all waiting for us as we came down *The Red Rose's* gangplank onto the wharf at Eastbay. Not that we could see them, because

Esmeralda was standing front and center, glowing, and smiling, and you could never look at anyone but Esmeralda.

I let Qrysta go ahead, and they embraced. "I want to hear all about it," Esmeralda said, and then grinned at the rest of us, "again and again and again, from all of you!" She looked us over, and noticed that we were eight now, not five. She saw Jess, and Evall, and Jenny Blunt. Being Esmeralda, she knew exactly what to do, which was nothing.

Qrysta said, "This is Jess. She is my pupil. One day, she will be as good as me."

Esmeralda gave Jess one of her irresistible smiles. "I expect you can prove that?" she challenged.

Jess couldn't help grinning. "Dunno," she said, "I can try."

Queen Esmeralda said, "Good idea! We'll have a tournament! And you can be a part of it, in a contest. How does that sound?"

"Will it be me against you?" Jess said.

Esmeralda shook her head, chuckling. "That wouldn't be much of a contest," she said, "I can't fight. I need people like you and Qrysta to do that for me."

Jess's face fell. Her opinion of this glowing girl had fallen.

Qrysta whispered in her ear.

Jess's eyes grew round.

"I'm sorry, Your Highness …" she said, curtseying. "… I didn't know—"

Esmeralda said, "Don't be, Jess! Any friend of Qrysta's is a friend of mine."

Jess fell silent, tongue-tied. I heard her mutter to Qrysta, as they left, and I led Jenny Blunt past them, "You didn't tell me she was the fucking queen!"

"Hello, Daxx," Esmeralda said. "Welcome home."

"Thank you, Highness," I said. And, because Esmeralda always knew what to do, she understood that she and I were now bystanders.

Commandant Blunt walked down from behind her, his eyes on the wife that he had not seen in twenty-four years. Marnie, I was glad to see, was standing quietly behind him.

He knew his Jenny, but frowned.

She was the age that she had been when he'd last seen her. *Exactly* how he remembered her.

But that couldn't be right …

I waited for him to look to me.

Which he did.

I told him, "That was then, Commandant. Since then, she has been through much, as have you. This is now." I cleansed the Glamour from Jenny Blunt.

Her face softened and settled into her true age. She was no longer the illusion that Malamyr had made her for her abuser. She was older, rounder, truer.

Commandant Bastard watched. He relaxed, understanding. He held his hands out to his long lost wife. "Ah," he said, smiling, "there you are, lass!"

"Jack," Jenny Blunt said, taking his hands, and that was all she could manage.

"You're home," he said. "And that's all I could ask for."

Jenny Blunt said, "Me too."

Epilogue

So many problems, such little time. Elun had told me what Jenny Blunt needed, and Marnie and I conferred. Marnie said that she and her Coven sisters, and the Apothecaries, would take it from there. It was a relief to know that Jenny would be in good hands.

Esmeralda was all for a celebration, and feasts, and a Royal Tournament; but I had to tell her, in private, that now wasn't the time—at least, not if she wanted me involved. She said that of *course* she did, and asked why not. Her eyes grew round as I told her of Graycote and what I had now become. She wanted to know more, so I Turned, in her private antechamber in My Lady of Eastbay's Castle, to show her. She was alarmed, staring up at me slavering above her, my claws outstretched—and I'd never smelled anything more delicious—but she did not recoil, as others had done. She studied me, thoughtfully. I re-Turned and slumped back down into my chair.

She looked over at me, considering. She was more curious than concerned. "So, what are you going to do?" she asked.

I didn't know how to answer.

Shift did. I felt her warmth through my back and brought her around to hold her in my hands.

She didn't have much to say. *We're in this together, Daxx. I'm with you all the way.*

All the way to where?

Even though she answered a question with another question, her reply was warm, and comforting—and, somehow, perfect. *Does it matter?*

I smiled.

Exactly, I felt her confirming. *As long as we're together.*

I patted her dark, rowan wood gratefully. Yes, we were in this together. We always would be. But as far as I knew, there was only one end to this tale.

I said aloud, to Shift as much as to Esmeralda, "Marnie says there's no cure. And …" I hesitated. "It gets worse. Every moon month it gets stronger, and your human side gets weaker."

"No cure? None?"

"None that anyone knows of. The thing is, Ez …" I faltered.

Esmeralda waited as I struggled with my thoughts and feelings. Eventually, I said, "Now that I've known this … *felt* this: I don't think I can bear to lose it."

I looked down at her, salt tears stinging my eyes. I was so, so lost. Such power. Such glory. Which I did not want, any more than I wanted to let go of it.

She reached out and took my hands in hers. "As long as *we* don't lose *you*," she said.

Silence fell between us.

"I need to find answers," I said. "And I need to be away from here before the full moon. You don't want … *that*, on the streets of Eastbay."

"No," she said. "Probably a good idea. I'll send word out. All over the realm. It'll take time for people to get here, for the tournament—weeks, even. You should be back in time for it." She smiled. "And if you aren't," she added, "whenever I look up at the full moon, I'll think of you."

Oller would handle our haul from the helldragon's hoard and Bartle's trove on *The Rose Revived*. He knew more about loot than the rest of us put together. Marnie would help him scry out the secrets of the magic items. I left the blood-red heartstone from Malamyr's snake staff, and the strange, twisted-headed staff I'd taken from the hoard, with her to study. I'd hear about it all, I knew, when I came back from where I'd be going.

If I came back.

Not that I knew where that might be.

I was confused. I had a problem. I had no idea how to solve it. Or even how to begin looking for a solution. I'd been Gifted. What to do about it? Where to start?

Esmeralda, together with My Lady of Eastbay, had laid on a feast to welcome us all home, a banquet as fine as any I'd attended—but my thoughts were elsewhere, on what lay ahead. I felt curiously detached from everyone—not just my companions, but those we'd met in this world: Nyrik, Horm, Marnie, Jess and Evall, Gelbert ...

Perhaps I was already Turning, inside, in anticipation of the next Moon Night. Perhaps I was just distracted. We'd done what we'd done. The results were in. Yes, I had a sense of completion, but it was small compared to the unease that I felt about what was yet to come.

My friends sensed my preoccupation and gave me space. They were only too aware of what was troubling me.

I remember little about that evening, but one moment stands out. We hadn't expected to see him, in the Great Hall of Eastbay Castle; but there he was, walking slowly towards us through the happy, feasting throng: Commandant Bastard. He was not alone. His son, whom he'd only met that day but looked so like him, was with him.

They both looked wary and tense. His long-lost wife, newly returned to him, was in his chambers, we knew. She was sleeping, he said, as he sat down across from me on a bench between Oller and Jess, who made room for him and his son to sit beside him. Marnie and the Superior of the Apothecaries were with his Jenny, he told us. He and his son had come to thank us.

I glanced at young Jack and felt the strain within him. *It would take time*, I thought, *to come to terms with what the lad had been through*.

Grell poured mugs of ale for them and refilled ours. We raised them to each other.

"You have my gratitude, all of you, more'n you or anyone can know," Jack Blunt said. His son glanced at him, surprised to see tears welling in the old man's eyes. "You gave me back my wife. My son. My *life*." Commandant Blunt continued, "If there's *ever a thing* I can do for you lads—why, all you need to do is ask."

"Actually, Commandant," Grell said, lowering his mug to the table, "there is."

"Name it," Commandant Bastard said.

"At this tourney, coming up," Grell began, then faltered.

Oller chuckled and elbowed Blunt in the ribs, who glared at him.

Oller winked. He knew what was coming.

Blunt slowly turned back to Grell and sipped at his ale.

He lowered his mug, his eyes never leaving Grell's. The Orc faltered under that steady gaze. It was a gaze that he knew all too well from his time in the training yard in Brigstowe Castle—a gaze that chilled the blood. You *really* didn't want that gaze on you, if you were one of Jack Blunt's recruits. He cleared his throat, and said, "*Yes*, well, ah—I was wondering, um, Commandant, if you'd be so kind, as to, er, consider, um, perhaps honoring me with, um, a, er, ah …" he tailed off.

Oller chuckled and came to his rescue. "If I may quote our large friend here, Commandant," he said, " '*when we see Commandant Bastard again, I'm gonna challenge him to a one-on-one, fighting two-handed. And I'm going to knock his fucking brains in for all the bruises he gave me in training!*' "

Commandant Bastard went still.

Grell quailed and gulped, embarrassed.

"Two-handed, against the best bloody Orc I've ever seen?" Blunt said at last. He studied Grell, his dark eyes brooding.

Grell, we could all see, was shifting in his seat, and far from comfortable. No one within earshot moved a muscle.

Commandant Bastard let him squirm, and then, nodding, said, "Yes, I'll oblige you with a turn, Master Grell,"

We all unfroze at that. A ripple of excitement ran through the listeners at our long table. Now *this* was going to be worth seeing!

I saw young Jack Blunt start, clearly surprised. He'd seen Grell in combat. And this old man, the father he'd never known about, was calmly agreeing to square up to *that* great brute?

Commandant Bastard chuckled, took a mouthful of ale, lowered his mug, and smiled across at Grell. "May the best man win, eh?" he said, with a smile.

Grell and Oller and I knew that smile of old. It meant trouble. Anyone on the end of it would end up flat on his back.

"Or Orc," Grell said, trying to sound convincing. Which he didn't.

Blunt shook his head. "He'll have to be an Orc who's improved a sight since he was last in my training yard."

Grell attempted a smile. "I believe I have, Commandant. Yes."

Blunt's eyebrows rose a fraction. We all could read *that* expression loud and clear. *Oh, is that so? Cocky, aren't we?*

"Do you?" he said, dismissively. "Well, I'll believe that when I see it, sonny." He raised his mug to Grell and drank, his dark eyes shining.

"Yes," Grell managed. "I believe you will. Thank you, Commandant."

"I'll be disappointed if you haven't, Graduate Grell," he said. "Seeing as you had a long way to go last time I looked."

Grell had no answer to that.

Oller was enjoying his discomposure. "Hehe, now look what you got yourself into, you big lunk!" he crowed, and reminded Grell, "An' I got ten o' my gold to your eight he has you flat on your hairy arse before you know what hit you! That's ten gold as good as in my cly already. Anyone want any more of it? Five-to-four against buggerlugs here?" He looked around theatrically, milking Grell's embarrassment. "Wot, no takers?" Too bloody fly, you lot—you know a dead duck when you see one." He turned to Grell. "Tell you what, matey, I'll give you seven to ten against, how's that sound? Just 'cos you're a pal. Your seven wins my ten."

Grell had had enough. He banged the table and glared at Oller. "Seventy more to your hundred, you little shitweasel!" He turned his glare at Commandant Bastard—projecting a confidence we didn't quite think he was actually feeling. It melted in the face of the hard smile that grew on Jack Blunt's face.

"Well," Commandant Bastard said, lowering his ale, his dark eyes boring into Grell's, "we can't have you losing your money, Master Pinches, now can we?"

Acknowledgements

Website: *www.richardsparks.com*

Editor: Lezli Robyn (*www.lezlirobyn.com*)

Map by Jenny Okun (*www.jennyokun.com*)

Representation: Julia Lord Literary Management (*www.julialordliterary.com*)

Coming next (winter 2025):

The Sequel: **NEW ROCK NEW RULES**
Book Three in the New Rock Series